S0-AFP-361

THE MACHINE STOPS—In the far-distant future, when people have become mere cogs in an Earth-spanning Machine, what happens when the Machine dies?

DAGON—Where a man encounters a monstrous god from the dawn of time!

THE TISSUE CULTURE KING—In darkest Africa, a British scientist continues his secret research with a bizarre cloning scheme.

THE FAITHFUL—After man's final Apocalypse, who shall inherit the Earth?

NIGHTFALL—Can the human mind ever adapt to a universe where darkness is forever?

These are but a few glimpses into the stories and ideas which through the years have helped to create THE ROAD TO SCIENCE FICTION.

> **JAMES GUNN** is a well-known science fiction author and a past president of the Science Fiction Writers of America. He was named Chairman of the prestigious John W. Campbell Memorial Award jury, and is currently teaching science fiction and literature courses at the University of Kansas, Lawrence, where he lives. *The Road to Science Fiction I—From Gilgamesh to Wells* is also available in a Mentor edition.

Other MENTOR and SIGNET Books You'll Enjoy

THE ROAD TO
SCIENCE FICTION #2

From Wells to Heinlein

Edited by James Gunn

A MENTOR BOOK

NEW AMERICAN LIBRARY

TIMES MIRROR

New York and Scarborough, Ontario
The New English Library Limited, London

To Robert A. Heinlein, Isaac Asimov,
A. E. van Vogt, Theodore Sturgeon,
and all the other writers
who created the golden age

ACKNOWLEDGMENTS

Isaac Asimov. "Nightfall." Copyright 1941 by Street &
Smith Publications, Inc. Copyright renewed 1968 by
Isaac Asimov. Reprinted by permission of author.

The following pages constitute an extension of the copyright page.

MENTOR TRADEMARK REG. U.S. PAT. OFF. AND FOREIGN COUNTRIES
REGISTERED TRADEMARK—MARCA REGISTRADA
HECHO.EN CHICAGO, U.S.A.

SIGNET, SIGNET CLASSICS, MENTOR, PLUME AND MERIDIAN BOOKS are published *in the United States* by The New American Library, Inc., 1301 Avenue of the Americas, New York, New York 10019, *in Canada* by The New American Library of Canada Limited, 81 Mack Avenue, Scarborough, Ontario M1L 1M8, *in the United Kingdom* by The New English Library Limited, Barnard's Inn, Holborn, London, EC1N 2JR, England

First Mentor Printing, February, 1979

1 2 3 4 5 6 7 8 9

PRINTED IN THE UNITED STATES OF AMERICA

Contents

Introduction

1

Science fiction began to take recognizable shape around the beginning of the twentieth century through the creation of the mass magazines and the work of a number of authors, but particularly that of H. G. Wells. Up to that time science fiction was a scattering of responses to new developments in science and technology and their impacts on society.

The origins of science fiction can be traced back at least as far as Mary Shelley's powerful gothic novel about the creation of artificial life, Hawthorne's fables of science, Poe's strange journeys and light-hearted speculations, and Verne's *voyages extraordinaires.* . . .

Wells saw science and technology becoming central facts in people's everyday lives, and he began to think of humanity as a species, even as a species whose survival was uncertain. His inquiring mind and his art assembled the various elements of a new fiction out of earlier fragments. For good reason Wells is called the father of modern science fiction.

He didn't call it "science fiction," of course. What he wrote were called "single-sitting stories of science" or "scientific romances." Hugo Gernsback, in 1929, would give the genre the name that would stick.

The Road to Science Fiction II: From Wells to Heinlein is the second volume in a three-volume series of anthologies whose purpose is to trace the evolution of science fiction from its earliest progenitors to what is presently being published in magazines and books. The first volume, *The Road to Science Fiction: From Gilgamesh to Wells,* contained the following definition of science fiction:

> Science fiction is the branch of literature that deals with the effects of change on people in the real world as it can be projected into the past, the future, or to distant places. It often concerns itself with scientific or technological change, and it usually involves matters whose

importance is greater than the individual or the community; often civilization or the race itself is in danger.

The first volume suggested that before science fiction could be written people had to learn to think in unaccustomed ways: (1) they had to learn to think of themselves not as a tribe, or as a people, or even as a nation, but as a species; (2) they had to adopt an open mind about the nature of the universe—its beginning and its end—and the fate of man; and (3) they had to discover the future, a future that would be different from the past or the present because of scientific advance and technological innovation.

The first volume was devoted largely to the third of these prerequisites: the discovery of the future and the ways in which life, and how people thought about it, was being changed, radically and irreversibly, by science and invention, and how this discovery and these changes inspired the fiction that a few writers began to create. The works described or reprinted in that first volume illustrated how humanity's world had changed through its own attitude toward it. Humanity was born into a universe that was mysterious and unknowable, in a condition of helplessness amid natural forces; slowly, through science, it began to perceive the universe as comprehensible, and to move from a reliance on magic or a resignation to the omnipotence of the gods to a growing independence from the tyranny of nature.

Gradually humanity learned that it could determine its own destiny through the use of its mind to understand and to change. The Industrial Revolution provided an illustration of how the process could work. The conversion of chemical energy into power, and the ingenious application of power to the innumerable tasks of humanity, showed how technology was translated into social change.

A few authors responded to this new force in human affairs, but almost a century would elapse after James Watt's invention before any meaningful recognition of this new world and its new way of thinking about the universe would show up in fiction. If humanity's future was in its own hands and not subject to the whims of cruel gods or to the grand design of some beneficent deity, humanity should devote some thought to the factors in the present that were shaping the future.

That was science fiction.

But science fiction was not simply futurism. It also could

be said to date from the publication of Charles Darwin's *Origin of Species* in 1859, which provided a scientific rationale for a process that had slowly enlarged the meaning of the word "human" until it encompassed the entire species. The view of humanity as a species was not only characteristic of science fiction but essential to it.

Because science fiction is so protean, every definition seems to cover only one aspect of its nature. Thus it has been called a literature of ideas or the literature of anticipation or the literature of change.

It could also be defined as the literature that concerns itself with the condition and fate of the human species.

2

Human society has evolved from the individual through the family unit, the tribe, the village, the city, the region, the nation, and, its most recent form, the alliance of nations. Next comes humanity as a species. All the way along that progression, full humanity has been denied to anyone who was not a member of the social group; outside the group were at best barbarians and at worst aliens, nonhumans. It was not only permissible but reasonable to treat these nonhumans inhumanly: to rob, rape, kill, or enslave. To make war on those outside the group, for whatever cause, was righteous, and to conquer was to enlarge the holy area where sanity and goodness prevailed, where "humanity" existed.

The literature of any period fulfills the needs of its social situation. Out of the tribal era came folk tales about the creation of the tribe and about its survival through flood and plague and battle. Out of the city-state came epics about heroes who built the city or repelled invaders, who won favor with the gods and interceded with them, or sometimes sacrificed themselves, for the people. Out of religious eras came devout drama to explicate doctrine and remind audiences of the place and function of godhead, and literature about good and evil, about the way to achieve transcendence, to discover divine will and live in consonance with it, to be saved. Out of times of nationalism came fiction about the way wars are won and lost. Out of an era of individualism came stories in which the sense of community is virtually absent and the major concern is with the discovery of self, with individual ad-

ventures rather than the victories of the culture hero, and
with the sometimes tragic discovery of the whatness of things.

In Wells's turn-of-the-century novels and stories, the focus
of concern became the species. In a period when other authors were writing about the small-scale tragedy of the individual or the social tragedy of the unfortunate, *The Time
Machine* and *The War of the Worlds* involved the fate of all
humanity. These broad strokes across the literary canvas, as
much as the fantastic plots, distinguished Wells's science fiction and his later utopian fiction from his so-called comedies;
the same kind of broad view displayed itself in his three en-
cyclopedic works, *The Outline of History* (1919), *The
Science of Life* (1930), and *The Work, Wealth, and Happiness of Mankind* (1931).

3

As science fiction built upon the splendid beginnings of
Wells's early fiction, its essential qualities emerged only
slowly from the many forms in which it was expressed.
Science fiction's proliferation of forms has always confused
definition. The murder mystery has an action and the western
has a place; science fiction has neither. It is capable of rang-
ing over all kinds and degrees of action, all time, from the
beginning of everything to its final end, and all space, from
the infinitely small to the universe itself.[1]

Science fiction, moreover, has freely adopted other modes
to suit its purpose—the adventure story, say, or the love
story. Even science-fiction sports stories are not uncommon,
and the science-fiction western, in which a lone hero ex-
changes his horse for a rocket ship and his six-gun for a blaster, became so prevalent that H. L. Gold, founding editor of
Galaxy, advertised that his magazine would never print such
stories. For many years the late John W. Campbell, editor of
Astounding/Analog, insisted that the science-fiction mystery
story was an impossibility, because the science-fiction detective
had such infinite potentials that the story could not play fair
with the reader; but Isaac Asimov proved him wrong with
such science-fiction detective novels as *The Caves of Steel*
(1954) and *The Naked Sun* (1957), and at least one volume
of short stories (*Asimov's Mysteries*, 1968).

Sometimes science fiction seems to fall naturally into one
mode, sometimes another. Asimov has divided the history of

modern science fiction (according to his definition, after 1926) into four periods: adventure-dominant between 1926 and 1938, science-dominant between 1938 and 1950, sociology-dominant between 1950 and 1965, and style-dominant since then. Though the terms are not all parallel, they can be useful ways of cataloging information. The problem of definition is to separate the unique qualities from those a genre may have adopted as a means of telling a story. In science fiction the traditional definition depends on subject matter: science fiction is "about" something such as science, technology, change. But another way of defining science fiction is by its attitude.

In the age of faith, humanity was urged to subordinate its earthly desires for the sake of an afterlife; the problem of the individual was not how to discover himself but how to become more like some ideal Christian. The age of faith gradually became the age of the individual. The Protestant Reformation made every person his own interpreter of God's word, the discoveries of science provided alternative explanations for creation, and accelerating technology destroyed the old social order that had provided traditional answers and left every person to find his own.

Out of the age of the individual came fiction that raised questions not about faith but about the individual: whether he/she would live or die, succeed or fail, find love or lose it, recognize the true nature of things or remain ignorant. In the midst of Conrad, James, and Bennett, Wells's concerns seemed not only out of step but unliterary.

4

The Time Machine (1895) and The War of the Worlds (1898) were unusual in many ways, but one unique aspect was their focus on the fate of humanity rather than the fate of any one person, and in a story such as Wells's "The Star" the fate of the planet is so much in the foreground that the individual scarcely exists. Even an apparently small-scale comedy such as "The New Accelerator" is not so much a story of an inventor's success or failure as a continual reminder of the social implications of the invention, including the sly satire at the end on the irresponsibility of the scientist.

E. M. Forster's "The Machine Stops" obviously is about all humanity, and the destruction at the end presumably is universal. Even the adventure fantasy of *Under the Moons of Mars* and its many sequels deals with the many races of Mars, the history of the planet, and the struggle to save remnants of civilization from the evaporation of its seas and the planet itself from the disappearance of its air. Merritt's "The People of the Pit" describes a race older than humanity, one against which humanity is virtually helpless. "Dragon" and Lovecraft's other horror stories are based on a mythology about elder gods and their relationships with contemporary men and women. London's "The Red One" describes one man's involvement with an alien spaceship but has implications beyond his individual fate. The analysis could continue through the entire contents of this volume.

If humanity-wide implications are not involved, or insufficiently involved, the piece of fiction may more appropriately be called something else. Perhaps it is more of a love story in a strange setting, an adventure story, a fable, a parable, or a study of character. Such questions of emphasis and attitude may help explain the controversy over "the New Wave" of the mid-1960s.

Whether or not this species-broad concern of science fiction can be elevated into a basic requirement of the genre, this way of looking at it can illuminate some of its characteristics. British critic, author, and anthologist Edmund Crispin, for instance, used this view of science fiction to help explain its treatment of character. Calling science fiction "origin of species fiction," he wrote:

> Its basic valuation of man is as just one of a horde of different animals sharing the same planet. Given this, it is not difficult to see that in science fiction individuals are apt to count for very little in their own right. The multitudinousness of the human species forbids us—if we are going to adopt such a standpoint—to take really seriously Madame Bovary or Strether or Leopold Bloom.[2]

In any case, in the first forty years of the twentieth century science fiction began to ask questions that had never before been asked: Will humanity progress or regress? Will its social forms change? Will humanity survive?

After the creation of the first science-fiction magazine in 1926 and particularly during the 1930s with its proliferating publications, its expanding audience, and its specialized authors, these questions began to sort themselves into categories: journeys, aliens, the past, the future.

Many early stories were long journeys of one kind or another. One purpose of the journey was to lend credibility to the strange creatures or civilizations encountered, or the events that happened. In "lost race" stories such as H. Rider Haggard's *She* or in the adventure stories of the early pulp magazines, the journeys were to unexplored places on the earth; occasionally they reached other worlds by astral projection. Writers turned to spaceflight when it became more believable than unexplored areas on the earth.

Other than a plausible narrative (as opposed to fantasy), such journeys offered the writer an opportunity to place people in strange environments, to confront humans with aliens and familiar civilizations and environments with those that were different in meaningful ways, and to compare contrasting moral and ethical principles, and physical and biological divergences, and their influences on humanity. The stories asked: Are the conditions we take for granted the same everywhere in the universe? Are people the same everywhere? How would life be changed if either were significantly different? Can humanity survive or thrive under extraterrestrial conditions? Underlying the theme of the extraterrestrial journey were the basic notions that humanity had the right to conquer as much of the universe as it could handle, and that placing human colonies on other worlds would increase humanity's chances for survival.

Other kinds of stories served to define humanity and to describe its prospects in other ways. Sometimes aliens were used directly to test humanity's characteristics or its right to survive. Stories about the distant past usually focused on the way humanity became human or the species evolved or contemporary civilization succeeded others (but may be repeating its fatal decisions). Stories about the future became more common and offered opportunities to deal with humanity's potential to improve or change its basic nature, or its fate. Sometimes the future held Armageddon, which questioned humanity's sanity or its ability to survive its own destructive impulses. Sometimes it held other threats, such as overpopulation, pollution, energy shortages, plagues, dehumanizing technology, dangerous discoveries, and such overwhelming natural phenomena as earthquakes, floods, ice ages, changes in solar output, stellar explosions. Sometimes it offered mysteries and the fundamental appeal of the unknown, the "sense of wonder" that is often mentioned in discussions of science fiction.

No other kind of fiction dealt with these kinds of problems. In the beginning the questions science fiction was asking seemed remote, fantastic, mere amusing speculation, but beginning in the late '30s and continuing into the present many of them became more real and more important than the questions other kinds of fiction could raise about the individual.

5

The development of science fiction was influenced by other factors. *The Road to Science Fiction: From Gilgamesh to Wells*, for instance, showed how the rise of science and technology had changed people's attitudes; these continued to help shape science fiction. During the Industrial Revolution, science and technology changed society surely but not always directly and perceptibly; from 1900 to 1940 they became part of the everyday life of the average person in western civilization.

Wells's vision of the future became reality during his lifetime. Medicine and public-health measures lengthened lifespans. Electricity brightened the night and provided convenient power at the end of two wires. Radio, the telephone, the automobile, and the airplane began to shorten distances, to provide new means of communication and a new kind of personal mobility, and to offer new uses for leisure time that factories and new production methods were supplying, along with unprecedented abundance that had to be shared with workers to be fully realized. The secrets of the universe were being probed with increasingly powerful telescopes and the atom was being divided into increasingly smaller particles that held the promise of inexhaustible sources of energy. Many of these scientific discoveries and inventions were being applied to warfare, to make it more deadly and more total.

For the first decade or so of the twentieth century, western belief in progress developed into a kind of religion. Humanity was perfectible, it said, and through the application of its intelligence to the obstacles that stood in the way of the millennium, particularly through the education of new scientists and engineers and through the application of the scientific method, the problems of humanity could all be solved. Day by day, in every way, humanity was getting better and better, to paraphrase Coué. Progress was its most important product, to paraphrase Dupont.

The fading of otherworldliness in Christianity and of the Renaissance reverence toward antiquity prepared the way for a belief in progress that developed out of the substantial accomplishments of Western Europe and the steady improvement in humanity's relationship with its physical and social environment. New continents were opened by the voyages of exploration; new views of the universe and humanity's place in it were revealed by Galileo and Newton. Agriculture and transportation improved spectacularly. After the fading of the Black Death and the end of the Hundred Years War, Europe became relatively free of plague and war. Artists like Michelangelo, Shakespeare, and Goethe produced works that rivaled or excelled those of the Greeks and Romans. Population increased steadily. Everything contributed to a growing confidence that all of humanity's problems that had not yet been solved were solvable.

Optimism about the future may have reached a peak in the late nineteenth and early twentieth centuries, and with some justice: the populations of Western Europe had nearly doubled in the century before 1914, in spite of the substantial emigration to the United States, where population had increased ten times in the same period. Industry had grown even faster: per capita income doubled in the thirty years preceding 1914. A new emphasis on education in England and the United States virtually eliminated illiteracy and created not only a new labor force to cope with the new technology but a new audience for newspapers and fiction in various forms.

World War I brought disillusionment about social progress, but the introduction of new weapons of war (both the tank and aircraft were foreseen by Wells, and the Martians in *The War of the Worlds* used a black poison gas as well as the heat rays that science has not yet, apparently, perfected) may have horrified mankind, yet at the same time they enhanced a faith in technology that the inventions of the next two and a half decades continued to feed. They also may have broadened the split between embittered literary traditionalists and the writers of the novels and stories that soon would be called science fiction, paralleling the division between "the two cultures" described by C. P. Snow. Even before World War I, E. M. Forster reacted to Wells's utopian phase with

"The Machine Stops," but the full-scale attacks on the belief in progress came later, with Aldous Huxley's *Brave New World* (1932) and George Orwell's *Nineteen Eighty-Four* (1949).

During the first forty years of the century, however, few science-fiction writers were pessimists. Not for them the melancholy of the lost generation. Like the founder of the first science-fiction magazine, Hugo Gernsback, early science-fiction writers generally were fascinated by the possibilities of science and invention, or they used those possibilities as a launching platform for their dreams about fantastic human adventures or achievements.

New inventions began to influence directly the way in which science fiction was made available to its readers. Foreshadowing McLuhan, the medium would shape the message. The railroad, the truck, and a system of national distribution brought magazines to every town within practical time limits. The rotary press and the halftone engraving made printing and illustration cheaper and the mass magazine possible. The general-education opportunities provided in England by the Education Act of 1871 and the compulsory primary-school movement in the United States after the Civil War provided new readers.

Then, in 1884, two new inventions—the linotype and the process for making paper from wood pulp—lowered the cost of printing still more and made possible the pulp magazine.

6

Popular literature would have seemed like a self-contradiction until the last century or so. The literature of the populace, the vulgate, the ordinary people,[3] existed only in oral form for most of humanity's history; only higher literature (officially approved by those who had the leisure and the skills to read) was written. Popular fiction emerged into the written tradition in the eighteenth century with the novel and later the short story.

With the growth in literacy and cheaper methods of publishing, fiction began to be produced for people with limited means to purchase it, limited time to read it, and limited backgrounds for understanding it. In Dickens's day many novels (including Dickens's) were serialized in penny newspapers or published in penny dreadfuls; their counterpart in the United States, beginning in 1860 and continuing in popularity until they began to be replaced by boys' magazines in the 1890s, was the dime novel.

New publishing enterprises brought forth a new kind of entrepreneur, like Frank A. Munsey. He came from Maine to New York in 1882 with the dream of becoming rich by publishing a boys' weekly to be called *Golden Argosy*. In 1888 the name was shortened to *Argosy*, and in 1896 it became an all-fiction magazine. The first pulp magazine offered 192 pages of fiction for a dime. The audience was conceived to be mainly the sons of working-class fathers and perhaps some members of the still-emerging middle class. What that audience wanted was adventure stories, and the new pulp magazines supplied all kinds of them: wild-west stories, sea stories, spy stories, war stories, travel stories, and fantasy stories and scientific romances as well.

Argosy was followed in 1903 by Street & Smith's *Popular Magazine*. In 1905 Munsey brought out *All-Story Magazine*. That same year *The Monthly Magazine* was started; two years later it was renamed *Blue Book*. In 1906 Street & Smith published *The People's Magazine*, and Munsey, *The Scrap Book*, whose fiction section was named *The Cavalier* in 1908; shortly thereafter it became an independent magazine.

The stories and novels of H. G. Wells were published in the United States in magazines like *Cosmopolitan*, but the pulp magazines serialized H. Rider Haggard's *Ayesha*, the sequel to *She*, and the stories and novels of such authors as Garrett P. Serviss, William Wallace Cook, George Allan England, and an author new to readers in 1912, Edgar Rice Burroughs.[4]

The pulp magazines were edited under the assumption that readers would as soon read one adventure story as another. A second possibility began to emerge from the letter columns that had become a part of every pulp magazine: some readers liked one kind of adventure story better than another. The response of the publishing entrepreneurs was to create the category pulp magazine.

Munsey published the first of them in 1906, *The Railroad Man's Magazine*, filled with the adventures of railroading, and in 1907, *The Ocean*, a magazine filled with sea stories; the latter lasted only a year. But the real beginning of the category pulps was in 1915 when Street & Smith created *Detective Story Monthly*, and followed it in 1919 with *Western Story Magazine* and in 1921 with *Love Stories*. Finally, in

1926, someone worked up enough courage to publish a science-fiction magazine. His name was Hugo Gernsback, and the magazine was *Amazing Stories.*

An immigrant from Luxembourg in 1904, an inventor, and a salesman not only of radios and electronic equipment but of the spirit of science and invention that lay behind them, Gernsback had been publishing popular science magazines since 1908, when he founded *Modern Electrics.* He sold the magazine in 1912 and started *Electrical Experimenter;* in 1920 he changed its name to *Science and Invention.* Beginning in 1911 with his own serialized novel about technological marvels of the future, *Ralph 124C 41+,* Gernsback started including an occasional science-fiction story, and in 1923 the August number of *Electrical Experimenter* was devoted entirely to "scientific fiction."

"Scientifiction" was what Gernsback called it in the first issue of *Amazing Stories,* and he described it as "the Jules Verne, H. G. Wells, and Edgar Allan Poe type of story—a charming romance intermingled with scientific fact and prophetic vision." At first the magazine contained only reprints, mostly from Verne, Wells, and Poe, but within a few months new stories began to appear. One of his finds was Edward Elmer Smith, Ph.D. (a doughnut-mix specialist whose first novel, *The Skylark of Space,* had been started in 1915, completed in 1920, and not published until 1928). Another was Philip Nowlan, creator of Buck Rogers.

In 1929 Gernsback lost control of his publishing empire and immediately started building another, including two science-fiction magazines, *Science Wonder Stories* and *Air Wonder Stories,* which he soon combined into *Wonder Stories.* In the first issue of *Science Wonder Stories* (June 1929), he described what he was going to publish as "science fiction."[5]

In 1930 a pulp magazine chain called Clayton Magazines added a science-fiction magazine called *Astounding Stories of Super-Science.* Now there were three magazines. Science fiction not only had been named; it began to be defined by the medium in which it was published. The new men of importance were not the writers but the editors; they defined what science fiction was, and what it was not, by what they were willing to publish.[6]

7

About the same time science fiction got a specialized magazine and a name, book publication of science fiction almost ceased. The fantasies of A. Merritt continued to be published, and in Tarzana, California, Edgar Rice Burroughs founded a company to publish his own work. The old standards were reprinted—Verne, Wells, Haggard, M. P. Shiel, Conan Doyle—and certain new books were published, books that belonged to the genre according to every criterion but one— they weren't published in the new magazines. They were books like Stapledon's *Last and First Men* (1930) and other novels, and Huxley's *Brave New World* (1932). The old pulp magazines had been mined by publishers for novels, but the new literature that was being created for the magazines was neither published in book form nor reviewed from 1926 until 1946.

It seemed as if the focus of the genre in the magazines had removed it from the literary view; it became subliterary, beneath critical consideration. Instead of establishing a science-fiction homeland, Gernsback had created a ghetto. It was, however, a ghetto filled with enthusiasm. Letters from readers arrived by the sackfuls. When these began to be printed in letter columns, along with addresses, readers started corrsponding, formed clubs, issued fanzines, and eventually organized conventions. In the ghetto readers created a fan subculture.

Writers had more problems. The editors were in charge, and their decision was final.

The early pulp editors had been men of influence, too. Robert H. Davis, identified with Munsey's *All-Story*, *Scrap Book*, and *Cavalier*, discovered and encouraged many new writers. Thomas Newell Metcalf, managing editor of *All-Story*, bought Edgar Rice Burroughs's first novel, *Under the Moons of Mars*, and then *Tarzan of the Apes*, but unaccountably lost *The Return of Tarzan* to Archibald Lowry Sessions, editor of Street & Smith's *New Story Magazine*.

The science-fiction magazines, however, were fewer and more particular. A good story was not enough; it had to fit a more precise gauge, not only in subject matter but sometimes in accuracy, development, and attitude as well. Even *Weird*

Tales, founded in 1923 and edited for many years by Farnsworth Wright, carved out its own little crypt.

Amazing Stories was edited by T. O'Conor Sloane, an elderly man whose chief claim to authority, besides possession of an M.A. and a Ph.D. proudly displayed on the masthead, was that he was a son-in-law to Thomas Alva Edison. But Gernsback himself laid down the requirements. He saw his new "scientifiction" as a way to promote understanding of science and technology through fiction, a kind of candy coating for a pill of instruction. His formula was "75 percent literature interwoven with 25 percent science." It was a formula that was more honored in the breach than the observance, but Gernsback retained his convictions to the end: in 1963 he complained to a science-fiction club that of the first nine Hugo winners of short fiction (the annual award for excellence presented by the World Science Fiction Convention and named in Gernsback's honor) only one deserved to be called science fiction. The rest were fantasy.

The editor of *Astounding Stories of Super-Science* was Harry Bates. He wanted well-plotted adventure stories that would fit into the pattern of the other Clayton pulp magazines. He had a major advantage over *Amazing Stories* and *Wonder Stories*; he could pay two cents a word on acceptance. The others paid as little as they could and no more than half a cent a word on publication, and sometimes, as H. L. Gold recalled, only on threat of lawsuit. But *Astounding* never made expenses as a Clayton magazine, and when the Clayton chain collapsed in 1933 *Astounding* was sold to Street & Smith.

A seventeen-year-old fan, Charles D. Hornig, was named editor of *Wonder Stories* in 1933; he was the first of a series of editors (and authors) who would emerge from fandom. His major accomplishment was the creation, with Gernsback, of the first nationwide fan organization, the Science Fiction League. In 1936 Gernsback sold *Wonder Stories* to Standard Magazines, where it was retitled *Thrilling Wonder Stories*; a couple of years later it got a companion magazine, *Startling Stories*. Their editor, another youthful fan named Mort Weisinger, became known for the ingenuity of his plotting and the way his fertile mind rolled out story ideas for his authors; he became more famous later as managing editor of *Superman Comics* and a prolific article writer.

The new editor at *Astounding* in 1933 was F. Orlin Tremaine. He was looking for good stories like the space epics of

E. E. Smith (now known to his fans as "Doc" Smith), and serialized Smith's *The Skylark of Valeron* in 1935. He also wanted bold new ideas for a series he labeled "thought-variant stories." And he published the work of a young writer who had been appearing in the other magazines; under his own name, John W. Campbell, Jr., he rivaled Doc Smith for popularity in the space-epic tradition, and under the pseudonym of Don A. Stuart, he began to write a new kind of story, gentler, more sophisticated, more concerned with philosophy and the behavioral sciences than the physical sciences and technology.

In 1937 Campbell was named editor of *Astounding Stories*. He became a new kind of gatekeeper: he worked with writers, encouraged them, gave them provocative ideas, helped reorganize their plots, demanded revisions—and through personal conversations, long letters, and stimulating editorials created a climate of intellectual excitement. Campbell made science fiction over in his own image.

8

Isaac Asimov has written that Campbell "de-emphasized the nonhuman and nonsocial in science fiction. . . . Campbell wanted businessmen, space-ship crewmen, young engineers, housewives, robots that were logical machines."[7] Elsewhere Asimov said that Campbell wanted stories in which the science was realistic, stories that represented the scientific culture accurately.[8]

A character identifiable as Robert Heinlein in Anthony Boucher's *roman à clef, Rocket to the Morgue* (1942), says about an editor identifiable as Campbell: "Grant your gadgets, and start your story from there. In other words, assume certain advances in civilization, then work out convincingly just how those would affect the lives of ordinary individuals like you and me. . . . to sum it all up in a phrase of Don's: 'I want a story that would be published in a magazine of the twenty-fifth century.' "[9]

Pragmatic, provoking, more at ease with ideas than with people, Campbell made his vision of science fiction into reality. He took ASTOUNDING STORIES and made it over into ASTOUNDING SCIENCE FICTION, then Astounding SCIENCE FICTION, astounding SCIENCE FICTION, and finally *Analog Science Fiction—Science Fact*. It was his influence, and the influence of the writers to whom he could communicate his vision, that created what has since become known as "the golden age of science fiction."

NOTES

1. For this reason John W. Campbell once remarked that all other fiction, including the mainstream, was a subcategory of science fiction.

2. *Times Literary Supplement*, Oct. 25, 1963.

3. In *Science-Fiction Studies*, Vol. 4, Part 3, November 1977, Darko Suvin calls popular literature "paraliterature," distinguishing it from "higher" or "canonical" literature that is officially approved by the upper class.

4. It was a period when virtually all authors (and many editors) used three names.

5. Brian M. Stableford, in *Foundation 10*, describes an earlier use of the words in William Wilson's *A Little Earnest Book Upon a Great Old Subject*, published in 1851, but Gernsback's invention was the meaningful one.

6. Frederik Pohl's working definition of science fiction when he was editor of *Galaxy*, he has said, was a story he could publish in the magazine without having too many readers cancel their subscriptions.

7. "Social Science Fiction," in *Modern Science Fiction*, edited by Reginald Bretnor (New York: Coward-McCann, 1953).

8. "The History of Science Fiction from 1938 to the Present" (film), University of Kansas, 1973.

9. *Rocket to the Morgue* (New York: Duell, Sloan & Pierce, 1942).

Science: The New Accelerator

By the latter half of the nineteenth century, science and technology were major forces for change, and they were changing society in ways that no one had imagined. Scientists such as Boole, Kekule, Maxwell, Mendel, Mendelejeff, Swan, Cantor, Arrhenius, Pasteur, Hertz, Marconi, Roentgen, Becquerel, and Thomson discovered basic properties of matter and energy, or of living things, or means of calculating or of thinking about them. Inventors such as Hunt, Otis, Bessemer, Lenoir, Nobel, Schultze, Hyatt, Muybridge, Isaacs, Gidden, Bell, Otto, Edison, Thomson, Daimler, Swan, Mergenthaler, Dohl, Parsons, Stanley, Ives, Hall, Berliner, Eastman, Walker, Dewar, Goodwin, Burroughs, and Hoffman applied earlier scientific discoveries to practical needs, or happened on a useful process. Philosophers such as Darwin and Marx suggested theories that revolutionized ways of thinking about society.

They applied increasing momentum to a world in motion.

The problem of coping with a static world is relatively simple; the nature of that world is implicit in the social structure, and the educational system, whatever it is, serves to indoctrinate as well as explicate. The individual need only find his place in that world and, as Plato recommends in *The Republic*, find satisfaction in it.

The first challenge of a changing world is to recognize that it is going to be different from whatever it is. The second challenge is to identify the forces causing change. The third challenge, and the most difficult, is to predict what the changes are going to be and to isolate the decisions that are going to affect the direction change takes.

Change encompasses the hope of utopia and the threat of extinction. The work of Herbert George Wells (1866–1946) ranged over the entire spectrum of possibilities. He recognized the nature of his world early, and to the realities of a changing world he owed his rise from near-poverty to wealth, fame, and influence over men's minds and possibly over the direction of events. In his *Experiment in Autobiography* (1934) he wrote:

> World forces were at work tending to disperse the aristocratic estate system in Europe, to abolish small traders, to make work in the retail trades less independent and satisfactory, to promote industrial co-ordination, increase productivity, necessitate new and better informed classes, evoke a new type of education and make it universal, break down political barriers everywhere and bring all men into one planetary community.

Wells felt the plight of the small trader with special keenness, since he had escaped that fate only through recalcitrance and good fortune. His mother still thought of the world as static and, with her new husband, bought an unsuccessful crockery shop near London; she hoped for her children the security of a trade, and apprenticed Wells twice as a draper, once as a pharmaceutical chemist. Books, education, and science were Wells's way out of that life, and his ability to make the new science comprehensible, first in textbooks and then in articles and encyclopedias, and to make its implications and its possibilities dramatic in his stories and novels, was his way into a new existence as a major author and a respected pundit.

In his early writing years, Wells was aiming his articles and stories at the new magazines that were springing up in England to reach a new middle-class audience. In 1891 George Newnes, who had founded a magazine called *Tit-Bits* ten years before, created the first mass magazine, *The Strand Magazine.* It was followed almost immediately by *Ludgate Monthly*, *Pall Mall*, and *The Idler*, and a bit later by *Pearson's Magazine* and others.

Wells's first stories were published in *The Pall Mall Budget*, but he soon broadened his market to include *The Pall Mall Gazette* and *The Strand. The National Observer* published a series of articles based on an idea about time traveling Wells had nursed through several versions in his Science School days, and then, when its editor found a new job at *The New Review*, rewrote the articles as a story called *The Time Machine* (1895).

The novella was an immediate success in serial form and as a book, and it won him such literary admirers as Joseph Conrad and Henry James. A series of novels followed: *The*

Island of Dr. Moreau (1896), *The Invisible Man* (1897), *The War of the Worlds* (1898), *When the Sleeper Wakes* (1899), and *The First Men in the Moon* (1901). His short stories were collected in such early volumes as *The Stolen Bacillus and Other Incidents* (1895), *The Plattner Story and Others* (1897), *Tales of Space and Time* (1899), and *Twelve Stories and a Dream* (1903).

With these Wells had virtually exhausted the threat of extinction as a possible result of change, he had imagined it in so many different ways: from alien invasion to wandering planets, civilized ants, cephalopods, undersea humanoids, social tyranny, war, human degeneration, and the death of the sun. Now he turned to the other side of change: the utopia. In among his novels about contemporary life and his encyclopedias, he scattered propaganda novels in which the message was foremost and the story secondary. Conrad and James (with whom he later had a celebrated quarrel about the function of the novel) had tempted him to emphasize the artistic in his writing, in spite of his inclination "to regard the novel as about as much an art form as a market place or a boulevard" and "to see it and to see it only in relation to something else—a story, a thesis." In his autobiography he wrote:

> In the end I revolted altogether and refused to play their game. "I am a journalist," I declared, "I refuse to play the artist. If sometimes I am an artist it is a freak of the gods. I am a journalist all the time and what I write *goes now*—and will presently die."

But what he wrote didn't die, especially the novels and short stories he wrote before the turn of the century. These were his science-fiction works, and they remain as alive today as when they first were published. "The New Accelerator" was published in *The Strand* in 1901; the dress and the manners have changed since then, but they are unimportant to the story.

"The New Accelerator" is an invention story, a "gadget" story. It only speculates about the possibilities of the new drug. As Isaac Asimov points out in his "Social Science Fiction" essay, an idea can be developed in several different ways. Wells could have written an adventure story in which the invention is used to steal military secrets, kidnap tyrants or crime leaders, or save the world from invasion by aliens or destruction by war. He could have written a sociological story in which the drug is an accepted reality but people, who have learned to live with variable time, must solve problems such as the control of crime, unfair labor practices, or unequal living rates.

Wells chose to treat the idea casually, as he did many of his notions, but his speculations show that he was aware of the implications. He could write the sociological story, as he demonstrated in *When the Sleeper Wakes* and others, but his readers had to be eased into a story, unlike modern readers educated to the subtleties and conventions of the genre.

The New Accelerator

by H. G. Wells

Certainly, if ever a man found a guinea when he was looking for a pin it is my good friend Professor Gibberne. I have heard before of investigators overshooting the mark, but never quite to the extent that he has done. He has really, this time at any rate, without any touch of exaggeration in the phrase, found something to revolutionise human life. And that when he was simply seeking an all-round nervous stimulant to bring languid people up to the stresses of these pushful days. I have tasted the stuff now several times, and I cannot do better than describe the effect the thing had on me. That there are astonishing experiences in store for all in search of new sensations will become apparent enough.

Professor Gibberne, as many people know, is my neighbour in Folkestone. Unless my memory plays me a trick, his portrait at various ages has already appeared in *The Strand Magazine*—I think late in 1899; but I am unable to look it up because I have lent that volume to someone who has never sent it back. The reader may, perhaps, recall the high forehead and the singularly long black eyebrows that give such a Mephistophelian touch to his face. He occupies one of those pleasant detached houses in the mixed style that make the western end of the Upper Sandgate Road so interesting.

His is the one with the Flemish gables and the Moorish portico, and it is in the room with the mullioned bay window that he works when he is down here, and in which of an evening we have so often smoked and talked together. He is a mighty jester, but, besides, he likes to talk to me about his work; he is one of those men who find a help and stimulus in talking, and so I have been able to follow the conception of the New Accelerator right up from a very early stage. Of course, the greater portion of his experimental work is not done in Folkestone, but in Gower Street, in the fine new laboratory next to the hospital that he has been the first to use.

As everyone knows, or at least as all intelligent people know, the special department in which Gibberne has gained so great and deserved a reputation among physiologists is the action of drugs upon the nervous system. Upon soporifics, sedatives, and anaesthetics he is, I am told, unequalled. He is also a chemist of considerable eminence, and I suppose in the subtle and complex jungle of riddles that centres about the ganglion cell and the axis fibre there are little cleared places of his making, glades of illumination, that, until he sees fit to publish his results, are inaccessible to every other living man. And in the last few years he has been particularly assiduous upon this question of nervous stimulants, and already, before the discovery of the New Accelerator, very successful with them. Medical science has to thank him for at least three distinct and absolutely safe invigorators of unrivalled value to practising men. In cases of exhaustion the preparation known as Gibberne's B Syrup has, I suppose, saved more lives already than any lifeboat round the coast.

"But none of these things begin to satisfy me yet," he told me nearly a year ago. "Either they increase the central energy without affecting the nerves or they simply increase the available energy by lowering the nervous conductivity; and all of them are unequal and local in their operation. One wakes up the heart and viscera and leaves the brain stupefied, one gets at the brain champagne fashion and does nothing good for the solar plexus, and what I want—and what, if it's an earthly possibility, I mean to have—is a stimulant that stimulates all round, that wakes you up for a time from the crown of your head to the tip of your great toe, and makes you go two—or even three to everybody else's one. Eh? That's the thing I'm after."

"It would tire a man," I said.

"Not a doubt of it. And you'd eat double or treble—and

all that. But just think what the thing would mean. Imagine yourself with a little phial like this"—he held up a bottle of green glass and marked his points with it—"and in this precious phial is the power to think twice as fast, move twice as quickly, do twice as much work in a given time as you could otherwise do."

"But is such a thing possible?"

"I believe so. If it isn't, I've wasted my time for a year. These various preparations of the hypophosphites, for example, seem to show that something of the sort . . . Even if it was only one and a half times as fast it would do."

"It *would* do," I said.

"If you were a statesman in a corner, for example, time rushing up against you, something urgent to be done, eh?"

"He could dose his private secretary," I said.

"And gain—double time. And think if *you,* for example, wanted to finish a book."

"Usually," I said, "I wish I'd never begun 'em."

"Or a doctor, driven to death, wants to sit down and think out a case. Or a barrister—or a man cramming for an examination."

"Worth a guinea a drop," said I, "and more—to men like that."

"And in a duel again," said Gibberne, "where it all depends on your quickness in pulling the trigger."

"Or in fencing," I echoed.

"You see," said Gibberne, "if I get it as an all-round thing it will really do you no harm at all—except perhaps to an infinitesimal degree it brings you nearer old age. You will just have lived twice to other people's once——"

"I suppose," I meditated, "in a duel—it would be fair?"

"That's a question for the seconds," said Gibberne.

I harked back further. "And you really think such a thing *is* possible?" I said.

"As possible," said Gibberne, and glanced at something that went throbbing by the window, "as a motorbus. As a matter of fact——"

He paused and smiled at me deeply, and tapped slowly on the edge of his desk with the green phial. "I think I know the stuff . . . Already I've got something coming." The nervous smile upon his face betrayed the gravity of his revelation. He rarely talked of his actual experimental work unless things were very near the end. "And it may be, it may be—I shouldn't be surprised—it may even do the thing at a greater rate than twice."

"It will be rather a big thing," I hazarded.

"It will be, I think, rather a big thing."

But I don't think he quite knew what a big thing it was to be, for all that.

I remember we had several subsequent talks about the stuff. "The New Accelerator" he called it, and his tone about it grew more confident on each occasion. Sometimes he talked nervously of unexpected physiological results its use might have, and then he would get a bit unhappy; at others he was frankly mercenary, and we debated long and anxiously how the preparation might be turned to commercial account. "It's a good thing," said Gibberne, "a tremendous thing. I know I'm giving the world something, and I think it only reasonable we should expect the world to pay. The dignity of science is all very well, but I think somehow I must have the monopoly of the stuff for, say, ten years. I don't see why *all* the fun in life should go to the dealers in ham."

My own interest in the coming drug certainly did not wane in the time. I have always had a queer twist towards metaphysics in my mind. I have always been given to paradoxes about space and time, and it seemed to me that Gibberne was really preparing no less than the absolute acceleration of life. Suppose a man repeatedly dosed with such a preparation: he would live an active and record life indeed, but he would be an adult at eleven, middle-aged at twenty-five, and by thirty well on the road to senile decay. It seemed to me that so far Gibberne was only going to do for anyone who took his drug exactly what Nature has done for the Jews and Orientals, who are men in their teens and aged by fifty, and quicker in thought and act than we are all the time. The marvel of drugs has always been great to my mind; you can madden a man, calm a man, make him incredibly strong and alert or a helpless log, quicken this passion and allay that, all by means of drugs, and here was a new miracle to be added to this strange armoury of phials the doctors use! But Gibberne was far too eager upon his technical points to enter very keenly into my aspect of the question.

It was the 7th or 8th of August, when he told me the distillation that would decide his failure or success for a time was going forward as we talked, and it was on the 10th that he told me the thing was done and the New Accelerator a tangible reality in the world. I met him as I was going up the

Sandgate Hill towards Folkestone—I think I was going to get
my hair cut; and he came hurrying down to meet me—I suppose he was coming to my house to tell me at once of his
success. I remember that his eyes were unusually bright and
his face flushed, and I noted even then the swift alacrity of
his step.

"It's done," he cried, and gripped my hand, speaking very
fast; "it's more than done. Come up to my house and see."

"Really?"

"Really!" he shouted. "Incredibly! Come up and see."

"And it does—twice!"

"It does more, much more. It scares me. Come up and see
the stuff. Taste it! Try it! It's the most amazing stuff on
earth." He gripped my arm and, walking at such a pace that
he forced me into a trot, went shouting with me up the hill.
A whole charabancful of people turned and stared at us in
unison after the manner of people in charabancs. It was one
of those hot, clear days that Folkestone sees so much of, every colour incredibly bright and every outline hard. There
was a breeze, of course, but not so much breeze as sufficed
under these conditions to keep me cool and dry. I panted for
mercy.

"I'm not walking fast, am I?" cried Gibberne, and slack-
ened his pace to a quick march.

"You've been taking some of this stuff," I puffed.

"No," he said. "At the utmost a drop of water that stood
in a beaker from which I had washed out the last traces of
the stuff. I took some last night, you know. But that is ancient history now."

"And it goes twice?" I said, nearing his doorway in a grateful perspiration.

"It goes a thousand times, many thousand times!" cried
Gibberne, with a dramatic gesture, flinging open his Early
English carved oak gate.

"Phew!" said I, and followed him to the door.

"I don't know how many times it goes," he said, with his
latchkey in his hand.

"And you——"

"It throws all sorts of light on nervous physiology, it kicks
the theory of vision into a perfectly new shape! . . . Heaven
knows how many thousand times. We'll try all that after—
The thing is to try the stuff now."

"Try the stuff?" I said, as we went along the passage.

"Rather," said Gibberne, turning on me in his study.

"There it is in that little green phial there! Unless you happen to be afraid?"

I am a careful man by nature, and only theoretically adventurous. I *was* afraid. But on the other hand there is pride.

"Well," I haggled. "You say you've tried it?"

"I've tried it," he said, "and I don't look hurt by it, do I? I don't even look livery and I *feel*——"

I sat down. "Give me the potion," I said. "If the worst comes to the worst it will save having my hair cut, and that I think is one of the most hateful duties of a civilised man. How do you take the mixture?"

"With water," said Gibberne, whacking down a carafe.

He stood up in front of his desk and regarded me in his easy chair; his manner was suddenly affected by a touch of the Harley Street specialist. "It's rum stuff, you know," he said.

I made a gesture with my hand.

"I must warn you in the first place as soon as you've got it down to shut your eyes, and open them very cautiously in a minute or so's time. One still sees. The sense of vision is a question of length of vibration, and not of multitude of impacts; but there's a kind of shock to the retina, a nasty giddy confusion just at the time if the eyes are open. Keep 'em shut."

"Shut," I said. "Good!"

"And the next thing is, keep still. Don't begin to whack about. You may fetch something a nasty rap if you do. Remember you will be going several thousand times faster than you ever did before, heart, lungs, muscles, brain—everything—and you will hit hard without knowing it. You won't know it, you know. You'll feel just as you do now. Only everything in the world will seem to be going ever so many thousand times slower than it ever went before. That's what makes it so deuced queer."

"Lor'," I said. "And you mean——"

"You'll see," said he, and took up a measure. He glanced at the material on his desk. "Glasses," he said, "water. All here. Mustn't take too much for the first attempt."

The little phial glucked out its precious contents. "Don't forget what I told you," he said, turning the contents of the measure into a glass in the manner of an Italian waiter measuring whisky. "Sit with the eyes tightly shut and in absolute stillness for two minutes," he said. "Then you will hear me speak."

He added an inch or so of water to the dose in each glass.

"By the bye," he said, "don't put your glass down. Keep it in your hand and rest your hand on your knee. Yes—so. And now——"

He raised his glass.

"The New Accelerator," I said.

"The New Accelerator," he answered, and we touched glasses and drank, and instantly I closed my eyes.

You know that blank non-existence into which one drops when one has taken "gas." For an indefinite interval it was like that. Then I heard Gibberne telling me to wake up, and I stirred and opened my eyes. There he stood as he had been standing, glass still in hand. It was empty, that was all the difference.

"Well?" said I.

"Nothing out of the way?"

"Nothing. A slight feeling of exhilaration, perhaps. Nothing more."

"Sounds?"

"Things are still," I said. "By Jove! yes! They *are* still. Except the sort of faint pat, patter, like rain falling on different things. What is it?"

"Analysed sounds," I think he said, but I am not sure. He glanced at the window. "Have you ever seen a curtain before a window fixed in that way before?"

I followed his eyes, and there was the end of the curtain, frozen, as it were, corner high, in the act of flapping briskly in the breeze.

"No," said I, "that's odd."

"And here," he said, and opened the hand that held the glass. Naturally I winced, expecting the glass to smash. But so far from smashing it did not even seem to stir; it hung in mid-air—motionless. "Roughly speaking," said Gibberne, "an object in these latitudes falls sixteen feet in the first second. This glass is falling sixteen feet in a second now. Only, you see, it hasn't been falling yet for the hundreth part of a second. That gives you some idea of the pace of my Accelerator." And he waved his hand round and round, over and under the slowly sinking glass. Finally he took it by the bottom, pulled it down and placed it very carefully on the table. "Eh?" he said to me, and laughed.

"That seems all right," I said, and began very gingerly to raise myself from my chair. I felt perfectly well, very light and comfortable, and quite confident in my mind. I was going fast all over. My heart, for example, was beating a thousand times a second, but that caused me no discomfort at all. I looked out of the window. An immovable cyclist, head down and with a frozen puff of dust behind his driving-wheel, scorched to overtake a galloping charabanc that did not stir. I gaped in amazement at this incredible spectacle. "Gibberne," I cried, "how long will this confounded stuff last?"

"Heaven knows!" he answered. "Last time I took it, I went to bed and slept it off. I tell you, I was frightened. It must have lasted some minutes, I think—it seemed like hours. But after a bit it slows down rather suddenly, I believe."

I was proud to observe that I did not feel frightened—I suppose because there were two of us. "Why shouldn't we go out?" I asked.

"Why not?"

"They'll see us."

"Not they. Goodness, no! Why, we shall be going a thousand times faster than the quickest conjuring trick that was ever done. Come along! Which way shall we go? Window, or door?"

And out by the window we went.

Assuredly of all the strange experiences that I have ever had, or imagined, or read of other people having or imagining, that little raid I made with Gibberne on the Folkestone Leas, under the influence of the New Accelerator, was the strangest and maddest of all. We went out by his gate into the road, and there we made a minute examination of the statuesque passing traffic. The tops of the wheels and some of the legs of the horses of this charabanc, the end of the whiplash and the lower jaw of the conductor—who was just beginning to yawn—were perceptibly in motion, but all the rest of the lumbering conveyance seemed still. And quite noiseless except for a faint rattling that came from one man's throat! And as parts of this frozen edifice there were a driver, you know, and a conductor, and eleven people! The effect as we walked about the thing began by being madly queer and ended by being—disagreeable. There they were, people like ourselves and yet not like ourselves, frozen in careless attitudes, caught in mid-gesture. A girl and a man smiled at one another, a leering smile that threatened to last for evermore; a woman in a floppy capelline rested her arm on the rail and stared at Gibberne's house with the unwinking stare of eternity; a man stroked his moustache like a figure of wax, and another stretched a tiresome stiff hand with extended fingers towards his loosened hat. We stared at them, we laughed at them, we made faces at them, and then a sort of disgust of them came upon us, and we turned away and walked round in front of the cyclist towards the Leas.

"Goodness!" cried Gibberne, suddenly, "look there!"

He pointed, and there at the tip of his finger and sliding down the air with wings flapping slowly and at the speed of an exceptionally languid snail—was a bee.

And so we came out upon the Leas. There the thing seemed madder than ever. The band was playing in the upper stand, though all the sound it made for us was a low-pitched, wheezy rattle, a sort of prolonged last sigh that passed at times into a sound like the slow, muffled ticking of some monstrous clock. Frozen people stood erect; strange, silent, self-conscious-looking dummies hung unstably in midstride, promenading upon the grass. I passed close to a poodle dog suspended in the act of leaping, and watched the slow movement of his legs as he sank to earth. "Lord, look *here!*" cried Gibberne, and we halted for a moment before a magnificent person in white faint-striped flannels, white shoes, and a Panama hat, who turned back to wink at two gaily-dressed ladies he had passed. A wink, studied with such deliberation as we could afford, is an unattractive thing. It loses any quality of alert gaiety, and one remarks that the winking eye does not completely close, that under its drooping lid appears the lower edge of an eyeball and a line of white. "Heaven give me memory," said I, "and I will never wink again."

"Or smile," said Gibberne, with his eye on the lady's answering teeth.

"It's infernally hot, somehow," said I. "Let's go slower."

"Oh, come along!" said Gibberne.

We picked our way among the Bath chairs in the path. Many of the people sitting in the chairs seemed almost natural in their passive poses, but the contorted scarlet of the bandsman was not a restful thing to see. A purple-faced gentleman was frozen in the midst of a violent struggle to refold his newspaper against the wind; there were many evidences that all these people in their sluggish way were exposed to a considerable breeze, a breeze that had no existence so far as our sensations went. We came out and walked a little way from the crowd, and turned and regarded it. To see all that multitude changed to a picture, smitten rigid, as it were, into the semblance of realistic wax, was impossibly wonderful. It was absurd, of course; but it filled me with an irrational, an exultant sense of superior advantage. Consider the wonder of it! All that I had said and thought and done since the stuff had begun to work in my veins had happened, so far as those people, so far as the world in general went, in the twinkling of an eye. "The New Accelerator—" I began, but Gibberne interrupted me.

"There's that infernal old woman!" he said.

"What old woman?"

"Lives next door to me," said Gibberne. "Has a lapdog that yaps. Gods! The temptation is strong!"

There is something very boyish and impulsive about Gibberne at times. Before I could expostulate with him he had dashed forward, snatched the unfortunate animal out of visible existence, and was running violently with its towards the cliff of the Leas. It was most extraordinary. The little brute, you know, didn't bark or wriggle or make the slightest sign of vitality. It kept quite stiffly in an attitude of somnolent repose, and Gibberne held it by the neck. It was like running about with a dog of wood. "Gibberne," I cried, "put it down!" Then I said something else. "If you run like that, Gibberne," I cried, "you'll set your clothes on fire. Your linen trousers are going brown as it is!"

He clapped his hand on his thigh and stood hesitating on the verge. "Gibberne," I cried, coming up, "put it down. This heat is too much! It's our running so! Two or three miles a second! Friction of the air!"

"What?" he said, glancing at the dog.

"Friction of the air," I shouted. "Friction of the air. Going too fast. Like meteorites and things. Too hot. And, Gibberne! Gibberne! I'm all over pricking and a sort of perspiration. You can see people stirring slightly. I believe the stuff's working off! Put that dog down."

"Eh?" he said.

"It's working off," I repeated. "We're too hot and the stuff's working off! I'm wet through."

He stared at me. Then at the band, the wheezy rattle of whose performance was certainly going faster. Then with a tremendous sweep of the arm he hurled the dog away from him and it went spinning upward, still inanimate, and hung at last over the grouped parasols of a knot of chattering people. Gibberne was gripping my elbow. "By Jove!" he cried. "I believe it is! A sort of hot pricking and—yes. That man's moving his pocket-handkerchief! Perceptibly. We must get out of this sharp."

But we could not get out of it sharply enough. Luckily, perhaps! For we might have run, and if we had run we should, I believe, have burst into flames. Almost certainly we should have burst into flames! You know we had neither of us thought of that . . . But before we could even begin to run the action of the drug had ceased. It was the business of a minute fraction of a second. The effect of the New Accelerator passed like the drawing of a curtain, vanished in the movement of a hand. I heard Gibberne's voice in infinite alarm. "Sit down," he said, and flop, down upon the turf at the edge of the Leas I sat—scorching as I sat. There is a patch of burnt grass there still where I sat down. The whole stagnation seemed to wake up as I did so, the disarticulated vibration of the band rushed together into a blast of music, the promenaders put their feet down and walked their ways, the papers and flags began flapping, smiles passed into words, the winker finished his wink and went on his way complacently, and all the seated people moved and spoke.

The whole world had come alive again, and was going as fast as we were, or rather we were going no faster than the rest of the world. It was like slowing down as one comes into a railway station. Everything seemed to spin round for a second or two, I had the most transient feeling of nausea, and that was all. And the little dog which had seemed to hang for a moment when the force of Gibberne's arm was expended fell with a swift acceleration clean through a lady's parasol!

That was the saving of us. Unless it was for one corpulent old gentleman in a Bath chair, who certainly did start at the sight of us and afterwards regarded us at intervals with a darkly suspicious eye, and finally, I believe, said something to his nurse about us, I doubt if a solitary person remarked our sudden appearance among them. Plop! We must have appeared abruptly. We ceased to smoulder almost at once, though the turf beneath me was uncomfortably hot. The attention of everyone—including even the Amusements' Association band, which on this occasion, for the only time in its history, got out of tune—was arrested by the amazing fact, and the still more amazing yapping and uproar caused by the fact, that a respectable, over-fed lapdog sleeping quietly to the east of the bandstand should suddenly fall through the parasol of a lady on the west—in a slightly singed condition due to the extreme velocity of its movements through the air. In these absurd days, too, when we are all trying to be as psychic and silly and superstitious as possible! People got up

and trod on other people, chairs were overturned, the Leas
policeman ran. How the matter settled itself, I do not
know—we were much too anxious to disentangle ourselves
from the affair and get out of range of the eye of the old
gentleman in the Bath chair to make minute inquiries. As
soon as we were sufficiently cool and sufficiently recovered
from our giddiness and nausea and confusion of mind to do
so we stood up and, skirting the crowd, directed our steps
back along the road below the Metropole towards Gibberne's
house. But amidst the din I heard very distinctly the gentleman who had been sitting beside the lady of the ruptured
sunshade using quite unjustifiable threats and language to one
of those chair-attendants who have "Inspector" written on
their caps. "If you didn't throw the dog," he said, "who *did?*"

The sudden return of movement and familiar noises, and
our natural anxiety about ourselves (our clothes were still
dreadfully hot, and the fronts of the thighs of Gibberne's
white trousers were scorched a drabbish brown), prevented
the minute observations I should have liked to make on all
these things. Indeed, I really made no observations of any
scientific value on that return. The bee, of course, had gone. I
looked for that cyclist, but he was already out of sight as we
came into the Upper Sandgate Road or hidden from us by
traffic; the charabanc, however, with its people now all alive
and stirring, was clattering along at a spanking pace almost
abreast of the nearer church.

We noted, however, that the window-sill on which we had
stepped in getting out of the house was slightly singed, and
that the impressions of our feet on the gravel of the path
were unusually deep.

So it was I had my first experience of the New Accelerator. Practically we had been running about and saying and
doing all sorts of things in the space of a second or so of time.
We had lived half an hour while the band had played, perhaps, two bars. But the effect it had upon us was that the
whole world had stopped for our convenient inspection. Considering all things, and particularly considering our rashness
in venturing out of the house, the experience might certainly
have been much more disagreeable than it was. It showed, no
doubt, that Gibberne has still much to learn before his
preparation is a manageable convenience, but its practicabil-
ity it certainly demonstrated beyond all cavil.

Since that adventure he has been steadily bringing its use

under control, and I have several times, and without the slightest bad result, taken measured doses under his direction; though I must confess I have not yet ventured abroad again while under its influence. I may mention, for example, that this story has been written at one sitting and without interruption, except for the nibbling of some chocolate, by its means. I began at 6:25, and my watch is now very nearly at the minute past the half-hour. The convenience of securing a long, uninterrupted spell of work in the midst of a day full of engagements cannot be exaggerated. Gibberne is now working at the quantitative handling of his preparation, with especial reference to its distinctive effects upon different types of constitution. He then hopes to find a Retarder with which to dilute its present rather excessive potency. The Retarder will, of course, have the reverse effect to the Accelerator; used alone it should enable the patient to spread a few seconds over many hours of ordinary time, and so to maintain an apathetic inaction, a glacierlike absence of alacrity, amidst the most animated or irritating surroundings. The two things together must necessarily work an entire revolution in civilised existence. It is the beginning of our escape from that Time Garment of which Carlyle speaks. While this Accelerator will enable us to concentrate ourselves with tremendous impact upon any moment or occasion that demands our utmost sense and vigour, the Retarder will enable us to pass in passive tranquillity through infinite hardship and tedium. Perhaps I am a little optimistic about the Retarder, which has indeed still to be discovered, but about the Accelerator there is no possible sort of doubt whatever. Its appearance upon the market in a convenient, controllable, and assimilable form is a matter of the next few months. It will be obtainable of all chemists and druggists, in small green bottles, at a high but, considering its extraordinary qualities, by no means excessive price. Gibberne's Nervous Accelerator it will be called, and he hopes to be able to supply it in three strengths: one in 200, one in 900, and one in 2000, distinguished by yellow, pink, and white labels respectively.

No doubt its use renders a great number of very extraordinary things possible; for, of course, the most remarkable and, possibly, even criminal proceedings may be effected with impunity by thus dodging, as it were, into the interstices of time. Like all potent preparations it will be liable to abuse. We have, however, discussed this aspect of the question very thoroughly, and we have decided that this is purely a matter of medical jurisprudence and altogether outside our province. We shall manufacture and sell the Accelerator, and, as for the consequences—we shall see.

The Literary Dissent

Byron and Shelley delighted in the prospects of the scientific enlightenment, although Mary Shelley's *Frankenstein* depicts a scientist daring too much. Goethe was a distinguished scientist as well as a literary genius. Poe celebrated technological advance. Tennyson foresaw a glorious future for humanity. But somewhere between the Industrial Revolution and World War I a substantial portion of the literary culture rebelled against the general belief in progress, denounced science and technology, and preached a return to old-fashioned virtues and eternal values.

Blake complained about "the dark satanic mills" that were despoiling the English countryside. Carlyle conceded that "in the management of external things we excel all other ages," but in "pure moral nature, in true dignity of soul and character, we are perhaps inferior to most civilised ages." Hawthorne's scientists destroyed whatever they loved. For Emerson "things are in the saddle and ride mankind."

"Literary intellectuals," C. P. Snow said in his 1959 "The Two Cultures" lecture, "are natural Luddites" who "have never tried, wanted, nor been able to understand the industrial revolution, much less accept it . . . Almost everywhere . . . intellectual persons didn't comprehend what was happening. Certainly the writers didn't. Plenty of them shuddered away, as though the right course for a man of feeling was to contract out; some . . . tried various kinds of fancies which were not in effect more than screams of horror."

The Cambridge critic F. R. Leavis responded that the human faculty above all others to which literature addresses itself is the moral consciousness, and maintained that great literature asks deeply important questions about the civilization around it, but "of course, to such questions there can't be, in any ordinary sense of the word, answers." The questions, moreover, will all be of the sort to make society hesitate, slow down, lose confidence in the future, distrust both social planning and technological advance.

The Snow-Leavis debate was virtually identical with a similar disagreement in the 1880s between T. H. Huxley and Matthew Arnold and in the second decade of the twentieth century between Wells and James. The response of the literary culture to Wells's belief in progress, particularly to the utopian vision of his later propaganda novels, was the antiutopia. More recently it has been called the "dystopia" from the Greek word meaning "ill" or "bad." Conditions are getting worse, not better, these works said, and rather than perfection the world may get destruction.

The anti-utopia, however, was not simply the literary reaction to the Wellsian vision of a beneficent future filled with machines and ruled over by scientists and engineers, even though Wells and his efforts to organize "an open conspiracy" to create a better world were the obvious targets of the opposition. George Orwell, whose *Nineteen Eighty-Four* (1949) was characterized by Snow as "the strongest possible wish that the future should not exist," wrote of Wells:

> Thinking people who were born about the beginning of this century are in some sense Wells's own creation. How much influence any mere writer has, and especially a "popular" writer whose work takes effect quickly, is questionable, but I doubt whether anyone who was writing books between 1900 and 1920, at any rate in the English language, influenced the young so much.

But two world wars and a depression also contributed their share of disillusionment to the literary atmosphere that produced Aldous Huxley's *Brave New World* (1932), Zamyatin's *We* (1924), C. S. Lewis's *Perelandra* trilogy (1938, 1943, and 1945), Gore Vidal's *Messiah* (1953), Evelyn Waugh's *Love Among the Ruins* (1953), Anthony Burgess's *A Clockwork Orange* (1962), and many others.

Anti-utopian visions sprang out of the science-fiction magazines themselves and the heads of such writers as Stanley Coblentz, David H. Keller, and S. Fowler Wright, and sometimes even of such basically optimistic writers as Jack Williamson. Frederik Pohl and Cyril Kornbluth brought the anti-utopia firmly into the mainstream of science fiction with their novel *The Space Merchants*, serialized in Galaxy in 1952 under the title of *Gravy Planet*.

The earliest and best-known of the anti-Wellsian dystopias,

however, was E. M. Forster's "The Machine Stops." Often
dated from its publication in his *The Eternal Moment*
(1928), it was first published in 1909 (Michaelmas Term,
Oxford and Cambridge Review).

Forster (1879–1970) was a novelist, essayist, and critic,
whose works and opinions commanded respect for several
decades. His best-known novels, particularly *A Passage to In-
dia* (1924), dealt with the problem of understanding between
cultures, but he also wrote fantasy such as that published in
The Eternal Moment and the much-anthologized "The Celestial Omnibus" published in the 1923 volume with the same
title.

In "The Machine Stops" Forster pushes the Wellsian future
city, as satire does, to the point where citizens are so dependent upon machines that life without them is not only barbaric
but impossible.

The Machine Stops

by E. M. Forster

Part I

THE AIR-SHIP

Imagine, if you can, a small room, hexagonal in shape, like
the cell of a bee. It is lighted neither by window nor by lamp,
yet it is filled with a soft radiance. There are no apertures for
ventilation, yet the air is fresh. There are no musical instruments, and yet, at the moment that my meditation opens, this
room is throbbing with melodious sounds. An arm-chair is in
the centre, by its side a reading-desk—that is all the furniture. And in the arm-chair there sits a swaddled lump of

flesh—a woman, about five feet high, with a face as white as a fungus. It is to her that the little room belongs.

An electric bell rang.

The woman touched a switch and the music was silent.

"I suppose I must see who it is," she thought, and set her chair in motion. The chair, like the music, was worked by machinery, and it rolled her to the other side of the room, where the bell still rang importunately.

"Who is it?" she called. Her voice was irritable, for she had been interrupted often since the music began. She knew several thousand people; in certain directions human intercourse had advanced enormously.

But when she listened into the receiver, her white face wrinkled into smiles, and she said:

"Very well, Let us talk, I will isolate myself. I do not expect anything important will happen for the next five minutes—for I can give you fully five minutes, Kuno. Then I must deliver my lecture on 'Music during the Australian Period.' "

She touched the isolation knob, so that no one else could speak to her. Then she touched the lighting apparatus, and the little room was plunged into darkness.

"Be quick!" she called, her irritation returning. "Be quick, Kuno; here I am in the dark wasting my time."

But it was fully fifteen seconds before the round plate that she held in her hands began to glow. A faint blue light shot across it, darkening to purple, and presently she could see the image of her son, who lived on the other side of the earth, and he could see her.

"Kuno, how slow you are."

He smiled gravely.

"I really believe you enjoy dawdling."

"I have called you before, Mother, but you were always busy or isolated. I have something particular to say."

"What is it, dearest boy? Be quick. Why could you not send it by pneumatic post?"

"Because I prefer saying such a thing. I want——"

"Well?"

"I want you to come and see me."

Vashti watched his face in the blue plate.

"But I can see you!" she exclaimed. "What more do you want?"

"I want to see you not through the Machine," said Kuno.

"I want to speak to you not through the wearisome Machine."

"Oh, hush!" said his mother, vaguely shocked. "You mustn't say anything against the Machine."

"Why not?"

"One mustn't."

"You talk as if a god had made the Machine," cried the other. "I believe that you pray to it when you are unhappy. Men made it, do not forget that. Great men, but men. The Machine is much, but it is not everything. I see something like you in this plate, but I do not see you. I hear something like you through this telephone, but I do not hear you. That is why I want you to come. Come and stop with me. Pay me a visit, so that we can meet face to face, and talk about the hopes that are in my mind."

She replied that she could scarcely spare the time for a visit.

"The air-ship barely takes two days to fly between me and you."

"I dislike air-ships."

"Why?"

"I dislike seeing the horrible brown earth, and the sea, and the stars when it is dark. I get no ideas in an air-ship."

"I do not get them anywhere else."

"What kind of ideas can the air give you?"

He paused for an instant.

"Do you not know four big stars that form an oblong, and three stars close together in the middle of the oblong, and hanging from these stars, three other stars?"

"No, I do not. I dislike the stars. But did they give you an idea? How interesting; tell me."

"I had an idea that they were like a man."

"I do not understand."

"The four big stars are the man's shoulders and his knees. The three stars in the middle are like the belts that men wore once, and the three stars hanging are like a sword."

"A sword?"

"Men carried swords about them, to kill animals and other men."

"It does not strike me as a very good idea, but it is certainly original. When did it come to you first?"

"In the air-ship——" He broke off, and she fancied that he looked sad. She could not be sure, for the Machine did not transmit *nuances* of expression. It only gave a general idea of people—an idea that was good enough for all practical purposes, Vashti thought. The imponderable bloom, declared by a discredited philosophy to be the actual essence of intercourse, was rightly ignored by the Machine, just as the imponderable bloom of the grape was ignored by the manufacturers of artificial fruit. Something "good enough" had long since been accepted by our race.

"The truth is," he continued, "that I want to see these stars again. They are curious stars. I want to see them not from the air-ship, but from the surface of the earth, as our ancestors did, thousands of years ago. I want to visit the surface of the earth."

She was shocked again.

"Mother, you must come, if only to explain to me what is the harm of visiting the surface of the earth."

"No harm," she replied, controlling herself. "But no advantage. The surface of the earth is only dust and mud, no life remains on it, and you would need a respirator, or the cold of the outer air would kill you. One dies immediately in the outer air."

"I know; of course I shall take all precautions."

"And besides——"

"Well?"

She considered, and chose her words with care. Her son had a queer temper, and she wished to dissuade him from the expedition.

"It is contrary to the spirit of the age," she asserted.

"Do you mean by that, contrary to the Machine?"

"In a sense, but——"

His image in the blue plate faded.

"Kuno!"

He had isolated himself.

For a moment Vashti felt lonely.

Then she generated the light, and the sight of her room, flooded with radiance and studded with electric buttons, revived her. There were buttons and switches everywhere—buttons to call for food, for music, for clothing. There was the hot-bath button, by pressure of which a basin of (imitation) marble rose out of the floor, filled to the brim with a warm deodorised liquid. There was the cold-bath button. There was the button that produced literature. And there were of course the buttons by which she communicated with her friends. The room, though it contained nothing, was in touch with all that she cared for in the world.

Vashti's next move was to turn off the isolation-switch, and all the accumulations of the last three minutes burst upon her. The room was filled with the noise of bells, and speaking-tubes. What was the new food like? Could she recommend it? Had she had any ideas lately? Might one tell her one's own ideas? Would she make an engagement to visit the public nurseries at an early date?—say this day month.

To most of these questions she replied with irritation—a growing quality in that accelerated age. She said that the new food was horrible. That she could not visit the public nurseries through press of engagements. That she had no ideas of her own but had just been told one—that four stars and three in the middle were like a man: she doubted there was much in it. Then she switched off her correspondents, for it was time to deliver her lecture on Australian music.

The clumsy system of public gatherings had been long since abandoned; neither Vashti nor her audience stirred from their rooms. Seated in her arm-chair she spoke, while they in their arm-chairs heard her, fairly well, and saw her, fairly well. She opened with a humorous account of music in the pre-Mongolian epoch, and went on to describe the great outburst of song that followed the Chinese conquest. Remote and primeval as were the methods of I-San-So and the Brisbane school, she yet felt (she said) that study of them might repay the musician of today: they had freshness; they had, above all, ideas.

Her lecture, which lasted ten minutes, was well received, and at its conclusion she and many of her audience listened to a lecture on the sea; there were ideas to be got from the sea; the speaker had donned a respirator and visited it lately. Then she fed, talked to many friends, had a bath, talked again, and summoned her bed.

The bed was not to her liking. It was too large, and she had a feeling for a small bed. Complaint was useless, for beds were of the same dimension all over the world, and to have had an alternative size would have involved vast alterations in the Machine. Vashti isolated herself—it was necessary, for neither day nor night existed under the ground—and reviewed all that had happened since she had summoned the bed last. Ideas? Scarcely any. Events—was Kuno's invitation an event?

By her side, on the little reading-desk, was a survival from the ages of litter—one book. This was the Book of the Machine. In it were instructions against every possible contingency. If she was hot or cold or dyspeptic or at loss for a word, she went to the book, and it told her which button to press. The Central Committee published it. In accordance with a growing habit, it was richly bound.

Sitting up in the bed, she took it reverently in her hands. She glanced round the glowing room as if someone might be watching her. Then, half ashamed, half joyful, she murmured "O Machine! O Machine!" and raised the volume to her lips. Thrice she kissed it, thrice inclined her head, thrice she felt the delirium of acquiescence. Her ritual performed, she turned to page 1367, which gave the times of the departure of the air-ships from the island in the southern hemisphere, under whose soil she lived, to the island in the northern hemisphere, whereunder lived her son.

She thought, "I have not the time."

She made the room dark and slept; she awoke and made the room light; she ate and exchanged ideas with her friends, and listened to music and attended lectures; she made the room dark and slept. Above her, beneath her, and around her, the Machine hummed eternally; she did not notice the noise, for she had been born with it in her ears. The earth, carrying her, hummed as it sped through silence, turning her now to the invisible sun, now to the invisible stars. She awoke and made the room light.

"Kuno!"

"I will not talk to you," he answered, "until you come."

"Have you been on the surface of the earth since we spoke last?"

His image faded.

Again she consulted the book. She became very nervous and lay back in her chair palpitating. Think of her as without teeth or hair. Presently she directed the chair to the wall, and pressed an unfamiliar button. The wall swung apart slowly. Through the opening she saw a tunnel that curved slightly, so that its goal was not visible. Should she go to see her son, here was the beginning of the journey.

Of course she knew all about the communication-system. There was nothing mysterious in it. She would summon a car and it would fly with her down the tunnel until it reached the lift that communicated with the air-ship station: the system had been in use for many, many years, long before the universal establishment of the Machine. And of course she had studied the civilisation that had immediately preceded her own—the civilisation that had mistaken the functions of the system, and had used it for bringing people to things, instead of for bringing things to people. Those funny old days, when men went for change of air instead of changing the air in their rooms! And yet—she was frightened of the tunnel: she had not seen it since her last child was born. It curved—but not quite as she remembered; it was brilliant—but not quite as brilliant as a lecturer had suggested. Vashti was seized with the terrors of direct experience. She shrank back into the room, and the wall closed up again.

"Kuno," she said, "I cannot come to see you. I am not well."

Immediately an enormous apparatus fell on to her out of the ceiling, a thermometer was automatically inserted between her lips, a stethoscope was automatically laid upon her heart. She lay powerless. Cool pads soothed her forehead. Kuno had telegraphed to her doctor.

So the human passions still blundered up and down in the Machine. Vashti drank the medicine that the doctor projected into her mouth, and the machinery retired into the ceiling. The voice of Kuno was heard asking how she felt.

"Better." Then with irritation: "But why do you not come to me instead?"

"Because I cannot leave this place."

"Why?"

"Because, any moment, something tremendous may happen."

"Have you been on the surface of the earth yet?"

"Not yet."

"Then what is it?"

"I will not tell you through the Machine."

She resumed her life.

But she thought of Kuno as a baby, his birth, his removal to the public nurseries, her one visit to him there, his visits to her—visits which stopped when the Machine had assigned him a room on the other side of the earth. "Parents, duties of," said the book of the Machine, "cease at the moment of birth. P. 422327483." True, but there was something special about Kuno—indeed there had been something special about all her children—and, after all, she must brave the journey if he desired it. And "something tremendous might happen." What did that mean? The nonsense of a youthful man, no doubt, but she must go. Again she pressed the unfamiliar button, again the wall swung back, and she saw the tunnel that curved out of sight. Clasping the Book, she rose, tottered on to the platform, and summoned the car. Her room closed behind her: the journey to the northern hemisphere had begun.

Of course it was perfectly easy. The car approached and in it she found arm-chairs exactly like her own. When she signalled, it stopped, and she tottered into the lift. One other passenger was in the lift, the first fellow creature she had seen face to face for months. Few travelled in these days, for, thanks to the advance of science, the earth was exactly alike all over. Rapid intercourse, from which the previous civilisation had hoped so much, had ended by defeating itself. What was the good of going to Pekin when it was just like Shrewsbury? Why return to Shrewsbury when it would be just like Pekin? Men seldom moved their bodies; all unrest was concentrated in the soul.

The air-ship service was a relic from the former age. It was kept up, because it was easier to keep it up than to stop it or to diminish it, but it now far exceeded the wants of the population. Vessel after vessel would rise from the vomitories of Rye or of Christchurch (I use the antique names), would sail into the crowded sky, and would draw up at the wharves of the south—empty. So nicely adjusted was the system, so independent of meteorology, that the sky, weather calm or cloudy, resembled a vast kaleidoscope whereon the same patterns periodically recurred. The ship on which Vashti sailed started now at sunset, now at dawn. But always, as it passed above Rheims, it would neighbour the ship that served between Helsingfors and the Brazils, and, every third time it surmounted the Alps, the fleet of Palermo would cross its track behind. Night and day, wind and storm, tide and earthquake, impeded man no longer. He had harnessed Leviathan. All the old literature, with its praise of Nature, and its fear of Nature, rang false as the prattle of a child.

Yet as Vashti saw the vast flank of the ship, stained with exposure to the outer air, her horror of direct experience returned. It was not quite like the air-ship in the cinematophote. For one thing it smelt—not strongly or unpleasantly, but it did smell, and with her eyes shut she should have known that a new thing was close to her. Then she had to walk to it from the lift, had to submit to glances from the other passengers. The man in front dropped his Book—no great matter, but it disquieted them all. In the rooms, if the Book was dropped, the floor raised it mechanically, but the gangway to the air-ship was not so prepared, and the sacred volume lay motionless. They stopped—the thing was unforeseen—and the man, instead of picking up his property, felt the muscles of his arm to see how they had failed him. Then someone actually said with direct utterance: "We shall be late"—and they trooped on board, Vashti treading on the pages as she did so.

Inside, her anxiety increased. The arrangements were old-fashioned and rough. There was even a female attendant, to whom she would have to announce her wants during the voyage. Of course a revolving platform ran the length of the boat, but she was expected to walk from it to her cabin. Some cabins were better than others, and she did not get the best. She thought the attendant had been unfair, and spasms of rage shook her. The glass valves had closed, she could not go back. She saw, at the end of the vestibule, the lift in which she had ascended going quietly up and down, empty. Beneath those corridors of shining tiles were rooms, tier below tier, reaching far into the earth, and in each room there sat a human being, eating, or sleeping, or producing ideas. And buried deep in the hive was her own room. Vashti was afraid.

"O Machine! O Machine!" she murmured, and caressed her Book, and was comforted.

Then the sides of the vestibule seemed to melt together, as do the passages that we see in dreams, the lift vanished, the Book that had been dropped slid to the left and vanished, polished tiles rushing by like a stream of water, there was a slight jar, and the air-ship, issuing from its tunnel, soared above the waters of a tropical ocean.

It was night. For a moment she saw the coast of Sumatra edged by the phosphorescence of waves, and crowned by lighthouses, still sending forth their disregarded beams. These also vanished, and only the stars distracted her. They were not motionless, but swayed to and fro above her head, thronging out of one skylight into another, as if the universe and not the air-ship was careening. And, as often happens on clear nights, they seemed now to be in perspective, now on a plane; now piled tier beyond tier into the infinite heavens, now concealing infinity, a roof limiting for ever the visions of men. In either case they seemed intolerable. "Are we to travel in the dark?" called the passengers angrily, and the attendant, who had been careless, generated the light, and pulled down the blinds of pliable metal. When the air-ships had been built, the desire to look direct at things still lingered in the world. Hence the extraordinary number of skylights and windows, and the proportionate discomfort to those who were civilised and refined. Even in Vashti's cabin one star peeped through a flaw in the blind, and after a few hours' uneasy slumber, she was disturbed by an unfamiliar glow, which was the dawn.

Quick as the ship had sped westwards, the earth had rolled eastwards quicker still, and had dragged back Vashti and her companions towards the sun. Science could prolong the night, but only for a little, and those high hopes of neutralising the earth's diurnal revolution had passed, together with hopes that were possibly higher. To "keep pace with the sun," or even to outstrip it, had been built for the purpose, capable of enormous speed, and steered by the greatest intellects of the epoch. Round the globe they went, round and round, westward, westward, round and round, amidst humanity's applause. In vain. The globe went eastward quicker still, horrible accidents occurred, and the Committee of the Machine, at the time rising into prominence, declared the pursuit illegal, unmechanical, and punishable by Homelessness.

Of Homelessness more will be said later.

Doubtless the Committee was right. Yet the attempt to "defeat the sun" aroused the last common interest that our race experienced about the heavenly bodies, or indeed about anything. It was the last time that men were compacted by thinking of a power outside the world. The sun had conquered, yet it was the end of his spiritual dominion. Dawn, midday, twilight, the zodiacal path, touched neither men's lives nor their hearts, and science retreated into the ground, to concentrate herself upon problems that she was certain of solving.

So when Vashti found her cabin invaded by a rosy finger of light, she was annoyed, and tried to adjust the blind. But the blind flew up altogether, and she saw through the skylight small pink clouds, swaying against a background of blue, and as the sun crept higher, its radiance entered direct, brimming down the wall, like a golden sea. It rose and fell with the air-ship's motion, just as waves rise and fall, but it advanced steadily, as a tide advances. Unless she was careful, it would strike her face. A spasm of horror shook her and she rang for the attendant. The attendant too was horrified, but she could do nothing; it was not her place to mend the blind. She could only suggest that the lady should change her cabin, which she accordingly prepared to do.

People were almost exactly alike all over the world, but the attendant of the air-ship, perhaps owing to her exceptional duties, had grown a little out of the common. She had often to address passengers with direct speech, and this had given her a certain roughness and originality of manner. When Vashti swerved away from the sunbeams with a cry, she behaved barbarically—she put out her hand to steady her.

"How dare you!" exclaimed the passenger. "You forget yourself!"

The woman was confused, and apologised for not having let her fall. People never touched one another. The custom had become obsolete, owing to the Machine.

"Where are we now?" asked Vashti haughtily.

"We are over Asia," said the attendant, anxious to be polite.

"Asia?"

"You must excuse my common way of speaking. I have got into the habit of calling places over which I pass by their unmechanical names."

"Oh, I remember Asia. The Mongols came from it."

"Beneath us, in the open air, stood a city that was once called Simla."

"Have you ever heard of the Mongols and of the Brisbane school?"

"No."

"Brisbane also stood in the open air."

"Those mountains to the right—let me show you them." She pushed back a metal blind. The main chain of the Himalayas was revealed. "They were once called the Roof of the World, those mountains."

"What a foolish name!"

"You must remember that, before the dawn of civilisation, they seemed to be an impenetrable wall that touched the stars. It was supposed that no one but the gods could exit above their summits. How we have advanced, thanks to the Machine!"

"How we have advanced, thanks to the Machine!" said Vashti.

"How we have advanced, thanks to the Machine!" echoed the passenger who had dropped his Book the night before, and who was standing in the passage.

"And that white stuff in the cracks?—what is it?"

"I have forgotten its name."

"Cover the window, please. These mountains give me no ideas."

The northern aspect of the Himalayas was in deep shadow:

on the Indian slope the sun had just prevailed. The forests had been destroyed during the literature epoch for the purpose of making newspaper-pulp, but the snows were awakening to their morning glory, and clouds still hung on the breasts of Kinchinjunga. In the plain were seen the ruins of cities, with diminished rivers creeping by their walls, and by the sides of these were sometimes the signs of vomitories, marking the cities of today. Over the whole prospect air-ships rushed, crossing and intercrossing with incredible *aplomb*, and rising nonchalantly when they desired to escape the perturbations of the lower atmosphere and to traverse the Roof of the World.

"We have indeed advanced, thanks to the Machine," repeated the attendant, and hid the Himalayas behind a metal blind.

The day dragged wearily forward. The passengers sat each in his cabin, avoiding one another with an almost physical repulsion and longing to be once more under the surface of the earth. There were eight or ten of them, mostly young males, sent out from the public nurseries to inhabit the rooms of those who had died in various parts of the earth. The man who had dropped his Book was on the homeward journey. He had been sent to Sumatra for the purpose of propagating the race. Vashti alone was travelling by her private will.

At midday she took a second glance at the earth. The airship was crossing another range of mountains, but she could see little, owing to clouds. Masses of black rock hovered below her, and merged indistinctly into grey. Their shapes were fantastic; one of them resembled a prostrate man.

"No ideas here," murmured Vashti, and hid the Caucasus behind a metal blind.

In the evening she looked again. They were crossing a golden sea, in which lay many small islands and one peninsula.

She repeated, "No ideas here," and hid Greece behind a metal blind.

Part II

THE MENDING APPARATUS

By a vestibule, by a lift, by a tubular railway, by a platform, by a sliding door—by reversing all the steps of her departure did Vashti arrive at her son's room, which exactly resembled her own. She might well declare that the visit was superfluous. The buttons, the knobs, the reading-desk with the Book, the temperature, the atmosphere, the illumination—all were exactly the same. And if Kuno himself, flesh of her flesh, stood close beside her at last, what profit was there in that? She was too well-bred to shake him by the hand.

Averting her eyes, she spoke as follows:

"Here I am. I have had the most terrible journey and greatly retarded the development of my soul. It is not worth it, Kuno, it is not worth it. My time is too precious. The sunlight almost touched me, and I have met with the rudest people. I can only stop a few minutes. Say what you want to say, and then I must return."

"I have been threatened with Homelessness," said Kuno.

She looked at him now.

"I have been threatened with Homelessness, and I could not tell you such a thing through the Machine."

Homelessness means death. The victim is exposed to the air, which kills him.

"I have been outside since I spoke to you last. The tremendous thing has happened, and they have discovered me."

"But why shouldn't you go outside!" she exclaimed. "It is perfectly legal, perfectly mechanical, to visit the surface of the earth. I have lately been to a lecture on the sea; there is no objection to that; one simply summons a respirator and gets an Egression-permit. It is not the kind of thing that spiritually-minded people do, and I begged you not to do it, but there is no legal objection to it."

"I did not get an Egression-permit."

"Then how did you get out?"

"I found out a way of my own."

The phrase conveyed no meaning to her, and he had to repeat it.

"A way of your own?" she whispered. "But that would be wrong."

"Why?"

The question shocked her beyond measure.

"You are beginning to worship the Machine," he said coldly. "You think it irreligious of me to have found a way of my own. It was just what the Committee thought, when they threatened me with Homelessness."

At this she grew angry. "I worship nothing!" she cried. "I am most advanced. I don't think you irreligious, for there is no such thing as religion left. All the fear and the superstition that existed once have been destroyed by the Machine. I only meant that to find out a way of your own was— Besides, there is no new way out."

"So it is always supposed."

"Except through the vomitories, for which one must have an Egression-permit, it is impossible to get out. The Book says so."

"Well, the Book's wrong, for I have been out on my feet."

For Kuno was possessed of a certain physical strength.

By these days it was a demerit to be muscular. Each infant was examined at birth, and all who promised undue strength were destroyed. Humanitarians may protest, but it would have been no true kindness to let an athlete live; he would never have been happy in that state of life to which the Machine had called him; he would have yearned for trees to climb, rivers to bathe in, meadows and hills against which he might measure his body. Man must be adapted to his surroundings, must he not? In the dawn of the world our weakly must be exposed on Mount Taygetus, in its twilight our strong will suffer euthanasia, that the Machine may progress, that the Machine may progress, that the Machine may progress eternally.

"You know that we have lost the sense of space. We say 'space is annihilated,' but we have annihilated not space, but the sense thereof. We have lost a part of ourselves. I determined to recover it, and I began by walking up and down the platform of the railway outside my room. Up and down, until I was tired, and so did recapture the meaning of 'Near' and 'Far.' 'Near' is a place to which I can get quickly *on my feet,* not a place to which the train or the air-ship will take me quickly. 'Far' is a place to which I cannot get quickly on my

feet; the vomitory is 'far,' though I could be there in thirty-
eight seconds by summoning the train. Man is the measure.
That was my first lesson. Man's feet are the measure for distance, his hands are the measure for ownership, his body is
the measure for all that is lovable and desirable and strong.
Then I went further: it was then that I called to you for the
first time, and you would not come.

"This city, as you know, is built deep beneath the surface
of the earth, with only the vomitories protruding. Having
paced the platform outside my own room, I took the lift to
the next platform and paced that also, and so with each in
turn, until I came to the topmost, above which begins the
earth. All the platforms were exactly alike, and all that I
gained by visiting them was to develop my sense of space and
my muscles. I think I should have been content with this—it
is not a little thing—but as I walked and brooded, it occurred
to me that our cities had been built in the days when men
still breathed the outer air, and that there had been ventilation shafts for the workmen. I could think of nothing but
these ventilation shafts. Had they been destroyed by all the
food-tubes and medicine-tubes and music-tubes that the
Machine has evolved lately? Or did traces of them remain?
One thing was certain. If I came upon them anywhere, it
would be in the railway-tunnels of the topmost story. Everywhere else, all space was accounted for.

"I am telling my story quickly, but don't think that I was
not a coward or that your answers never depressed me. It is
not the proper thing, it is not mechanical, it is not decent to
walk along a railway-tunnel. I did not fear that I might tread
upon a live rail and be killed. I feared something far more in-
tangible—doing what was not contemplated by the Machine.
Then I said to myself, 'Man is the measure,' and I went, and
after many visits I found an opening.

"The tunnels, of course, were lighted. Everything is light,
artificial light; darkness is the exception. So when I saw a
black gap in the tiles, I knew that it was an exception, and
rejoiced. I put in my arm—I could put in no more at first—
and waved it round and round in ecstasy. I loosened another
tile, and put in my head, and shouted into the darkness: 'I
am coming, I shall do it yet,' and my voice reverberated
down endless passages. I seemed to hear the spirits of those
dead workmen who had returned each evening to the starlight and to their wives, and all the generations who had lived

in the open air called back to me, 'You will do it yet, you are coming.'"

He paused, and, absurd as he was, his last words moved her. For Kuno had lately asked to be a father, and his request had been refused by the Committee. His was not a type that the Machine desired to hand on.

"Then a train passed. It brushed by me, but I thrust my head and arms into the hole. I had done enough for one day, so I crawled back to the platform, went down in the lift, and summoned my bed. Ah, what dreams! And again I called you, and again you refused."

She shook her head and said:

"Don't. Don't talk of these terrible things. You make me miserable. You are throwing civilisation away."

"But I had got back the sense of space and a man cannot rest then. I determined to get in at the hole and climb the shaft. And so I exercised my arms. Day after day I went through ridiculous movements, until my flesh ached, and I could hang by my hands and hold the pillow on my bed outstretched for many minutes. Then I summoned a respirator, and started.

"It was easy at first. The mortar had somehow rotted, and I soon pushed some more tiles in, and clambered after them into the darkness, and the spirits of the dead comforted me. I don't know what I mean by that. I just say what I felt. I felt, for the first time, that a protest had been lodged against corruption, and that even as the dead were comforting me, so I was comforting the unborn. I felt that humanity existed, and that it existed without clothes. How can I possibly explain this? It was naked, humanity seemed naked, and all these tubes and buttons and machineries neither came into the world with us, nor will they follow us out, nor do they matter supremely while we are here. Had I been strong, I would have torn off every garment I had, and gone out into the outer air unswaddled. But this is not for me, nor perhaps for my generation. I climbed with my respirator and my hygienic clothes and my dietetic tabloids! Better thus than not at all.

"There was a ladder, made of some primaeval metal. The light from the railway fell upon its lowest rungs, and I saw that it led straight upwards out of the rubble at the bottom of the shaft. Perhaps our ancestors ran up and down it a dozen times daily, in their building. As I climbed, the rough edges cut through my gloves so that my hands bled. The light helped me for a little, and then came darkness and, worse still, silence which pierced my ears like a sword. The Machine hums! Did you know that? Its hum penetrates our blood, and may even guide our thoughts. Who knows! I was getting beyond its power. Then I thought: 'This silence means that I am doing wrong.' But I heard voices in the silence, and again they strengthened me." He laughed. "I had need of them. The next moment I cracked my head against something."

She sighed.

"I had reached one of those pneumatic stoppers that defend us from the outer air. You may have noticed them on the air-ship. Pitch dark, my feet on the rungs of an invisible ladder, my hands cut; I cannot explain how I lived through this part, but the voices still comforted me, and I felt for fastenings. The stopper, I suppose, was about eight feet across. I passed my hand over it as far as I could reach. It was perfectly smooth. I felt it almost to the center. Not quite to the centre, for my arm was too short. Then the voice said: 'Jump. It is worth it. There may be a handle in the centre, and you may catch hold of it and so come to us your own way. And if there is no handle, so that you may fall and are dashed to pieces—it is still worth it: you will still come to us your own way.' So I jumped. There was a handle, and——"

He paused. Tears gathered in his mother's eyes. She knew that he was fated. If he did not die today he would die tomorrow. There was not room for such a person in the world. And with her pity disgust mingled. She was ashamed at having borne such a son, she who had always been so respectable and so full of ideas. Was he really the little boy to whom she had taught the use of his stops and buttons, and to whom she had given his first lessons in the Book? The very hair that disfigured his lip showed that he was reverting to some savage type. On atavism the Machine can have no mercy.

"There was a handle, and I did catch it. I hung tranced over the darkness and heard the hum of these workings as the last whisper in a dying dream. All the things I had cared about and all the people I had spoken to through tubes appeared infinitely little. Meanwhile the handle revolved. My weight had set something in motion and I spun slowly, and then——

"I cannot describe it. I was lying with my face to the sunshine. Blood poured from my nose and ears and I heard a tremendous roaring. The stopper, with me clinging to it, had simply been blown out of the earth, and the air that we make down here was escaping through the vent into the air above. It burst up like a fountain. I crawled back to it—for the upper air hurts—and, as it were, I took great sips from the edge. My respirator had flown goodness knows where, my clothes were torn. I just lay with my lips close to the hole, and I sipped until the bleeding stopped. You can imagine nothing so curious. This hollow in the grass—I will speak of it in a minute,—the sun shining into it, not brilliantly but through marbled clouds,—the peace, the nonchalance, the sense of space, and, brushing my cheek, the roaring fountain of our artificial air! Soon I spied my respirator, bobbing up and down in the current high above my head, and higher still were many air-ships. But no one ever looks out of air-ships, and in my case they could not have picked me up. There I was, stranded. The sun shone a little way down the shaft, and revealed the topmost rung of the ladder, but it was hopeless trying to reach it. I should either have been tossed up again by the escape, or else have fallen in, and died. I could only lie on the grass, sipping and sipping, and from time to time glancing around me.

"I knew that I was in Wessex, for I had taken care to go to a lecture on the subject before starting. Wessex lies above the room in which we are talking now. It was once an important state. Its kings held all the southern coast from the Andredswald to Cornwall, while the Wansdyke protected them on the north, running over the high ground. The lecturer was only concerned with the rise of Wessex, so I do not know how long it remained an international power, nor would the knowledge have assisted me. To tell the truth I could do nothing but laugh, during this part. There was I, with a pneumatic stopper by my side and a respirator bobbing over my head, imprisoned, all three of us, in a grass-grown hollow that was edged with fern."

Then he grew grave again.

"Lucky for me that it was a hollow. For the air began to fall back into it and to fill it as water fills a bowl. I could crawl about. Presently I stood. I breathed a mixture, in which the air that hurts predominated whenever I tried to climb the sides. This was not so bad. I had not lost my tabloids and remained ridiculously cheerful, and as for the Machine, I forgot about it altogether. My one aim now was to get to the top, where the ferns were, and to view whatever objects lay beyond.

"I rushed the slope. The new air was still too bitter for me and I came rolling back, after a momentary vision of something grey. The sun grew very feeble, and I remembered that he was in Scorpio—I had been to a lecture on that too. If the sun is in Scorpio and you are in Wessex, it means that you must be as quick as you can, or it will get too dark. (This is the first bit of useful information I have ever got from a lecture, and I expect it will be the last.) It made me try frantically to breath the new air, and to advance as far as I dared out of my pond. The hollow filled so slowly. At times I thought that the fountain played with less vigour. My respirator seemed to dance nearer the earth; the roar was decreasing."

He broke off.

"I don't think this is interesting you. The rest will interest you even less. There are no ideas in it, and I wish that I had not troubled you to come. We are too different, mother."

She told him to continue.

"It was evening before I climbed the bank. The sun had very nearly slipped out of the sky by this time, and I could not get a good view. You, who have just crossed the Roof of the World, will not want to hear an account of the little hills that I saw—low colourless hills. But to me they were living and the turf that covered them was a skin, under which their muscles rippled, and I felt that those hills had called with incalculable force to men in the past, and that men had loved them. Now they sleep—perhaps for ever. They commune with humanity in dreams. Happy the man, happy the woman, who awakes the hills of Wessex. For though they sleep, they will never die."

His voice rose passionately.

"Cannot you see, cannot all your lecturers see, that it is we who are dying, and that down here the only thing that really lives is the Machine? We created the Machine, to do our will, but we cannot make it do our will now. It has robbed us of the sense of space and of the sense of touch, it has blurred every human relation and narrowed down love to a carnal act, it has paralysed our bodies and our wills, and now it compels us to worship it. The Machine develops—but not on our lines. The Machine proceeds—but not to our goal. We only exist as the blood corpuscles that course through its arteries, and if it could work without us, it would let us die. Oh, I have no remedy—or, at least, only one—to tell men again and again that I have seen the hills of Wessex as Ælfrid saw them when he overthrew the Danes.

"So the sun set. I forgot to mention that a belt of mist lay between my hill and other hills, and that it was the colour of pearl."

He broke off for the second time.

"Go on," said his mother wearily.

He shook his head.

"Go on. Nothing that you say can distress me now. I am hardened."

"I had meant to tell you the rest, but I cannot: I know that I cannot: good-bye."

Vashti stood irresolute. All her nerves were tingling with his blasphemies. But she was also inquisitive.

"This is unfair," she complained. "You have called me across the world to hear your story, and hear it I will. Tell me—as briefly as possible, for this is a disastrous waste of time—tell me how you returned to civilisation."

"Oh—that!" he said, starting. "You would like to hear about civilisation. Certainly. Had I got to where my respirator fell down?"

"No—but I understand everything now. You put on your respirator, and managed to walk along the surface of the earth to a vomitory, and there your conduct was reported to the Central Committee."

"By no means."

He passed his hand over his forehead, as if dispelling some strong impression. Then, resuming his narrative, he warmed to it again.

"My respirator fell about sunset. I had mentioned that the fountain seemed feebler, had I not."

"Yes."

"About sunset, it let the respirator fall. As I said, I had entirely forgotten about the Machine, and I paid no great attention at the time, being occupied with other things. I had my pool of air, into which I could dip when the outer keenness became intolerable, and which would possibly remain for days, provided that no wind sprang up to disperse it. Not until it was too late, did I realize what the stoppage of the escape implied. You see—the gap in the tunnel had been mended; the Mending Apparatus, the Mending Apparatus, was after me.

"One other warning I had, but I neglected it. The sky at night was clearer than it had been in the day, and the moon, which was about half the sky behind the sun, shone into the dell at moments quite brightly. I was in my usual place—on the boundary between the two atmospheres—when I thought I saw something dark move across the bottom of the dell, and vanish into the shaft. In my folly, I ran down. I bent over and listened, and I thought I heard a faint scraping noise in the depths.

"At this—but it was too late—I took alarm. I determined to put on my respirator and to walk right out of the dell. But my respirator had gone. I knew exactly where it had fallen— between the stopper and the aperture—and I could even feel the mark that it had made in the turf. It had gone, and I re- alised that something evil was at work, and I had better es- cape to the other air, and, if I must die, die running towards the cloud that had been the colour of the pearl. I never started. Out of the shaft—it is too horrible. A worm, a long white worm, had crawled out of the shaft and was gliding over the moonlit grass.

"I screamed. I did everything that I should not have done, I stamped upon the creature instead of flying from it, and it at once curled round the ankle. Then we fought. The worm let me run all over the dell, but edged up my leg as I ran. 'Help!' I cried. (That part is too awful. It belongs to the part that you will never know.) 'Help!' I cried. (Why cannot we suffer in silence?) 'Help!' I cried. Then my feet were wound together, I fell, I was dragged away from the dear ferns and the living hills, and past the great metal stopper (I can tell you this part), and I thought it might save me again if I caught hold of the handle. It also was enwrapped, it also. Oh, the whole dell was full of the things. They were searching it in all directions, they were denuding it, and the white snouts of others peeped out of the hole, ready if needed. Everything that could be moved they brought—brushwood, bundles of fern, everything, and down we all went intertwined into hell. The last things that I saw, ere the stopper closed after us, were certain stars, and I felt that a man of my sort lived in the sky. For I did fight, I fought till the very end, and it was only my head hitting against the ladder that quieted me. I woke up in this room. The worms had vanished. I was sur- rounded by artificial air, artificial light, artificial peace, and my friends were calling to me down speaking tubes to know wheher I had come across any new ideas lately."

Here his story ended. Discussion of it was impossible, and Vashti turned to go.

"It will end in Homelessness," she said quietly.

"I wish it would," retorted Kuno.

"The Machine has been most merciful."

"I prefer the mercy of God."

"By that superstitious phrase, do you mean that you could live in the outer air?"

"Yes."

"Have you ever seen, round the vomitories, the bones of those who were extruded after the Great Rebellion?"

"Yes."

"They were left where they perished for our edification. A few crawled away, but they perished, too—who can doubt it? And so with the Homeless of our own day. The surface of the earth supports life no longer."

"Indeed."

"Ferns and a little grass may survive, but all higher forms have perished. Has any air-ship detected them?"

"No."

"Has any lecturer dealt with them?"

"No."

"Then why this obstinacy?"

"Because I have seen them," he exploded.

"Seen *what?*"

"Because I have seen her in the twilight—because she came to my help when I called—because she, too, was entangled by the worms, and, luckier than I, was killed by one of them piercing her throat."

He was mad. Vashti departed, nor, in the troubles that followed, did she ever see his face again.

Part III

THE HOMELESS

During the years that followed Kuno's escapade, two important developments took place in the Machine. On the surface they were revolutionary, but in either case men's minds had been prepared beforehand, and they did but express tendencies that were latent already.

The first of these was the abolition of respirators.

Advanced thinkers, like Vashti, had always held it foolish to visit the surface of the earth. Air-ships might be necessary,

but what was the good of going out for mere curiosity and
crawling along for a mile or two in a terrestrial motor? The
habit was vulgar and perhaps faintly improper: it was as un-
productive of ideas, and had no connection with the habits
that really mattered. So respirators were abolished, and with
them, of course, the terrestrial motors, and except for a few
lecturers, who complained that they were debarred access to
their subject-matter, the development was accepted quietly.
Those who still wanted to know what the earth was like had
after all only to listen to some gramophone, or to look into
some cinematophote. And even the lecturers acquiesced when
they found that a lecture on the sea was none the less stimulating when compiled out of other lectures that had already
been delivered on the same subject. "Beware of first-hand
ideas!" exclaimed one of the most advanced of them. "First-
hand ideas do not really exist. They are but the physical impressions produced by love and fear, and on this gross
foundation who could erect a philosophy? Let your ideas be
secondhand, and if possible tenth-hand, for then they will be
far removed from that disturbing element—direct observation. Do not learn anything about this subject of mine—the
French Revolution. Learn instead what I think that Enicharmon thought Urizen thought Gutch thought Ho-Yung
thought Chi-Bo-Sing thought Lafcadio Hearn thought Carlyle
thought Mirabeau said about the French Revolution. Through
the medium of these eight great minds, the blood that was
shed at Paris and the windows that were broken at Versailles
will be clarified to an idea which you may employ most
profitably in your daily lives. But be sure that the intermedi-
ates are many and varied, for in history one authority exists
to counteract another. Urizen must counteract the scepticism
of Ho-Yung and Enicharmon, I must myself counteract the
impetuosity of Gutch. You who listen to me are in a better
position to judge about the French Revolution than I am.
Your descendants will be even in a better position than you,
for they will learn what you think, and yet another intermedi-
ate will be added to the chain. And in time"—his voice
rose—"there will come a generation that has got beyond
facts, beyond impressions, a generation absolutely colourless,
a generation

             'seraphically free
        From taint of personality,'
which will see the French Revolution not as it happened, nor

as they would like it to have happened, but as it would have happened, had it taken place in the days of the Machine."

Tremendous applause greeted this lecture, which did but voice a feeling already latent in the minds of men—a feeling that terrestrial facts must be ignored, and that the abolition of respirators was a positive gain. It was even suggested that air-ships should be abolished too. This was not done, because air-ships had somehow worked themselves into the Machine's system. But year by year they were used less, and mentioned less by thoughtful men.

The second great development was the reestablishment of religion.

This, too, had been voiced in the celebrated lecture. No one could mistake the reverent tone in which the peroration had concluded, and it awakened a responsive echo in the heart of each. Those who had long worshipped silently, now began to talk. They described the strange feeling of peace that came over them when they handled the Book of the Machine, the pleasure that it was to repeat certain numerals out of it, however little meaning those numerals conveyed to the outward ear, the ecstasy of touching a button, however unimportant, or of ringing an electric bell, however superfluously.

"The Machine," they exclaimed, "feeds us and clothes us and houses us; through it we speak to one another, through it we see one another, in it we have our being. The Machine is the friend of ideas and the enemy of superstition: the Machine is omnipotent, eternal; blessed is the Machine." And before long this allocution was printed on the first page of the Book, and in subsequent editions the ritual swelled into a complicated system of praise and prayer. The word "religion" was sedulously avoided, and in theory the Machine was still the creation and the implement of man. But in practice all, save a few retrogrades, worshipped it as divine. Nor was it worshipped in unity. One believer would be chiefly impressed by the blue optic plates, through which he saw other believers; another by the mending apparatus, which sinful Kuno had compared to worms; another by the lifts, another by the Book. And each would pray to this or to that, and ask it to intercede for him with the Machine as a whole. Persecution—that also was present. It did not break out, for reasons that will be set forward shortly. But it was latent, and all who did not accept the minimum known as "undenominational

Mechanism" lived in danger of Homelessness, which means death, as we know.

To attribute these two great developments to the Central Committee, is to take a very narrow view of civilisation. The Central Committee announced the developments, it is true, but they were no more the cause of them than were the kings of the imperialistic period the cause of war. Rather did they yield to some invincible pressure, which came no one knew whither, and which, when gratified, was succeeded by some new pressure equally invincible. To such a state of affairs it is convenient to give the name of progress. No one confessed the Machine was out of hand. Year by year it was served with increased efficiency and decreased intelligence. The better a man knew his own duties upon it, the less he understood the duties of his neighbour, and in all the world there was not one who understood the monster as a whole. Those master brains had perished. They had left full directions, it is true, and their successors had each of them mastered a portion of those directions. But Humanity, in its desire for comfort, had over-reached itself. It had exploited the riches of nature too far. Quietly and complacently, it was sinking into decadence, and progress had come to mean the progress of the Machine.

As for Vashti, her life went peacefully forward until the final disaster. She made her room dark and slept; she awoke and made the room light. She lectured and attended lectures. She exchanged ideas with her innumerable friends and believed she was growing more spiritual. At times a friend was granted Euthanasia, and left his or her room for the homelessness that is beyond all human conception. Vashti did not much mind. After an unsuccessful lecture, she would sometimes ask for Euthanasia herself. But the death-rate was not permitted to exceed the birth-rate, and the Machine had hitherto refused it to her.

The troubles began quietly, long before she was conscious of them.

One day she was astonished at receiving a message from her son. They never communicated, having nothing in common, and she had only heard indirectly that he was still alive, and had been transferred from the northern hemisphere, where he had behaved so mischievously, to the southern—indeed, to a room not far from her own.

"Does he want me to visit him?" she thought. "Never again, never. And I have not the time."

No, it was madness of another kind.

He refused to visualize his face upon the blue plate, and speaking out of the darkness with solemnity said:

"The Machine stops."

"What do you say?"

"The Machine is stopping, I know it, I know the signs."

She burst into a peal of laughter. He heard her and was angry, and they spoke no more.

"Can you imagine anything more absurd?" she cried to a friend. "A man who was my son believes that the Machine is stopping. It would be impious if it was not mad."

"The Machine is stopping?" her friend replied. "What does that mean? The phrase conveys nothing to me."

"Nor to me."

"He does not refer, I suppose, to the trouble there has been lately with the music?"

"Oh no, of course not. Let us talk about music."

"Have you complained to the authorities?"

"Yes, and they say it wants mending, and referred me to the Committee of the Mending Apparatus. I complained of those curious gasping sighs that disfigure the symphonies of the Brisbane school. They sound like some one in pain. The Committee of the Mending Apparatus say that it shall be remedied shortly."

Obscurely worried, she resumed her life. For one thing, the defect in the music irritated her. For another thing, she could not forget Kuno's speech. If he had known that the music was out of repair—he could not know it, for he detested music—if he had known that it was wrong, "the Machine stops" was exactly the venomous sort of remark he would have made. Of course he had made it at a venture, but the coincidence annoyed her, and she spoke with some petulance to the Committee of the Mending Apparatus.

They replied, as before, that the defect would be set right shortly.

"Shortly! At once!" she retorted. "Why should I be worried by imperfect music? Things are always put right at once. If you do not mend it at once, I shall complain to the Central Committee."

"No personal complaints are received by the Central Committee," the Committee of the Mending Apparatus replied.

"Through whom am I to make my complaint, then?"

"Through us."

"I complain then."

"Your complaint shall be forwarded in its turn."

"Have others complained?"

This question was unmechanical, and the Committee of the Mending Apparatus refused to answer it.

"It is too bad!" she exclaimed to another of her friends. "There never was such an unfortunate woman as myself. I can never be sure of my music now. It gets worse and worse each time I summon it."

"I too have my troubles," the friend replied. "Sometimes my ideas are interrupted by a slight jarring noise."

"What is it?"

"I do not know whether it is inside my head, or inside the wall."

"Complain, in either case."

"I have complained, and my complaint will be forwarded in its turn to the Central Committee."

Time passed, and they resented the defects no longer. The defects had not been remedied, but the human tissues in that latter day had become so subservient, that they readily adapted themselves to every caprice of the Machine. The sigh at the crisis of the Brisbane symphony no longer irritated Vashti: she accepted it as part of the melody. The jarring noise, whether in the head or in the wall, was no longer resented by her friend. And so with the mouldy artificial fruit, so with the bath water that began to stink, so with the defective rhymes that the poetry machine had taken to emit. All were bitterly complained of at first, and then acquiesced in and forgotten. Things went from bad to worse unchallenged.

It was otherwise with the failure of the sleeping apparatus. That was a more serious stoppage. There came a day when over the whole world—in Sumatra, in Wessex, in the innumerable cities of Courland and Brazil—the beds, when summoned by their tired owners, failed to appear. It may seem a ludicrous matter, but from it we may date the collapse of humanity. The Committee responsible for the failure was assailed by complainants, whom it referred, as usual, to the Committee of the Mending Apparatus, who in its turn assured them that their complaints would be forwarded to the Central Committee. But the discontent grew, for mankind was not yet sufficiently adaptable to do without sleeping.

"Some one is meddling with the Machine——" they began.

"Some one is trying to make himself king, to reintroduce the personal element."

"Punish that man with Homelessness."

"To the rescue! Avenge the Machine! Avenge the Machine!"

"War! Kill the man!"

But the Committee of the Mending Apparatus now came forward, and allayed the panic with well-chosen words. It confessed that the Mending Apparatus was itself in need of repair.

The effect of this frank confession was admirable.

"Of course," said a famous lecturer—he of the French Revolution, who gilded each new decay with splendour—"of course we shall not press our complaints now. The Mending Apparatus has treated us so well in the past that we all sympathize with it, and will wait patiently for its recovery. In its own good time it will resume its duties. Meanwhile let us do without our beds, our tabloids, our other little wants. Such, I feel sure, would be the wish of the Machine."

Thousands of miles away his audience applauded. The Machine still linked them. Under the sea, beneath the roots of the mountains, ran the wires through which they saw and heard, the enormous eyes and ears that were their heritage, and the hum of many workings clothed their thoughts in one garment of subserviency. Only the old and the sick remained ungrateful, for it was rumoured that Euthanasia, too, was out of order, and that pain had reappeared among men.

It became difficult to read. A blight entered the atmosphere and dulled its luminosity. At times Vashti could scarcely see across her room. The air, too, was foul. Loud were the complaints, impotent the remedies, heroic the tone of the lecturer as he cried: "Courage, courage! What matter so long as the Machine goes on? To it the darkness and the light are one." And though things improved again after a time, the old brilliancy was never recaptured, and humanity never recovered from its entrance into twilight. There was an hysterical talk of "measures," of "provisional dictatorship," and the inhabitants of Sumatra were asked to familiarize themselves with the workings of the central power station, the said power station being situated in France. But for the most part panic reigned, and men spent their strength praying to their Books, tangible proofs of the Machine's omnipotence. There were gradations of terror—at times came rumours of hope—the Mending Apparatus was almost mended—the enemies of the Machine had been got under—new "nerve-centres" were evolving which would do the work even more magnificently than before. But there came a day when, without the slightest warning, without any previous hint of feebleness, the entire communication-system broke down, all over the world, and the world, as they understood it, ended.

Vashti was lecturing at the time and her earlier remarks had been punctuated with applause. As she proceeded the audience became silent, and at the conclusion there was no sound. Somewhat displeased, she called to a friend who was a specialist in sympathy. No sound: doubtless the friend was sleeping. And so with the next friend whom she tried to summon, and so with the next, until she remembered Kuno's cryptic remark, "The Machine stops."

The phrase still conveyed nothing. If Eternity was stopping it would of course be set going shortly.

For example, there was still a little light and air—the atmosphere had improved a few hours previously. There was still the Book, and while there was the Book there was security.

Then she broke down, for with the cessation of activity came an unexpected terror—silence.

She had never known silence, and the coming of it nearly killed her—it did kill many thousands of people outright. Ever since her birth she had been surrounded by the steady hum. It was to the ear what artificial air was to the lungs, and agonizing pains shot across her head. And scarcely knowing what she did, she stumbled forward and pressed the unfamiliar button, the one that opened the door of her cell.

Now the door of the cell worked on a simple hinge of its own. It was not connected with the central power station, dying far away in France. It opened, rousing immoderate hopes in Vashti, for she thought that the Machine had been mended. It opened, and she saw the dim tunnel that curved far away towards freedom. One look, and then she shrank back. For the tunnel was full of people—she was almost the last in that city to have taken alarm.

People at any time repelled her, and these were nightmares from her worst dreams. People were crawling about, people were screaming, whimpering, gasping for breath, touching each other, vanishing in the dark, and ever and anon being pushed off the platform on the live rail. Some were fighting round the electric bells, trying to summon trains which could not be summoned. Others were yelling for Euthanasia or for respirators, or blaspheming the Machine. Others stood at the doors of their cells fearing, like herself, either to stop in them or to leave them. And behind all the uproar was silence—the silence which is the voice of the earth and of the generations who have gone.

No—it was worse than solitude. She closed the door again and sat down to wait for the end. The disintegration went on, accompanied by horrible cracks and rumbling. The valves that restrained the Medical Apparatus must have been weakened, for it ruptured and hung hideously from the ceiling. The floor heaved and fell and flung her from her chair. A tube oozed towards her serpent fashion. And at last the final horror approached—light began to ebb, and she knew that civilisation's long day was closing.

She whirled round, praying to be saved from this, at any rate, kissing the Book, pressing button after button. The uproar outside was increasing, and even penetrated the wall. Slowly the brilliancy of her cell was dimmed, the reflections faded from her metal switches. Now she could not see the reading-stand, now not the Book, though she held it in her hand. Light followed the flight of sound, air was following light, and the original void returned to the cavern from which it had been so long excluded. Vashti continued to whirl, like the devotees of an earlier religion, screaming, praying, striking at the buttons with bleeding hands.

It was thus that she opened her prison and escaped—escaped in the spirit: at least so it seems to me, ere my meditation closes. That she escaped in the body—I cannot perceive that. She struck, by chance, the switch that released the door, and the rush of foul air on her skin, the loud throbbing whispers in her ears, told her that she was facing the tunnel again, and that tremendous platform on which she had seen men fighting. They were not fighting now. Only the whispers remained, and the little whimpering groans. They were dying by hundreds out in the dark.

She burst into tears.

Tears answered her.

They wept for humanity, those two, not for themselves. They could not bear that this should be the end. Ere silence was completed their hearts were opened, and they knew what had been important on the earth. Man, the flower of all flesh, the noblest of all creatures visible, man who had once made god in his image, and had mirrored his strength on the constellations, beautiful naked man was dying, strangled in the garments that he had woven. Century after century had he toiled, and here was his reward. Truly the garment had seemed heavenly at first, shot with the colours of culture, sewn with the threads of self-denial. And heavenly it had been so long as it was a garment and no more, so long as man could shed it at will and live by the essence that is his soul, and the essence, equally divine, that is his body. The sin against the body—it was for that they wept in chief; the centuries of wrong against the muscles and the nerves, and those five portals by which we can alone apprehend—glozing it over with talk of evolution, until the body was white pap, the home of ideas as colourless, last sloshy stirrings of a spirit that had grasped the stars.

"Where are you?" she sobbed.

His voice in the darkness said, "Here."

"Is there any hope, Kuno?"

"None for us."

"Where are you?"

She crawled towards him over the bodies of the dead. His blood spurted over her hands.

"Quicker," he gasped, "I am dying—but we touch, we talk, not through the Machine."

He kissed her.

"We have come back to our own. We die, but we have recaptured life, as it was in Wessex, when Ælfrid overthrew the Danes. We know what they know outside, they who dwelt in the cloud that is the colour of a pearl."

"But, Kuno, is it true? Are there still men on the surface of the earth? Is this—this tunnel, this poisoned darkness—really not the end?"

He replied:

"I have seen them, spoken to them, loved them. They are hiding in the mist and the ferns until our civilization stops. To-day they are the Homeless—to-morrow—"

"Oh, to-morrow—some fool will start the Machine again, to-morrow."

"Never," said Kuno, "never. Humanity has learnt its lesson."

As he spoke, the whole city was broken like a honeycomb. An air-ship had sailed in through the vomitory into a ruined wharf. It crashed downwards, exploding as it went, rending gallery after gallery with its wings of steel. For a moment they saw the nations of the dead, and, before they joined them, scraps of the untainted sky.

Island in the Sky,
Or Romance Triumphant

The great period of African exploration was the middle of the nineteenth century, climaxed by Stanley's "Dr. Livingstone, I presume." Robert Peary reached the North Pole in 1909, and Roald Amundsen the South Pole in 1911. By 1912 the last inaccessible area on the planet earth (with the exceptions of the ocean depths and the Himalayan heights) had been touched by humanity, if not thoroughly explored.

Few plausible places remained where a lost race could be discovered or where unusual activities could go unnoticed: a hidden valley in the Canadian northwest or in Antarctica, an isolated island in the South Pacific, the impenetrable jungles of darkest Africa, the Siberian tundra, or inside a hollow earth, a notion popularized early in the nineteenth century by Captain John Cleves Symmes of Ohio. But gradually all except the inside of the earth were being visited, described, rendered increasingly familiar and less mysterious. Authors of romances who wanted to retain both credibility and the appeal of the contemporary had to look elsewhere.

The Italian astronomer Schiaparelli (1835–1910) mapped the surface of Mars during the opposition of 1877 and by 1881 described a complicated pattern of straight lines that he called *canali* or "channels," a word mistranslated into English as "canals." Percival Lowell (1855–1916) built his own observatory in Arizona. Beginning in 1894 he began observations of Mars that resulted in detailed drawings of Martian "canals" and the "oases" at which they met, as well as in such books as *Mars and Its Canals* (1906) and *Mars as the Abode of Life* (1908), popularizing the notion of an inhabited Mars with a civilization capable of building a network of canals to carry enough moisture from the melting icecaps to ease the desiccation of a dying planet.

Venus, more nearly a sister planet to Earth, remained more a planet of mystery. Its eternal white shroud of clouds offered fewer evidences of livability but provided unlimited opportu-

nities for speculation. Most of them pictured a watery world
with gigantic flora and fauna like earth's Mesozoic era. More
recent observations, especially Russian probes, have indicated
that the clouds are really a shroud, that the surface of Venus
is dead, cremated by the hothouse effect of the carbon dioxide in the atmosphere. After that the science-fiction author
(as well as scientists such as Carl Sagan) has speculated
about terraforming Venus.

The other planets have remained less likely places for life
or adventure. Mercury is too small and too hot, and the outer
planets are too big and too cold, though occasionally stories
have been placed on all of them, or on one of the large satellites of Jupiter or Saturn.

Mars, though, remained the planet of choice. Wells had
described it as inhabited and civilized in "The Crystal Egg"
(1897) and as an envious invader in *The War of the Worlds*
(1898). After the moon, it became the most likely island in
the sky.

Certainly it was to Edgar Rice Burroughs (1875–1950).
Burroughs is important to the development of science fiction
not so much because of the excellence of his writing or his
innovations in idea, theme, or technique, but because he was
so prolific and so successful, and because his brand of romantic adventure was so appealing to succeeding generations of
readers that his influence must be reckoned with. Almost every author of science fiction and many readers credit Burroughs with their introduction, at an early age, to "the sense
of wonder."

Burroughs himself was thirty-five years old before he
turned to writing. He had failed at several occupations before
he decided he could write stories for the pulp magazines that
were proliferating in the first decade of the twentieth century.
In 1929 he recalled, "If people were paid for writing rot such
as I read I could write stories just as rotten," though this suggests a disdain that was never evident in his writing.

His first manuscript was a novel serialized beginning in the
February 1912 *All-Story*, under the title of *Under the Moons
of Mars*, and appeared in book form as *A Princess of Mars*.
Burroughs was an immediate success, and in the next thirty-
eight years he completed sixty-nine books, twenty-six featuring
the most popular character created in the twentieth century,
Tarzan. He published eleven books in his Martian series, including the fourth book in the series, *The Chessmen of Mars*
(1922), seven in his Pellucidar series about a hollow earth,

and four in his Venus series. In the process he made a fortune (at least $10 million during his lifetime), founded a town, and created his own publishing house. His books continue to be reprinted around the world, and he retains his basic appeal to the young.

Burroughs may have written with some haste and with little concern for literary niceties; what interested him, and apparently his readers, was a good story with a strong romantic interest and lots of action, especially hand-to-hand combat. The use of coincidence didn't bother him (as it did not bother Verne, who considered it an acknowledgment of a divine presence in human affairs). Although he may have done little if any rewriting, Burroughs worked out in advance details of environment, history, and culture, even alien geographies and languages.

Burroughs's novels—and he wrote mostly in the novel form—belong to a category that might best be called "adventure fantasy." (The term "heroic fantasy," used for a contemporary genre, carries other connotations.) He was not all that concerned with plausibility, as later science fiction would be; when he transports John Carter to Mars, Carter literally wishes upon a star. But, as Prof. R. D. Mullen has pointed out, once Carter gets there, the Mars he finds is the Mars popularized by Percival Lowell, a Mars that Burroughs then peoples with strange creatures out of his prolific imagination.

Burroughs was not the first to write "adventure fantasy"—one might mention the names of Garrett P. Serviss and George Allan England, certainly H. Rider Haggard, perhaps M. P. Shiel, A. Conan Doyle, and others—and he may have drawn inspiration not only from Lowell but, as Richard Lupoff speculates, from earlier novels by Edwin Lester Arnold, *Phra the Phoenician* (1890) and *Lieut. Gullivar Jones: His Vacation* (1905). But Burroughs captured so well the spirit of the genre that it was his work later writers imitated, and the imitations continue down to the present.

From The Chessmen of Mars

by *Edgar Rice Burroughs*

Chapter II

AT THE GALE'S MERCY

Tara of Helium did not return to her father's guests, but awaited in her own apartments the word from Djor Kantos which she knew must come, begging her to return to the gardens. She would then refuse, haughtily. But no appeal came from Djor Kantos. At first Tara of Helium was angry, then she was hurt, and always she was puzzled. She could not understand. Occasionally she thought of the Jed of Gathol and then she would stamp her foot, for she was very angry indeed with Gahan. The presumption of the man! He had insinuated that he read love for him in her eyes. Never had she been so insulted and humiliated. Never had she so thoroughly hated a man. Suddenly she turned toward Uthia.

"My flying leather!" she commanded.

"But the guests!" exclaimed the slave girl. "Your father, The Warlord, will expect you to return."

"He will be disappointed," snapped Tara of Helium.

The slave hesitated. "He does not approve of your flying alone," she reminded her mistress.

The young princess sprang to her feet and seized the unhappy slave by the shoulders, shaking her. "You are becoming unbearable, Uthia," she cried. "Soon there will be no alternative than to send you to the public slave-market. Then possibly you will find a master to your liking."

70

Tears came to the soft eyes of the slave girl. "It is because I love you, my princess," she said softly. Instantly Tara of Helium melted. She took the slave in her arms and kissed her.

"I have the disposition of a thoat, Uthia," she said. "Forgive me! I love you and there is nothing that I would not do for you and nothing would I do to harm you. Again, as I have so often in the past, I offer you your freedom."

"I do not wish my freedom if it will separate me from you, Tara of Helium," replied Uthia. "I am happy here with you—I think that I should die without you."

Again the girls kissed. "And you will not fly alone, then?" questioned the slave.

Tara of Helium laughed and pinched her companion. "You persistent little pest," she cried. "Of course I shall fly—does not Tara of Helium always do that which pleases her?"

Uthia shook her head sorrowfully. "Alas! she does," she admitted. "Iron is the Warlord of Barsoom to the influences of all but two. In the hands of Dejah Thoris and Tara of Helium he is as potters' clay."

"Then run and fetch my flying leather like the sweet slave you are," directed the mistress.

Far out across the ochre sea-bottoms beyond the twin cities of Helium raced the swift flier of Tara of Helium. Thrilling to the speed and the buoyancy and the obedience of the little craft the girl drove toward the northwest. Why she should choose that direction she did not pause to consider. Perhaps because in that direction lay the least known areas of Barsoom, and, *ergo*, Romance, Mystery, and Adventure. In that direction also lay far Gathol; but to that fact she gave no conscious thought.

She did, however, think occasionally of the jed of that distant kingdom, but the reaction to these thoughts was scarcely pleasurable. They still brought a flush of shame to her cheeks and a surge of angry blood to her heart. She was very angry with the Jed of Gathol, and though she should never see him again she was quite sure that hate of him would remain fresh in her memory forever. Mostly her thoughts revolved about another—Djor Kantos. And when she thought of him she thought also of Olvia Marthis of Hastor. Tara of Helium thought that she was jealous of the fair Olvia and it made her very angry to think that. She was angry with Djor Kantos and herself, but she was not angry at all with Olvia Marthis,

whom she loved, and so of course she was not jealous really.
The trouble was, that Tara of Helium had failed for once to
have her own way. Djor Kantos had not come running like a
willing slave when she had expected him; and, ah, here was
the nub of the whole thing! Gahan, Jed of Gathol, a stranger,
had been a witness to her humiliation. He had seen her un-
claimed at the beginning of a great function and he had had
to come to her rescue to save her, as he doubtless thought,
from the inglorious fate of a wallflower. At the recurring
thought, Tara of Helium could feel her whole body burning
with scarlet shame and then she went suddenly white and
cold with rage; whereupon she turned her flier about so
abruptly that she was all but torn from her lashings upon the
flat, narrow deck. She reached home just before dark. The
guests had departed. Quiet had descended upon the palace.
An hour later she joined her father and mother at the evening meal.

"You deserted us, Tara of Helium," said John Carter. "It is
not what the guests of John Carter should expect."

"They did not come to see me," replied Tara of Helium. "I
did not ask them."

"They were no less your guests," replied her father.

The girl rose, and came and stood beside him and put her
arms about his neck.

"My proper old Virginian," she cried, rumpling his shock
of black hair.

"In Virginia you would be turned over your father's knee
and spanked," said the man smiling.

She crept into his lap and kissed him. "You do not love me
any more," she announced. "No one loves me," but she could
not compose her features into a pout because bubbling laughter insisted upon breaking through.

"The trouble is there are too many who love you," he said.
"And now there is another."

"Indeed!" she cried. "What do you mean?"

"Gahan of Gathol has asked permission to woo you."

The girl sat up very straight and tilted her chin in the air.
"I would not wed with a walking diamond-mine," she said. "I
will not have him."

"I told him as much," replied her father, "and that you
were as good as betrothed to another. He was very courteous
about it; but at the same time he gave me to understand that
he was accustomed to getting what he wanted and that he
wanted you very much. I suppose it will mean another war.

Your mother's beauty kept Helium at war for many years, and—well, Tara of Helium, if I were a young man I should doubtless be willing to set all Barsoom afire to win you, as I still would to keep your divine mother," and he smiled across the sorapus table and its golden service at the undimmed beauty of Mars' most beautiful woman.

"Our little girl should not yet be troubled with such matters," said Dejah Thoris. "Remember, John Carter, that you are not dealing with an Earth child whose span of life would be more than half completed before a daughter of Barsoom reached actual maturity."

"But do not the daughters of Barsoom sometimes marry as early as twenty?" he insisted.

"Yes, but they may still be desirable in the eyes of men after forty generations of Earth folk have returned to dust—there is no hurry, at least, upon Barsoom. We do not fade and decay here as you tell me those of your planet do, though you, yourself, belie your own words. When the time seems proper Tara of Helium shall wed with Djor Kantos, and until then let us give the matter no further thought."

"No," said the girl, "the subject irks me, and I shall not marry Djor Kantos, or another—I do not intend to wed."

Her father and mother looked at her and smiled. "When Gahan of Gathol returns he may carry you off," said the former.

"He has gone?" asked the girl.

"His flier departs for Gathol in the morning," John Carter replied.

"I have seen the last of him then," remarked Tara of Helium with a sigh of relief.

"He says not," returned John Carter.

The girl dismissed the subject with a shrug and the conversation passed to other topics. A letter had arrived from Thuvia of Ptarth, who was visiting at her father's court while Carthoris, her mate, hunted in Okar. Word had been received that the Tharks and Warhoons were again at war, or rather that there had been an engagement, for war was their habitual state. In the memory of man there had been no peace between these two savage green hordes—and only a single temporary truce. Two new battleships had been launched at Hastor. A little band of holy therns was attempting to revive the ancient and discredited religion of Issus, who they claimed still lived in spirit and had communicated with them. There were rumors of war from Dusar. A scientist claimed to have discovered human life on the further moon. A madman had attempted to destroy the atmosphere plant. Seven people had been assassinated in Greater Helium during the last ten zodes (the equivalent of an Earth day).

Following the meal Dejah Thoris and The Warlord played at jetan, the Barsoomian game of chess, which is played upon a board of a hundred alternate black and orange squares. One player has twenty black pieces, the other, twenty orange pieces. A brief description of the game may interest those Earth readers who care for chess, and will not be lost upon those who pursue this narrative to its conclusion, since before they are done they will find that a knowledge of jetan will add to the interest and the thrills that are in store for them.

The men are placed upon the board as in chess upon the first two rows next the players. In order from left to right on the line of squares nearest the players, the jetan pieces are Warrior, Padwar, Dwar, Flier, Chief, Princess, Flier, Dwar, Padwar, Warrior. In the next line all are Panthans except the end pieces, which are called Thoats, and represent mounted warriors.

The Panthans, which are represented as warriors with one feather, may move one space in any direction except backward; the Thoats, mounted warriors with three feathers, may move one straight and one diagonal, and may jump intervening pieces; Warriors, foot soldiers with two feathers, straight in any direction, or diagonally, two spaces; Padwars, lieutenants wearing two feathers, two diagonal in any direction, or combination; Dwars, captains wearing three feathers, three spaces straight in any direction, or combination; Fliers, represented by a propellor with three blades, three spaces in any direction, or combination, diagonally, and may jump intervening pieces; the Chief, indicated by a diadem with ten jewels, three spaces in any direction, straight, or diagonal; Princess, diadem with a single jewel, same as Chief, and can jump intervening pieces.

The game is won when a player places any of his pieces on the same square with his opponent's Princess, or when a Chief takes a Chief. It is drawn when a Chief is taken by any opposing piece other than the opposing Chief; or when both sides have been reduced to three pieces, or less, of equal value, and the game is not terminated in the following ten moves, five apiece. This is but a general outline of the game, briefly stated.

It was this game that Dejah Thoris and John Carter were

playing when Tara of Helium bid them good night, retiring to her own quarters and her sleeping silks and furs. "Until morning, my beloved," she called back to them as she passed from the apartment, nor little did she guess, nor her parents, that this might indeed be the last time that they would ever set eyes upon her.

The morning broke dull and gray. Ominous clouds billowed restlessly and low. Beneath them torn fragments scudded toward the northwest. From her window Tara of Helium looked out upon this unusual scene. Dense clouds seldom overcast the Barsoomian sky. At this hour of the day it was her custom to ride one of those small thoats that are the saddle animals of the red Martians, but the sight of the billowing clouds lured her to a new adventure. Uthia still slept and the girl did not disturb her. Instead, she dressed quietly and went to the hangar upon the roof of the palace directly above her quarters where her own swift flier was housed. She had never driven through the clouds. It was an adventure that always she had longed to experience. The wind was strong and it was with difficulty that she maneuvered the craft from the hangar without accident, but once away it raced swiftly out above the twin cities. The buffeting winds caught and tossed it, and the girl laughed aloud in sheer joy of the resultant thrills. She handled the little ship like a veteran, though few veterans would have faced the menace of such a storm in so light a craft. Swiftly she rose toward the clouds, racing with the scudding streamers of the storm-swept fragments, and a moment later she was swallowed by the dense masses billowing above. Here was a new world, a world of chaos unpeopled except for herself; but it was a cold, damp, lonely world and she found it depressing after the novelty of it had been dissipated, by an overpowering sense of the magnitude of the forces surging about her. Suddenly she felt very lonely and very cold and very little. Hurriedly, therefore, she rose until presently her craft broke through into the glorious sunlight that transformed the upper surface of the somber element into rolling masses of burnished silver. Here it was still cold, but without the dampness of the clouds, and in the eye of the brilliant sun her spirits rose with the mounting needle of her altimeter. Gazing at the clouds, now far beneath, the girl experienced the sensation of hanging stationary in midheaven; but the whirring of her propeller, the wind beating upon her, the high figures that rose and fell beneath the glass

of her speedometer, these told her that her speed was terrific.
It was then that she determined to turn back.

The first attempt she made above the clouds, but it was unsuccessful. To her surprise she discovered that she could not
even turn against the high wind, which rocked and buffeted
the frail craft. Then she dropped swiftly to the dark and
wind-swept zone between the hurtling clouds and the gloomy
surface of the shadowed ground. Here she tried again to
force the nose of the flier back toward Helium, but the tempest seized the frail thing and hurled it remorselessly about,
rolling it over and over and tossing it as it were a cork in a
cataract. At last the girl succeeded in righting the flier, perilously close to the ground. Never before had she been so
close to death, yet she was not terrified. Her coolness had
saved her, that and the strength of the deck lashings that held
her. Traveling with the storm she was safe, but where was it
bearing her? She pictured the apprehension of her father and
mother when she failed to appear at the morning meal. They
would find her flier missing and they would guess that somewhere in the path of the storm it lay a wrecked and tangled
mass upon her dead body, and then brave men would go out
in search of her, risking their lives; and that lives would be
lost in the search, she knew, for she realized now that never
in her lifetime had such a tempest raged upon Barsoom.

She must turn back! She must reach Helium before her
mad lust for thrills had cost the sacrifice of a single coura-
geous life! She determined that greater safety and likelihood
of success lay above the clouds, and once again she rose
through the chilling, wind-tossed vapor. Her speed again was
terrific, for the wind seemed to have increased rather than to
have lessened. She sought gradually to check the swift flight
of her craft, but though she finally succeeded in reversing her
motor the wind but carried her on as it would. Then it was
that Tara of Helium lost her temper. Had her world not always bowed in acquiescence to her every wish? What were
these elements that they dared to thwart her? She would
demonstrate to them that the daughter of The Warlord was
not to be denied! They would learn that Tara of Helium
might not be ruled even by the forces of nature!

And so she drove her motor forward again and then with
her firm, white teeth set in grim determination she drove the
steering lever far down to port with the intention of forcing
the nose of her craft straight into the teeth of the wind, and
the wind seized the frail thing and toppled it over upon its

back, and twisted and turned it and hurled it over and over; the propellor raced for an instant in an air pocket and then the tempest seized it again and twisted it from its shaft, leaving the girl helpless upon an unmanageable atom that rose and fell, and rolled and tumbled—the sport of the elements she had defied. Tara of Helium's first sensation was one of surprise—that she had failed to have her own way. Then she commenced to feel concern—not for her own safety but for the anxiety of her parents and the dangers that the inevitable searchers must face. She reproached herself for the thoughtless selfishness that had jeopardized the peace and safety of others. She realized her own grave danger, too; but she was still unterrified, as befitted the daughter of Dejah Thoris and John Carter. She knew that her buoyancy tanks might keep her afloat indefinitely, but she had neither food nor water, and she was being borne toward the least-known area of Barsoom. Perhaps it would be better to land immediately and await the coming of the searchers, rather than to allow herself to be carried still further from Helium, thus greatly reducing the chances of early discovery; but when she dropped toward the ground she discovered that the violence of the wind rendered an attempt to land tantamount to destruction and she rose again, rapidly.

Carried along a few hundred feet above the ground she was better able to appreciate the Titanic proportions of the storm than when she had flown in the comparative serenity of the zone above the clouds, for now she could distinctly see the effect of the wind upon the surface of Barsoom. The air was filled with dust and flying bits of vegetation and when the storm carried her across an irrigated area of farm land she saw great trees and stone walls and buildings lifted high in air and scattered broadcast over the devastated country; and then she was carried swiftly on to other sights that forced in upon her consciousness a rapidly growing conviction that after all Tara of Helium was a very small and insignificant and helpless person. It was quite a shock to her self-pride while it lasted, and toward evening she was ready to believe that it was going to last forever. There had been no abatement in the ferocity of the tempest, nor was there indication of any. She could only guess at the distance she had been carried for she could not believe in the correctness of the high figures that had been piled upon the record of her odometer. They seemed unbelievable and yet, had she known it, they were quite true—in twelve hours she had flown and been carried by the storm full seven thousand haads. Just before dark she was carried over one of the deserted cities of ancient Mars. It was Torquas, but she did not know it. Had she, she might readily have been forgiven for abandoning the last vestige of hope, for to the people of Helium Torquas seems as remote as do the South Sea Islands to us. And still the tempest, its fury unabated, bore her on.

All that night she hurtled through the dark beneath the clouds, or rose to race through the moonlit void beneath the glory of Barsoom's two satellites. She was cold and hungry and altogether miserable, but her brave little spirit refused to admit that her plight was hopeless even though reason proclaimed the truth. Her reply to reason, sometimes spoken aloud in sudden defiance, recalled the Spartan stubbornness of her sire in the face of certain annihilation: "I still live!"

That morning there had been an early visitor at the palace of The Warlord. It was Gahan, Jed of Gathol. He had arrived shortly after the absence of Tara of Helium had been noted, and in the excitement he had remained unannounced until John Carter had happened upon him in the great reception corridor of the palace as The Warlord was hurrying out to arrange for the dispatch of ships in search of his daughter.

Gahan read the concern upon the face of The Warlord. "Forgive me if I intrude, John Carter," he said. "I but came to ask the indulgence of another day since it would be foolhardy to attempt to navigate a ship in such a storm."

"Remain, Gahan, a welcome guest until you choose to leave us," replied The Warlord; "but you must forgive any seeming inattention upon the part of Helium until my daughter is restored to us."

"Your daughter! Restored! What do you mean?" exclaimed the Gatholian. "I do not understand."

"She is gone, together with her light flier. That is all we know. We can only assume that she decided to fly before the morning meal and was caught in the clutches of the tempest. You will pardon me, Gahan, if I leave you abruptly—I am arranging to send ships in search of her"; but Gahan, Jed of Gathol, was already speeding in the direction of the palace gate. There he leaped upon a waiting thoat and followed by two warriors in the metal of Gathol, he dashed through the avenues of Helium toward the palace that had been set aside for his entertainment.

Chapter III

THE HEADLESS HUMANS

Above the roof of the palace that housed the Jed of Gathol and his entourage, the cruiser *Vanator* tore at her stout moorings. The groaning tackle bespoke the mad fury of the gale, while the worried faces of those members of the crew whose duties demanded their presence on the straining craft gave corroborative evidence of the gravity of the situation. Only stout lashings prevented these men from being swept from the deck, while those upon the roof below were constantly compelled to cling to rails and stanchions to save themselves from being carried away by each new burst of meteoric fury. Upon the prow of the *Vanator* was painted the device of Gathol, but no pennants were displayed in the upper works since the storm had carried away several in rapid succession, just as it seemed to the watching men that it must carry away the ship itself. They could not believe that any tackle could withstand for long this Titanic force. To each of the twelve lashings clung a brawny warrior with drawn short-sword. Had but a single mooring given to the power of the tempest eleven short-swords would have cut the others; since, partially moored, the ship was doomed, while free in the tempest it stood at least some slight chance for life.

"By the blood of Issus, I believe they will hold!" screamed one warrior to another.

"And if they do not hold may the spirits of our ancestors reward the brave warriors upon the *Vanator*," replied another of those upon the roof of the palace, "for it will not be long from the moment her cables part before her crew dons the leather of the dead; but yet, Tanus, I believe they will hold. Give thanks at least that we did not sail before the tempest fell, since now each of us has a chance to live."

"Yes," replied Tanus, "I should hate to be abroad today upon the stoutest ship that sails the Barsoomian sky."

It was then that Gahan the Jed appeared upon the roof. With him were the balance of his own party and a dozen warriors of Helium. The young chief turned to his followers.

79

"I sail at once upon the *Vanator*," he said, "in search of Tara of Helium who is thought to have been carried away upon a one-man flier by the storm. I do not need to explain to you the slender chances the *Vanator* has to withstand the fury of the tempest, nor will I order you to your deaths. Let those who wish remain behind without dishonor. The others will follow me," and he leaped for the rope ladder that lashed wildly in the gale.

The first man to follow him was Tanus and when the last reached the deck of the cruiser there remained upon the palace roof only the twelve warriors of Helium, who, with naked swords, had taken the posts of the Gatholians at the moorings.

Not a single warrior who had remained aboard the *Vanator* would leave her now.

"I expected no less," said Gahan, as with the help of those already on the deck he and the others found secure lashings. The commander of the *Vanator* shook his head. He loved his trim craft, the pride of her class in the little navy of Gathol. It was of her he thought—not of himself. He saw her lying torn and twisted upon the ochre vegetation of some distant sea-bottom, to be presently overrun and looted by some savage, green horde. He looked at Gahan.

"Are you ready, San Tothis?" asked the Jed.

"All is ready."

"Then cut away!"

Word was passed across the deck and over the side to the Heliumetic warriors below that at the third gun they were to cut away. Twelve keen swords must strike simultaneously and with equal power, and each must sever completely and instantly three strands of heavy cable that no loose end fouling a block bring immediate disaster upon the *Vanator*.

Boom! The voice of the signal gun rolled down through the screaming wind to the twelve warriors upon the roof. *Boom!* Twelve swords were raised above twelve brawny shoulders. *Boom!* Twelve keen edges severed twelve complaining moorings clean and as one.

The *Vanator*, her propellors whirling, shot forward with the storm. The tempest struck her in the stern as with a mailed fist and stood the great ship upon her nose, and then it caught her and spun her as a child's top spins; and upon the palace roof the twelve men looked on in silent helplessness and prayed for the souls of the brave warriors who were going to their death. And others saw, from Helium's lofty

landing stages and from a thousand hangars upon a thousand
roofs; but only for an instant did the preparations stop that
would send other brave men into the frightful maelstrom of
that apparently hopeless search, for such is the courage of the
warriors of Barsoom.

But the *Vanator* did not fall to the ground, within sight of
the city at least, though as long as the watchers could see her
never for an instant did she rest upon an even keel. Sometime
she lay upon one side or the other, or again she hurtled along
keel up, or rolled over and over, or stood upon her nose or
her tail at the caprice of the great force that carried her
along. And the watchers saw that this great ship was merely
being blown away with the other bits of débris great and
small that filled the sky. Never in the memory of man or the
annals of recorded history had such a storm raged across the
face of Barsoom.

And in another instant was the *Vanator* forgotten as the
lofty, scarlet tower that had marked Lesser Helium for ages
crashed to ground, carrying death and demolition upon the
city beneath. Panic reigned. A fire broke out in the ruins. The
city's every force seemed crippled, and it was then that The
Warlord ordered the men that were about to set forth in
search of Tara of Helium to devote their energies to the salvation of the city, for he too had witnessed the start of the
Vanator and realized the futility of wasting men who were
needed sorely if Lesser Helium was to be saved from utter
destruction.

Shortly after noon of the second day the storm commenced
to abate, and before the sun went down, the little craft upon
which Tara of Helium had hovered between life and death
these many hours drifted slowly before a gentle breeze above
a landscape of rolling hills that once had been lofty mountains upon a Martian continent. The girl was exhausted from
loss of sleep, from lack of food and drink, and from the nervous reaction consequent to the terrifying experiences
through which she had passed. In the near distance, just top-
ping an intervening hill, she caught a momentary glimpse of
what appeared to be a dome-capped tower. Quickly she
dropped the flier until the hill shut it off from the view of the
possible occupants of the structure she had seen. The tower
meant to her the habitation of man, suggesting the presence
of water and perhaps, of food. If the tower was the deserted
relic of a bygone age she would scarcely find food there, but
there was still a chance that there might be water. If it was

inhabited, then must her approach be cautious, for only enemies might be expected to abide in so far distant a land. Tara
of Helium knew that she must be far from the twin cities of
her grandfather's empire, but had she guessed within even a
thousand haads of the reality, she had been stunned by realization of the utter hopelessness of her state.

Keeping the craft low, for the buoyancy tanks were still in-
tact, the girl skimmed the ground until the gently-moving
wind had carried her to the side of the last hill that inter-
vened between her and the structure she had thought a man-
built tower. Here she brought the flier to the ground among
some stunted trees, and dragging it beneath one where it
might be somewhat hidden from craft passing above, she
made it fast and set forth to reconnoiter. Like most women
of her class she was armed only with a single slender blade,
so that in such an emergency as now confronted her she must
depend almost solely upon her cleverness in remaining undiscovered by enemies. With utmost caution she crept warily
toward the crest of the hill, taking advantage of every natural
screen that the landscape afforded to conceal her approach
from possible observers ahead, while momentarily she cast
quick glances rearward lest she be taken by surprise from
that quarter.

She came at last to the summit, where, from the conceal-
ment of a low bush, she could see what lay beyond. Beneath
her spread a beautiful valley surrounded by low hills. Dotting
it were numerous circular towers, dome-capped, and surrounding each tower was a stone wall enclosing several acres
of ground. The valley appeared to be in a high state of cultivation. Upon the opposite side of the hill and just beneath
her was a tower and enclosure. It was the roof of the former
that had first attracted her attention. In all respects it seemed
identical in construction with those further out in the valley—a high, plastered wall of massive construction surrounding a similarly constructed tower, upon whose gray surface
was painted in vivid colors a strange device. The towers were
about forty sofads in diameter, approximately forty earth-
feet, and sixty in height to the base of the dome. To an Earth
man they would have immediately suggested the silos in
which dairy farmers store ensilage for their herds, but closer
scrutiny, revealing an occasional embrasured opening together
with the strange construction of the domes, would have altered such a conclusion. Tara of Helium saw that the domes
seemed to be faced with innumerable prisms of glass, those

that were exposed to the declining sun scintillating so gorge-
ously as to remind her suddenly of the magnificent trappings
of Gahan of Gathol. As she thought of the man she shook
her head angrily, and moved cautiously forward a foot or
two that she might get a less obstructed view of the nearer
tower and its enclosure.

As Tara of Helium looked down into the enclosure surrounding the nearest tower, her brows contracted momentarily in frowning surprise, and then her eyes went wide in an
expression of incredulity tinged with horror, for what she saw
was a score or two of human bodies—naked and headless.
For a long moment she watched, breathless; unable to believe
the evidence of her own eyes—that these gruesome things
moved and had life! She saw them crawling about on hands
and knees over and across one another, searching about with
their fingers. And she saw some of them at troughs, for which
the others seemed to be searching, and those at the troughs
were taking something from these receptacles and apparently
putting it in a hole where their necks should have been. They
were not far beneath her—she could see them distinctly and
she saw that there were the bodies of both men and women,
and that they were beautifully proportioned, and that their
skin was similar to hers, but of a slightly lighter red. At first
she had thought that she was looking upon a shambles and
that the bodies, but recently decapitated, were moving under
the impulse of muscular reaction; but presently she realized
that this was their normal condition. The horror of them fascinated her, so that she could scarce take her eyes from them.
It was evident from their groping hands that they were eye-
less, and their sluggish movements suggested a rudimentary
nervous system and a correspondingly minute brain. The girl
wondered how they subsisted for she could not, even by the
wildest stretch of imagination, picture these imperfect creatures as intelligent tillers of the soil. Yet that the soil of the
valley was tilled was evident and that these things had food
was equally so. But who tilled the soil? Who kept and fed
these unhappy things, and for what purpose? It was an
enigma beyond her powers of deduction.

The sight of food aroused again a consciousness of her
own gnawing hunger and the thirst that parched her throat.
She could see both food and water within the enclosure; but
would she dare enter even should she find means of ingress?
She doubted it, since the very thought of possible contact

with these gruesome creatures sent a shudder through her
frame.

Then her eyes wandered again out across the valley until
presently they picked out what appeared to be a tiny stream
winding its way through the center of the farm lands—a
strange sight upon Barsoom. Ah, if it were but water! Then
she might hope with a real hope, for the fields would give her
sustenance which she could gain by night, while by day she
hid among the surrounding hills, and sometime, yes, sometime she knew, the searchers would come, for John Carter,
Warlord of Barsoom, would never cease to search for his
daughter until every square haad of the planet had been
combed again and again. She knew him and she knew the
warriors of Helium and so she knew that could she but manage to escape harm until they came, they would indeed come
at last.

She would have to wait until dark before she dare venture
into the valley, and in the meantime she thought it well to
search out a place of safety nearby where she might be reasonably safe from savage beasts. It was possible that the dis-
trict was free from carnivora, but one might never be sure in
a strange land. As she was about to withdraw behind the
brow of the hill her attention was again attracted to the enclosure below. Two figures had emerged from the tower.
Their beautiful bodies seemed identical with those of the
headless creatures among which they moved, but the newcomers were not headless. Upon their shoulders were heads
that seemed human, yet which the girl intuitively sensed were
not human. They were just a trifle too far away for her to see
them distinctly in the waning light of the dying day, but she
knew that they were too large, they were out of proportion to
the perfectly proportioned bodies, and they were oblate in
form. She could see that the men wore some manner of
harness to which were slung the customary long-sword and
short-sword of the Barsoomian warrior, and that about their
short necks were massive leather collars cut to fit closely over
the shoulders and snugly to the lower part of the head. Their
features were scarce discernible, but there was a suggestion of
grotesqueness about them that carried to her a feeling of re-
vulsion.

The two carried a long rope to which were fastened, at intervals of about two sofads, what she later guessed were light
manacles, for she saw the warriors passing among the poor
creatures in the enclosure and about the right wrist of each

they fastened one of the manacles. When all had been thus
fastened to the rope one of the warriors commenced to pull
and tug at the loose end as though attempting to drag the
headless company toward the tower, while the other went
among them with a long, light whip with which he flicked
them upon the naked skin. Slowly, dully, the creatures rose to
their feet and between the tugging of the warrior in front and
the lashing of him behind the hopeless band was finally
herded within the tower. Tara of Helium shuddered as she
turned away. What manner of creatures were these?

Suddenly it was night. The Barsoomian day had ended,
and then the brief period of twilight that renders the transition from daylight to darkness almost as abrupt as the
switching off of an electric light, and Tara of Helium had
found no sanctuary. But perhaps there were no beasts to fear,
or rather to avoid—Tara of Helium liked not the word fear.
She would have been glad, however, had there been a cabin,
even a very tiny cabin, upon her small flier; but there was no
cabin. The interior of the hull was completely taken up by
the buoyancy tanks. Ah, she had it! How stupid of her not to
have thought of it before. She could moor the craft to the
tree beneath which it rested and let it rise the length of the
rope. Lashed to the deck rings she would then be safe from
any roaming beast of prey that chanced along. In the morning she could drop to ground again before the craft was discovered.

As Tara of Helium crept over the brow of the hill down
toward the valley, her presence was hidden by the darkness
of the night from the sight of any chance observer who might
be loitering by a window in the nearby tower. Cluros, the farther moon, was just rising above the horizon to commence his
leisurely journey through the heavens. Eight zodes later he
would set—a trifle over nineteen and a half Earth hours—
and during that time Thuria, his vivacious mate, would have
circled the planet twice and be more than half way around
on her third trip. She had but just set. It would be more than
three and a half hours before she shot above the opposite
horizon to hurtle, swift and low, across the face of the dying
planet. During this temporary absence of the mad moon Tara
of Helium hoped to find both food and water, and gain again
the safety of her flier's deck.

She groped her way through the darkness, giving the tower
and its enclosure as wide a berth as possible. Sometimes she
stumbled, for in the long shadows cast by the rising Cluros

objects were grotesquely distorted, though the light from the
moon was still not sufficient to be of much assistance to her.
Nor, as a matter of fact, did she want light. She could find
the stream in the dark, by the simple expedient of going
down hill until she walked into it and she had seen that bearing trees and many crops grew throughout the valley, so that
she would pass food in plenty ere she reached the stream. If
the moon showed her the way more clearly and thus saved
her from an occasional fall, he would, too, show her more
clearly to the strange denizens of the towers, and that, of
course, must not be. Could she have waited until the following night conditions would have been better, since Cluros
would not appear in the heavens at all and so, during
Thuria's absence, utter darkness would reign; but the pangs
of thirst and the gnawing of hunger could be endured no
longer with food and drink both in sight, and so she had decided to risk discovery rather than suffer longer.

Safely past the nearest tower, she moved as rapidly as she
felt consistent with safety, choosing her way wherever possible so that she might take advantage of the shadows of the
trees that grew at intervals and at the same time discover
those which bore fruit. In this latter she met with almost immediate success, for the very third tree beneath which she
halted was heavy with ripe fruit. Never, thought Tara of Helium, had aught so delicious impinged upon her palate, and
yet it was naught else than the almost tasteless usa, which is
considered to be palatable only after having been cooked and
highly spiced. It grows easily with little irrigation and the
trees bear abundantly. The fruit, which ranks high in food
value, is one of the staple foods of the less well-to-do, and because of its cheapness and nutritive value forms one of the
principal rations of both armies and navies upon Barsoom, a
use which has won for it a Martian *sobriquet* which, freely
translated into English, would be, The Fighting Potato. The
girl was wise enough to eat but sparingly, but she filled her
pocket-pouch with the fruit before she continued upon her
way.

Two towers she passed before she came at last to the
stream and here again she was temperate, drinking but little
and that very slowly, contenting herself with rinsing her
mouth frequently and bathing her face, her hands, and her
feet; and even though the night was cold, as Martian nights
are, the sensation of refreshment more than compensated for
the physical discomfort of the low temperature. Replacing

her sandals she sought among the growing truck near the stream for whatever edible berries or tubers might be planted there, and found a couple of varieties that could be eaten raw. With these she replaced some of the usa in her pocket-pouch, not only to insure a variety but because she found them more palatable. Occasionally she returned to the stream to drink, but each time moderately. Always were her eyes and ears alert for the first signs of danger, but she had neither seen nor heard aught to disturb her. And presently the time approached when she felt she must return to her flier lest she be caught in the revealing light of low swinging Thuria. She dreaded leaving the water for she knew that she must become very thirsty before she could hope to come again to the stream. If she only had some little receptacle in which to carry water, even a small amount would tide her over until the following night; but she had nothing and so she must content herself as best she could with the juices of the fruit and tubers she had gathered.

After a last drink at the stream, the longest and deepest she had allowed herself, she rose to retrace her steps toward the hills; but even as she did so she became suddenly tense with apprehension. What was that? She could have sworn that she saw something move in the shadows beneath a tree not far away. For a long minute the girl did not move—she scarce breathed. Her eyes remained fixed upon the dense shadows below the tree, her ears strained through the silence of the night. A low moaning came down from the hills where her flier was hidden. She knew it well—the weird note of the hunting banth. And the great carnivore lay directly in her path. But he was not so close as this other thing, hiding there in the shadows just a little way off. What was it? It was the strain of uncertainty that weighed heaviest upon her. Had she known the nature of the creature lurking there half its menace would have vanished. She cast quickly about her in search of some haven of refuge should the thing prove dangerous.

Again arose the moaning from the hills, but this time closer. Almost immediately it was answered from the opposite side of the valley, behind her, and then from the distance to the right of her, and twice upon her left. Her eyes had found a tree, quite near. Slowly, and without taking her eyes from the shadows of that other tree, she moved toward the overhanging branches that might afford her sanctuary in the event of need, and at her first move a low growl rose from the spot she had been watching and she heard the sudden moving of a big body. Simultaneously the creature shot into the moonlight in full charge upon her, its tail erect, its tiny ears laid flat, its great mouth with its multiple rows of sharp and powerful fangs already yawning for its prey, its ten legs carrying it forward in great leaps, and now from the beast's throat issued the frightful roar with which it seeks to paralyze its prey. It was a banth—the great, maned lion of Barsoom. Tara of Helium saw it coming and leaped for the tree toward which she had been moving, and the banth realized her intention and redoubled his speed. As his hideous roar awakened the echoes in the hills, so too it awakened echoes in the valley; but these echoes came from the living throats of others of his kind, until it seemed to the girl that Fate had thrown her into the midst of a countless multitude of these savage beasts.

Almost incredibly swift is the speed of a charging banth, and fortunate it was that the girl had not been caught farther in the open. As it was, her margin of safety was next to negligible, for as she swung nimbly to the lower branches the creature in pursuit of her crashed among the foliage almost upon her as it sprang upward to seize her. It was only a combination of good fortune and agility that saved her. A stout branch deflected the raking talons of the carnivore, but so close was the call that a giant forearm brushed her flesh in the instant before she scrambled to the higher branches.

Baffled, the banth gave vent to his rage and disappointment in a series of frightful roars that caused the very ground to tremble, and to these were added the roarings and the growlings and the moanings of his fellows as they approached from every direction, in the hope of wresting from him whatever of his kill they could take by craft or prowess. And now he turned snarling upon them as they circled the tree, while the girl, huddled in a crotch above them, looked down upon the gaunt, yellow monsters padding on noiseless feet in a restless circle about her. She wondered now at the strange freak of fate that had permitted her to come down this far into the valley by night unharmed; but even more she wondered how she was to return to the hills. She knew that she would not dare venture it by night and she guessed, too, that by day she might be confronted by even graver perils. To depend upon this valley for sustenance she now saw to be beyond the pale of possibility because of the banths that would keep her from food and water by night, while the dwellers in the towers would doubtless make it equally impossible for her to forage by day. There was but one solution of her difficulty and that was to return to her flier and pray that the wind would waft her to some less terrorful land; but when might she return to the flier? The banths gave little evidence of relinquishing hope of her, and even if they wandered out of sight would she dare risk the attempt? She doubted it.

Hopeless indeed seemed her situation—hopeless it was.

More Things Under Heaven and Earth

The adventure-fantasy genre received new spurts of vigor from each Burroughs success, and from the success of other authors, such as A. Conan Doyle, whose *The Lost World* was published in 1912, and George Allan England, whose best-known novel, *Darkness and Dawn* (later to become a trilogy), was serialized in *Cavalier* the same year.

It was a time of series and sequels and trilogies. It was a time also of events in the real world, with the discovery of cosmic rays, the planetary atom, and atomic number, and the invention of the X-ray tube, the tank, the radio-tube oscillator, stainless steel, and the mass spectroscope, and the outbreak of World War I. Charles B. Stilson's trilogy about a lost race in an Antarctic volcanic valley began in *All-Story* in 1915 with *Polaris of the Snows*, and J. U. Giesy's trilogy about the adventures of a man who projects his astral self to a planet of Sirius began in *All-Story* in 1918 with *Palos of the Dog Star Pack*. Other authors working in the genre include Austin Hall, Homer Eon Flint, Ray Cummings, Victor Rousseau, Francis Stevens, and Garrett Smith.

Then, in 1917, a new talent appeared in the pulp-magazine field, and a new variation in the adventure-fantasy genre. The variation was toward even more fantastic situations and toward an epic quality of struggle between ultimate good and ultimate evil. The author was A. (for Abraham) Merritt (1884–1943).

Merritt spent most of his working career as associate editor and eventually editor of William Randolph Hearst's Sunday magazine section, *The American Weekly*. The job paid well, but Merritt apparently needed some creative release. The avenues for that release may have been opened by the articles that crossed his desk. Strange happenings, mysterious places, romantic episodes were staples in the Sunday diet Hearst fed his readers.

The first Merritt story, an oriental fantasy entitled

"Through the Dragon Glass," appeared in *All-Story* in 1917; the second, a year later, was "The People of the Pit." In 1918, also, appeared the classic novelette "The Moon Pool." It was followed a year later by a sequel, Merritt's first novel, *The Conquest of the Moon Pool*. The two were reprinted the same year as *The Moon Pool*.

Merritt became a steady producer of romantic novels, as successful in his way as Burroughs, though never as prolific. In succeeding years he wrote *The Metal Monster* (1920), *The Ship of Ishtar* (1926), *Seven Footprints to Satan* (1928), *The Face in the Abyss* (1931), *Dwellers in the Mirage* (1932), *Burn Witch Burn!* (1933), and *Creep, Shadow* (1934). All were serialized, mostly in *Argosy*, frequently reprinted, and almost immediately published in book form. They maintained substantial sales for decades, first in hardcover, two by Putnam, one by the Doubleday Crime Club, the remainder by Liveright, and then in paperback by Avon. They sold by the millions and still remain in print.

Merritt's importance in the history of science fiction rests as much upon his influence on other writers and on the tastes of readers as upon the value of the work itself. Merritt's work was reprinted in Gernsback's *Amazing Stories*, and such early science-fiction writers as Jack Williamson and Edmond Hamilton modeled their first stories after his fantastic environments, his ultimate menaces, and his lush prose. His strain of romantic fantasy runs through the early science-fiction magazines.

Where Burroughs's novels were adventure stories in fantastic settings, Merritt's tales ended with good and evil locked in mortal combat. The outcomes of these conflicts did not depend simply on strength of arm, skill in combat, courage, honor, or ingenuity. They turned on the ability of the soul to remain steadfast, to resist temptation or to endure hardship; often the strength to rise to the ultimate challenge was made possible by unselfish love.

Burroughs's heroes never admit the possibility of defeat. "I still live," says John Carter. Merritt's heroes and heroines continually doubt their abilities to succeed against insuperable obstacles, as well they might, and are continually faced, literally, with a fate worse than death.

Merritt placed his lost races in remote places of the earth: caverns and hidden valleys were particular favorites, and great distances usually were involved. Within the hidden places were uniquely fantastic creatures: energy beings,

Krakens, gigantic faces that wept tears of blood, snake mothers; satanic leaders of criminals . . . In those places heroic
men and women were tested by forces beyond their imaginings and often immeasurably beyond their powers, forces that
combined the horrible and the marvelous in equal quantities.

In describing these places and these forces Merritt often
succumbed to excess: he delighted in the exotic adjective and
noun, such as "amethyst," "cusped," "cornute," "chimerically
angled," "opalescence," "luminescence," and so forth; and in
such contradictory mixtures as "mingled ecstasy and horror,"
"fantastic yet disquietingly symmetrical." But the contradictory traits of Merritt's alien creatures, as well as his inventiveness, kept them fresh, somehow more credible than
unalloyed evil, even appealing. Here was the sense of wonder
at its most wonderful.

Merritt's lush prose was beloved in his time but is not
much in favor these days. But what he was trying to evoke
was a feeling of the utterly fantastic, and if he tried too hard
to describe the ineffable he might well be forgiven his
excesses as Burroughs is forgiven his coincidences.

The People of the Pit

by A. Merritt

North of us a shaft of light shot half way to the zenith. It
came from behind the five peaks. The beam drove up
through a column of blue haze whose edges were marked as
sharply as the rain that streams from the edges of a thunder
cloud. It was like the flash of a searchlight through an azure
mist. It cast no shadows.

As it struck upward the summits were outlined hard and
black and I saw that the whole mountain was shaped like a
hand. As the light silhouetted it, the gigantic fingers stretched,
the hand seemed to thrust itself forward. It was exactly as
though it moved to push something back. The shining beam
held steady for a moment; then broke into myriads of little
luminous globes that swung to and fro and dropped gently.
They seemed to be searching.

The forest had become very still. Every wood noise held its breath. I felt the dogs pressing against my legs. They too were silent; but every muscle in their bodies trembled, their hair was stiff along their backs and their eyes, fixed on the falling lights, were filmed with the terror glaze.

I looked at Anderson. He was staring at the North where once more the beam had pulsed upward.

"It can't be the aurora," I spoke without moving my lips. My mouth was as dry as though Lao T'zai had poured his fear dust down my throat.

"If it is I never saw one like it," he answered in the same tone. "Besides who ever heard of an aurora at this time of the year?"

He voiced the thought that was in my own mind.

"It makes me think something is being hunted up there," he said, "an unholy sort of hunt—it's well for us to be out of range."

"The mountain seems to move each time the shaft shoots up," I said. "What's it keeping back, Starr? It makes me think of the frozen hand of cloud that Shan Nadour set before the Gate of Ghouls to keep them in the lairs that Eblis cut for them."

He raised a hand—listening.

From the North and high overhead there came a whispering. It was not the rustling of the aurora, that rushing, crackling sound like the ghosts of winds that blew at Creation racing through the skeleton leaves of ancient trees that sheltered Lilith. It was a whispering that held in it a demand. It was eager. It called us to come up where the beam was flashing. It drew. There was in it a note of inexorable insistence. It touched my heart with a thousand tiny fear-tipped fingers and it filled me with a vast longing to race on and merge myself in the light. It must have been so that Ulysses felt when he strained at the mast and strove to obey the crystal sweet singing of the Sirens.

The whispering grew louder.

"What the hell's the matter with those dogs?" cried Anderson savagely. "Look at them!"

The malemutes, whining, were racing away toward the light. We saw them disappear among the trees. There came back to us a mournful howling. Then that too died away and left nothing but the insistent murmuring overhead.

The glade we had camped in looked straight to the North. We had reached I suppose three hundred miles above the first great bend of the Koskokwim toward the Yukon. Certainly we were in an untrodden part of the wilderness. We had pushed through from Dawson at the breaking of the Spring, on a fair lead to the lost five peaks between which, so the Athabasean medicine man had told us, the gold streams out like putty from a clenched fist. Not an Indian were we able to get to go with us. The land of the Hand Mountain was accursed they said. We had sighted the peaks the night before, their tops faintly outlined against a pulsing glow. And now we saw the light that had led us to them.

Anderson stiffened. Through the whispering had broken a curious pad-pad and a rustling. It sounded as though a small bear were moving towards us. I threw a pile of wood on the fire and, as it blazed up, saw something break through the bushes. It walked on all fours, but it did not walk like a bear. All at once it flashed upon me—it was like a baby crawling upstairs. The forepaws lifted themselves in grotesquely infantile fashion. It was grotesque but it was—terrible. It grew closer. We reached for our guns—and dropped them. Suddenly we knew that this crawling thing was a man!

It was a man. Still with the high climbing pad-pad he swayed to the fire. He stopped.

"Safe," whispered the crawling man, in a voice that was an echo of the murmur overhead. "Quite safe here. They can't get out of the blue, you know. They can't get you—unless you go to them——"

He fell over on his side. We ran to him. Anderson knelt.

"God's love!" he said. "Frank, look at this!"

He pointed to the hands. The wrists were covered with torn rags of a heavy shirt. The hands themselves were stumps! The fingers had been bent into the palms and the flesh had been worn to the bone. They looked like the feet of a little black elephant! My eyes traveled down the body. Around the waist was a heavy band of yellow metal. From it fell a ring and a dozen links of shining white chain!

"What is he? Where did he come from?" said Anderson. "Look, he's fast asleep—yet even in his sleep his arms try to climb and his feet draw themselves up one after the other! And his knees—how in God's name was he ever able to move on them?"

It was even as he said. In the deep sleep that had come upon the crawler arms and legs kept raising in a deliberate, dreadful climbing motion. It was as though they had a life of their own—they kept their movement independently of the motionless body. They were semaphoric motions. If you have ever stood at the back of a train and had watched the semaphores rise and fall you will know exactly what I mean.

Abruptly the overhead whispering ceased. The shaft of light dropped and did not rise again. The crawling man became still. A gentle glow began to grow around us. It was dawn, and the short Alaskan summer night was over. Anderson rubbed his eyes and turned to me a haggard face.

"Man!" he exclaimed. "You look as though you have been through a spell of sickness!"

"No more than you, Starr," I said: "What do you make of it all?"

"I'm thinking our only answer lies there," he answered, pointing to the figure that lay so motionless under the blankets we had thrown over him. "Whatever it was—that's what it was after. There was no aurora about that light, Frank. It was like the flaring up of some queer hell the preacher folk never frightened us with."

"We'll go no further today," I said. "I wouldn't wake him for all the gold that runs between the fingers of the five peaks—nor for all the devils that may be behind them."

The crawling man lay in a sleep as deep as the Styx. We bathed and bandaged the pads that had been his hands. Arms and legs were as rigid as though they were crutches. He did not move while we worked over him. He lay as he had fallen, the arms a trifle raised, the knees bent.

"Why did he crawl?" whispered Anderson. "Why didn't he walk?"

I was filing the band about the waist. It was gold, but it was like no gold I had ever handled. Pure gold is soft. This was soft, but it had an unclean, viscid life of its own. It clung to the file. I gashed through it, bent it away from the body and hurled it far off. It was—loathsome!

All that day he slept. Darkness came and still he slept. That night there was no shaft of light, no questing globe, no whispering. Some spell of horror seemed lifted from the land. It was noon when the crawling man awoke. I jumped as the pleasant drawling voice sounded.

"How long have I slept?" he asked. His pale blue eyes grew quizzical as I stared at him.

"A night—and almost two days," I said.

"Was there any light up there last night?" He nodded to the North eagerly. "Any whispering?"

"Neither," I answered. His head fell back and he stared up at the sky.

"They've given it up, then?" he said at last.

"Who have given it up?" asked Anderson.

"Why, the people of the pit," replied the crawling man quietly.

We stared at him.

"The people of the pit," he said. "Things that the Devil made before the Flood and that somehow have escaped God's vengeance. You weren't in any danger from them—unless you had followed their call. They can't get any further than the blue haze. I was their prisoner," he added simply. "They were trying to whisper me back to them!"

Anderson and I looked at each other, the same thought in both our minds.

"You're wrong," said the crawling man. "I'm not insane. Give me a very little to drink. I'm going to die soon, but I want you to take me as far South as you can before I die, and afterwards I want you to build a big fire and burn me. I want to be in such shape that no infernal spell of theirs can drag my body back to them. You'll do it too, when I've told you about them——" he hesitated. "I think their chain is off me?" he said.

"I cut it off," I answered shortly.

"Thank God for that too," whispered the crawling man.

He drank the brandy and water we lifted to his lips.

"Arms and legs quite dead," he said. "Dead as I'll be soon. Well, they did well for me. Now I'll tell you what's up there behind that hand. Hell!"

"Now listen. My name is Stanton—Sinclair Stanton. Class 1900, Yale. Explorer. I started away from Dawson last year to hunt for five peaks that rise like a hand in a haunted country and run pure gold between them. Same thing you were after? I thought so. Late last fall my comrade sickened. Sent him back with some Indians. Little later all my Indians ran away from me. I decided I'd stick, built a cabin, stocked myself with food and lay down to winter it. In the Spring I started off again. Little less than two weeks ago I sighted the five peaks. Not from this side though—the other. Give me some more brandy.

"I'd made too wide a detour," he went on. "I'd gotten too far North. I beat back. From this side you see nothing but forest straight up to the base of the Hand Mountain. Over on the other side——"

He was silent for a moment.

"Over there is forest too. But it doesn't reach so far. No! I came out of it. Stretching miles in front of me was a level plain. It was as worn and ancient looking as the desert around the ruins of Babylon. At its end rose the peaks. Between me and them—far off—was what looked like a low dike of rocks. Then—I ran across the road!"

"The road!" cried Anderson incredulously.

"The road," said the crawling man. "A fine smooth stone road. It ran straight on to the mountain. Oh, it was road all right—and worn as though millions and millions of feet had passed over it for thousands of years. On each side of it were sand and heaps of stones. Afterwhile I began to notice these stones. They were cut, and the shape of the heaps somehow gave me the idea that a hundred thousand years ago they might have been houses. I sensed man about them and at the same time they smelled of immemorial antiquity. Well——

"The peaks grew closer. The heaps of ruins thicker. Something inexpressibly desolate hovered over them; something reached from them that struck my heart like the touch of ghosts so old that they could be only the ghosts of ghosts. I went on.

"And now I saw that what I had thought to be the low rock range at the base of the peaks was a thicker litter of ruins. The Hand Mountain was really much farther off. The road passed between two high rocks that raised themselves like a gateway."

The crawling man paused.

"They were a gateway," he said. "I reached them. I went between them. And then I sprawled and clutched the earth in sheer awe! I was on a broad stone platform. Before me was—sheer space! Imagine the Grand Canyon five times as wide and with the bottom dropped out. That is what I was looking into. It was like peeping over the edge of a cleft world down into the infinity where the planets roll! On the far side stood the five peaks. They looked like a gigantic warning hand stretched up to the sky. The lip of the abyss curved away on each side of me.

"I could see down perhaps a thousand feet. Then a thick blue haze shut out the eye. It was like the blue you see gather on the high hills at dusk. And the pit—it was awesome; awesome as the Maori Gulf of Ranalak, that sinks between the living and the dead and that only the freshly released soul has strength to leap—but never strength to cross again.

"I crept back from the verge and stood up, weak. My hand rested against one of the pillars of the gateway. There was carving upon it. It bore in still sharp outlines the heroic figure of a man. His back was turned. His arms were outstretched. There was an odd peaked headdress upon him. I looked at the opposite pillar. It bore a figure exactly similar. The pillars were triangular and the carvings were on the side away from the pit. The figures seemed to be holding something back. I looked closer. Behind the outstretched hands I seemed to see other shapes.

"I traced them out vaguely. Suddenly I felt unaccountably sick. There had come to me an impression of enormous upright slugs. Their swollen bodies were faintly cut—all except the heads which were well marked globes. They were—unutterably loathsome. I turned from the gates back to the void. I stretched myself upon the slab and looked over the edge.

"A stairway led down into the pit!"

"A stairway!" we cried.

"A stairway," repeated the crawling man as patiently as before. "It seemed not so much carved out of the rock as built into it. The slabs were about six feet long and three feet wide. It ran down from the platform and vanished into the blue haze."

"But who could build such a stairway as that?" I said. "A stairway built into the wall of a precipice and leading down into a bottomless pit!"

"Not bottomless," said the crawling man quietly. "There was a bottom. I reached it!"

"Reached it?" we repeated.

"Yes, by the stairway," answered the crawling man. "You see—I went down it!

"Yes," he said. "I went down the stairway. But not that day. I made my camp back of the gates. At dawn I filled my knapsack with food, my two canteens with water from a spring that wells up there by the gateway, walked between the carved monoliths and stepped over the edge of the pit.

"The steps ran along the side of the rock at a forty degree pitch. As I went down and down I studied them. They were of a greenish rock quite different from the granitic porphyry that formed the wall of the precipice. At first I thought that the builders had taken advantage of an outcropping stratum, and had carved from it their gigantic flight. But the regularity of the angle at which it fell made me doubtful of this theory.

"After I had gone perhaps half a mile I stepped out upon a

landing. From this landing the stairs made a V shaped turn and ran on downward, clinging to the cliff at the same angle as the first flight; it was a zig-zag, and after I had made three of these turns I knew that the steps dropped straight down in a succession of such angles. No strata could be so regular as that. No, the stairway was built by hands! But whose? The answer is in those ruins around the edge, I think—never to be read.

"By noon I had lost sight of the five peaks and the lip of the abyss. Above me, below me, was nothing but the blue haze. Beside me, too, was nothingness, for the further breast of rock had long since vanished. I felt no dizziness, and any trace of fear was swallowed in a vast curiosity. What was I to discover? Some ancient and wonderful civilization that had ruled when the Poles were tropical gardens? Nothing living, I felt sure—all was too old for life. Still, a stairway so wonderful must lead to something quite as wonderful I knew. What was it? I went on.

"At regular intervals I had passed the mouths of small caves. There would be two thousand steps and then an opening, two thousand more steps and an opening—and so on and on. Late that afternoon I stopped before one of these clefts. I suppose I had gone then three miles down the pit, although the angles were such that I had walked in all fully ten miles. I examined the entrance. On each side were carved the figures of the great portal above, only now they were standing face forward, the arms outstretched as though to hold something back from the outer depths. Their faces were covered with veils. There were no hideous shapes behind them. I went inside. The fissure ran back for twenty yards like a burrow. It was dry and perfectly light. Outside I could see the blue haze rising upward like a column, its edges clearly marked. I felt an extraordinary sense of security, although I had not been conscious of any fear. I felt that the figures at the entrance were guardians—but against what?

"The blue haze thickened and grew faintly luminescent. I fancied that it was dusk above. I ate and drank a little and slept. When I awoke the blue had lightened again, and I fancied it was dawn above. I went on. I forgot the gulf yawning at my side. I felt no fatigue and little hunger or thirst, although I had drunk and eaten sparingly. That night I spent within another of the caves, and at dawn I descended again.

"It was late that day when I first saw the city——"

He was silent for a time.

"The city," he said at last, "there is a city you know. But
not such a city as you have ever seen—nor any other man
who has lived to tell of it. The pit, I think, is shaped like a
bottle; the opening before the five peaks is the neck. But how
wide the bottom is I do not know—thousands of miles
maybe. I had begun to catch little glints of light far down in
the blue. Then I saw the tops of—trees, I suppose they are.
But not our kind of trees—unpleasant, snaky kind of trees.
They reared themselves on high thin trunks and their tops
were nests of thick tendrils with ugly little leaves like arrow
heads. The trees were red, a vivid angry red. Here and there
I glimpsed spots of shining yellow. I knew these were water
because I could see things breaking through their surface—or
at least I could see the splash and ripple, but what it was that
disturbed them I never saw.

"Straight beneath me was the—city. I looked down upon
mile after mile of closely packed cylinders. They lay upon
their sides in pyramids of three, of five—of dozens—piled
upon each other. It is hard to make you see what that city is
like—look, suppose you have water pipes of a certain length
and first you lay three of them side by side and on top of
them you place two and on these two one; or suppose you
take five for a foundation and place on these four and then
three, then two and then one. Do you see? That was the way
they looked. But they were topped by towers, by minarets, by
flares, by fans, and twisted monstrosities. They gleamed as
though coated with pale rose flames. Beside them the venomous red trees raised themselves like the heads of hydras
guarding nests of gigantic, jeweled and sleeping worms!

"A few feet beneath me the stairway jutted out into a Titanic arch, unearthly as the span that bridges Hell and leads
to Asgard. It curved out and down straight through the top of
the highest pile of carven cylinders and then it vanished
through it. It was appalling—it was demonic——"

The crawling man stopped. His eyes rolled up into his
head. He trembled and his arms and legs began their horrible
crawling movement. From his lips came a whispering. It was
an echo of the high murmuring we had heard the night he
came to us. I put my hands over his eyes. He quieted.

"The Things Accursed!" he said. "The People of the Pit!
Did I whisper? Yes—but they can't get me now—they can't!"

After a time he began as quietly as before.

"I crossed the span. I went down through the top of
that—building. Blue darkness shrouded me for a moment and

I felt the steps twist into a spiral. I wound down and then—I was standing high up in—I can't tell you in what, I'll have to call it a room. We have no images for what is in the pit. A hundred feet below me was the floor. The walls sloped down and out from where I stood in a series of widening crescents. The place was colossal—and it was filled with a curious mottled red light. It was like the light inside a green and gold flecked fire opal. I went down to the last step. Far in front of me rose a high, columned altar. Its pillars were carved in monstrous scrolls—like mad octopuses with a thousand drunken tentacles; they rested on the backs of shapeless monstrosities carved in crimson stone. The altar front was a gigantic slab of purple covered with carvings.

"I can't describe these carvings! No human being could— the human eye cannot grasp them any more than it can grasp the shapes that haunt the fourth dimension. Only a subtle sense in the back of the brain sensed them vaguely. They were formless things that gave no conscious image, yet pressed into the mind like small hot seals—ideas of hate—of combats between unthinkable monstrous things—victories in a nebulous hell of steaming, obscene jungles—aspirations and ideals immeasurably loathsome——

"And as I stood I grew aware of something that lay behind the lip of the altar fifty feet above me. I knew it was there—I felt it with every hair and every tiny bit of my skin. Something infinitely malignant, infinitely horrible, infinitely ancient. It lurked, it brooded, it threatened and it—was invisible!

"Behind me was a circle of blue light. I ran for it. Something urged me to turn back, to climb the stairs and make away. It was impossible. Repulsion for that unseen Thing raced me onward as though a current had my feet. I passed through the circle. I was out on a street that stretched on into dim distance between rows of the carven cylinders.

"Here and there the red trees arose. Between them rolled the stone burrows. And now I could take in the amazing ornamentation that clothed them. They were like the trunks of smooth skinned trees that had fallen and had been clothed with high reaching noxious orchids. Yes—those cylinders were like that—and more. They should have gone out with the dinosaurs. They were—monstrous. They struck the eyes like a blow and they passed across the nerves like a rasp. And nowhere was there sight or sound of living thing.

"There were circular openings in the cylinders like the

circle in the Temple of the Stairway. I passed through one of them. I was in a long, bare vaulted room whose curving sides half closed twenty feet over my head, leaving a wide slit that opened into another vaulted chamber above. There was absolutely nothing in the room save the same mottled reddish light that I had seen in the Temple. I stumbled. I still could see nothing, but there was something on the floor over which I had tripped. I reached down—and my hand touched a thing cold and smooth—that moved under it—I turned and ran out of that place—I was filled with a loathing that had in it something of madness—I ran on and on blindly—wringing my hands—weeping with horror——

"When I came to myself I was still among the stone cylinders and red trees. I tried to retrace my steps; to find the Temple. I was more than afraid. I was like a new loosed soul panic-stricken with the first terrors of hell. I could not find the Temple! Then the haze began to thicken and glow; the cylinders to shine more brightly. I knew that it was dusk in the world above and I felt that with dusk my time of peril had come; that the thickening of the haze was the signal for the awakening of whatever things lived in this pit.

"I scrambled up the sides of one of the burrows. I hid behind a twisted nightmare of stone. Perhaps, I thought, there was a chance of remaining hidden until the blue lightened, and the peril passed. There began to grow around me a murmur. It was everywhere—and it grew and grew into a great whispering. I peeped from the side of the stone down into the street. I saw lights passing and repassing. More and more lights—they swam out of the circular doorways and they thronged the street. The highest were eight feet above the pave; the lowest perhaps two. They hurried, they sauntered, they bowed, they stopped and whispered—and there was nothing under them!"

"Nothing under them!" breathed Anderson.

"No," he went on, "that was the terrible part of it—there was nothing under them. Yet certainly the lights were living things. They had consciousness, volition, thought—what else I did not know. They were nearly two feet across—the largest. Their center was a bright nucleus—red, blue, green. This nucleus faded off, gradually, into a misty glow that did not end abruptly. It too seemed to face off into nothingness—but a nothingness that had under it a somethingness. I strained my eyes trying to grasp this body into which the lights merged and which one could only feel was there, but could not see.

"And all at once I grew rigid. Something cold, and thin like a whip, had touched my face. I turned my head. Close behind were three of the lights. They were a pale blue. They looked at me—if you can imagine lights that are eyes. Another whiplash gripped my shoulder. Under the closest light came a shrill whispering. I shrieked. Abruptly the murmuring in the street ceased. I dragged my eyes from the pale blue globe that held them and looked out—the lights in the streets were rising by myriads to the level of where I stood! There they stopped and peered at me. They crowded and jostled as though they were a crowd of curious people—on Broadway. I felt a score of the lashes touch me——

"When I came to myself I was again in the great Place of the Stairway, lying at the foot of the altar. All was silent. There were no lights—only the mottled red glow. I jumped to my feet and ran toward the steps. Something jerked me back to my knees. And then I saw that around my waist had been fastened a yellow ring of metal. From it hung a chain and this chain passed up over the lip of the high ledge. I was chained to the altar!

"I reached into my pockets for my knife to cut through the ring. It was not there! I had been stripped of everything except one of the canteens that I had hung around my neck and which I suppose They had thought was—part of me. I tried to break the ring. It seemed alive. It writhed in my hands and it drew itself closer around me! I pulled at the chain. It was immovable. There came to me the consciousness of the unseen Thing above the altar. I groveled at the foot of the slab and wept. Think—alone in that place of strange light with the brooding ancient Horror above me—a monstrous Thing, a Thing unthinkable—an unseen Thing that poured forth horror——

"After awhile I gripped myself. Then I saw beside one of the pillars a yellow bowl filled with a thick white liquid. I drank it. If it killed I did not care. But its taste was pleasant and as I drank my strength came back to me with a rush. Clearly I was not to be starved. The lights, whatever they were, had a conception of human needs.

"And now the reddish mottled gleam began to deepen. Outside arose the humming and through the circle that was the entrance came streaming the globes. They ranged themselves in ranks until they filled the Temple. Their whispering grew into a chant, a cadenced whispering chant that rose and fell, rose and fell, while to its rhythm the globes lifted and sank, lifted and sank.

"All that night the lights came and went—and all that night the chant sounded as they rose and fell. At the last I felt myself only an atom of consciousness in a sea of cadenced whispering; an atom that rose and fell with the bowing globes. I tell you that even my heart pulsed in unison with them! The red glow faded, the lights streamed out; the whispering died. I was again alone and I knew that once again day had broken in my own world.

"I slept. When I awoke I found beside the pillar more of the white liquid. I scrutinized the chain that held me to the altar. I began to rub two of the links together. I did this for hours. When the red began to thicken there was a ridge worn in the links. Hope rushed up within me. There was, then, a chance to escape.

"With the thickening the lights came again. All through that night the whispering chant sounded, and the globes rose and fell. The chant seized me. It pulsed through me until every nerve and muscle quivered to it. My lips began to quiver. They strove like a man trying to cry out on a nightmare. And at last they too were whispering the chant of the people of the pit. My body bowed in unison with the lights—I was, in movement and sound, one with the nameless things while my soul sank back sick with horror and powerless. While I whispered I—saw Them!"

"Saw the lights?" I asked stupidly.

"Saw the Things under the lights," he answered. "Great transparent snail-like bodies—dozens of waving tentacles stretching from them—round gaping mouths under the luminous seeing globes. They were like the ghosts of inconceivably monstrous slugs! I could see through them. And as I stared, still bowing and whispering, the dawn came and they streamed to and through the entrance. They did not crawl or walk—they floated! They floated and were—gone!

"I did not sleep. I worked all that day at my chain. By the thickening of the red I had worn it a sixth through. And all that night I whispered and bowed with the pit people, joining in their chant to the Thing that brooded above me!

"Twice again the red thickened and the chant held me— then on the morning of the fifth day I broke through the worn links of the chain. I was free! I drank from the bowl of white liquid and poured what was left in my flask. I ran to the Stairway. I rushed up and past that unseen Horror behind

the altar ledge and was out upon the Bridge. I raced across
the span and up the Stairway.

"Can you think what it is to climb straight up the verge of
a cleft-world—with hell behind you? Hell was behind me and
terror rode me. The city had long been lost in the blue haze
before I knew that I could climb no more. My heart beat
upon my ears like a sledge. I fell before one of the little
caves feeling that here at last was sanctuary. I crept far back
within it and waited for the haze to thicken. Almost at once
it did so. From far below me came a vast and angry murmur.
At the mouth of the rift I saw a light pulse up through the
blue; die down and as it dimmed I saw myriads of the globes
that are the eyes of the pit people swing downward into the
abyss. Again and again the light pulsed and the globes fell.
They were hunting me. The whispering grew louder, more insistent.

"There grew in me the dreadful desire to join in the whispering as I had done in the Temple. I bit my lips through and
through to still them. All that night the beam shot up through
the abyss, the globes swung and the whispering sounded—and
now I knew the purpose of the caves and of the sculptured
figures that still had power to guard them. But what were the
people who had carved them? Why had they built their city
around the verge and why had they set that Stairway in the
pit? What had they been to those Things that dwelt at the
bottom and what use had the Things been to them that they
should live beside their dwelling place? That there had been
some purpose was certain. No work so prodigious as the
Stairway would have been undertaken otherwise. But what
was the purpose? And why was it that those who had dwelt
about the abyss had passed away ages gone, and the dwellers
in the abyss still lived? I could find no answer—nor can I
find any now. I have not the shred of a theory.

"Dawn came as I wondered and with it silence. I drank
what was left of the liquid in my canteen, crept from the
cave and began to climb again. That afternoon my legs gave
out. I tore off my shirt, made from it pads for my knees and
coverings for my hands. I crawled upward. I crawled up and
up. And again I crept into one of the caves and waited until
again the blue thickened, the shaft of light shot through it
and the whispering came.

"But now there was a new note in the whispering. It was
no longer threatening. It called and coaxed. It drew. A new
terror gripped me. There had come upon me a mighty desire

to leave the cave and go out where the lights swung; to let them do with me as they pleased, carry me where they wished. The desire grew. It gained fresh impulse with every rise of the beam until at last I vibrated with the desire as I had vibrated to the chant in the Temple. My body was a pendulum. Up would go the beam and I would swing toward it! Only my soul kept steady. It held me fast to the floor of the cave. And all that night it fought with my body against the spell of the pit people.

"Dawn came. Again I crept from the cave and faced the Stairway. I could not rise. My hands were torn and bleeding; my knees an agony. I forced myself upward step by step. After a while my hands became numb, the pain left my knees. They deadened. Step by step my will drove my body upward upon them.

"And then—a nightmare of crawling up infinite stretches of steps—memories of dull horror while hidden within caves with the lights pulsing without and whisperings that called and called me—memory of a time when I awoke to find that my body was obeying the call and had carried me half way out between the guardians of the portals while thousands of gleaming globes rested in the blue haze and watched me. Glimpses of bitter fights against sleep and always, always—a climb up and up along infinite distances of steps that led from Abaddon to a Paradise of blue sky and open world!

"At last a consciousness of the clear sky close above me, the lip of the pit before me—memory of passing between the great portals of the pit and of steady withdrawal from it—dreams of giant men with strange peaked crowns and veiled faces who pushed me onward and onward and held back Roman Candle globules of light that sought to draw me back to a gulf wherein planets swam between the branches of red trees that had snakes for crowns.

"And then a long, long sleep—how long God alone knows—in a cleft of rocks; an awakening to see far in the North the beam still rising and falling, the lights still hunting, the whispering high above me calling.

"Again crawling on dead arms and legs that moved—that moved—like the Ancient Mariner's ship—without volition of mine, but that carried me from a haunted place. And then— your fire—and this—safety!"

The crawling man smiled at us for a moment. Then swiftly life faded from his face. He slept.

That afternoon we struck camp and carrying the crawling

man started back South. For three days we carried him and still he slept. And on the third day, still sleeping, he died. We built a great pile of wood and we burned his body as he had asked. We scattered his ashes about the forest with the ashes of the trees that had consumed him. It must be a great magic indeed that could disentangle those ashes and draw him back in a rushing cloud to the pit he called Accursed. I do not think that even the People of the Pit have such a spell. No.

But we did not return to the five peaks to see.

The Call of the Fantastic

Any discussion of the generic roots of science fiction may overstress the role of the pulp magazines and of those who wrote for the pulp magazines. In the early part of the century, at least, the magazines were not the unifying force they would later become, and influential science fiction was being published in books and general-interest magazines. Non-genre readers had not yet learned to look down upon science fiction, and the science-fiction reader was so starved for material to satisfy his as-yet-unspecified need that he looked everywhere.

Even after the creation of the science-fiction magazine, for several years only a single new magazine was available each month, plus a quarterly after the first year and a half. These appeased the reader's appetite for only a day or two at most, and then he (almost always a "he") would search elsewhere. He leafed through other pulp magazines for something resembling science fiction; he ran his eyes across the new books at the library; he rummaged through dusty library stacks for familiar authors or promising titles on old, neutrally rebound volumes.

The 1930s brought two more magazines, but readers still picked up such hero pulp magazines as *Doc Savage*, discovered Olaf Stapledon, Aldous Huxley, and Philip Wylie as their books came out, and unearthed Jules Verne, H. Rider Haggard, M. P. Shiel, H. G. Wells, and A. Conan Doyle.

Doyle (1859–1930) had become rich and famous as the creator of Sherlock Holmes and abandoned an unpromising medical career for the life of a freelance writer. His personal favorites were his historical romances, but he also contributed science-fiction and fantasy stories to the magazines that competed for his work: usually *The Strand* in England, *Lippincott's*, *The Saturday Evening Post*, and other general-interest magazines in the United States. His most famous science-fiction novels featured Prof. George Edward Challenger in *The*

Lost World (1912) and *The Poison Belt* (1913); another well-known science fiction novella was *The Maracot Deep* (1927).

Another literary figure who wrote science fiction regularly, though not as a major part of his output, was Jack London (1876–1916). He was the illegitimate son of an itinerant Irish astrologer and an ardent spiritualist. His father deserted his mother before London's birth and never acknowledged his paternity. London was born and raised in Oakland, California, in poverty; he took his name from John London, the man his mother married when Jack was not yet a year old.

London worked at a wide variety of manual jobs at low wages while growing up, including stints in a cannery, and as oyster pirate, longshoreman, and sailor. He headed east briefly as a member of Coxey's Army to march to Washington, D.C., continued the journey as a hobo, was arrested for vagrancy in Niagara Falls, N.Y., and served a month in the penitentiary. In 1897 he joined the Klondike Gold Rush and returned the next year, unsuccessful. He became an enthusiastic convert to socialism.

During these years of travel, labor, and education, he had been writing with some success. The novel based on his Alaskan experience, *The Call of the Wild* (1903), sold a million and a half copies in hardcovers and brought him some security, but his baronial and spendthrift ways kept him writing constantly to pay his bills. At the age of forty, perhaps feeling the diminution of his writing powers as well as the pressure of finances and the ravages of heavy drinking, he died, perhaps of uremic poisoning, perhaps of a purposeful overdose of morphine and atrophine sulphate.

Among his twenty-two novels are two that are clearly science fiction—*Before Adam* (1906) and *The Star Rover* (1914)—and one that is primarily a propaganda novel for socialism, but a futuristic political work nevertheless, *The Iron Heel* (1907). In addition, his other novels contained speculative and even fantasy elements that made them congenial reading for science-fiction fans, particularly *The Call of the Wild* and *The Sea Wolf* (1904).

One of the earliest of his science-fiction stories, "A Thousand Deaths," was published in an unusual fantasy magazine, H. D. Umbstaetter's *The Black Cat*, but London's stories soon were appearing in *Collier's*, *The Atlantic Monthly*, *McClure's*, *Redbook*, *Cosmopolitan*, and *The Saturday Evening Post*. Perhaps his best-known short piece of science fiction is his novelette "The Scarlet Plague" (1912), which was reprinted in a volume of his stories by the same name in 1915.

London's major novels were well known to the science-fiction audience that developed in the 30's and '40s, but his shorter science-fiction work, with the exception of "The Scarlet Plague" and "The Shadow and the Flash," which were reprinted in *Famous Fantastic Mysteries* in the late '40s, as well as the novel *The Star Rover,* were little known. Among them was "The Red One" (1918), published in *Cosmopolitan* almost two years after London's death and reprinted the same year in a collection of his stories by that name.

"The Red One" illustrates the early level of sophistication writers of sixty years ago were capable of achieving, and their readers of accepting. Similar stories in which extraterrestrial visitation would play so casually integrated a part would not be published until at least the golden age.

The Red One

by Jack London

There it was! The abrupt liberation of sound, as he timed it with his watch, Bassett likened to the trump of an archangel. Walls of cities, he meditated, might well fall down before so vast and compelling a summons. For the thousandth time vainly he tried to analyze the tone-quality of that enormous peal that dominated the land far into the strongholds of the surrounding tribes. The mountain gorge which was its source rang to the rising tide of it until it brimmed over and flooded earth and sky and air. With the wantonness of a sick man's fancy, he likened it to the mighty cry of some Titan of the Elder World vexed with misery or wrath. Higher and higher it arose, challenging and demanding in such profounds of volume that it seemed intended for ears beyond the narrow confines of the solar system. There was in it, too, the clamor of protest in that there were no ears to hear and comprehend its utterance.

—Such the sick man's fancy. Still he strove to analyze the

sound. Sonorous as thunder was it, mellow as a golden bell, thin and sweet as a thrummed taut cord of silver—no; it was none of these, nor a blend of these. There were no words nor semblances in his vocabulary and experience with which to describe the totality of that sound.

Time passed. Minutes merged into quarters of hours, and quarters of hours into half hours, and still the sound persisted, ever changing from its initial vocal impulse yet never receiving fresh impulse—fading, dimming, dying as enormously as it had sprung into being. It became a confusion of troubled mutterings and babblings and colossal whisperings. Slowly it withdrew, sob by sob, into whatever great bosom had birthed it, until it whimpered deadly whispers of wrath and as equally seductive whispers of delight, striving still to be heard, to convey some cosmic secret, some understanding of infinite import and value. It dwindled to a ghost of sound that had lost its menace and promise, and became a thing that pulsed on in the sick man's consciousness for minutes after it had ceased. When he could hear it no longer, Bassett glanced at his watch. An hour had elapsed ere that archangel's trump had subsided into tonal nothingness.

Was this, then, *his* dark tower?—Bassett pondered, remembering his Browning and gazing at his skeleton-like and fever-wasted hands. And the fancy made him smile—of Childe Roland bearing a slug-horn to his lips with an arm as feeble as his was. Was it months, or years, he asked himself, since he first heard that mysterious call on the beach at Ringmanu? To save himself he could not tell. The long sickness had been most long. In conscious count of time he knew of months, many of them; but he had no way of estimating the long intervals of delirium and stupor. And how fared Captain Bateman of the blackbirder *Nari?* he wondered; and had Captain Bateman's drunken mate died of delirium tremens yet?

From which vain speculations, Bassett turned idly to review all that had occurred since that day on the beach of Ringmanu when he first heard the sound and plunged into the jungle after it. Sagawa had protested. He could see him yet, his queer little monkeyish face eloquent with fear, his back burdened with specimen cases, in his hands Bassett's butterfly net and naturalist's shotgun, as he quavered in Bêche-de-mer English: "Me fella too much fright along bush. Bad fella boy too much stop'm along bush."

Bassett smiled sadly at the recollection. The little New

Hanover boy had been frightened, but had proved faithful, following him without hesitancy into the bush in the quest after the source of the wonderful sound. No fire-hollowed tree-trunk, that, throbbing war through the jungle depths, had been Bassett's conclusion. Erroneous had been his next conclusion, namely, that the source or cause could not be more distant than an hour's walk and that he would easily be back by mid-afternoon to be picked up by the *Nari's* whaleboat.

"That big fella noise no good, all the same devil-devil," Sagawa had adjudged. And Sagawa had been right. Had he not had his head hacked off within the day? Bassett shuddered. Without doubt Sagawa had been eaten as well by the bad fella boys too much that stopped along the bush. He could see him, as he had last seen him stripped of the shot-gun and all the naturalist's gear of his master, lying on the narrow trail where he had been decapitated barely the moment before. Yes, within a minute the thing had happened. Within a minute, looking back, Bassett had seen him trudging patiently along under his burdens. Then Bassett's own trouble had come upon him. He looked at the cruelly healed stumps of the first and second fingers of his left hand, then rubbed them softly into the indentation in the back of his skull. Quick as had been the flash of the long-handled tomahawk, he had been quick enough to duck away his head and partially to deflect the stroke with his up-flung hand. Two fingers and a nasty scalp-wound had been the price he paid for his life. With one barrel of his ten-gauge shotgun he had blown the life out of the bushman who had so nearly got him; with the other barrel he had peppered the bushmen bending over Sagawa, and had had the pleasure of knowing that the major portion of the charge had gone into the one who leaped away with Sagawa's head. Everything had occurred in a flash. Only himself, the slain bushman, and what remained of Sagawa, were in the narrow wild-pig run of a path. From the dark jungle on either side came no rustle of movement or sound of life. And he had suffered distinct and dreadful shock. For the first time in his life he had killed a human being, and he knew nausea as he contemplated the mess of his handiwork.

Then had begun the chase. He retreated up the pig-run before his hunters, who were between him and the beach. How many there were, he could not guess. There might have been one, or a hundred, for aught he saw of them. That some of them took to the trees and travelled along through the jungle roof he was certain; but at the most he never glimpsed more than an occasional flitting of shadows. No bowstrings twanged that he could hear; but every little while, whence discharged he knew not, tiny arrows whispered past him or struck tree-boles and fluttered to the ground beside him. They were bone-tipped and feather-shafted, and the feathers, torn from the breasts of humming-birds, iridesced like jewels.

Once—and now, after the long lapse of time, he chuckled gleefully at the recollection—he had detected a shadow above him that came to instant rest as he turned his gaze upward. He could make out nothing, but, deciding to chance it, had fired at it a heavy charge of number five shot. Squalling like an infuriated cat, the shadow crashed down through tree-ferns and orchids and thudded upon the earth at his feet, and, still squalling its rage and pain, had sunk its human teeth into the ankle of his stout tramping boot. He, on the other hand, was not idle, and with his free foot had done what reduced the squalling to silence. So inured to savagery had Bassett since become, that he chuckled again with the glee of the recollection.

What a night had followed! Small wonder that he had accumulated such a virulence and variety of fevers, he thought, as he recalled that sleepless night of torment, when the throb of his wounds was as nothing compared with the myriad stings of the mosquitoes. There had been no escaping them, and he had not dared to light a fire. They had literally pumped his body full of poison, so that, with the coming of day, eyes swollen almost shut, he had stumbled blindly on, not caring much when his head should be hacked off and his carcass started on the way of Sagawa's to the cooking fire. Twenty-four hours had made a wreck of him—of mind as well as body. He had scarcely retained his wits at all, so maddened was he by the tremendous inoculation of poison he had received. Several times he fired his shotgun with effect into the shadows that dogged him. Stinging day insects and gnats added to his torment, while his bloody wounds attracted hosts of loathsome flies that clung sluggishly to his flesh and had to be brushed off and crushed off.

Once, in that day, he heard again the wonderful sound, seemingly more distant, but rising imperiously above the nearer war-drums in the bush. Right there was where he had made his mistake. Thinking that he had passed beyond it and that, therefore, it was between him and the beach of Ringmanu, he had worked back toward it when in reality he was penetrating deeper and deeper into the mysterious heart of the unexplored island. That night, crawling in among the twisted roots of a banyan tree, he had slept from exhaustion while the mosquitoes had had their will of him.

Followed days and nights that were vague as nightmares in his memory. One clear vision he remembered was of suddenly finding himself in the midst of a bush village and watching the old men and children fleeing into the jungle. All had fled but one. From close at hand and above him, a whimpering as of some animal in pain and terror had startled him. And looking up he had seen her—a girl, or young woman, rather, suspended by one arm in the cooking sun. Perhaps for days she had so hung. Her swollen protruding tongue spoke as much. Still alive, she gazed at him with eyes of terror. Past help, he decided, as he noted the swellings of her legs which advertised that the joints had been crushed and the great bones broken. He resolved to shoot her, and there the vision terminated. He could not remember whether he had or not, any more than could he remember how he chanced to be in that village or how he succeeded in getting away from it.

Many pictures, unrelated, came and went in Bassett's mind as he reviewed that period of his terrible wanderings. He remembered invading another village of a dozen houses and driving all before him with his shotgun save for one old man, too feeble to flee, who spat at him and whined and snarled as he dug open a ground-oven and from amid the hot stones dragged forth a roasted pig that steamed its essence deliciously through its green-leaf wrappings. It was at this place that a wantonness of savagery had seized upon him. Having feasted, ready to depart with a hind quarter of the pig in his hand, he deliberately fired the grass thatch of a house with his burning glass.

But seared deepest of all in Bassett's brain, was the dank and noisome jungle. It actually stank with evil, and it was always twilight. Rarely did a shaft of sunlight penetrate its matted roof a hundred feet overhead. And beneath that roof was an aerial ooze of vegetation, a monstrous, parasitic dripping of decadent lifeforms that rooted in death and lived on death. And through all this he drifted, ever pursued by the flitting shadows of the anthropophagi, themselves ghosts of evil that dared not face him in battle but that knew, soon or late, that they would feed on him. Bassett remembered that at the time, in lucid moments, he had likened himself to a wounded bull pursued by plains' coyotes too cowardly to

battle with him for the meat of him, yet certain of the inevitable end of him when they would be full gorged. As the
bull's horns and stamping hoofs kept off the coyotes, so his
shotgun kept off these Solomon Islanders, these twilight
shades of bushmen of the island of Guadalcanal.

Came the day of the grass lands. Abruptly, as if cloven by
the sword of God in the hand of God, the jungle terminated.
The edge of it, perpendicular and as black as the infamy of
it, was a hundred feet up and down. And, beginning at the
edge of it, grew the grass—sweet, soft, tender, pasture grass
that would have delighted the eyes and beasts of any husbandman and that extended, on and on, for leagues and
leagues of velvet verdure, to the backbone of the great island,
the towering mountain range flung up by some ancient earthcataclysm, serrated and gullied but not yet erased by the erosive tropic rains. But the grass! He had crawled into it a
dozen yards, buried his face in it, smelled it, and broken
down in a fit of involuntary weeping.

And, while he wept, the wonderful sound had pealed
forth—if by *peal*, he had often thought since, an adequate
description could be given of the enunciation of so vast a
sound so melting sweet. Sweet it was as no sound ever heard.
Vast it was, of so mighty a resonance that it might have
proceeded from some brazen-throated monster. And yet it
called to him across that leagues-wide savannah, and was like
a benediction to his long-suffering, pain-wracked spirit.

He remembered how he lay there in the grass, wet-cheeked
but no longer sobbing, listening to the sound and wondering
that he had been able to hear it on the beach of Ringmanu.
Some freak of air pressures and air currents, he reflected, had
made it possible for the sound to carry so far. Such conditions might not happen again in a thousand days or ten thousand days; but the one day it had happened had been the day
he landed from the *Nari* for several hours' collecting. Especially had he been in quest of the famed jungle butterfly, a
foot across from wing-tip to wing-tip, as velvet-dusky of lack
of color as was the gloom of the roof, of such lofty arboreal
habits that it resorted only to the jungle roof and could be
brought down only by a dose of shot. It was for this purpose
that Sagawa had carried the twenty-gauge shotgun.

Two days and nights he had spent crawling across that belt
of grass land. He had suffered much, but pursuit had ceased
at the jungle-edge. And he would have died of thirst had not
a heavy thunderstorm revived him on the second day.

And then had come Balatta. In the first shade, where the savannah yielded to the dense mountain jungle, he had collapsed to die. At first she had squealed with delight at sight of his helplessness, and was for beating his brain out with a stout forest branch. Perhaps it was his very utter helplessness that had appealed to her, and perhaps it was her human curiosity that made her refrain. At any rate, she had refrained, for he opened his eyes again under the impending blow, and saw her studying him intently. What especially struck her about him were his blue eyes and white skin. Coolly she had squatted on her hams, spat on his arm, and with her fingertips scrubbed away the dirt of days and nights of muck and jungle that sullied the pristine whiteness of his skin.

And everything about her had struck him especially, although there was nothing conventional about her at all. He laughed weakly at the recollection, for she had been as innocent of garb as Eve before the fig-leaf adventure. Squat and lean at the same time, asymmetrically limbed, string-muscled as if with lengths of cordage, dirt caked from infancy save for casual showers, she was as unbeautiful a prototype of woman as he, with a scientist's eye, had ever gazed upon. Her breasts advertised at the one time her maturity and youth; and, if by nothing else, her sex was advertised by the one article of finery with which she was adorned, namely a pig's tail, thrust through a hole in her left ear-lobe. So lately had the tail been severed, that its raw end still oozed blood that dried upon her shoulder like so much candle-droppings. And her face! A twisted and wizened complex of apish features, perforated by upturned, sky-open, Mongolian nostrils, by a mouth that sagged from a huge upper-lip and faded precipitately into a retreating chin, and by peering querulous eyes that blinked as blink the eyes of denizens of monkey-cages.

Not even the water she brought him in a forest-leaf, and the ancient and half-putrid chunk of roast pig, could redeem in the slightest the grotesque hideousness of her. When he had eaten weakly for a space, he closed his eyes in order not to see her, although again and again she poked them open to peer at the blue of them. Then had come the sound. Nearer, much nearer, he knew it to be; and he knew equally well, despite the weary way he had come, that it was still many hours distant. The effect of it on her had been startling. She cringed under it, with averted face, moaning and chattering with fear. But after it had lived its full life of an hour, he closed his eyes and fell asleep with Balatta brushing the flies from him.

When he awoke it was night, and she was gone. But he was aware of renewed strength, and, by then too thoroughly inoculated by the mosquito poison to suffer further inflammation, he closed his eyes and slept an unbroken stretch till sun-up. A little later Balatta had returned, bringing with her a half dozen women who, unbeautiful as they were, were patently not so unbeautiful as she. She evidenced by her conduct that she considered him her find, her property, and the pride she took in showing him off would have been ludicrous had his situation not been so desperate.

Later, after what had been to him a terrible journey of miles, when he collapsed in front of the devil-devil house in the shadow of the breadfruit tree, she had shown very lively ideas on the matter of retaining possession of him. Ngurn, whom Bassett was to know afterward as the devil-devil doctor, priest, or medicine man of the village, had wanted his head. Others of the grinning and chattering monkey-men, all as stark of clothes and bestial of appearance as Balatta, had wanted his body for the roasting oven. At that time he had not understood their language, if by *language* might be dignified the uncouth sounds they made to represent ideas. But Bassett had thoroughly understood the matter of debate, especially when the men pressed and prodded and felt of the flesh of him as if he were so much commodity in a butcher's stall.

Balatta had been losing the debate rapidly, when the accident happened. One of the men, curiously examining Bassett's shotgun, managed to cock and pull a trigger. The recoil of the butt into the pit of the man's stomach had not been the most sanguinary result, for the charge of shot, at a distance of a yard, had blown the head of one of the debaters into nothingness.

Even Balatta joined the others in flight, and, ere they returned, his senses already reeling from the oncoming fever-attack, Bassett had regained possession of the gun. Whereupon, although his teeth chattered with the ague and his swimming eyes could scarcely see, he held onto his fading consciousness until he could intimidate the bushmen with the simple magics of compass, watch, burning glass, and matches. At the last, with due emphasis of solemnity and awfulness, he had killed a young pig with his shotgun and promptly fainted.

Bassett flexed his arm muscles in quest of what possible

strength might reside in such weakness, and dragged himself slowly and totteringly to his feet. He was shockingly emaciated; yet, during the various convalescences of the many months of his long sickness, he had never regained quite the same degree of strength as this time. What he feared was another relapse such as he had already frequently experienced. Without drugs, without even quinine, he had managed so far to live through a combination of the most pernicious and most malignant of malarial and black-water fevers. But could he continue to endure? Such was his everlasting query. For, like the genuine scientist he was, he would not be content to die until he had solved the secret of the sound.

Supported by a staff, he staggered the few steps to the devil-devil house where death and Ngurn reigned in gloom. Almost as infamously dark and evil-stinking as the jungle was the devil-devil house—in Bassett's opinion. Yet therein was usually to be found his favorite crony and gossip, Ngurn, always willing for a yarn or a discussion, the while he sat in the ashes of death and in a slow smoke shrewdly revolved curing human heads suspended from the rafters. For, through the months' interval of consciousness of his long sickness, Bassett had mastered the psychological simplicities and lingual difficulties of the language of the tribe of Ngurn and Balatta, and Gngngn—the latter the addle-headed young chief who was ruled by Ngurn, and who, whispered intrigue had it, was the son of Ngurn.

"Will the Red One speak to-day?" Bassett asked, by this time so accustomed to the old man's gruesome occupation as to take even an interest in the progress of the smoke-curing.

With the eye of an expert Ngurn examined the particular head he was at work upon.

"It will be ten days before I can say 'finish,' " he said. "Never has any man fixed heads like these."

Bassett smiled inwardly at the old fellow's reluctance to talk with him of the Red One. It had always been so. Never, by any chance, had Ngurn or any other member of the weird tribe divulged the slightest hint of any physical characteristic of the Red One. Physical the Red One must be, to emit the wonderful sound, and though it was called the Red One, Bassett could not be sure that red represented the color of it. Red enough were the deeds and powers of it, from what abstract clues he had gleaned. Not alone, had Ngurn informed him, was the Red One more bestial powerful than the neighbor tribal gods, ever a-thirst for the red blood of living hu-

man sacrifices, but the neighbor gods themselves were
sacrificed and tormented before him. He was the god of a
dozen allied villages similar to this one, which was the central
and commanding village of the federation. By virtue of the
Red One many alien villages had been devastated and even
wiped out, the prisoners sacrificed to the Red One. This was
true to-day, and it extended back into old history carried
down by word of mouth through the generations. When he,
Ngurn, had been a young man, the tribes beyond the grass
lands had made a war raid. In the counter raid, Ngurn and
his fighting folk had made many prisoners. Of children alone
over five score living had been bled white before the Red
One, and many, many more men and women.

The Thunderer, was another of Ngurn's names for the
mysterious deity. Also at times was he called The Loud
Shouter, The God-Voiced, The Bird-Throated, The One with
the Throat Sweet as the Throat of the Honey-Bird, The Sun
Singer, and The Star-Born.

Why The Star-Born? In vain Bassett interrogated Ngurn.
According to that old devil-devil doctor, the Red One had always been, just where he was at present, forever singing and
thundering his will over men. But Ngurn's father, wrapped in
decaying grass-matting and hanging even then over their
heads among the smoky rafters of the devil-devil house, had
held otherwise. That departed wise one had believed that the
Red One came from out of the starry night, else why—so his
argument had run—had the old and forgotten ones passed his
name down as the Star-Born? Bassett could not but recognize
something cogent in such argument. But Ngurn affirmed the
long years of his long life, wherein he had gazed upon many
starry nights, yet never had he found a star on grass land or
in jungle depth—and he had looked for them. True, he had
beheld shooting stars (this in reply to Bassett's contention);
but likewise had he beheld the phosphorescence of fungoid
growths and rotten meat and fireflies on dark nights, and the
flames of wood-fires and of blazing candle-nuts; yet what
were flame and blaze and glow when they had flamed, and
blazed and glowed? Answer: memories, memories only, of
things which had ceased to be, like memories of matings accomplished, of feasts forgotten, of desires that were the
ghosts of desires, flaring, flaming, burning, yet unrealized in
achievement of easement and satisfaction. Where was the appetite of yesterday? the roasted flesh of the wild pig the

hunter's arrow failed to slay? the maid, unwed and dead, ere the young man knew her?

A memory was not a star, was Ngurn's contention. How could a memory be a star? Further, after all his long life he still observed the starry night-sky unaltered. Never had he noted the absence of a single star from its accustomed place. Besides, stars were fire, and the Red One was not fire—which last involuntary betrayal told Bassett nothing.

"Will the Red One speak to-morrow?" he queried.

Ngurn shrugged his shoulders as who should say.

"And the day after?—and the day after that?" Bassett persisted.

"I would like to have the curing of your head," Ngurn changed the subject. "It is different from any other head. No devil-devil has a head like it. Besides, I would cure it well. I would take months and months. The moons would come and the moons would go, and the smoke would be very slow, and I should myself gather the materials for the curing smoke. The skin would not wrinkle. It would be as smooth as your skin now."

He stood up, and from the dim rafters grimed with the smoking of countless heads, where day was no more than a gloom, took down a matting-wrapped parcel and began to open it.

"It is a head like yours," he said, "but it is poorly cured."

Bassett had pricked up his ears at the suggestion that it was a white man's head; for he had long since come to accept that these jungle-dwellers, in the midmost center of the great island, had never had intercourse with white men. Certainly he had found them without the almost universal Bêche-de-mer English of the west South Pacific. Nor had they knowledge of tobacco, nor of gunpowder. Their few precious knives, made from lengths of hoop-iron, and their few and more precious tomahawks, made from cheap trade hatchets, he had surmised they had captured in war from the bushmen of the jungle beyond the grass lands, and that they, in turn, had similarly gained them from the salt water men who fringed the coral beaches of the shore and had contact with the occasional white men.

"The folk in the out beyond do not know how to cure heads," old Ngurn explained, as he drew forth from the filthy matting and placed in Bassett's hands an indubitable white man's head.

Ancient it was beyond question; white it was as the blond

hair attested. He could have sworn it once belonged to an Englishman, and to an Englishman of long before by token of the heavy gold circlets still threaded in the withered ear-lobes.

"Now your head . . ." the devil-devil doctor began on his favorite topic.

"I'll tell you what," Bassett interrupted, struck by a new idea. "When I die I'll let you have my head to cure, if, first, you take me to look upon the Red One."

"I will have your head anyway when you are dead," Ngurn rejected the proposition. He added, with the brutal frankness of the savage: "Besides, you have not long to live. You are almost a dead man now. You will grow less strong. In not many months I shall have you here turning and turning in the smoke. It is pleasant, through the long afternoons, to turn the head of one you have known as well as I know you. And I shall talk to you and tell you the many secrets you want to know. Which will not matter, for you will be dead."

"Ngurn," Bassett threatened in sudden anger. "You know the Baby Thunder in the Iron that is mine." (This was in reference to his all-potent and all-awful shotgun.) "I can kill you any time, and then you will not get my head."

"Just the same, will Gngngn, or some one else of my folk get it," Ngurn complacently assured him. "And just the same will it turn and turn here in the devil-devil house in the smoke. The quicker you slay me with your Baby Thunder, the quicker will your head turn in the smoke."

And Bassett knew he was beaten in the discussion.

What was the Red One?—Bassett asked himself a thousand times in the succeeding week, while he seemed to grow stronger. What was the source of the wonderful sound? What was this Sun Singer, this Star-Born One, this mysterious deity, as bestial-conducted as the black and kinky-headed and mon-key-like human beasts who worshiped it, and whose silver-sweet, bull-mouthed singing and commanding he had heard at the taboo distance for so long?

Ngurn had he failed to bribe with the inevitable curing of his head when he was dead. Gngngn, imbecile and chief that he was, was too imbecilic, too much under the sway of Ngurn, to be considered. Remained Balatta, who, from the time she found him and poked his blue eyes open to re-crudescence of her grotesque, female hideousness, had contin-ued his adorer. Woman she was, and he had long known that the only way to win from her treason to her tribe was through the woman's heart of her.

Bassett was a fastidious man. He had never recovered from the initial horror caused by Balatta's female awfulness. Back in England, even at best, the charm of woman, to him, had never been robust. Yet now, resolutely, as only a man can do who is capable of martyring himself for the cause of science, he proceeded to violate all the fineness and delicacy of his nature by making love to the unthinkably disgusting bush-woman.

He shuddered, but with averted face hid his grimaces and swallowed his gorge as he put his arm around her dirt-crusted shoulders and felt the contact of her rancid-oily and kinky hair with his neck and chin. But he nearly screamed when she succumbed to that caress so at the very first of the courtship and mowed and gibbered and squealed little, queer, pig-like gurgly noises of delight. It was too much. And the next he did in the singular courtship was to take her down to the stream and give her a vigorous scrubbing.

From then on he devoted himself to her like a true swain as frequently and for as long at a time as his will could override his repugnance. But marriage, which she ardently suggested, with due observance of tribal custom, he balked at. Fortunately, taboo rule was strong in the tribe. Thus, Ngurn could never touch bone, or flesh, or hide of crocodile. This had been ordained at his birth. Gngngn was denied ever the touch of woman. Such pollution, did it chance to occur, could be purged only by the death of the offending female. It had happened once, since Bassett's arrival, when a girl of nine, running in play, stumbled and fell against the sacred chief. And the girl-child was seen no more. In whispers, Balatta told Bassett that she had been three days and nights in dying before the Red One. As for Balatta, the breadfruit was taboo to her. For which Bassett was thankful. The taboo might have been water.

For himself, he fabricated a special taboo. Only could he marry, he explained, when the Southern Cross rode highest in the sky. Knowing his astronomy, he thus gained a reprieve of nearly nine months; and he was confident that within that time he would either be dead or escaped to the coast with full knowledge of the Red One and of the source of the Red One's wonderful voice. At first he had fancied the Red One to be some colossal statue, like Memnon, rendered vocal under certain temperature conditions of sunlight. But when, af-

ter a war raid, a batch of prisoners was brought in and the
sacrifice made at night, in the midst of rain, when the sun
could play no part, the Red One had been more vocal than
usual, Bassett discarded that hypothesis.

In company with Balatta, sometimes with men and parties
of women, the freedom of the jungle was his for three
quadrants of the compass. But the fourth quadrant, which
contained the Red One's abiding place, was taboo. He made
more thorough love to Balatta—also saw to it that she
scrubbed herself more frequently. Eternal female she was, capable of any treason for the sake of love. And, though the
sight of her was provocative of nausea and the contact of her
provocative of despair, although he could not escape her awfulness in his dream-haunted nightmares of her, he nevertheless was aware of the cosmic verity of sex that animated her
and that made her own life of less value than the happiness
of her lover with whom she hoped to mate. Juliet or Balatta?
Where was the intrinsic difference? The soft and tender product of ultra-civilization, or her bestial prototype of a hundred
thousand years before her?—there was no difference.

Bassett was a scientist first, a humanist afterward. In the
jungle-heart of Guadalcanal he put the affair to the test, as in
the laboratory he would have put to the test any chemical
reaction. He increased his feigned ardor for the bushwoman,
at the same time increasing the imperiousness of his will of
desire over her to be led to look upon the Red One face to
face. It was the old story, he recognized, that the woman
must pay, and it occurred when the two of them, one day,
were catching the unclassified and unnamed little black fish,
an inch long, half-eel and half-scaled, rotund with salmon-
golden roe, that frequented the fresh water and that were esteemed, raw and whole, fresh or putrid, a perfect delicacy.
Prone in the muck of the decaying jungle-floor, Balatta threw
herself, clutching his ankles with her hands, kissing his feet
and making slubbery noises that chilled his backbone up and
down again. She begged him to kill her rather than exact this
ultimate love-payment. She told him of the penalty of breaking the taboo of the Red One—a week of torture, living, the
details of which she yammered out from her face in the mire
until he realized that he was yet a tyro in knowledge of the
frightfulness the human was capable of wreaking on the human.

Yet did Bassett insist on having his man's will satisfied, at
the woman's risk, that he might solve the mystery of the Red

One's singing, though she should die long and horribly and screaming. And Balatta, being mere woman, yielded. She led him into the forbidden quadrant. An abrupt mountain shouldering in from the north to meet a similar intrusion from the south, tormented the stream in which they had fished into a deep and gloomy gorge. After a mile along the gorge, the way plunged sharply upward until they crossed a saddle of raw limestone which attracted his geologist's eye. Still climbing, although he paused often from sheer physical weakness, they scaled forest-clad heights until they emerged on a naked mesa of tableland. Bassett recognized the stuff of its composition as black volcanic sand, and knew that a pocket magnet could have captured a full load of the sharply angular grains he trod upon.

And then, holding Balatta by the hand and leading her onward, he came to it—a tremendous pit, obviously artificial, in the heart of the plateau. Old history, the South Seas Sailing Directions, scores of remembered data and connotations swift and furious, surged through his brain. It was Mendana who had discovered the islands and named them Solomon's, believing that he had found that monarch's fabled mines. They had laughed at the old navigator's childlike credulity; and yet here stood himself, Bassett, on the rim of an excavation for all the world like the diamond pits of South Africa.

But no diamond this that he gazed upon. Rather was it a pearl, with the depth of iridescence of a pearl; but of a size all pearls of earth and time welded into one, could not have totalled; and of a color undreamed of any pearl, or of anything else, for that matter, for it was the color of the Red One. And the Red One himself Bassett knew it to be on the instant. A perfect sphere, fully two hundred feet in diameter, the top of it was a hundred feet below the level of the rim. He likened the color quality of it to lacquer. Indeed, he took it to be some sort of lacquer applied by man, but a lacquer too marvelously clever to have been manufactured by the bush-folk. Brighter than bright cherry-red, its richness of color was as if it were red builded upon red. It glowed and iridesced in the sunlight as if gleaming up from underlay under underlay of red.

In vain Balatta strove to dissuade him from descending. She threw herself in the dirt; but, when he continued down the trail that spiralled the pit-wall, she followed, cringing and whimpering her terror. That the red sphere had been dug out as a precious thing, was patent. Considering the paucity of members of the federated twelve villages and their primitive tools and methods, Bassett knew that the toil of a myriad generations could scarcely have made that enormous excavation.

He found the pit bottom carpeted with human bones, among which, battered and defaced, lay village gods of wood and stone. Some, covered with obscene totemic figures and designs, were carved from solid tree trunks forty or fifty feet in length. He noted the absence of the shark and turtle gods, so common among the shore villages, and was amazed at the constant recurrence of the helmet motive. What did these jungle savages of the dark heart of Guadalcanal know of helmets? Had Mendana's men-at-arms worn helmets and penetrated here centuries before? And if not, then whence had the bush-folk caught the motive?

Advancing over the litter of gods and bones, Balatta whimpering at his heels, Bassett entered the shadow of the Red One and passed on under its gigantic overhand until he touched it with his finger-tips. No lacquer that. Nor was the surface smooth as it should have been in the case of lacquer. On the contrary, it was corrugated and pitted, with here and there patches that showed signs of heat and fusing. Also, the substance of it was metal, though unlike any metal or combination of metals he had ever known. As for the color itself, he decided it to be no application. It was the intrinsic color of the metal itself.

He moved his finger-tips, which up to that had merely rested, along the surface, and felt the whole gigantic sphere quicken and live and respond. It was incredible! So light a touch on so vast a mass! Yet did it quiver under the finger-tip caress in rhythmic vibrations that became whisperings and rustlings and mutterings of sound—but of sound so different; so elusive thin that it was shimmeringly sibillant; so mellow that it was maddening sweet, piping like an elfin horn, which last was just what Bassett decided would be like a peal from some bell of the gods reaching earthward from across space.

He looked to Balatta with swift questioning; but the voice of the Red One he had evoked had flung her face-downward and moaning among the bones. He returned to contemplation of the prodigy. Hollow it was, and of no metal known on earth, was his conclusion. It was right-named by the ones of old-time as the Star-Born. Only from the stars could it have come, and no thing of chance was it. It was a creation of artifice and mind. Such perfection of form, such hollowness that it certainly possessed, could not be the result of mere fortuitousness. A child of intelligences, remote and unguessable, working corporally in metals, it indubitably was. He stared at it in amaze, his brain a racing wild-fire of hypotheses to account for this far-journeyer who had adventured the night of space, threaded the stars, and now rose before him and above him, exhumed by patient anthropophagi, pitted and lacquered by its fiery bath in two atmospheres.

But was the color a lacquer of heat upon some familiar metal? Or was it an intrinsic quality of the metal itself? He thrust in the blade-point of his pocket-knife to test the constitution of the stuff. Instantly the entire sphere burst into a mighty whispering, sharp with protest, almost twanging goldenly if a whisper could possibly be considered to twang, rising higher, sinking deeper, the two extremes of the registry of sound threatening to complete the circle and coalesce into the bull-mouthed thundering he had so often heard beyond the taboo distance.

Forgetful of safety, of his own life itself, entranced by the wonder of the unthinkable and unguessable thing, he raised his knife to strike heavily from a long stroke, but was prevented by Balatta. She upreared on her knees in an agony of terror, clasping his knees and supplicating him to desist. In the intensity of her desire to impress him, she put her forearm between her teeth and sank them to the bone.

He scarcely observed her act, although he yielded automatically to his gentler instincts and withheld the knife-hack. To him, human life had dwarfed to microscopic proportions before this colossal portent of higher life from within the distances of the sidereal universe. As had she been a dog, he kicked the ugly little bushwoman to her feet and compelled her to start with him on an encirclement of the base. Part way around, he encountered horrors. Even, among the others, did he recognize the sun-shrivelled remnant of the nine-years girl who had accidentally broken Chief Gngngn's personality taboo. And, among what was left of these that had passed, he encountered what was left of one who had not yet passed. Truly had the bush-folk named themselves into the name of the Red One, seeing in him their own image which they strove to placate and please with such red offerings.

Farther around, always treading the bones and images of humans and gods that constituted the floor of this ancient charnel house of sacrifice, he came upon the device by which the Red One was made to send his call singing thunderingly across the jungle-belts and grass lands to the far beach of Ringmanu. Simple and primitive was it as was the Red One's consummate artifice. A great king-post, half a hundred feet in length, seasoned by centuries of superstitious care, carven into dynasties of gods, each superimposed, each helmeted, each seated in the open mouth of a crocodile, was slung by ropes, twisted of climbing vegetable parasites, from the apex of a tripod of three great forest trunks, themselves carved into grinning and grotesque adumbrations of man's modern concepts of art and god. From the striker king-post, were suspended ropes of climbers to which men could apply their strength and direction. Like a battering ram, the king-post could be driven end-onward against the mighty, red-iridescent sphere.

Here was where Ngurn officiated and functioned religiously for himself and the twelve tribes under him. Bassett laughed aloud, almost with madness, at the thought of this wonderful messenger, winged with intelligence across space, to fall into a bushman stronghold and be worshiped by apelike, man-eating and head-hunting savages. It was as if God's Word had fallen into the muck mire of the abyss underlying the bottom of hell; as if Jehovah's Commandments had been presented on carved stone to the monkeys of the monkey cage at the Zoo; as if the Sermon on the Mount had been preached in a roaring bedlam of lunatics.

The slow weeks passed. The nights, by election, Bassett spent on the ashen floor of the devil-house, beneath the ever-swinging, slow-curing heads. His reason for this was that it was taboo to the lesser sex of woman, and therefore, a refuge for him from Balatta, who grew more persecutingly and perilously loverly as the Southern Cross rode higher in the sky and marked the imminence of her nuptials. His days Bassett spent in a hammock swung under the shade of the great breadfruit tree before the devil-devil house. There were breaks in this program, when, in the comas of his devastating fever-attacks, he lay for days and nights in the house of heads. Ever he struggled to combat the fever, to live, to continue to live, to grow strong and stronger against the day when he would be strong enough to dare the grass lands and the belted jungle beyond, and win to the beach, and to some labor-recruiting, blackbirding ketch or schooner, and on to civilization and the men of civilization, to whom he could give news of the message from other worlds that lay, darkly worshiped by beastmen, in the black heart of Guadalcanal's midmost center.

On other nights, lying late under the breadfruit tree, Bassett spent long hours watching the slow setting of the western stars beyond the black wall of jungle where it had been thrust back by the clearing for the village. Possessed of more than a cursory knowledge of astronomy, he took a sick man's pleasure in speculating as to the dwellers on the unseen worlds of those incredibly remote suns, to haunt whose houses of light, life came forth, a shy visitant, from the rayless crypts of matter. He could no more apprehend limits to time than bounds to space. No subversive radium speculations had shaken his steady scientific faith in the conversation of energy and the indestructibility of matter. Always and forever must there have been stars. And surely, in that cosmic ferment, all must be comparatively alike, comparatively of the same substance, or substances, save for the freaks of the ferment. All must obey, or compose, the same laws that ran without infraction through the entire experience of man. Therefore, he argued and agreed, must worlds and life be appanages to all the suns as they were appanages to the particular sun of his own solar system.

Even as he lay here, under the breadfruit tree, an intelligence that stared across the starry gulfs, so must all the universe be exposed to the ceaseless scrutiny of innumerable eyes, like his, though grantedly different, with behind them, by the same token, intelligences that questioned and sought the meaning and the construction of the whole. So reasoning, he felt his soul go forth in kinship with that august company, that multitude whose gaze was forever upon the arras of infinity.

Who were they, what were they, those far distant and superior ones who had bridged the sky with their gigantic, red-iridescent, heaven-singing message? Surely, and long since, had they, too, trod the path on which man had so recently, by the calendar of the cosmos, set his feet. And to be able to send such a message across the pit of space, surely they had reached those heights to which man, in tears and travail and bloody sweat, in darkness and confusion of many counsels, was so slowly struggling. And what were they on their heights? Had they won Brotherhood? Or had they learned that the law of love imposed the penalty of weakness and decay? Was strife, life? Was the rule of all the universe the pit-

iless rule of natural selection? And, and most immediately
and poignantly, were their far conclusions, their long-won
wisdoms, shut even then in the huge, metallic heart of the
Red One, waiting for the first earth-man to read? Of one
thing he was certain: No drop of red dew shaken from the
lion-mane of some sun in torment, was the sounding sphere.
It was of design, not chance, and it contained the speech and
wisdom of the stars.

What engines and elements and mastered forces, what lore
and mysterious and destiny-controls, might be there! Undoubtedly, since so much could be enclosed in so little a thing as
the foundation stone of a public building, this enormous
sphere should contain vast histories, profounds of research
achieved beyond man's wildest guesses, laws and formulae
that, easily mastered, would make man's life on earth, individual and collective, spring up from its present mire to inconceivable heights of purity and power. It was Time's
greatest gift to blindfold, insatiable, and sky-aspiring man.
And to him, Bassett, had been vouchsafed the lordly fortune
to be the first to receive this message from man's interstellar
kin!

No white man, much less no outland man of the other
bush-tribes, had gazed upon the Red One and lived. Such the
law expounded by Ngurn to Bassett. There was such a thing
as blood brotherhood, Bassett, in return, had often argued in
the past. But Ngurn had stated solemnly no. Even the blood
brotherhood was outside the favor of the Red One. Only a
man born within the tribe could look upon the Red One and
live. But now, his guilty secret known only to Balatta, whose
fear of immolation before the Red One fast-sealed her lips,
the situation was different. What he had to do was recover
from the abominable fevers that weakened him and gain to
civilization. Then would he lead an expedition back, and, although the entire population of Gaudalcanal be destroyed,
extract from the heart of the Red One the message of the
world from other worlds.

But Bassett's relapses grew more frequent, his brief convalescences less and less vigorous, his periods of coma longer,
until he came to know, beyond the last promptings of the optimism inherent in so tremendous a constitution as his own,
that he would never live to cross the grass lands, perforate
the perilous coast jungle, and reach the sea. He faded as the
Southern Cross rose higher in the sky, till even Balatta knew
that he would be dead ere the nuptial date determined by his

taboo. Ngurn made pilgrimage personally and gathered the smoke materials for the curing of Bassett's head, and to him made proud announcement and exhibition of the artistic perfectness of his intention when Bassett should be dead. As for himself, Bassett was not shocked. Too long and too deeply had life ebbed down in him to bite him with fear of its impending extinction. He continued to persist, alternating periods of unconsciousness with periods of semi-consciousness, dreamy and unreal, in which he idly wondered whether he had ever truly beheld the Red One or whether it was a nightmare fancy of delirium.

Came the day when all mists and cobwebs dissolved, when he found his brain clear as a bell, and took just appraisement of his body's weakness. Neither hand nor foot could he lift. So little control of his body did he have, that he was scarcely aware of possessing one. Lightly indeed his flesh sat upon his soul, and his soul, in its briefness of clarity, knew by its very clarity, that the black of cessation was near. He knew the end was close; knew that in all truth he had with his eyes beheld the Red One, the messenger between the worlds; knew that he would never live to carry that message to the world—that message, for aught to the contrary, which might already have waited man's hearing in the heart of Gaudalcanal for ten thousand years. And Bassett stirred with resolve, calling Ngurn to him, out under the shade of the breadfruit tree, and with the old devil-devil doctor discussing the terms and arrangements of his last life effort, his final adventure in the quick of the flesh.

"I know the law, O Ngurn," he concluded the matter. "Whoso is not of the folk may not look upon the Red One and live. I shall not live anyway. Your young men shall carry me before the face of the Red One, and I shall look upon him, and hear his voice, and thereupon die, under your hand, O Ngurn. Thus will the three things be satisfied: the law, my desire, and your quicker possession of my head for which all your preparations wait."

To which Ngurn consented, adding:

"It is better so. A sick man who cannot get well is foolish to live on for so little a while. Also, is it better for the living that he should go. You have been much in the way of late. Not but what it was good for me to talk to such a wise one. But for moons of days we have held little talk. Instead, you have taken up room in the house of heads, making noises like a dying pig, or talking much and loudly in your own language which I do not understand. This has been a confusion to me, for I like to think on the great things of the light and dark as I turn the heads in the smoke. Your much noise has thus been a disturbance to the long-learning and hatching of the final wisdom thât will be mine before I die. As for you, upon whom the dark has already brooded, it is well that you die now. And I promise you, in the long days to come when I turn your head in the smoke, no man of the tribe shall come in to disturb us. And I will tell you many scerets, for I am an old man and very wise, and I shall be adding wisdom to wisdom as I turn your head in the smoke."

So a litter was made, and, borne on the shoulders of half a dozen of the men, Bassett departed on the last little adventure that was to cap the total adventure, for him, of living. With a body of which he was scarcely aware, for even the pain had been exhausted out of it, and with a bright clear brain that accommodated him to a quiet ecstasy of sheer lucidness of thought, he lay back on the lurching litter and watched the fading of the passing world, beholding for the last time the breadfruit tree before the devil-devil house, the dim day beneath the matted jungle roof, the gloomy gorge between the shouldering mountains, the saddle of raw limestone, and the mesa of black, volcanic sand.

Down the spiral path of the pit they bore him, encircling the sheening glowing Red One that seemed ever imminent to iridesce from color and light into sweet singing and thunder. And over bones and logs of immolated men and gods they bore him, past the horror of other immolated ones that yet lived, to the three-king-post tripod and the huge king-post striker.

Here Bassett, helped by Ngurn and Balatta, weakly sat up, swaying weakly from the hips, and with clear, unfaltering, all-seeing eyes gazed upon the Red One.

"Once, O Ngurn," he said, not taking his eyes from the sheening, vibrating surface whereon and wherein all the shades of cherry-red played unceasingly, ever a-quiver to change into sound, to become silken rustlings, silvery whisperings, golden thrummings of chords, velvet pipings of elfland, mellow-distances of thunderings.

"I wait," Ngurn prompted after a long pause, the long-handled tomahawk unassumingly ready in his hand.

"Once, O Ngurn," Bassett repeated, "let the Red One speak so that I may see it speak as well as hear it. Then strike, thus, when I raise my hand; for, when I raise my hand, I shall drop my head forward and make place for the stroke at the base of my neck. But, O Ngurn, I, who am about to pass out of the light of day forever, would like to pass with the wonder-voice of the Red One singing greatly in my ears."

"And I promise you that never will a head be so well cured as yours," Ngurn assured him, at the same time signalling the tribesmen to man the propelling ropes suspended from the king-post striker. "Your head shall be my greatest piece of work in the curing of heads."

Bassett smiled quietly at the old one's conceit, as the great carved log, drawn back through two-score feet of space, was released. The next moment he was lost in ecstasy at the abrupt and thunderous liberation of sound. But such thunder! Mellow it was with preciousness of all sounding metals. Archangels spoke in it; it was magnificently beautiful before all other sounds; it was invested with the intelligence of supermen of planets of other suns; it was the voice of God, seducing and commanding to be heard. And—the everlasting miracle of that interstellar metal. Bassett, with his own eyes, saw color and colors transform into sound till the whole visible surface of the vast sphere was a-crawl and titillant and vaporous with what he could not tell was color or was sound. In that moment the interstices of matter were his, and the interfusings and intermating transfusings of matter and force.

Time passed. At the last Bassett was brought back from his ecstasy by an impatient movement of Ngurn. He had quite forgotten the old devil-devil one. A quick flash of fancy brought a husky chuckle into Bassett's throat. His shotgun lay beside him in the litter. All he had to do, muzzle to head, was press the trigger and blow his head into nothingness.

But why cheat him? was Bassett's next thought. Head-hunting, cannibal beast of a human that was as much ape as human, nevertheless Old Ngurn had, according to his lights, played squarer than square. Ngurn was in himself a fore-runner of ethics and contract, of consideration, and gentleness in man. No, Bassett decided; it would be a ghastly pity and an act of dishonor to cheat the old fellow at the last. His head was Ngurn's, and Ngurn's head to cure it would be.

And Bassett, raising his hand in signal, bending forward his head as agreed so as to expose cleanly the articulation to his taut spinal cord, forgot Balatta, who was merely a woman, a woman merely and only and undesired. He knew, without seeing, when the razor-edged hatchet rose in the air behind him. And for that instant, ere the end, there fell upon Bassett the shadow of the Unknown, a sense of impending marvel of the rending of walls before the imaginable. Almost, when he knew the blow had started and just ere the edge of steel bit the flesh and nerves, it seemed that he gazed upon the serene face of the Medusa, Truth.—And, simultaneous with the bite of the steel on the onrush of the dark, in a flashing instant of fancy, he saw the vision of his head turning slowly, always turning, in the devil-devil house beside the breadfruit tree.

The Horror Out of Providence

A companion thread of strangeness wove through the more commonplace fabric of literature alongside the speculations of science fiction. It was the thread of supernatural horror.

Actually, the horror story, in its broadest sense, antedated science fiction by at least fifty years, perhaps one hundred years, and, according to choice of definition, perhaps by millennia. In a slender volume titled *Supernatural Horror in Literature* (1927, revised 1939), H. P. Lovecraft (1890–1937), now considered himself as the supreme practitioner of the art of terrifying readers, traced its roots to the ceremonial magic of Egypt and the Semitic nations, and then through what he called "the most revolting fertility-rites of immemorial antiquity" into the medieval witch cults.

Out of these and other medieval myths about werewolves, ghosts, sorcerors, and the dead arisen, including the dual vision of reality that they implied, came the gothic novel. Horace Walpole created the first gothic with *The Castle of Otranto* (1764). The most popular novels in this tradition were William Beckford's *Vathek* (1784), Mrs. Ann Radcliffe's *The Mysteries of Udolpho* (1784), M. G. "Monk" Lewis's *The Monk* (1796), and Charlotte Dacre's *Zofloya* (1806). Their formula featured a young woman in peril, haunted castles, clanking chains, ghostly apparitions, and sometimes the threat of a fate worse than death.

Mary Shelley's *Frankenstein* (1818), considered by some critics the first science-fiction novel, was influenced by the gothics and shared many of their characteristics.

Lovecraft listed Bulwer-Lytton, LeFanu, Wilkie Collins, Haggard, Doyle, Wells, and Stevenson as writing in the "romantic, semi-gothic, quasi-moral tradition," but saved his greatest admiration for Poe, O'Brien, and Bierce. He also mentions the work of F. Marion Crawford, Robert W. Chambers, Henry James, Oscar Wilde, M. P. Shiel, Bram Stoker, Sax Rohmer, William Hope Hodgson, and others, and gives particular attention to Arthur Machen, Algernon Blackwood, M. R. James, and Lord Dunsany.

But Lovecraft himself came to represent the fiction of horror that he described, and the magazine that published most of his work, *Weird Tales,* its contemporary expression. *Weird Tales* was founded in 1923 by Clark Henneberger, but he sold it after a year and the person most closely identified with the magazine, editor Farnsworth Wright, took charge until 1938, when the magazine was sold again; Dorothy McIlwraith edited the magazine until its last issue in 1954. It never made money, and a recent revival was equally unsuccessful.

The number of readers who wanted to be terrified seemed to be limited, but *Weird Tales* readers were loyal. So were its authors, though their pay was low and slow. Among them was Lovecraft, whose first *Weird Tales* story was published six months after the magazine's March 1923 initial issue. The story was "Dagon," which had been published earlier in the November 1919 issue of a little magazine called *The Vagrant.*

Lovecraft soon became a *Weird Tales* regular, and, in fact, when his stories were occasionally rejected he seldom sent them elsewhere. Once friends had to smuggle two manuscripts to *Astounding.* Actually, few other magazines published such fiction. *All-Story, Argosy,* or *Cavalier* would publish an occasional story like Irwin S. Cobb's "Fishhead," but *Weird Tales* was alone in its category. The later *Horror Tales* and *Terror Tales* specialized in sadism, and *The Thrill Book, Strange Tales,* and *Ghost Stories* either disappeared quickly or had little influence.

Lovecraft's importance rests on two aspects of his career: he carved out a special niche for himself in pulp literature, and he created an army of followers. That niche was supernatural horror, and in his analysis he distinguished it from similar kinds of appeals, from mere physical fear, say, or "the mundanely gruesome." What he called for was fear of the unknown:

> The one test of the really weird is simply this—whether or not there be excited in the reader a profound sense of dread, and of contact with unknown spheres and powers; a subtle attitude of awed listening, as if for the beating of black wings or the scratching of outside shapes and entities on the known universe's utmost rim.

Lovecraft himself seemed almost as strange as his fiction. His father died in a mental institution of paresis when Lovecraft was only eight; his mother also was hospitalized for several years before her death, and suffered from a mental disturbance. Except for a brief and unsuccessful marriage to a Brooklyn businesswoman, Lovecraft lived with aunts in Providence, inadequately supported by a dwindling family income and by ghost writing and revising. He spent much of his time on amateur journalism and contributed freely to other publications. His fiction brought him little money.

But he befriended many young writers by mail, sending them letters of incredible length and detail. Often he criticized and encouraged their work. Sometimes he collaborated with them. They responded with worship and adoption of his prose style and his mythos. They included E. Hoffman Price, Clark Ashton Smith, Donald and Howard Wandrei, Robert Bloch, Henry Kuttner, C. L. Moore, Frank Belknap Long, and Carl Jacobi. August Derleth was so taken with Lovecraft's writing and the Chtulhu mythos that he invented as a background for many of his stories that Derleth and Donald Wandrei founded Arkham House to publish, posthumously, Lovecraft's *The Outsider, and Others* (1939), other Lovecraft work, and then other fantasy work, early Ray Bradbury, and such science-fiction authors as A. E. Van Vogt.

Lovecraft died in 1937 of Bright's disease and intestinal cancer. He left one novel, *The Case of Charles Dexter Ward* (serialized in 1941), and a body of short stories, a number of them built around a myth about evil elder powers who once ruled the earth, were exiled, wish to return, and still are worshiped in ancient, dark, stagnant corners of the world. His best-known stories are "The Shadow Out of Time," "At the Mountains of Madness," "The Colour Out of Space," "The Shadow Over Innsmouth," "The Dunwich Horror," "The Whisperer in Darkness," "The Call of Cthulhu," "The Rats in the Wall," and "The Outsider."

One of his earliest stories, "Dagon" is based on established myth rather than Lovecraft's mythos, and it lacks some of the later extremes of language and style Lovecraft developed in his attempts to raise the hairs on the back of his reader's neck.

Horror stories, and fantasy of any kind, are difficult to distinguish from science fiction, since both involve the fantastic. Many critics don't attempt to distinguish between them; some maintain that no meaningful distinction exists. But fantasy enchants or horrifies by the power of its vision or the rapture of its words; science fiction persuades with logic and explanation. Science fiction presents a strangeness the reader did not imagine could exist in his world; fantasy tells the reader that the world is strange beyond his belief.

Dagon

by H. P. Lovecraft

I am writing this under an appreciable mental strain, since by tonight I shall be no more. Penniless, and at the end of my supply of the drug which alone makes life endurable, I can bear the torture no longer; and shall cast myself from this garret window into the squalid street below. Do not think from my slavery to morphine that I am a weakling or a degenerate. When you have read these hastily scrawled pages you may guess, though never fully realise, why it is that I must have forgetfulness or death.

It was in one of the most open and least frequented parts of the broad Pacific that the packet of which I was supercargo fell a victim to the German sea-raider. The great war was then at its very beginning, and the ocean forces of the Hun had not completely sunk to their later degradation; so that our vessel was made a legitimate prize, whilst we of her crew were treated with all the fairness and consideration due us as naval prisoners. So liberal, indeed, was the discipline of our captors, that five days after we were taken I managed to escape alone in a small boat with water and provisions for a good length of time.

When I finally found myself adrift and free, I had but little idea of my surroundings. Never a competent navigator, I could only guess vaguely by the sun and stars that I was somewhat south of the equator. Of the longitude I knew nothing, and no island or coastline was in sight. The weather kept fair, and for uncounted days I drifted aimlessly beneath the scorching sun; waiting either for some passing ship, or to be cast on the shores of some habitable land. But neither ship nor land appeared, and I began to despair in my solitude upon the heaving vastnesses of unbroken blue.

The change happened whilst I slept. Its details I shall never know; for my slumber, though troubled and dream-infested, was continuous. When at last I awaked, it was to discover myself half sucked into a slimy expanse of hellish black mire which extended about me in monotonous undulations as far as I could see, and in which my boat lay grounded some distance away.

Though one might well imagine that my first sensation would be of wonder at so prodigious and unexpected a transformation of scenery, I was in reality more horrified than astonished; for there was in the air and in the rotting soil a sinister quality which chilled me to the very core. The region was putrid with the carcasses of decaying fish, and of other less describable things which I saw protruding from the nasty mud of the unending plain. Perhaps I should not hope to convey in mere words the unutterable hideousness that can dwell in absolute silence and barren immensity. There was nothing within hearing, and nothing in sight save a vast reach of black slime; yet the very completeness of the stillness and the homogeneity of the landscape oppressed me with a nauseating fear.

The sun was blazing down from a sky which seemed to me almost black in its cloudless cruelty; as though reflecting the inky marsh beneath my feet. As I crawled into the stranded boat I realised that only one theory could explain my position. Through some unprecedented volcanic upheaval, a portion of the ocean floor must have been thrown to the surface, exposing regions which for innumerable millions of years had lain hidden under unfathomable watery depths. So great was the extent of the new land which had risen beneath me, that I could not detect the faintest noise of the surging ocean, strain my ears as I might. Nor were there any sea-fowl to prey upon the dead things.

For several hours I sat thinking or brooding in the boat, which lay upon its side and afforded a slight shade as the sun moved across the heavens. As the day progressed, the ground lost some of its stickiness, and seemed likely to dry sufficiently for travelling purposes in a short time. That night I slept but little, and the next day I made for myself a pack containing food and water, preparatory to an overland journey in search of the vanished sea and possible rescue.

On the third morning I found the soil dry enough to walk

upon with ease. The odour of the fish was maddening; but I
was too much concerned with graver things to mind so slight
an evil, and set out boldly for an unknown goal. All day I
forged steadily westward, guided by a far-away hummock
which rose higher than any other elevation on the rolling
desert. That night I encamped, and on the following day still
travelled toward the hummock, though that object seemed
scarcely nearer than when I had first espied it. By the fourth
evening I attained the base of the mound, which turned out
to be much higher than it had appeared from a distance; an
intervening valley setting it out in sharper relief from the
general surface. Too weary to ascend, I slept in the shadow
of the hill.

I know not why my dreams were so wild that night; but
ere the waning and fantastically gibbous moon had risen far
above the eastern plain, I was awake in a cold perspiration,
determined to sleep no more. Such visions as I had experienced were too much for me to endure again. And in the
glow of the moon I saw how unwise I had been to travel by
day. Without the glare of the parching sun, my journey
would have cost me less energy; indeed, I now felt quite able
to perform the ascent which had deterred me at sunset. Picking up my pack, I started for the crest of the eminence.

I have said that the unbroken monotony of the rolling
plain was a source of vague horror to me; but I think my
horror was greater when I gained the summit of the mound
and looked down the other side into an immeasurable pit or
canyon, whose black recesses the moon had not yet soared
high enough to illumine. I felt myself on the edge of the
world; peering over the rim into a fathomless chaos of eternal
night. Through my terror ran curious reminiscences of *Paradise Lost*, and Satan's hideous climb through the unfashioned
realms of darkness.

As the moon climbed higher in the sky, I began to see that
the slopes of the valley were not quite so perpendicular as I
had imagined. Ledges and outcroppings of rock afforded
fairly easy footholds for a descent, whilst after a drop of a
few hundred feet, the declivity became very gradual. Urged
on by an impulse which I cannot definitely analyse, I
scrambled with difficulty down the rocks and stood on the
gentler slope beneath, gazing into the Stygian deeps where no
light had yet penetrated.

All at once my attention was captured by a vast and singular object on the opposite slope, which rose steeply about a

hundred yards ahead of me; an object that gleamed whitely in the newly bestowed rays of the ascending moon. That it was merely a gigantic piece of stone, I soon assured myself; but I was conscious of a distinct impression that its contour and position were not altogether the work of Nature. A closer scrutiny filled me with sensations I cannot express; for despite its enormous magnitude, and its position in an abyss which had yawned at the bottom of the sea since the world was young, I perceived beyond a doubt that the strange object was a well-shaped monolith whose massive bulk had known the workmanship and perhaps the worship of living and thinking creatures.

Dazed and frightened, yet not without a certain thrill of the scientist's or archaeologist's delight, I examined my surroundings more closely. The moon, now near the zenith, shone weirdly and vividly above the towering steeps that hemmed in the chasm, and revealed the fact that a far-flung body of water flowed at the bottom, winding out of sight in both directions, and almost lapping my feet as I stood on the slope. Across the chasm, the wavelets washed the base of the Cyclopean monolith, on whose surface I could now trace both inscriptions and crude sculptures. The writing was in a system of hieroglyphics unknown to me, and unlike anything I had ever seen in books, consisting for the most part of conventionalised aquatic symbols such as fishes, eels, octopi, crustaceans, molluscs, whales and the like. Several characters obviously represented marine things which are unknown to the modern world, but whose decomposing forms I had observed on the ocean-risen plain.

It was the pictorial carving, however, that did most to hold me spellbound. Plainly visible across the intervening water on account of their enormous size was an array of bas-reliefs whose subjects would have excited the envy of a Doré. I think that these things were supposed to depict men—at least, a certain sort of men; though the creatures were shown disporting like fishes in the waters of some marine grotto, or paying homage at some monolithic shrine which appeared to be under the waves as well. Of their faces and forms I dare not speak in detail; for the mere remembrance makes me grow faint. Grotesque beyond the imagination of a Poe or a Bulwer, they were damnably human in general outline despite webbed hands and feet, shockingly wide and flabby lips, glassy, bulging eyes, and other features less pleasant to recall. Curiously enough, they seemed to have been chiselled badly out of proportion with their scenic background; for one of the creatures was shown in the act of killing a whale represented as but little larger than himself. I remarked, as I say, their grotesqueness and strange size; but in a moment decided that they were merely the imaginary gods of some primitive fishing or seafaring tribe; some tribe whose last descendant had perished eras before the first ancestor of the Piltdown or Neanderthal Man was born. Awestruck at this unexpected glimpse into a past beyond the conception of the most daring anthropologist, I stood musing whilst the moon cast queer reflections on the silent channel before me.

Then suddenly I saw it. With only a slight churning to mark its rise to the surface, the thing slid into view above the dark waters. Vast, Polyphemus-like, and loathsome, it darted like a stupendous monster of nightmares to the monolith, about which it flung its gigantic scaly arms, the while it bowed its hideous head and gave vent to certain measured sounds. I think I went mad then.

Of my frantic ascent of the slope and cliff, and of my delirious journey back to the stranded boat, I remember little. I believe I sang a great deal, and laughed oddly when I was unable to sing. I have indistinct recollections of a great storm some time after I reached the boat; at any rate, I know that I heard peals of thunder and other tones which Nature utters only in her wildest moods.

When I came out of the shadows I was in a San Francisco hospital; brought thither by the captain of the American ship which had picked up my boat in mid-ocean. In my delirium I had said much, but found that my words had been given scant attention. Of any land upheaval in the Pacific, my rescuers knew nothing; nor did I deem it necessary to insist upon a thing which I knew they could not believe. Once I sought out a celebrated ethnologist, and amused him with peculiar questions regarding the ancient Philistine legend of Dagon, the Fish-God; but soon perceiving that he was hopelessly conventional, I did not press my inquiries.

It is at night, especially when the moon is gibbous and waning, that I see the thing. I tried morphine; but the drug has given only transient surcease, and has drawn me into its clutches as a hopeless slave. So now I am to end it all, having written a full account for the information or the contemptuous amusement of my fellow-men. Often I ask myself if it could not all have been a pure phantasm—a mere freak of fever as I lay sun-stricken and raving in the open boat after my escape from the German man-of-war. This I ask myself, but ever does there come before me a hideously vivid vision in reply. I cannot think of the deep sea without shuddering at the nameless things that may at this very moment be crawling and floundering on its slimy bed, worshipping their ancient stone idols and carving their own detestable likenesses on submarine obelisks of water-soaked granite. I dream of a day when they may rise above the billows to drag down in their reeking talons the remnants of puny, war-exhausted mankind—of a day when the land shall sink, and the dark ocean floor shall ascend amidst universal pandemonium.

The end is near. I hear a noise at the door, as of some immense slippery body lumbering against it. It shall not find me. God, *that hand!* The window! The window!

The Science-Fiction Magazine
Begins Its Amazing Career

The first science-fiction magazine could have been published in 1924, the year after the creation of *Weird Tales*. Hugo Gernsback (1884–1967) had been publishing science-fiction stories, including some he wrote himself, in his popular science magazines since 1911, and published a "scientific fiction number" of *Science and Invention* in 1923. In 1924 he mailed out a prospectus to potential subscribers describing a magazine to be called *Scientifiction*, but the response was not encouraging.

Gernsback persevered, however, and in April 1926 produced *Amazing Stories*. In his opening editorial he preached his vision of an exciting, rewarding future through science and technology, and promoted the magazine for its novelty: ". . . new kind of fiction magazine . . . entirely new, entirely different . . . never been done before . . . deserves your attention. . . ."

But he had decided that "scientifiction" was too intimidating to be used as a title; it smacked too much of science. "Amazing" was more like it, but "scientifiction" served as a definition and a subtitle: AMAZING STORIES—SCIENTIFICTION ran across the spine.

For the first three issues the readers got reprints from Jules Verne, H. G. Wells, and Edgar Allan Poe, and a few others. Jack Williamson, who began reading the magazine in its first year, believes that perhaps its greatest accomplishment was to bring the stories and novels of Wells back into circulation. For the first year and a half, the magazine carried the names of Verne or Wells or Poe on its cover, sometimes two of them, sometimes all three.

Beginning with the fourth issue, new stories began to appear. By the October 1927 issue, readers were complaining about Wells's wordiness. Gernsback began to downplay the reprints and eliminate the cover names for the sake of new writers.

The man responsible for establishing the medium and setting its tone was an entrepreneur who immigrated to the United States at the age of eighteen, with $200 and the plans for a battery in his pocket. At first his enterprises did not run smoothly, but after several false starts Gernsback founded a store to import electrical equipment, designed a home radio (that sent as well as received), and created catalogs and then a magazine to publicize his wares.

The early stories he published in his popular science magazines, as well as those published in *Amazing*, were distinguished more for their enthusiasm than their narrative skill. Occasionally, however, a new kind of story would appear, such as "The Tissue-Culture King." It would be distinguished not only by its more expert use of language but by its concern with biology.

Biology provided inspiration for few stories in the '30s or '40s—writers and readers were more fascinated by the physical sciences—and only in the '60s would new and surprising developments in biology turn writers in that direction. But significant biological discoveries came in the last part of the nineteenth century and the first part of the twentieth: Pasteur's discovery of the germ theory of disease, Lister's sterilization processes, the rediscovery of Mendel's laws of inheritance, further developments in genetics and evolution, and so on.

The Alexis Carrel referred to in "The Tissue-Culture King" was the most direct inspiration for the story. Carrel earned a Nobel Prize in 1912 for his work in blood-vessel suturing, but even more fascinating were his studies on the transplantation of organs and his efforts to keep them alive and healthy by perfusing them with blood and nutrients. He kept a piece of embryonic chicken heart alive and growing for thirty-four years. He also worked with Charles Lindbergh to develop an artificial heart.

Julian Huxley (1887–1975) was a man ahead of his time. But then he came from a family in the vanguard of several movements. His grandfather, T. H. Huxley, was Darwin's champion in England (and H. G. Wells's biology teacher). His great-uncle was Matthew Arnold. His brother, Aldous (of whom more later), became a distinguished novelist and social critic.

Julian Huxley was a biologist and science writer. He taught zoology and physiology in the U.S. and England, served on an exploring party, lived in Africa, was director of the Regent's Park Zoo and biology editor for the *Encyclopedia Britannica,* collaborated with Wells and his son G. P. on *The Science of Life,* and wrote many more books about science and society in collaboration and alone. He was the first director-general of UNESCO.

"The Tissue-Culture King" apparently is his only science-fiction story. Why he wrote it and how it ended up in *Amazing* in 1927 is still a mystery. But his example—a scientist writing science fiction—would be followed by many others such as John Taine (Eric Temple Bell), Philip Latham (Robert S. Richardson), Isaac Asimov, Fred Hoyle, Gregory Benford, and many others.

Note that Huxley was raising questions long before the atomic bomb about the social value of science and the social responsibility of the scientist.

The Tissue-Culture King

by Julian Huxley

We had been for three days engaged in crossing a swamp. At last we were out on dry ground, winding up a gentle slope. Near the top the brush grew thicker. The look of a rampart grew as we approached; it had the air of having been deliberately planted by men. We did not wish to have to hack our way through the spiky barricade, so turned to the right along the front of the green wall. After three or four hundred yards we came on a clearing which led into the bush, narrowing down to what seemed a regular passage or trackway. This made us a little suspicious. However, I thought we had better make all the progress we could, and so ordered the caravan to turn into the opening, myself taking second place behind the guide.

Suddenly the tracker stopped with a guttural exclamation. I looked, and there was one of the great African toads, hopping with a certain ponderosity across the path. But it had a second head growing upwards from its shoulders! I had never seen anything like this before, and wanted to secure such a remarkable monstrosity for our collections; but as I moved forward, the creature took a couple of hops into the shelter of the prickly scrub.

We pushed on, and I became convinced that the gap we were following was artificial. After a little, a droning sound came to our ears, which we very soon set down as that of a human voice. The party was halted, and I crept forward with the guide. Peeping through the last screen of brush we looked down into a hollow and were immeasurably startled at what we saw there. The voice proceeded from an enormous Negro man at least eight feet high, the biggest man I had ever seen outside a circus. He was squatting, from time to time prostrating the forepart of his body, and reciting some prayer or incantation. The object of his devotion was before him on the ground; it was a small flat piece of glass held on a little carved ebony stand. By his side was a huge spear, together with a painted basket with a lid.

After a minute or so, the giant bowed down in silence, then took up the ebony-and-glass object and placed it in the basket. Then to my utter amazement he drew out a two-headed toad like the first I had seen, but in a cage of woven grass, placed it on the ground, and proceeded to more genuflection and ritual murmurings. As soon as this was over, the toad was replaced, and the squatting giant tranquilly regarded the landscape.

Beyond the hollow or dell lay an undulating country, with clumps of bush. A sound in the middle distance attracted attention; glimpses of color moved through the scrub; and a party of three or four dozen men were seen approaching, most of them as gigantic as our first acquaintance. All marched in order, armed with great spears, and wearing colored loin straps with a sort of sporran, it seemed, in front. They were preceded by an intelligent-looking Negro of ordinary stature armed with a club, and accompanied by two figures more remarkable than the giants. They were undersized, almost dwarfish, with huge heads, and enormously fat and brawny both in face and body. They wore bright yellow cloaks over their black shoulders.

At sight of them, our giant rose and stood stiffly by the side of his basket. The party approached and halted. Some order was given, a giant stepped out from the ranks towards ours, picked up the basket, handed it stiffly to the newcomer, and fell into place in the little company. We were clearly witnessing some regular routine of relieving guard, and I was racking my brains to think what the whole thing might signify—guards, giants, dwarfs, toads—when to my dismay I heard an exclamation at my shoulder.

It was one of those damned porters, a confounded fellow who always liked to show his independence. Bored with waiting, I suppose, he had self-importantly crept up to see what it was all about, and the sudden sight of the company of giants had been too much for his nerves. I made a signal to lie quiet, but it was too late. The exclamation had been heard; the leader gave a quick command, and the giants rushed up and out in two groups to surround us.

Violence and resistance were clearly out of the question. With my heart in my mouth, but with as much dignity as I could muster, I jumped up and threw out my empty hands, at the same time telling the tracker not to shoot. A dozen spears seemed towering over me, but none were launched; the leader ran up the slope and gave a command. Two giants came up and put my hands through their arms. The tracker and the porter were herded in front at the spear point. The other porters now discovered there was something amiss, and began to shout and run away, with half the spearmen after them. We three were gently but firmly marched down and across the hollow.

I understood nothing of the language, and called to my tracker to try his hand. It turned out that there was some dialect of which he had a little understanding, and we could learn nothing save the fact that we were being taken to some superior authority.

For two days we were marched through pleasant park-like country, with villages at intervals. Every now and then some new monstrosity in the shape of a dwarf or an incredibly fat woman or a two-headed animal would be visible, until I thought I had stumbled on the original source of supply of circus freaks.

The country at last began to slope gently down to a pleasant river-valley; and presently we neared the capital. It turned out to be a really large town for Africa, its mud walls of strangely impressive architectural form, with their heavy, slabby buttresses, and giants standing guard upon them. Seeing us approach, they shouted, and a crowd poured out of the nearest gate. My God, what a crowd! I was getting used to giants by this time, but here was a regular Barnum and Bailey show; more semi-dwarfs; others like them but more

so—one could not tell whether the creatures were precociously mature children or horribly stunted adults; others
portentously fat, with arms like sooty legs of mutton, and
rolls and volutes of fat crisping out of their steatopygous pos-
teriors; still others precociously senile and wizened, others
hateful and imbecile in looks. Of course, there were plenty of
ordinary Negroes too, but enough of the extraordinary to
make one feel pretty queer. Soon after we got inside, I suddenly noted something else which appeared inexplicable—a
telephone wire, with perfectly good insulators, running across
from tree to tree. A telephone—in an unknown African
town. I gave it up.

But another surprise was in store for me. I saw a figure
pass across from one large building to another—a figure unmistakably that of a white man. In the first place, it was
wearing white ducks and sun helmet; in the second, it had a
pale face.

He turned at the sound of our cavalcade and stood looking
a moment; then walked towards us.

"Halloa!" I shouted. "Do you speak English?"

"Yes," he answered, "but keep quiet a moment," and began talking quickly to our leaders, who treated him with the
greatest deference. He dropped back to me and spoke rapidly: "You are to be taken into the council hall to be examined: but I will see to it that no harm comes to you. This is a
forbidden land to strangers, and you must be prepared to be
held up for a time. You will be sent down to see me in the
temple buildings as soon as the formalities are over, and I'll
explain things. They want a bit of explaining," he added with
a dry laugh. "By the way, my name is Hascombe, lately
research worker at Middlesex Hospital, now religious adviser
to His Majesty King Mgobe." He laughed again and pushed
ahead. He was an interesting figure—perhaps fifty years old,
spare body, thin face, with a small beard, and rather sunken,
hazel eyes. As for his expression, he looked cynical, but also
as if he were interested in life.

By this time we were at the entrance to the hall. Our giants
formed up outside, with my men behind them, and only I
and the leader passed in. The examination was purely formal,
and remarkable chiefly for the ritual and solemnity which
characterized all the actions of the couple of dozen fine-looking men in long robes who were our examiners. My men
were herded off to some compound. I was escorted down to a

little hut, furnished with some attempt at European style, where I found Hascombe.

As soon as we were alone I was after him with my questions. "Now you can tell me. Where are we? What is the meaning of all this circus business and this menagerie of monstrosities? And how do you come here?" He cut me short. "It's a long story, so let me save time by telling it my own way."

I am not going to tell it as he told it; but will try to give a more connected account, the result of many later talks with him, and of my own observations.

Hascombe had been a medical student of great promise; and after his degree had launched out into research. He had first started on parasitic protozoa, but had given that up in favor of tissue culture; from these he had gone off to cancer research, and from that to a study of developmental physiology. Later a big Commission on sleeping sickness had been organized, and Hascombe, restless and eager for travel, had pulled wires and got himself appointed as one of the scientific staff sent to Africa. He was much impressed with the view that wild game acted as a reservoir for the *Trypanosoma gambiense*. When he learned of the extensive migrations of game, he saw here an important possible means of spreading the disease and asked leave to go up country to investigate the whole problem. When the Commission as a whole had finished its work, he was allowed to stay in Africa with one other white man and a company of porters to see what he could discover. His white companion was a laboratory technician, a taciturn non-commissioned officer of science called Aggers.

There is no object in telling of their experiences here. Suffice it that they lost their way and fell into the hands of this same tribe. That was fifteen years ago: and Aggers was now long dead—as the result of a wound inflicted when he was caught, after a couple of years, trying to escape.

On their capture, they too had been examined in the council chamber, and Hascombe (who had interested himself in a dilettante way in anthropology as in most other subjects of scientific inquiry) was much impressed by what he described as the exceedingly religious atmosphere. Everything was done with an elaboration of ceremony; the chief seemed more priest than king, and performed various rites at intervals, and priests were busy at some sort of altar the whole time. Among other things, he noticed that one of their rites was connected with blood. First the chief and then the councillors were in turn requisitioned for a drop of vital fluid pricked from their finger-tips, and the mixture, held in a little vessel, was slowly evaporated over a flame.

Some of Hascombe's men spoke a dialect not unlike that of their captors, and one was acting as interpreter. Things did not look too favorable. The country was a "holy place," it seemed, and the tribe a "holy race." Other Africans who trespassed there, if not killed, were enslaved, but for the most part they let well alone, and did not trespass. White men they had heard of, but never seen till now, and the debate was what to do—to kill, let go, or enslave? To let them go was contrary to all their principles: the holy place would be defiled if the news of it were spread abroad. To enslave them—yes; but what were they good for? and the Council seemed to feel an instinctive dislike for these other-colored creatures. Hascombe had an idea. He turned to the interpreter. "Say this: 'You revere the Blood. So do we white men; but we do more—we can render visible the blood's hidden nature and reality, and with permission I will show this great magic.'" He beckoned to the bearer who carried his precious microscope, set it up, drew a drop of blood from the tip of his finger with his knife, and mounted it on a slide under a coverslip. The bigwigs were obviously interested. They whispered to each other. At length, "Show us," commanded the chief.

Hascombe demonstrated his preparation with greater interest than he had ever done to first-year medical students in the old days. He explained that the blood was composed of little people of various sorts, each with their own lives, and that to spy upon them thus gave us new powers over them. The elders were more or less impressed. At any rate the sight of these thousands of corpuscles where they could see nothing before made them think, made them realize that the white man had power which might make him a desirable servant.

They would not ask to see their own blood for fear that the sight would put them into the power of those who saw it. But they had blood drawn from a slave. Hascombe asked too for a bird, and was able to create a certain interest by showing how different were the little people of its blood.

"Tell them," he said to the interpreter, "that I have many other powers and magics which I will show them if they will give me time."

The long and short of it was that he and his party were spared—He said he knew then what one felt when the magistrate said: "Remanded for a week."

He had been attracted by one of the elder statesmen of the tribe—a tall, powerful-looking man of middle-age; and was agreeably surprised when this man came round next day to see him. Hascombe later nicknamed him the Prince-Bishop, for his combination of the qualities of the statesman and the ecclesiastic: his real name was Bugala. He was as anxious to discover more about Hascombe's mysterious powers and resources as Hascombe was to learn what he could of the people into whose hands he had fallen, and they met almost every evening and talked far into the night.

Bugala's inquiries were as little prompted as Hascombe's by a purely academic curiosity. Impressed himself by the microscope, and still more by the effect which it had had on his colleagues, he was anxious to find out whether by utilizing the powers of the white man he could not secure his own advancement. At length, they struck a bargain. Bugala would see to it that no harm befell Hascombe. But Hascombe must put his resources and powers at the disposal of the Council; and Bugala would take good care to arrange matters so that he himself benefited. So far as Hascombe could make out, Bugala imagined a radical change in the national religion, a sort of reformation based on Hascombe's conjuring tricks; and that he would emerge as the High Priest of this changed system.

Hascombe had a sense of humor, and it was tickled. It seemed pretty clear that they could not escape, at least for the present. That being so, why not take the opportunity of doing a little research work at state expense—an opportunity which he and his like were always clamoring for at home? His thoughts began to run away with him. He would find out all he could of the rites and superstitions of the tribe. He would, by the aid of his knowledge and his scientific skill, exalt the details of these rites, the expression of those superstitions, the whole physical side of their religiosity, on to a new level which should to them appear truly miraculous.

It would not be worth my troubling to tell all the negotiations, the false starts, the misunderstandings. In the end he secured what he wanted—a building which could be used as a laboratory; an unlimited supply of slaves for the lower and priests for the higher duties of laboratory assistants, and the promise that when his scientific stores were exhausted they

would do their best to secure others from the coast—a
promise which was scrupulously kept, so that he never went
short for lack of what money could buy.

He next applied himself diligently to a study of their religion and found that it was built round various main motifs.
Of these, the central one was the belief in the divinity and
tremendous importance of the Priest-King. The second was a
form of ancestor-worship. The third was an animal cult, in
particular of the more grotesque species of the African fauna.
The fourth was sex, *con variazioni.* Hascombe reflected on
these facts. Tissue culture; experimental embryology; endocrine treatment; artificial parthenogenesis. He laughed and
said to himself: "Well, at least I can try, and it ought to be
amusing."

That was how it all started. Perhaps the best way of giving
some idea of how it had developed will be for me to tell my
own impressions when Hascombe took me round his laboratories. One whole quarter of the town was devoted entirely to
religion—it struck me as excessive, but Hascombe reminded
me that Tibet spends one-fifth of its revenues on melted but-
ter to burn before its shrines. Facing the main square was the
chief temple, built impressively enough of solid mud. On either side were the apartments where dwelt the servants of the
gods and administrators of the sacred rites. Behind were Hascombe's laboratories, some built of mud, others, under his
later guidance, of wood. They were guarded night and day by
patrols of giants, and were arranged in a series of quadran-
gles. Within one quadrangle was a pool which served as an
aquarium; in another, aviaries and great hen-houses; in yet
another, cages with various animals; in the fourth a little
botanic garden. Behind were stables with dozens of cattle and
sheep, and a sort of experimental ward for human beings.

He took me into the nearest of the buildings. "This," he
said, "is known to the people as the Factory (it is difficult to
give the exact sense of the word, but it literally means pro-
ducing-place), the Factory of Kingship or Majesty, and the
Wellspring of Ancestral Immortality." I looked round, and
saw platoons of buxom and shining African women, becom-
ingly but unusually dressed in tight-fitting white dresses and
caps, and wearing rubber gloves. Microscopes were much in
evidence, also various receptacles from which steam was
emerging. The back of the room was screened off by a
wooden screen in which were a series of glass doors; and

these doors opened into partitions, each labelled with a name in that unknown tongue, and each containing a number of objects like the one I had seen taken out of the basket by the giant before we were captured. Pipes surrounded this chamber, and appeared to be distributing heat from a fire in one corner.

"Factory of Majesty!" I exclaimed. "Wellspring of Immortality! What the dickens do you mean?"

"If you prefer a more prosaic name," said Hascombe, "I should call this the Institute of Religious Tissue Culture." My mind went back to a day in 1918 when I had been taken by a biological friend in New York to see the famous Rockefeller Institute; and at the word tissue culture I saw again before me Dr. Alexis Carrel and troops of white-garbed American girls making cultures, sterilizing, microscopizing, incubating and the rest of it. The Hascombe Institute was, it is true, not so well equipped, but it had an even larger, if differently colored, personnel.

Hascombe began his explanations. "As you probably know, Frazer's 'Golden Bough'* introduced us to the idea of a sacred priest-king, and showed how fundamental it was in primitive societies. The welfare of the tribe is regarded as inextricably bound up with that of the King, and extraordinary precautions are taken to preserve him from harm. In this kingdom, in the old days, the King was hardly allowed to set his foot to the ground in case he should lose divinity; his cut hair and nail-parings were entrusted to one of the most important officials of state, whose duty it was to bury them secretly, in case some enemy should compass the King's illness or death by using them in black magic rites. If anyone of base blood trod on the King's shadow, he paid the penalty with his life. Each year a slave was made mock-king for a week, allowed to enjoy all the king's privileges, and was decapitated at the close of his brief glory; and by this means it was supposed that the illnesses and misfortunes that might befall the King were vicariously got rid of.

"I first of all rigged up my apparatus, and with the aid of Aggers, succeeded in getting good cultures, first of chick tissues and later, by the aid of embryo-extract, of various and adult mammalian tissues. I then went to Bugala, and told him that I could increase the safety, if not of the King as an indi-

* A very elaborate treatise on a division of Roman mythology, especially on the cult of Diana.

vidual, at least of the life which was in him, and that I
presumed that this would be equally satisfactory from a theo-
logical point of view. I pointed out that if he chose to be
made guardian of the King's subsidiary lives, he would be in
a much more important position than the chamberlain or the
burier of the sacred nail-parings, and might make the post the
most influential in the realm.

"Eventually I was allowed (under threats of death if anything untoward occurred) to remove small portions of His
Majesty's subcutaneous connective tissue under a local anaes-
thetic. In the presence of the assembled nobility I put fragments of this into culture medium, and showed it to them
under the microscope. The cultures were then put away in
the incubator, under a guard—relieved every eight hours—of
half a dozen warriors. After three days, to my joy they had
all taken and showed abundant growth. I could see that the
Council was impressed, and reeled off a magnificent speech,
pointing out that this growth constituted an actual increase in
the quantity of the divine principle inherent in royalty; and
what was more, that I could increase it indefinitely. With that
I cut each of my cultures into eight, and sub-cultured all the
pieces. They were again put under guard, and again examined after three days. Not all of them had taken this time,
and there were some murmurings and angry looks, on the
ground that I had killed some of the King; but I pointed out
that the King was still the King, that his little wound had
completely healed, and that any successful cultures represented so much extra sacredness and protection to the state. I
must say that they were very reasonable, and had good theo-
logical acumen, for they at once took the hint.

"I pointed out to Bugala, and he persuaded the rest without much difficulty, that they could now disregard some of
the older implications of the doctrines of kingship. The most
important new idea which I was able to introduce was *mass-
production*. Our aim was to multiply the King's tissues indefinitely, to ensure that some of their protecting power should
reside everywhere in the country. Thus by concentrating upon
quantity, we could afford to remove some of the restrictions
upon the King's mode of life. This was of course agreeable to
the King; and also to Bugala, who saw himself wielding un-
dreamt-of power. One might have supposed that such an innovation would have met with great resistance simply on
account of its being an innovation; but I must admit that

these people compared very favorably with the average businessman in their lack of prejudice.

"Having thus settled the principle, I had many debates with Bugala as to the best methods for enlisting the mass of the population in our scheme. What an opportunity for scientific advertising! But, unfortunately, the population could not read. However, war propaganda worked very well in more or less illiterate countries—why not here?"

Hascombe organized a series of public lectures in the capital, at which he demonstrated his regal tissues to the multitude, who were bidden to the place by royal heralds. An impressive platform group was always supplied from the ranks of the nobles. The lecturer explained how important it was for the community to become possessed of greater and greater stores of the sacred tissues. Unfortunately, the preparation was laborious and expensive, and it behooved them all to lend a hand. It had accordingly been arranged that to everyone subscribing a cow or buffalo, or its equivalent—three goats, pigs, or sheep—a portion of the royal anatomy should be given, handsomely mounted in an ebony holder. Sub-culturing would be done at certain hours and days, and it would be obligatory to send the cultures for renewal. If through any negligence the tissue died, no renewal would be made. The subscription entitled the receiver to subculturing rights for a year, but was of course renewable. By this means not only would the totality of the King be much increased, to the benefit of all, but each cultureholder would possess an actual part of His Majesty, and would have the infinite joy and privilege of aiding by his own efforts the multiplication of divinity.

Then they could also serve their country by dedicating a daughter to the state. These young women would be housed and fed by the state, and taught the technique of the sacred culture. Candidates would be selected according to general fitness, but would of course, in addition, be required to attain distinction in an examination on the principles of religion. They would be appointed for a probationary period of six months. After this they would receive a permanent status, with the title of Sisters of the Sacred Tissue. From this, with age, experience, and merit, they could expect promotion to the rank of mothers, grandmothers, great-grandmothers, and grand ancestresses of the same. The merit and benefit they would receive from their close contact with the source of all benefits would overflow on to their families.

The scheme worked like wildfire. Pigs, goats, cattle, buffaloes, and Negro maidens poured in. Next year the scheme was extended to the whole country, a peripatetic laboratory making the rounds weekly.

By the close of the third year there was hardly a family in the country which did not possess at least one sacred culture. To be without one would have been like being without one's trousers—or at least without one's hat*—on Fifth Avenue. Thus did Bugala effect a reformation in the national religion, enthrone himself as the most important personage in the country, and entrench applied science and Hascombe firmly in the organization of the state.

Encouraged by his success, Hascombe soon set out to capture the ancestry-worship branch of the religion as well. A public proclamation was made pointing out how much more satisfactory it would be if worship could be made not merely to the charred bones of one's forbears, but to bits of them still actually living and growing. All who were desirous of profiting by the enterprise of Bugala's Department of State should therefore bring their older relatives to the laboratory at certain specified hours, and fragments would be painlessly extracted for culture.

This, too, proved very attractive to the average citizen. Occasionally, it is true, grandfathers or aged mothers arrived in a state of indignation and protest. However, this did not matter, since, according to the law, once children were twenty-five years of age, they were not only assigned the duty of worshipping their ancestors, alive or dead, but were also given complete control over them, in order that all rites might be duly performed to the greater safety of the commonweal. Further, the ancestors soon found that the operation itself was trifling, and, what was more, that once accomplished, it had the most desirable results. For their descendants preferred to concentrate at once upon the culture which they would continue to worship after the old folks were gone, and so left their parents and grandparents much freer than before from the irksome restrictions which in all ages have beset the officially holy.

Thus, by almost every hearth in the kingdom, instead of the old-fashioned rows of red jars containing the incinerated

---

* This was written before the year 1927.

remains of one or other of the family forbears, the new generation saw growing up a collection of family slides. Each would be taken out and reverently examined at the hour of prayer. "Grandpapa is not growing well this week," you would perhaps hear the young black devotee say; the father of the family would pray over the speck of tissue; and if that failed, it would be taken back to the factory for rejuvenation. On the other hand, what rejoicing when a rhythm of activity stirred in the cultures! A spurt on the part of great-grandmother's tissues would bring her wrinkled old smile to mind again; and sometimes it seemed as if one particular generation were all stirred simultaneously by a pulse of growth, as if combining to bless their devout descendants.

To deal with the possibility of cultures dying out, Hascombe started a central storehouse, where duplicates of every strain were kept, and it was this repository of the national tissues which had attracted my attention at the back of the laboratory. No such collection had ever existed before, he assured me. Not a necropolis, but a histopolis, if I may coin a word: not a cemetery, but a place of eternal growth.

The second building was devoted to endocrine products—an African Armour's—and was called by the people the "Factory of Ministers to the Shrines"

"Here," he said, "you will not find much new. You know the craze for 'glands' that was going on at home years ago, and its results, in the shape of pluriglandular preparations, a new genre of patent medicines, and a popular literature that threatened to outdo the Freudians, and explain human beings entirely on the basis of glandular make-up, without reference to the mind at all.

"I had only to apply my knowledge in a comparatively simple manner. The first thing was to show Bugala how, by repeated injections of prepituitary, I could make an ordinary baby grow up into a giant. This pleased him, and he introduced the idea of a sacred bodyguard, all of really gigantic stature, quite overshadowing Frederick's Grenadiers.

"I did, however, extend knowledge in several directions. I took advantage of the fact that their religion holds in reverence monstrous and imbecile forms of human beings. That is, of course, a common phenomenon in many countries, where half-wits are supposed to be inspired, and dwarfs the object of superstitious awe. So I went to work to create various new types. By employing a particular extract of adrenal cortex, I produced children who would have been a match for the Infant Hercules, and, indeed, looked rather like a cross between him and a brewer's drayman. By injecting the same extract into adolescent girls I was able to provide them with the most copious mustaches, after which they found ready employment as prophetesses.

"Tampering with the post-pituitary gave remarkable cases of obesity. This, together with the passion of the men for fatness in their women, Bugala took advantage of, and I believe made quite a fortune by selling as concubines female slaves treated in this way. Finally, by another pituitary treatment, I at last mastered the secret of true dwarfism, in which perfect proportions are retained.

"Of these productions, the dwarfs are retained as acolytes in the temple; a band of the obese young ladies form a sort of Society of Vestal Virgins, with special religious duties, which, as the embodiment of the national ideal of beauty, they are supposed to discharge with peculiarly propitious effect; and the giants form our Regular Army.

"The Obese Virgins have set me a problem which I confess I have not yet solved. Like all races who set great store by sexual enjoyment, these people have a correspondingly exaggerated reverence for virginity. It therefore occurred to me that if I could apply Jacques Loeb's great discovery of artificial parthenogenesis to man, or, to be precise, to these young ladies, I should be able to grow a race of vestals, self-reproducing yet ever virgin, to whom in concentrated form should attach that reverence of which I have just spoken. You see, I must always remember that it is no good proposing any line of work that will not benefit the national religion. I suppose state-aided research would have much the same kinds of difficulties in a really democratic state. Well this, as I say, has so far beaten me. I have taken the matter a step further than Bataillon with his fatherless frogs, and I have induced parthenogesesis in the eggs of reptiles and birds; but so far I have failed with mammals. However, I've not given up yet!"

Then we passed to the next laboratory, which was full of the most incredible animal monstrosities. "This laboratory is the most amusing," said Hascombe. "Its official title is 'Home of the Living Fetishes.' Here again I have simply taken a prevalent trait of the populace, and used it as a peg on which to hang research. I told you that they always had a fancy for the grotesque in animals, and used the most bizarre forms, in the shape of little clay or ivory statuettes, for fetishes.

"I thought I would see whether art could not improve upon

nature, and set myself to recall my experimental embryology. I use only the simplest methods. I utilize the plasticity of the earliest stages to give double-headed and cyclopean monsters. That was, of course, done years ago in newts by Spemann and fish by Stockard; and I have merely applied the mass-production methods of Mr. Ford to their results. But my specialties are three-headed snakes, and toads with an extra heaven-pointing head. The former are a little difficult, but there is a great demand for them, and they fetch a good price. The frogs are easier: I simply apply Harrison's methods to embryo tadpoles."

He then showed me into the last building. Unlike the others, this contained no signs of research in progress, but was empty. It was draped with black hangings, and lit only from the top. In the center were rows of ebony benches, and in front of them a glittering golden ball on a stand.

"Here I am beginning my work on reinforced telepathy," he told me. "Some day you must come and see what it's all about, for it really is interesting."

You may imagine that I was pretty well flabbergasted by this catalogue of miracles. Every day I got a talk with Hascombe, and gradually the talks became recognized events of our daily routine. One day I asked if he had given up hope of escaping. He showed a queer hesitation in replying. Eventually he said, "To tell you the truth, my dear Jones, I have really hardly thought of it these last few years. It seemed so impossible at first that I deliberately put it out of my head and turned with more and more energy, I might almost say fury, to my work. And now, upon my soul, I'm not quite sure whether I want to escape or not."

"Not *want* to!" I exclaimed; "surely you can't mean that!"

"I am not so sure," he rejoined. "What I most want is to get ahead with this work of mine. Why, man, you don't realize what a chance I've got! And it is all growing so fast—I can see every kind of possibility ahead"; and he broke off into silence.

However, although I was interested enough in his past achievements, I did not feel willing to sacrifice my future to his perverted intellectual ambitions. But he would not leave his work.

The experiments which most excited his imagination were those he was conducting into mass telepathy. He had received his medical training at a time when abnormal psychology was still very unfashionable in England, but had luckily been thrown in contact with a young doctor who was a keen student of hypnotism, through whom he had been introduced to some of the great pioneers, like Bramwell and Wingfield. As a result, he had become a passable hypnotist himself, with a fair knowledge of the literature.

In the early days of his captivity he became interested in the sacred dances which took place every night of full moon, and were regarded as propitiations of the celestial powers. The dancers all belong to a special sect. After a series of exciting figures, symbolizing various activities of the chase, war, and love, the leader conducts his band to a ceremonial bench. He then begins to make passes at them; and what impressed Hascombe was this, that a few seconds sufficed for them to fall back in deep hypnosis against the ebony rail. It recalled, he said, the most startling cases of collective hypnosis recorded by the French scientists. The leader next passed from one end of the bench to the other, whispering a brief sentence into each ear. He then, according to immemorial rite, approached the Priest-King, and, after having exclaimed aloud, "Lord of Majesty, command what thou wilt for thy dancers to perform," the King would thereupon command some action which had previously been kept secret. The command was often to fetch some object and deposit it at the moon-shrine; or to fight the enemies of the state; or (and this was what the company most liked) to be some animal, or bird. Whatever the command, the hypnotized men would obey it, for the leader's whispered words had been an order to hear and carry out only what the King said; and the strangest scenes would be witnessed as they ran, completely oblivious of all in their path, in search of the gourds or sheep they had been called on to procure, or lunged in a symbolic way at invisible enemies, or threw themselves on all fours and roared as lions, or galloped as zebras, or danced as cranes. The command executed, they stood like stocks or stones, until their leader, running from one to the other, touched each with a finger and shouted "Wake." They woke, and limp, but conscious of having been the vessels of the unknown spirit, danced back to their special hut or clubhouse.

This susceptibility to hypnotic suggestion struck Hascombe, and he obtained permission to test the performers more closely. He soon established that the people were, as a race, extremely prone to dissociation, and could be made to lapse into deep hypnosis with great ease, but a hypnosis in which the subconscious, though completely cut off from the waking self, comprised portions of the personality not retained in the hypnotic selves of Europeans. Like most who have fluttered round the psychological candle, he had been interested in the notion of telepathy; and now, with this supply of hypnotic subjects under his hands, began some real investigation of the problem.

By picking his subjects, he was soon able to demonstrate the existence of telepathy, by making suggestions to one hypnotized man who transferred them without physical intermediation to another at a distance. Later—and this was the culmination of his work—he found that when he made a suggestion to several subjects at once, the telepathic effect was much stronger than if he had done it to one at a time—the hypnotized minds were reinforcing each other. "I'm after the super-consciousness," Hascombe said, "and I've already got the rudiments of it."

I must confess that I got almost as excited as Hascombe over the possibilities thus opened up. It certainly seemed as if he were right in principle. If all the subjects were in practically the same psychological state, extraordinary reinforcing effects were observed. At first the attainment of this similarity of condition was very difficult; gradually, however, we discovered that it was possible to tune hypnotic subjects to the same pitch, if I may use the metaphor, and then the fun really began.

First of all we found that with increasing reinforcement, we could get telepathy conducted to greater and greater distances, until finally we could transmit commands from the capital to the national boundary, nearly a hundred miles. We next found that it was not necessary for the subject to be in hypnosis to receive the telepathic command. Almost everybody, but especially those of equable temperament, could thus be influenced. Most extraordinary of all, however, were what we at first christened "near effects," since their transmission to a distance was not found possible until later. If, after Hascombe had suggested some simple command to a largish group of hypnotized subjects, he or I went right up among them, we would experience the most extraordinary sensation, as of some superhuman personality repeating the command in a menacing and overwhelming way and, whereas with one part of ourselves we felt that we must carry out the command, with another we felt, if I may say so, as if we were only a part of the command, or of something much bigger than ourselves which was commanding. And this, Hascombe claimed, was the first real beginning of the super-consciousness.

Bugala, of course, had to be considered. Hascombe, with the old Tibetan prayer-wheel at the back of his mind, suggested that eventually he would be able to induce hypnosis in the whole population, and then transmit a prayer. This would ensure that the daily prayer, for instance, was really said by the whole population, and, what is more, simultaneously, which would undoubtedly much enhance its efficacy. And it would make it possible in times of calamity or battle to keep the whole praying force of the nation at work for long spells together.

Bugala was deeply interested. He saw himself, through this mental machinery, planting such ideas as he wished in the brain-cases of his people. He saw himself willing an order; and the whole population rousing itself out of trance to execute it. He dreamt dreams before which those of the proprietor of a newspaper syndicate, even those of a director of propaganda in wartime, would be pale and timid. Naturally, he wished to receive personal instruction in the methods himself; and, equally naturally, we could not refuse him, though I must say that I often felt a little uneasy as to what he might choose to do if he ever decided to override Hascombe and to start experimenting on his own. This, combined with my constant longing to get away from the place, led me to cast about again for means of escape. Then it occurred to me that this very method about which I had such gloomy presentiments, might itself be made the key to our prison.

So one day, after getting Hascombe worked up about the loss to humanity it would be to let this great discovery die with him in Africa, I set to in earnest. "My dear Hascombe," I said, "you must get home out of this. What is there to prevent you saying to Bugala that your experiments are nearly crowned with success, but that for certain tests you must have a much greater number of subjects at your disposal? You can then get a battery of two hundred men, and after you have tuned them, the reinforcment will be so great that you will have at your disposal a mental force big enough to affect the whole population. Then, of course, one fine day we should raise the potential of our mind-battery to the highest possible level, and send out through it a general hypnotic influence. The whole country, men, women, and children, would sink into stupor. Next we should give our experimental squad the suggestion to broadcast 'sleep for a week.' The telepathic message would be relayed to each of the thousands of minds waiting receptively for it, and would take root in them, until the whole nation became a single super-consciousness, conscious only of the one thought 'sleep' which we had thrown into it."

The reader will perhaps ask how we ourselves expected to escape from the clutches of the super-consciousness we had created. Well, we had discovered that metal was relatively impervious to the telepathic effect, and had prepared for ourselves a sort of tin pulpit, behind which we could stand while conducting experiments. This, combined with caps of metal foil, enormously reduced the effects on ourselves. We had not informed Bugala of this property of metal.

Hascombe was silent. At length he spoke. "I like the idea," he said; "I like to think that if I ever do get back to England and to scientific recognition, my discovery will have given me the means of escape."

From that moment we worked assiduously to perfect our method and our plans. After about five months everything seemed propitious. We had provisions packed away, and compasses. I had been allowed to keep my rifle, on promise that I would never discharge it. We had made friends with some of the men who went trading to the coast, and had got from them all the information we could about the route, without arousing their suspicions.

At last, the night arrived. We assembled our men as if for an ordinary practice, and after hypnosis had been induced, started to tune them. At this moment Bugala came in, unannounced. This was what we had been afraid of; but there had been no means of preventing it. "What shall we do?" I whispered to Hascombe, in English. "Go right ahead and be damned to it," was his answer; "we can put him to sleep with the rest."

So we welcomed him, and gave him a seat as near as possible to the tightly packed ranks of the performers. At length the preparations were finished. Hascombe went into the pulpit and said, "Attention to the words which are to be suggested." There was a slight stiffening of the bodies. "Sleep" said Hascombe. "*Sleep* is the command: command all in this land to sleep unbrokenly." Bugala leapt up with an exclamation; but the induction had already begun.

We with our metal coverings were immune. But Bugala

was struck by the full force of the mental current. He sank back on his chair, helpless. For a few minutes his extraordinary will resisted the suggestion. Although he could not move, his angry eyes were open. But at length he succumbed, and he too slept.

We lost no time in starting, and made good progress through the silent country. The people were sitting about like wax figures. Women sat asleep by their milk-pails, the cow by this time far away. Fat-bellied naked children slept at their games. The houses were full of sleepers sleeping upright round their food, recalling Wordsworth's famous "party in a parlor."

So we went on, feeling pretty queer and scarcely believing in this morphic state into which we had plunged a nation. Finally the frontier was reached, where with extreme elation, we passed an immobile and gigantic frontier guard. A few miles further we had a good solid meal, and a doze. Our kit was rather heavy, and we decided to jettison some superfluous weight, in the shape of some food, specimens, and our metal headgear, or mind-protectors, which at this distance, and with the hypnosis wearing a little thin, were, we thought, no longer necessary.

About nightfall on the third day, Hascombe suddenly stopped and turned his head.

"What's the matter?" I said. "Have you seen a lion?" His reply was completely unexpected. "No. I was just wondering whether really I ought not to go back again."

"Go back again," I cried. "What in the name of God Almighty do you want to do that for?"

"It suddenly struck me that I ought to," he said, "about five minutes ago. And really, when one comes to think of it, I don't suppose I shall ever get such a chance at research again. What's more, this is a dangerous journey to the coast, and I don't expect we shall get through alive."

I was thoroughly upset and put out, and told him so. And suddenly, for a few moments, I felt I must go back too. It was like that old friend of our boyhood, the voice of conscience.

"Yes, to be sure, we ought to go back," I thought with fervor. But suddenly checking myself as the thought came under the play of reason—"*Why* should we go back?" All sorts of reasons were proffered, as it were, by unseen hands reaching up out of the hidden parts of me.

And then I realized what had happened. Bugala had waked up; he had wiped out the suggestion we had given to the super-consciousness, and in its place put in another. I could see him thinking it out, the cunning devil (one must give him credit for brains!), and hear him, after making his passes, whisper to the nation in prescribed form his new suggestion: "Will to return!" "Return!" For most of the inhabitants the command would have no meaning, for they would have been already at home. Doubtless some young men out on the hills, or truant children, or girls run off in secret to meet their lovers, were even now returning, stiffly and in somnambulistic trance, to their homes. It was only for them that the new command of the super-consciousness had any meaning—and for us.

I am putting it in a long and discursive way; at the moment I simply *saw* what had happened in a flash. I told Hascombe, I showed him it *must* be so, that nothing else would account for the sudden change. I begged and implored him to use his reason, to stick to his decision and to come on. How I regretted that, in our desire to discard all useless weight, we had left behind our metal telepathy-proof head coverings!.

But Hascombe would not, or could not, see my point. I suppose he was much more imbued with all the feelings and spirit of the country, and so more susceptible. However that may be, he was immovable. He must go back; he knew it; he saw it clearly; it was his sacred duty; and much other similar rubbish. All this time the suggestion was attacking me too; and finally I felt that if I did not put more distance between me and that unisonic battery of will, I should succumb as well as he.

"Hascombe," I said, "I am going on. For God's sake, come with me." And I shouldered my pack, and set off. He was shaken, I saw, and came a few steps after me. But finally he turned, and, in spite of my frequent pauses and shouts to him to follow, made off in the direction we had come. I can assure you that it was with a gloomy soul that I continued my solitary way. I shall not bore you with my adventures. Suffice it to say that at last I got to a white outpost, weak with fatigue and poor food and fever.

I kept very quiet about my adventures, only giving out that our expedition had lost its way and that my men had run away or been killed by the local tribes. At last I reached England. But I was a broken man, and a profound gloom had invaded my mind at the thought of Hascombe and the way he had been caught in his own net. I never found out what happened to him, and I do not suppose that I am likely to find out now. You may ask why I did not try to organize a rescue expedition; or why, at least, I did not bring Hascombe's discoveries before the Royal Society or the Metaphysical Institute. I can only repeat that I was a broken man. I did not expect to be believed; I was not at all sure that I could repeat our results, even on the same human material, much less with men of another race; I dreaded ridicule; and finally I was tormented by doubts as to whether the knowledge of mass-telepathy would not be a curse rather than a blessing to mankind.

However, I am an oldish man now and, what is more, old for my years. I want to get the story off my chest. Besides, old men like sermonizing and you must forgive, gentle reader, the sermonical turn which I now feel I must take. The question I want to raise is this: Dr. Hascombe attained to an unsurpassed power in a number of the applications of science—but _to what end did all this power serve?_ It is the merest cant and twaddle to go on asserting, as most of our press and people continue to do, that increase of scientific knowledge and power must in itself be good. I commend to the great public the obvious moral of my story and ask them to think what they propose to do with the power which is gradually being accumulated for them by the labors of those who labor because they like power, or because they want to find the truth about how things work.

Pedestrian Words, Soaring Concepts

Now that there was a science-fiction magazine (within four years, three science-fiction magazines), where would the writers be found who would fill it with their stories? Several answers emerged: some authors already had been contributing science fiction and fantasy to Gernsback's popular science magazines or to the unspecialized pulps; others found *Amazing Stories* just one more market for stories that they wrote in many categories; still others discovered in themselves a spirit of enthusiasm, speculation, or inspiration that responded to *Amazing*'s unique tone.

Edgar Rice Burroughs was willing to write an original novel, *The Mastermind of Mars* (1927), for Gernsback's *Amazing Annual*. Ray Cummings, whose long writing career began with "The Girl in the Golden Atom" (*All-Story*, 1919), wrote dozens of stories for all the science-fiction magazines. Murray Leinster (Will F. Jenkins) broke into print in 1918 and published "The Runaway Skyscraper" in *Argosy* in 1919, but he was busy with other markets and contributed to science-fiction magazines only occasionally until the '40s.

Some full-time writers wrote in many categories. If they wrote fast enough and successfully enough, they could make a good income even at a half-cent to a cent a word. The fabulous Frederick Faust is the best-known author of this type. He wrote and sold millions of words under many pseudonyms, but particularly that of Max Brand. Apparently he never wrote directly for the sf magazines, although several of his earlier Munsey-magazine stories were reprinted in the '40s by the *Famous Fantastic Mysteries* magazines. A prolific author who did write for the sf magazines, beginning in 1930, was Arthur J. Burks, who is reputed to have written 10,000 words every day and to have sold most of it to all sorts of pulp magazines.

Some writers wrote prolifically mostly or entirely for the sf magazines. Captain S. P. Meek published thirty-four stories between 1929 and 1932. Harl Vincent (H. V. Schoeplin) published seventy-three stories between 1928 and 1941. Stanton A. Coblentz, whose first and abiding love was poetry, published sixty-one stories in various magazines between 1928 and 1950; he found science fiction an excellent vehicle for social satire.

Then came the new writers. Science fiction was something novel, idealistic, open—and it attracted people fascinated by the future and its possibilities or by humanity and its potential. They would spend much of their lives writing fantasy and science fiction, though seldom as full-time writers; the field was too small to support them.

There was Edward Elmer Smith, Ph.D. (doughnut-mix specialist). He completed his first space epic (The Skylark of Space) in 1919 and had to wait until 1928 to see it published in Amazing. Philip Nowlan wrote two science-fiction stories about a character named Anthony Rogers; when they were published in Amazing in 1928 and 1929 they led to a long relationship with Buck Rogers. Dr. Miles J. Breuer published the first of his thirty-nine stories in a 1927 Amazing. P. Schuyler Miller published thirty-seven stories before taking over the book-review column for Astounding. There were others, such as Arthur K. Barnes, Raymond Z. Gallun, Neil R. Jones, Nathan (Nat) Schachner, and Arthur Leo Zagat.

Getting special mention later in this anthology are writers such as John W. Campbell, Edmond Hamilton, and Jack Williamson.

Among the authors who found science fiction a homeland was David H. Keller, M.D. (1880–1966). Keller was a physician who specialized in psychoanalysis and worked in a series of hospitals for the mentally ill. He wrote extensively about medicine (700 articles, ten books) and much science fiction and weird fiction. Oddly enough, until he was forty-seven he wrote his fiction for himself and bound his stories for his own library.

His first published story, "The Revolt of the Pedestrians," ran in Amazing in 1928. His sixty-six stories published in sf magazines appeared mostly in the next half-dozen years, although some were published as late as 1941. He also wrote a number of stories for Weird Tales. Among his best-known works are the stories "The Thing in the Cellar," "A Piece of Linoleum," "Stenographer's Hands," and "The Ivy War," and the novels Life Everlasting, The Solitary Hunters, and The Abyss.

"The Revolt of the Pedestrians" exhibits some sophisticated techniques surprising for its time: the calm acceptance of change, the casual division of humanity into automobilists and pedestrians, and the emergence of satire from the story itself. It resembles "The Machine Stops," but differs in revealing ways. In Keller's story there is recognition of the situation, if only by a few people, and they attempt to change things. In *Brave New World*, the Savage hangs himself. In *Nineteen Eighty-Four*, Winston Smith's mind is wiped clean. Not until Williamson's "With Folded Hands . . ." does the science-fiction anti-utopia reach complete hopelessness, and even then the ellipsis suggests the possibility of change.

In 1928 the sf magazines still nursed the belief that if the problem was recognized thinking men and women could find a solution.

The Revolt of the Pedestrians

by David H. Keller, M.D.

A young pedestrian mother was walking slowly down a country road holding her little son by his hand. They were beautiful examples of pedestrians, though tired and dusty from long days spent on their journey from Ohio to Arkansas, where the pitiful remnant of the doomed species was gathering for the final struggle. For several days these two had walked the roads westward, escaping instant death again and again by repeated miracles. Yet this afternoon, tired, hungry and hypnotized by the setting sun in her face, the woman slept even as she walked and only woke screaming, when she realized that escape was impossible. She succeeded in pushing her son to safety in the gutter, and then died instantly beneath the wheels of a skilfully driven car, going at sixty miles an hour.

The lady in the sedan was annoyed at the jolt and spoke rather sharply to the chauffeur through the speaking tube.

"What was that jar, William?"

"Madam, we have just run over a pedestrian."

"Oh, is that all? Well, at least you should be careful." The lady added to her little daughter, "William just ran over a pedestrian and there was only the slightest jar."

The little girl looked with pride on her new dress. It was her eighth birthday and they were going to her grandmother's for the day. Her twisted atrophied legs moved in slow rhythmic movements. It was her mother's pride to say that her little daughter had never tried to walk. She could think, however, and something was evidently worrying her. She looked up.

"Mother!" she asked. "Do pedestrians feel pain the way we do?"

"Why, of course not, Darling," said the mother. "They are not like us, in fact some say they are not human beings at all."

"Are they like monkeys?"

"Well, perhaps higher than apes, but much lower than automobiles."

The machine sped on.

Miles behind a terror-stricken lad lay sobbing on the bleeding body of his mother, which he somehow had found strength to drag to the side of the road. He remained there till another day dawned and then left her and walked slowly up the hills into the forest. He was hungry and tired, sleepy and heartbroken but he paused for a moment on the crest of the hill and shook his fist in inarticulate rage.

That day, a deep hatred was formed in his soul.

The world had gone automobile wild. Traffic cops had no time for the snail-like movements of walkers—they were a menace to civilization—a drawback to progress—a defiance to the development of science. Nothing mattered in a man's body but his brains.

Gradually machinery had replaced muscle as a means of attaining man's desire on earth. Life consisted only of a series of explosions of gasoline or alcohol—air mixtures or steam expansion in hollow cylinders and turbines, and this caused power to be applied wherever the mind of man dictated. All mankind was accomplishing their desires by mechanical energy made in small amounts transmitted over wires as electricity for the use of vast centers of population.

The sky always had its planes; the higher levels for the inter-city express service, the lower for individual suburban traffic—the roads, all of reinforced concrete, were often one-way roads, exacted by the number of machines in order to avoid continual collisions. While part of the world had taken readily to the skies, the vast proportion had been forced, by insufficient development of the semi-circular canals, to remain on earth.

The automobile had developed as legs had atrophied. No longer content to use it constantly outdoors, the successors of Ford had perfected the smaller individual machine for use indoors, all steps being replaced by curving ascending passages. Men thus came to live within metal bodies, which they left only for sleep. Gradually, partly through necessity and partly through inclination, the automobile was used in sport as well as in play. Special types were developed for golf; children seated in autocars rolled hoops through shady parks; lazily, prostrate on one, a maiden drifted through the tropical waters of a Florida resort. Mankind had ceased to use their lower limbs.

With disuse came atrophy: with atrophy came progressive and definite changes in the shapes of mankind; with these changes came new conceptions of feminine beauty. All this happened not in one generation, nor in ten, but gradually in the course of centuries.

Customs changed; so laws changed. No longer were laws for everyone's good but only for the benefit of the automobilist. The roads, formerly for the benefit of all, were finally restricted to those in machines. At first it was merely dangerous to walk on the highways; later it became a crime. Like all changes, this came slowly. First came a law restricting certain roads to automobilists; then came a law prohibiting pedestrians from the use of roads; then a law giving them no legal recourse if injured while walking on a public highway; later it became a felony to do so.

Then came the final law providing for the legal murder of all pedestrians on the highway, wherever or whenever they could be hit by an auto.

No one was content to go slowly—all the world was crazed by a desire for speed. There was also a desire, no matter where an automobilist was, to go to some other city. Thus Sundays and holidays were distinguished by thousands and millions of automobilists going "somewhere," none being content to spend the hours of leisure quietly where they were. Rural landscapes consisted of long lines of machines passing between walls of advertisements at the rate of eighty miles an hour, pausing now and then at gasoline filling stations, at road houses or to strip an occasional tree of its blooms. The air was filled with vapors from the exhausts of machinery and the raucous noise of countless horns of all description. No one saw anything: no one wanted to see anything: the desire of each driver was to drive faster than the car ahead of his. It was called in the vernacular of the day—"A quiet Sunday in the country."

There were no pedestrians; that is, almost none. Even in the rural districts mankind was on wheels mechanically propelled. Such farming as was done was done by machinery. Here and there, clinging like mountain sheep to inaccessible mountainsides, remained a few pedestrians who, partly from choice, but mainly from necessity, had retained the desire to use their legs. These people were always poor. At first the laws had no terror for them. Every state had some families who had never ceased to be pedestrians. On these the automobilists looked first with amusement and then with alarm. No one realized the tremendous depth of the chasm between the two groups of the Genus Homo till the national law was passed forbidding the use of all highways to pedestrians. At once, all over the United States, the revolt of the Walkers began. Although Bunker Hill was hundreds of years away, the spirit of Bunker Hill survived, and the prohibition of walking on the roads only increased the desire to do so. More pedestrians than ever were accidentally killed. Their families retaliated by using every effort to make automobiling unpleasant and dangerous—nails, tacks, glass, logs, barbed wire, huge rocks were used as weapons. In the Ozarks, backwoodsmen took delight in breaking windshields and puncturing tires with well-directed rifle shots. Others walked the roads and defied the automobilists. Had the odds been equal, a condition of anarchy would have resulted; being unequal, the pedestrians were simply a nuisance. Class-consciousness reached its acme when Senator Glass of New York rose in the Senate Chambers and said in part:

"A race that ceases to develop must die out. For centuries mankind has been on wheels, and thus has advanced towards a state of mechanical perfection. The pedestrian, careless of his inherent right to ride, has persisted not only in walking, but even has gone so far as to claim equal rights with the higher type of automobilist. Patience has ceased to be a virtue. Nothing more can be done for these miserable degenerates of our race. The kindest thing to do now is to inaugurate a process of extermination. Only thus can we prevent a continuation of the disorders which have marked the otherwise uniform peaceful history of our fair land. There is, therefore, nothing for me to do save to urge the passage of the 'Pedestrian Extermination Act.' This as you know provides for the instant death of all pedestrians, wherever and whenever they are found by the Constabulary of each State. The last census shows there are only about ten thousand left and these are mostly in a few of the mid-western states. I am proud to state that my own constituency, which up to yesterday had only one pedestrian, an old man over ninety years of age, has now a clear record. A telegram just received states that fortunately he tottered on a public road in a senile effort to visit his wife's grave and was instantly killed by an automobilist. But though New York has at present none of these vile degenerates, we are anxious to aid our less fortunate states."

The law was instantly passed, being opposed only by the Senators from Kentucky, Tennessee and Arkansas. To promote interest, a bounty was placed on each pedestrian killed. A silver star was given to each county reporting complete success. A gold star to each state containing only autoists. The pedestrian, like the carrier pigeon, was doomed.

It is not to be expected that the extermination was immediate or complete. There was some unexpected resistance. It had been in effect one year when the pedestrian child swore vengeance on the mechanical means of destroying humanity.

Sunday afternoon a hundred years later, the Academy of Natural Sciences in Philadelphia was filled with the usual throng of pleasure seekers, each in his own auto-car. Noiselessly, on rubber-tired wheels, they journeyed down the long aisles, pausing now and then before this exhibit or that which attracted their individual attention. A father was taking his little boy through and each was greatly interested: the boy in the new world of wonders, the father in the boy's intelligent questions and observations. Finally the boy stopped his auto-car in front of a glass case.

"What is that, Father? They look as we do, only what peculiar shapes."

"That, my son, is a family of pedestrians. It was long ago it all happened and I know of it only because my mother told me about them. This family was shot in the Ozark Mountains. It is believed they were the last in the world."

"I am sorry," said the boy, slowly. "If there were more, I would like you to get a little one for me to play with."

"There are no more," said the father. "They are all dead."

The man thought he was telling the truth to his son. In fact, he prided himself on always being truthful to children. Yet he was wrong. For a few pedestrians remained, and their leader, in fact, their very brains, was the great-grandson of the little boy who had stood up on the hill with hatred in his heart long before.

Irrespective of climatic conditions, environment and all varieties of enemies, man has always been able to exist. With the race of pedestrians it was in very truth the survival of the fittest. Only the most agile, intelligent and sturdy were able to survive the systematic attempt made to exterminate them. Though reduced in numbers they survived; though deprived of all the so-called benefits of modern civilization, they existed. Forced to defend not only their individual existence, but also the very life of their race, they gained the cunning of their backwoodsmen ancestors and kept alive. They lived, hunted, loved, and died and for two generations the civilized world was unaware of their very existence. They had their political organization, their courts of law. Justice, based on Blackstone and the Constitution, ruled. Always a Miller ruled: first the little boy with hatred in his heart, grown to manhood; then his son, trained from childhood to the sole task of hatred of all things mechanical; then the grandson, wise, cunning, a dream-builder; and finally the great-grandson, Abraham Miller, prepared by three generations for the ultimate revenge.

Abraham Miller was the hereditary president of the Colony of Pedestrians hidden in the Ozark Mountains. They were isolated, but not ignorant; few in number but adaptive. The first fugitives had many brilliant men: inventors, college professors, patriots and even a learned jurist. These men kept their knowledge and transmitted it. They dug in the fields, hunted in the woods, fished in the streams, and builded in their laboratories. They even had automobiles, and now and then, with limbs tied close to their bodies, would travel as spies into the land of the enemy. Certain of the children were trained from childhood to act in this capacity. There is even evidence that for some years one of these spies lived in St. Louis.

It was a colony with a single ambition—a union of individuals for one purpose only; the children lisped it, the school children spoke it daily; the young folks whispered it to each other in the moonlight; in the laboratories it was carved on every wall; the senile gathered their children around and swore them to it; every action of the colony was bent toward one end—

"We will go back."

They were paranoiac in their hatred. Without exception, all of their ancestors had been hunted like wild beasts, exterminated without mercy—like vermin. It was not revenge they desired, but liberty—the right to live as they wished, to go and come as they pleased.

For three generations the colony had preserved the secret of their existence. Year by year as a unit they had lived, worked and died for a single ambition. Now the time had come for the execution of their plans, the fulfillment of their desires. Meanwhile the world of automobilists lived on, materialistic, mechanical, selfish. Socialism had provided comfort for the masses but had singularly failed to provide happiness. All lived, everyone had an income, no one but was provided with a home, food and clothes. But the homes were of concrete; they were uniform, poured out by the million; the furniture was concrete; poured with the houses. The clothing was paper, water-proofed: it was all in one design and was furnished—four suits a year to each person. The food was sold in bricks, each brick containing all the elements necessary for the continuation of life; on every brick was stamped the number of calories. For centuries, inventors had invented till finally life became uniform and work a matter of push buttons. Yet the world of the autoists was an unhappy one, for no one worked with muscles. In summer time it was, of course, necessary to perspire, but for generations no one had sweated. The words "toil," "labor," "work" were marked obsolete in the dictionaries.

Yet no one was happy because it was found to be a mechanical impossibility to invent an automobile that would travel over one hundred and fifty miles an hour and stay on the ordinary country road. The automobilists could not go as fast as they wanted to. Space could not be annihilated; time could not be destroyed.

Besides, everyone was toxic. The air was filled with the dangerous vapors generated by the combustion of millions of gallons of gasoline and its substitutes, even though many machines were electrified. The greatest factor contributing to this toxemia, however, was the greatly reduced excretion of toxins through the skin and the almost negative production of energy through muscular contraction. The automobilists had ceased to work, using the term in its purely archaic form, and having ceased to work, they had ceased to sweat. A few hours a day on a chair in a factory or at a desk was sufficient to earn the necessaries of life. The automobilist never being tired, nature demanded a lesser number of hours spent in sleep. The remaining hours were spent in automobiles, going somewhere; it mattered not where they went so long as they went fast. Babies were raised in machines; in fact, all life was lived in them. The American Home had disappeared—it was replaced by the automobile.

The automobilists were going somewhere but were not sure where. The pedestrians were confident of where they were going.

Society in its modern sense was socialistic. This implied that all classes were comfortable. Crime, as such, had ceased to exist some generations previous, following the putting into force of Bryant's theory that all crime was due to two per cent of the population and that if these were segregated and sterilized, crime would cease in one generation. When Bryant first promulgated his thesis, it was received with some scepticism, but its practical application was hailed with delight by everyone who was not directly affected.

Yet even in this apparently perfect society there were defects. Though everyone had all the necessities of life, such equality was not true of luxuries. In other words, there were still rich men and poor men, and the wealthy still dominated the government and made the laws.

Among the rich there were none more exclusive, aristocratic and dominant than the Heislers. Their estate on the Hudson was enclosed by thirty miles of twelve-foot iron fence. Few could boast of having visited there, of having week-ended in the stone palace surrounded by a forest of pine, beech and hemlock. They were so powerful that none of the family had ever held a public office. They made Presidents, but never cared to have one in the family. Their enemies said that their wealth came from fortunate marriages with the Ford and Rockefeller families but, no doubt, this was a falsehood based on jealousy. The Heislers had banks and real estate; they owned factories and office buildings. It was definitely stated that they owned the President of the United States and the Judges of the Supreme Court. One of their possessions was rarely spoken of, or mentioned in the newspapers. The only child of the ruling branch of the family walked.

William Henry Heisler was an unusual millionaire. When

told that his wife had presented him with a daughter he promised his Gods (though he was not certain who they were) that he would spend at least an hour a day with his child supervising her care.

For some months nothing unusual was noticed about this little girl baby, though at once all the nurses commented on her ugly legs. Her father simply considered that probably all baby legs were ugly.

At the age of one year, the baby tried to stand and take a step. Even this was passed over, as the pediatricians were united in the opinion that all children tried to use their legs for a few months, but it was a bad habit usually easily broken—like thumb-sucking. They gave the usual advice to the nurses which would have been followed had it not been for her father who merely stated, "Every child has a personality. Let her alone, see what she will do." And in order to insure obedience, he selected one of his private secretaries, who was to be in constant attendance and make daily written reports.

The child grew. There came the time when she was no longer called "baby" but dignified by the name of "Margaretta." As she grew, her legs grew. The more she walked, the stronger they became. There was no one to help her, for none of the adults had ever walked, nor had they seen anyone walk. She not only walked but she objected in her own baby way to mechanical locomotion. She screamed like a baby wild cat at her first introduction to an automobile and never could become reconciled even to the auto-cars for house use.

When it was too late, her father consulted everyone who could possibly know anything about the situation and its remedy. Heisler wanted his child to develop her own personality, but he did not want her to be odd. He therefore gathered in consultation, neurologists, anatomists, educators, psychologists, students of child behavior and obtained no satisfaction from them. All agreed that it was a pitiful case of atavism, a throwback. As for cure, there were a thousand suggestions from psycho-analysis to the brutal splinting and bandaging of the little girl's lower extremities. Finally, in disgust, Heisler paid them all for their trouble and bribed them all for their silence and told them sharply to go to Hell. He had no idea where this place was, or just what he meant, but found some relief in saying it.

They all left promptly except one who, in addition to his other vocations, followed genealogy as an avocation. He was an old man, and they made an interesting contrast as they sat facing each other in their auto-cars. Heisler was middle aged, vigorous, a real leader of men, gigantic save for his shrunken legs. The other man was old, gray haired, withered, a dreamer. They were alone in the room, save for the child who played happily in the sunshine of the large bay windows.

"I thought I told you to go to Hell with the rest," growled the leader of men.

"How can I?" was the mild reply. "Those others did not obey you. They simply autoed out of your home. I am waiting for you to tell me how to go there. Where is this Hell you order us to? Our submarines have explored the ocean bed five miles below sea level. Our aeroplanes have gone some miles towards the stars. Mount Everest has been conquered. I read all these journeyings, but nowhere do I read of a Hell. Some centuries ago theologians said it was a place that sinners went to when they died, but there has been no sin since Bryant's two per cent were identified and sterilized. You with your millions and limitless power are as near Hell as you will ever be, when you look at your abnormal child."

"But she is bright mentally, Professor," protested Heisler; "only seven years old but tested ten years by the Binet-Simon Scale. If only she would stop this damned walking. Oh! I am proud of her but I want her to be like other girls. Who will want to marry her? It's positively indecent. Look at her. What is she doing?"

"Why, bless me!" exclaimed the old man. "I read of that in a book three hundred years old just the other day. Lots of children used to do that."

"But what is it?"

"Why, it used to be called 'turning somersaults.' "

"But what does it mean? Why does she do it?"

Heisler wiped the sweat off his face.

"It will make us ridiculous if it becomes known."

"Oh, well, with your power you can keep it quiet—but have you studied your family history? Do you know what blood strains are in her?"

"No. I never was interested. Of course, I belong to the Sons of the American Revolution, and all that sort of thing. They brought me the papers and I signed on the dotted line. I never read them though I paid well to have a book published about it all."

"So you had a Revolutionary ancestor? Where's the book?"

Heisler rang for his private secretary, who autoed in, received his curt orders and soon returned with the Heisler family history which the old man opened eagerly. Save for the noise made by the child, who was playing with a small stuffed bear, the room was deadly still. Suddenly the old man laughed.

"It is all as plain as can be. Your Revolutionary ancestor was a Miller; Abraham Miller of Hamilton Township. His mother was captured and killed by Indians. They were pedestrians of the most pronounced strain; of course, every one was a pedestrian in those days. The Millers and the Heislers intermarried. That was some hundred years ago. Your Great Grandfather Heisler had a sister who married a Miller. She is spoken of here on page 330. Let me read it to you.

" 'Margaretta Heisler was the only sister of William Heisler. Independent and odd in many ways, she committed the folly of marrying a farmer by the name of Abraham Miller, who was one of the most noted leaders in the pedestrian riots in Pennsylvania. Following his death, his widow and only child, a boy eight years old, disappeared and no doubt were destroyed in the general process of pedestrian extermination. An old letter written by her to her brother, prior to her marriage, contained the boast that she never had ridden in an automobile and never would; that God had given her legs and she intended to use them and that she was fortunate in finally finding a man who also had legs and the desire to live on them, as God had planned men and women to do.'

"There is the secret of this child of yours. She is a reversal to the sister of your great grandfather. That lady died a hundred years ago rather than follow the fashion. You say yourself that this little one nearly died from convulsions when the attempt was made to put her in an automobile. It is a clear case of heredity. If you try to break the child of the habit, you will probably kill her. The only thing to do is to leave her alone. Let her develop as she wishes. She is your daughter. Her will is your will. The probability is that neither can change the other. Let her use her legs. She probably will climb trees, run, swim, wander where she will."

"So that is the way of it," sighed Heisler. "That means the end of our family. No one would want to marry a monkey no matter how intelligent she is. So you think she will some day climb a tree? If there is a Hell, this is mine, as you suggest."

"But she is happy!"

"Yes, if laughter is an index. But will she be as she grows

older? She will be different. How can she have associates? Of course they won't apply that extermination law in her case; my position will prevent that. I could even have it repealed. But she will be lonely—so lonely!"

"Perhaps she will learn to read—then she won't be lonely."

They both looked at the child.

"What is she doing now?" demanded Heisler. "You seem to know more than anyone I ever met about such things."

"Why, she is hopping. Is that not remarkable? She never saw anyone hop and yet she is doing it. I never saw a child do it and yet I can identify it and give it a name. In Kate Greenaway's illustrations, I have seen pictures of children hopping."

"Confound the Millers anyway!" growled Heisler.

After that conversation, Heisler engaged the old man, whose sole duty was to investigate the subject of pedestrian children and find how they played and used their legs. Having investigated this, he was to instruct the little girl.

The entire matter of her exercise was left to him. Thus from that day on a curious spectator from an aeroplane might have seen an old man sitting on the lawn showing a golden-haired child pictures from very old books and talking together about the same pictures. Then the child would do things that no child had done for a hundred years—bounce a ball, skip rope, dance folk dances and jump over a bamboo stick supported by two upright bars. Long hours were spent in reading and always the old man would begin by saying:

"Now this is the way they used to do."

Occasionally a party would be given for her and other little girls from the neighboring rich would come and spend the day. They were polite—so was Margaretta Heisler—but the parties were not successful. The company could not move except in their auto-cars, and they looked on their hostess with curiosity and scorn. They had nothing in common with the curious walking child, and these parties always left Margaretta in tears.

"Why can't I be like other girls?" she demanded of her father. "Is it always going to be this way? Do you know that girls laugh at me because I walk?"

Heisler was a good father. He held to his vow to devote one hour a day to his daughter, and during that time gave of his intelligence as eagerly and earnestly as he did to his business in the other hours. Often he talked to Margaretta as though she were his equal, an adult with full mental development.

"You have your own personality," he would say to her. "The mere fact that you are different from other people does not of necessity mean that they are right and you are wrong. Perhaps you are both right—at least you are both following out your natural proclivities. You are different in desires and physique from the rest of us, but perhaps you are more normal than we are. The professor shows us pictures of ancient peoples and they all had legs developed like yours. How can I tell whether man has degenerated or improved? At times when I see you run and jump, I envy you. I and all of us are tied down to earth—dependent on a machine for every part of our daily life. You can go where you please. You can do this and all you need is food and sleep. In some ways this is an advantage. On the other hand, the professor tells me that you can only go about four miles an hour while I can go over one hundred."

"But why should I want to go so fast when I do not want to go anywhere?"

"That is just the astonishing thing. Why don't you want to go? It seems that not only your body but also your mind, your personality, your desires are old-fashioned, hundreds of years old-fashioned. I try to be here in the house or garden every day—at least an hour—with you, but during the other waking hours I want to go. You do the strangest things. The professor tells me about it all. There is your bow and arrow, for instance. I bought you the finest firearms and you never use them, but you get a bow and arrow from some museum and finally succeed in killing a duck, and the professor said you built a fire out of wood and roasted it and ate it. You even made him eat some."

"But it was good, father—much better than the synthetic food. Even the professor said the juice made him feel younger."

Heisler laughed, "You are a savage—nothing more than a savage."

"But I can read and write!"

"I admit that. Well, go ahead and enjoy yourself. I only wish I could find another savage for you to play with, but there are no more."

"Are you sure?"

"As much so as I can be. In fact, for the last five years my agents have been scouring the civilized world for a pedestrian colony. There are a few in Siberia and the Tartar Plateau, but they are impossible. I would rather have you associate with apes."

"I dream of one, father," whispered the girl shyly. "He is a nice boy and he can do everything I can. Do dreams ever come true?"

Heisler smiled. "I trust this one will, and now I must hurry back to New York. Can I do anything for you?"

"Yes—find some one who can teach me how to make candles."

"Candles? Why, what are they?"

She ran and brought an old book and read it to him. It was called, "The Gentle Pirate," and the hero always read in bed by candle light.

"I understand," he finally said as he closed the book. "I remember now that I once read of their having something like that in the Catholic Churches. So you want to make some? See the professor and order what you need. Hum— candles—why, they would be handy at night if the electricity failed, but then it never does."

"But I don't want electricity. I want candles and matches to light them with."

"Matches?"

"Oh, father! In some ways you are ignorant. I know lots of words you don't, even though you are so rich."

"I admit it. I will admit anything and we will find how to make your candles. Shall I send you some ducks?"

"Oh, no. It is so much more fun to shoot them."

"You are a real barbarian!"

"And you are a dear ignoramus."

So it came to pass that Margaretta Heisler reached her seventeenth birthday, tall, strong, agile, brown from constant exposure to wind and sun, able to run, jump, shoot accurately with bow and arrow, an eater of meat, a reader of books by candle light, a weaver of carpets and a lover of nature. Her associates had been mainly elderly men: only occasionally would she see the ladies of the neighborhood. She tolerated the servants, the maids and housekeeper. The love she gave her father she also gave to the old professor, but he had taught her all she knew and the years had made him senile and sleepy.

There came to her finally the urge to travel. She wanted to see New York with its twenty million automobilists; its hundred-story office buildings; its smokeless factories; its standardized houses. There were difficulties in the way of such a trip, and no one knew these better than her father. The roads were impossible and all of New York was now either streets or houses. There being no pedestrians, there was no need of sidewalks. Besides, even Heisler's wealth would not be able to prevent the riot sure to result from the presence in a large city of such a curiosity as a pedestrian. Heisler was powerful, but he dreaded the result of allowing his daughter the freedom of New York. Furthermore, up to this time, her deformity was known only to a few. Once she was in New York, the city papers would publish his disgrace to the world.

Several of the office buildings in New York City were one hundred stories high. There were no stairways but as a safety precaution circular spiral ramps had been built in each structure for the use of auto-cars in case the elevators failed to work. This, however, never happened, and few of the tenants ever knew of their existence. The were used at night by the scrub women busily auto-carring from one floor to another cleaning up. The higher the floor the purer was the air and the more costly was the yearly rental. Below, in the canyon and the street, an ozone machine was necessary every few feet to purify the air and make unnecessary the use of gas masks. On the upper floors, however, there were pure breezes from off the Atlantic. Noticeable was the absence of flies and mosquitoes; pigeons built their nests in the crevices, and on the highest roof a pair of American eagles nested year after year in haughty defiance of the mechanical auto, a thousand feet below.

It was in the newest building in New York and on the very highest floor that a new office was opened. On the door was the customary gilded sign, "New York Electrical Co." Boxes had been left there, decorators had embellished the largest room, the final result being that it was simply a standardized office. A stenographer had been installed and sat at a noiseless machine, answering, if need be, the automatic telephone.

To this roomy suite one day in June came, by invitation, a dozen of the leaders of industry. They came, each thinking he was the only one invited to the conference. Surprise as well as suspicion was the marked feature of the meeting. There were three men there who were secretly and independently trying to undermine Heisler and tear him from his financial throne. Heisler himself was there, apparently quiet, but inwardly a seething flame of repressed electricity. The stenographer seated them as they arrived, in order around a long table. They remained in their auto-cars. No one used chairs. One or two of the men joked with each other. All nodded to Heisler, but none spoke to him.

The furniture, surroundings, stenographer were all part of the standard office in the business section. Only one small portion of the room aroused their curiosity. At the head of the table was an armchair. None of the men around the table had ever used a chair; none had seen one save in the Metropolitan Museum. The auto-car had replaced the chair even as the automobile had replaced the human leg.

The chimes in the tower rang out the two-o'clock message. All of the twelve looked at their watches. One man frowned. His watch was some minutes slow. In another minute all were frowning. They had a two-o'clock appointment with this stranger and he had not kept it. To them, time was valuable.

Then a door opened and the man walked in. That was the first astonishing thing—and then they marveled at the size and shape of him. There was something uncanny about it—peculiar, weird.

Then the man sat down—in the chair. He did not seem much larger now than the other men, though he was younger than any of them, and had a brown complexion which contrasted peculiarly with the dead gray-white pallor of the others. Then, gravely, almost mechanically, with clear distinct enunciation, he began to speak.

"I see, gentlemen, that you have all honored me by accepting my invitation to be present this afternoon. You will pardon my not informing any of you that the others were also invited. Had I done so, several of you would have refused to come and without any one of you the meeting would not be as successful as I intended it to be.

"The name of this company is the 'New York Electrical Co.' That is just a name assumed as a mask. In reality, there is no company. I am the representative of the nation of pedestrians. In fact, I am their president and my name is Abraham Miller. Four generations ago, as, no doubt, you know, Congress passed the Pedestrian Extermination Act. Following that, those who continued to walk were hunted like wild animals, slaughtered without mercy. My great-grandfather, Abraham Miller, was killed in Pennsylvania; his wife was run down on the public highway in Ohio as she was attempting to join the other pedestrians in the Ozarks. There were no battles, there was no conflict. At that time there were only ten thousand pedestrians in all the United States. Within a few years there were none—at least so your ancestors thought. The race of pedestrians, however, survived. We lived on. The trials of those early years are written in our histories and taught to our children. We formed a colony and continued our existence although we disappeared from the world as you know it.

"Year by year we lived on until now we number over two hundred persons in our Republic. We are not, in fact never have been, ignorant. Always we worked for one purpose and that was the right to return to the world. Our motto for one hundred years has been: 'We will go back.'

"So I have come to New York and called you into conference. While you were selected for your influence, wealth and ability, there was present in every instance another important reason. Each of you is a lineal descendant of a United States Senator who voted for the Pedestrian Extermination Act. You can readily see the significance of that. You have the power to undo a great injustice done to a branch of American citizens. Will you let us come back? We want to come back as pedestrians, to come and go as we please, safely. Some of us can drive automobiles and aeroplanes, but we don't want to. We want to walk, and if a mood strikes us to walk in the highway, we want to do it without constant danger of death. We do not hate you, we pity you. There is no desire to antagonize you; rather we want to coöperate with you.

"We believe in work—muscle work. No matter what our young people are trained for, they are taught to work—to do manual work. We understand machinery, but do not like to use it. The only help we accept is from domestic animals, horses, and oxen. In several places we use water power to run our grist mills and saw our timbers. For pleasure we hunt, fish, play tennis, swim in our mountain lake. We keep our bodies clean and try to do the same with our minds. Our boys marry at twenty-one—our girls at eighteen. Occasionally a child grows up to be abnormal—degenerate. I frankly say that such children disappear. We eat meat and vegetables, fish, and grain raised in our valley. The time has come when we cannot care for a continued increase in population. The time has come when we must come back into the world. What we desire is a guarantee of safety. I will now leave you in conference for fifteen minutes, and at the end of such time

I will return for an answer. If you have any questions; I will answer them then."

He left the room. One of the men rolled over to the telephone, found the wire cut; another went over to the door and found it locked. The stenographer had disappeared. There followed sharp discussion marked by temper and lack of logic. One man only kept silent. Heisler sat motionless; so much so that the cigar, clenched between his teeth, went out.

Then Miller came back. A dozen questions were hurled at him. One man swore at him. Finally there was silence.

"Well!" questioned Miller.

"Give us time—a week in which to discuss it—to ascertain public opinion," urged one of them.

"No," said Heisler, "let us give our answer now."

"Oh, of course," sneered one of his bitter opponents. "Your reason for giving a decision is plain, though it has never been in the newspapers."

"For that," said Heisler, "I am going to get you. You are a cur and you know it or you would not drag my family into this."

"Oh, Hell! Heisler—you can't bluff me any more!"

Miller hit the table with his fist——

"What's your answer?"

One of the men held up his hand for an audience.

"We all know the history of pedestrianism: the two groups represented here cannot live together. There are two hundred million of us and two hundred of them. Let them stay in their valley. That is what I think. If this man is their leader, we can judge what the colony is like. They are ignorant anarchists. There is no telling what they would demand if we listened to them. I think we should have this man arrested. He is a menace to society."

That broke the ice. One after another they spoke, and when they finished, it was plain that all save Heisler were hostile, antagonistic and merciless. Miller turned to him——

"What is your verdict?"

"I am going to keep quiet. These men know it all. You have heard them. They are a unit. What I would say can make no difference. In fact, I don't care. For some time I have ceased to care about anything."

Miller turned in his swivel chair and looked out over the city. In some ways it was a pretty city, if one liked such a place. Under him, in the city streets, in the bee-hives, over twenty million automobilists spent their lives on wheels. Not one in a million had a desire beyond the city limits; the roads connecting the metropolis with other cities were but urban arteries wherein the automobiles passed like corpuscles, the auto-trucks proceeded like plasma. Miller feared the city, but he pitied the legless pigmies inhabiting it.

Then he turned again and asked for silence.

"I wanted to make a peaceful adjustment. We desire no more bloodshed, no more internecine strife. You who lead public sentiment have by your recent talk shown me that the pedestrian can expect no mercy at the hands of the present Government. You know and I know that this is no longer a nation where the people rule. You rule. You elect whom you please for senators, for presidents; you snap your whip and they dance. That is why I came to you men, instead of making a direct appeal to the Government. Feeling confident what your action would be, I have prepared this short paper which I will ask you to sign. It contains a single statement: 'The Pedestrians cannot return.'

"When you have all signed this, I will explain to you just what we will do."

"Why sign it?" said the first man, the one seated to the right of Miller. "Now my idea is this!" and he crumpled the paper to a tight ball and threw it under the table. His conduct was at once followed by applause. Only Heisler sat still. Miller looked out the window till all was quiet.

Finally he spoke again:

"In our colony we have perfected a new electro-dynamic principle. Released, it at once separates the atomic energy which makes possible all movement, save muscle movement. We have tested this out with smaller machines in limited space and know exactly what we can do. We do not know how to restore the energy in any territory where we have once destroyed it. Our electricians are waiting for my signal transmitted by radio. In fact, they have been listening to all this conversation, and I will now give them the signal to throw the switch. The signal is our motto: 'We will come back.' "

"So that is the signal?" sneered one of the men. "What happened?"

"Nothing much," replied Heisler, "at least I see no difference. What was supposed to happen, Abraham Miller?"

"Nothing much," said Miller, "only the destruction of all mankind except the pedestrians. We tried to imagine what would happen when our electricians threw the switch and released this new principle, but even our sociologists could not fully imagine what would be the result. We do not know whether you can live or die—whether any of you can survive. No doubt the city dwellers will die speedily in their artificial bee-hives. Some in the country may survive."

"Hello, hello!" exclaimed a multi-millionaire, "I feel no different. You are a dreamer of dreams. I am leaving and will report you at once to the police. Open your damn door and let us out!"

Miller opened the door.

Most of the men pressed their starting button and took hold of the steering rod. Not a machine moved. The others, startled, tried to leave. Their auto-cars were dead. Then one, with a hysterical curse, raised an automatic at Miller and pulled the trigger. There was a click—and nothing more.

Miller pulled out his watch.

"It is now 2:40 P.M. The automobiles are beginning to die. They do not know it yet. When they do, there will be a panic. We cannot give any relief. There are only a few hundred of us and we cannot feed and care for hundreds of millions of cripples. Fortunately there is a circular-inclined plane or ramp in this building and your auto-cars are all equipped with brakes. I will push you one at a time to the plane, if you will steer your cars. Obviously you do not care to remain here and equally obviously the elevators are not running. I will call on my stenographer to help me. Perhaps you suspected before that he was a pedestrian trained from boyhood to take female parts. He is one of our most efficient spies. And now we will say goodbye. A century ago you knowingly and willingly tried to exterminate us. We survived. We do not want to exterminate you, but I fear for your future."

Thereupon he went behind one of the auto-cars and started pushing it towards the doorway. The stenographer, who had reappeared as a pedestrian, and in trousers, took hold of another car. Soon only Heisler was left. He held up his hand in protest.

"Would you mind pushing me over to that window?"

Miller did so. The automobilist looked out curiously.

"There are no aeroplanes in the sky. There should be hundreds."

"No doubt," replied Miller, "they have all planed down to earth. You see they have no power."

"Then everything has stopped?"

"Almost. There is still muscle power. There is still power produced by the bending of woods as in a bow and arrow—also that produced by a metal coil like the main spring in a watch. You notice your watch is still running. Of course, domestic animals can still produce power—that is just a form of muscle power. In our valley we have grist mills and saw mills running by water power. We can see no reason why they should not keep on; all other power is destroyed. Do you realize it? There is no electricity, no steam, no explosions of any kind. All those machines are dead."

Heisler pulled out a handkerchief, slowly, automatically and wiped the sweat from his face as he said:

"I can hear a murmur from the city. It rises up to this window like distant surf beating rhythmically against a sandy shore. I can hear no other noise, only this murmur. It recalls to my mind the sound of a swarm of bees leaving their old hive and flying compactly through the air with their queen in the center, trying to find a new home. There is a sameness to the noise like a distant waterfall. What does it mean? I think I know, but I cannot bear to say it with words."

"It means," said Miller, "that below us and around us twenty million people are beginning to die in office buildings, stores and homes; in subways, elevators and trains; in tubes and ferry boats; on the street, and in the restaurants, twenty million people suddenly realize that they cannot move. No one can help them. Some have left their cars and are trying to pull themselves along on their hands, their withered legs helplessly trailing behind them. They are calling to each other for help, but even now they cannot know the full extent of the disaster. By tomorrow each man will be a primitive animal. In a few days there will be no food, no water. I hope they will die quickly—before they eat each other. The nation will die and no one will know about it, for there will be no newspapers, no telephones, no wireless. I will communicate with my people by carrier pigeons. It will be months before I can rejoin them. Meanwhile I can live. I can go from place to place. The sound you hear from the city is the cry of a soul in despair."

Heisler grabbed Miller's hand convulsively. "But if you made it stop, you can make it start?"

"No—we stopped it with electricity. There is now no more electricity. I presume our own machines were at once put out of power."

"So we are going to die?"

"I believe so. Perhaps your scientists can invent a remedy. We did a hundred years ago. We lived. Your nation tried by every known scientific art to destroy us, but we lived. Perhaps you can. How can I tell? We wanted to arbitrate. All we asked for was equality. You saw how those other men voted and how they thought. If they had had the power, they would instantly have destroyed my little colony. What we did was simply done in self-protection."

Heisler tried to light his cigar. The electric lighter would not work, so he held it dry in his mouth, in one corner, chewing it.

"You say your name is Abraham Miller? I believe we are cousins of some sort. I have a book that tells about it."

"I know all about that. Your great-grandfather and my great-grandmother were brother and sister."

"I believe that is what the professor said, except that at that time we did not know about you. What I want to talk about, however, is my daughter."

The two men talked on and on. The murmur continued to mount from the city, unceasing, incessant, full of notes new to the present generation. Yet at the distance—from the earth below to the hundredth story above, it was all one sound. Though composed of millions of variants, it blended into unity. Miller finally began walking up and down, from one office wall to the window and back again.

"I thought no one more free from nerves than I was. My whole life has been schooled in preparation for this moment. We had right, justice, even our forgotten God on our side. I still can see no other way, no other way, but this makes me sick, Heisler; it nauseates me. When I was a boy I found a mouse caught in a barn door, almost torn in two. I tried to help it and the tortured animal bit my finger so I simply had to break its neck. It couldn't live—and when I tried to help it, it bit me, so I had to kill it. Do you understand? I had to, but, though I was justified, I grew deadly sick; I vomited on the barn floor. Something like that is going on below there. Twenty million deformed bodies all around us are beginning to die. They might have been men and women like those we have in the colony but they became obsessed with the idea of mechanical devices of all kinds. If I tried to help—went into the street now—they would kill me. I couldn't keep them off me—I couldn't kill them fast enough. We were justified— man—we were justified, but it makes me sick."

"It does not affect me that way," replied Heisler, "I am accustomed to crushing out my opponents. I had to, or they would crush me. I look on all this as a wonderful experiment. For years I have thought about our civilization—on account of my daughter. I have lost interest. In many ways I have lost my fighting spirit. I don't seem to care what happens, but I would like to follow that cur down the circular plane and wrap my hands around his neck. I don't want him to die of hunger."

"No. You stay here. I want you to write a history of it all—just how it happened. We want an accurate record to justify our action. You stay here and work with my stenographer. I am going to find your daughter. We cannot let a pedestrian suffer. We will take you back with us. With suitable apparatus you could learn to ride a horse."

"You want me to live?"

"Yes, but not for yourself. There are a dozen reasons. For the next twenty years you can lecture to our young people. You can tell them what happened when the world ceased to work, to sweat, when they deliberately exchanged the home for the automobile and toil and labor for machinery. You can tell them that and they will believe you."

"Wonderful!" exclaimed Heisler. "I have made Presidents and now I become a legless example for a new world."

"You will attain fame. You will be the last automobilist."

"Let's start," urged Heisler. "Call your stenographer!"

The stenographer had been in New York one month prior to the meeting of Miller and the representatives of the auto-mobilists. During that time, thanks to his early training in mimicry as a spy, he had been absolutely successful in de-ceiving all he came in contact with. In his auto-car, dressed as a stenographer, his face perfumed and painted, and rings on his fingers, he passed unnoticed amid the other thousands of similar women. He went to their restaurants and to their theatres. He even visited them in their homes. He was the perfect spy; but he was a man.

He had been trained to the work of a spy. For years he had been imbued with loyalty to an enthusiasm for his repub-lic of pedestrians. He had sworn to the oath—that the repub-lic should come first. Abraham Miller had selected him because he could trust him. The spy was young, with hardly a down on his cheeks. He was celibate. He was patriotic.

But for the first time in his life, he was in a big city. The firm on the floor below employed a stenographer. She was a very efficient worker in more ways than one and there was

that about the new stenographer that excited her interest.
They met and arranged to meet again. They talked about
love, the new love between women. The spy did not understand this, having never heard of such a passion, but he did
understand eventually, the caresses and kisses. She proposed
that they room together, but he naturally found objections.
However, they had spent much of their spare time together.
More than once the pedestrian had been on the point of con-
fiding to her, not only concerning the impending calamity,
but also his real sex and his true love.

In such cases where a man falls in love with a woman the
explanation is hard to find. It is always hard to find. Here
there was something twisted, a pathological perversion. It was
a monstrous thing that he should fall in love with a legless
woman when he might, by waiting, have married a woman
with columns of ivory and knees of alabaster. Instead, he
loved and desired a woman who lived in a machine. It was
equally pathological that she should love a woman. Each was
sick—soul-sick, and each to continue the intimacy deceived
the other. Now with the city dying beneath him, the stenographer felt a deep desire to save this legless woman. He felt
that a way could be found, somehow, to persuade Abraham
Miller to let him marry this stenographer—at least let him
save her from the debacle.

So in soft shirt and knee trousers he cast a glance at Miller
and Heisler engaged in earnest conversation and then tiptoed
out the door and down the inclined plane to the floor below.
Here all was confusion. Boldly striding into the room where
the stenographer had her desk, he leaned over her and started
to talk. He told her that he was a man, a pedestrian. Rapidly
came the story of what it all meant, the cries from below, the
motionless auto-cars, the useless elevators, the silent telephones. He told her that the world of automobilists would die
because of this and that, but that she would live because of
his love for her. All he asked was the legal right to care for
her, to protect her. They would go somewhere and live, out
in the country. He would roll her around the meadows. She
could have geese, baby geese that would come to her chair
when she cried, "Weete, weete."

The legless woman listened. What pallor there might be in
her cheeks was skillfully covered with rouge. She listened and
looked at him, a man, a man with legs, walking. He said he
loved her, but the person she had loved was a woman; a

woman with dangling, shrunken, beautiful legs like her own, not muscular monstrosities.

She laughed hysterically, said she would marry him, go wherever he wanted her to go, and then she clasped him to her and kissed him full on the mouth, and then kissed his neck over the jugular vein, and he died, bleeding into her mouth, and the blood mingled with rouge made her face a vivid carmine. She died some days later from hunger.

Miller never knew where his stenographer died. Had he time he might have hunted for him, but he began to share Heisler's anxiety about the pedestrian girl isolated and alone amid a world of dying automobilists. To the father she was a daughter, the only child, the remaining and sole branch of his family. To Miller, however, she was a symbol. She was a sign of nature's revolt, an indication of her last spasmodic effort to restore mankind to his former place in the world. Her father wanted her saved because she was his daughter, the pedestrian because she was one of them, one of the race of pedestrians.

On that hundredth floor kegs of water, stores of food had been provided. Every provision had been made to sustain life in the midst of death. Heisler was shown all these. He was made comfortable and then Miller, with some provisions, a canteen of water, a road map, and a stout club in his grasp, left that place of peace and quiet and started down the spiral ramp. At the best it was simply difficult walking, the spirals being wide enough to prevent dizziness. What Miller feared was the obstruction of the entire passage at some point by a tangled mass of auto-cars, but evidently all cars which had managed to reach the plane had been able to descend. He paused now and then at this floor or that, shuddered at the cries he heard and then went on, down, down into the street.

Here it was even worse than he expected. On the second the electro-dynamic energy had been released from the Ozark valley—on that very second all machinery had ceased. In New York City twenty million people were in automobiles or auto-cars at that particular second. Some were working at desks, in shops; some were eating in restaurants, loafing at their clubs; others were going somewhere. Suddenly everyone was forced to stay where he was. There was no communication save within the limits of each one's voice; the phone, radio, newspapers were useless. Every auto-car stopped; every automobile ceased to move. Each man and woman was dependent on his own body for existence; no one could help the

other, no one could help himself. Transportation died and no
one knew it had happened save in his own circle, as far as
the eye could see or the ear could hear, because communication had died with the death of transportation. Each automobilist stayed where he happened to be at that particular
moment.

Then slowly as the thought came to them that movement
was impossible, there came fear and with fear, panic. But it
was a new kind of panic. All previous panics consisted in the
sudden movement of large numbers of people in the same
direction, fleeing from a real or an imaginary fear. This panic
was motionless and for a day the average New Yorker, while
gripped with fear, crying with fright, remained within his car.
Then came mass-movement but not the movement of previous panics. It was the slow tortuous movement of crippled
animals dragging legless bodies forward by arms unused to
muscular exercise. It was not the rapid, wind-like movement
of the frenzied panic-stricken mob, but a slow, convulsive,
worm-like panic. Word was passed from one to another in
hoarse whisperings that the city was a place of death, would
become a morgue, that in a few days there would be no food.
While no one knew what had happened everyone knew that
the city could not live long unless food came regularly from
the country, and the country suddenly became more than
long cement roads between sign-boards. It was a place where
food could be procured and water. The city had become dry.
The mammoth pump throwing millions of gallons of water to
a careless population had ceased to pump. There was no
more water save in the rivers encircling the city and these
were filthy, man-polluted. In the country there must be water
somewhere.

So, on the second day began the flight from New York—a
flight of cripples, not of eagles; a passage of humanity shaped
like war-maimed soldiers. Their speed was not uniform, but
the fastest could only crawl less than a mile an hour. Philosophers would have stayed where they were and died. Animals,
thus tortured, would quietly wait the end, but these automobilists were neither philosophers nor animals, and they had to
move. All their life they had been moving. The bridges were
the first spaces to show congestion. On all of them were some
automobiles, but traffic is not heavy at two in the afternoon.
Gradually, by noon of the second day, these river highways
were black with people crawling to get away from the city.
There came congestion, and with congestion, stasis, and with

stasis, simply a writhing without progression. Then on top of this stationary layer of humanity crawled another layer which in its turn reached congestion, and on top of the second layer a third layer. A dozen streets led to each bridge but each bridge was only as wide as a street. Gradually the outer rows of the upper layer began falling into the river beneath. Ultimately many sought this termination. From the bridges came, ultimately, a roar like surf beating against a rock-bound shore. In it was the beginnings of desperate madness. Men died quickly on the bridges, but before they died they started to bite each other. Within the city certain places showed the same congestion. Restaurants and cafes became filled with bodies almost to the ceiling. There was food here but no one could reach it save those next to it and these were crushed to death before they could profit by their good fortune, and dying, blocked with bodies, those who remained alive and able to eat.

Within twenty-four hours mankind had lost its religion, its humanity, its high ideals. Every one tried to keep himself alive even though by doing so he brought death sooner to others. Yet in isolated instances, individuals rose to heights of heroism. In the hospitals an occasional nurse remained with her patients, giving them food till she with them died of hunger. In one of the maternity wards a mother gave birth to a child. Deserted by everyone she placed the child to her breast and kept it there till hunger pulled down her lifeless arms.

It was into this world of horror that Miller walked as he emerged from the office building. He had provided himself with a stout club but hardly any of the crawling automobilists noticed him. So he walked slowly over to Fifth Avenue and then headed north, and as he walked he prayed, though on that first day he saw but little of what he was to see later on.

On and on he went till he came to water and that he swam and then again he went on and by night he was out in the country where he ceased to pray continuously. Here he met an occasional autoist, who was simply annoyed at his machine breaking down. No one in the country realized at first what had really happened; no one ever fully realized before he died in his farm house, just what it all meant. It was only the city dwellers who knew, and they did not understand.

The next day Miller rose early from the grass and started again, after carefully consulting the road map. He avoided the towns, circling them. He had learned the desire, constant, incessant, inescapable, to share his provisions with those starving cripples, and he had to keep his strength and save food for her, that pedestrian girl, alone among helpless servants, within an iron fence thirty miles long. It was near the close of the second day of his walk. For some miles he had seen no one. The sun, low in the forest of oaks, threw fantastic shadows over the concrete road.

Down the road, ever nearing him, came a strange caravan. There were three horses tied to each other. On the backs of two were bundles and jugs of water fastened stoutly but clumsily. On the third horse an old man rested in a chair-like saddle and at this time he slept, his chin resting on his chest, his hands clutching, even in sleep, the sides of the chair. Leading the first horse walked a woman, tall, strong, lovely in her strength, striding with easy pace along the cement road. On her back was slung a bow with a quiver of arrows and in her right hand she carried a heavy cane. She walked on fearlessly, confidently; she seemed filled with power, confidence and pride.

Miller paused in the middle of the road. The caravan came near him. Then it stopped in front of him.

"Well," said the woman, and her voice blended curiously with the sunlit shadows and the flickering leaves.

"Well! Who are you and why do you block our way?"

"Why, I am Abraham Miller and you are Margaretta Heisler. I am hunting for you. Your father is safe and he sent me for you."

"And you are a pedestrian?"

"Just as truly as you are!" and so on and on—

The professor woke from his nap. He looked down on the young man and woman, standing, talking, already forgetting that there was anything else in the world.

"Now, that is the way it was in the old days," mused the professor to himself.

It was a Sunday afternoon some hundred years later. A father and his little son were sightseeing in the Museum of Natural Sciences in the reconstructed city of New York. The whole city was now simply a vast museum. Folks went there to see it but no one wanted to live there. In fact, no one wanted to live in such a place as a city when he could live on a farm.

It was a part of every child's education to spend a day or more in an automobilist's city, so on this Sunday afternoon the father and his little son walked slowly through the large buildings. They saw the mastodon, the bison, the pterodactyl. They paused for some time before a glass case containing a wigwam of the American Indian with a typical Indian family. Finally they came to a large wagon, on four rubber wheels, but there was no shaft and no way that horses or oxen could be harnessed to it. In the wagon on seats were men, women and little children. The boy looked at them curiously and pulled at his father's sleeve.

"Look, daddy. What are that wagon and those funny people without legs. What does it mean?"

"That, my son, is a family of automobilists," and there and then he paused and gave his son the little talk that all pedestrian fathers are required by law to give to their children.

The Philosopher of Time and Space

By 1930 the science-fiction magazines were proliferating. Gernsback had passed through bankruptcy—"bankruptcy deluxe," *The New York Times* called it when each creditor was paid $1.08 for each $1 owed—and had created an entire new spectrum of magazines without skipping an issue, and in the process had invented the term "science fiction." Then, in January 1930, *Astounding Stories of Super-Science* appeared on the newsstands.

William Clayton was the publisher. The new magazine had been suggested to him by editor Harry Bates to fill one of three holes in a gigantic printer's sheet of four-color covers, which already contained thirteen covers of the action-adventure pulp magazines published by the Clayton chain. *Astounding Stories* openly imitated the *Amazing* name, but Bates and Clayton wanted stories with more action and adventure, like Clayton's other magazines.

Bates was able to pay a magnificent two cents a word for stories, and on acceptance rather than on publication, or even later; but the supply was limited. There weren't enough science-fiction writers to provide good stories for three magazines, and converting the chain's action-adventure writers only gave Bates different problems with unsatisfactory rewrites, extensive editing, or writing or co-authoring stories himself under pseudonyms.

Astounding Stories never made money as a Clayton magazine, but came close to breaking even; the Clayton chain itself folded in 1933 because of financial difficulties brought on by Clayton's attempts to buy out a partner. In 1933 *Astounding* was bought by Street & Smith, the old dime-novel, boys'-magazine publisher turned pulp-magazine chain.

The influence of the magazines on the reading and writing of science fiction was beginning to develop in ways that would change the nature of the genre, but significant work— mostly novels—was being published outside the magazines and largely in ignorance of them. Wells was still publishing his occasional propaganda work, such as *The Shape of Things to Come* (1933) and *The Holy Terror* (1939), and speculative romance such as *Star Begotten* (1937); Philip Wylie published *Gladiator* in 1930, *The Murderer Invisible* in 1931, and *When Worlds Collide* (with Edwin Balmer) in *Blue Book* in 1932; and Sinclair Lewis published *It Can't Happen Here* in 1935.

An unexpected author of science fiction emerged in 1930 from the ranks of professional philosophers. Olaf Stapledon (1886–1950) earned his doctorate in philosophy from the University of Liverpool, and taught there and elsewhere for a brief time. He published *A Modern Theory of Ethics* in 1929, *Philosophy and Living* in 1938, *Saints and Revolutionaries* in 1939, and *New Hope for Britain* in 1939.

While he was working on his first philosophy book, he also launched himself on the vast flight of imagination that produced his first science-fiction work, *Last and First Men* (1930). On the strength of its success, he gave up his university position and undertook a writing career that produced, among others, *Last Men in London* (1932), *Odd John* (1935), *Star Maker* (1937), and *Sirius* (1944).

His fiction reached a broad general audience as well as the developing science-fiction readership, and his speculations influenced those who were writing for the magazines and the readers, soon to be called fans, who would develop into writers. *Odd John* was acclaimed the definitive treatment of the superman theme. *Star Maker* was staggering in its description of the creation of the universe, galactic civilizations and empires, intelligent stars and nebulae. *Sirius* concerned a super-dog and his relationships with the people who developed his intelligence.

Of Stapledon's four major works, two were small-scale novels, focusing on individual details and character development, and two were sweeping fictional essays. *Last and First Men* covers a period from 1930 to a period some two billion years in the future, through some seventeen evolutionary races of man, who emigrate to Venus and finally to Neptune, where what humanity has become faces its final doom with dignity and the hope of casting human spores upon the solar wind to reach other parts of the galaxy. J. B. Priestley called it a masterpiece; Hugh Walpole called it "as original as the solar system."

Though he may have known nothing of the sf magazines,

Stapledon knew what kind of fiction he was writing. In the preface to *Last and First Men* he wrote:

> To romance of the future may seem to be indulgence in ungoverned speculation for the sake of the marvelous. Yet controlled imagination in this sphere can be a very valuable exercise for minds bewildered about the present and its potentialities. Today we should welcome, and even study, every serious attempt to envisage the future of our race; not merely in order to grasp the very diverse and often tragic possibilities that confront us, but also that we may familiarize ourselves with the certainty that many of our most cherished ideals would seem puerile to more developed minds. To romance of the far future, then, is to attempt to see the human race in its cosmic setting, and to mould our hearts to entertain new values.
>
> But if such imaginative construction of possible futures is to be at all potent, our imagination must be strictly disciplined.

He was writing not fantasy but "imaginative construction of possible futures," what he could have called science fiction. "The merely fantastic has only minor power," he wrote, and "we must select with a purpose. . . . We must achieve neither mere history, nor mere fiction, but myth." *Last and First Men* was a major contribution to the myth of the future that "Doc" Smith, Ed Hamilton, and others already had begun to shape, and to which writers yet to roll paper into typewriter, notably Robert Heinlein and Isaac Asimov, would work into a kind of consensus future history.

From Last and First Men

by Olaf Stapledon

Chapter XIII

HUMANITY ON VENUS

I. TAKING ROOT AGAIN

Man's sojourn on Venus lasted somewhat longer than his whole career on the Earth. From the days of Pithecanthropus to the final evacuation of his native planet he passed, as we have seen, through a bewildering diversity of form and circumstance. On Venus, though the human type was somewhat more constant biologically, it was scarcely less variegated in culture.

To give an account of this period, even on the minute scale that has been adopted hitherto, would entail another volume. I can only sketch its bare outline. The sapling, humanity, transplanted into foreign soil, withers at first almost to the root, slowly readjusts itself, grows into strength and a certain permanence of form, burgeons, season by season, with leaf and flower of many successive civilizations and cultures, sleeps winter by winter, through many ages of reduced vitality, but at length (to force the metaphor), avoids this recurrent defeat by attaining an evergreen constitution and a continuous efflorescence. Then once more, through the whim of Fate, it is plucked up by the roots and cast upon another world.

The first human settlers on Venus knew well that life would be a sorry business. They had done their best to alter the planet to suit human nature, but they could not make Venus into another Earth. The land surface was minute. The climate was almost unendurable. The extreme difference of temperature between the protracted day and night produced incredible storms, rain like a thousand contiguous waterfalls, terrifying electrical disturbances, and fogs in which a man

could not see his own feet. To make matters worse, the oxygen supply was as yet barely enough to render the air
breathable. Worse still, the liberated hydrogen was not always
successfully ejected from the atmosphere. It would sometimes
mingle with the air to form an explosive mixture, and sooner
or later there would occur a vast atmospheric flash. Recurrent
disasters of this sort destroyed the architecture and the human inhabitants of many islands, and further reduced the
oxygen supply. In time, however, the increasing vegetation
made it possible to put an end to the dangerous process of
electrolysis.

Meanwhile, these atmospheric explosions crippled the race
so seriously that it was unable to cope with a more mysterious trouble which beset it some time after the migration. A
new and inexplicable decay of the digestive organs, which
first occurred as a rare disease, threatened within a few centuries to destroy mankind. The physical effects of this plague
were scarcely more disastrous than the psychological effects
of the complete failure to master it; for, what with the mystery of the moon's vagaries and the deep-seated, unreasoning,
sense of guilt produced by the extermination of the Veneri-
ans, man's self-confidence was already seriously shaken, and
his highly organized mentality began to show symptoms of
derangement. The new plague was, indeed, finally traced to
something in the Venerian water, and was supposed to be due
to certain molecular groupings, formerly rare, but subsequently fostered by the presence of terrestrial organic matter
in the ocean. No cure was discovered.

And now another plague seized upon the enfeebled race.
Human tissues had never perfectly assimilated the Martian
units which were the means of "telepathic" communication.
The universal ill-health now favoured a kind of "cancer" of
the nervous system, which was due to the ungoverned proliferation of these units. The harrowing results of this disease
may be left unmentioned. Century by century it increased;
and even those who did not actually contract the sickness
lived in constant terror of madness.

These troubles were aggravated by the devastating heat.
The hope that, as the generations passed, human nature
would adapt itself even to the more sultry regions, seemed to
be unfounded. Far otherwise, within a thousand years the
once-populous arctic and antarctic islands were almost
deserted. Out of each hundred of the great pylons, scarcely
more than two were inhabited, and these only by a few

plague-stricken and broken-spirited human relics. These alone
were left to turn their telescopes upon the earth and watch the
unexpectedly delayed bombardment of their native world by
the fragments of the moon.

Population decreased still further. Each brief generation
was slightly less well developed than its parents. Intelligence
declined. Education became superficial and restricted. Contact with the past was no longer possible. Art lost its significance, and philosophy its dominion over the minds of men.
Even applied science began to be too difficult. Unskilled control of the sub-atomic sources of power led to a number of
disasters, which finally gave rise to a superstition that all
"tampering with nature" was wicked, and all the ancient wisdom a snare of Man's Enemy. Books, instruments, all the
treasures of human culture, were therefore burnt. Only the
perdurable buildings resisted destruction. Of the incomparable
world-order of the Fifth Men nothing was left but a few island tribes cut off from one another by the ocean, and from
the rest of space-time by the depths of their own ignorance.

After many thousands of years human nature did begin to
adapt itself to the climate and to the poisoned water without
which life was impossible. At the same time a new variety of
the fifth species now began to appear, in which the Martian
units were not included. Thus at last the race regained a certain mental stability, at the expense of its faculty of "telepathy," which man was not to regain until almost the last phase
of his career. Meanwhile, though he had recovered somewhat
from the effects of an alien world, the glory that had been
was no more. Let us therefore hurry through the ages that
passed before noteworthy events again occurred.

In early days on Venus men had gathered their foodstuff
from the great floating islands of vegetable matter which had
been artificially produced before the migration. But as the
oceans became populous with modifications of the terrestrial
fauna, the human tribes turned more and more to fishing.
Under the influence of its marine environment, one branch of
the species assumed such an aquatic habit that in time it actually began to develop biological adaptations for marine life.
It is perhaps surprising that man was still capable of spontaneous variation; but the fifth human species was artificial,
and had always been prone to epidemics of mutation. After
some millions of years of variation and selection there appeared a very successful species of seal-like sub-men. The
whole body was moulded to stream-lines. The lung capacity

was greatly developed. The spine had elongated, and increased in flexibility. The legs were shrunken, grown together, and flattened into a horizontal rudder. The arms also were diminutive and fin-like, though they still retained the manipulative forefinger and thumb. The head had shrunk into the body and looked forward in the direction of swimming. Strong carnivorous teeth, emphatic gregariousness, and a new, almost human, cunning in the chase, combined to make these seal-men lords of the ocean. And so they remained for many million years, until a more human race, annoyed at their piscatorial success, harpooned them out of existence.

For another branch of the degenerated fifth species had retained a more terrestrial habit and the ancient human form. Sadly reduced in stature and in brain, these abject beings were so unlike the original invaders that they are rightly considered a new species, and may therefore be called the Sixth Men. Age after age they gained a precarious livelihood by grubbing roots upon the forest-clad islands, trapping the innumerable birds, and catching fish in the tidal inlets with ground bait. Not infrequently they devoured, or were devoured by, their seal-like relatives. So restricted and constant was the environment of these human remnants, that they remained biologically and culturally stagnant for some millions of years.

At length, however, geological events afforded man's nature once more the opportunity of change. A mighty warping of the planet's crust produced an island almost as large as Australia. In time this was peopled, and from the clash of tribes a new and versatile race emerged. Once more there was methodical tillage, craftsmanship, complex social organization, and adventure in the realm of thought.

During the next two hundred million years all the main phases of man's life on earth were many times repeated on Venus with characteristic differences. Theocratic empires; free and intellectualistic island cities; insecure overlordship of feudal archipelagos; rivalries of high priest and emperor; religious feuds over the interpretation of sacred scriptures; recurrent fluctuations of thought from naïve animism, through polytheism, conflicting monotheisms, and all the desperate "isms" by which mind seeks to blur the severe outline of truth; recurrent fashions of comfort-seeking fantasy and cold intelligence; social disorders through the misuse of volcanic or wind power in industry; business empires and pseudo-communistic empires—all these forms flitted over the changing substance of mankind again and again, as in an enduring hearth fire there appear and vanish the infinitely diverse forms of flame and smoke. But all the while the brief spirits, in whose massed configurations these forms inhered, were intent chiefly on the primitive needs of food, shelter, companionship, crowd-lust, love-making, the two-edged relationship of parent and child, the exercise of muscle and intelligence in facile sport. Very seldom, only in rare moments of clarity, only after ages of misapprehension, did a few of them, here and there, now and again, begin to have the deeper insight into the world's nature and man's. And no sooner had this precious insight begun to propagate itself, than it would be blotted out by some small or great disaster, by epidemic disease, by the spontaneous disruption of society, by an access of racial imbecility, by a prolonged bombardment of meteorites, or by the mere cowardice and vertigo that dared not look down the precipice of fact.

2. THE FLYING MEN

We need not dwell upon these multitudinous reiterations of culture, but must glance for a moment at the last phase of this sixth human species, so that we may pass on to the artificial species which it produced.

Throughout their career the Sixth Men had often been fascinated by the idea of flight. The bird was again and again their most sacred symbol. Their monotheism was apt to be worship not of a god-man, but of a god-bird, conceived now as the divine sea-eagle, winged with power, now as the giant swift, winged with mercy, now as a disembodied spirit of air, and once as the bird-god that became man to endow the human race with flight, physical and spiritual.

It was inevitable that flight should obsess man on Venus, for the planet afforded but a cramping home for groundlings; and the riotous efflorescence of avian species shamed man's pedestrian habit. When in due course the Sixth Men attained knowledge and power comparable to that of the First Men at their height, they invented flying-machines of various types. Many times, indeed, mechanical flight was rediscovered and lost again with the downfall of civilization. But at its best it was regarded only as a makeshift. And when at length, with the advance of the biological sciences, the Sixth Men were in a position to influence the human organism itself, they determined to produce a true flying man. Many civilizations strove vainly for this result, sometimes half-heartedly, sometimes with religious earnestness. Finally the most enduring and brilliant of all the civilizations of the Sixth Men actually attained the goal.

The Seventh Men were pigmies, scarcely heavier than the largest of terrestrial flying birds. Through and through they were organized for flight. A leathery membrane spread from the foot to the tip of the immensely elongated and strengthened "middle" finger. The three "outer" fingers, equally elongated, served as ribs to the membrane; while the index and thumb remained free for manipulation. The body assumed the stream-lines of a bird, and was covered with a deep quilt of feathery wool. This, and the silken down of the flight-membranes, varied greatly from individual to individual in colouring and texture. On the ground the Seventh Men walked much as other human beings, for the flight-membranes were folded close to the legs and body, and hung from the arms like exaggerated sleeves. In flight the legs were held extended as a flattened tail, with the feet locked together by the big toes. The breastbone was greatly developed as a keel, and as a base for the muscles of flight. The other bones were hollow, for lightness, and their internal surfaces were utilized as supplementary lungs. For, like the birds, these flying men had to maintain a high rate of oxidation. A state which others would regard as fever was normal to them.

Their brains were given ample tracts for the organization of prowess in flight. In fact, it was found possible to equip the species with a system of reflexes for aerial balance, and a true, though artificial, instinctive aptitude for flight, and interest in flight. Compared with their makers their brain volume was of necessity small, but their whole neural system was very carefully organized. Also it matured rapidly, and was extremely facile in the acquirement of new modes of activity. This was very desirable; for the individual's natural life period was but fifty years, and in most cases it was deliberately cut short by some impossible feat at about forty, or whenever the symptoms of old age began to be felt.

Of all human species these bat-like Flying Men, the Seventh Men, were probably the most care-free. Gifted with harmonious physique and gay temperament, they came into a social heritage well adapted to their nature. There was no occasion for them, as there had often been for some others, to regard the world as fundamentally hostile to life, or themselves as essentially deformed. Of quick intelligence in respect of daily personal affairs and social organization, they were untroubled by the insatiable lust of understanding. Not that they were an unintellectual race, for they soon formulated a beautifully systematic account of experience. They clearly perceived, however, that the perfect sphere of their thought was but a bubble adrift in chaos. Yet it was an elegant bubble. And the system was true, in its own gay and frankly insincere manner, true as significant metaphor, not literally true. What more, it was asked, could be expected of human intellect? Adolescents were encouraged to study the ancient problems of philosophy, for no reason but to convince themselves of the futility of probing beyond the limits of the orthodox system. "Prick the bubble of thought at any point," it was said, "and you shatter the whole of it. And since thought is one of the necessities of human life, it must be preserved."

Natural science was taken over from the earlier species with half-contemptuous gratitude, as a necessary means of sane adjustment to the environment. Its practical applications were valued as the ground of the social order; but as the millennia advanced, and society approached that remarkable perfection and stability which was to endure for many million years, scientific inventiveness became less and less needful, and science itself was relegated to the infant schools. History also was given in outline during childhood, and subsequently ignored.

This curiously sincere intellectual insincerity was due to the fact that the Seventh Men were chiefly concerned with matters other than abstract thought. It is difficult to give to members of the first human species an inkling of the great preoccupation of these Flying Men. To say that it was flight would be true, yet far less than the truth. To say that they sought to live dangerously and vividly, to crowd as much experience as possible into each moment, would again be a caricature of the truth. On the physical plane indeed "the universe of flight" with all the variety of peril and skill afforded by a tempestuous atmosphere, was every individual's chief medium of self-expression. Yet it was not flight itself, but the spiritual aspect of flight, which obsessed the species.

In the air and on the ground the Seventh Men were different beings. Whenever they exercised themselves in flight they suffered a remarkable change of spirit. Much of their time had to be spent on the ground, since most of the work upon which civilization rested was impossible in the air. Moreover, life in the air was life at high pressure, and necessitated spells

of recuperation on the ground. In their pedestrian phase the
Seventh Men were sober folk, mildly bored, yet in the main
cheerful, humorously impatient of the drabness and irk of
pedestrian affairs, but ever supported by memory and anticipation of the vivid life of the air. Often they were tired, after
the strain of that other life, but seldom were they despondent
or lazy. Indeed, in the routine of agriculture and industry
they were industrious as the wingless ants. Yet they worked
in a strange mood of attentive absentmindedness; for their
hearts were ever in the air. So long as they could have frequent periods of aviation, they remained bland even on the
ground. But if for any reason such as illness they were con-
fined to the ground for a long period, they pined, developed
acute melancholia, and died. Their makers had so contrived
them that with the onset of any very great pain or misery
their hearts should stop. Thus they were to avoid all serious
distress. But, in fact, this merciful device worked only on the
ground. In the air they assumed a very different and more
heroic nature, which their makers had not foreseen, though
indeed it was a natural consequence of their design.

In the air the flying man's heart beat more powerfully. His
temperature rose. His sensation became more vivid and more
discriminate, his intelligence more agile and penetrating. He
experienced a more intense pleasure or pain in all that happened to him. It would not be true to say that he became
more emotional; rather the reverse, if by emotionality is
meant enslavement to the emotions. For the most remarkable
feature of the aerial phase was that this enhanced power of
appreciation was dispassionate. So long as the individual was
in the air, whether in lonely struggle with the storm, or in the
ceremonial ballet with sky-darkening hosts of his fellows;
whether in the ecstatic love dance with a sexual partner, or in
solitary and meditative circlings far above the world; whether
his enterprise was fortunate, or he found himself dismem-
bered by the hurricane, and crashing to death; always the gay
and the tragic fortunes of his own person were regarded
equally with detached aesthetic delight. Even when his
dearest companion was mutilated or destroyed by some aerial
disaster, he exulted; though also he would give his own life in
the hope of effecting a rescue. But very soon after he had returned to the ground he would be overwhelmed with grief,
would strive vainly to recapture the lost vision, and would
perhaps die of heart failure.

Even when, as happened occasionally in the wild climate

of Venus, a whole aerial population was destroyed by some world-wide atmospheric tumult, the few broken survivors, so long as they could remain in the air, exulted. And actually while at length they sank exhausted toward the ground, toward certain disillusionment and death, they laughed inwardly. Yet an hour after they had alighted, their constitution would be changed, their vision lost. They would remember only the horror of the disaster, and the memory would kill them.

No wonder the Seventh Men grudged every moment that was passed on the ground. While they were in the air, of course, the prospect of a pedestrian interlude, or indeed of endless pedestrianism, though in a manner repugnant, would be accepted with unswerving gaiety; but while they were on the ground, they grudged bitterly to be there. Early in the career of the species the proportion of aerial to terrestrial hours was increased by a biological invention. A minute foodplant was produced which spent the winter rooted in the ground, and the summer adrift in the sunlit upper air, engaged solely in photosynthesis. Henceforth the populations of the Flying Men were able to browse upon the bright pastures of the sky, like swallows. As the ages passed, material civilization became more and more simplified. Needs which could not be satisfied without terrestrial labour tended to be outgrown. Manufactured articles became increasingly rare. Books were no longer written or read. In the main, indeed, they were no longer necessary; but to some extent their place was taken by verbal tradition and discussion, in the upper air. Of the arts, music, spoken lyric and epic verse, and the supreme art of winged dance, were constantly practised. The rest vanished. Many of the sciences inevitably faded into tradition; yet the true scientific spirit was preserved in a very exact meteorology, a sufficient biology, and a human psychology surpassed only by the second and fifth species at their height. None of these sciences, however, was taken very seriously, save in its practical applications. For instance, psychology explained the ecstasy of flight very neatly as a febrile and "irrational" beatitude. But no one was disconcerted by this theory; for every one, while on the wing, felt it to be merely an amusing half-truth.

The social order of the Seventh Men was in essence neither utilitarian, nor humanistic, nor religious, but aesthetic. Every act and every institution were to be justified as contributing to the perfect form of the community. Even social prosperity was conceived as merely the medium in which beauty should be embodied, the beauty, namely, of vivid individual lives harmoniously related. Yet not only for the individual, but even for the race itself (so the wise insisted), death on the wing was more excellent than prolonged life on the ground. Better, far better, would be racial suicide than a future of pedestrianism. Yet though both the individual and the race were conceived as instrumental to objective beauty, there was nothing religious, in any ordinary sense, in this conviction. The Seventh Men were completely without interest in the universal and the unseen. The beauty which they sought to create was ephemeral and very largely sensuous. And they were well content that it should be so. Personal immortality, said a dying sage, would be as tedious as an endless song. Equally so with the race. The lovely flame, of which we all are members, must die, he said, must die; for without death she would fall short of beauty.

For close on a hundred million terrestrial years this aerial society endured with little change. On many of the islands throughout this period stood even yet a number of the ancient pylons, though repaired almost beyond recognition. In these nests the men and women of the seventh species slept through the long Venerian nights, crowded like roosting swallows. By day the same great towers were sparsely peopled with those who were serving their turn in industry, while in the fields and on the sea others laboured. But most were in the air. Many would be skimming the ocean, to plunge, gannetlike, for fish. Many, circling over land or sea, would now and again swoop like hawks upon the wild-fowl which formed the chief meat of the species. Others, forty or fifty thousand feet above the waves, where even the plentiful atmosphere of Venus was scarcely capable of supporting them, would be soaring, circling, sweeping, for pure joy of flight. Others, in the calm and sunshine of high altitudes, would be hanging effortless upon some steady up-current of air for meditation and the rapture of mere percipience. Not a few love-intoxicated pairs would be entwining their courses in aerial patterns, in spires, cascades, and true love-knots of flight, presently to embrace and drop ten thousand feet in bodily union. Some would be driving hither and thither through the green mists of vegetable particles, gathering the manna in their open mouths. Companies, circling together, would be discussing matters social or aesthetic; others would be singing together, or listening to recitative epic verse. Thousands, gathering in the sky like migratory birds, would perform massed convolutions, reminiscent of the vast mechanical aerial choreography of the First World State, but more vital and expressive, as a bird's flight is more vital than the flight of any machine. And all the while there would be some, solitary or in companies, who, either in the pursuit of fish and wildfowl, or out of pure devilment, pitted their strength and skill against the hurricane, often tragically, but never without zest, and laughter of the spirit.

It may seem to some incredible that the culture of the Seventh Men should have lasted so long. Surely it must either have decayed through mere monotony and stagnation or have advanced into richer experience. But no. Generation succeeded generation, and each was too short-lived to outlast its young delight and discover boredom. Moreover, so perfect was the adjustment of these beings to their world, that even if they had lived for centuries they would have felt no need of change. Flight provided them with intense physical exhilaration, and with the physical basis of a genuine and ecstatic, though limited, spiritual experience. In this their supreme attainment they rejoiced not only in the diversity of flight itself, but also in the perceived beauties of their variegated world, and most of all, perhaps, in the thousand lyric and epic ventures of human intercourse in an aerial community.

The end of this seemingly everlasting elysium was nevertheless involved in the very nature of the species. In the first place, as the ages lengthened into aeons, the generations preserved less and less of the ancient scientific lore. For it became insignificant to them. The aerial community had no need for it. This loss of mere information did not matter so long as their condition remained unaltered; but in due course biological changes began to undermine them. The species had always been prone to a certain biological instability. A proportion of infants, varying with circumstances, had always been misshapen; and the deformity had generally been such as to make flight impossible. The normal infant was able to fly early in its second year. If some accident prevented it from doing so, it invariably fell into a decline and died before its third year was passed. But many of the deformed types, being the result of a partial reversion to the pedestrian nature, were able to live on indefinitely without flight. According to a merciful custom these cripples had always to be destroyed. But at length, owing to the gradual exhaustion of a certain marine salt essential to the high-strung nature of the

Seventh Men, infants were more often deformed than true to type. The world population declined so seriously that the organized aerial life of the community could no longer be carried on according to the time-honoured aesthetic principles. No one knew how to check this racial decay, but many felt that with greater biological knowledge it might be avoided. A disastrous policy was now adopted. It was decided to spare a carefully selected proportion of the deformed infants, those namely which, though doomed to pedestrianism, were likely to develop high intelligence. Thus it was hoped to raise a specialized group of persons whose work should be biological research untrammelled by the intoxication of flight.

The brilliant cripples that resulted from this policy looked at existence from a new angle. Deprived of the supreme experience for which their fellows lived, envious of a bliss which they knew only by report, yet contemptuous of the naïve mentality which cared for nothing (it seemed) but physical exercise, love-making, the beauty of nature, and the elegances of society, these flightless intelligences sought satisfaction almost wholly in the life of research and scientific control. At the best, however, they were a tortured and resentful race. For their natures were fashioned for the aerial life which they could not lead. Although they received from the winged folk just treatment and a certain compassionate respect, they writhed under this kindness, locked their hearts against all the orthodox values, and sought out new ideals. Within a few centuries they had rehabilitated the life of intellect, and, with the power that knowledge gives, they had made themselves masters of the world. The amiable fliers were surprised, perplexed, even pained; and yet withal amused. Even when it became evident that the pedestrians were determined to create a new world-order in which there would be no place for the beauties of natural flight, the fliers were only distressed while they were on the ground.

The islands were becoming crowded with machinery and flightless industrialists. In the air itself the winged folk found themselves outstripped by the base but effective instruments of mechanical flight. Wings became a laughing stock, and the life of natural flight was condemned as a barren luxury. It was ordained that in future every flier must serve the pedestrian world-order, or starve. And as the cultivation of wind-borne plants had been abandoned, and fishing and fowling rights were strictly controlled, this law was no empty form. At first it was impossible for the fliers to work on the ground for long hours, day after day, without incurring serious ill-health and an early death. But the pedestrian physiologists invented a drug which preserved the poor wage-slaves in something like physical health, and actually prolonged their life. No drug, however, could restore their spirit, for their normal aerial habit was reduced to a few tired hours of recreation once a week. Meanwhile, breeding experiments were undertaken to produce a wholly wingless large-brained type. And finally a law was enacted by which all winged infants must be either mutilated or destroyed. At this point the fliers made an heroic but ineffectual bid for power. They attacked the pedestrian population from the air. In reply the enemy rode them down in his great aeroplanes and blew them to pieces with high explosive.

The fighting squadrons of the natural fliers were finally driven to the ground in a remote and barren island. Thither the whole flying population, a mere remnant of its former strength, fled out of every civilized archipelago in search of freedom: the whole population—save the sick, who committed suicide, and all infants that could not yet fly. These were stifled by their mothers or next-of-kin, in obedience to a decree of the leaders. About a million men, women and children, some of whom were scarcely old enough for the prolonged flight, now gathered on the rocks, regardless that there was not food in the neighbourhood for a great company.

Their leaders, conferring together, saw clearly that the day of Flying Man was done, and that it would be more fitting for a high-souled race to die at once than to drag on in subjection to contemptuous masters. They therefore ordered the population to take part in an act of racial suicide that should at least make death a noble gesture of freedom. The people received the mssage while they were resting on the stony moorland. A wail of sorrow broke from them. It was checked by the speaker, who bade them strive to see, even on the ground, the beauty of the thing that was to be done. They could not see it; but they knew that if they had the strength to take wing again they would see it clearly, almost as soon as their tired muscles bore them aloft. There was no time for waste, for many were already faint with hunger, and anxious lest they should fail to rise. At the appointed signal the whole population rose into the air with a deep roar of wings. Sorrow was left behind. Even the children, when their mothers explained what was to be done, accepted their fate with zest; though, had they learned of it on the ground, they would have been terror-stricken. The company now flew steadily West, forming themselves into a double file many miles long. The cone of a volcano appeared over the horizon, and rose as they approached. The leaders pressed on towards its ruddy smoke plume; and unflinchingly, couple by couple, the whole multitude darted into its fiery breath and vanished. So ended the career of Flying Men.

3. A MINOR ASTRONOMICAL EVENT

The flightless yet still half avian race that now possessed the planet settled down to construct a society based on industry and science. After many vicissitudes of fortune and of aim, they produced a new human species, the Eighth Men. These long-headed and substantial folk were designed to be strictly pedestrian, physically and mentally. Apt for manipulation, calculation and invention, they very soon turned Venus into an engineer's paradise. With power drawn from the planet's central heat, their huge electric ships bored steadily through the perennial monsoons and hurricanes, which also their aircraft treated with contempt. Islands were joined by tunnels and by millepede bridges. Every inch of land served some industrial or agricultural end. So successfully did the generations amass wealth that their rival races and rival castes were able to indulge, every few centuries, in vast revelries of mutual slaughter and material destruction without, as a rule, impoverishing their descendants. And so insensitive had man become that these orgies shamed him not at all. Indeed, only by ardours of physical violence could this most philistine species wrench itself for a while out of its complacency. Strife which to nobler beings would have been a grave spiritual disaster, was for these a tonic, almost a religious exercise. These cathartic paroxysms, it should be observed, were but the rare and brief crises which automatically punctuated ages of stolid peace. At no time did they threaten the existence of the species; seldom did they even destroy its civilization.

It was after a lengthy period of peace and scientific advancement that the Eighth Men made a startling astronomical discovery. Ever since the First Men had learned that in the life of every star there comes a critical moment when the great orb collapses, shrinking to a minute, dense grain with feeble radiation, man had periodically suspected that the sun was about to undergo this change, and become a typical

"White Dwarf." The Eighth Men detected sure signs of the catastrophe, and predicted its date. Twenty thousand years they gave themselves before the change should begin. In another fifty thousand years, they guessed, Venus would probably be frozen and uninhabitable. The only hope was to migrate to Mercury during the great change, when that planet was already ceasing to be intolerably hot. It was necessary then to give Mercury an atmosphere, and to breed a new species which should be capable of adapting itself finally to a world of extreme cold.

This desperate operation was already on foot when a new astronomical discovery rendered it futile. Astronomers detected, some distance from the solar system, a volume of nonluminous gas. Calculation showed that this object and the sun were approaching one another at a tangent, and that they would collide. Further calculation revealed the probable results of this event. The sun would flare up and expand prodigiously. Life would be quite impossible on any of the planets save, just possibly, Uranus, and more probably Neptune. The three planets beyond Neptune would escape roasting, but were unsuitable for other reasons. The two outermost would remain glacial, and, moreover, lay beyond the range of the imperfect etherships of the Eighth Men. The innermost was practically a bald globe of iron, devoid not merely of atmosphere and water, but also of the normal covering of rock. Neptune alone might be able to support life; but how could even Neptune be populated? Not only was its atmosphere very unsuitable, and its gravitational pull such as to make man's body an intolerable burden, but also up to the time of the collision it would remain excessively cold. Not till after the collision could it support any kind of life known to man.

How these difficulties were overcome I have no time to tell, though the story of man's attack upon his final home is well worthy of recording. Nor can I tell in detail of the conflict of policy which now occurred. Some, realizing that the Eighth Men themselves could never live on Neptune, advocated an orgy of pleasure-living till the end. But at length the race excelled itself in an almost unanimous resolve to devote its remaining centuries to the production of a human being capable of carrying the torch of mentality into a new world.

Ether-vessels were able to reach that remote world and set up chemical changes for the improvement of the atmosphere. It was also possible, by means of the lately rediscovered process of automatic annihilation of matter, to produce a constant supply of energy for the warming of an area where life might hope to survive until the sun should be rejuvenated.

When at last the time for migration was approaching, a specially designed vegetation was shipped to Neptune and established in the warm area to fit it for man's use. Animals, it was decided, would be unnecessary. Subsequently a specially designed human species, the Ninth Men, was transported to man's new home. The giant Eighth Men could not themselves inhabit Neptune. The trouble was not merely that they could scarcely support their own weight, let alone walk, but that the atmospheric pressure on Neptune was unendurable. For the great planet bore a gaseous envelope thousands of miles deep. The solid globe was scarcely more than the yolk of a huge egg. The mass of the air itself combined with the mass of the solid to produce a gravitational pressure greater than that upon the Venerian ocean floor. The Eighth Men, therefore, dared not emerge from their ether-ships to tread the surface of the planet save for brief spells in steel diving suits. For them there was nothing else to do but to return to the archipelagos of Venus, and make the best of life until the end. They were not spared for long. A few centuries after the settlement of Neptune had been completed by transferring thither all the most precious material relics of humanity, the great planet itself narrowly missed collision with the dark stranger from space. Uranus and Jupiter were at the time well out of its track. Not so Saturn, which, a few years after Neptune's escape, was engulfed with all its rings and satellites. The sudden incandescence which resulted from this minor collision was but a prelude. The huge foreigner rushed on. Like a finger poked into a spider's web, it tangled up the planetary orbits. Having devoured its way through the asteroids, it missed Mars, caught Earth and Venus in its blazing hair, and leapt at the sun. Henceforth the centre of the solar system was a star nearly as wide as the old orbit of Mercury, and the system was transformed.

Ford's in His Flivver

By 1932 the world had passed through one disillusioning crisis and was deep in another. World War I had shattered carefully nurtured notions of progress in human affairs, had virtually destroyed a generation of European men, and had created the Communist Revolution and a persistent mood of cynicism.

Progress, nevertheless, was evident to the discerning. Population (it had not yet begun to seem a liability) was expanding in the Western world as public-health measures and better nutrition began to reduce the death rate and lengthen the life span: in the United States between 1900 and 1960 it increased from 47.3 years to 69.7. The U.S. gross national product increased over the same period from $17 billion to $500 billion.

A significant part of the improvement in productiveness came through invention, particularly in agriculture, where new machinery, hybrid grains, and chemical fertilizers brought further efficiencies to a process that had already reduced the labor of producing an acre of wheat from sixty-one hours to three hours. Meanwhile energy became cheap and plentiful with the discovery of oil and processes for fractionating it, and the increasing application of electricity to all sorts of tasks; steel-making was improved; transportation by ship, train, truck, and eventually airplane got produce and the abundance flowing out of new factories to the markets of the world; radio and the telephone improved and speeded communication. . . .

During this period factories became efficient means of producing goods for mass consumption. The process began in 1798 when Eli Whitney invented a means for mass-producing guns through interchangeable parts; it culminated in 1916 with Henry Ford's invention of the production line. Instead of workers taking parts to a chassis, Ford moved the chassis past a series of workers who performed a single task, thus en-

abling him to replace skilled mechanics with unskilled la-
borers. It also enabled him to reduce the price of his "tin
lizzie" from $850 to $360, in spite of the fact that in 1914 he
had reduced the work day from nine hours to eight and more
than doubled the wages of his workers. His innovations
brought the automobile into the mass market; it was the only
market that could justify his production methods.

Abundance doesn't necessarily produce happiness, but poverty almost always brings misery.

But the system that produced abundance, that gave the
working class an unprecedented standard of living and the
time to enjoy it, had other consequences. Work became less
satisfying, life became more frantic, people had more unoccupied time to reflect upon their condition, and the trend of civilization seemed to be toward increasing mechanization,
increasing population, and increasing urbanization in the pursuit of greater efficiency and the more abundant life.

From the vantage point of a year or two into the economic
disorder called the Depression, Aldous Huxley (1894-1963)
saw in the complex tendencies symbolized by Ford's innovations an ambiguous future. It is not the sterile underground
world of Forster's "The Machine Stops." The citizens are not
occupied with esoteric thoughts; indeed, they hardly think at
all. They perform tasks for which they are bred, from ova, in
bottles; they enjoy indiscriminate sex ("orgy-porgy") without
consequences; they have the all-purpose happiness drug
"soma" for moments of discomfort, VPS (violent passion surrogate) once a month to clean out their systems, and a world
without disease, decay, want, or strong emotion.

As they put it, "Ford's in his flivver."

It is not an unattractive world except to those who, like the
Savage, prefer poetry, religion, sin, and freedom, who are
willing to suffer—no, want to suffer—for them; who demand,
with the Savage, the right to be unhappy. In the pages repro-
duced here, Huxley sets up no straw man in the Controller,
Mustapha Mond.

The author of *Brave New World* was a member of the English literary establishment, though not a typical member. In
his lean, tall body he combined the literary culture and the
scientific culture of the nineteenth century represented by his
great-uncle, Matthew Arnold, and his grandfather, T. H.
Huxley, the two-culture antagonists of half a century before.
In the mixture Huxley's uniquely contradictory characteristics
found some explanation.

The most important single event of his life, he recalled, was the loss of his eyesight as a result of keratitis contracted at Eton. When he went on to Oxford, he gave up an earlier ambition to become a physician and took up English literature and philology. Gradually he regained the ability to read with one eye aided by a magnifying glass, taught, worked on the staff of the *Athenaeum*, did literary journalism for many periodicals, and turned to writing novels.

He has been called more an essayist than a novelist, but his novels were acclaimed as prime examples of the skeptical brilliance that burst forth after World War I, beginning with *Limbo* (1920), *Chrome Yellow* (1921), *Mortal Coils* (1922), and *Antic Hay* (1923) before reaching a peak in *Point Counter Point* (1928). *Brave New World* (1932) was his first science-fiction novel, though not his last; it was followed by *After Many a Summer Dies the Swan* (1940) and *Ape and Essence* (1948), and, the year before his death, by a utopia that found hope in much that he had found dangerous to the spirit in 1932, *Island* (1962).

After spending much of his novel-writing years in Italy and France (he was a good friend and neighbor of the D. H. Lawrences), Huxley lived out his last thirty years in southern California, where he found hope and tranquillity. For a brilliant skeptic and a social critic, he was a surprising optimist and a mystic, pursuing the discredited Bates eye exercises and the transcendental experiences of mescalin, LSD, and Eastern religions that he wrote about in *Doors of Perception* (1954) and *The Perennial Philosophy*.

In *Brave New World Revisited* (1958) he returned to his best-known work to see how its ideas had been realized. The techniques and their results are those that behavioral psychologist B. H. Skinner described in *Beyond Freedom and Dignity* (1971) and idealized in his utopian novel *Walden Two* (1948).

Brian Aldiss has called *Brave New World* "arguably the Western world's most famous science fiction novel."

From Brave New World

by Aldous Huxley

CHAPTER SIXTEEN

The room into which the three were ushered was the Controller's study.

"His fordship will be down in a moment." The Gamma butler left them to themselves.

Helmholtz laughed aloud.

"It's more like a caffeine-solution party than a trial," he said, and let himself fall into the most luxurious of the pneumatic arm-chairs. "Cheer up, Bernard," he added, catching sight of his friend's green unhappy face. But Bernard would not be cheered; without answering, without even looking at Helmholtz, he went and sat down on the most uncomfortable chair in the room, carefully chosen in the obscure hope of somehow deprecating the wrath of the higher powers.

The Savage meanwhile wandered restlessly round the room, peering with a vague superficial inquisitiveness at the books in the shelves, at the soundtrack rolls and the reading machine bobbins in their numbered pigeon-holes. On the table under the window lay a massive volume bound in limp black leather-surrogate, and stamped with large golden T's. He picked it up and opened it. MY LIFE AND WORK, BY OUR FORD. The book had been published at Detroit by the Society for the Propagation of Fordian Knowledge. Idly he turned the pages, read a sentence here, a paragraph there, and had just come to the conclusion that the book didn't interest him, when the door opened, and the Resident World Controller for Western Europe walked briskly into the room.

Mustapha Mond shook hands with all three of them; but it was to the Savage that he addressed himself. "So you don't much like civilization, Mr. Savage," he said.

The Savage looked at him. He had been prepared to lie, to bluster, to remain sullenly unresponsive; but, reassured by the good-humoured intelligence of the Controller's face, he decided to tell the truth, straightforwardly. "No." He shook his head.

Bernard started and looked horrified. What would the Controller think? To be labelled as the friend of a man who said that he didn't like civilization—said it openly and, of all people, to the Controller—it was terrible. "But, John," he began. A look from Mustapha Mond reduced him to an abject silence.

"Of course," the Savage went on to admit, "there are some very nice things. All that music in the air, for instance . . ."

"Sometimes a thousand twangling instruments will hum about my ears and sometimes voices."

The Savage's face lit up with a sudden pleasure. "Have you read it too?" he asked. "I thought nobody knew about that book here, in England."

"Almost nobody. I'm one of the very few. It's prohibited, you see. But as I make the laws here, I can also break them. With impunity, Mr. Marx," he added, turning to Bernard. "Which I'm afraid you *can't* do."

Bernard sank into a yet more hopeless misery.

"But why is it prohibited?" asked the Savage. In the excitement of meeting a man who had read Shakespeare he had momentarily forgotten everything else.

The Controller shrugged his shoulders. "Because it's old; that's the chief reason. We haven't any use for old things here."

"Even when they're beautiful?"

"Particularly when they're beautiful. Beauty's attractive, and we don't want people to be attracted by old things. We want them to like the new ones."

"But the new ones are so stupid and horrible. Those plays, where there's nothing but helicopters flying about and you *feel* the people kissing." He made a grimace. "Goats and monkeys!" Only in Othello's words could he find an adequate vehicle for his contempt and hatred.

"Nice tame animals, anyhow," the Controller murmured parenthetically.

"Why don't you let them see *Othello* instead?"

"I've told you; it's old. Besides, they couldn't understand it."

Yes, that was true. He remembered how Helmholtz had laughed at *Romeo and Juliet*. "Well then," he said, after a pause, "something new that's like *Othello*, and that they could understand."

"That's what we've all been wanting to write," said Helmholtz, breaking a long silence.

"And it's what you never will write," said the Controller. "Because, if it were really like *Othello* nobody could understand it, however new it might be. And if it were new, it couldn't possibly be like *Othello*."

"Why not?"

"Yes, why not?" Helmholtz repeated. He too was forgetting the unpleasant realities of the situation. Green with anxiety and apprehension, only Bernard remembered them; the others ignored him. "Why not?"

"Because our world is not the same as Othello's world. You can't make flivvers without steel—and you can't make tragedies without social instability. The world's stable now. People are happy; they get what they want, and they never want what they can't get. They're well off; they're safe; they're never ill; they're not afraid of death; they're blissfully ignorant of passion and old age; they're plagued with no mothers or fathers; they've got no wives, or children, or lovers to feel strongly about; they're so conditioned that they practically can't help behaving as they ought to behave. And if anything should go wrong, there's *soma*. Which you go and chuck out of the window in the name of liberty, Mr. Savage. *Liberty!*" He laughed. "Expecting Deltas to know what liberty is! And now expecting them to understand *Othello!* My good boy!"

The Savage was silent for a little. "All the same," he insisted obstinately, "*Othello's* good, *Othello's* better than those feelies."

"Of course it is," the Controller agreed. "But that's the price we have to pay for stability. You've got to choose between happiness and what people used to call high art. We've sacrificed the high art. We have the feelies and the scent organ instead."

"But they don't mean anything."

"They mean themselves; they mean a lot of agreeable sensations to the audience."

"But they're . . . they're told by an idiot."

The Controller laughed. "You're not being very polite to your friend, Mr. Watson. One of our most distinguished Emotional Engineers . . ."

"But he's right," said Helmholtz gloomily. "Because it *is* idiotic. Writing when there's nothing to say . . ."

"Precisely. But that requires the most enormous ingenuity. You're making flivvers out of the absolute minimum of steel—works of art out of practically nothing but pure sensation."

The Savage shook his head. "It all seems to me quite horrible."

"Of course it does. Actual happiness always looks pretty squalid in comparison with the over-compensations for misery. And, of course, stability isn't nearly so spectacular as instability. And being contented has none of the glamour of a good fight against misfortune, none of the picturesqueness of a struggle with temptation, or a fatal overthrow by passion or doubt. Happiness is never grand."

"I suppose not," said the Savage after a silence. "But need it be quite so bad as those twins?" He passed his hand over his eyes as though he were trying to wipe away the remembered image of those long rows of identical midgets at the assembling tables, those queued-up twin-herds at the entrance to the Brentford monorail station, those human maggots swarming round Linda's bed of death, the endless repeated face of his assailants. He looked at his bandaged left hand and shuddered. "Horrible!"

"But how useful! I see you don't like our Bokanovsky Groups; but, I assure you, they're the foundation on which everything else is built. They're the gyroscope that stabilizes the rocket plane of state on its unswerving course." The deep voice thrillingly vibrated; the gesticulating hand implied all space and the onrush of the irresistible machine. Mustapha Mond's oratory was almost up to synthetic standards.

"I was wondering," said the Savage, "why you had them at all—seeing that you can get whatever you want out of those bottles. Why don't you make everybody an Alpha Double Plus while you're about it?"

Mustapha Mond laughed. "Because we have no wish to have our throats cut," he answered. "We believe in happiness and stability. A society of Alphas couldn't fail to be unstable and miserable. Imagine a factory staffed by Alphas—that is to say by separate and unrelated individuals of good heredity and conditioned so as to be capable (within limits) of making a free choice and assuming responsibilities. Imagine it!" he repeated.

The Savage tried to imagine it, not very successfully.

"It's an absurdity. An Alpha-decanted, Alpha-conditioned man would go mad if he had to do Epsilon Semi-Moron work—go mad, or start smashing things up. Alphas can be completely socialized—but only on condition that you make them do Alpha work. Only an Epsilon can be expected to make Epsilon sacrifices, for the good reason that for him they aren't sacrifices; they're the line of least resistance. His conditioning has laid down rails along which he's got to run. He can't help himself; he's foredoomed. Even after decanting, he's still inside a bottle—an invisible bottle of infantile and embryonic fixations. Each one of us, of course," the Controller meditatively continued, "goes through life inside a bottle. But if we happen to be Alphas, our bottles are, relatively speaking, enormous. We should suffer acutely if we were continued in a narrow space. You cannot pour upper-caste champagne-surrogate into lower-caste bottles. It's obvious theoretically. But it has also been proved in actual practice. The result of the Cyprus experiment was convincing."

"What was that?" asked the Savage.

Mustapha Mond smiled. "Well, you can call it an experiment in rebottling if you like. It began in A.F. 473. The Controllers had the island of Cyprus cleared of all its existing inhabitants and re-colonized with a specially prepared batch of twenty-two thousand Alphas. All agricultural and industrial equipment was handed over to them and they were left to manage their own affairs. The result exactly fulfilled all the theoretical predictions. The land wasn't properly worked; there were strikes in all the factories; the laws were set at naught, orders disobeyed; all the people detailed for a spell of low-grade work were perpetually intriguing for high-grade jobs, and all the people with high-grade jobs were counter-intriguing at all costs to stay where they were. Within six years they were having a first-class civil war. When nineteen out of the twenty-two thousand had been killed, the survivors unanimously petitioned the World Controllers to resume the government of the island. Which they did. And that was the end of the only society of Alphas that the world has ever seen."

The Savage sighed, profoundly.

"The optimum population," said Mustapha Mond, "is modelled on the iceberg—eight-ninths below the water line, one-ninth above."

"And they're happy below the water line?"

"Happier than above it. Happier than your friend here, for example." He pointed.

"In spite of that awful work?"

"Awful? *They* don't find it so. On the contrary, they like it. It's light, it's childishly simple. No strain on the mind or the muscles. Seven and a half hours of mild, unexhausting labour, and then the *soma* ration and games and unrestricted copulation and the feelies. What more can they ask for? True," he added, "they might ask for shorter hours. And of course we could give them shorter hours. Technically, it would be perfectly simple to reduce all lower-caste working hours to three or four a day. But would they be any the happier for that? No, they wouldn't. The experiment was tried, more than a century and a half ago. The whole of Ireland was put on to the four-hour day. What was the result? Unrest and a large increase in the consumption of *soma*; that was all. Those three and half hours of extra leisure were so far from being a source of happiness, that people felt constrained to take a holiday from them. The Inventions Office is stuffed with plans for labour-saving processes. Thousands of them." Mustapha Mond made a lavish gesture. "And why don't we put them into execution? For the sake of the labourers; it would be sheer cruelty to afflict them with excessive leisure. It's the same with agriculture. We could synthesize every morsel of food, if we wanted to. But we don't. We prefer to keep a third of the population on the land. For their own sakes—because it takes *longer* to get food out of the land than out of a factory. Besides, we have our stability to think of. We don't want to change. Every change is a menace to stability. That's another reason why we're so chary of applying new inventions. Every discovery in pure science is potentially subversive; even science must sometimes be treated as a possible enemy. Yes, even science."

Science? The Savage frowned. He knew the word. But what it exactly signified he could not say. Shakespeare and the old men of the pueblo had never mentioned science, and from Linda he had only gathered the vaguest hints: science was something you made helicopters with, something that caused you to laugh at the Corn Dances, something that prevented you from being wrinkled and losing your teeth. He made a desperate effort to take the Controller's meaning.

"Yes," Mustapha Mond was saying, "that's another item in the cost of stability. It isn't only art that's incompatible with happiness; it's also science. Science is dangerous; we have to keep it most carefully chained and muzzled."

"What?" said Helmholtz, in astonishment. "But we're always saying that science is everything. It's a hypnopædic platitude."

"Three times a week between thirteen and seventeen," put in Bernard.

"And all the science propaganda we do at the College . . ."

"Yes; but what sort of science?" asked Mustapha Mond sarcastically. "You've had no scientific training, so you can't judge. I was a pretty good physicist in my time. Too good— good enough to realize that all our science is just a cookery book, with an orthodox theory of cooking that nobody's allowed to question, and a list of recipes that mustn't be added to except by special permission from the head cook. I'm the head cook now. But I was an inquisitive young scullion once. I started doing a bit of cooking on my own. Unorthodox cooking, illicit cooking. A bit of real science, in fact." He was silent.

"What happened?" asked Helmholtz Watson.

The Controller sighed. "Very nearly what's going to happen to you young men. I was on the point of being sent to an island."

The words galvanized Bernard into a violent and unseemly activity. "Send *me* to an island?" He jumped up, ran across the room and stood gesticulating in front of the Controller. "You can't send *me*. I haven't done anything. It was the others. I swear it was the others." He pointed accusingly to Helmholtz and the Savage. "Oh, please don't send me to Iceland. I promise I'll do what I ought to do. Give me another chance. Please give me another chance." The tears began to flow. "I tell you, it's their fault," he sobbed. "And not to Iceland. Oh please, your fordship, please . . ." And in a paroxysm of abjection he threw himself on his knees before the Controller. Mustapha Mond tried to make him get up; but Bernard persisted in his grovelling; the stream of words poured out inexhaustibly. In the end the Controller had to ring for his fourth secretary.

"Bring three men," he ordered, "and take Mr. Marx into a bedroom. Give him a good *soma* vaporization and then put him to bed and leave him."

The fourth secretary went out and returned with three green-uniformed twin footmen. Still shouting and sobbing, Bernard was carried out.

"One would think he was going to have his throat cut," said the Controller, as the door closed. "Whereas, if he had the smallest sense, he'd understand that his punishment is really a reward. He's being sent to an island. That's to say, he's being sent to a place where he'll meet the most interesting set of men and women to be found anywhere in the world. All the people who, for one reason or another, have got too self-consciously individual to fit into community-life. All the people who aren't satisfied with orthodoxy, who've got independent ideas of their own. Every one, in a word, who's any one. I almost envy you, Mr. Watson."

Helmholtz laughed. "Then why aren't you on an island yourself?"

"Because, finally, I preferred this," the Controller answered. "I was given the choice: to be sent to an island, where I could have got on with my pure science, or to be taken on to the Controllers' Council with the prospect of succeeding in due course to an actual Controllership. I chose this and let the science go." After a silence, "Sometimes," he added, "I rather regret the science. Happiness is a hard master—particularly other people's happiness. A much harder master, if one isn't conditioned to accept it unquestioningly, than truth." He sighed, fell silent again, then continued in a brisker tone, "Well, duty's duty. One can't consult one's own preferences. I'm interested in truth, I like science. But truth's a menace, science is a public danger. As dangerous as it's been beneficent. It has given us the stablest equilibrium in history. China's was hopelessly insecure by comparison; even the primitive matriarchies weren't steadier than we are. Thanks, I repeat, to science. But we can't allow science to undo its own good work. That's why we so carefully limit the scope of its researches—that's why I almost got sent to an island. We don't allow it to deal with any but the most immediate problems of the moment. All other enquiries are most sedulously discouraged. It's curious," he went on after a little pause, "to read what people in the time of Our Ford used to write about scientific progress. They seemed to have imagined that it could be allowed to go on indefinitely, regardless of everything else. Knowledge was the highest good, truth the supreme value; all the rest was secondary and subordinate. True, ideas were beginning to change even then. Our Ford himself did a great deal to shift the emphasis from truth and beauty to comfort and happiness. Mass production demanded the shift. Universal happiness keeps the wheels steadily turning; truth and beauty can't. And, of course, whenever the masses seized political power, then it was happiness rather than truth and beauty that mattered. Still, in spite of everything, unrestricted scientific research was still permitted. People still went on talking about truth and beauty as though they were the sovereign goods. Right up to the time of the Nine Years' War. *That* made them change their

tune all right. What's the point of truth or beauty or
knowledge when the anthrax bombs are popping all around
you? That was when science first began to be controlled—after the Nine Years' War. People were ready to have even
their appetites controlled then. Anything for a quiet life.
We've gone on controlling ever since. It hasn't been very
good for truth, of course. But it's been very good for happiness. One can't have something for nothing. Happiness has
got to be paid for. You're paying for it, Mr. Watson—paying
because you happen to be too much interested in beauty. I
was too much interested in truth; I paid too."

"But *you* didn't go to an island," said the Savage, breaking
a long silence.

The Controller smiled. "That's how I paid. By choosing to
serve happiness. Other people's—not mine. It's lucky," he
added, after a pause, "that there are such a lot of islands in
the world. I don't know what we should do without them. Put
you all in the lethal chamber, I suppose. By the way, Mr.
Watson, would you like a tropical climate? The Marquesas,
for example; or Samoa? Or something rather more bracing?"

Helmholtz rose from his pneumatic chair. "I should like a
thoroughly bad climate," he answered. "I believe one would
write better if the climate were bad. If there were a lot of
wind and storms, for example . . ."

The Controller nodded his approbation. "I like your spirit,
Mr. Watson. I like it very much indeed. As much as I offi-
cially disapprove of it." He smiled. "What about the Falkland
Islands?"

"Yes, I think that will do," Helmholtz answered. "And
now, if you don't mind, I'll go and see how poor Bernard's
getting on."

CHAPTER SEVENTEEN

"Art, science—you seem to have paid a fairly high price for
your happiness," said the Savage, when they were alone.
"Anything else?"

"Well, religion, of course," replied the Controller. "There
used to be something called God—before the Nine Years'
War. But I was forgetting; you know all about God, I suppose."

"Well . . ." The Savage hesitated. He would have liked to
say something about solitude, about night, about the mesa ly-

ing pale under the moon, about the precipice, the plunge into shadowy darkness, about death. He would have liked to speak; but there were no words. Not even in Shakespeare.

The Controller, meanwhile, had crossed to the other side of the room and was unlocking a large safe let into the wall between the bookshelves. The heavy door swung open. Rummaging in the darkness within, "It's a subject," he said, "that has always had a great interest for me." He pulled out a thick black volume. "You've never read this, for example."

The Savage took it. *"The Holy Bible, containing the Old and New Testaments,"* he read aloud from the title-page.

"Nor this." It was a small book and had lost its cover.

"The Imitation of Christ."

"Nor this." He handed out another volume.

"The Varieties of Religious Experience. By William James."

"And I've got plenty more," Mustapha Mond continued, resuming his seat. "A whole collection of pornographic old books. God in the safe and Ford on the shelves." He pointed with a laugh to his avowed library—to the shelves of books, the racks full of reading-machine bobbins and sound-track rolls.

"But if you know about God, why don't you tell them?" asked the Savage indignantly. "Why don't you give them these books about God?"

"For the same reason as we don't give them *Othello*: they're old; they're about God hundreds of years ago. Not about God now."

"But God doesn't change."

"Men do, though."

"What difference does that make?"

"All the difference in the world," said Mustapha Mond. He got up again and walked to the safe. "There was a man called Cardinal Newman," he said. "A cardinal," he exclaimed parenthetically, "was a kind of Arch-Community-Songster."

" 'I Pandulph, of fair Milan, cardinal.' I've read about them in Shakespeare."

"Of course you have. Well, as I was saying, there was a man called Cardinal Newman. Ah, here's the book." He pulled it out. "And while I'm about it I'll take this one too. It's by a man called Maine de Biran. He was a philosopher, if you know what that was."

"A man who dreams of fewer things than there are in heaven and earth," said the Savage promptly.

"Quite so. I'll read you one of the things he *did* dream of in a moment. Meanwhile, listen to what this old Arch-Community-Songster said." He opened the book at the place marked by a slip of paper and began to read. " 'We are not our own any more than what we possess is our own. We did not make ourselves, we cannot be supreme over ourselves. We are not our own masters. We are God's property. Is it not our happiness thus to view the matter? Is it any happiness or any comfort, to consider that we *are* our own? It may be thought so by the young and prosperous. These may think it a great thing to have everything, as they suppose, their own way—to depend on no one—to have to think of nothing out of sight, to be without the irksomeness of continual acknowledgment, continual prayer, continual reference of what they do to the will of another. But as time goes on, they, as all men, will find that independence was not made for man—that it is an unnatural state—will do for a while, but will not carry us on safely to the end . . . ' " Mustapha Mond paused, put down the first book and, picking up the other, turned over the pages. "Take this, for example," he said, and in his deep voice once more began to read: " 'A man grows old; he feels in himself that radical sense of weakness, of listlessness, of discomfort, which accompanies the advance of age; and, feeling thus, imagines himself merely sick, lulling his fears with the notion that this distressing condition is due to some particular cause, from which, as from an illness, he hopes to recover. Vain imaginings! That sickness is old age; and a horrible disease it is. They say that it is the fear of death and of what comes after death that makes men turn to religion as they advance in years. But my own experience has given me the conviction that, quite apart from any such terrors or imaginings, the religious sentiment tends to develop as we grow older; to develop because, as the passions grow calm, as the fancy and sensibilities are less excited and less excitable, our reason becomes less troubled in its working, less obscured by the images, desires and distractions, in which it used to be absorbed; whereupon God emerges as from behind a cloud; our soul feels, sees, turns towards the source of all light; turns naturally and inevitably; for now that all that gave to the world of sensation its life and charm has begun to leak away from us, now that phenomenal existence is no more bolstered up by impressions from within or from without, we feel the need to lean on something that abides, something that will never play us false—a reality, an absolute and everlasting truth. Yes, we inevitably turn to God; for this religious sentiment is of its nature so pure, so delightful to the soul that experiences it, that it makes up to us for all our other losses.'" Mustapha Mond shut the book and leaned back in his chair. "One of the numerous things in heaven and earth that these philosophers didn't dream about was this" (he waved his hand), "us, the modern world. 'You can only be independent of God while you've got youth and prosperity; independence won't take you safely to the end.' Well, we've now got youth and prosperity right up to the end. What follows? Evidently, that we can be independent of God. 'The religious sentiment will compensate us for all our losses.' But there aren't any losses for us to compensate; religious sentiment is superfluous. And why should we go hunting for a substitute for youthful desires, when youthful desires never fail? A substitute for distractions, when we go on enjoying all the old fooleries to the very last? What need have we to repose when our minds and bodies continue to delight in activity? of consolation, when we have *soma?* of something immovable, when there is the social order?"

"Then you think there is no God?"

"No, I think there quite possibly is one."

"Then why? . . ."

Mustapha Mond checked him. "But he manifests himself in different ways to different men. In premodern times he manifested himself as the being described in these books. Now . . ."

"How does he manifest himself now?" asked the Savage.

"Well, he manifests himself as an absence; as though he weren't there at all."

"That's your fault."

"Call it the fault of civilization. God isn't compatible with machinery and scientific medicine and universal happiness. You must make your choice. Our civilization has chosen machinery and medicine and happiness. That's why I have to keep these books locked up in the safe. They're smut. People would be shocked if . . ."

The Savage interrupted him. "But isn't it *natural* to feel there's a God?"

"You might as well ask if it's natural to do up one's trousers with zippers," said the Controller sarcastically. "You remind me of another of those old fellows called Bradley. He defined philosophy as the finding of bad reason for what one believes by instinct. As if one believed anything by instinct! One believes things because one has been conditioned to believe them. Finding bad reasons for what one believes for other bad reasons—that's philosophy. People believe in God because they've been conditioned to believe in God."

"But all the same," insisted the Savage, "it is natural to believe in God when you're alone—quite alone, in the night, thinking about death . . ."

"But people never are alone now," said Mustapha Mond. "We make them hate solitude; and we arrange their lives so that it's almost impossible for them ever to have it."

The Savage nodded gloomily. At Malpais he had suffered because they had shut him out from the communal activities of the pueblo, in civilized London he was suffering because he could never escape from those communal activities, never be quietly alone.

"Do you remember that bit in *King Lear?*" said the Savage at last. " 'The gods are just and of our pleasant vices make instruments to plague us; the dark and vicious place where thee he got cost him his eyes,' and Edmund answers—you remember, he's wounded, he's dying—'Thou hast spoken right; 'tis true. The wheel come full circle; I am here.' What about that now? Doesn't there seem to be a God managing things, punishing, rewarding?"

"Well, does there?" questioned the Controller in his turn. "You can indulge in any number of pleasant vices with a freemartin and run no risks of having your eyes put out by your son's mistress. 'The wheel has come full circle; I am here.' But where would Edmund be nowadays? Sitting in a pneumatic chair, with his arm round a girl's waist, sucking away at his sex-hormone chewing-gum and looking at the feelies. The gods are just. No doubt. But their code of law is dictated, in the last resort, by the people who organize society; Providence takes its cue from men."

"Are you sure?" asked the Savage. "Are you quite sure that the Edmund in that pneumatic chair hasn't been just as heavily punished as the Edmund who's wounded and bleeding to death? The gods are just. Haven't they used his pleasant vices as an instrument to degrade him?"

"Degrade him from what position? As a happy, hard-working, goods-consuming citizen he's perfect. Of course, if you choose some other standard than ours, then perhaps you might say he was degraded. But you've got to stick to one set of postulates. You can't play Electro-magnetic Golf according to the rules of Centrifugal Bumble-puppy."

"But value dwells not in particular will," said the Savage. "It holds his estimate and dignity as well wherein 'tis precious of itself as in the prizer."

"Come, come," protested Mustapha Mond, "that's going rather far, isn't it?"

"If you allowed yourselves to think of God, you wouldn't allow yourselves to be degraded by pleasant vices. You'd have a reason for bearing things patiently, for doing things with courage. I've seen it with the Indians."

"I'm sure you have," said Mustapha Mond. "But then we aren't Indians. There isn't any need for a civilized man to bear anything that's seriously unpleasant. And as for doing things—Ford forbid that he should get the idea into his head. It would upset the whole social order if men started doing things on their own."

"What about self-denial, then? If you had a God, you'd have a reason for self-denial."

"But industrial civilization is only possible when there's no self-denial. Self-indulgence up to the very limits imposed by hygiene and economics. Otherwise the wheels stop turning."

"You'd have a reason for chastity!" said the Savage, blushing a little as he spoke the words.

"But chastity means passion, chastity means neurasthenia. And passion and neurasthenia mean instability. And instability means the end of civilization. You can't have a lasting civilization without plenty of pleasant vices."

"But God's the reason for everything noble and fine and heroic. If you had a God . . ."

"My dear young friend," said Mustapha Mond, "civilization has absolutely no need of nobility or heroism. These things are symptoms of political inefficiency. In a properly organized society like ours, nobody has any opportunities for being noble or heroic. Conditions have got to be thoroughly unstable before the occasion can arise. Where there are wars, where there are divided allegiances, where there are temptations to be resisted, objects of love to be fought for or defended—there, obviously, nobility and heroism have some sense. But there aren't any wars nowadays. The greatest care is taken to prevent you from loving any one too much. There's no such thing as a divided allegiance; you're so conditioned that you can't help doing what you ought to do. And what you ought to do is on the whole so pleasant, so many of the natural impulses are allowed free play, that there really aren't any temptations to resist. And if ever, by some unlucky chance, anything unpleasant should somehow happen, why, there's always *soma* to give you a holiday from the facts. And there's always *soma* to calm your anger, to reconcile you to your enemies, to make you patient and long-suffering. In the past you could only accomplish these things by making a great effort and after years of hard moral training. Now, you swallow two or three half-gramme tablets, and there you are. Anybody can be virtuous now. You can carry at least half your morality about in a bottle. Christianity without tears—that's what *soma* is."

"But the tears are necessary. Don't you remember what Othello said? 'If after every tempest came such calms, may the winds blow till they have wakened death.' There's a story one of the old Indians used to tell us, about the Girl of Mátaski. The young men who wanted to marry her had to do a morning's hoeing in her garden. It seemed easy; but there were flies and mosquitoes, magic ones. Most of the young men simply couldn't stand the biting and stinging. But the one that could—he got the girl."

"Charming! But in civilized countries," said the Controller, "you can have girls without hoeing for them; and there aren't any flies or mosquitoes to sting you. We got rid of them all centuries ago."

The Savage nodded, frowning. "You got rid of them. Yes, that's just like you. Getting rid of everything unpleasant instead of learning to put up with it. Whether 'tis better in the mind to suffer the slings and arrows of outrageous fortune, or to take arms against a sea of troubles and by opposing end them . . . But you don't do either. Neither suffer nor oppose. You just abolish the slings and arrows. It's too easy."

He was suddenly silent, thinking of his mother. In her room on the thirty-seventh floor, Linda had floated in a sea of singing lights and perfumed caresses—floated away, out of space, out of time, out of the prison of her memories, her habits, her aged and bloated body. And Tomakin, ex-Director of Hatcheries and Conditioning, Tomakin was still on holiday—on holiday from humiliation and pain, in a world where he could not hear those words, that derisive laughter, could not see that hideous face, feel those moist and flabby arms round his neck, in a beautiful world . . .

"What you need," the Savage went on, "is something *with* tears for a change. Nothing costs enough here."

("Twelve and a half million dollars," Henry Foster had protested when the Savage told him that. "Twelve and a half million—that's what the new Conditioning Centre cost. Not a cent less.")

"Exposing what is mortal and unsure to all that fortune, death and danger dare, even for an eggshell. Isn't there something in that?" he asked, looking up at Mustapha Mond. "Quite apart from God—though of course God would be a reason for it. Isn't there something in living dangerously?"

"There's a great deal in it," the Controller replied. "Men and women must have their adrenals stimulated from time to time."

"What?" questioned the Savage, uncomprehending.

"It's one of the conditions of perfect health. That's why we've made the V.P.S. treatments compulsory."

"V.P.S.?"

"Violent Passion Surrogate. Regularly once a month. We flood the whole system with adrenalin. It's the complete physiological equivalent of fear and rage. All the tonic effects of murdering Desdemona and being murdered by Othello, without any of the inconveniences."

"But I like the inconveniences."

"We don't," said the Controller. "We prefer to do things comfortably."

"But I don't want comfort. I want God, I want poetry, I want real danger, I want freedom, I want goodness. I want sin."

"In fact," said Mustapha Mond, "you're claiming the right to be unhappy."

"All right then," said the Savage defiantly, "I'm claiming the right to be unhappy."

"Not to mention the right to grow old and ugly and impotent; the right to have syphilis and cancer; the right to have too little to eat; the right to be lousy; the right to live in constant apprehension of what may happen to-morrow; the right to catch typhoid; the right to be tortured by unspeakable pains of every kind."

There was a long silence.

"I claim them all," said the Savage at last.

Mustapha Mond shrugged his shoulders. "You're welcome," he said.

The Alien from Milwaukee

By 1934, science fiction was settling into its niche, a comfortable corner in the local drugstore, a row in the pulp-laden rack at the occasional newsstand. What had seemed strikingly original in the late '20s was becoming traditional, and some ideas were beginning to seem outmoded or even worn out. Something new was demanded by readers, and anything new—like F. Orlin Tremaine's "thought variant" category in *Astounding*—automatically got some praise.

Fandom was becoming an influence. It had created itself out of the letter columns in the magazines as letter writers began to write each other. Where a community enjoyed more than a single fan—as in Philadelphia, New York and Los Angeles—a club was formed. They were usually clubs of readers, although the entry level into the magazines was sufficiently low that every reader could dream of becoming a writer.

The clubs began to issue magazines; in the developing argot of the fan movement, these became known as clubzines. Individual fans issued fanzines of varying degrees of quality in appearance and contents; sometimes the mail was their only contact with other fans. They solicited responses to their publishing efforts, and cherished—and often published in their next issue—these letters of comment (locs).

The earliest clubs organized themselves, but in 1934 Hugo Gernsback and Charles D. Hornig, the seventeen-year-old fan who had been named editor of Gernsback's *Wonder Stories* less than a year before, announced the creation of the Science Fiction League. The successes, failures, and power struggles of the early fan movement would fill several books—and have: Sam Moskowitz's *The Immortal Storm* (1954) and Harry Warner's *All Our Yesterdays* (1969) are the two major works, although a recent book, Damon Knight's *The Futurians* (1977), describes in detail one particular fan group in New York whose members went on to contribute significantly not only to the writing of science fiction (Asimov, Blish, Knight, Kornbluth, Merril, Pohl, Wilson) and its editing (Knight, Lowndes, Merril, Pohl, Shaw, Wollheim), but also its publishing (Kyle, Wollheim) and its agenting (Dockweiler, Kidd, Pohl, Shaw).

Fandom was an overheated teapot, boiling with its internal conflicts. An early debate, for instance, focused on whether a clubzine should emphasize science or science fiction; later in the '30s two factions battled over the issue of communism in fandom; and in 1939 a group of Futurians was excluded from the Moskowitz-organized first World Science Fiction Convention, in Manhattan.

But fandom also meant a force for greater sophistication in the fiction that was published, even if that meant that fans had to write the stories themselves. The appearance, then, of a story entitled "A Martian Odyssey" in the July 1934 issue of *Wonder Stories* was greeted with surprise and joy. It was over the name of an author nobody had heard of before because it was his first science-fiction story. He was Stanley Weinbaum (1902–1935), and he lived in Milwaukee, where he belonged to an organization of hopeful writers called the Fictioneers, which also included Raymond A. Palmer, Ralph Milne Farley (Roger Sherman Hoar), Arthur Tofte, and, a year later, Robert Bloch.

What fans saw in "A Martian Odyssey" was a certain ingenuity in plotting and some skill in dialog and characterization, but mostly sympathetically drawn aliens who were truly different from humans. They had different appearances, different cultures, different thought processes, even different biologies. Up to this time aliens had traced their origins to the drooling, tentacled, rubbery menaces that crawled out of H. G. Wells's Martian capsules. They were either dangerous enemies who wanted what humans had for reasons that humans could understand, or they were simply humans on other planets.

Weinbaum came to science fiction a bit late in life—in his short life, at least. He had earned a degree in chemical engineering from the University of Wisconsin in 1923, but made little use of his degree. He managed motion-picture theaters for a while, then tried writing novel-length romances, at least one of which was serialized by a newspaper syndicate.

In spite of the acclaim for "A Martian Odyssey," his stories weren't snapped up by the magazines, nor was his writing particularly remunerative. The magazines were paying only a penny a word at best, and they rejected several of Weinbaum's efforts to follow up his first success. Gradually, however, other stories began to appear: "Valley of Dreams," a sequel to "A Martian Odyssey" in *Wonder Stories;* "Flight on Titan," "Parasite Planet," and "The Lotus Eaters" in *Astounding.* All were stories of alien worlds and alien life forms.

Weinbaum broadened his repertoire to encompass such stories as the frequently reprinted (and dramatized) "The Adaptive Ultimate" and "Dawn of Flame" and "The Black Flame," published posthumously and later reprinted as a novel, *The Black Flame* (1948). But before the end of 1935 Weinbaum was dead of throat cancer, and his brief science-fiction career—numbered in a dozen or so stories rather than in novels—was over, only a year and a half after it had begun.

Weinbaum brought nothing new to space—his Mars was the Mars of Lowell and Burroughs, and his other planets reflected the best knowledge of science at that time, which since then has been proved incorrect in important ways. What he had to contribute was skillful writing with some effort at characterization, sometimes a light romantic aspect, and a plot in which everything revolved around the idea, not action. Most of all he created credible extraterrestrials who existed for their own reasons and convincing ecologies in which they could logically exist.

Isaac Asimov has written that there were three novas in science fiction, talents who burst like exploding stars upon the science-fiction scene and instantly captured the imaginations of the readers: E. E. Smith, Robert Heinlein, and Stanley Weinbaum. Weinbaum's brilliance may have been the greatest; certainly it was the shortest.

A Martian Odyssey

by Stanley G. Weinbaum

Jarvis stretched himself as luxuriously as he could in the cramped general quarters of the *Ares.*

"Air you can breathe!" he exulted. "It feels as thick as soup after the thin stuff out there!" He nodded at the Martian landscape stretching flat and desolate in the light of the nearer moon, beyond the glass of the port.

The other three stared at him sympathetically—Putz, the engineer, Leroy, the biologist, and Harrison, the astronomer and captain of the expedition. Dick Jarvis was chemist of the famous crew, the *Ares* expedition, first human beings to set foot on the mysterious neighbor of the earth, the planet Mars. This, of course, was in the old days, less than twenty years after the mad American Doheny perfected the atomic blast at the cost of his life, and only a decade after the equally mad Cardoza rode on it to the moon. They were true pioneers, these four of the *Ares*. Except for a half-dozen moon expeditions and the ill-fated de Lancey flight aimed at the seductive orb of Venus, they were the first men to feel other gravity than earth's, and certainly the first successful crew to leave the earth-moon system. And they deserved that success when one considers the difficulties and discomforts— the months spent in acclimatization chambers back on earth, learning to breathe the air as tenuous as that of Mars, the challenging of the void in the tiny rocket driven by the cranky reaction motors of the twenty-first century, and mostly the facing of an absolutely unknown world.

Jarvis stretched and fingered the raw and peeling tip of his frost-bitten nose. He sighed again contentedly.

"Well," exploded Harrison abruptly, "are we going to hear what happened? You set out all shipshape in an auxiliary rocket, we don't get a peep for ten days, and finally Putz here picks you out of a lunatic ant-heap with a freak ostrich as your pal! Spill it, man!"

"Speel?" queried Leroy perplexedly. "Speel what?"

"He means '*spiel*'," explained Putz soberly. "It iss to tell."

Jarvis met Harrison's amused glance without the shadow of a smile. 'That's right, Karl," he said in grave agreement with Putz. "*Ich spiel es!*" He grunted comfortably and began.

"According to orders," he said, "I watched Karl here take off toward the North, and then I got into my flying sweat-box and headed South. You'll remember, Cap—we had orders not to land, but just scout about for points of interest. I set the two cameras clicking and buzzed along, riding pretty high— about two thousand feet—for a couple of reasons. First, it gave the cameras a greater field, and second, the under-jets travel so far in this half-vacuum they call air here that they stir up dust if you move low."

"We know all that from Putz," grunted Harrison. "I wish you'd saved the films, though. They'd have paid the cost of this junket; remember how the public mobbed the first moon pictures?"

"The films are safe," retorted Jarvis. "Well," he resumed, "as I said, I buzzed along at a pretty good clip; just as we figured, the wings haven't much lift in the air at less than a hundred miles per hour, and even then I had to use the under-jets.

"So, with the speed and the altitude and the blurring caused by the under-jets, the seeing wasn't any too good. I could see enough, though, to distinguish that what I sailed over was just more of this grey plain that we'd been examining the whole week since our landing—same blobby growths and the same eternal carpet of crawling little planet-animals, or biopods, as Leroy calls them. So I sailed along, calling back my position every hour as instructed, and not knowing whether you heard me."

"I did!" snapped Harrison.

"A hundred and fifty miles south," continued Jarvis imperturbably, "the surface changed to a sort of low plateau, nothing but desert and orange-tinted sand. I figured that we were right in our guess, then, and this grey plain we dropped on was really the Mare Cimmerium which would make my orange desert the region called Xanthus. If I were right, I ought to hit another grey plain, the Mare Chronium, in another couple of hundred miles, and then another orange desert, Thyle I or II. And so I did."

"Putz verified our position a week and a half ago!" grumbled the captain. "Let's get to the point."

"Coming!" remarked Jarvis. "Twenty miles into Thyle—believe it or not—I crossed a canal!"

"Putz photographed a hundred! Let's hear something new!"

"And did he also see a city?"

"Twenty of 'em, if you call those heaps of mud cities!"

"Well," observed Jarvis, "from here on I'll be telling a few things Putz didn't see!" He rubbed his tingling nose, and continued. "I knew that I had sixteen hours of daylight at this season, so eight hours—eight hundred miles—from here, I decided to turn back. I was still over Thyle, whether I or II I'm not sure, not more than twenty-five miles into it. And right there, Putz's pet motor quit!"

"Quit? How?" Putz was solicitous.

"The atomic blast got weak. I started losing altitude right away, and suddenly there I was with a thump right in the middle of Thyle! Smashed my nose on the window, too!" He rubbed the injured member ruefully.

"Did you maybe try vashing der combustion chamber mit acid sulphuric?" inquired Putz. "Sometimes der lead giffs a secondary radiation—"

"Naw!" said Jarvis disgustedly. "I wouldn't try that, of course—not more than ten times! Besides, the bump flattened the landing gear and busted off the under-jets. Suppose I got the thing working—what then? Ten miles with the blast coming right out of the bottom and I'd have melted the floor from under me!" He rubbed his nose again. "Lucky for me a pound only weighs seven ounces here, or I'd have been mashed flat!"

"I could have fixed!" ejaculated the engineer. "I bet it was not serious."

"Probably not," agreed Jarvis sarcastically. "Only it wouldn't fly. Nothing serious, but I had the choice of waiting to be picked up or trying to walk back—eight hundred miles, and perhaps twenty days before we had to leave! Forty miles a day! Well," he concluded, "I chose to walk. Just as much chance of being picked up, and it kept me busy."

"We'd have found you," said Harrison.

"No doubt. Anyway, I rigged up a harness from some seat straps, and put the water tank on my back, took a cartridge belt and revolver, and some iron rations, and started out."

"Water tank!" exclaimed the little biologist, Leroy. "She weigh one-quarter ton!"

"Wasn't full. Weighed about two hundred and fifty pounds earthweight, which is eighty-five here. Then, besides, my own personal two hundred and ten pounds is only seventy on Mars, so, tank and all, I grossed a hundred and fifty-five, or fifty-five pounds less than my everyday earthweight. I figured on that when I undertook the forty-mile daily stroll. Oh—of course I took a thermo-skin sleeping bag for these wintry Martian nights.

"Off I went, bouncing along pretty quickly. Eight hours of daylight meant twenty miles or more. It got tiresome, of course —plugging along over a soft sand desert with nothing to see, not even Leroy's crawling biopods. But an hour or so brought me to the canal—just a dry ditch about four hundred feet wide, and straight as a railroad on its own company map.

"There'd been water in it sometime, though. The ditch was covered with what looked like a nice green lawn. Only, as I approached, the lawn moved out of my way!"

"Eh?" said Leroy.

"Yeah, it was a relative of your biopods. I caught one—a little grasslike blade about as long as my finger, with two thin, stemmy legs."

"He is where?" Leroy was eager.

"He is let go! I had to move, so I plowed along with the walking grass opening in front and closing behind. And then I was out on the orange desert of Thyle again.

"I plugged steadily along, cussing the sand that made going so tiresome, and, incidentally, cussing that cranky motor of yours, Karl. It was just before twilight that I reached the edge of Thyle, and looked down over the grey Mare Chronium. And I knew there was seventy-five miles of *that* to be walked over, and then a couple of hundred miles of that Xanthus desert, and about as much more Mare Cimmerium. Was I pleased? I started cussing you fellows for not picking me up!"

"We were trying, you sap!" said Harrison.

"That didn't help. Well, I figured I might as well use what was left of daylight in getting down the cliff that bounded Thyle. I found an easy place, and down I went. Mare Chronium was just the same sort of place as this—crazy leafless plants and a bunch of crawlers; I gave it a glance and hauled out my sleeping bag. Up to that time, you know, I hadn't seen anything worth worrying about on this half-dead world—nothing dangerous, that is."

"Did you?" queried Harrison.

"*Did I!* You'll hear about it when I come to it. Well, I was just about to turn in when suddenly I heard the wildest sort of shenanigans!"

"Vot iss shenanigans?" inquired Putz.

"He says, 'Je ne sais quoi'," explained Leroy. "It is to say, 'I don't know what'."

"That's right," agreed Jarvis. "I didn't know what, so I sneaked over to find out. There was a racket like a flock of crows eating a bunch of canaries—whistles, cackles, caws, trills, and what have you. I rounded a clump of stumps, and there was Tweel!"

"Tweel?" said Harrison, and "Tveel?" said Leroy and Putz.

"That freak ostrich," explained the narrator. "At least,

Tweel is as near as I can pronounce it without sputtering. He called it something like 'Trrrweerrlll'."

"What was he doing?" asked the captain.

"He was being eaten! And squealing, of course, as any one would."

"Eaten! By what?"

"I found out later. All I could see then was a bunch of black ropy arms tangled around what looked like, as Putz described it to you, an ostrich. I wasn't going to interfere, naturally; if both creatures were dangerous, I'd have one less to worry about.

"But the bird-like thing was putting up a good battle, dealing vicious blows with an eighteen-inch beak, between screeches. And besides, I caught a glimpse or two of what was on the end of those arms!" Jarvis shuddered. "But the clincher was when I noticed a little black bag or case hung about the neck of the bird-thing! It was intelligent! That or tame, I assumed. Anyway, it clinched my decision. I pulled out my automatic and fired into what I could see of its antagonist.

"There was a flurry of tentacles and a spurt of black corruption, and then the thing, with a disgusting sucking noise, pulled itself and its arms into a hole in the ground. The other let out a series of clacks, staggered around on legs about as thick as golf sticks, and turned suddenly to face me. I held my weapon ready, and the two of us stared at each other.

"The Martian wasn't a bird, really. It wasn't even birdlike, except just at first glance. It had a beak all right, and a few feathery appendages, but the beak wasn't really a beak. It was somewhat flexible; I could see the tip bend slowly from side to side; it was almost like a cross between a beak and a trunk. It had four-toed feet, and four-fingered things—hands, you'd have to call them, and a little roundish body, and a long neck ending in a tiny head—and that beak. It stood an inch or so taller than I, and—well, Putz saw it!"

The engineer nodded. "*Ja!* I saw!"

Jarvis continued. "So—we stared at each other. Finally the creature went into a series of clackings and twitterings and held out its hands toward me, empty. I took that as a gesture of friendship."

"Perhaps," suggested Harrison, "it looked at that nose of yours and thought you were its brother!"

"Huh! You can be funny without talking! Anyway, I put

up my gun and said 'Aw, don't mention it,' or something of the sort, and the thing came over and we were pals.

"By that time, the sun was pretty low and I knew that I'd better build a fire or get into my thermo-skin. I decided on the fire. I picked a spot at the base of the Thyle cliff where the rock could reflect a little heat on my back. I started breaking off chunks of this desiccated Martian vegetation, and my companion caught the idea and brought in an armful. I reached for a match, but the Martian fished into his pouch and brought out something that looked like a glowing coal; one touch of it, and the fire was blazing—and you all know what a job we have starting a fire in this atmosphere!

"And that bag of his!" continued the narrator. "That was a manufactured article, my friends; press an end and she popped open—press the middle and she sealed so perfectly you couldn't see the line. Better than zippers.

"Well, we stared at the fire for a while and I decided to attempt some sort of communication with the Martian. I pointed at myself and said 'Dick'; he caught the drift immediately, stretched a bony claw at me and repeated 'Tick.' Then I pointed at him, and he gave that whistle I called Tweel; I can't imitate his accent. Things were going smoothly; to emphasize the names, I repeated 'Dick,' and then, pointing at him, 'Tweel.'

'There we stuck! He gave some clacks that sounded negative, and said something like 'P-p-p-root.' And that was just the beginning; I was always 'Tick,' but as for him—part of the time he was 'Tweel,' and part of the time he was 'P-p-p-proot,' and part of the time he was sixteen other noises!

"We just couldn't connect. I tried 'rock,' and I tried 'star,' and 'tree,' and 'fire,' and Lord knows what else, and try as I would, I couldn't get a single word! Nothing was the same for two successive minutes, and if that's a language, I'm an alchemist! Finally I gave it up and called him Tweel, and that seemed to do.

"But Tweel hung on to some of my words. He remembered a couple of them, which I suppose is a great achievement if you're used to a language you have to make up as you go along. But I couldn't get the hang of his talk; either I missed some subtle point or we just didn't *think* alike—and I rather believe the latter view.

"I've other reasons for believing that. After a while I gave up the language business, and tried mathematics. I scratched two plus two equals four on the ground, and demonstrated it with pebbles. Again Tweel caught the idea, and informed me that three plus three equals six. Once more we seemed to be getting somewhere.

"So, knowing that Tweel had at least a grammar school education, I drew a circle for the sun, pointing first at it, and then at the last glow of the sun. Then I sketched in Mercury, and Venus, and Mother Earth, and Mars, and finally, pointing to Mars, I swept my hand around in a sort of inclusive gesture to indicate that Mars was our current environment. I was working up to putting over the idea that my home was on the earth.

"Tweel understood my diagram all right. He poked his beak at it, and with a great deal of trilling and clucking, he added Deimos and Phobos to Mars, and then sketched in the earth's moon!

"Do you see what that proves? It proves that Tweel's race uses telescopes—that they're civilized!"

"Does not!" snapped Harrison. "The moon is visible from here as a fifth magnitude star. They could see its revolution with the naked eye."

"The moon, yes!" said Jarvis. "You've missed my point. Mercury isn't visible! And Tweel knew of Mercury because he placed the Moon at the *third* planet, not the second. If he didn't know Mercury, he'd put the earth second, and Mars third, instead of fourth! See?"

"Humph!" said Harrison.

"Anyway," proceeded Jarvis, "I went on with my lesson. Things were going smoothly, and it looked as if I could put the idea over. I pointed at the earth on the diagram, and then at myself, and then, to clinch it, I pointed to myself and then to the earth itself shining bright green almost at the zenith.

"Tweel set up such an excited clacking that I was certain he understood. He jumped up and down, and suddenly he pointed at himself and then at the sky, and then at himself and at the sky again. He pointed at his middle and then at Arcturus, at his head and then at Spica, at his feet and then at half a dozen stars, while I just gaped at him. Then, all of a sudden, he gave a tremendous leap. Man, what a hop! He shot straight up into the starlight, seventy-five feet if an inch! I saw him silhouetted against the sky, saw him turn and come down at me head first, and land smack on his beak like a javelin! There he stuck square in the center of my sun-circle in the sand—a bull's eye!"

"Nuts!" observed the captain. "Plain nuts!"

"That's what I thought, too! I just stared at him open-mouthed while he pulled his head out of the sand and stood up. Then I figured he'd missed my point, and I went through the whole blamed rigamarole again, and it ended the same way, with Tweel on his nose in the middle of my picture!"

"Maybe it's a religious rite," suggested Harrison.

"Maybe," said Jarvis dubiously. "Well, there we were. We could exchange ideas up to a certain point, and then—blooey! Something in us was different, unrelated; I don't doubt that Tweel thought me just as screwy as I thought him. Our minds simply looked at the world from different viewpoints, and perhaps his viewpoint is as true as ours. But—we couldn't get together, that's all. Yet, in spite of all difficulties, I *liked* Tweel, and I have a queer certainty that he liked me."

"Nuts!" repeated the captain. "Just daffy!"

"Yeah? Wait and see. A couple of times I've thought that perhaps we—" He paused, and then resumed his narrative. "Anyway, I finally gave it up, and got into my thermo-skin to sleep. The fire hadn't kept me any too warm, but that damned sleeping bag did. Got stuffy five minutes after I closed myself in. I opened it a little and bingo! Some eighty-below-zero air hit my nose, and that's when I got this pleasant little frostbite to add to the bump I acquired during the crash of my rocket.

"I don't know what Tweel made of my sleeping. He sat around, but when I woke up, he was gone. I'd just crawled out of my bag, though, when I heard some twittering, and there he came, sailing down from that three-story Thyle cliff to alight on his beak beside me. I pointed to myself and toward the north, and he pointed at himself and toward the south, and when I loaded up and started away, he came along.

"Man, how he traveled! A hundred and fifty feet at a jump, sailing through the air stretched out like a spear, and landing on his beak. He seemed surprised at my plodding, but after a few moments he fell in beside me, only every few minutes he'd go into one of his leaps, and stick his nose into the sand a block ahead of me. Then he'd come shooting back at me; it made me nervous at first to see that beak of his coming at me like a spear, but he always ended in the sand at my side.

"So the two of us plugged along across the Mare Chronium. Same sort of place as this—same crazy plants and same little green biopods growing in the sand, or crawling out of your way. We talked—not that we understood each other, you know, but just for company. I sang songs, and I suspected Tweel did too; at least, some of his trillings and twitterings had a subtle sort of rhythm.

"Then, for variety, Tweel would display his smattering of English words. He'd point to an outcropping and say 'rock,' and point to a pebble and say it again; or he'd touch my arm and say 'Tick,' and then repeat it. He seemed terrifically amused that the same word meant the same thing twice in succession, or that the same word could apply to two different objects. It set me wondering if perhaps his language wasn't like the primitive speech of some earth people—you know, Captain, like the Negritoes, for instance, who haven't any generic words. No word for food or water or man—words for good food and bad food, or rain water and sea water, or strong man and weak man—but no names for general classes. They're too primitive to understand that rain water and sea water are just different aspects of the same thing. But that wasn't the case with Tweel; it was just that we were somehow mysteriously different—our minds were alien to each other. And yet—we *liked* each other!"

"Looney, that's all," remarked Harrison. "That's why you two were so fond of each other."

"Well, I like *you!*" countered Jarvis wickedly. "Anyway," he resumed, "don't get the idea that there was anything screwy about Tweel. In fact, I'm not so sure but that he couldn't teach our highly praised human intelligence a trick or two. Oh, he wasn't an intellectual superman, I guess; but don't overlook the point that he managed to understand a little of my mental workings, and I never even got a glimmering of his."

"Because he didn't have any!" suggested the captain, while Putz and Leroy blinked attentively.

"You can judge of that when I'm through," said Jarvis. "Well, we plugged along across the Mare Chronium all that day, and all the next. Mare Chronium—Sea of Time! Say, I was willing to agree with Schiaparelli's name by the end of that march! Just that grey, endless plain of weird plants, and never a sign of any other life. It was so monotonous that I was even glad to see the desert of Xanthus toward the evening of the second day.

"I was fair worn out, but Tweel seemed as fresh as ever, for all I never saw him drink or eat. I think he could have crossed the Mare Chronium in a couple of hours with those block-long nose dives of his, but he stuck along with me. I offered him some water once or twice; he took the cup from me and sucked the liquid into his beak, and then carefully squirted it all back into the cup and gravely returned it.

"Just as we sighted Xanthus, or the cliffs that bounded it, one of those nasty sand clouds blew along, not as bad as the one we had here, but mean to travel against. I pulled the transparent flap of my thermo-skin bag across my face and managed pretty well, and I noticed that Tweel used some feathery appendages growing like a mustache at the base of his beak to cover his nostrils, and some similar fuzz to shield his eyes."

"He is a desert creature!" ejaculated the little biologist, Leroy.

"Huh? Why?"

"He drink no water—he is adapt for sand storm—"

"Proves nothing! There's not enough water to waste any where on this desiccated pill called Mars. We'd call all of it desert on earth, you know." He paused. "Anyway, after the sand storm blew over, a little wind kept blowing in our faces, not strong enough to stir the sand. But suddenly things came drifting along from the Xanthus cliffs—small, transparent spheres, for all the world like glass tennis balls! But light—they were almost light enough to float even in this thin air—empty, too; at least, I cracked open a couple and nothing came out but a bad smell. I asked Tweel about them, but all he said was 'No, no no,' which I took to mean that he knew nothing about them. So they went bouncing by like tumbleweeds, or like soap bubbles, and we plugged on toward Xanthus. Tweel pointed at one of the crystal balls once and said 'rock,' but I was too tired to argue with him. Later I discovered what he meant.

"We came to the bottom of the Xanthus cliffs finally, when there wasn't much daylight left. I decided to sleep on the plateau if possible; anything dangerous, I reasoned, would be more likely to prowl through the vegetation of the Mare Chronium than the sand of Xanthus. Not that I'd seen a single sign of menace, except the rope-armed black thing that had trapped Tweel, and apparently that didn't prowl at all, but lured its victims within reach. It couldn't lure me while I slept, especially as Tweel didn't seem to sleep at all, but simply sat patiently around all night. I wondered how the creature had managed to trap Tweel, but there wasn't any way of asking him. I found that out too, later; it's devilish!

"However, we were ambling around the base of the Xanthus barrier looking for an easy spot to climb. At least, I was! Tweel could have leaped it easily, for the cliffs were lower than Thyle—perhaps sixty feet. I found a place and started up, swearing at the water tank strapped to my back—it didn't bother me except when climbing—and suddenly I heard a sound that I thought I recognized!

"You know how deceptive sounds are in this thin air. A shot sounds like the pop of a cork. But this sound was the drone of a rocket, and sure enough, there went our second auxiliary about ten miles to westward, between me and the sunset!"

"Vas me!" said Putz. "I hunt for you."

"Yeah; I knew that, but what good did it do me? I hung on to the cliff and yelled and waved with one hand. Tweel saw it too, and set up a trilling and twittering, leaping to the top of the barrier and then high into the air. And while I watched the machine droned on into the shadows to the south.

"I scrambled to the top of the cliff. Tweel was still pointing and trilling excitedly, shooting up toward the sky and coming down head-on to stick upside down on his back in the sand. I pointed toward the south, and at myself, and he said, 'Yes—Yes—Yes'; but somehow I gathered that he thought the flying thing was a relative of mine, probably a parent. Perhaps I did his intellect an injustice; I think now that I did.

"I was bitterly disappointed by the failure to attract attention. I pulled out my thermo-skin and crawled into it, as the night chill was already apparent. Tweel stuck his beak into the sand and drew up his legs and arms and looked for all the world like one of those leafless shrubs out there. I think he stayed that way all night."

"Protective mimicry!" ejaculated Leroy. "See? He is desert creature!"

"In the morning," resumed Jarvis, "we started off again. We hadn't gone a hundred yards into Xanthus when I saw something queer! This is one thing Putz didn't photograph, I'll wager!

"There was a line of little pyramids—tiny ones, not more than six inches high, stretching across Xanthus as far as I could see! Little buildings made of pygmy bricks, they were hollow inside and truncated, or at least broken at the top and empty. I pointed at them and said 'What?' to Tweel, but he gave some negative twitters to indicate, I suppose, that he didn't know. So off we went, following the row of pyramids because they ran north, and I was going north.

"Man we trailed that line for hours! After a while, I noticed another queer thing: they were getting larger. Same number of bricks in each one, but the bricks were larger.

"By noon they were shoulder high. I looked into a couple—all just the same, broken at the top and empty. I examined a brick or two as well; they were silica, and old as creation itself!"

"They were weathered—edges rounded. Silica doesn't weather easily even on earth, and in this climate—!"

"How old you think?"

"Fifty thousand—a hundred thousand years. How can I tell? The little ones we saw in the morning were older—perhaps ten times as old. Crumbling. How old would that make *them?* Half a million years? Who knows?" Jarvis paused a moment. "Well," he resumed, "we followed the line. Tweel pointed at them and said 'rock' once or twice, but he'd done that many times before. Besides, he was more or less right about these.

"I tried questioning him. I pointed at a pyramid and asked 'People?' and indicated the two of us. He set up a negative sort of clucking and said, 'No, no, no. No one-one-two. No two-two-four,' meanwhile rubbing his stomach. I just stared at him and he went through the business again. 'No one-one-two. No two-two-four.' I just gaped at him."

"That proves it!" exclaimed Harrison. "Nuts!"

"You think so?" queried Jarvis sardonically. "Well, I figured it out different! 'No one-one-two!' You don't get it, of course, do you?"

"Nope—nor do you!"

"I think I do! Tweel was using the few English words he knew to put over a very complex idea. What, let me ask, does mathematics make you think of?"

"Why—of astronomy. Or—or logic!"

"That's it! 'No one-one-two!' Tweel was telling me that the builders of the pyramids weren't people—or that they weren't intelligent, that they weren't reasoning creatures! Get it?"

"Huh! I'll be damned!"

"You probably will."

"Why," put in Leroy, "he rub his belly?"

"Why? Because, my dear biologist, that's where his brains are! Not in his tiny head—in his middle!"

"*C'est* impossible!"

"Not on Mars, it isn't! This flora and fauna aren't earthly; your biopods prove that!" Jarvis grinned and took up his narrative. "Anyway, we plugged along across Xanthus and in about the middle of the afternoon, something else queer happened. The pyramids ended."

"Ended!"

"Yeah; the queer part was that the last one—and now they were ten-footers—was capped! See? Whatever built it was still inside; we'd trailed 'em from their half-million-year-old origin to the present.

"Tweel and I noticed it about the same time. I yanked out my automatic (I had a clip of Boland explosive bullets in it) and Tweel, quick as a sleight-of-hand trick, snapped a queer little glass revolver out of his bag. It was much like our weapons, except that the grip was larger to accommodate his four-taloned hand. And we held our weapons ready while we sneaked up along the lines of empty pyramids.

"Tweel saw the movement first. The top tiers of bricks were heaving, shaking, and suddenly slid down the sides with a thin crash. And then—something—something was coming out!

"A long, silver-grey arm appeared, dragging after it an armored body. Armored, I mean, with scales, silver-grey and dull-shining. The arm heaved the body out of the hole; the beast crashed to the sand.

"It was a nondescript creature—body like a big grey cask, arm and a sort of mouth-hole at one end; stiff, pointed tail at the other—and that's all. No other limbs, no eyes, ears, nose—nothing! The thing dragged itself a few yards, inserted its pointed tail in the sand, pushed itself upright, and just sat.

"Tweel and I watched it for ten minutes before it moved. Then, with a creaking and rustling like—oh, like crumpling stiff paper—its arm moved to the mouth-hole and out came a brick! The arm placed the brick carefully on the ground, and the thing was still again.

"Another ten minutes—another brick. Just one of Nature's bricklayers. I was about to slip away and move on when Tweel pointed at the thing and said 'rock'! I went 'huh?' and he said it again. Then, to the accompaniment of some of his trilling, he said, 'No—no—,' and gave two or three whistling breaths.

"Well, I got his meaning, for a wonder! I said, 'No breathe?' and demonstrated the word. Tweel was ecstatic; he said, 'Yes, yes, yes! No, no, no breet!' Then he gave a leap and sailed out to land on his nose about one pace from the monster!

"I was startled, you can imagine! The arm was going up for a brick, and I expected to see Tweel caught and mangled, but—nothing happened! Tweel pounded on the creature, and the arm took the brick and placed it neatly beside the first. Tweel rapped on its body again, and said 'rock,' and I got up nerve enough to take a look myself.

"Tweel was right again. The creature *was* rock, and it didn't breathe!"

"How you know?" snapped Leroy, his black eyes blazing interest.

"Because I'm a chemist. The beast was made of silica! There must have been pure silicon in the sand, and it lived on that. Get it? We, and Tweel, and those plants out there, and even the biopods are *carbon* life; this thing lived by a different set of chemical reactions. It was silicon life!"

"*La vie silicieuse!*" shouted Leroy. "I have suspect, and now it is proof! I must go see! *Il faut que je—*"

"All right! All right!" said Jarvis. "You can go see. Anyhow, there the thing was, alive and yet not alive, moving every ten minutes, and then only to remove a brick. Those bricks were its waste matter. See, Frenchy? We're carbon, and our waste is carbon dioxide, and this thing is silicon and *its* waste is silicon dioxide—silica. But silica is a solid, hence the bricks. And it builds itself in, and when it is covered, it moves over to a fresh place to start over. No wonder it creaked! A living creature a half a million years old!"

"How you know how old?" Leroy was frantic.

"We trailed its pyramids from the beginning, didn't we? If this weren't the original pyramid builder, the series would have ended somewhere before we found him, wouldn't it?—ended and started over with the small ones. That's simple enough, isn't it?

"But he reproduces, or tries to. Before the third brick came out, there was a little rustle and out popped a whole stream of those little crystal balls. They're his spores, or seeds—call 'em what you want. They went bouncing by across Xanthus just as they'd bounced by us back in the Mare Chronium. I've a hunch how they work, too—this is for your information, Leroy. I think the crystal shell of silica is no more than protective covering, like an eggshell, and that the active principle is the smell inside. It's some sort of gas that attacks silicon, and if the shell is broken near a supply of that element, some reaction starts that ultimately develops into a beast like that one."

"You should try!" exclaimed the little Frenchman. "We must break one to see!"

"Yeah? Well, I did. I smashed a couple against the sand. Would you like to come back in about ten thousand years to see if I planted some pyramid monsters? You'd most likely be able to tell by that time!" Jarvis paused and drew a deep breath. "Lord! That queer creature! Do you picture it? Blind, deaf, nerveless, brainless—just a mechanism, and yet—immortal! Bound to go on making bricks, building pyramids, as long as silicon and oxygen exist, and even afterwards it'll just stop. It won't be dead. If the accidents of a million years bring it its food again, there it'll be, ready to run again, while brains and civilizations are part of the past. A queer beast—yet I met a stranger one!"

"If you did, it must have been in your dreams!" growled Harrison.

"You're right!" said Jarvis soberly. "In a way, you're right. The dream-beast! That's the best name for it—and it's the most fiendish, terrifying creation one could imagine! More dangerous than a lion, more insidious than a snake!"

"Tell me!" begged Leroy. "I must go see!"

"Not this devil!" He paused again. "Well," he resumed, "Tweel and I left the pyramid creature and plowed along through Xanthus. I was tired and a little disheartened by Putz's failure to pick me up, and Tweel's trilling got on my nerves, as did his flying nosedives. So I just strode along without a word, hour after hour across that monotonous desert.

"Toward mid-afternoon we came in sight of a low dark line on the horizon. I knew what it was. It was a canal; I'd crossed it in the rocket and it meant that we were just one-third of the way across Xanthus. Pleasant thought, wasn't it? And still, I was keeping up to schedule.

"We approached the canal slowly; I remembered that this one was bordered by a wide fringe of vegetation and that Mudheap City was on it.

"I was tired, as I said. I kept thinking of a good hot meal, and then from that I jumped to reflections of how nice and home-like even Borneo would seem after this crazy planet, and from that, to thoughts of little old New York, and then to thinking about a girl I know there—Fancy Long. Know her?"

"Vision entertainer," said Harrison. "I've tuned her in. Nice blonde—dances and sings on the *Yerba Mate* hour."

"That's her," said Jarvis ungrammatically. "I know her pretty well—just friends, get me?—though she came down to see us off in the *Ares*. Well, I was thinking about her, feeling pretty lonesome, and all the time we were approaching that line of rubbery plants.

"And then—I said, 'What 'n Hell!' and stared. And there she was—Fancy Long, standing plain as day under one of those crack-brained trees, and smiling and waving just the way I remembered her when we left!"

"Now you're nuts, too!" observed the captain.

"Boy, I almost agreed with you! I stared and pinched myself and closed my eyes and then stared again—and everytime, there was Fancy Long smiling and waving! Tweel saw something, too; he was trilling and clucking away, but I scarcely heard him. I was bounding toward her over the sand, too amazed even to ask myself questions.

"I wasn't twenty feet from her when Tweel caught me with one of his flying leaps. He grabbed my arm, yelling, 'No—no—no!' in his squeaky voice. I tried to shake him off—he was as light as if he were built of bamboo—but he dug his claws in and yelled. And finally some sort of sanity returned to me and I stopped less than ten feet from her. There she stood, looking as solid as Putz's head!"

"Vot?" said the engineer.

"She smiled and waved, and waved and smiled, and I stood there dumb as Leroy, while Tweel squeaked and chattered. I *knew* it couldn't be real, yet—there she was!

"Finally I said, 'Fancy! Fancy Long!' She just kept on smiling and waving, but looking as real as if I hadn't left her thirty-seven million miles away.

"Tweel had his glass pistol out, pointing it at her. I grabbed his arm, but he tried to push me away. He pointed at her and said, 'No breet! No breet!' and I understood that he meant that the Fancy Long thing wasn't alive. Man, my head was whirling!

"Still, it gave me the jitters to see him pointing his weapon at her. I don't know why I stood there watching him take careful aim, but I did. Then he squeezed the handle of his weapon; there was a little puff of steam, and Fancy Long was gone! And in her place was one of those writhing, black rope-armed horrors like the one I'd saved Tweel from!

"The dream-beast! I stood there dizzy, watching it die

while Tweel trilled and whistled. Finally he touched my arm, pointed at the twisting thing, and said, 'You one-one-two, he one-one-two.' After he'd repeated it eight or ten times, I got it. Do any of you?"

"*Oui!*" shrilled Leroy. "*Moi—je le comprends!* He mean you think of something, the beast he know, and you see it! *Un chien*—a hungry dog, he would see the big bone with meat! Or smell it—not?"

"Right!" said Jarvis. "The dream-beast uses its victim's longings and desires to trap its prey. The bird at nesting season would see its mate, the fox, prowling for its own prey, would see a helpless rabbit!"

"How he do?" queried Leroy.

"How do I know? How does a snake back on earth charm a bird into its very jaws? And aren't there deep-sea fish that lure their victims into their mouths? Lord!" Jarvis shuddered, "Do you see how insidious the monster is? We're warned now—but henceforth we can't trust even our eyes. You might see me—I might see one of you—and back of it may be nothing but another of those black horrors!"

"How'd your friend know?" asked the captain abruptly.

"Tweel? I wonder! Perhaps he was thinking of something that couldn't possibly have interested me, and when I started to run, he realized that I saw something different and was warned. Or perhaps the dream-beast can only project a single vision, and Tweel saw what I saw—or nothing. I couldn't ask him. But it's just another proof that his intelligence is equal to ours or greater."

"He's daffy, I tell you!" said Harrison. "What makes you think his intellect ranks with the human?"

"Plenty of things! First the pyramid-beast. He hadn't seen one before; he said as much. Yet he recognized it as a dead-alive automaton of silicon."

"He could have heard of it," objected Harrison. "He lives around here, you know."

"Well how about the language? I couldn't pick up a single idea of his and he learned six or seven words of mine. And do you realize what complex ideas he put over with no more than those six or seven words? The pyramid-monster—the dream-beast! In a single phrase he told me that one was a harmless automaton and the other a deadly hypnotist. What about that?"

"Huh!" said the captain.

"*Huh* if you wish! Could you have done it knowing only

six words of English? Could you go even further, as Tweel did, and tell me that another creature was of a sort of intelligence so different from ours that understanding was impossible—even more impossible than that between Tweel and me?"

"Eh? What was that?"

"Later. The point I'm making is that Tweel and his race are worthy of our friendship. Somewhere on Mars—and you'll find I'm right—is a civilization and culture equal to ours, and maybe more than equal. And communication is possible between them and us; Tweel proves that. It may take years of patient trial, for their minds are alien, but less alien than the next minds we encountered—if they *are* minds."

"The next ones? What next ones?"

"The people of the mud cities along the canals." Jarvis frowned, then resumed his narrative. "I thought the dream-beast and the silicon-monster were the strangest beings conceivable, but I was wrong. These creatures are still more alien, less understandable than either and far less comprehensible than Tweel, with whom friendship is possible, and even, by patience and concentration, the exchange of ideas.

"Well," he continued, "we left the dream-beast dying, dragging itself back into its hole, and we moved toward the canal. There was a carpet of that queer walking-grass scampering out of our way, and when we reached the bank, there was a yellow trickle of water flowing. The mound city I'd noticed from the rocket was a mile or so to the right and I was curious enough to want to take a look at it.

"It had seemed deserted from my previous glimpse of it, and if any creatures were lurking in it—well, Tweel and I were both armed. And by the way, that crystal weapon of Tweel's was an interesting device; I took a look at it after the dream-beast episode. It fired a little glass splinter, poisoned, I suppose, and I guess it held at least a hundred of 'em to a load. The propellant was steam—just plain steam!"

"Shteam!" echoed Putz. "From vot come, shteam?"

"From water, of course! You could see the water through the transparent handle and about a gill of another liquid, thick and yellowish. When Tweel squeezed the handle—there was no trigger—a drop of water and a drop of the yellow stuff squirted into the firing chamber, and the water vaporized—pop!—like that. It's not so difficult; I think we could develop the same principle. Concentrated sulphuric acid will heat water almost to boiling, and so will quicklime, and there's potassium and sodium—

"Of course, his weapon hadn't the range of mine, but it wasn't so bad in this thin air, and it *did* hold as many shots as a cowboy's gun in a Western movie. It was effective, too, at least against Martian life; I tried it out, aiming at one of the crazy plants, and darned if the plant didn't wither up and fall apart! That's why I think the glass splinters were poisoned.

"Anyway, we trudged along toward the mud-heap city and I began to wonder whether the city builders dug the canals. I pointed to the city and then at the canal, and Tweel said 'No—no—no!' and gestured toward the south. I took it to mean that some other race had created the canal system, perhaps Tweel's people. I don't know; maybe there's still another intelligent race on the planet, or a dozen others. Mars is a queer little world.

"A hundred yards from the city we crossed a sort of road—just a hard-packed mud trail, and then, all of a sudden, along came one of the mound builders!

"Man, talk about fantastic beings! It looked rather like a barrel trotting along on four legs with four other arms or tentacles. It had no head, just body and members and a row of eyes completely around it. The top end of the barrel-body was a diaphragm stretched as tight as a drum head, and that was all. It was pushing a little coppery cart and tore right past us like the proverbial bat out of Hell. It didn't even notice us, although I thought the eyes on my side shifted a little as it passed.

"A moment later another came along, pushing another empty cart. Same thing—it just scooted past us. Well, I wasn't going to be ignored by a bunch of barrels playing train, so when the third one approached, I planted myself in the way—ready to jump, of course, if the thing didn't stop.

"But it did. It stopped and set up a sort of drumming from the diaphragm on top. And I held out both hands and said, 'We are friends!' And what do you suppose the thing did?"

"Said, 'Pleased to meet you,' I'll bet!" suggested Harrison.

"I couldn't have been more surprised if it had! It drummed on its diaphragm, and then suddenly boomed out, 'We are v-r-r-iends!' and gave its pushcart a vicious poke at me! I jumped aside, and away it went while I stared dumbly after it.

"A minute later another one came hurrying along. This

one didn't pause, but simply drummed out, 'We are
v-r-r-iends!' and scurried by. How did it learn the phrase?
Were all of the creatures in some sort of communication with
each other? Were they all parts of some central organism? I
don't know, though I think Tweel does.

"Anyway, the creatures went sailing past us, every one
greeting us with the same statement. It got to be funny; I
never thought to find so many friends on this Godforsaken
ball! Finally I made a puzzled gesture to Tweel; I guess he
understood, for he said, 'One-one-two—yes!—two-two-four
—no!' Get it?"

"Sure," said Harrison. "It's a Martian nursery rhyme."

"Yeah! Well, I was getting used to Tweel's symbolism, and
I figured it out this way. 'One-one-two—yes!' The creatures
were intelligent. 'Two-two-four—no!' Their intelligence was
not of our order, but something different and beyond the
logic of two and two is four. Maybe I missed his meaning.
Perhaps he meant that their minds were of low degree, able
to figure out the simple things—'One-one-two—yes!'—but not
more difficult things—'Two-two-four—no!' But I think from
what we saw later that he meant the other.

"After a few moments, the creatures came rushing back—
first one, then another. Their pushcarts were full of stones,
sand, chunks of rubbery plants, and such rubbish as that.
They droned out their friendly greeting, which didn't really
sound so friendly, and dashed on. The third one I assumed to
be my first acquaintance and I decided to have another chat
with him. I stepped into his path again and waited.

"Up he came, booming out his 'We are v-r-r-riends' and
stopped. I looked at him; four or five of his eyes looked at
me. He tried his password again and gave a shove on his cart
but I stood firm. And then the—the dashed creature reached
out one of his arms, and two finger-like nippers tweaked my
nose!"

"Haw!" roared Harrison. "Maybe the things have a sense of
beauty!"

"Laugh!" grumbled Jarvis. "I'd already had a nasty bump
and a mean frostbite on that nose. Anyway, I yelled 'Ouch!'
and jumped aside and the creature dashed away; but from
then on, their greeting was 'We are v-r-r-riends! Ouch!' Queer
beasts!

"Tweel and I followed the road squarely up to the nearest
mound. The creatures were coming and going, paying us not
the slightest attention, fetching their loads of rubbish. The

road simply dived into an opening, and slanted down like an old mine, and in and out darted the barrel-people, greeting us with their eternal phrase.

"I looked in; there was a light somewhere below, and I was curious to see it. It didn't look like a flame or torch, you understand, but more like a civilized light, and I thought that I might get some clue as to the creatures' development. So in I went and Tweel tagged along, not without a few trills and twitters, however.

"The light was curious; it sputtered and flared like an old arc light, but came from a single black rod set in the wall of the corridor. It was electric, beyond doubt. The creatures were fairly civilized, apparently.

"Then I saw another light shining on something that glittered and I went on to look at that, but it was only a heap of shiny sand. I turned toward the entrance to leave, and the Devil take me if it wasn't gone!

"I supposed the corridor had curved, or I'd stepped into a side passage. Anyway, I walked back in that direction I thought we'd come, and all I saw was more dim-lit corridor. The place was a labyrinth! There was nothing but twisting passages running every way, lit by occasional lights, and now and then a creature running by, sometimes with a pushcart, sometimes without.

"Well, I wasn't much worried at first. Tweel and I had only come a few steps from the entrance. But every move we made after that seemed to get us in deeper. Finally I tried following one of the creatures with an empty cart, thinking that he'd be going out for his rubbish, but he ran around aimlessly, into one passage and out another. When he started dashing around a pillar like one of these Japanese waltzing mice, I gave up, dumped my water tank on the floor, and sat down.

"Tweel was as lost as I. I pointed up and he said 'No—no—no!' in a sort of helpless trill. And we couldn't get any help from the natives. They paid no attention at all, except to assure us they were friends—ouch!

"Lord! I don't know how many hours or days we wandered around there! I slept twice from sheer exhaustion; Tweel never seemed to need sleep. We tried following only the upward corridors, but they'd run uphill a ways and then curve downwards. The temperature in that damned ant hill was constant; you couldn't tell night from day and after my first sleep I didn't know whether I'd slept one hour or thirteen, so

I couldn't tell from my watch whether it was midnight or noon.

"We saw plenty of strange things. There were machines running in some of the corridors, but they didn't seem to be doing anything—just wheels turning. And several times I saw two barrel-beasts with a little one growing between them, joined to both."

"Parthenogenesis!" exulted Leroy. "Parthenogenesis by budding like *les tulipes!*"

"If you say so, Frenchy," agreed Jarvis. "The things never noticed us at all, except, as I say, to greet us with 'We are v-r-r-riends! Ouch!' They seemed to have no homelife of any sort, but just scurried around with their pushcarts, bringing in rubbish. And finally I discovered what they did with it.

"We'd had a little luck with a corridor, one that slanted upwards for a great distance. I was feeling that we ought to be close to the surface when suddenly the passage debouched into a domed chamber, the only one we'd seen. And man!—I felt like dancing when I saw what looked like daylight through a crevice in the roof.

"There was a—a sort of machine in the chamber, just an enormous wheel that turned slowly, and one of the creatures was in the act of dumping his rubbish below it. The wheel ground it with a crunch—sand, stones, plants, all into powder that sifted away somewhere. While we watched, others filed in, repeating the process, and that seemed to be all. No rhyme nor reason to the whole thing—but that's characteristic of this crazy planet. And there was another fact that's almost too bizarre to believe.

"One of the creatures, having dumped his load, pushed his cart aside with a crash and calmly shoved himself under the wheel! I watched him being crushed, too stupefied to make a sound, and a moment later, another followed him! They were perfectly methodical about it, too; one of the cartless creatures took the abandoned pushcart.

"Tweel didn't seem surprised; I pointed out the next suicide to him, and he just gave the most human-like shrug imaginable, as much as to say, 'What can I do about it?' He must have known more or less about these creatures.

"Then I saw something else. There was something beyond the wheel, something shining on a sort of low pedestal. I walked over; there was a little crystal about the size of an egg, fluorescing to beat Tophet. The light from it stung my hands and face, almost like a static discharge, and then I noticed another funny thing. Remember that wart I had on my left thumb? Look!" Jarvis extended his hand. "It dried up and fell off—just like that! And my abused nose—say, the pain went out of it like magic! The thing had the property of hard ex-rays of gamma radiations, only more so; it destroyed diseased tissue and left healthy tissue unharmed!

"I was thinking what a present *that'd* be to take back to Mother Earth when a lot of racket interrupted. We dashed back to the other side of the wheel in time to see one of the pushcarts ground up. Some suicide had been careless, it seems.

"Then suddenly the creatures were booming and drumming all round us and their noise was decidedly menacing. A crowd of them advanced toward us; we backed out of what I thought was the passage we'd entered by, and they came rumbling after us, some pushing carts and some not. Crazy brutes! There was a whole chorus of 'We are v-r-r-riends! Ouch!' I didn't like the 'ouch'; it was rather suggestive.

"Tweel had his glass gun out and I dumped my water tank for greater freedom and got mine. We backed up the corridor with the barrel-beasts following—about twenty of them. Queer thing—the ones coming in with loaded carts moved past us inches away without a sign.

"Tweel must have noticed that. Suddenly, he snatched out that glowing cigar-lighter of his and touched a cart-load of plant limbs. Puff! The whole load was burning—and the crazy beast pushing it went right along without a change of pace! It created some disturbance among our 'v-r-r-riends,' however—and then I noticed the smoke eddying and swirling past us, and sure enough, there was the entrance!

"I grabbed Tweel and out we dashed and after us our twenty pursuers. The daylight felt like Heaven, though I saw at first glance that the sun was all but set, and that was bad, since I couldn't live outside my thermo-skin bag in a Martian night—at least, without a fire.

"And things got worse in a hurry. They cornered us in an angle between two mounds, and there we stood. I hadn't fired nor had Tweel; there wasn't any use in irritating the brutes. They stopped a little distance away and began their booming about friendship and ouches.

"Then things got still worse! A barrel-brute came out with a pushcart and they all grabbed into it and came out with handfuls of foot-long copper darts—sharp-looking ones—and all of a sudden one sailed past my ear—zing! And it was shoot or die then.

"We were doing pretty well for a while. We picked off the ones next to the pushcart and managed to keep the darts at a minimum, but suddenly there was a thunderous booming of 'v-r-r-riends' and 'ouches,' and a whole army of 'em came out of their hole.

"Man! We were through and I knew it! Then I realized that Tweel wasn't. He could have leaped the mound behind us as easily as not. He was staying for me!

"Say, I could have cried if there'd been time! I'd liked Tweel from the first, but whether I'd have had gratitude to do what he was doing—suppose I *had* saved him from the first dream-beast—he'd done as much for me, hadn't he? I grabbed his arm, and said 'Tweel,' and pointed up, and he understood. He said, 'No—no—no, Tick!' and popped away with his glass pistol.

"What could I do? I'd be a goner anyway when the sun set, but I couldn't explain that to him. I said, 'Thanks, Tweel, You're a man!' and felt that I wasn't paying him any compliment at all. A man! There are mighty few men who'd do that.

"So I went 'bang' with my gun and Tweel went 'puff' with his, and the barrels were throwing darts and getting ready to rush us, and booming about being friends. I had given up hope. Then suddenly an angel dropped right down from Heaven in the shape of Putz, with his underjets blasting the barrels into very small pieces!

"Wow! I let out a yell and dashed for the rocket; Putz opened the door and in I went, laughing and crying and shouting! It was a moment or so before I remembered Tweel; I looked around in time to see him rising in one of his nosedives over the mound and away.

"I had a devil of a job arguing Putz into following! By the time we got the rocket aloft, darkness was down; you know how it comes here—like turning off a light. We sailed out over the desert and put down once or twice. I yelled 'Tweel!' and yelled it a hundred times, I guess. We couldn't find him; he could travel like the wind and all I got—or else I imagined it—was a faint trilling and twittering drifting out of the south. He'd gone, and damn it! I wish—I wish he hadn't!"

The four men of the *Ares* were silent—even the sardonic Harrison. At last Leroy broke the stillness.

"I should like to see," he murmured.

"Yeah," said Harrison. "And the wart-cure. Too bad you missed that; it might be the cancer cure they've been hunting for a century and a half."

"Oh, that!" muttered Jarvis gloomily. "That's what started the fight!" He drew a glistening object from his pocket.

"Here it is."

Who Went There?

The history of the physical sciences in the first half of the twentieth century might be summed up as the expansion of the very large and the subdivision of the very small.

In 1918, Harlow Shapley announced that earth's local galaxy, the Milky Way, was ten times larger than previously believed; a bit later the size, somewhat reduced, was estimated as 25,000 by 100,000 light-years. In 1924, Edwin F. Hubble proved the existence of other galaxies. In the process the earth, which for millennia had been considered the center of the universe, and its solar system, which for centuries had been considered virtually unique, were shunted to a peripheral location in one of its galaxy's spiral arms, and the Milky Way was diminished to only one of billions of galaxies in the universe, some of them a billion light-years away from the sun and at the edges of perception hurtling away at nearly the speed of light.

At the same time the atom, which once had been pictured as the irreducible form of matter, was being shattered into smaller and smaller particles for whose behavior new laws had to be discovered. Thomson's discovery of the electron in 1896 was followed by Rutherford's discovery of the nature of radioactive disintegration in 1904, Gockel's discovery of cosmic rays in 1910, and Coolidge's development of the x-ray tube and Bohr's model of the planetary atom in 1913. Between 1924 and 1926, De Broglie and Schroedinger announced their theory of wave mechanics in atomic theory, and Heisinger, his quantum mechanics. Lawrence built the first cyclotron in 1930, Pauli postulated the neutrino in 1931, and in 1932 Chadwick discovered the neutron and Anderson the positron. In 1934, Fermi began the creation of transuranic elements, and in 1938, Meitner, Hahn, and Strassman announced the nuclear fission of uranium.

In this expanding universe where even the reality of the matter in it was dissolving away, humanity was displaced from its unique role at the center of creation to a position not much different from that of the ant or the microbe. In the '30s, this reduction in importance was reinforced by the failure of humanity to control its own institutions in the Depression and its inability to cope with the weather that created the Dust Bowl.

Two forces, then, worked from different directions to propel the imaginations of science-fiction writers into space: the diminution in the status of humanity demanded correction—if people were less significant, they needed to grow larger in ambition and courage and ability to cope with these greater challenges; and the ingenuity of science in perceiving the obscure suggested the capacity of humanity to master it.

Stories had been written about atomic energy, and even atomic warfare, since H. G. Wells's *The World Set Free* (1914). Now, as science began to decipher the structure of the atom and the nature of the radioactive process, such stories appeared in the magazines with increasing frequency.

Stories about spaceflight had been around much longer, since Lucian of Samosata's "A True Story" (c. A.D. 165-175). They began to be published with more conviction in the early adventure pulp magazines. The preferred method for getting to another planet or another star, however, was astral projection, the way Burroughs's John Carter got to Mars or Giesy's Jason Croft got to Sirius. Then, in 1928, *Weird Tales* serialized Edmond Hamilton's *Crashing Suns* and *Amazing Stories* published Edward Elmer Smith's novel *The Skylark of Space.* When Burroughs sent Carson Napier to Venus (he started for Mars but ended up on Venus because the moon threw him off course) in *Pirates of Venus* (1934, magazine serial 1932), he sent him in a spaceship.

This new genre of stories was built upon the assumption that humanity would conquer space through science and engineering—not by spirit but by machine. Once into space, the stories went on, man would conquer his solar system and then expand into the galaxy, meeting physical problems and alien threats, sometimes setting up an empire, which had to be governed and policed.

Hamilton wrote a series of stories about a Council of Suns and an Interstellar Patrol. Smith (1890-1965) wrote a series of novels (seldom anything shorter) in which good and evil usually battled for control of the universe: first in the *Skylark* tetralogy, then in a six-volume series named after its major character, the *Lensman.*

Smith became a fan favorite, and the fan publishing movement that got going after World War II seemed to be motivated mostly by a desire to reprint Doc Smith's space operas: the *Lensman* series, for instance, was published by Fantasy Press in a uniform boxed set under the title *The History of Civilization*. But a young writer who sold stories to *Amazing Stories* while still a student at M.I.T. soon challenged Smith for the affections of the fans.

John W. Campbell, Jr. (1910–1971), had two stories published in *Amazing* in 1930. The fact has frequently been noted, as one of life's curious coincidences, that his first story appeared the same month as the first issue of *Astounding Stories*, a magazine with which he would be intimately associated.

Campbell flunked out of M.I.T. because he couldn't pass German, completed a degree in physics a year later at Duke University, and tried to make a living at various jobs during the difficult early years of the Depression, including one six-month period writing technical literature and editing texts for Carleton Ellis. But he kept up his output of fiction, and contributed a series of monthly articles on astronomy to *Astounding*.

For the first few years Campbell specialized in space opera. By 1934, when his first novel, *The Mightiest Machine*, was serialized in *Astounding*, he was ranked by many as Smith's equal in these far-flung romances. But even before *The Mightiest Machine* reached print, Campbell had begun to work on a different kind of story, less frantic, more poetic, more concerned with sociology, psychology, and philosophy than with astronomy and physics. These stories were at the same time more realistic in their portrayal of the scientific culture and more romantic in their treatment of ultimate themes. The first of these, "Twilight," was published in *Astounding* under the pseudonym Don A. Stuart the month before *The Mightiest Machine* began.

Campbell followed "Twilight" with a series of stories similar in style and quality. By 1937 the name of Stuart (taken from the maiden name of his first wife) was more admired by discriminating readers than Campbell's own. One of the classic novelettes of science fiction, "Who Goes There?" was published under the Stuart byline in 1938 and later became the basis for a badly mauled film adaptation, "The Thing" (1951).

By 1937, however, Campbell had been hired as the editor of *Astounding*, and within a year his own fiction writing was

virtually over, at the age of twenty-eight. From then on his
energies would be devoted to getting from other authors the
kind of science fiction he wanted. In the role of author he
had marked one transition in science fiction; in the role of
editor he would guide the next.

Twilight

by John W. Campbell

"Speaking of hitch-hikers," said Jim Bendell in a rather bewildered way, "I picked up a man the other day that certainly was a queer cuss." He laughed, but it wasn't a real
laugh. "He told me the queerest yarn I ever heard. Most of
them tell you how they lost their good jobs and tried to find
work out here in the wide spaces of the West. They don't
seem to realize how many people we have out here. They
think all this great beautiful country is uninhabited."

Jim Bendell's a real estate man, and I knew how he could
go on. That's his favorite line, you know. He's real worried
because there's a lot of homesteading plots still open out in
our state. He talks about the beautiful country, but he never
went further into the desert than the edge of town. 'Fraid of
it actually. So I sort of steered him back on the track.

"What did he claim, Jim? Prospector who couldn't find
land to prospect?"

"That's not very funny, Bart. No; it wasn't only what he
claimed. He didn't even claim it, just said it. You know, he
didn't say it was true, he just said it. That's what gets me. I
know it ain't true, but the way he said it—Oh, I don't know."

By which I knew he didn't. Jim Bendell's usually pretty
careful about his English—real proud of it. When he slips,
that means he's disturbed. Like the time he thought the rat-
tlesnake was a stick of wood and wanted to put it on the fire.

Jim went on: And he had funny clothes, too. They looked
like silver, but they were soft as silk. And at night they
glowed just a little.

I picked him up about dusk. Really picked him up. He was
lying off about ten feet from the South Road. I thought, at

first, somebody had hit him, and then hadn't stopped. Didn't see him very clearly, you know. I picked him up, put him in the car, and started on. I had about three hundred miles to go, but I thought I could drop him at Warren Spring with Doc Vance. But he came to in about five minutes, and opened his eyes. He looked straight off, and he looked first at the car, then at the Moon. "Thank God!" he says, and then looks at me. It gave me a shock. He was beautiful. No; he was handsome.

He wasn't either one. He was magnificent. He was about six feet two, I think, and his hair was brown, with a touch of red-gold. It seemed like fine copper wire that's turned brown. It was crisp and curly. His forehead was wide, twice as wide as mine. His features were delicate, but tremendously impressive; his eyes were gray, like etched iron, and bigger than mine—a lot.

That suit he wore—it was more like a bathing suit with pajama trousers. His arms were long and muscled smoothly as an Indian's. He was white, though, tanned lightly with a golden, rather than a brown, tan.

But he was magnificent. Most beautiful man I ever saw. I don't know, damn it!

"Hello!" I said. "Have an accident?"

"No; not this time, at least."

And his voice was magnificent, too. It wasn't an ordinary voice. It sounded like an organ talking, only it was human.

"But maybe my mind isn't quite steady yet. I tried an experiment. Tell me what the date is, year and all, and let me see," he went on.

"Why—December 9, 1932," I said.

And it didn't please him. He didn't like it a bit. But the wry grin that came over his face gave way to a chuckle.

"Over a thousand—" he says reminiscently. "Not as bad as seven million. I shouldn't complain."

"Seven million what?"

"Years," he said, steadily enough. Like he meant it. "I tried an experiment once. Or I will try it. Now I'll have to try again. The experiment was—in 3059. I'd just finished the release experiment. Testing space then. Time—it wasn't that, I still believe. It was space. I felt myself caught in that field, but I couldn't pull away. Field gamma-H 481, intensity 935 in the Pellman range. It sucked me in, and I went out.

"I think it took a short cut through space to the position the solar system will occupy. Through a higher dimension, effecting a speed exceeding light and throwing me into the future plane."

He wasn't telling me, you know. He was just thinking out loud. Then he began to realize I was there.

"I couldn't read their instruments, seven million years of evolution changed everything. So I overshot my mark a little coming back. I belong in 3059.

"But tell me, what's the latest scientific invention of this year?"

He startled me so, I answered almost before I thought.

"Why, television, I guess. And radio and airplanes."

"Radio—good. They will have instruments."

"But see here—who are you?"

"Ah—I'm sorry. I forgot," he replied in that organ voice of his. "I am Ares Sen Kenlin. And you?"

"James Waters Bendell."

"Waters—what does that mean? I do not recognize it."

"Why—it's a name, of course. Why should you recognize it?"

"I see—you have not the classification, then. 'Sen' stands for science."

"Where did you come from, Mr. Kenlin?"

"Come from?" He smiled, and his voice was slow and soft. "I came out of space across seven million years or more. They had lost count—the men had. The machines had eliminated the unneeded service. They didn't know what year it was. But before that—my home is in Neva'th City in the year 3059."

That's when I began to think he was a nut.

"I was an experimenter," he went on. "Science, as I have said. My father was a scientist, too, but in human genetics. I myself experiment. He proved his point, and all the world followed suit. I was the first of the new race.

"The new race—oh, holy destiny—what has—what will—

"What is its end? I have seen it—almost. I saw them—the little men—bewildered—lost. And the machines. Must it be—can't anything sway it?

"Listen—I heard this song."

He sang the song. Then he didn't have to tell me about the people. I knew them. I could hear their voices, in the queer, crackling, un-English words. I could read their bewildered longings. It was in a minor key, I think. It called, it called and asked, and hunted hopelessly. And over it all the steady rumble and whine of the unknown, forgotten machines.

The machines that couldn't stop, because they had been started, and the little men had forgotten how to stop them, or even what they were for, looking at them and listening—and wondering. They couldn't read or write any more, and the language had changed, you see, so that the phonic records of their ancestors meant nothing to them.

But that song went on, and they wondered. And they looked out across space and they saw the warm, friendly stars—too far away. Nine planets they knew and inhabited. And locked by infinite distance, they couldn't see another race, a new life.

And through it all—two things. The machines. Bewildered forgetfulness. And maybe one more. Why?

That was the song, and it made me cold. It shouldn't be sung around people of today. It almost killed something. It seemed to kill hope. After that song—I—well, I believed him.

When he finished the song, he didn't talk for a while. Then he sort of shook himself.

You won't understand (he continued). Not yet—but I have seen them. They stand about, like misshapen men with huge heads. But their heads contain only brains. They had machines that could think—but somebody turned them off a long time ago, and no one knew how to start them again. That was the trouble with them. They had wonderful brains. Far better than yours or mine. But it must have been millions of years ago when they were turned off, too, and they just haven't thought since then. Kindly little people. That was all they knew.

When I slipped into that field it grabbed me like a gravitational field whirling a space transport down to a planet. It sucked me in—and through. Only the other side must have been seven million years in the future. That's where I was. It must have been in exactly the same spot on Earth's surface, but I never knew why.

It was night then, and I saw the city a little way off. The Moon was shining on it, and the whole scene looked wrong. You see, in seven million years, men had done a lot with the positions of the planetary bodies, what with moving space liners, clearing lanes through the asteroids, and such. And seven million years is long enough for natural things to change positions a little. The Moon must have been fifty thousand miles farther out. And it was rotating on its axis. I lay there awhile and watched it. Even the stars were different.

There were ships going out of the city. Back and forth, like things sliding along a wire, but there was only a wire of force, of course. Part of the city, the lower part, was brightly lighted with what must have been mercury vapor glow, I decided. Blue-green. I felt sure men didn't live there—the light was wrong for eyes. But the top of the city was so sparsely lighted.

Then I saw something coming down out of the sky. It was brightly lighted. A huge globe, and it sank straight to the center of the great black-and-silver mass of the city.

I don't know what it was, but even then I knew the city was deserted. Strange that I could even imagine that, I who had never seen a deserted city before. But I walked the fifteen miles over to it and entered it. There were machines going about the streets, repair machines, you know. They couldn't understand that the city didn't need to go on functioning, so they were still working. I found a taxi machine that seemed fairly familiar. It had a manual control that I could work.

I don't know how long that city had been deserted. Some of the men from the other cities said it was a hundred and fifty thousand years. Some went as high as three hundred thousand years. Three hundred thousand years since human foot had been in that city. The taxi machine was in perfect condition, functioned at once. It was clean, and the city was clean and orderly. I saw a restaurant and I was hungry. Hungrier still for humans to speak to. There were none, of course, but I didn't know.

The restaurant had the food displayed directly, and I made a choice. The food was three hundred thousand years old, I suppose; I didn't know, and the machines that served it to me didn't care, for they made things synthetically, you see, and perfectly. When the builders made those cities, they forgot one thing. They didn't realize that things shouldn't go on forever.

It took me six months to make my apparatus. And near the end I was ready to go; and, from seeing those machines go blindly, perfectly, on in orbits of their duties with the tireless, ceaseless perfection their designers had incorporated in them, long after those designers and their sons, and their sons' sons had no use for them—

When Earth is cold, and the Sun has died out, those machines will go on. When Earth begins to crack and break, those perfect, ceaseless machines will try to repair her—

I left the restaurant and cruised about the city in the taxi.

The machine had a little, electric-power motor, I believe, but it gained its power from the great central power radiator. I knew before long that I was far in the future. The city was divided into two sections, a section of many strata where machines functioned smoothly, save for a deep humming beat that echoed through the whole city like a vast unending song of power. The entire metal framework of the place echoed with it, transmitted it, hummed with it. But it was soft and restful, a reassuring beat.

There must have been thirty levels above ground, and twenty more below, a solid block of metal walls and metal floors and metal and glass and force machines. The only light was the blue-green glow of the mercury vapor arcs. The light of mercury vapor is rich in high-energy-quanta, which stimulate the alkali metal atoms to photo-electric activity. Or perhaps that is beyond the science of your day? I have forgotten.

But they had used that light because many of their worker machines needed sight. The machines were marvelous. For five hours I wandered through the vast power plant on the very lowest level, watching them, and because there was motion, and that pseudo-mechanical life, I felt less alone.

The generators I saw were a development of the release I had discovered—when? The release of the energy of matter, I mean, and I knew when I saw that for what countless ages they could continue.

The entire lower block of the city was given over to the machines. Thousands. But most of them seemed idle, or, at most, running under light load. I recognized a telephone apparatus, and not a single signal came through. There was no life in the city. Yet when I pressed a little stud beside the screen on one side of the room, the machine began working instantly. It was ready. Only no one needed it any more. The men knew how to die, and be dead, but the machines didn't.

Finally I went up to the top of the city, the upper level. It was a paradise.

There were shrubs and trees and parks, glowing in the soft light that they had learned to make in the very air. They had learned it five million years or more before. Two million years ago they forgot. But the machines didn't, and they were still making it. It hung in the air, soft, silvery light, slightly rosy, and the gardens were shadowy with it. There were no machines here now, but I knew that in daylight they must come out and work on those gardens, keeping them a paradise for masters who had died, and stopped moving, as they could not.

In the desert outside the city it had been cool, and very dry. Here the air was soft, warm and sweet with the scent of blooms that men had spent several hundreds of thousands of years perfecting.

Then somewhere music began. It begun in the air, and spread softly through it. The Moon was just setting now, and as it set, the rosy-silver glow waned and the music grew stronger.

It came from everywhere and from nowhere. It was within me. I do not know how they did it. And I do not know how such music could be written.

Savages make music too simple to be beautiful, but it is stirring. Semisavages write music beautifully simple, and simply beautiful. Your Negro music was your best. They knew music when they heard it and sang it as they felt it. Semicivilized people write great music. They are proud of their music, and make sure it is known for great music. They make it so great it is top-heavy.

I had always thought our music good. But that which came through the air was the song of triumph, sung by a mature race, the race of man in its full triumph! It was man singing his triumph in majestic sound that swept me up; it showed me what lay before me; it carried me on.

And it died in the air as I looked at the deserted city. The machines should have forgotten that song. Their masters had, long before.

I came to what must have been one of their homes; it was a dimly-seen doorway in the dusky light, but as I stepped up to it, the lights which had not functioned in three hundred thousand years illuminated it for me with a green-white glow, like a firefly, and I stepped into the room beyond. Instantly something happened to the air in the doorway behind me; it was as opaque as milk. The room in which I stood was a room of metal and stone. The stone was some jet-black substance with the finish of velvet, and the metals were silver and gold. There was a rug on the floor, a rug of just such material as I am wearing now, but thicker and softer. There were divans about the room, low and covered with these soft metallic materials. They were black and gold and silver, too.

I had never seen anything like that. I never shall again, I suppose, and my language and yours were not made to describe it.

The builders of that city had right and reason to sing that song of sweeping triumph, triumph that swept them over the nine planets and the fifteen habitable moons.

But they weren't there any more, and I wanted to leave. I thought of a plan and went to a subtelephone office to examine a map I had seen. The old World looked much the same. Seven or even seventy million years don't mean much to old Mother Earth. She may even succeed in wearing down those marvelous machine cities. She can wait a hundred million or a thousand million years before she is beaten.

I tried calling different city centers shown on the map. I had quickly learned the system when I examined the central apparatus.

I tried once—twice—thrice—a round dozen times. Yawk City, Lunon City, Paree, Shkago, Singpor, others. I was beginning to feel that there were no more men on all earth. And I felt crushed, as at each city the machines replied and did my bidding. The machines were there in each of those far vaster cities, for I was in the Neva City of their time. A small city. Yawk City was more than eight hundred kilometers in diameter.

In each city I tried several numbers. Then I tried San Frisco. There was some one there, and a voice answered and the picture of a human appeared on the little glowing screen. I could see him start and stare in surprise at me. Then he started speaking to me. I couldn't understand, of course. I can understand your speech, and you mine, because your speech of this day is largely recorded on records of various types and has influenced our pronunciation.

Some things are changed; names of cities, particularly because the names of cities are apt to be polysyllabic, and used a great deal. People tend to elide them, shorten them. I am in—Nee-vah-dah—as you would say? We say only Neva. And Yawk State. But it is Ohio and Iowa still. Over a thousand years, effects were small on words, because they were recorded.

But seven million years had passed, and the men had forgotten the old records, used them less as time went on, and their speech varied till the time came when they could no longer understand the records. They were not written any more, of course.

Some men must have arisen occasionally among that last of the race and sought for knowledge, but it was denied them. An ancient writing can be translated if some basic rule is found. An ancient voice though—and when the race has forgotten the laws of science and the labor of mind.

So his speech was strange to me as he answered over that circuit. His voice was high in pitch, his words liquid, his tones sweet. It was almost a song as he spoke. He was excited and called others. I could not understand them, but I knew where they were. I could go to them.

So I went down from the paradise gardens, and as I prepared to leave, I saw dawn in the sky. The strange-bright stars winked and twinkled and faded. Only one bright rising star was familiar—Venus. She shone golden now. Finally, as I stood watching for the first time that strange heaven, I began to understand what had first impressed me with the wrongness of the view. The stars, you see, were all different.

In my time—and yours, the solar system is a lone wanderer that by chance is passing across an intersection point of Galactic traffic. The stars we see at night are the stars of moving clusters, you know. In fact our system is passing through the heart of the Ursa Major group. Half a dozen other groups center within five hundred light-years of us.

But during those seven millions of years, the Sun had moved out of the group. The heavens were almost empty to the eye. Only here and there shone a single faint star. And across the vast sweep of black sky swung the band of the Milky Way. The sky was empty.

That must have been another thing those men meant in their songs—felt in their hearts. Loneliness—not even the close, friendly stars. We have stars within half a dozen light-years. They told me that their instruments, which gave directly the distance to any star, showed that the nearest was one hundred and fifty light-years away. It was enormously bright. Brighter even than Sirius of our heavens. And that made it even less friendly, because it was a blue-white supergiant. Our sun would have served as a satellite for that star.

I stood there and watched the lingering rose-silver glow die as the powerful blood-red light of the Sun swept over the horizon. I knew by the stars now, that it must have been several millions of years since my day; since I had last seen the Sun sweep up. And that blood-red light made me wonder if the Sun itself was dying.

An edge of it appeared, blood-red and huge. It swung up, and the color faded, till in half an hour it was the familiar yellow-gold disk.

It hadn't changed in all that time.

I had been foolish to think that it would. Seven million years—that is nothing to Earth, how much less to the Sun? Some two thousand thousand thousand times it had risen since I last saw it rise. Two thousand thousand thousand days. If it had been that many years—I might have noticed a change.

The universe moves slowly. Only life is not enduring; only life changes swiftly. Eight short millions of years. Eight days in the life of Earth—and the race was dying. It had left something: machines. But they would die, too, even though they could not understand. So I felt. I—may have changed that. I will tell you. Later.

For when the Sun was up, I looked again at the sky and the ground, some fifty floors below. I had come to the edge of the city.

Machines were moving on that ground, leveling it, perhaps. A great wide line of gray stretched off across the level desert straight to the east. I had seen it glowing faintly before the Sun rose—a roadway for ground machines. There was no traffic on it.

I saw an airship slip in from the east. It came with a soft, muttering whine of air. like a child complaining in sleep; it grew to my eyes like an expanding balloon. It was huge when it settled in a great port-slip in the city below. I could hear now the clang and mutter of machines, working on the materials brought in, no doubt. The machines had ordered raw materials. The machines in other cities had supplied. The freight machines had carried them here.

San Frisco and Jacksville were the only two cities on North America still used. But the machines went on in all the others, because they couldn't stop. They hadn't been ordered to.

Then high above, something appeared, from the city beneath me, from a center section, three small spheres rose. They, like the freight ship, had no visible driving mechanisms. The point in the sky above, like a black star in a blue space, had grown to a moon. The three spheres met it high above. Then together they descended and lowered into the center of the city, where I could not see them.

It was freight transport from Venus. The one I had seen land the night before had come from Mars, I learned.

I moved after that and looked for some sort of a taxi-plane. They had none that I recognized in scouting about the city. I searched the higher levels, and here and there saw deserted ships, but far too large for me, and without controls.

It was nearly noon—and I ate again. The food was good.

I knew then that this was a city of the dead ashes of human hopes. The hopes not of *a* race, not the whites, nor the yellow, nor the blacks, but the human race. I was mad to leave the city. I was afraid to try the ground road to the west, for the taxi I drove was powered from some source in the city, and I knew it would fail before many miles.

It was afternoon when I found a small hangar near the outer wall of the vast city. It contained three ships. I had been searching through the lower strata of the human section—the upper part. There were restaurants and shops and theaters there. I entered one place where, at my entrance, soft music began, and colors and forms began to rise on a screen before me.

They were the triumph songs in form and sound and color of a mature race, a race that had marched steadily upward through five millions of years—and didn't see the path that faded out ahead, when they were dead and stopped, and the city itself was dead—but hadn't stopped. I hastened out of there—and the song that had not been sung in three hundred thousand years died behind me.

But I found the hangar. It was a private one, likely. Three ships. One must have been fifty feet long and fifteen in diameter. It was a yacht, a space yacht, probably. One was some fifteen feet long and five feet in diameter. That must have been the family air machine. The third was a tiny thing, little more than ten feet long and two in diameter. I had to lie down within it, evidently.

There was a periscope device that gave me a view ahead and almost directly above. A window that permitted me to see what lay below—and a device that moved a map under a frosted-glass screen and projected it onto the screen in such a way that the cross-hairs of the screen always marked my position.

I spent half an hour attempting to understand what the makers of that ship had made. But the men who made that were men who held behind them the science and knowledge of five million years and the perfect machines of those ages. I saw the release mechanism that powered it. I understood the principles of that and, vaguely, the mechanics. But there were no conductors, only pale beams that pulsed so swiftly you could hardly catch the pulsations from the corner of the eye.

They had been glowing and pulsating, some half dozen of them, for three hundred thousand years at least; probably more.

I entered the machine, and instantly half a dozen more beams sprang into being; there was a slight suggestion of a quiver, and a queer strain ran through my body. I understood in an instant, for the machine was resting on gravity nullifiers. That had been my hope when I worked on the space fields I discovered after the release.

But they had had it for millions of years before they built that perfect deathless machine. My weight entering it had forced it to readjust itself and simultaneously to prepare for operation. Within, an artificial gravity equal to that of Earth had gripped me, and the neutral zone between the outside and the interior had caused the strain.

The machine was ready. It was fully fueled. You see they were equipped to tell automatically their wants and needs. They were almost living things, every one. A caretaker machine kept them supplied, adjusted, even repaired them when need be, and when possible. If it was not, I learned later, they were carried away in a service truck that came automatically; replaced by an exactly similar machine; and carried to the shops where they were made, and automatic machines made them over.

The machine waited patiently for me to start. The controls were simple, obvious. There was a lever at the left that you pushed forward to move forward, pulled back to go back. On the right a horizontal, pivoted bar. If you swung it left, the ship spun left; if right, the ship spun right. If tipped up, the ship followed it, and likewise for all motions other than backward and forward. Raising it bodily raised the ship, as depressing it depressed the ship.

I lifted it slightly, a needle moved a bit on a gauge comfortably before my eyes as I lay there, and the floor dropped beneath me. I pulled the other control back, and the ship gathered speed as it moved gently out into the open. Releasing both controls into neutral, the machine continued till it stopped at the same elevation, the motion absorbed by air friction. I turned it about, and another dial before my eyes moved, showing my position. I could not read it, though. The map did not move, as I had hoped it would. So I started toward what I felt was west.

I could feel no acceleration in that marvelous machine. The ground simply began leaping backward, and in a moment the city was gone. The map unrolled rapidly beneath me now, and I saw that I was moving south of west. I turned northward slightly, and watched the compass. Soon I understood that, too, and the ship sped on.

I had become too interested in the map and compass, for suddenly there was a sharp buzz and, without my volition, the machine rose and swung to the north. There was a mountain ahead of me; I had not seen, but the ship had.

I noticed then what I should have seen before—two little knobs that could move the map. I started to move them and heard a sharp clicking, and the pace of the ship began decreasing. A moment and it had steadied at a considerably lower speed, the machine swinging to a new course. I tried to right it, but to my amazement the controls did not affect it.

It was the map, you see. It would either follow the course, or the course would follow it. I had moved it and the machine had taken over control of its own accord. There was a little button I could have pushed—but I didn't know. I couldn't control the ship until it finally came to rest and lowered itself to a stop six inches from the ground in the center of what must have been the ruins of a great city. Sacramento, probably.

I understood now, so I adjusted the map for San Frisco, and the ship went on at once. It steered itself around a mass of broken stone, turned back to its course, and headed on, a bullet-shaped, self-controlled dart.

It didn't descend when it reached San Frisco. It simply hung in the air and sounded a soft musical hum. Twice. Then I waited, too, and looked down.

There were people here. I saw the humans of that age for the first time. They were little men—bewildered—dwarfed, with heads disproportionately large. But not extremely so.

Their eyes impressed me most. They were huge, and when they looked at me there was a power in them that seemed sleeping, but too deeply to be roused.

I took the manual controls then and landed. And no sooner had I got out, than the ship rose automatically and started off by itself. They had automatic parking devices. The ship had gone to a public hangar, the nearest, where it would be automatically serviced and cared for. There was a little call set I should have taken with me when I got out. Then I could have pressed a button and called it to me—wherever I was in that city.

The people about me began talking—singing almost—

among themselves. Others were coming up leisurely. Men and women—but there seemed no old and few young. What few young there were, were treated almost with respect, carefully taken care of lest a careless footstep on their toes or a careless step knock them down.

There was reason, you see. They lived a tremendous time. Some lived as long as three thousand years. Then—they simply died. They didn't grow old, and it never had been learned why people died as they did. The heart stopped, the brain ceased thought—and they died. But the young children, children not yet mature, were treated with the utmost care. But one child was born in the course of a month in that city of one hundred thousand people. The human race was growing sterile.

And I have told you that they were lonely? Their loneliness was beyond hope. For, you see, as man strode toward maturity, he destroyed all forms of life that menaced him. Disease. Insects. Then the last of the insects, and finally the last of the man-eating animals.

The balance of nature was destroyed then, so they had to go on. It was like the machines. They started them—and now they can't stop. They started destroying life—and now it wouldn't stop. So they had to destroy weeds of all sorts, then many formerly harmless plants. Then the herbivora, too, the deer and the antelope and the rabbit and the horse. They were a menace, they attacked man's machine-tended crops. Man was still eating natural foods.

You can understand. The thing was beyond their control. In the end they killed off the denizens of the sea, also, in self-defense. Without the many creatures that had kept them in check, they were swarming beyond bounds. And the time had come when synthetic foods replaced natural. The air was purified of all life about two and a half million years after our day, all microscopic life.

That meant that the water, too, must be purified. It was— and then came the end of life in the ocean. There were minute organisms that lived on bacterial forms, and tiny fish that lived on the minute organisms, and small fish that lived on the tiny fish, and the big fish that lived on the small fish— and the beginning of the chain was gone. The sea was devoid of life in a generation. That meant about one thousand and five hundred years to them. Even the sea plants had gone.

And on all Earth there was only man and the organisms he had protected—the plants he wanted for decoration, and certain ultra-hygienic pets, as long-lived as their masters. Dogs. They must have been remarkable animals. Man was reaching his maturity then, and his animal friend, the friend that had followed him through a thousand millenniums to your day and mine, and another four thousand millenniums to the day of man's early maturity, had grown in intelligence. In an ancient museum—a wonderful place, for they had, perfectly preserved, the body of a great leader of mankind who had died five and a half million years before I saw him—in that museum, deserted then, I saw one of those canines. His skull was nearly as large as mine. They had simple ground machines that dogs could be trained to drive, and they held races in which the dogs drove those machines.

Then man reached his full maturity. It extended over a period of a full million years. So tremendously did he stride ahead, the dog ceased to be a companion. Less and less were they wanted. When the million years had passed, and man's decline began, the dog was gone. It had died out.

And now this last dwindling group of men still in the system had no other life form to make its successor. Always before when one civilization toppled, on its ashes rose a new one. Now there was but one civilization, and all other races, even other species, were gone save in the plants. And man was too far along in his old age to bring intelligence and mobility from the plants. Perhaps he could have in his prime.

Other worlds were flooded with man during that million years—the million years. Every planet and every moon of the system had its quota of men. Now only the planets had their populations, the moons had been deserted. Pluto had been left before I landed, and men were coming from Neptune, moving in toward the Sun, and the home planet, while I was there. Strangely quiet men, viewing, most of them, for the first time, the planet that had given their race life.

But as I stepped from that ship and watched it rise away from me, I saw why the race of man was dying. I looked back at the faces of those men, and on them I read the answer. There was one single quality gone from the still-great minds—minds far greater than yours or mine. I had to have the help of one of them in solving some of my problems. In space, you know, there are twenty coordinates, ten of which are zero, six of which have fixed values, and the four others represent our changing, familiar dimensions in space-time. That means that integrations must proceed in not double, or triple, or quadruple—but ten integrations.

It must have taken me too long. I would never have solved all the problems I must work out. I could not use their mathematics machines; and mine, of course, were seven million years in the past. But one of those men was interested and helped me. He did quadruple and quintuple integration, even quadruple integration between varying exponential limits—in his head.

When I asked him to. For the one thing that had made man great had left him. As I looked in their faces and eyes on landing I knew it. They looked at me, interested at this rather unusual-looking stranger—and went on. They had come to see the arrival of a ship. A rare event, you see. But they were merely welcoming me in a friendly fashion. They were not curious! Man had lost the instinct of curiosity.

Oh, not entirely! They wondered at the machines, they wondered at the stars. But they did nothing about it. It was not wholly lost to them yet, but nearly. It was dying. In the six short months I stayed with them, I learned more than they had learned in the two or even three thousand years they had lived among the machines.

Can you appreciate the crushing loneliness it brought to me? I, who love science, who see in it, or have seen in it, the salvation, the raising of mankind—to see those wondrous machines, of man's triumphant maturity, forgotten and misunderstood. The wondrous, perfect machines that tended, protected, and cared for those gentle, kindly people who had—forgotten.

They were lost among it. The city was a magnificent ruin to them, a thing that rose stupendous about them. Something not understood, a thing that was of the nature of the world. It was. It had not been made; it simply was. Just as the mountains and the deserts and the waters of the seas.

Do you understand—can you see that the time since those machines were new was longer than the time from our day to the birth of the race? Do we know the legends of our first ancestors? Do we remember their lore of forest and cave? The secret of chipping a flint till it had a sharp-cutting edge? The secret of trailing and killing a saber-toothed tiger without being killed oneself?

They were now in similar straits, though the time had been longer, because the language had taken a long step toward perfection, and because the machines maintained everything for them through generation after generation.

Why, the entire planet of Pluto had been deserted—yet on

Pluto the largest mines of one of their metals were located; the machines still functioned. A perfect unity existed throughout the system. A unified system of perfect machines.

And all those people knew was that to do a certain thing to a certain lever produced certain results. Just as men in the Middle Ages knew that to take a certain material, wood, and place it in contact with other pieces of wood heated red, would cause the wood to disappear, and become heat. They did not understand that wood was being oxidized with the release of the heat of formation of carbon dioxide and water. So those people did not understand the things that fed and clothed and carried them.

I stayed with them there for three days. And then I went to Jacksville. Yawk City, too. That was enormous. It stretched over—well, from well north of where Boston is today to well south of Washington—that was what they called Yawk City.

I never believed that, when he said it, said Jim, interrupting himself. I knew he didn't. If he had I think he'd have bought land somewhere along there and held for a rise in value. I know Jim. He'd have the idea that seven million years was something like seven hundred, and maybe his great-grandchildren would be able to sell it.

Anyway, went on Jim, he said it was all because the cities had spread so. Boston spread south. Washington, north. And Yawk City spread all over. And the cities between grew into them.

And it was all one vast machine. It was perfectly ordered and perfectly neat. They had a transportation system that took me from the North End to the South End in three minutes. I timed it. They had learned to neutralize acceleration.

Then I took one of the great space lines to Neptune. There were still some running. Some people, you see, were coming the other way.

The ship was huge. Mostly it was a freight liner. It floated up from Earth, a great metal cylinder three quarters of a mile long, and a quarter of a mile in diameter. Outside the atmosphere it began to accelerate. I could see Earth dwindle. I have ridden one of our own liners to Mars, and it took me, in 3048, five days. In half an hour on this liner Earth was just a star, with a smaller, dimmer star near it. In an hour we passed Mars. Eight hours later we landed on Neptune.

M'reen was the city. Large as the Yawk City of my day—and no one living there.

The planet was cold and dark—horribly cold. The sun was a tiny, pale disk, heatless and almost lightless. But the city was perfectly comfortable. The air was fresh and cool, moist with the scent of growing blossoms, perfumed with them. And the whole giant metal framework trembled just slightly with the humming, powerful beat of the mighty machines that had made and cared for it.

I learned from records I deciphered, because of my knowledge of the ancient tongue that their tongue was based on, and the tongue of that day when man was dying, that the city was built three million, seven hundred and thirty thousand, one hundred and fifty years after my birth. Not a machine had been touched by the hand of man since that day.

Yet the air was perfect for man. And the warm, rose-silver glow hung in the air here and supplied the only illumination.

I visited some of their other cities where there were men. And there, on the retreating outskirts of man's domain, I first heard The Song of Longings, as I called it.

And another, The Song of Forgotten Memories. Listen:

He sang another of those songs. There's one thing I know, declared Jim. That bewildered note was stronger in his voice, and by that time I guess I pretty well understood his feelings. Because, you have to remember, I heard it only secondhand from an ordinary man, and Jim had heard it from an eye-and-ear witness that was not ordinary, and heard it in that organ voice. Anyway, I guess Jim was right when he said: "He wasn't any ordinary man." No ordinary man could think of those songs. They weren't right. When he sang that song, it was full of more of those plaintive minors. I could feel him searching his mind for something he had forgotten, something he desperately wanted to remember—something he knew he should have known—and I felt it eternally elude him. I felt it get further away from him as he sang. I heard that lonely, frantic searcher attempting to recall that thing—that thing that would save him.

And I heard him give a little sob of defeat—and the song ended. Jim tried a few notes. He hasn't a good ear for music—but that was too powerful to forget. Just a few hummed notes. Jim hasn't much imagination, I guess, or when that man of the future sang to him he would have gone mad. It shouldn't be sung to modern men; it isn't meant for them.

You've heard those heart-rendering cries some animals give, like human cries, almost? A loon, now—he sounds like a lunatic being murdered horribly.

That's just unpleasant. That song made you feel just exactly what the singer meant—because it didn't just sound human—it was human. It was the essence of humanity's last defeat, I guess. You always feel sorry for the chap who loses after trying hard. Well, you could feel the whole of humanity trying hard—and losing. And you knew they couldn't afford to lose, because they couldn't try again.

He said he'd been interested before. And still not wholly upset by these machines that couldn't stop. But that was too much for him.

I knew after that, he said, that these weren't men I could live among. They were dying men, and I was alive with the youth of the race. They looked at me with the same longing, hopeless wonder with which they looked at the stars and the machines. They knew what I was, but couldn't understand.

I began to work on leaving.

It took six months. It was hard because my instruments were gone, of course, and theirs didn't read in the same units. And there were few instruments, anyway. The machines didn't read instruments; they acted on them. They were sensory organs to them.

But Reo Lantal helped where he could. And I came back.

I did just one thing before I left that may help. I may even try to get back there sometime. To see, you know.

I said they had machines that could really think? But that someone had stopped them a long time ago, and no one knew how to start them?

I found some records and deciphered them. I started one of the last and best of them and started it on a great problem. It is only fitting it should be done. The machine can work on it, not for a thousand years, but for a million, if it must.

I started five of them actually, and connected them together as the records directed.

They are trying to make a machine with something that man had lost. It sounds rather comical. But stop to think before you laugh. And remember that Earth as I saw it from the ground level of Neva City just before Reo Lantal threw the switch.

Twilight—the sun has set. The desert out beyond, in its mystic, changing colors. The great, metal city rising straight-walled to the human city above, broken by spires and towers and great trees with scented blossoms. The silvery-rose glow in the paradise of gardens above.

And all the great city-structure throbbing and humming to the steady gentle beat of perfect, deathless machines built more than three million years before—and never touched since that time by human hands. And they go on. The dead city. The men that have lived, and hoped, and built—and died to leave behind them those little men who can only wonder and look and long for a forgotten kind of companionship. They wander through the vast cities their ancestors built, knowing less of them than the machines themselves.

And the songs. Those tell the story best, I think. Little, hopeless, wondering men amid vast unknowing, blind machines that started three million years before—and just never know how to stop. They are dead—and can't die and be still.

So I brought another machine to life, and set it to a task which, in time to come, it will perform.

I ordered it to make a machine which would have what man had lost. A curious machine.

And then I wanted to leave quickly and go back. I had been born in the first full light of man's day. I did not belong in the lingering, dying glow of man's twilight.

So I came back. A little too far back. But it will not take me long to return—accurately this time.

"Well, that was his story." Jim said. "He didn't *tell* me it was true—didn't say anything about it. And he had me thinking so hard I didn't even see him get off in Reno when we stopped for gas.

"But—he wasn't an ordinary man," repeated Jim, in a rather belligerent tone.

Jim claims he doesn't believe the yarn, you know. But he does; that's why he always acts so determined about it when he says the stranger wasn't an ordinary man.

No, he wasn't, I guess. I think he lived and died, too, probably, sometime in the thirty-first century. And I think he saw the twilight of the race, too.

The Idea Machine

Science fiction has been called a literature of ideas.

The audience for science fiction in the '30s and the '40s, even a part of the audience (or all of the audience part of the time) up to the present, has been interested primarily in the ideas rather than in the other qualities of the stories. A new idea aedquately written often was acclaimed a breakthrough, while an old idea presented with unusual narrative skill sometimes was discounted as unimportant.

Characters never have been as important to science fiction as to fantasy and traditional fiction. In fantasy, unusual things happen to the individual and often because that individual is unusual; with the exception of the totally fantastic world, the events do not happen to everyone or the stories would not be fantasy. In traditional fiction the unique reactions of the individual become all important. In science fiction the character is more important as a representative of humanity than as an idiosyncratic individual; the more typical he is, the clearer the society-wide or even species-wide significance and the easier the reader can transfer the meaning into his own world.

Most of science fiction has been written in what Prof. Robert Scholes calls "journeyman's prose, serviceable but inelegant." Some of the most revered authors wrote as awkwardly as Dreiser. Occasionally a writer would be admired for a skill with words or an ability to create a mood, a setting, or a character, sometimes far beyond the writer's deserts, perhaps because the attempt was so unusual. But such characteristics are not necessarily handicaps: simplicity itself is not a flaw and when accurately used can be effective, particularly when the ideal language of ideas is clarity, even transparency. As Scholes went on to observe: "If to use English as well as Swift or Wells might suffice, then sf has an adequate language."

The ideas came first, and a good part of the science fiction of the '30s was distinguished by its ideas: speeded-up evolu-

287

tion, cryogenics, robots with protoplasmic brains, reduction in size and submicroscopic people, nonhumanoid aliens, time travel to the end of the world, the enslavement of humanity by aliens from Venus, aliens on the moon, the inspection of the future through long periods of self-induced coma, the universe as an atom, the planets as eggs laid around the sun that begin to hatch, alternate universes, the universe expanding because other worlds are fleeing from earth's contamination with protoplasmic life, the shrinking of a scientist through smaller and smaller planetary atoms, aliens who can imitate anything and read minds, the devolution of intelligent one-celled interstellar colonists into multicellular creatures and finally men, antimatter, cities enclosed within impenetrable walls, and many others.

Such ideas originated with a writer—sometimes even with a scientist or philosopher outside the field—and were built upon or refuted by other writers. The house of science fiction was constructed communally and ideas were its bricks.

The idea story was symbolized by F. Orlin Tremaine's "thought-variant" designation in *Astounding*. He recognized the heart of reader interest, and he urged writers to come up with intriguing notions that would merit the label. Among the writers he approached was William Fitzgerald Jenkins (1896–1975).

Jenkins, better known to science-fiction readers under his pseudonym Murray Leinster, had ambitions to be a scientist and a writer but never completed the eighth grade. As a scientist he was primarily an inventor and patented many devices, including the front-projection system used for making background shots and special effects for motion pictures. He held a variety of jobs until his twenty-first birthday, when he turned to writing full-time.

His success came early. His first piece, though unpaid, was accepted when he was only thirteen, he began to place fillers with *The Smart Set* at seventeen, and soon he was selling stories to the pulp magazines, particularly *Argosy*, where his first science-fiction story, "The Runaway Skyscraper," was published in 1919. He continued to write successfully for the next five decades, and earned the title of "the dean of science fiction writers," although he wrote much that was not science fiction.

Over the years he wrote nearly 1,500 stories for a great variety of magazines and nearly a hundred books. He used the name Will F. Jenkins for his non-science-fiction work and for his stories in the slick magazines even if they were science fiction. His sf stories and novels were largely under the name Murray Leinster.

Theodore Sturgeon wrote of him that he "wrote few great stories and no bad ones." His prose was workmanlike, his characters were functional, but his ideas were ingenious. He also had the knack of turning most of his ideas into novelettes, novellas, or novels—there are few Leinster short stories compared to his total output. It was an ability that made sense when many of his publishers paid by the word.

Mostly he was distinguished by his originality: he was a first-class idea man in a business that dealt in ideas, and he originated many of the concepts that later would become the mutual property of the genre. His 1920 story "The Mad Planet" described a world in which plants and insects have grown huge, leaving humanity dwarfed and hunted. "Sidewise in Time" (1934) fathered a generation of alternate-universe stories. "First Contact" (1945) was the definitive treatment of the problem of alien meeting. His 1945 novel *Murder of the USA* may have been the first of the atomic-attack treatments. "A Logic Named Joe" (1946) dealt with the problems that might be caused by home-computer terminals. "The Strange Case of John Kingman" (1948) involved a man who had been locked in an insane asylum for 162 years and was discovered to be an alien. His novelette "Exploration Team" won a Hugo in 1962.

There were many others, among them a 1935 story in *Astounding* titled "Proxima Centauri." It dealt, probably for the first time, with the problem of travel between the stars at the limit set by Einstein's Theory of Relativity—the speed of light. The trip to the nearest star would take at least fourteen years, so the ship was planned as a self-contained, self-sustaining world.

It was a concept that would be used many times again, definitively in Robert Heinlein's "Universe" (1941). Harlan Ellison's star-crossed syndicated television series "The Starlost" (1974) was based on the same idea.

"Proxima Centauri" presents an alien race with whom there is no possibility of commerce or compromise. Perhaps illustrative of the flexibility of the idea business is the fact that Leinster's best-known novelette, "First Contact," makes the point that creatures of good will can find an accommodation that is more profitable to each than an attempt at conquest.

Proxima Centauri

by Murray Leinster

The *Adastra*, from a little distance, already shone in the light of the approaching sun. The vision disks which scanned the giant space ship's outer skin relayed a faint illumination to the visiplates within. They showed the monstrous, rounded bulk of the metal globe, crisscrossed with girders too massive to be transported by any power less than that of the space ship itself. They showed the whole, five-thousand-foot globe as an ever so faintly glowing object, seemingly motionless in mid-space.

In that seeming, they lied. Monstrous as the ship was, and apparently too huge to be stirred by any conceivable power, she was responding to power now. At a dozen points upon her faintly glowing side there were openings. From those openings there flowed out tenuous purple flames. They gave little light, those flames—less than the star ahead—but they were the disintegration blasts from the rockets which had lifted the *Adastra* from the surface of Earth and for seven years had hurled it on through interstellar space toward Proxima Centauri, nearest of the fixed stars to humanity's solar system.

Now they hurled it forward no more. The mighty ship was decelerating. Thirty-two and two-tenths feet per second, losing velocity at the exact rate to maintain the effect of Earth's gravity within its bulk, the huge globe showed. For months braking had been going on. From a peak-speed measurably near the velocity of light, the first of all vessels to span the distance between two solar systems had slowed and slowed, and would reach a speed of maneuver some sixty million miles from the surface of the star.

Far, far ahead, Proxima Centauri glittered invitingly. The vision disks that showed its faint glow upon the space ship's hull had counterparts which carried its image within the hull, and in the main control room it appeared enlarged very many times. An old, white-bearded man in uniform regarded

290

it meditatively. He said slowly, as if he had said the same thing often before:

"Quaint, that ring. It is double, like Saturn's. And Saturn has nine moons. One wonders how many planets this sun will have."

The girl said restlessly: "We'll find out soon, won't we? We're almost there. And we already know the rotation period of one of them! Jack said that——"

Her father turned deliberately to her. "Jack?"

"Gary," said the girl. "Jack Gary."

"My dear," said the old man mildly, "he seems well-disposed, and his abilities are good, but he is a Mut. Remember!"

The girl bit her lip.

The old man went on, quite slowly and without rancor: "It is unfortunate that we have had this division among the crew of what should have been a scientific expedition conducted in the spirit of a crusade. You hardly remember how it began. But we officers know only too well how many efforts have been made by the Muts to wreck the whole purpose of our voyage. This Jack Gary is a Mut. He is brilliant, in his way. I would have brought him into the officers' quarters, but Alstair investigated and found undesirable facts which made it impossible."

"I don't believe Alstair!" said the girl evenly. "And, anyhow, it was Jack who caught the signals. And he's the one who's working with them, officer or Mut! And he's human, anyhow. It's time for the signals to come again and you depend on him to handle them."

The old man frowned. He walked with a careful steadiness to a seat. He sat down with an old man's habitual and rather pathetic caution. The *Adastra*, of course, required no such constant vigilance at the controls as the interplanetary space ships require. Out here in emptiness there was no need to watch for meteors, for traffic, or for those queer and yet inexplicable force fields which at first made interplanetary flights so hazardous.

The ship was so monstrous a structure, in any case, that the tinier meteorites could not have harmed her. And at the speed she was now making greater ones would be notified by the induction fields in time for observation and if necessary the changing of her course.

A door at the side of the control room opened briskly and

a man stepped in. He glanced with conscious professionalism at the banks of indicators. A relay clicked, and his eyes darted to the spot. He turned and saluted the old man with meticulous precision. He smiled at the girl.

"Ah, Alstair," said the old man. "You are curious about the signals, too?"

"Yes, sir. Of course! And as second in command I rather like to keep an eye on signals. Gary is a Mut, and I would not like him to gather information that might be kept from the officers."

"That's nonsense!" said the girl hotly.

"Probably," agreed Alstair. "I hope so. I even think so. But I prefer to leave out no precaution."

A buzzer sounded. Alstair pressed a button and a vision plate lighted. A dark, rather grim young face stared out of it.

"Very well, Gary," said Alstair curtly.

He pressed another button. The vision plate darkened and lighted again to show a long corridor down which a solitary figure came. It came close and the same face looked impassively out. Alstair said even more curtly:

"The other doors are open, Gary. You can come straight through."

"I think that's monstrous!" said the girl angrily as the plate clicked off. "You know you trust him! You have to! Yet every time he comes into officers' quarters you act as if you thought he had bombs in each hand and all the rest of the men behind him!"

Alstair shrugged and glanced at the old man, who said tiredly:

"Alstair is second in command, my dear, and he will be commander on the way back to Earth. I could wish you would be less offensive."

But the girl deliberately withdrew her eyes from the brisk figure of Alstair with its smart uniform, and rested her chin in her hands to gaze broodingly at the farther wall. Alstair went to the banks of indicators, surveying them in detail. The ventilator hummed softly. A relay clicked with a curiously smug, self-satisfied note. Otherwise there was no sound.

The *Adastra*, mightiest work of the human race, hurtled on through space with the light of a strange sun shining faintly upon her enormous hull. Twelve lambent purple flames glowed from holes in her forward part. She was decelerating, lessening her speed by thirty-two point two feet per second per second, maintaining the effect of Earth's gravity within her bulk.

Earth was seven years behind and uncounted millions of billions of miles. Interplanetary travel was a commonplace in the solar system now, and a thriving colony on Venus and a precariously maintained outpost on the largest of Jupiter's moons promised to make space commerce thrive even after the dead cities of Mars had ceased to give up their incredibly rich loot. But only the *Adastra* had ever essayed space beyond Pluto.

She was the greatest of ships, the most colossal structure ever attempted by men. In the beginning, indeed, her design was derided as impossible of achievement by the very men who later made her building a fact. Her framework beams were so huge that, once cast, they could not be moved by any lifting contrivance at her builders' disposal. Therefore the molds for them were built and the metal poured in their final position as a part of the ship. Her rocket tubes were so colossal that the necessary supersonic vibrations—to neutralize the disintegration effect of the Caldwell field—had to be generated at thirty separate points on each tube, else the disintegration of her fuel would have spread to the tubes themselves and the big ship afterward, with even the mother planet following in a burst of lambent purple flame. At full acceleration a set of twelve tubes disintegrated five cubic centimeters of water per second.

Her diameter was a shade over five thousand feet. Her air tanks carried a reserve supply without purification. Her stores, her shops, her supplies of raw and finished materials, were in such vast quantities that to enumerate them would be merely to recite meaningless figures.

There were even four hundred acres of food-growing space within her, where crops were grown under sun lamps. Those crops used waste organic matter as fertilizer and restored exhaled carbon dioxide to use, in part as oxygen and in part as carbohydrate foodstuffs.

The *Adastra* was a world in herself. Given power, she could subsist her crew forever, growing her food supplies, purifying her own internal atmosphere without loss and without fail, and containing space within which every human need could be provided, even solitude.

And starting out upon the most stupendous journey in human history, she had formally been given the status of a world, with her commander empowered to make and enforce all needed laws. Bound for a destination four light-years distant, the minimum time for her return was considered to be fourteen years. No crew could possibly survive so long a voyage undecimated. Therefore the enlistments for the voyage had not been by men, but by families.

There were fifty children on board when the *Adastra* lifted from Earth's surface. In the first year of her voyage ten more were born. It had seemed to the people of Earth that not only could the mighty ship subsist her crew forever, but that the crew itself, well-nourished and with more than adequate facilities both for amusement and education, could so far perpetuate itself as to make a voyage of a thousand years as practicable as the mere journey to Proxima Centauri.

And so it could, but for a fact at once so needless and so human that nobody anticipated it. The fact was tedium. In less than six months the journey had ceased to become a great adventure. To the women in particular, the voyage of the big ship became deadly routine.

The *Adastra* itself took on the semblance of a gigantic apartment house without newspapers, department stores, new film plays, new faces, or even the relieving annoyances of changeable weather. The sheer completeness of all preparations for the voyage made the voyage itself uneventful. That meant tedium.

Tedium meant restlessness. And restlessness, with women on board who had envisioned high adventure, meant the devil to pay. Their husbands no longer appeared as glamorous heroes. They were merely human beings. The men encountered similar disillusionments. Pleas for divorce flooded the commander's desk, he being legally the fount of all legal action. During the eighth month there was one murder, and in the three months following, two more.

A year and a half out from Earth, and the crew was in a state of semimutiny originating in sheer boredom. By two years out, the officers' quarters were sealed off from the greater part of the *Adastra's* interior, the crew was disarmed, and what work was demanded of the mutineers was enforced by force guns in the hands of the officers. By three years out, the crew was demanding a return to Earth. But by the time the *Adastra* could be slowed and stopped from her then incredible velocity, she would be so near her destination as to make no appreciable difference in the length of her total voyage. For the rest of the time the members of the crew strove to relieve utter monotony by such vices and such pastimes as could be improvised in the absence of any actual need to work.

The officers' quarters referred to the underlings by a term become habitual, a contraction of the word "mutineers." The crew came to have a queer distaste for all dealing with the officers. But, despite Alstair, there was no longer much danger of an uprising. A certain mental equilibrium had—very late—developed.

From the nerve-racked psychology of dwellers in an isolated apartment house, the greater number of the *Adastra's* complement came to have the psychology of dwellers in an isolated village. The difference was profound. In particular the children who had come to maturity during the long journey through space were well-adjusted to the conditions of isolation and of routine.

Jack Gary was one of them. He had been sixteen when the trip began, son of a rocket-tube engineer whose death took place the second year out. Helen Bradley was another. She had been fourteen when her father, as designer and commanding officer of the mighty globe, pressed the control key that set the huge rockets into action.

Her father had been past maturity at the beginning. Aged by responsibility for seven uninterrupted years, he was an old man now. And he knew, and even Helen knew without admitting it, that he would never survive the long trip back. Alstair would take his place and the despotic authority inherent in it, and he wanted to marry Helen.

She thought of these things, with her chin cupped in her hand, brooding in the control room. There was no sound save the humming of the ventilator and the infrequent smug click of a relay operating the automatic machinery to keep the *Adastra* a world in which nothing ever happened.

A knock on the door. The commander opened his eyes a trifle vaguely. He was very old now, the commander. He had dozed.

Alstair said shortly, "Come in!" and Jack Gary entered.

He saluted, pointedly to the commander. Which was according to regulations, but Alstair's eyes snapped.

"Ah, yes," said the commander. "Gary. It's about time for more signals, isn't it?"

"Yes, sir."

Jack Gary was very quiet, very businesslike. Only once, when he glanced at Helen, was there any hint of anything but the formal manner of a man intent on his job. Then his eyes told her something, in an infinitely small fraction of a second, which changed her expression to one of flushed content.

Short as the glance was, Alstair saw it. He said harshly:

"Have you made any progress in deciphering the signals, Gary?"

Jack was setting the dials of a panwave receptor, glancing at penciled notes on a calculator pad. He continued to set up the reception pattern.

"No, sir. There is still a sequence of sounds at the beginning which must be a form of call, because a part of the same sequence is used as a signature at the close. With the commander's permission I have used the first part of that call sequence as a signature in our signals in reply. But in looking over the records of the signals I've found something that looks important."

The commander said mildly: "What is it, Gary?"

"We've been sending signals ahead of us on a tight beam, sir, for some months. Your idea was to signal ahead, so that if there were any civilized inhabitants on planets about the sun, they'd get an impression of a peaceful mission."

"Of course!" said the commander. "It would be tragic for the first of interstellar communications to be unfriendly!"

"We've been getting answers to our signals for nearly three months. Always at intervals of a trifle over thirty hours. We assumed, of course, that a fixed transmitter was sending them, and that it was signaling once a day when the station was in the most favorable position for transmitting to us."

"Of course," said the commander gently. "It gave us the period of rotation of the planet from which the signals come."

Jack Gary set the last dial and turned on the switch. A low-pitched hum arose, which died away. He glanced at the dials again, checking them.

"I've been comparing the records, sir, making due allowance for our approach. Because we cut down the distance between us and the star so rapidly, our signals to-day take several seconds less to reach Proxima Centauri than they did yesterday. Their signals should show the same shortening of interval, if they are actually sent out at the same instant of planetary time every day."

The commander nodded benevolently.

"They did, at first," said Jack. "But about three weeks ago

the time interval changed in a brand-new fashion. The signal strength changed, and the wave form altered a little, too, as if a new transmitter was sending. And the first day of that change the signals came through one second earlier than our velocity of approach would account for. The second day they were three seconds earlier, the third day six, the fourth day ten, and so on. They kept coming earlier by a period indicating a linear function until one week ago. Then the rate of change began to decrease again."

"That's nonsense!" said Alstair harshly.

"It's records," returned Jack curtly.

"But how do you explain it, Gary?" asked the commander mildly.

"They're sending now from a space ship, sir," replied Jack briefly, "which is moving toward us at four times our maximum acceleration. And they're flashing us a signal at the same interval, according to their clocks, as before."

A pause. Helen Bradley smiled warmly. The commander thought carefully. Then he admitted:

"Very good, Gary! It sounds plausible. What next?"

"Why, sir," said Jack, "since the rate of change shifted, a week ago, it looks as if that other space ship started to decelerate again. Here are my calculations, sir. If the signals are sent at the same interval they kept up for over a moment, there is another space ship headed toward us, and she is decelerating to stop and reverse and will be matching our course and speed in four days and eighteen hours. They'll meet and surprise us, they think."

The commander's face lighted up. "Marvelous, Gary! They must be far advanced indeed in civilization! Intercourse between two such peoples, separated by four light-years of distance! What marvels we shall learn! And to think of their sending a ship far beyond their own system to greet and welcome us!"

Jack's expression remained grim.

"I hope so, sir," he said dryly.

"What now, Gary?" demanded Alstair angrily.

"Why," said Jack deliberately, "they're still pretending that the signals come from their planet, by signaling at what they think are the same times. They could exchange signals for twenty-four hours a day, if they chose, and be working out a code for communication. Instead, they're trying to deceive us. My guess is that they're coming at least prepared to fight.

And if I'm right, their signals will begin in three seconds, exactly."

He stopped, looking at the dials of the receptor. The tape which photographed the waves as they came in, and the other which recorded the modulations, came out of the receptor blank. But suddenly, in just three seconds, a needle kicked over and tiny white lines appeared on the rushing tapes. The speaker uttered sounds.

It was a voice which spoke. So much was clear. It was harsh yet sibilant, more like the stridulation of an insect than anything else. But the sounds it uttered were modulated as no insect can modulate its outcry. They formed what were plainly words, without vowels or consonants, yet possessing expression and varying in pitch and tone quality.

The three men in the control room had heard them many times before, and so had the girl. But for the first time they carried to her an impression of menace, of threat, of a concealed lust for destruction that made her blood run cold.

II

The space ship hurtled on through space, her rocket tubes sending forth small and apparently insufficient purple flames which emitted no smoke, gave off no gas, and were seemingly nothing but small marsh fires inexplicably burning in emptiness.

There was no change in her outer appearance. There had been none to speak of in years. At long, infrequent intervals men had emerged from air locks and moved about her sides, bathing the steel they walked on and themselves alike with fierce glares from heat lamps lest the cold of her plating transmit itself through the material of the suits and kill the men like ants on red-hot metal. But for a long time no such expedition had been needed.

Only now, in the distant faint light of Proxima Centauri, a man in a space suit emerged from such a tiny lock. Instantly he shot out to the end of a threadlike life line. The constant deceleration of the ship not only simulated gravity within. Anything partaking of its motion showed the same effect. The man upon its decelerating forward side was flung away from the ship by his own momentum, the same force which, within it, had pressed his feet against the floors.

He hauled himself back laboriously, moving with an exaggerated clumsiness in his bloated space suit. He clung to handholds and hooked himself in place, while he worked an electric drill. He moved still more clumsily to another place and drilled again. A third, and fourth, and fifth. For half an hour or more, then, he labored to set up on the vast steel surface, which seemed always above him, an intricate array of wires and framework. In the end he seemed content. He hauled himself back to the air lock and climbed within. The *Adastra* hurtled onward, utterly unchanged save for a very tiny fretwork of wire, perhaps thirty feet across, which looked more like a microscopic barbed-wire entanglement than anything else.

Within the *Adastra*, Helen Bradley greeted Jack warmly as he got out of his space suit.

"It was horrible!" she told him, "to see you dangling like that! With millions of miles of empty space below you!"

"If my line had parted," said Jack quietly, "your father'd have turned the ship and caught up to me. Let's go turn on the inductor and see how the new reception grid works."

He hung up the space suit. As they turned to go through the doorway their hands touched accidentally. They looked at each other and faltered. They stopped, Helen's eyes shining. They unconsciously swayed toward each other. Jack's hands lifted hungrily.

Footsteps sounded close by. Alstair, second in command of the space ship, rounded a corner and stopped short.

"What's this?" he demanded savagely. "Just because the commander's brought you into officers' quarters, Gary, it doesn't follow that your Mut methods of romance can come, too!"

"You dare!" cried Helen furiously.

Jack, from a hot dull flush, was swiftly paling to the dead-white of rage.

"You'll take that back," he said very quietly indeed, "or I'll show you Mut methods of fighting with a force gun! As an officer, I carry one, too, now!"

Alstair snarled at him.

"Your father's been taken ill," he told Helen angrily. "He feels the voyage is about over. Anticipation has kept his strength for months past, but now he's——"

With a cry, the girl fled.

Alstair swung upon Jack. "I take back nothing," he snapped. "You're an officer, by order of the commander. But you're a Mut besides, and when I'm commander of the *Adas-*

tra you don't stay an officer long! I'm warning you! What were you doing here?"

Jack was deathly pale, but the status of officer on the *Adastra*, with its consequent opportunity of seeing Helen, was far too precious to be given up unless at the last extremity. And, besides, there was the work he had in hand. His work, certainly, could not continue unless he remained an officer.

"I was installing an interference grid on the surface," he said, "to try to discover the sending station of the messages we've been getting. It will also act, as you know, as an inductor up to a certain range, and in its range is a good deal more accurate than the main inductors of the ship."

"Then get to your damned work," said Alstair harshly, "and pay full attention to it and less to romance!"

Jack plugged in the lead wire from his new grid to the pan-wave receptor. For an hour he worked more and more grimly. There was something very wrong. The inductors showed blank for all about the *Adastra*. The interference grid showed an object of considerable size not more than two million miles distant and to one side of the *Adastra's* course. Suddenly, all indication of that object's existence blanked out. Every dial on the pan-wave receptor went back to zero.

"Damnation!" said Jack under his breath.

He set up a new pattern on the controls, calculated a moment and deliberately changed the pattern on the spare bank of the main inductors, and then simultaneously switched both instruments to their new frequencies. He waited, almost holding his breath, for nearly half a minute. It would take so long for the inductor waves of the new frequency to reach out the two million miles and then collapse into the analyzers and give their report of any object in space which had tended to deform them.

Twenty-six, twenty-seven, twenty-eight seconds. Every alarm bell on the monstrous ship clanged furiously! Emergency doors hissed into place all over the vessel, converting every doorway into an air lock. Seconds later, the visiplates in the main control room began to flash alight.

"Reporting, Rocket Control!" "Reporting, Air Service!" "Reporting, Power Supply."

Jack said crisply: "The main inductors report an object two million miles distant with velocity in our direction. The commander is ill. Please find Vice Commander Alstair."

Then the door of the control room burst open and Alstair himself raged into the room.

"What the devil!" he rasped. "Ringing a general alarm? Have you gone mad? The inductors——"

Jack pointed to the main inductor bank. Every dial bore out the message of the still-clanging alarms. Alstair stared blankly at them. As he looked, every dial went back to zero.

And Alstair's face went as blank as the dials.

"They felt out our inductor screens," said Jack grimly, "and put out some sort of radiation which neutralized them. So I set up two frequencies, changed both, and they couldn't adjust their neutralizers in time to stop our alarms."

Alstair stood still, struggling with the rage which still possessed him. Then he nodded curtly.

"Quite right. You did good work. Stand by."

And, quite cool and composed, he took command of the mighty space ship, even if there was not much for him to do. In five minutes, in fact, every possible preparation for emergency had been made and he turned again to Jack.

"I don't like you," he said coldly. "As one man to another, I dislike you intensely. But as vice commander and acting commander at the moment, I have to admit that you did good work in uncovering this little trick of our friends to get within striking distance without our knowing they were anywhere near."

Jack said nothing. He was frowning, but it was because he was thinking of Helen. The *Adastra* was huge and powerful, but she was not readily maneuverable. She was enormously massive, but she could not be used for ramming. And she possessed within herself almost infinite destructiveness, in the means of producing Caldwell fields for the disintegration of matter, but she contained no weapon more dangerous than a two-thousand-kilowatt vortex gun for the destruction of dangerous animals or vegetation where she might possibly land.

"What's your comment?" demanded Alstair shortly. "How do you size up the situation?"

"They act as if they're planning hostilities," replied Jack briefly, "and they've got four times our maximum acceleration so we can't get away. With that acceleration they ought to be more maneuverable, so we can't dodge them. We've no faintest idea of what weapons they carry, but we know that we can't fight them unless their weapons are very puny indeed. There's just one chance that I can see."

"What's that?"

"They tried to slip up on us. That looks as if they intended to open fire without warning. But maybe they are frightened and only expected to examine us without our getting a chance to attack them. In that case, our only bet is to swing over our signaling beam to the space ship. When they realize we know they're there and still aren't getting hostile, they may not guess we can't fight. They may think we want to be friendly and they'd better not start anything with a ship our size that's on guard."

"Very well. You're detailed to communication duty," said Alstair. "Go ahead and carry out that program. I'll consult the rocket engineers and see what they can improvise in the way of fighting equipment. Dismiss!"

His tone was harsh. It was arrogant. It rasped Jack's nerves and made him bristle all over. But he had to recognize that Alstair wasn't letting his frank dislike work to the disadvantage of the ship. Alstair was, in fact, one of those ambitious officers who are always cordially disliked by everybody, at all times, until an emergency arises. Then their competence shows up.

Jack went to the communications-control room. It did not take long to realign the transmitter beam. Then the sender began to repeat monotonously the recorded last message from the *Adastra* to the distant and so far unidentified planet of the ringed star. And while the signal went out, over and over again, Jack called on observations control for a sight of the strange ship.

They had a scanner on it now and by stepping up illumination to the utmost, and magnification to the point where the image was as rough as an old-fashioned half-tone cut, they brought the strange ship to the visiplate as a six-inch miniature.

It was egg-shaped and perfectly smooth. There was no sign of external girders, of protruding atmospheric-navigation fins, of escape-boat blisters. It was utterly featureless save for tiny spots which might be portholes, and rocket tubes in which intermittent flames flickered. It was still decelerating to match the speed and course of the *Adastra*.

"Have you got a spectroscope report on it?" asked Jack.

"Yeh," replied the observations orderly. "An' I don't believe it. They're using fuel rockets—some organic compound. An' the report says the hull of that thing is cellulose, not metal. It's wood, on the outside."

Jack shrugged. No sign of weapons. He went back to his own job. The space ship yonder was being penetrated through and through by the message waves. Its receptors could not fail to be reporting that a tight beam was upon it, following its every movement, and that its presence and probable mission were therefore known to the mighty ship from out of space.

But Jack's own receptors were silent. The tape came out of them utterly blank. No—a queer, scrambled, blurry line, as if the analyzers were unable to handle the frequency which was coming through. Jack read the heat effect. The other space ship was sending with a power which meant five thousand kilowatts pouring into the *Adastra*. Not a signal. Grimly, Jack heterodyned the wave on a five-meter circuit and read off its frequency and type. He called the main control.

"They're pouring short stuff into us," he reported stiffly to Alstair. "About five thousand kilowatts of thirty-centimeter waves, the type was used on Earth to kill weevils in wheat. It ought to be deadly to animal life, but of course our hull simply absorbs it."

Helen. Impossible to stop the *Adastra*. They'd started for Proxima Centauri. Decelerating though they were, they couldn't check much short of the solar system, and they were already attacked by a ship with four times their greatest acceleration. Pouring a deadly frequency into them—a frequency used on Earth to kill noxious insects. Helen was—

"Maybe they think we're dead! They'll know our transmitter's mechanical."

The G.C. phone snapped suddenly, in Alstair's voice.

"Attention, all officers! The enemy space ship has poured what it evidently considers a deadly frequency into us, and is now approaching at full acceleration! Orders are that absolutely no control of any sort is to be varied by a hair's breath. Absolutely no sign of living intelligence within the *Adastra* is to be shown. You will stand by all operative controls, prepared for maneuver if it should be necessary. But we try to give the impression that the *Adastra* is operating on automatic controls alone! Understood?"

Jack could imagine the reports from the other control rooms. His own receptor sprang suddenly into life. The almost hooted sounds of the call signal, so familiar that they seemed words. Then an extraordinary jumble of noises—words in a human voice. More stridulated sounds. More words in perfectly accurate English. The English words were in the tones and accents of an officer of the *Adastra*, plainly recorded and retransmitted.

"Communications!" snapped Alstair. "You will not answer this signal! It is an attempt to find out if we survived their ray attack!"

"Check," said Jack.

Alstair was right. Jack watched and listened as the receptor babbled on. It stopped. Silence for ten minutes. It began again. The *Adastra* hurtled on. The babble from space came to an end. A little later the G.C. phone snapped once more:

"The enemy space ship has increased its acceleration, evidently convinced that we are all dead. It will arrive in approximately four hours. Normal watches may be resumed for three hours unless an alarm is given."

Jack leaned back in his chair, frowning. He began to see the tactics Alstair planned to use. They were bad tactics, but the only ones a defenseless ship like the *Adastra* could even contemplate. It was at least ironic that the greeting the *Adastra* received at the end of a seven-years' voyage through empty space be a dose of a type of radiation used on Earth to exterminate vermin.

But the futility of this attack did not mean that all attacks would be similarly useless. And the *Adastra* simply could not be stopped for many millions of miles, yet. Even if Alstair's desperate plan took care of this particular assailant and this particular weapon, it would not mean—it could not!—that the *Adastra* or the folk within had any faintest chance of defending themselves. And there was Helen—

III

The visiplates showed the strange space ship clearly, now, even without magnification. It was within five miles of the *Adastra* and it had stopped. Perfectly egg-shaped, without any protuberance whatever except the rocket tubes in its rear, it hung motionless with relation to the Earth ship, which meant that its navigators had analyzed her rate of decleration long since and had matched all the constants of her course with precision.

Helen, her face still tear-streaked, watched as Jack turned up the magnification, and the illumination with it. Her father had collapsed very suddenly and very completely. He was resting quietly now, dozing almost continuously, with his face wearing an expression of utter contentment.

He had piloted the *Adastra* to its first contact with the civilization of another solar system. His lifework was done and he was wholly prepared to rest. He had no idea, of course, that the first actual contact with the strange space ship was a burst of short waves of a frequency deadly to all animal life.

The space ship swelled on the visiplate as Jack turned the knob. He brought it to an apparent distance of a few hundred yards only. With the illumination turned up, even the starlight on the hull would have been sufficient to show any surface detail. But there was literally none. No rivet, no bolt, no line of joining plates. A row of portholes were dark and dead within.

"And it's wood!" repeated Jack. "Made out of some sort of cellulose which stands the cold of space!"

Helen said queerly: "It looks to me as if it had been grown, rather than built."

Jack blinked. He opened his mouth as if to speak, but the receptor at his elbow suddenly burst into the hootlike stridulations which were the signals from the egglike ship. Then English words, from recordings of previous signals from the *Adastra*. More vowelless, modulated phrases. It sounded exactly as if the beings in the other space ship were trying urgently to open communication and were insisting that they had the key to the *Adastra's* signals. The temptation to reply was great.

"They've got brains, anyhow," said Jack grimly.

The signals were cut off. Silence. Jack glanced at the wave tape. It showed the same blurring as before.

"More short stuff. At this distance, it ought not only to kill us, but even sterilize the interior of the whole ship. Lucky our hull is heavy alloy with a high hysteresis-rate. Not a particle of that radiation can get through."

Silence for a long, long time. The wave tape showed that a terrific beam of thirty-centimeter waves continued to play upon the *Adastra*. Jack suddenly plugged in observations and asked a question. Yes, the outer hull was heating. It had gone up half a degree in fifteen minutes.

"Nothing to worry about in that," grunted Jack. "Fifteen degrees will be the limit they can put it up, with this power."

The tape came out clear. The supposed death radiation was cut off. The egg-shaped ship darted forward. And then for twenty minutes or more Jack had to switch from one outside vision disk to another to keep it in sight. It hovered about the huge bulk of the *Adastra* with a wary inquisitiveness. Now half a mile away, now no more than two hundred yards, the thing darted here and there with an amazing acceleration and as amazing a braking power. It had only the rocket tubes at the smaller end of its egg-shaped form. It was necessary for it to fling its whole shape about to get a new direction, and the gyroscopes within it must have been tremendously powerful. Even so, the abruptness of its turns were startling.

"I wouldn't like to be inside that thing!" said Jack. "We'd be crushed to a pulp by their normal navigation methods. They aren't men like us. They can stand more than we can."

The thing outside seemed sentient, seemed alive. And by the eagerness of its movements it seemed the more horrible, flitting about the gigantic space ship it now believed was a monstrous coffin.

It suddenly reversed itself and shot back toward the *Adastra*. Two hundred yards, one hundred yards, a hundred feet. It came to a cushioned stop against the surface to the Earth vessel.

"Now we'll see something of them," said Jack crisply. "They landed right at an air lock. They know what that is, evidently. Now we'll see them in their space suits."

But Helen gasped. A part of the side of the strange ship seemed to swell suddenly. It bulged out like a blister. It touched the surface of the *Adastra*. It seemed to adhere. The point of contact grew larger.

"Good Lord!" said Jack blankly. "Is it alive? And is it going to try to eat our ship?"

The general-communication phone rasped sharply:

"Officers with arms to the air lock GH41 immediately! The Centaurians are opening the air lock from the outside. Wait orders there! The visiplate in the air lock is working and you will be informed. Go ahead!"

The phone clicked off. Jack seized a heavy gun, one of the force rifles which will stun a man at anything up to eighteen hundred yards and kill at six, when used at full power. His side arm hung in its holster. He swung for the door.

"Jack!" said Helen desperately.

He kissed her. It was the first time their lips had touched, but it seemed the most natural thing in the world, just then. He went racing down the long corridors of the *Adastra* to the rendezvous. And as he raced, his thoughts were not at all those of a scientist and an officer of Earth's first expedition into interstellar space. Jack was thinking of Helen's lips touching his desperately, of her soft body pressed close to him.

A G. C. speaker whispered overhead as he ran:

"They're inside the air lock. They opened it without trouble. They're testing our air, now. Apparently it suits them all."

The phone fell behind. Jack ran on, panting. Somebody else was running ahead. There were half a dozen, a dozen men grouped at the end of the corridor. A murmur from the side wall.

". . . rking at the inner air-lock door. Only four or five of them, apparently, will enter the ship. They are to be allowed to get well away from the air lock. You will keep out of sight. When the emergency locks go on it will be your signal. Use your heavy force guns, increasing power from minimum until they fall paralyzed. It will probably take a good deal of power to subdue them. They are not to be killed if it can be avoided. Ready!"

There were a dozen or more officers on hand. The fat rocket chief. The lean air officer. Subalterns of the other departments. The rocket chief puffed audibly as he wedged himself out of sight. Then the clicking of the inner air-lock door. It opened into the anterroom. Subdued, muffled hootings came from the door. The Things—whatever they were—were inspecting the space suits there. The hootings were distinctly separate and distinctly intoned. But they suddenly came as a babble. More than one Thing was speaking at once. There was excitement, eagerness, an extraordinary triumph in these voices.

Then something stirred in the doorway of the air-lock anteroom. A shadow crossed the threshold. And then the Earthmen saw the creatures who were invading the ship.

For an instant they seemed almost like men. They had two legs, and two dangling things—tentacles—which apparently served as arms and tapered smoothly to ends which split into movable, slender filaments. The tentacles and the legs alike seemed flexible in their entire lengths. There were no "joints" such as men use in walking, and the result was that the Centaurians walked with a curiously rolling gait.

Most startling, though, was the fact that they had no heads. They came wabbling accustomedly out of the air lock, and at the end of one "arm" each carried a curious, semi-cylindrical black object which they handled as if it might be a weapon. They wore metallic packs fastened to their bodies.

The bodies themselves were queerly "grained." There was a tantalizing familiarity about the texture of their skin.

Jack, staring incredulously, looked for eyes, for nostrils, for a mouth. He saw twin slits only. He guessed at them for eyes. He saw no sign of any mouth at all. There was no hair. But he saw a scabrous, brownish substance on the back of one of the Things which turned to hoot excitedly at the rest. It looked like bark, like tree bark. And a light burst upon Jack. He almost cried out, but instead reached down and quietly put the lever of his force gun at full power at once.

The Things moved on. They reached a branching corridor and after much arm waving and production of their apparently articulated sounds they separated into two parties. They vanished. Their voices dwindled. The signal for an attack upon them had not yet been given. The officers, left behind, stirred uneasily. But a G. C. phone whispered.

"Steady! They think we're all dead. They're separating again. We may be able to close emergency doors and have each one sealed off from all the rest and then handle them in detail. You men watch the air lock!"

Silence. The humming of a ventilator somewhere near by. Then, suddenly, a man screamed shrilly a long distance off, and on the heels of his outcry there came a new noise from one of the Things. It was a highpitched squealing noise, triumphant and joyous and unspeakably horrible.

Other squealings answered it. There were rushing sounds, as if the other Things were running to join the first. And then came a hissing of compressed air and a hum of motors. Doors snapped shut everywhere, sealing off every part of the ship from every other part. And in the dead silence of their own sealed compartment, the officers on guard suddenly heard inquiring hoots.

Two more of the Things came out of the air lock. One of the men moved. The Thing saw him and turned its half-cylindrical object upon him. The man—it was the communications officer—shrieked suddenly and leaped convulsively. He was stone dead even as his muscles tensed for that incredible leap.

And the Thing emitted a high-pitched triumphant note which was exactly like the other horrible sound they had heard, and sped eagerly toward the body. One of the long, tapering arms lashed out and touched the dead man's hand.

Then Jack's force gun began to hum. He heard another and another open up. In seconds the air was filled with a sound like that of a hive of angry bees. Three more of the

Things came out of the air lock, but they dropped in the barrage of force-gun beams. It was only when there was a sudden rush of air toward the lock, showing that the enemy ship had taken alarm and was darting away, that the men dared cease to fill that doorway with their barrage. Then it was necessary to seal the air lock in a hurry. Only then could they secure the Things that had invaded the *Adastra*.

Two hours later, Jack went into the main control room and saluted with an exact precision. His face was rather white and his expression entirely dogged and resolved. Alstair turned to him, scowling.

"I sent for you," he said harshly, "because you're likely to be a source of trouble. The commander is dead. You heard it?"

"Yes, sir," said Jack grimly. "I heard it."

"In consequence, I am commander of the *Adastra*," said Alstair provocatively. "I have, you will recall, the power of life and death in cases of mutinous conduct, and it is also true that marriage on the *Adastra* is made legal only by executive order bearing my signature."

"I am aware of the fact, sir," said Jack more grimly still.

"Very well," said Alstair deliberately. "For the sake of discipline, I order you to refrain from all association with Miss Bradley. I shall take disobedience of the order as mutiny. I intend to marry her myself. What have you to say to that?"

Jack said as deliberately: "I shall pay no attention to the order, sir, because you aren't fool enough to carry out such a threat! Are you such a fool that you don't see we've less than one chance in five hundred of coming out of this? If you want to marry Helen, you'd better put all your mind on giving her a chance to live!"

A savage silence held for a moment. The two men glared furiously at each other, the one near middle age, the other still a young man, indeed. Then Alstair showed his teeth in a smile that had no mirth whatever in it.

"As man to man I dislike you extremely," he said harshly. "But as commander of the *Adastra* I wish I had a few more like you. We've had seven years of routine on this damned ship, and every officer in quarters is rattled past all usefulness because an emergency has come at last. They'll obey orders, but there's not one fit to give them. The communications officer was killed by one of those devils, wasn't he?"

"Yes, sir."

"Very well. You're brevet communications officer. I hate your guts, Gary, and I do not doubt that you hate mine, but you have brains. Use them now. What have you been doing?"

"Adjusting a dictawriter, sir, to get a vocabulary of one of these Centaurian's speech, and hooking it up as a two-way translator, sir."

Alstair stared in momentary surprise, and then nodded. A dictawriter, of course, simply analyzes a word into its phonetic parts, sets up the analysis and picks out a card to match its formula. Normally, the card then actuates a printer. However, instead of a type-choosing record, the card can contain a record of an equivalent word in another language, and then operates a speaker.

Such machines have been of only limited use on Earth because of the need for so large a stock of vocabulary words, but have been used to some extent for literal translations both of print and speech. Jack proposed to record a Centaurian's vocabulary with English equivalents, and the dictawriter, hearing the queer hoots the strange creature uttered, would pick out a card which would then cause a speaker to enunciate its English synonym.

The reverse, of course, would also occur. A conversation could be carried on with such a prepared vocabulary without awaiting practice in understanding or imitating the sounds of another language.

"Excellent!" said Alstair curtly. "But put some one else on the job if you can. It should be reasonably simple, once it's started. But I need you for other work. You know what's been found out about these Centaurians, don't you?"

"Yes, sir. Their hand weapon is not unlike our force guns, but it seems to be considerably more effective. I saw it kill the communications officer."

"But the creatures themselves!"

"I helped tie one of them up."

"What do you make of it? I've a physician's report, but he doesn't believe it himself!"

"I don't blame him, sir," said Jack grimly. "They're not our idea of intelligent beings at all. We haven't any word for what they are. In one sense they're plants, apparently. That is, their bodies seem to be composed of cellulose fibers where ours are made of muscle fibers. But they are intelligent, fiendishly intelligent.

"The nearest we have to them on Earth are certain carnivorous plants, like pitcher plants and the like. But they're as far above a pitcher plant as a man is above a sea anemone, which is just as much an animal as a man is. My guess, sir, would be that they're neither plant nor animal. Their bodies are built up of the same materials as earthly plants, but they move about like animals do on Earth. They surprise us, but we may surprise them, too. It's quite possible that the typical animal form on their planet is sessile like the typical plant form on ours."

Alstair said bitterly: "And they look on us, animals, as we look on plants!"

Jack said without expression: "Yes, sir. They eat through holes in their arms. The one who killed the communications officer seized his arm. It seemed to exude some fluid that liquefied his flesh instantly. It sucked the liquid back in at once. If I may make a guess, sir—"

"Go ahead," snapped Alstair. "Everybody else is running around in circles, either marveling or sick with terror."

"The leader of the party, sir, had on what looked like an ornament. It was a band of leather around one of its arms."

"Now, what the devil—"

"We had two men killed. One was the communications officer and the other was an orderly. When we finally subdued the Centaurian who'd killed that orderly, it had eaten a small bit of him, but the rest of the orderly's body had undergone some queer sort of drying process, from chemicals the Thing seemed to carry with it."

Alstair's throat worked as if in nausea. "I saw it."

"It's a fanciful idea," said Jack grimly, "but if a man was in the position of that Centaurian, trapped in a space ship belonging to an alien race, with death very probably before him, well, about the only thing a man would strap to his body, as the Centaurian did the dried, preserved body of that orderly—"

"Would be gold," snapped Alstair. "Or platinum, or jewels which he would hope to fight clear with!"

"Just so," said Jack. "Now, I'm only guessing, but those creatures are not human, nor even animals. Yet they eat animal food. They treasure animal food as a human being would treasure diamonds. An animal's remains—leather—they wear as an ornament. It looks to me as if animal tissue was rather rare on their planet, to be valued so highly. In consequence—"

Alstair stood up, his features working. "Then our bodies would be the same as gold to them! As diamonds! Gary, we haven't the ghost of a chance to make friends with these fiends!"

Jack said dispassionately: "No; I don't think we have. If a race of beings with tissues of metallic gold landed on Earth, I rather think they'd be murdered. But there's another point, too. There's Earth. From our course, these creatures can tell where we came from, and their space ships are rather good. I think I'll put somebody else on the dictawriter job and see if I can flash a message back home. No way to know whether they get it, but they ought to be watching for one by the time it's there. Maybe they've improved their receptors. They intended to try, anyhow."

"Men could meet these creatures' ships in space," said Alstair harshly, "if they were warned. And guns might answer, but if they didn't handle these devils Caldwell torpedoes would. Or a suicide squad, using their bodies for bait. We're talking like dead men, Gary."

"I think, sir," said Jack, "we are dead men." Then he added: "I shall put Helen Bradley on the dictawriter, with a guard to handle the Centaurian. He'll be bound tightly."

The statement tacitly assumed that Alstair's order to avoid her was withdrawn. It was even a challenge to him to repeat it. And Alstair's eyes glowed and he controlled himself with difficulty.

"Damn you, Gary," he said savagely, "get out!"

He turned to the visiplate which showed the enemy ship as Jack left the control room.

The egg-shaped ship was two thousand miles away now, and just decelerating to a stop. In its first flight it had rocketed here and there like a mad thing. It would have been impossible to hit it with any projectile, and difficult in the extreme even to keep radiation on it in anything like a tight beam. Now, stopped stock-still with regard to the *Adastra*, it hung on, observing, very probably devising some new form of devilment. So Alstair considered, anyhow. He watched it somberly.

The resources of the *Adastra*, which had seemed so vast when she took off from Earth, were pitifully inadequate to handle the one situation which had greeted her, hostility. She could have poured out the treasures of man's civilization to the race which ruled this solar system. Savages, she could have uplifted. Even to a race superior to men she could have

offered man's friendship and eager pupilage. But these creatures that—

The space ship stayed motionless. Probably signaling back
to its home planet, demanding orders. Reports came in to the
Adastra's main control room and Alstair read them. The
Centaurians were unquestionably extracting carbon dioxide
from the air. That compound was to their metabolism what
oxygen is to men, and in pure air they could not live.

But their metabolic rate was vastly greater than that of any
plant on Earth. It compared with the rate of earthly animals.
They were not plants by any definition save that of constitution, as a sea anemone is not an animal except by the test of
chemical analysis.

The Centaurians had a highly organized nervous system,
the equivalent of brains, and both great intelligence and a
language. They produced sounds by a stridulating organ in a
special body cavity. And they felt emotion.

A captive creature when presented with various objects
showed special interest in machinery, showing an acute realization of the purpose of a small sound recorder and uttering
into it an entire and deliberate series of sounds. Human
clothing it fingered eagerly. Cloth it discarded, when of cotton or rayon, but it displayed great excitement at the feel of
a woolen shirt and even more when a leather belt was given
to it. It placed the belt about its middle, fastening the buckle
without a fumble after a single glance at its working.

It unraveled a thread from the shirt and consumed it, rocking to and fro as if in ecstasy. When meat was placed before
it, it seemed to become almost delirious with excitement. A
part of the meat it consumed instantly, to ecstatic swayings.
The rest it preserved by a curious chemical process, using
substances from a small metal pack it had worn and for
which it made gestures.

Its organs of vision were behind two slits in the upper part
of its body, and no precise examination of the eyes themselves had been made. But the report before Alstair said spe-
cifically that the Centaurian displayed an avid eagerness
whenever it caught sight of a human being. And that the eagerness was not of a sort to be reassuring.

It was the sort of excitement—only much greater—which
it had displayed at the sight of wool and leather. As if by instinct, said the report, the captive Centaurian had several
times made a gesture as if turning some weapon upon a human when first it sighted him.

Alstair read this report and others. Helen Bradley reported barely two hours after Jack had assigned her to the work.

"I'm sorry, Helen," said Alstair ungraciously. "You shouldn't have been called on for duty. Gary insisted on it. I'd have left you alone."

"I'm glad he did," said Helen steadily. "Father is dead, to be sure, but he was quite content. And he died before he found out what these Centaurians are like. Working was good for me. I've succeeded much better than I even hoped. The Centaurian I worked with was the leader of the party which invaded this ship. He understood almost at once what the dictawriter was doing, and we've a good vocabulary recorded already. If you want to talk to him, you can."

Alstair glanced at the visiplate. The enemy ship was still motionless. Easily understandable, of course. The *Adastra's* distance from Proxima Centauri could be measured in hundreds of millions of miles, now, instead of millions of billions, but in another terminology it was light-hours away still. If the space ship had signaled its home planet for orders, it would still be waiting for a reply.

Alstair went heavily to the biology laboratory, of which Helen was in charge, just as she was in charge of the biological specimens—rabbits, sheep, and a seemingly endless array of small animals—which on the voyage had been bred for a food supply and which it had been planned to release should a planet suitable for colonizing revolve about the ringed star.

The Centaurian was bound firmly to a chair with a myriad of cords. He—she—it, was utterly helpless. Beside the chair the dictawriter and its speaker were coupled together. From the Centaurian came hooted notes which the machine translated with a rustling sound between words.

"You—are—commander—this—ship?" the machine translated without intonation.

"I am," said Alstair, and the machine hooted musically.

"This—woman—man—dead," said the machine tonelessly again, after more sounds from the extraordinary living thing which was not an animal.

Helen interjected swiftly: "I told him my father was dead."

The machine went on: "I—buy—all—dead—man—on—ship—give—metal—gold—you—like—"

Alstair's teeth clicked together. Helen went white. She tried to speak, and choked upon the words.

"This," said Alstair in mirthless bitterness, "is the beginning of the interstellar friendship we hoped to institute!"

Then the G. C. phone said abruptly:

"Calling Commander Alstair! Radiation from ahead! Several wave lengths, high intensity! Apparently several space ships are sending, though we can make out no signals!"

And then Jack Gary came into the biology laboratory. His face was set in grim lines. It was very white. He saluted with great precision.

"I didn't have to work hard, sir," he said sardonically. "The last communications officer had been taking his office more or less as a sinecure. We'd had no signals for seven years, and he didn't expect any. But they're coming through and have been for months.

"They left Earth three years after we did. A chap named Callaway, it seems, found that a circularly polarized wave makes a tight beam that will hold together forever. They've been sending to us for years past, no doubt, and we're getting some of the first messages now.

"They've built a second *Adastra*, sir, and it's being manned—hell, no! It was manned four years ago! It's on the way out here now! It must be at least three years on the way, and it has no idea of these devils waiting for it. Even if we blow ourselves to bits, sir, there'll be another ship from Earth coming, unarmed as we are, to run into these devils when it's too late to stop—"

The G. C. phone snapped again:

"Commander Alstair! Observations reporting! The external hull temperature has gone up five degrees in the past three minutes and is still climbing. Something's pouring heat into us at a terrific rate!"

Alstair turned to Jack. He said with icy politeness:

"Gary, after all there's no use in our continuing to hate each other. Here is where we all die together. Why do I still feel inclined to kill you?"

But the questioon was rhetorical only. The reason was wholly clear. At the triply horrible news, Helen had begun to cry softly. And she had gone blindly into Jack's arms to do it.

IV

The situation was, as a matter of fact, rather worse than the first indications showed. The external hull temperature, for instance, was that of the generalizing thermometer, which averaged for all the external thermometers. A glance at the thermometer bank, through a visiphone connection, showed the rearmost side of the *Adastra* at practically normal. It was the forward hemisphere, the side nearest Proxima Centauri, which was heating. And that hemisphere was not heating equally. The indicators which flashed red lights were closely grouped.

Alstair regarded them with a stony calm in the visiplate.

"Squarely in the center of our disk, as they see it," he said icily. "It will be that fleet of space ships, of course."

Jack Gary said crisply: "Sir, the ship from which we took prisoners made contact several hours earlier than we expected. It must be that, instead of sending one vessel with a transmitter on board, they sent a fleet, and a scout ship on ahead. That scout ship has reported that we laid a trap for some of her crew, and consequently they've opened fire!"

Alstair said sharply into a G. C. transmitter:

"Sector G90 is to be evacuated at once. It is to be sealed off immediately and all occupants will emerge from air locks. Adjoining sectors are to be evacuated except by men on duty, and they will don space suits immediately."

He clicked off the phone and added calmly: "The external temperature over part of G90 is four hundred degrees now. Dull-red heat. In five minutes it should melt. They'll have a hole bored right through us in half an hour."

Jack said urgently: "Sir! I'm pointing out that they've attacked because the scout ship reported we laid a trap for some of its crew! We have just the ghost of a chance—"

"What?" demanded Alstair bitterly. "We've no weapons!"

"The dictawriter, sir!" snapped Jack. "We can talk to them now!"

Alstair said harshly: "Very well, Gary. I appoint you ambassador. Go ahead!"

He swung on his heel and went swiftly from the control room. A moment later his voice came out of the G. C. phone: "Calling the Rocket Chief! Report immediately on personal visiphone. Emergency!"

His voice was cut off, but Jack was not aware of it. He was plugging in to communications and demanding full power on the transmission beam and a widening of its arc. He snapped one order after another and explained to Helen in swift asides.

She grasped the idea at once. The Centaurian in the biology laboratory was bound, of course. No flicker of expression could be discovered about the narrow slits which were his vision organs. But Helen—knowing the words of the vocabulary cards—spoke quietly and urgently into the dictawriter microphone. Hootlike noises came out of the speaker in their place, and the Centaurian stirred. Sounds came from him in turn, and the speaker said woodenly:

"I—speak—ship—planet. Yes."

And as the check-up came through from communications control, the eerie, stridulated, unconsonanted noises of his language filled the biology laboratory and went out on the widened beam of the main transmitter.

Ten thousand miles away the Centaurian scout ship hovered. The *Adastra* bored on toward the ringed sun which had been the goal of mankind's most daring expedition. From ten thousand miles she would have seemed a mere dot, but the telescopes of the Centaurians would show her every detail. From a thousand miles she would seem a toy, perhaps, intricately crisscrossed with strengthening members.

From a distance of a few miles only, though, her gigantic size could be realized fully. Five thousand feet in diameter, she dwarfed the hugest of those distant, unseen shapes in emptiness which made up a hostile fleet now pouring deadly beams upon her.

From a distance of a few miles, too, the effect of that radiation could be seen. The *Adastra*'s hull was alloy steel; tough and necessarily with a high hysteresis rate. The alternating currents of electricity induced in that steel by the Centaurian radiation would have warmed even a copper hull. But the alloy steel grew hot. It changed color. It glowed faintly red over an area a hundred feet across.

A rocket tube in that area abruptly ceased to emit its purple, lambent flame. It had been cut off. Other rockets increased their power a trifle to make up for it. The dull red glow of the steel increased. It became carmine. Slowly, inexorably, it heated to a yellowish tinge. It became canary in color. It tended toward blue.

Vapor curled upward from its surface, streaming away from the tortured, melting surface as if drawn by the distant sun. That vapor grew thick; dazzlingly bright; a veritable cloud of metallic steam. And suddenly there was a violent eruption from the center of the *Adastra*'s lighted hemisphere. The outer hull was melted through. Air from the interior burst out into the void, flinging masses of molten, vaporizing metal before it. It spread with an incredible rapidity, flaring instantly into the attenuated, faintly glowing mist of a comet's tail.

The visiplate images inside the *Adastra* grew dim. Stars paled ahead. The Earth ship had lost a part of her atmosphere and it fled on before her, writhing. Already it had spread into so vast a space that its density was immeasurable, but it was still so much more dense than the infinite emptiness of space that it filled all the cosmos before the *Adastra* with a thinning nebulosity.

And at the edges of the huge gap in the big ship's hull, the thick metal bubbled and steamed, and the interior partitions began to glow with an unholy light of dull-red heat, which swiftly went up to carmine and began to turn faintly yellow.

In the main control room, Alstair watched bitterly until the visiplates showing the interior of section G90 fused. He spoke very calmly into the microphone before him.

"We've got less time than I thought," he said deliberately. "You'll have to hurry. It won't be sure at best, and you've got to remember that these devils will undoubtedly puncture us from every direction and make sure there's absolutely nothing living on board. You've got to work something out, and in a hurry, to do what I've outlined!"

A half-hysterical voice came back to him.

"But, sir, if I cut the sonic vibrations in the rockets we'll go up in a flare! A single instant! The disintegration of our fuel will spread to the tubes and the whole ship will simply explode! It will be quick!"

"You fool!" snarled Alstair. "There's another ship from Earth on the way! Unwarned! And unarmed like we are! And from our course these devils can tell where we came from! We're going to die, yes! We won't die pleasantly! But we're going to make sure these fiends don't start out a space fleet for Earth! There's to be no euthanasia for us! We've got to make our dying do some good! We've got to protect humanity!"

Alstair's face, as he snarled into the visiplate, was not that of a martyr or a person making a noble self-sacrifice. It was the face of a man overawing and bullying a subordinate into obedience.

With a beam of radiation playing on his ship which the metal hull absorbed and transformed into heat, Alstair raged at this department and that. A second bulkhead went, and there was a second eruption of vaporized metal and incandescent gas from the Monster vessel. Millions of miles away, a wide-flung ring of egg-shaped space ships lay utterly motionless, giving no sign of life and looking like monsters asleep. But from them the merciless beams of radiation sped out and focused upon one spot upon the *Adastra*'s hull, and it spewed forth frothing metal and writhing gases and now and again some still recognizable object which flared and exploded as it emerged.

And within the innumerable compartments of the mighty ship, human beings reacted to their coming doom in manners as various as the persons themselves. Some screamed. A few of the more sullen members of the crew seemed to go mad, to become homicidal maniacs. Still others broke into the stores and proceeded systematically but in some haste to drink themselves comatose. Some women clutched their children and wept over them. And some of them went mad.

But Alstair's snarling, raging voice maintained a semblance of discipline in a few of the compartments. In a machine shop men worked savagely, cursing, and making mistakes as they worked which made their work useless. The lean air officer strode about his domain, a huge spanner in his hand, and smote with a righteous anger at any sign of panic. The rocket chief, puffing, manifested an unexpected genius for sustained profanity, and the rockets kept their pale purple flames out in space without a sign of flickering.

But in the biology laboratory the scene was one of quiet, intense concentration. Bound to helplessness, the Centaurian, featureless and inscrutable, filled the room with its peculiar form of speech. The dictawriter rustled softly, senselessly analyzing each of the sounds and senselessly questing for vocabulary cards which would translate them into English wordings. Now and again a single card did match up. Then the machine translated a single word of the Centaurian's speech.

"—ship—" A long series of sounds, varying rapidly in pitch, in intensity, and in emphasis. "—men—" Another long series. "—talk men—"

The Centaurian ceased to make its hootlike noises. Then, very carefully, it emitted new ones. The speaker translated them all. The Centaurian had carefully selected words recorded with Helen.

"He understands what we're trying to do," said Helen, very pale.

The machine said: "You—talk—machine—talk—ship."

Jack said quietly into the transmitter: "We are friends. We have much you want. We want only friendship. We have killed none of your men except in self-defense. We ask peace. If we do not have peace, we will fight. But we wish peace."

He said under his breath to Helen, as the machine rustled and the speaker hooted: "Bluff, that war talk. I hope it works!"

Silence. Millions of miles away, unseen space ships aimed a deadly radiation in close, tight beams at the middle of the *Adastra*'s disk. Quaintly enough, that radiation would have been utterly harmless to a man's body. It would have passed through, undetected.

But the steel of the Earth ship's hull stopped and absorbed it as eddy currents. The eddy currents became heat. And a small volcano vomited out into space the walls, the furnishing, the very atmosphere of the *Adastra* through the hole that the heat had made.

It was very quiet indeed in the biology laboratory. The receptor was silent. One minute. Two minutes. Three. The radio waves carrying Jack's voice traveled at the speed of light, but it took no less than ninety seconds for them to reach the source of the beams which were tearing the *Adastra* to pieces. And there was a time loss there, and ninety seconds more for other waves to hurtle through space at one hundred and eighty-six thousand miles each second with the reply.

The receptor hooted unmusically. The dictawriter rustled softly. Then the speaker said without expression:

"We—friends—now—no—fight—ships—come—to—take —you—planet."

And simultaneously the miniature volcano on the *Adastra*'s hull lessened the violence of its eruption, and slowly its molten, bubbling edges ceased first to steam, and then to bubble, and from the blue-white of vaporizing steel they cooled to yellow, and then to carmine, and more slowly to a dull red, and more slowly still to the glistening, infinitely white metallic surface of steel which cools where there is no oxygen.

Jack said crisply into the control-room microphone: "Sir, I have communicated with the Centaurians and they have ceased fire. They say they are sending a fleet to take us to their planet."

"Very good," said Alstair's voice bitterly, "especially since nobody seems able to make the one contrivance that would do some good after our death. What next?"

"I think it would be a good idea to release the Centaurian here," said Jack. "We can watch him, of course, and paralyze him if he acts up. It would be a diplomatic thing to do, I believe."

"You're ambassador," said Alstair sardonically. "We've got time to work, now. But you'd better put somebody else on the ambassadorial work and get busy again on the job of sending a message back to Earth, if you think you can adapt a transmitter to the type of wave they'll expect."

His image faded. And Jack turned to Helen. He felt suddenly very tired.

"That is the devil of it," he said drearily. "They'll expect a wave like they sent us, and with no more power than we have, they'll hardly pick up anything else! But we picked up in the middle of a message and just at the end of their description of the sending outfit they're using on Earth. Undoubtedly they'll describe it again, or rather they did describe it again, four years back, and we'll pick it up if we live long enough. But we can't even guess when that will be. You're going to keep on working with this—creature, building up a vocabulary?"

Helen regarded him anxiously. She put her hand upon his arm.

"He's intelligent enough," she said urgently. "I'll explain to him and let somebody else work with him. I'll come with you. After all, we—we may not have long to be together."

"Perhaps ten hours," said Jack tiredly.

He waited, somberly, while she explained in carefully chosen words—which the dictawriter translated—to the Centaurian. She got an assistant and two guards. They released the headless Thing. It offered no violence. Instead, it manifested impatience to continue the work of building up in the translator files a vocabulary through which a complete exchange of ideas could take place.

Jack and Helen went together to the communications room. They ran the Earth message, as received so far. It was an extraordinary hodgepodge. Four years back, Earth had been enthusiastic over the thought of sending word to its most daring adventures. A flash of immaterial energy could travel tirelessly through uncountable millions of billions of miles of space and overtake the explorers who had started three years before. By its text, this message had been sent some time after the first message of all. In the sending, it had been broadcast all over the Earth, and many millions of people undoubtedly had thrilled to the thought that they heard words which would span the space between two suns.

But the words were not helpful to those on the *Adastra*. The message was a "cheer-up" program, which began with lusty singing by a popular quartet, continued with wisecracks by Earth's most highly paid comedian—and his jokes were all very familiar to those on the *Adastra*—and then a congratulatory address by an eminent politician, and other drivel. In short, it was a hodgepodge of trash designed to gain publicity by means of the Earth broadcast for those who took part in it.

It was not helpful to those on the *Adastra*, with the hull of the ship punctured, death before them, and probably destruction for the whole human race to follow as a consequence of their voyage.

Jack and Helen sat quietly and listened. Their hands clasped unconsciously. Rather queerly, the extreme brevity of the time before them made extravagant expressions of affection seem absurd. They listened to the unspeakably vulgar message from Earth without really hearing it. Now and again they looked at each other.

In the biology laboratory the building-up of a vocabulary went on swiftly. Pictures came into play. A second Centaurian was released, and by his skill in delineation—which proved that the eyes of the plant men functioned almost identically with those of Earth men—added both to the store of definitions and equivalents and to knowledge of the Centaurian civilization.

Piecing the information together, the civilization began to take on a strange resemblance to that of humanity. The Centaurians possessed artificial structures which were undoubtedly dwelling houses. They had cities, laws, arts—the drawing of the second Centaurian was proof of that—and sciences. The science of biology in particular was far advanced, taking to some extent the place of metallurgy in the civilization of men. Their structures were grown, not built. Instead of metals to shape to their own ends, they had forms of protoplasm whose rate and manner of growth they could control.

Houses, bridges, vehicles—even space ships were formed of living matter which was thrown into a quiescent nonliving state when it had attained the form and size desired. And it could be caused to become active again at will, permitting such extraordinary features as the blisterlike connection that had been made by the space ship with the hull of the *Adastra*.

So far, the Centaurian civilization was strange enough, but still comprehensible. Even men might have progressed in some such fashion had civilization developed on Earth from a different point of departure. It was the economics of the Centaurians which was at once understandable and horrifying to the men who learned of it.

The Centaurian race had developed from carnivorous plants, as men from carnivorous forebears. But at some early date in man's progression, the worship of gold began. No such diversion of interest occurred upon the planets of Proxima Centauri. As men have devastated cities for gold, and have cut down forests and gutted mines and ruthlessly destroyed all things for gold or for other things which could be exchanged for gold, so the Centaurians had quested animals.

As men exterminated the buffalo in America, to trade his hide for gold, so the Centaurians had ruthlessly exterminated the animal life of their planet. But to Centaurians, animal tissue itself was the equivalent of gold. From sheer necessity, ages since, they had learned to tolerate vegetable foodstuffs. But the insensate lust for flesh remained. They had developed methods for preserving animal food for indefinite periods. They had dredged their seas for the last and smallest crustacean. And even space travel became a desirable thing in their eyes, and then a fact, because telescopes showed them vegetation on other planets of their sun, and animal life as a probability.

Three planets of Proxima Centauri were endowed with climates and atmospheres favorable to vegetation and animal life, but only on one planet now, and that the smallest and most distant, did any trace of animal life survive. And even there the Centaurians hunted feverishly for the last and dwindling colonies of tiny quadrupeds which burrowed hundreds of feet below a frozen continent.

It became clear that the *Adastra* was an argosy of such treasure—in the form of human beings—as no Centuarian could ever have imagined to exist. And it became more than ever clear that a voyage to Earth would command all the resources of the race. Billions of human beings! Trillions of lesser animals! Uncountable creatures in the seas! All the

Centaurian race would go mad with eagerness to invade this kingdom of riches and ecstasy, the ecstasy felt by any Centaurian when consuming the prehistoric foodstuff of his race.

V

Egg-shaped, featureless ships of space closed in from every side at once. The thermometer banks showed a deliberate, painstaking progression of alarm signals. One dial glowed madly red and faded, and then another, and yet another, as the Centaurian ships took up their positions. Each such alarm, of course, was from the momentary impact of a radiation beam on the *Adastra*'s hull.

Twenty minutes after the last of the beams had proved the *Adastra*'s helplessness, an egglike ship approached the Earth vessel and with complete precision made contact with its forward side above an air lock. Its hull bellied out in a great blister which adhered to the steel.

Alstair watched the visiplate which showed it, his face very white and his hands clenched tightly. Jack Gary's voice, strained and hoarse, came from the biology-laboratory communicator.

"Sir, a message from the Centaurians. A ship has landed on our hull and its crew will enter through the air lock. A hostile move on our part, of course, will mean instant destruction."

"There will be no resistance to the Centaurians," said Alstair harshly. "It is my order! It would be suicide!"

"Even so, sir," said Jack's voice savagely, "I still think it would be a good idea!"

"Stick to your duty!" rasped Alstair. "What progress has been made in communication?"

"We have vocabulary cards for nearly five thousand words. We can converse on nearly any subject, and all of them are unpleasant. The cards are going through a duplicator now and will be finished in a few minutes. A second dictawriter with the second file will be sent you as soon as the cards are complete."

In a visiplate, Alstair saw the headless figures of Centaurians emerging from the entrance to an air lock in the *Adastra*'s hull.

"Those Centaurians have entered the ship," he snapped as

an order to Jack. "You're communications officer! Go meet them and lead their commanding officer here!"

"Check!" said Jack grimly.

It sounded like a sentence of death, that order. In the laboratory he was very pale indeed. Helen pressed close to him.

The formerly captive Centaurian hooted into the dictawriter, inquiringly. The speaker translated.

"What—command?"

Helen explained. So swiftly does humanity accustom itself to the incredible that it seemed almost natural to address a microphone and hear the hoots and stridulations of a nonhuman voice fill the room with her meaning.

"I—go—also—they—no—kill—yet."

The Centaurian rolled on before. With an extraordinary dexterity, he opened the door. He had merely seen it opened. Jack took the lead. His side-arm force gun remained in its holster beside him, but it was useless. He could probably kill the plant man behind him, but that would do no good.

Dim hootings ahead. The plant man made sounds—loud and piercing sounds. Answers came to him. Jack came in view of the new group of invaders. There were twenty or thirty of them, every one armed with half-cylindrical objects, larger than the first creatures had carried.

At sight of Jack there was excitement. Eager trembling of the armlike tentacles at either side of the headless trunks. There were instinctive, furtive movements of the weapons. A loud hooting as of command. The Things were still. But Jack's flesh crawled from the feeling of sheer, carnivorous lust that seemed to emanate from them.

His guide, the former captive, exchanged incomprehensible noises with the newcomers. Again a ripple of excitement in the ranks of the plant men.

"Come," said Jack curtly.

He led the way to the main control room. Once they heard someone screaming monotonously. A woman cracked under the coming of doom. A hooting babble broke the silence among the ungainly Things which followed Jack. Again an authoritative note silenced it.

The control room. Alstair looked like a man of stone, of marble, save that his eyes burned with a fierce and almost maniacal flame. A visiplate beside him showed a steady stream of Centaurians entering through a second air lock. There were hundreds of them, apparently. The dictawriter came in, under Helen's care. She cried out in instinctive horror at sight of so many of the monstrous creatures at once in the control room.

"Set up the dictawriter," said Alstair in a voice so harsh, so brittle that it seemed pure ice.

Trembling, Helen essayed to obey.

"I am ready to talk," said Alstair harshly into the dictawriter microphone.

The machine, rustling softly, translated. The leader of the new party hooted in reply. An order for all officers to report here at once, after setting all controls for automatic operations of the ship. There was some difficulty with the translation of the Centaurian equivalent of "automatic." It was not in the vocabulary file. It took time.

Alstair gave the order. Cold sweat stood out upon his face, but his self-control was iron.

A second order, also understood with a certain amount of difficulty. Copies of all technical records, and all—again it took time to understand—all books bearing on the construction of this ship were to be taken to the air lock by which these plant men had entered. Samples of machinery, generators, and weapons to the same destination.

Again Alstair gave the order. His voice was brittle, was even thin, but it did not falter or break.

The Centaurian leader hooted an order over which the dictawriter rustled in vain. His followers swept swiftly to the doors of the control room. They passed out, leaving but four of their number behind. And Jack went swiftly to Alstair. His force gun snapped out and pressed deep into the commander's middle. The Centaurians made no movement of protest.

"Damn you!" said Jack, his voice thick with rage. "You've let them take the ship! You plan to bargain for your life! Damn you, I'm going to kill you and fight my way to a rocket tube and send this ship up in a flare of clean flame that'll kill these devils with us!"

But Helen cried swiftly: "Jack! Don't! I know!"

Like an echo her words—because she was near the dictawriter microphone—were repeated in the hooting sounds of the Centaurian language. And Alstair, livid and near to madness, nevertheless said harshly in the lowest of tones:

"You fool! These devils can reach Earth, now they know it's worth reaching! So even if they kill every man on the ship but the officers—and they may—we've got to navigate to their planet and land there." His voice dropped to a rasping whisper and he raged almost soundlessly: "And if you think I want to live through what's coming, shoot!"

Jack stood rigid for an instant. Then he stepped back. He saluted with an elaborate, mechanical precision.

"I beg your pardon, sir," he said unsteadily. "You can count on me hereafter."

One of the officers of the *Adastra* stumbled into the control room. Another. Still another. They trickled in. Six officers out of thirty.

A Centaurian entered with the curious rolling gait of his race. He went impatiently to the dictawriter and made noises.

"These—all—officers?" asked the machine tonelessly.

"The air officer shot his family and himself," gasped a subaltern of the air department. "A bunch of Muts charged a rocket tube and the rocket chief fought them off. Then he bled to death from a knife in his throat. The stores officer was—"

"Stop!" said Alstair in a thin, high voice. He tore at his collar. He went to the microphone and said thinly: "These are all the officers still alive. But we can navigate the ship."

The Centaurian—he wore a wide band of leather about each of his arms and another about his middle—waddled to the G. C. phone. The tendrils at the end of one arm manipulated the switch expertly. He emitted strange, formless sounds—and hell broke loose!

The visiplates all over the room emitted high-pitched squealing sounds. They were horrible. They were ghastly. They were more terrible than the sounds of a wolf pack hard on the heels of a fear-mad deer. They were the sounds Jack had heard when one of the first invaders of the *Adastra* saw a human being and killed him instantly. And other sounds came out of the visiplates, too. There were human screams. There were even one or two explosions.

But then there was silence. The five Centaurians in the control room quivered and trembled. A desperate bloodlust filled them, the unreasoning, blind, instinctive craving which came of evolution from some race of carnivorous plants become capable of movement through the desperate need for food.

The Centaurian with the leather ornaments went to the dictawriter again. He hooted in it:

"Want—two—men—go—from—ship—learn—from—them
—now."

There was an infinitely tiny sound in the main control
room. It was a drop of cold sweat, falling from Alstair's face
to the floor. He seemed to have shriveled. His face was as
ashy gray. His eyes were closed. But Jack looked steadily
from one to the other of the surviving officers.

"That will mean vivisection, I suppose," he said harshly.
"It's certain they plan to visit Earth, else—intelligent as they
are—they wouldn't have wiped out everybody but us. Even
for treasure. They'll want to try out weapons on a human
body, and so on. Communications is about the most useless
of all the departments now, sir, I volunteer."

Helen gasped: "No, Jack! No!"

Alstair opened his eyes. "Gary has volunteered. One more
man to volunteer for vivisection." He said it in the choked
voice of one holding to sanity by the most terrible of efforts.
"They'll want to find out how to kill men. Their thirty-centimeter waves didn't work. They know the beams that melted
our hull wouldn't kill men. I can't volunteer! I've got to stay
with the ship!" There was despair in his voice. "One more
man to volunteer for these devils to kill slowly!"

Silence. The happenings of the past little while, and the
knowledge of what still went on within the *Adastra*'s innumerable compartments, had literally stunned most of the six.
They could not think. They were mentally dazed, emotionally
paralyzed by the sheer horrors they had encountered.

Then Helen stumbled into Jack's arms. "I'm—going, too!"
she gasped. "We're—all going to die! I'm not needed! And I
can—die with Jack."

Alstair groaned. "Please!"

"I'm—going!" she panted. "You can't stop me! With Jack!
Whither thou goest—"

Then she choked. She pressed close. The Centaurian of the
leather belts hooted impatiently into the dictawriter.

"These—two—come."

Alstair said in a strange voice: "Wait!" Like an automaton, he moved to his desk. He took up an electropen. He
wrote, his hands shaking. "I am mad," he said thinly. "We
are all mad. I think we are dead and in hell. But take this."

Jack stuffed the official order slip in his pocket. The Centaurian of the leather bands hooted impatiently. He led them,
with his queer, rolling gait, toward the air lock by which the

plant men had entered. Three times they were seen by roving Things, which emitted that triply horrible shrill squeal. And each time the Centaurian of the leather bands hooted authoritatively and the plant men withdrew.

Once, too, Jack saw four creatures swaying backward and forward about something on the floor. He reached out his hands and covered Helen's eyes until they were past.

They came to the air lock. Their guide pointed through it. The man and the girl obeyed. Long, rubbery tentacles seized them and Helen gasped and was still. Jack fought fiercely, shouting her name. Then something struck him savagely. He collapsed.

He came back to consciousness with a feeling of tremendous weight upon him. He stirred, and with his movement some of the oppression left him. A light burned, not a light such as men know on Earth, but a writhing flare which beat restlessly at the confines of a transparent globe which contained it. There was a queer smell in the air, too, an animal smell. Jack sat up. Helen lay beside him, unconfined and apparently unhurt. None of the Centaurians seemed to be near.

He chafted her wrists helplessly. He heard a stuttering sound and with each of the throbs of noise felt a momentary acceleration. Rockets, fuel rockets.

"We're on one of their damned ships!" said Jack coldly. He felt for his force gun. It was gone.

Helen opened her eyes. She stared vaguely about. Her eyes fell upon Jack. She shuddered suddenly and pressed close to him.

"What—what happened?"

"We'll have to find out," replied Jack grimly.

The floor beneath his feet careened suddenly. Instinctively, he glanced at a porthole which until then he had only subconsciously noted. He gazed out into the utterly familiar blackness of space, illumined by very many tiny points of light which were stars. He saw a ringed sun and points of light which were planets.

One of those points of light was very near. Its disk was perceptible, and polar snow caps, and the misty alternation of greenish areas which would be continents with the indescribable tint which is ocean bottom when viewed from beyond a planet's atmosphere.

Silence. No hootings of that strange language without vowels or consonants which the Centaurians used. No sound of any kind for a moment.

"We're heading for that planet, I suppose," said Jack quietly. "We'll have to see if we can manage to get ourselves killed before we land."

Then a murmur in the distance. It was a strange, muted murmur, in nothing resembling the queer notes of the plant men. With Helen clinging to him, Jack explored cautiously, out of the cubby-hole in which they had awakened. Silence save for that distant murmur. No movement anywhere. Another faint stutter of the rockets, with a distinct accelerative movement of the whole ship. The animal smell grew stronger. They passed through a strangely shaped opening and Helen cried out:

"The animals!"

Heaped higgledy-piggledy were cages from the *Adastra*, little compartments containing specimens of each of the animals which had been bred from for food, and which it had been planned to release if a planet suitable for colonization revolved about Proxima Centauri. Farther on was an indescribable mass of books, machines, cases of all sorts—the materials ordered to be carried to the air lock by the leader of the plant men. Still no sign of any Centaurian.

But the muted murmur, quite incredibly sounding like a human voice, came from still farther ahead. Bewildered, now, Helen followed as Jack went still cautiously toward the source of the sound.

They found it. It came from a bit of mechanism cased in with the same lusterless, dull-brown stuff which composed the floor and walls and every part of the ship about them. And it was a human voice. More, it was Alstair's, racked and harsh and half hysterical.

"—you must have recovered consciousness by now dammit, and these devils want some sign of it! They cut down your acceleration when I told them the rate they were using would keep you unconscious! Gary! Helen! Set off that signal!"

A pause. The voice again:

"I'll tell it again. You're in a space ship these fiends are guiding by a tight beam which handles the controls. You're going to be set down on one of the planets which once contained animal life. It's empty now, unoccupied except by plants. And you and the space ship's cargo of animals and books and so on are the reserved, special property of the high arch-fiend of all these devils. He had you sent in an outside-controlled ship because none of his kind could be trusted with such treasure as you and the other animals!

"You're a reserve of knowledge, to translate our books, explain our science, and so on. It's forbidden for any other space ship than his own to land on your planet. Now will you send that signal? It's a knob right above the speaker my voice is coming out of. Pull it three times, and they'll know you're all right and won't send another ship with preservatives for your flesh lest a priceless treasure go to waste!"

The tinny voice—Centaurian receptors were not designed to reproduce the elaborate phonetics of the human voice—laughed hysterically.

Jack reached up and pulled the knob, three times. Alstair's voice went on:

"This ship is hell, now. It isn't a ship any more, but a sort of brimstone pit. There are seven of us alive, and we're instructing Centaurians in the operation of the controls. But we've told them that we can't turn off the rockets to show their inner workings, because to be started they have to have a planet's mass near by, for deformation of space so the reaction can be started. They're keeping us alive until we've shown them that. They've got some method of writing, too, and they write down everything we say, when it's translated by a dictawriter. Very scientific—"

The voice broke off.

"Your signal just came," it said an instant later. "You'll find food somewhere about. The air ought to last you till you land. You've got four more days of travel. I'll call back later. Don't worry about navigation. It's attended to."

The voice died again, definitely.

The two of them, man and girl, explored the Centaurian space ship. Compared to the *Adastra*, it was miniature. A hundred feet long, or more, by perhaps sixty feet at its greatest diameter. They found cubby-holes in which there was now nothing at all, but which undoubtedly at times contained the plant men packed tightly.

These rooms could be refrigerated, and it was probable that at a low temperature the Centaurians reacted like vegetation on Earth in winter and passed into a dormant, hibernating state. Such an arrangement would allow of an enormous crew being carried, to be revived for landing or battle.

"If they refitted the *Adastra* for a trip back to Earth on that basis," said Jack grimly, "they'd carry a hundred and fifty thousand Centaurians at least. Probably more."

The thought of an assault upon mankind by these creatures was an obsession. Jack was tormented by it. Womanlike, Helen tried to cheer him by their own present safety.

"We volunteered for vivisection," she told him pitifully, the day after their recovery of consciousness, "and we're safe for a while, anyhow. And—we've got each other—"

"It's time for Alstair to communicate again," said Jack harshly. It was nearly thirty hours after the last signing off. Centaurian routine, like Earth discipline or terrestrial space ships, maintained a period equal to a planet's daily rotation as the unit of time. "We'd better go listen to him."

They did. And Alstair's racked voice came from the queerly shaped speaker. It was more strained, less sane, than the day before. He told them of the progress of the Things in the navigation of the *Adastra*. The six surviving officers already were not needed to keep the ship's apparatus functioning. The air-purifying apparatus in particular was shut off, since in clearing the air of carbon dioxide it tended to make the air unbreathable for the Centaurians.

The six men were now permitted to live that they might satisfy the insatiable desire of the plant men for information. They lived a perpetual third degree, with every resource of their brains demanded for record in the weird notation of their captors. The youngest of the six, a subaltern of the air department, went mad under the strain alike of memory and of anticipation. He screamed senselessly for hours, and was killed and his body promptly mummified by the strange, drying chemicals of the Centaurians. The rest were living shadows, starting at a sound.

"Our deceleration's been changed," said Alstair, his voice brittle. "You'll land just two days before we settle down, on the planet these devils call home. Queer they've no colonizing instinct. Another one of us is about to break, I think. They've taken away our shoes and belts now, by the way. They're leather. We'd take a gold band from about a watermelon, wouldn't we? Consistent, these—"

And he raged once, in sudden hysteria:

"I'm a fool! I sent you two off together while I'm living in hell! Gary, I order you to have nothing to do with Helen! I order that the two of you shan't speak to each other! I order that—"

Another day passed. And another. Alstair called twice more. Each time, by his voice, he was more desperate, more nerve-racked, closer to the bounds of madness. The second time he wept, the while he cursed Jack for being where there were none of the plant men.

"We're not interesting to the devils, now, except as animals. Our brains don't count! They're gutting the ship systematically. Yesterday they got the earthworms from the growing area where we grew crops! There's a guard on each of us now. Mine pulled out some of my hair this morning and ate it, rocking back and forth in ecstasy. We've no woolen shirts. They're animals!"

Another day still. Then Alstair was semihysterical. There were only three men left alive on the ship. He had instructions to give Jack in the landing of the egg-shaped vessel on the uninhabited world. Jack was supposed to help. His destination was close now. The disk of the planet which was to be his and Helen's prison filled half the heavens. And the other planet toward which the *Adastra* was bound was a full-sized disk to Alstair.

Beyond the rings of Proxima Centauri there were six planets in all, and the prison planet was next outward from the home of the plant men. It was colder than was congenial to them, though for a thousand years their flesh-hunting expeditions had searched its surface until not a mammal or a bird, no fish or even a crustacean was left upon it. Beyond it again an ice-covered world lay, and still beyond there were frozen shapes whirling in emptiness.

"You know, now, how to take over when the beam releases the atmospheric controls," said Alstair's voice. It wavered as if he spoke through teeth which chattered from pure nerve strain. "You'll have quiet. Trees and flowers and something like grass, if the pictures they've made mean anything. We're running into the greatest celebration in the history of all hell. Every space ship called home. There won't be a Centaurian on the planet who won't have a tiny shred of some sort of animal matter to consume. Enough to give him that beastly delight they feel when they get hold of something of animal origin.

"Damn them! Every member of the race! We're the greatest store of treasure ever dreamed of! They make no bones of talking before me, and I'm mad enough to understand a good bit of what they say to each other. Their most high panjandrum is planning bigger space ships than were ever grown before. He'll start out for Earth with three hundred space ships, and most of the crews asleep or hibernating. There'll be three million devils straight from hell on those ships, and they've those damned beams that will fuse an earthly ship at ten million miles."

Talking helped to keep Alstair sane, apparently. The next day Jack's and Helen's egg-shaped vessel dropped like a plummet from empty space into an atmosphere which screamed wildly past its smooth sides. Then Jack got the ship under control and it descended slowly and ever more slowly and at last came to a cushioned stop in a green glade hard by a forest of strange but wholly reassuring trees. It was close to sunset on this planet, and darkness fell before they could attempt exploration.

They did little exploring, however, either the next day or the day after. Alstair talked almost continuously.

"Another ship coming from Earth," he said, and his voice cracked. "Another ship! She started at least four years ago. She'll get here in four years more. You two may see her, but I'll be dead or mad by to-morrow night! And here's the humorous thing! It seems to me that madness is nearest when I think of you, Helen, letting Jack kiss you! I loved you, you know, Helen, when I was a man, before I became a corpse watching my ship being piloted into hell. I loved you very much. I was jealous, and when you looked at Gary with shining eyes I hated him. I still hate him, Helen! Ah, how I hate him!" But Alstair's voice was the voice of a ghost, now, a ghost in purgatory. "And I've been a fool, giving him that order"

Jack walked about with abstracted, burning eyes. Helen put her hands on his shoulders and he spoke absently to her, his voice thick with hatred. A desperate, passionate lust to kill Centaurians filled him. He began to hunt among the machines. He became absorbed, assembling a ten-kilowatt vortex gun from odd contrivances. He worked at it for many hours. Then he heard Helen at work, somewhere. She seemed to be struggling. It disturbed him. He went to see.

She had just dragged the last of the cages from the *Adastra* out into the open. She was releasing the little creatures within. Pigeons soared eagerly above her. Rabbits, hardly hopping out of her reach, munched delightedly upon the unfamiliar but satisfactory leafed vegetation underfoot.

She browsed. There were six of them besides a tiny, wabbly-legged lamb. Chickens pecked and scratched. But there were no insects in this world. They would find only seeds and green stuff. Four puppies rolled ecstatically on scratchy green things in the sunlight.

"Anyhow," said Helen defiantly. "They can be happy for a while! They're not like us! We have to worry! And this world could be a paradise for humans!"

Jack looked somberly out across the green and beautiful world. No noxious animals. No harmful insects. There could be no diseases on this planet, unless men introduced them of set purpose. It would be a paradise.

The murmur of a human voice came from within the space ship. He went bitterly to listen. Helen came after him. They stood in the strangely shaped cubby-hole which was the control room. Walls, floors, ceiling, instrument cases—all were made of the lusterless dark-brown stuff which had grown into the shapes the Centaurians desired. Alstair's voice was strangely more calm, less hysterical, wholly steady.

"I hope you're not off exploring somewhere, Helen and Gary," it said from the speaker. "They've had a celebration here to-day. The *Adastra*'s landed. I landed it. I'm the only man left alive. We came down in the center of a city of these devils, in the middle of buildings fit to form the headquarters of hell. The high panjandrum has a sort of palace right next to the open space where I am now.

"And to-day they celebrated. It's strange how much animal matter there was on the *Adastra*. They even found horsehair stiffening in the coats of our uniforms. Woolen blankets. Shoes. Even some of the soaps had an animal origin, and they 'refined' it. They can recover any scrap of animal matter as cleverly as our chemists can recover gold and radium. Queer, eh?"

The speaker was silent a moment.

"I'm sane, now," the voice said steadily. "I think I was mad for a while. But what I saw to-day cleared my brain. I saw millions of these devils dipping their arms into great tanks, great troughs, in which solutions of all the animal tissues from the *Adastra* were dissolved. The high panjandrum kept plenty for himself! I saw the things they carried into his palace through lines of guards. Some of those things had been my friends. I saw a city gone crazy with beastly joy, the devils swaying back and forth in ecstasy as they absorbed the loot from Earth. I heard the high panjandrum hoot a sort of imperial address from the throne. And I've learned to understand quite a lot of those hootings.

"He was telling them that Earth is packed with animals. Men. Beasts. Birds. Fish in the oceans. And he told them that the greatest space fleet in history will soon be grown, which will use the propulsion methods of men, our rockets, Gary, and the first fleet will carry uncountable swarms of them to occupy Earth. They'll send back treasure, too, so that every one of his subjects will have such ecstasy, frequently, as they had to-day. And the devils, swaying crazily back and forth, gave out that squealing noise of theirs. Millions of them at once."

Jack groaned softly. Helen covered her eyes as if to shut out the sight her imagination pictured.

"Now, here's the situation from your standpoint," said Alstair steadily, millions of miles away and the only human being upon a planet of bloodlusting plant men. "They're coming here now, their scientists, to have me show them the inside workings of the rockets. Some others will come over to question you two to-morrow. But I'm going to show these devils our rockets. I'm sure—perfectly sure—that every space ship of the race is back on this planet.

"They came to share the celebration when every one of them got as a free gift from the grand panjandrum as much animal tissue as he could hope to acquire in a lifetime of toil. Flesh is a good bit more precious than gold, here. It rates, on a comparative scale, somewhere between platinum and radium. So they all came home. Every one of them! And there's a space ship on the way here from Earth. It'll arrive in four years more. Remember that!"

An impatient, distant hooting came from the speaker.

"They're here," said Alstair steadily. "I'm going to show them the rockets. Maybe you'll see the fun. It depends on the time of day where you are. But remember, there's a sister ship to the *Adastra* on the way! And Gary, that order I gave you last thing was the act of a madman, but I'm glad I did it. Good-by, you two!"

Small hooting sounds, growing fainter, came from the speaker. Far, far away, amid the city of fiends, Alstair was going with the plant men to show them the rockets' inner workings. They wished to understand every aspect of the big ship's propulsion, so that they could build—or grow—ships as large and carry multitudes of their swarming myriads to a solar system where animals were to be found.

"Let's go outside," said Jack harshly. "He said he'd do it,

since he couldn't get a bit of a machine made that could be depended on to do it. But I believed he'd go mad. It didn't seem possible to live to their planet. We'll go outside and look at the sky."

Helen stumbled. They stood upon the green grass, looking up at the firmament above them. They waited, staring. And Jack's mind pictured the great rocket chambers of the *Adastra*. He seemed to see the strange procession enter it; a horde of the ghastly plant men and then Alstair, his face like marble and his hands as steady.

He'd open up the breech of one of the rockets. He'd explain the disintegration field, which collapses the electrons of hydrogen so that it rises in atomic weight to helium, and the helium to lithium, while the oxygen of the water is split literally into neutronium and pure force. Alstair would answer hooted questions. The supersonic generators he would explain as controls of force and direction. He would not speak of the fact that only the material of the rocket tubes, when filled with exactly the frequency those generators produced, could withstand the effect of the disintegration field.

He would not explain that a tube started without those generators in action would catch from the fuel and disintegrate, and that any other substance save one, under any other condition save that one rate of vibration, would catch also and that tubes, ship, and planet alike would vanish in a lambent purple flame.

No; Alstair would not explain that. He would show the Centaurians how to start the Caldwell field.

The man and the girl looked at the sky. And suddenly there was a fierce purple light. It dwarfed the reddish tinge of the ringed sun overhead. For one second, for two, for three, the purple light persisted. There was no sound. There was a momentary blast of intolerable heat. Then all was as before.

The ringed sun shone brightly. Clouds like those of Earth floated serenely in a sky but a little less blue than that of home. The small animals from the *Adastra* munched contentedly at the leafy stuff underfoot. The pigeons soared joyously, exercising their wings in full freedom.

"He did it," said Jack. "And every space ship was home. There aren't any more plant men. There's nothing left of their planet, their civilization, or their plans to harm our Earth."

Even out in space, there was nothing where the planet of

the Centaurians had been. Not even steam or cooling gases. It was gone as if it had never existed. And the man and woman of Earth stood upon a planet which could be a paradise for human beings, and another ship was coming presently, with more of their kind.

"He did it!" repeated Jack quietly. "Rest his soul! And we—we can think of living, now, instead of death."

The grimness of his face relaxed slowly. He looked down at Helen. Gently, he put his arm about her shoulders.

She pressed close, gladly, thrusting away all thoughts of what had been. Presently she asked softly: "What was that last order Alstair gave you?"

"I never looked," said Jack.

He fumbled in his pocket. Pocketworn and frayed, the order slip came out. He read it and showed it to Helen. By statutes passed before the *Adastra* left Earth, laws and law enforcement on the artificial planet were intrusted to the huge ship's commander. It had been specially provided that a legal marriage on the *Adastra* would be constituted by an official order of marriage signed by the commander. And the slip handed to Jack by Alstair, as Jack went to what he'd thought would be an agonizing death, was such an order. It was, in effect, a marriage certificate.

They smiled at each other, those two.

"It—wouldn't have mattered," said Helen uncertainly. "I love you. But I'm glad!"

One of the freed pigeons found a straw upon the ground. He tugged at it. His mate inspected it solemnly. They made pigeon noises to each other. They flew away with the straw. After due discussion, they had decided that it was an eminently suitable straw with which to begin the building of a nest.

The World-Wrecker on Mars

The science fiction of the '30s and the '40s, or even the science fiction up to the present, can't be explained without the understanding that it was a commercial genre. From Gernsback on, publishers were mostly trying to make a buck, editors were looking for stories that would sell magazines, and the full-time writers, at least, were trying to sell stories to editors and in sufficient quantity to make a living.

To be sure, all fiction—indeed, all writing intended for sale or for performance to a paying audience—has some aspects of the commercial. Shakespeare left Stratford to make his fortune, and Samuel Johnson pointed out that "no man but a blockhead ever wrote, except for money." The most avant-garde author appreciated by only a few wishes it were otherwise, that his novel would sell a million copies and bring him the recognition and the economic rewards his work deserves.

But science-fiction writers were playing for smaller stakes, and the few who were trying to make a living out of the magazines were working for pennies. A cent a word was the best wages they could hope for. In *Hell's Cartographers*, Brian Aldiss noted that "the smaller the payment, the larger it looms." The motivation of the writers, however, could not have been entirely mercenary; they could have written more profitably in other fields, but they chose to write science fiction because they liked its freedom, or they enjoyed the ambience, the feedback, or the companionship, or because they loved what they wrote.

If they wanted to make a living at it, however, they had to write constantly, swiftly, hastily, and with little, if any, revision. Their virtues were glibness and narrative instinct, and, occasionally, the ability to let the submerged artist, if there, break the surface for a breath of air. Sometimes, though, in light of the market, that was a mistake.

The writing, then, tended toward adventure and action, because these were easy to write and used up a great many words, and besides, the readers liked them best. The editors preferred them, too. Algis Budrys said in *Nebula Winners Twelve* that all editors believe, and have the sales figures to prove, that "a storyteller will outsell a writer." Campbell was not completely in that camp. He liked adventure stories, all right, and published Doc Smith's *Lensman* series and other adventure serials, but he wanted them written, if possible, around an original idea or a series of ideas, like van Vogt's *Null-A* series or Hal Clement's *Mission of Gravity*.

Partly because of Campbell's influence, partly because of the modifications of reality, science-fiction adventure stories became harder to write; today the out-and-out adventure is more likely to be a fantasy without the pressure of accommodation to the real world. Occasionally, too, the role of the adventure writer would wear thin, and the writer's desire to write something more subtle or more meaningful, never completely absent, would result in fiction of a different sort.

The most surprising aspect of the science fiction of the '30s is not that so much of it was poorly written but that out of this process came stories with vitality, stories with originality and some skill, stories that surpassed the circumstances of their creation.

The writers most admired in the '30s, however, were adventure writers. One of them was Edmond Hamilton (1904-1977). He was prolific with ideas, as science-fiction writers of the times had to be, but most of his writing fell into the adventure mode.

Hamilton broke into publication in 1926 with a story in *Weird Tales,* inspired by A. Merritt's fantasies, entitled "The Monster-God of Mamurth." The twenty-two-year-old author was the only son in a Pennsylvania family; he had three sisters. He finished high school at the age of fourteen, but was expelled from college in his junior year for missing chapel. He worked for a time as a railway-yard clerk, then turned, for good, to full-time writing.

Jack Williamson, a long-time friend of Hamilton's, has said that *Weird Tales* never rejected a Hamilton story. He became one of its most frequent and popular authors under his own name and half a dozen pseudonyms. In particular he created a series of stories about an Interstellar Patrol made up of creatures from many different worlds to defend the civilized galaxy. "They helped shape the myth of man's coming conquest of the stars that is still a major science fiction theme," Williamson has written.

One of Hamilton's favorite plots concerned a threat to a solar system or the galaxy by evil forces that were thwarted by one man. From this he earned the nickname of "world-wrecker" or sometimes "world-saver" Hamilton. He sold stories to many magazines, including *Amazing Stories, Wonder Stories* and its successors, and the early *Astounding*. He may never have sold a story to John Campbell, however. One of his stories appeared in the December 1938 *Astounding*, but may have been in inventory when Campbell took over as editor.

In 1939, Leo Margulies, editorial director of Standard Magazines (publisher of *Startling Stories* and *Thrilling Wonder Stories*), created *Captain Future* magazine and recruited Hamilton to write it; he wrote all but three of the twenty-one novels and novelettes in the series. In 1969–70 the series was reprinted in paperback.

Hamilton married another science-fiction writer, Leigh Brackett, (1915-1978), in 1946. She, too, wrote romantic adventure stories, but she also wrote screenplays, including (with William Faulkner) *The Big Sleep* and later many others, including several John Wayne films. She also wrote suspense novels and in recent years returned to a favorite early hero, Eric John Stark, for a series of sf novels.

For many years Hamilton ground out *Superman* scripts, but he continued to write science fiction. *The Star Kings* was published in 1949 and *City at the World's End* in 1951. "What's It Like Out There?" was published in *Thrilling Wonder Stories* in 1952, but it is not out of place in this period. The original version was written in 1933, rejected by several editors, and put away for nearly twenty years before it was revised and found acceptance in another era.

The story represents the modification of the myth of man's conquest of space by the reality of space flight and by the discoveries that science was beginning to make about the real nature of the other planets. It also illustrates the artistic skills that often lurked beneath the surface of the pulps.

What's It Like Out There?

by Edmond Hamilton

I hadn't wanted to wear my uniform when I left the hospital, but I didn't have any other clothes there and I was too glad to get out to argue about it. But as soon as I got on the local plane I was taking to Los Angeles, I was sorry I had it on.

People gawked at me and began to whisper. The stewardess gave me a special big smile. She must have spoken to the pilot, for he came back and shook hands, and said, "Well, I guess a trip like this is sort of a comedown for *you.*"

A little man came in, looked around for a seat, and took the one beside me. He was a fussy, spectacled guy of fifty or sixty, and he took a few minutes to get settled. Then he looked at me, and stared at my uniform and at the little brass button on it that said "TWO."

"Why," he said, "you're one of those Expedition Two men!" And then, as though he'd only just figured it out, "Why, you've been to Mars!"

"Yeah," I said. "I was there."

He beamed at me in a kind of wonder. I didn't like it, but his curiosity was so friendly that I couldn't quite resent it.

"Tell me," he said, "what's it like out there?"

The plane was lifting, and I looked out at the Arizona desert sliding by close underneath.

"Different," I said. "It's different."

The answer seemed to satisfy him completely. "I'll just bet it is," he said. "Are you going home, Mr. . . ."

"Haddon. Sergeant Frank Haddon."

"You going home, Sergeant?"

"My home's back in Ohio," I told him. "I'm going in to L.A. to look up some people before I go home."

"Well, that's fine. I hope you have a good time, Sergeant. You deserve it. You boys did a great job out there. Why, I read in the newspapers that after the U.N. sends out a couple more expeditions, we'll have cities out there, and regular passenger lines, and all that."

"Look," I said, "that stuff is for the birds. You might as

342

well build cities down there in Mojave, and have them a lot closer. There's only one reason for going to Mars now, and that's uranium."

I could see he didn't quite believe me. "Oh, sure," he said, "I know that's important too, the uranium we're all using now for our power stations—but that isn't all, is it?"

"It'll be all, for a long, long time," I said.

"But look, Sergeant, this newspaper article said . . ."

I didn't say anything more. By the time he'd finished telling about the newspaper article, we were coming down into L.A. He pumped my hand when we got out of the plane.

"Have yourself a time, Sergeant! You sure rate it. I hear a lot of chaps on Two didn't come back."

"Yeah," I said. "I heard that."

I was feeling shaky again by the time I got to downtown L.A. I went in a bar and had a double bourbon and it made me feel a little better.

I went out and found a cabby and asked him to drive me out to San Gabriel. He was a fat man with a broad red face.

"Hop right in, buddy," he said. "Say, you're one of those Mars guys, aren't you?"

I said, "That's right."

"Well, well," he said. "Tell me, how was it out there?"

"It was a pretty dull grind, in a way," I told him.

"I'll bet it was!" he said, as we started through traffic. "Me, I was in the Army in World War Two, twenty years ago. That's just what it was, a dull grind nine tenths of the time. I guess it hasn't changed any."

"This wasn't any Army expedition," I explained. "It was a United Nations one, not an Army one—but we had officers and rules of discipline like the Army."

"Sure, it's the same thing," said the cabby. "You don't need to tell me what it's like, buddy. Why, back there in 'forty-two, or was it 'forty-three?—anyway, back there I remember that . . ."

I leaned back and watched Huntington Boulevard slide past. The sun poured in on me and seemed very hot, and the air seemed very thick and soupy. It hadn't been so bad up on the Arizona plateau, but it was a little hard to breathe down here.

The cabby wanted to know what address in San Gabriel. I got the little packet of letters out of my pocket and found the one that had "Martin Valinez" and a street address on the back. I told the cabby and put the letters back into my pocket.

I wished now that I'd never answered them.

But how could I keep from answering when Joe Valinez' parents wrote to me at the hospital? And it was the same with Jim's girl, and Walter's family. I'd had to write back, and the first thing I knew I'd promised to come and see them, and now if I went back to Ohio without doing it I'd feel like a heel. Right now, I wished I'd decided to be a heel.

The address was on the south side of San Gabriel, in a section that still had a faintly Mexican tinge to it. There was a little frame grocery store with a small house beside it, and a picket fence around the yard of the house; very neat, but a queerly homely place after all the slick California stucco.

I went into the little grocery, and a tall, dark man with quiet eyes took a look at me and called a woman's name in a low voice and then came around the counter and took my hand.

"You're Sergeant Haddon," he said. "Yes. Of course. We've been hoping you'd come."

His wife came in a hurry from the back. She looked a little too old to be Joe's mother, for Joe had been just a kid; but then she didn't look so old either, but just sort of worn.

She said to Valinez, "Please, a chair. Can't you see he's tired? And just from the hospital."

I sat down and looked between them at a case of canned peppers, and they asked me how I felt, and wouldn't I be glad to get home, and they hoped all my family were well.

They were gentlefolk. They hadn't said a word about Joe, just waited for me to say something. And I felt in a spot, for I hadn't known Joe well, not really. He'd been moved into our squad only a couple of weeks before take-off, and since he'd been our first casualty, I'd never got to know him much.

I finally had to get it over with, and all I could think to say was, "They wrote you in detail about Joe, didn't they?"

Valinez nodded gravely. "Yes—that he died from shock within twenty-four hours after take-off. The letter was very nice."

His wife nodded too. "Very nice," she murmured. She looked at me, and I guess she saw that I didn't know quite what to say, for she said, "You can tell us more about it. Yet you must not if it pains you."

I could tell them more. Oh, yes, I could tell them a lot more, if I wanted to. It was all clear in my mind, like a movie film you run over and over till you know it by heart.

I could tell them all about the take-off that had killed their son. The long lines of us, uniformed backs going up into Rocket Four and all the other nineteen rockets—the lights flaring up there on the plateau, the grind of machinery and blast of whistles and the inside of the big rocket as we climbed up the ladders of its center well.

The movie was running again in my mind, clear as crystal, and I was back in Cell Fourteen of Rocket Four, with the minutes ticking away and the walls quivering every time one of the other rockets blasted off, and us ten men in our hammocks, prisoned inside that odd-shaped windowless metal room, waiting. Waiting, till that big, giant hand came and smacked us down deep into our recoil springs, crushing the breath out of us, so that you fought to breathe, and the blood roared into your head, and your stomach heaved in spite of all the pills they'd given you, and you heard the giant laughing, *b-r-r-room! b-r-r-room! b-r-r-oom!*

Smash, smash, again and again, hitting us in the guts and cutting our breath and someone being sick, and someone else sobbing, and the *b-r-r-oom! b-r-r-oom!* laughing as it killed us; and then the giant quit laughing, and quit slapping us down, and you could feel your sore and shaky body and wonder if it was still all there.

Walter Millis cursing a blue streak in the hammock underneath me, and Breck Jergen, our sergeant then, clambering painfully out of his straps to look us over, and then through the voices a thin, ragged voice saying uncertainly, "Breck, I think I'm hurt . . ."

Sure, that was their boy Joe, and there was blood on his lips, and he'd had it—we knew when we first looked at him that he'd had it. A handsome kid, turned waxy now as he held his hand on his middle and looked up at us. Expedition One had proved that take-off would hit a certain percentage with internal injuries every time, and in our squad, in our little windowless cell, it was Joe that had been hit.

If only he'd died right off. But he couldn't die right off, he had to lie in the hammock all those hours and hours. The medics came and put a strait-jacket around his body and doped him up, and that was that, and the hours went by. And we were so shaken and deathly sick ourselves that we didn't have the sympathy for him we should have had—not till he started moaning and begging us to take the jacket off.

Finally Walter Millis wanted to do it, and Breck wouldn't

allow it, and they were arguing and we were listening when the moaning stopped, and there was no need to do anything about Joe Valinez any more. Nothing but to call the medics, who came into our little iron prison and took him away.

Sure, I could tell the Valinezes all about how their Joe died, couldn't I?

"Please," whispered Mrs. Valinez, and her husband looked at me and nodded silently.

So I told them.

I said, "You know Joe died in space. He'd been knocked out by the shock of take-off, and he was unconscious, not feeling a thing. And then he woke up, before he died. He didn't seem to be feeling any pain, not a bit. He lay there, looking out the window at the stars. They're beautiful, the stars out there in space, like angels. He looked, and then he whispered something and lay back and was gone."

Mrs. Valinez began to cry softly. "To die out there, looking at stars like angels . . ."

I got up to go, and she didn't look up. I went out the door of the little grocery store, and Valinez came with me.

He shook my hand. "Thank you, Sergeant Haddon. Thank you very much."

"Sure," I said.

I got into the cab. I took out my letters and tore that one into bits. I wished to God I'd never got it. I wished I didn't have any of the other letters I still had.

2

I took the early plane for Omaha. Before we got there I fell asleep in my seat, and then I began to dream, and that wasn't good.

A voice said, "We're coming down."

And we were coming down, Rocket Four was coming down, and there we were in our squad cell, all of us strapped into our hammocks, waiting and scared, wishing there was a window so we could see out, hoping our rocket wouldn't be the one to crack up, hoping none of the rockets cracked up, but if one does, don't let it be *ours*. . . .

"We're coming down. . . ."

Coming down, with the blasts starting to boom again underneath us, hitting us hard, not steady like at take-off, but blast-blast-blast, and then again, blast-blast.

Breck's voice, calling to us from across the cell, but I couldn't hear for the roaring that was in my ears between blasts. No, it was *not* in my ears, that roaring came from the wall beside me: we had hit atmosphere, we were coming in.

The blasts in lightning succession without stopping, crash-crash-crash-crash-crash! Mountains fell on me, and this was it, and don't let it be ours, please, God, don't let it be ours. . . .

Then the bump and the blackness, and finally somebody yelling hoarsely in my ears, and Breck Jergen, his face deathly white, leaning over me.

"Unstrap and get out, Frank! All men out of hammocks—all men out!"

We'd landed, and we hadn't cracked up, but we were half dead and they wanted us to turn out, right this minute, and we couldn't.

Breck yelling to us, "Breathing masks on! Masks on! We've got to go out!"

"My God, we've just landed, we're torn to bits, we can't!"

"We've got to! Some of the other rockets cracked up in landing and we've got to save whoever's still living in them! Masks on! Hurry!"

We couldn't, but we did. They hadn't given us all those months of discipline for nothing. Jim Clymer was already on his feet, Walter was trying to unstrap underneath me, whistles were blowing like mad somewhere and voices shouted hoarsely.

My knees wobbled under me as I hit the floor. Young Lassen, beside me, tried to say something and then crumpled up. Jim bent over him, but Breck was at the door yelling, "Let him go! Come on!"

The whistles screeching at us all the way down the ladders of the well, and the mask clip hurting my nose, and down at the bottom a disheveled officer yelling at us to get out and join Squad Five, and the gangway reeling under us.

Cold. Freezing cold, and a wan sunshine from the shrunken little sun up there in the brassy sky, and a rolling plain of ocherous red and sand stretching around us, sand that slid away under our feet as our squads followed Captain Wall toward the distant metal bulk that lay oddly canted and broken in a little shallow valley.

"Come on, men—hurry! Hurry!"

Sure, all of it a dream, the dreamlike way we walked with our lead-soled shoes dragging our feet back after each step, and the voices coming through the mask resonators muffled and distant.

Only not a dream, but a nightmare, when we got up to the canted metal bulk and saw what had happened to Rocket Seven—the metal hull ripped like paper, and a few men crawling out of the wreck with blood on them, and a gurgling sound where shattered tanks were emptying, and voices whimpering, "First aid! First aid!"

Only it hadn't happened, it hadn't happened yet at all, for we were still back in Rocket Four coming in, we hadn't landed yet at all but we were going to any minute.

"We're coming down. . . ."

I couldn't go through it all again. I yelled and fought my hammock straps and woke up, and I was in my plane seat and a scared hostess was a foot away from me, saying, "This is Omaha, Sergeant. We're coming down."

They were all looking at me, all the other passengers, and I guessed I'd been talking in the dream—I still had the sweat down my back like all those nights in the hospital when I'd keep waking up.

I sat up, and they all looked away from me quick and pretended they hadn't been staring.

We came down to the airport. It was midday, and the hot Nebraska sun felt good on my back when I got out. I was lucky, for when I asked at the bus depot about going to Cuffington, there was a bus all ready to roll.

A farmer sat down beside me, a big young fellow who offered me cigarettes and told me it was only a few hours' ride to Cuffington.

"Your home there?" he asked.

"No, my home's back in Ohio," I said. "A friend of mine came from there. Name of Clymer."

He didn't know him, but he remembered that one of the town boys had gone on that second expedition to Mars.

"Yeah," I said. "That was Jim."

He couldn't keep it in any longer. "What's it like out there, anyway?"

I said, "Dry. Terrible dry."

"I'll bet it is," he said. "To tell the truth, it's too dry here, this year, for good wheat weather. Last year it was fine. Last year . . ."

Cuffington, Nebraska, was a wide street of stores, and other streets with trees and old houses, and yellow wheat fields all around as far as you could see. It was pretty hot, and I was glad to sit down in the bus depot while I went through the thin little phone book.

There were three Graham families in the book, but the first one I called was the right one—Miss Ila Graham. She talked fast and excited, and said she'd come right over, and I said I'd wait in front of the bus depot.

I stood underneath the awning, looking down the quiet street and thinking that it sort of explained why Jim Clymer had always been such a quiet, slow-moving sort of guy. The place was sort of relaxed, like he'd been.

A coupé pulled up, and Miss Graham opened the door. She was a brown-haired girl, not especially good-looking, but the kind you think of as a nice girl, a very nice girl.

She said, "You look so tired that I feel guilty now about asking you to stop."

"I'm all right," I said. "And it's no trouble stopping over a couple of places on my way back to Ohio."

As we drove across the little town, I asked her if Jim hadn't had any family of his own here.

"His parents were killed in a car crash years ago," Miss Graham said. "He lived with an uncle on a farm outside Grandview, but they didn't get along, and Jim came into town and got a job at the power station."

She added, as we turned a corner, "My mother rented him a room. That's how we got to know each other. That's how we—how we got engaged."

"Yeah, sure," I said.

It was a big square house with a deep front porch, and some trees around it. I sat down in a wicker chair, and Miss Graham brought her mother out. Her mother talked a little about Jim, how they missed him, and how she declared he'd been just like a son.

When her mother went back in, Miss Graham showed me a little bunch of blue envelopes. "These were the letters I got from Jim. There weren't very many of them, and they weren't very long."

"We were only allowed to send one thirty-word message every two weeks," I told her. "There were a couple of thousand of us out there, and they couldn't let us jam up the message transmitter all the time."

"It was wonderful how much Jim could put into just a few words," she said, and handed me some of them.

I read a couple. One said, "I have to pinch myself to realize that I'm one of the first Earthmen to stand on an alien world. At night, in the cold, I look up at the green star that's Earth and can't quite realize I've helped an age-old dream come true."

Another one said, "This world's grim and lonely, and mysterious. We don't know much about it yet. So far, nobody's seen anything living but the lichens that Expedition One reported, but there might be anything here."

Miss Graham asked me, "Was that all there was, just lichens?"

"That, and two or three kinds of queer cactus things," I said. "And rock and sand. That's all."

As I read more of those little blue letters, I found that now that Jim was gone I knew him better than I ever had. There was something about him I'd never suspected. He was romantic inside. We hadn't suspected it, he was always so quiet and slow, but now I saw that all the time he was more romantic about the thing we were doing than any of us.

He hadn't let on. We'd have kidded him, if he had. Our name for Mars, after we got sick of it, was the Hole. We always talked about it as the Hole. I could see now that Jim had been too shy of our kidding to ever let us know that he glamorized the thing in his mind.

"This was the last one I got from him before his sickness," Miss Graham said.

That one said, "I'm starting north tomorrow with one of the mapping expeditions. We'll travel over country no human has ever seen before."

I nodded. "I was on that party myself. Jim and I were on the same half-track."

"He was thrilled by it, wasn't he, Sergeant?"

I wondered. I remembered that trip, and it was hell. Our job was simply to run a preliminary topographical survey, checking with Geigers for possible uranium deposits.

It wouldn't have been so bad, if the sand hadn't started to blow.

It wasn't sand like Earth sand. It was ground to dust by billions of years of blowing around that dry world. It got inside your breathing mask, and your goggles, and the engines of the half-tracks, in your food and water and clothes. There was nothing for three days but cold, and wind, and sand.

Thrilled? I'd have laughed at that before. But now I didn't know. Maybe Jim had been, at that. He had lots if patience, a lot more than I ever had. Maybe he glamorized that hellish trip into wonderful adventure on a foreign world.

"Sure, he was thrilled," I said. "We all were. Anybody would be."

Miss Graham took the letters back, and then said, "You had Martian sickness too, didn't you?"

I said, yes, I had, just a touch, and that was why I'd had to spend a stretch in reconditioning hospital when I got back.

She waited for me to go on, and I knew I had to. "They don't know yet if it's some sort of virus or just the effect of Martian conditions on Earthmen's bodies. It hit forty per cent of us. It wasn't really so bad—fever and dopiness, mostly."

"When Jim got it, was he well cared for?" she asked. Her lips were quivering a little.

"Sure, he was well cared for. He got the best care there was," I lied.

The best care there was? That was a laugh. The first cases got decent care, maybe. But they'd never figured on so many coming down. There wasn't any room in our little hospital—they just had to stay in their bunks in the aluminum Quonsets when it hit them. All our doctors but one were down, and two of them died.

We'd been on Mars six months when it hit us, and the loneliness had already got us down. All but four of our rockets had gone back to Earth, and we were alone on a dead world, our little town of Quonsets huddled together under that hateful, brassy sky, and beyond it the sand and rocks that went on forever.

You go up to the North Pole and camp there, and find out how lonely that is. It was worse out there, a lot worse. The first excitement was gone long ago, and we were tired, and homesick in a way nobody was ever homesick before—we wanted to see green grass, and real sunshine, and women's faces, and hear running water; and we wouldn't until Expedition Three came to relieve us. No wonder guys blew their top out there. And then came Martian sickness, on top of it.

"We did everything for him that we could," I said.

Sure we had. I could still remember Walter and me tramping through the cold night to the hospital to try to get a medic, while Breck stayed with him, and how we couldn't get one.

I remember how Walter had looked up at the blazing sky as we tramped back, and shaken his fist at the big green star of Earth.

"People up there are going to dances tonight, watching shows, sitting around in warm rooms laughing! Why should good men have to die out here to get them uranium for cheap power?"

"Can it," I told him tiredly. "Jim's not going to die. A lot of guys got over it."

The best care there was? That was real funny. All we could do was wash his face, and give him the pills the medic left, and watch him get weaker every day till he died.

"Nobody could have done more for him than was done," I told Miss Graham.

"I'm glad," she said. "I guess—it's just one of those things."

When I got up to go she asked me if I didn't want to see Jim's room. They'd kept it for him just the same, she said.

I didn't want to, but how are you going to say so? I went up with her and looked and said it was nice. She opened a big cupboard. It was full of neat rows of old magazines.

"They're all the old science fiction magazines he read when he was a boy," she said. "He always saved them."

I took one out. It had a bright cover, with a space ship on it, not like our rockets but a streamlined thing, and the rings of Saturn in the background.

When I laid it down, Miss Graham took it up and put it back carefully into its place in the row, as though somebody was coming back who wouldn't like to find things out of order.

She insisted on driving me back to Omaha, and out to the airport. She seemed sorry to let me go, and I suppose it was because I was the last real tie to Jim, and when I was gone it was all over then for good.

I wondered if she'd get over it in time, and I guessed she would. People do get over things. I suppose she'd marry some other nice guy, and I wondered what they'd do with Jim's things—with all those old magazines nobody was ever coming back to read.

3

I would never have stopped at Chicago at all if I could have got out of it, for the last person I wanted to talk to anybody about was Walter Millis. It would be too easy for me to make a slip and let out stuff nobody was supposed to know.

But Walter's father had called me at the hospital, a couple of times. The last time he called, he said he was having

Breck's parents come down from Wisconsin so they could see me, too, so what could I do then but say, yes, I'd stop. But I didn't like it at all, and I knew I'd have to be careful.

Mr. Millis was waiting at the airport and shook hands with me and said what a big favor I was doing them all, and how he appreciated my stopping when I must be anxious to get back to my own home and parents.

"That's all right," I said. "My dad and mother came out to the hospital to see me when I first got back."

He was a big, fine-looking important sort of man, with a little bit of the stuffed shirt about him, I thought. He seemed friendly enough, but I got the feeling he was looking at me and wondering why I'd come back and his son Walter hadn't. Well, I couldn't blame him for that.

His car was waiting, a big car with a driver, and we started north through the city. Mr. Millis pointed out a few things to me to make conversation, especially a big atomic-power station we passed.

"It's only one of thousands, strung all over the world," he said. "They're going to transform our whole economy. This Martian uranium will be a big thing, Sergeant."

I said, yes, I guessed it would.

I was sweating blood, waiting for him to start asking about Walter, and I didn't know yet just what I could tell him. I could get myself in Dutch plenty if I opened my big mouth too wide, for that one thing that had happened to Expedition Two was supposed to be strictly secret, and we'd all been briefed on why we had to keep our mouths shut.

But he let it go for the time being, and just talked over stuff. I gathered that his wife wasn't too well, and that Walter had been their only child. I also gathered that he was a very big shot in business, and dough-heavy.

I didn't like him. Walter I'd liked plenty, but his old man seemed a pretty pompous person, with his heavy business talk.

He wanted to know how soon I thought Martian uranium would come through in quantity, and I said I didn't think it'd be very soon.

"Expedition One only located the deposits," I said, "and Two just did mapping and setting up a preliminary base. Of course, the thing keeps expanding, and I hear Four will have a hundred rockets. But Mars is a tough setup."

Mr. Millis said decisively that I was wrong, that the world

was power-hungry, that it would be pushed a lot faster than I expected.

He suddenly quit talking business and looked at me and asked, "Who was Walter's best friend out there?"

He asked it sort of apologetically. He was a stuffed shirt; but all my dislike of him went away then.

"Breck Jergen," I told him. "Breck was our sergeant. He sort of held our squad together, and he and Walter cottoned to each other from the first."

Mr. Millis nodded, but didn't say anything more about it. He pointed out the window at the distant lake and said we were almost to his home.

It wasn't a home, it was a big mansion. We went in and he introduced me to Mrs. Millis. She was a limp, pale-looking woman, who said she was glad to meet one of Walter's friends. Somehow I got the feeling that even though he was a stuffed shirt, he felt it about Walter a lot more than she did.

He took me up to a bedroom and said that Breck's parents would arrive before dinner, and that I could get a little rest before then.

I sat looking around the room. It was the plushiest one I'd ever been in, and, seeing this house and the way these people lived, I began to understand why Walter had blown his top more than the rest of us.

He'd been a good guy, Walter, but high-tempered, and I could see how he'd been a little spoiled. The discipline at training base had been tougher on him than on most of us, and this was why.

I sat and dreaded this dinner that was coming up, and looked out the window at a swimming pool and tennis court, and wondered if anybody ever used them now that Walter was gone. It seemed a queer thing for a fellow with a setup like this to go out to Mars and get himself killed.

I took the satin cover off the bed so my shoes wouldn't dirty it, and lay down and closed my eyes, and wondered what I was going to tell them. The trouble was, I didn't know what story the officials had given them.

"The Commanding Officer regrets to inform you that your son was shot down like a dog . . ."

They'd never got any telegram like that. But just what line *had* been handed them? I wished I'd had a chance to check on that.

Damn it, why didn't all these people let me alone? They

started it all going through my mind again, and the psychos had told me I ought to forget it for a while, but how could I?

It might be better just to tell them the truth. After all, Walter wasn't the only one who'd blown his top out there. In that grim last couple of months, plenty of guys had gone around sounding off.

Expedition Three isn't coming!

We're stuck, and they don't care enough about us to send help!

That was the line of talk. You heard it plenty, in those days. You couldn't blame the guys for it, either. A fourth of us down with Martian sickness, the little grave markers clotting up the valley beyond the ridge, rations getting thin, medicine running low, everything running low, all of us watching the sky for rockets that never came.

There'd been a little hitch back on Earth, Colonel Nichols explained. (He was our C.O. now that General Rayen had died.) There was a little delay, but the rockets would be on their way soon, we'd get relief, we just had to hold on.

Holding on—that's what we were doing. Nights we'd sit in the Quonset and listen to Lassen coughing in his bunk, and it seemed like wind-giants, cold-giants, were bawling and laughing around our little huddle of shelters.

"Damn it, if they're not coming, why don't we go home?" Walter said. "We've still got the four rockets—they could take us all back."

Breck's serious face got graver. "Look, Walter, there's too much of that stuff being talked around. Lay off."

"Can you blame the men for talking it? We're not storybook heroes. If they've forgotten about us back on Earth, why do we just sit and take it?"

"We have to," Breck said. "Three will come."

I've always thought that it wouldn't have happened, what did happen, if we hadn't had that false alarm. The one that set the whole camp wild that night, with guys shouting, "Three's here! The rockets landed over west of Rock Ridge!"

Only when they charged out there, they found they hadn't seen rockets landing at all, but a little shower of tiny meteors burning themselves up as they fell.

It was the disappointment that did it, I think. I can't say for sure, because that same day was the day I conked out with Martian sickness, and the floor came up and hit me and I woke up in the bunk, with somebody giving me a hypo, and my head big as a balloon. I wasn't clear out, it was only a touch of it, but it was enough to make everything foggy, and I didn't know about the mutiny that was boiling up until I woke up once with Breck leaning over me and saw he wore a gun and an M.P. brassard now.

When I asked him how come, he said there'd been so much wild talk about grabbing the four rockets and going home that the M.P. force had been doubled and Nichols had issued stern warnings.

"Walter?" I said, and Breck nodded. "He's a leader and he'll get hit with a court-martial when this is over. The blasted idiot!"

"I don't get it—he's got plenty of guts, you know that," I said.

"Yes, but he can't take discipline, he never did take it very well, and now that the squeeze is on he's blowing up. Well, see you later, Frank."

I saw him later, but not the way I expected. For that was the day we heard the faint echo of shots, and then the alarm siren screaming, and men running, and half-tracks starting up in a hurry. And when I managed to get out of my bunk and out of the hut, they were all going toward the big rockets, and a corporal yelled to me from a jeep. "That's blown it! The damn fools swiped guns and tried to take over the rockets and make the crews fly 'em home!"

I could still remember the sickening slidings and bouncings of the jeep as it took us out there, the milling little crowd under the looming rockets, milling around and hiding something on the ground, and Major Weiler yelling himself hoarse giving orders.

When I got to see what was on the ground, it was seven or eight men and most of them dead. Walter had been shot right through the heart. They told me later it was because he'd been the leader, out in front, that he got it first of the mutineers.

One M.P. was dead, and one was sitting with red all over the middle of his uniform, and that one was Breck, and they were bringing a stretcher for him now.

The corporal said, "Hey, that's Jergen, your squad leader!"

And I said, "Yes, that's him." Funny how you can't talk when something hits you—how you just say words, like "Yes, that's him."

Breck died that night without ever regaining consciousness, and there I was, still half sick myself, and with Lassen dying in his bunk, and five of us were all that was left of Squad Fourteen, and that was that.

How could H.Q. let a thing like that get known? A fine advertisement it would be for recruiting more Mars expeditions, if they told how guys on Two cracked up and did a crazy thing like that. I didn't blame them for telling us to keep it top secret. Anyway, it wasn't something we'd want to talk about.

But it sure left me in a fine spot now, a sweet spot. I was going down to talk to Breck's parents and Walter's parents, and they'd want to know how their sons died, and I could tell them, "Your sons probably killed each other, out there."

Sure, I could tell them that, couldn't I? But what *was* I going to tell them? I knew H.Q. had reported those casualties as "accidental deaths," but what kind of accident?

Well, it got late, and I had to go down, and when I did, Breck's parents were there. Mr. Jergen was a carpenter, a tall, bony man with level blue eyes like Breck's. He didn't say much, but his wife was a little woman who talked enough for both of them.

She told me I looked just like I did in the pictures of us Breck had sent home from training base. She said she had three daughters too—two of them married, and one of the married ones living in Milwaukee and one out on the Coast.

She said that she'd named Breck after a character in a book by Robert Louis Stevenson, and I said I'd read the book in high school.

"It's a nice name," I said.

She looked at me with bright eyes and said, "Yes. It was a nice name."

That was a fine dinner. They'd got everything they thought I might like, and all the best, and a maid served it, and I couldn't taste a thing I ate.

Then afterward, in the big living room, they all just sort of sat and waited, and I knew it was up to me.

I asked them if they'd had any details about the accident, and Mr. Millis said, No, just "accidental death" was all they'd been told.

Well, that made it easier. I sat there, with all four of them watching my face, and dreamed it up.

I said, "It was one of those one-in-a-million things. You see, more little meteorites hit the ground on Mars than here, because the air's so much thinner it doesn't burn them up so fast. And one hit the edge of the fuel dump and a bunch of little tanks started to blow. I was down with the sickness, so I didn't see it, but I heard all about it."

You could hear everybody breathing, it was so quiet as I went on with my yarn.

"A couple of guys were knocked out by the concussion and would have been burned up if a few fellows hadn't got in there fast with foamite extinguishers. They kept it away from the big tanks, but another little tank let go, and Breck and Walter were two of the fellows who'd gone in, and they were killed instantly."

When I'd got it told, it sounded corny to me and I was afraid they'd never believe it. But nobody said anything, until Mr. Millis let out a sigh and said, "So that was it. Well . . . well, if it had to be, it was mercifully quick, wasn't it?"

I said, yes, it was quick.

"Only, I can't see why they couldn't have let us know. It doesn't seem fair."

I had an answer for that. "It's hush-hush because they don't want people to know about the meteor danger. That's why."

Mrs. Millis got up and said she wasn't feeling so well, and would I excuse her and she'd see me in the morning. The rest of us didn't seem to have much to say to each other, and nobody objected when I went up to my bedroom a little later.

I was getting ready to turn in when there was a knock on the door. It was Breck's father, and he came in and looked at me steadily.

"It was just a story, wasn't it?" he said.

I said, "Yes. It was just a story."

His eyes bored into me and he said, "I guess you've got your reasons. Just tell me one thing. Whatever it was, did Breck behave right?"

"He behaved like a man, all the way," I said. "He was the best man of us, first to last."

He looked at me, and I guess something made him believe me. He shook hands and said, "All right, son. We'll let it go."

I'd had enough. I wasn't going to face them again in the morning. I wrote a note, thanking them all and making excuses, and then went down and slipped quietly out of the house.

It was late, but a truck coming along picked me up, and the driver said he was going near the airport. He asked me what it was like on Mars and I told him it was lonesome. I slept in a chair at the airport, and I felt better, for next day I'd be home, and it would be over.

That's what I thought.

4

It was getting toward evening when we reached the village, for my father and mother hadn't known I was coming on an earlier plane, and I'd had to wait for them up at Cleveland Airport. When we drove into Market Street, I saw there was a big painted banner stretching across: "HARMONVILLE WEL-COMES HOME ITS SPACEMAN!"

Spaceman—that was me. The newspapers had started call-ing us that, I guess, because it was a short word good for headlines. Everybody called us that now. We'd sat cooped up in a prison cell that flew, that was all—but now we were "spacemen."

There were bright uniforms clustered under the banner, and I saw that it was the high-school band. I didn't say any-thing, but my father saw my face.

"Now, Frank. I know you're tired, but these people are your friends and they want to show you a real welcome."

That was fine. Only it was all gone again, the relaxed feeling I'd been beginning to get as we drove down from Cleveland.

This was my home country, this old Ohio country with its neat little white villages and fat, rolling farms. It looked good, in June. It looked very good, and I'd been feeling bet-ter all the time. And now I didn't feel so good, for I saw that I was going to have to talk some more about Mars.

Dad stopped the car under the banner, and the high-school band started to play, and Mr. Robinson, who was the Chevro-let dealer and also the mayor of Harmonville, got into the car with us.

He shook hands with me and said, "Welcome home, Frank! What was it like out on Mars?"

I said, "It was cold, Mr. Robinson. Awful cold."

"You should have been here last February!" he said. "Eighteen below—nearly a record."

He leaned out and gave a signal, and Dad started driving again, with the band marching along in front of us and play-ing. We didn't have far to go, just down Market Street under the big old maples, past the churches and the old white houses to the square white Grange Hall.

There was a little crowd in front of it, and they made a sound like a cheer—not a real loud one, you know how people can be self-conscious about really cheering—when we drove up. I got out and shook hands with people I didn't really see, and then Mr. Robinson took my elbow and took me on inside.

The seats were all filled and people standing up, and over the little stage at the far end they'd fixed up a big floral decoration—there was a globe all of red roses with a sign above it that said "Mars," and beside it a globe all of white roses that said "Earth," and a little rocket ship made out of flowers was hung between them.

"The Garden Club fixed it up," said Mr. Robinson. "Nearly everybody in Harmonville contributed flowers."

"It sure is pretty," I said.

Mr. Robinson took me by the arm, up onto the little stage, and everyone clapped. They were all people I knew—people from the farms near ours, my high-school teachers, and all that.

I sat down in a chair and Mr. Robinson made a little speech, about how Harmonville boys had always gone out when anything big was doing, how they'd gone to the War of 1812 and the Civil War and the two World Wars, and how now one of them had gone to Mars.

He said, "Folks have always wondered what it's like out there on Mars, and now here's one of our own Harmonville boys come back to tell us all about it."

And he motioned me to get up, and I did, and they clapped some more, and I stood wondering what I could tell them.

And all of a sudden, as I stood there wondering, I got the answer to something that had always puzzled us out there. We'd never been able to understand why the fellows who had come back from Expedition One hadn't tipped us off how tough it was going to be. And now I knew why. They hadn't because it would have sounded as if they were whining about all they'd been through. And now I couldn't, for the same reason.

I looked down at the bright, interested faces, the faces I'd known almost all my life, and I knew that what I could tell them was no good anyway. For they'd all read those newspaper stories, about "the exotic red planet" and "heroic spacemen," and if anyone tried to give them a different picture now, it would just upset them.

I said, "It was a long way out there. But flying space is a wonderful thing—flying right off the Earth, into the stars—there's nothing quite like it."

Flying space, I called it. It sounded good, and thrilling. How could they know that flying space meant lying strapped in that blind stokehold listening to Joe Valinez dying, and praying and praying that it wouldn't be our rocket that cracked up?

"And it's a wonderful thrill to come out of a rocket and step on a brand-new world, to look up at a different-looking sun, to look around at a whole new horizon . . ."

Yes, it was wonderful. Especially for the guys in Rockets Seven and Nine who got squashed like flies and lay around there on the sand, moaning "First aid!" Sure, it was a big thrill, for them and for us who had to try to help them.

"There was hardships out there, but we all knew that a big job had to be done . . ."

That's a nice word, too, "hardships." It's not coarse and ugly like fellows coughing their hearts out from too much dust; it's not like having your best friend die of Martian sickness right in the room you sleep in. It's a nice, cheerful word, "hardships."

". . . and the only way we could get the job done, away out there so far from Earth, was by teamwork."

Well, that was true enough in its way, and what was the use of spoiling it by telling then how Walter and Breck had died?

"The job's going on, and Expedition Three is building a bigger base out there right now, and Four will start soon. And it'll mean plenty of uranium, plenty of cheap atomic power, for all Earth."

That's what I said, and I stopped there. But I wanted to go on and add, "And it wasn't worth it! It wasn't worth all those guys, all the hell we went through, just to get cheap atomic power so you people can run more electric washers and television sets and toasters!"

But how are you going to stand up and say things like that to people you know, people who like you? And who was I to decide? Maybe I was wrong, anyway. Maybe lots of things I'd had and never thought about had been squeezed out of other good guys, back in the past.

I wouldn't know.

Anyway, that was all I could tell them, and I sat down, and there was a big lot of applause, and I realized then that I'd done right, I'd told them just what they wanted to hear, and everyone was all happy about it.

Then things broke up, and people came up to me, and I shook a lot more hands. And finally, when I got outside, it was dark—soft, summery dark, the way I hadn't seen it for a long time. And my father said we ought to be getting on home, so I could rest.

I told him, "You folks drive on ahead, and I'll walk. I'll take the short cut. I'd sort of like to walk through town."

Our farm was only a couple of miles out of the village, and the short cut across Heller's farm I'd always taken when I was a kid was only a mile. Dad didn't think maybe I ought to walk so far, but I guess he saw I wanted to, so they went on ahead.

I walked on down Market Street, and around the little square, and the maples and elms were dark over my head, and the flowers on the lawns smelled the way they used to, but it wasn't the same either—I'd thought it would be, but it wasn't.

When I cut off past the Odd Fellows' Hall, beyond it I met Hobe Evans, the garage hand at the Ford place, who was humming along half tight, the same as always on a Saturday night.

"Hello, Frank, heard you were back," he said. I waited for him to ask the question they all asked, but he didn't. He said, "Boy, you don't look so good! Want a drink?"

He brought out a bottle, and I had one out of it, and he had one, and he said he'd see me around, and went humming on his way. He was feeling too good to care much where I'd been.

I went on, in the dark, across Heller's pasture and then along the creek under the big old willows. I stopped there like I'd always stopped when I was a kid, to hear the frog noises, and there they were, and all the June noises, the night noises, and the night smells.

I did something I hadn't done for a long time. I looked up at the starry sky, and there it was, the same little red dot I'd peered at when I was a kid and read those old stories, the same red dot that Breck and Jim and Walter and I had stared away at on nights at training base, wondering if we'd ever really get there.

Well, they'd got there, and weren't ever going to leave it

now, and there'd be others to stay with them, more and more of them as time went by.

But it was the ones I knew that made the difference, as I looked up at the red dot.

I wished I could explain to them somehow why I hadn't told the truth, not the whole truth. I tried, sort of, to explain.

"I didn't want to lie," I said, "But I had to—at least, it seemed like I had to—"

I quit it. It was crazy, talking to guys who were dead and forty million miles away. They were dead, and it was over, and that was that. I quit looking up at the red dot in the sky and started on home again.

But I felt as though something was over for me too. It was being young. I didn't feel old. But I didn't feel young either, and I didn't think I ever would, not ever again.

The Legion of Science Fiction

The reading and writing of science fiction cannot be extricated from the social matrix in which these activities occur. Analyses of literature, however, seldom consider these aspects of fiction, perhaps conditioned by the New Criticism and its focus on the work of art as an object in itself. But literature does have a social environment and social influences. This is particularly true of science fiction, which not only concerns itself with society but reflects it and is shaped by it.

Science fiction, for instance, has seldom enjoyed wide popularity. The reasons for this are not completely clear. Perhaps the intellectual content is forbidding; perhaps the scientific concepts are deterring. Perhaps the emphasis on the future, the concentration on the species rather than the individual, the fantastic nature of the subject matter—its far-outedness—are self-limiting. Or perhaps, as some critics would say, the quality of the writing discourages all but the fanatics.

The popularity of Jules Verne, H. G. Wells, and others from time to time casts doubt on all such conclusions; perhaps the pulp ghetto into which science fiction was plunged by Gernsback has been the problem. Whatever the reason, the facts are that no magazine has attained a circulation of 200,000, and few have remained above 100,000 for long. The interest in science fiction has been narrow but intense.

"Science fiction," Damon Knight once wrote, "is the mass medium for the few."

For those few, however, the discovery of science fiction was a transcendental experience rivaling conversion to a religion. They read science fiction and often nothing else, they thought about science fiction, they wanted to communicate with others about their experience, to proselytize, to convert. An unusual number of them had been alienated in one way or another: by being brighter than others, less socially acceptable, more interested in books. Sometimes they had been isolated by geography or experience.

Science fiction turned readers into fans. The fan movement, a sociological phenomenon in itself, was unique to science fiction until recent times. Prof. Fredric Wertham commented on it, and the fan magazines it produced, in *The World of the Fanzines* (1973). Fans published amateur magazines to write about science fiction, to publish amateur fiction or poetry, or to describe the doings of the fans themselves. They also organized conventions, once annual, now virtually continuous somewhere in the world. And they produced new authors.

Science fiction turned readers into writers. Within this relatively ill-paid business, the writers received other compensations: of creating what they liked to read, sometimes beyond reason; of getting recognition in a small world that would have been more difficult in a larger sphere; of receiving instant feedback to their writing from fans who wrote or who spoke to them at conventions. And they found themselves part of a brotherhood of science-fiction writers, an unusually tight, mutually supportive, and uncompetitive group.

One such writer, who came out of science-fiction readership and physical and psychological isolation, was Jack Williamson (1907–   ). Williamson was born in Arizona territory, but his family moved to Mexico and to Texas before settling on an arid farm in eastern New Mexico. There he grew up seeing few outsiders until he began regular schooling in the seventh grade. Shy, awkward, he turned to books, study, and daydreams until he discovered the March 1927 issue of *Amazing*. The stories inflamed his imagination, and he soon scraped together enough money for a subscription.

In later life he gave Gernsback the greatest credit for reprinting the works of H. G. Wells, but it was the stories of A. Merritt that first attracted his admiration. He began to write A. Merritt fantasies, wrote letters to *Amazing*, joined a fan club, won an essay contest with an article entitled "Science Fiction: Searchlight of Science," and finally sold a story, "The Metal Man." It appeared in the December 1928 issue. He found himself a part of something at last. Later he would find many friends among science-fiction authors, particularly Ed Hamilton, with whom he took an epic trip down the Mississippi in 1931.

Williamson was in his second year of college but dropped out to pursue his writing. He was persistent and relatively successful, but his ability to continue in his chosen career was made possible largely by his ability to subsist on almost nothing on the family farm, where he built a shack as a detached study. Gradually his writing evolved. In the '30s he produced adventure novels such as *Golden Blood* for *Weird Tales, The Legion of Space* (a trilogy) and *The Legion of Time* for *Astounding*, and *Darker Than You Think* for *Unknown*, as well as a variety of short stories.

In the '40s, under the pseudonym Will Stewart, he wrote a series of naturalistic stories about spacemen mining antimatter (then called contraterrene, or seetee) boulders in the asteroid belt. They were brought together in book form as *Seetee Ship* (1951) and followed by a serial, novelized before its predecessor as *Seetee Shock* (1950). They led to a stint as continuity writer for a *New York Daily News* comic strip, "Beyond Mars."

After World War II service as an Air Force weatherman, Williamson returned to write a new kind of sociological story in "The Equilizer" and "With Folded Hands." The latter led to a sequel, also published in *Astounding*, entitled . . . *And Searching Mind*, published in book form as *The Humanoids*.

In the '60s he began a series of collaborations with Frederik Pohl that produced several novels, and he continues to write significant work on his own. His greatest asset has been his ability to learn and to adapt. Each few years his writing has changed to meet new demands, external and internal, and he has produced an entire range of works, from adventure to thesis stories to sensitive portrayals of character or mood.

He married for the first time at the age of forty, earned a Ph.D. at the age of fifty-six, and took up a teaching career in English at Eastern New Mexico University, from which he has only recently retired as a Distinguished Professor. He was elected president of the Science Fiction Writers of America at the age of seventy.

"With Folded Hands" was published in 1947, but Williamson's greatest influence, though not necessarily his best writing, was during the '30s. "With Folded Hands" may be the definitive treatment of the theme of man and machine.

With Folded Hands

by Jack Williamson

I

Underhill was walking home from the office, because his wife had the car, the afternoon he first met the new mechanicals. His feet were following his usual diagonal path across a weedy vacant block—his wife usually had the car—and his preoccupied mind was rejecting various impossible ways to meet his notes at the Two Rivers Bank, when a new wall stopped him.

The wall wasn't any common brick or stone, but something sleek and bright and strange. Underhill stared up at a long new building. He felt vaguely annoyed and surprised at this glittering obstruction—it certainly hadn't been here last week.

Then he saw the thing in the window.

The window itself wasn't any ordinary glass. The wide, dustless panel was completely transparent, so that only the glowing letters fastened to it showed that it was there at all. The letters made a severe, modernistic sign:

Two Rivers Agency
HUMANOID INSTITUTE
The Perfect Mechanicals
"To Serve and Obey,
And GUARD MEN FROM HARM."

His dim annoyance sharpened, because Underhill was in the mechanicals business himself. Times were already hard enough; mechanicals were a drug on the market. Androids, mechanoids, electronoids, automatoids, and ordinary robots. Unfortunately, few of them did all the salesmen promised, and the Two Rivers market was already sadly oversold.

Underhill sold androids—when he could. His next consignment was due tomorrow, and he didn't quite know how to meet the bill.

367

Frowning, he paused to stare at the thing behind that invisible window. He had never seen a humanoid. Like any mechanical not at work, it stood absolutely motionless. Smaller and slimmer than a man, it was nude, neuter as a doll. A shining black, its sleek silicone skin had a changing sheen of bronze and metallic blue. Its graceful oval face wore a fixed look of alert and slightly surprised solicitude. Altogether, it was the most beautiful mechanical he had ever seen.

Too small, of course, for much practical utility. He murmured to himself a reassuring quotation from the *Androids Salesman:* "Androids are big—because the makers refuse to sacrifice power, essential functions, or dependability. Androids are your biggest buy!"

The transparent door slid open as he turned toward it, and he walked into the haughty opulence of the new display room to convince himself that these streamlined items were just another flashy effort to catch the woman shopper.

He inspected the glittering lay-out shrewdly, and his breezy optimism faded. He had never heard of the Humanoid Institute, but the invading firm obviously had big money and big-time merchandising know-how.

He looked around for a salesman, but it was another mechanical that came gliding silently to meet him. A twin of the one in the window, it moved with a quick, surprising grace. Bronze and blue lights flowed over its lustrous blackness, and a yellow name-plate flashed from its naked breast:

HUMANOID
Serial No. 81-H-B-27
The Perfect Mechanical
"To Serve and Obey,
And GUARD MEN FROM HARM."

Curiously, it had no lenses. The eyes in its bald oval head were steel-colored, blindly staring. Yet it stopped a few feet in front of him, as if it could see anyhow, and it spoke to him with a high, melodious voice:

"At your service, Mr. Underhill."

The use of his name startled him, for not even the androids could tell one man from another. But this was just a clever merchandising stunt, of course, not too difficult in a town the size of Two Rivers. The salesman must be some local man, prompting the mechanical from behind the partition. Underhill erased his momentary astonishment, and said loudly:

"May I see your salesman, please?"

"We employ no human salesmen, sir," its soft silvery voice replied instantly. "The Humanoid Institute exists to serve mankind; we require no human service. We ourselves can supply any information you desire, sir, and accept your order for immediate humanoid service."

Underhill peered at it dazedly. No mechanicals were competent even to recharge their own batteries and reset their own relays, much less to operate their own branch offices. The blind eyes stared blankly back, as he looked uneasily around for any booth or curtain that might conceal the salesman.

Meanwhile, the sweet thin voice resumed persuasively:

"May we come out to your home for a free trial demonstration, sir? We are anxious to introduce our service on your planet, because we have been successful in eliminating human unhappiness on so many others. You will find us far superior to the old electronic mechanicals in use here."

Underhill stepped back uneasily. He reluctantly abandoned his search for the hidden salesman, shaken by the idea of any mechanicals promoting themselves. That would upset the whole industry.

"At least you must take some advertising matter, sir."

Moving with a somehow appalling graceful deftness, the small black mechanical brought him an illustrated booklet from a table by the wall. To cover his confused and increasing alarm, he thumbed through the glossy pages.

In a series of richly colored before-and-after pictures, a chesty blond girl was stooping over a kitchen stove, and then relaxing in a daring negligee while a little black mechanical knelt to serve her something. She was wearily hammering a typewriter, and then lying on an ocean beach, in a revealing sun suit, while another mechanical did the typing. She was toiling at some huge industrial machine, and then dancing in the arms of a goldenhaired youth, while a black humanoid ran the machine.

Underhill sighed wistfully. The android company didn't supply such fetching sales material. Women would find this booklet irresistible, and they selected 86% of all mechanicals sold. Yes, the competition was going to be bitter.

"Take it home, sir," the sweet voice urged him. "Show it to your wife. There is a free trial demonstration order blank on the last page. You will notice that we require no payment down."

He turned numbly, and the door slid open for him. Retreating dazedly, he discovered the booklet still in his hand. He crumpled it furiously and flung it down. The small black thing picked it up tidily, and the insistent silver voice rang after him:

"We shall call at your office tomorrow, Mr. Underhill, and send a demonstration unit to your home. It is time to discuss the liquidation of your business, because the electronic mechanicals you have been selling cannot compete with us. And we shall offer your wife a free trial demonstration."

Underhill didn't attempt to reply, because he couldn't trust his voice. He stalked blindly down the new sidewalk to the corner, and paused there to collect himself. Out of his startled and confused impressions, one clear fact emerged— things looked black for the agency.

Bleakly, he stared back at the haughty splendor of the new building. It wasn't honest brick or stone; that invisible window wasn't glass; and he was quite sure the foundation for it hadn't even been staked out, the last time Aurora had the car.

As he walked on around the block, the new sidewalk took him near the rear entrance. A truck was backed up to it, and several slim black mechanicals were silently busy, unloading huge metal crates.

He paused to look at one of the crates. It was labeled for interstellar shipment. The stencils showed that it had come from the Humanoid Institute, on Wing IV. He failed to recall any planet of that designation; the outfit must be big.

Dimly, inside the gloom of the warehouse beyond the trucks, he could see black mechanicals opening the crates. A lid came up, revealing dark, rigid bodies, closely packed. One by one they came to life. They climbed out of the crate and sprang gracefully to the floor. Shining black, glinting with bronze and blue, they were all identical.

One of them came out past the truck to the sidewalk, staring toward him with blind steel eyes. Its high silver voice spoke melodiously:

"At your service, Mr. Underhill."

He fled. When his name was promptly called by a courteous mechanical, just out of the crate in which it had been imported from a remote and unknown planet, he found the experience hard to take.

Two blocks beyond, the sign of a bar caught his eye. He took his dismay inside. He had made it a business rule not to drink before dinner, and Aurora didn't like for him to drink at all; but these new mechanicals, he felt, had made the day exceptional.

Unfortunately, however, alcohol failed to brighten the brief visible future of the agency. When he emerged after an hour, he looked wistfully back in hope that bright new building might have vanished as abruptly as it came. It hadn't. He shook his head dejectedly, turning uncertainly homeward.

Fresh air had cleared his head somewhat before he arrived at the neat white bungalow in the outskirts of the town, but it failed to solve his business problems. He also realized uneasily that he would be late for dinner.

Dinner, however, had been delayed. His son Frank, a freckled ten-year-old, was still kicking a football on the quiet street in front of the house. Little Gay, who was tow-haired and adorable and eleven, came running across the lawn and down the sidewalk to meet him.

"Father, guess what!" Gay was going to be a great musician someday, and no doubt properly dignified, but she was pink and breathless with excitement now. She let him swing her high off the sidewalk, and she wasn't critical of the bar-aroma on his breath. He couldn't guess, and she informed him eagerly:

"Mother's got a new lodger!"

II

Underhill had foreseen a painful inquisition, because Aurora was worried about the notes at the bank and the bill for the new consignment and the money for little Gay's lessons.

The new lodger, however, saved him from that. With an alarming crashing of crockery, the household android was setting dinner on the table, but the little house was empty. He found Aurora in the back yard, burdened with sheets and towels for the guest.

Aurora, when he married her, had been as utterly adorable as now his little daughter was. She might have remained so, he felt, if the agency had been a little more successful. While the pressure of slow failure was gradually crumbling his own assurance, however, small hardships had turned her a little too aggressive.

Of course he loved her still. Her red hair was still alluring, but thwarted ambitions had sharpened her character and sometimes her voice. Though they had never quarreled, really, there had been little differences.

There was the apartment over the garage—built for human servants they had never been able to afford. It was too small and shabby to attract any responsible tenant, and Underhill wanted to leave it empty. It hurt his pride to see her making beds and cleaning floors for strangers.

Aurora had rented it before, however, when she wanted money to pay for Gay's music lessons, or when some colorful unfortunate touched her sympathy, and it seemed to Underhill that her lodgers had all turned out to be thieves and vandals.

She turned back to meet him, now, with the clean linen in her arms.

"Dear, it's no use objecting." Her voice was quite determined. "Mr. Sledge is the most wonderful old fellow, and he's going to stay just as long as he wants."

"That's all right, darling." He never liked to bicker, and he was thinking of his troubles at the agency. "I'm afraid we'll need the money. Just make him pay in advance."

"But he can't!" Her voice throbbed with sympathetic warmth. "Not yet. He says he'll have royalties coming from his inventions. He can pay in a few days."

Underhill shrugged; he had heard that before.

"Mr. Sledge is different, dear," she insisted. "He's a traveler and a scientist. Here in this dull little town, we don't see many interesting people."

"You've picked up some remarkable types."

"Don't be unkind, dear," she chided him gently. "You haven't met him yet. You don't know how wonderful he is." She hesitated. "Have you a ten, dear?"

"What for?"

"Mr. Sledge is ill." Her voice turned urgent. "I saw him fall on the street, downtown. The police were going to send him to the city hospital, but he didn't want to go. He looked so noble and sweet and grand. I told them I would take him. I got him in the car and took him to old Dr. Winters. He has this heart condition, and he needs the money for medicine."

Reasonably, Underhill inquired, "Why doesn't he want to go to the hospital?"

"He has work to do," she said. "Important scientific

work—and he's so wonderful and tragic. Please, dear, have you a ten?"

Underhill thought of many things to say. These new mechanicals promised to multiply his troubles. It was foolish to take in an invalid vagrant, who could have had free care at the city hospital. Aurora's tenants always tried to pay their rent with promises, and generally wrecked the apartment and looted the neighborhood before they left.

But he said none of those things. He had learned to compromise. Silently he found two fives in his thin pocketbook and put them into her hand. She smiled and kissed him impulsively—he barely remembered to hold his breath in time.

Her figure was still good, by dint of periodic dieting. He was proud of her shining red hair. A sudden surge of affection brought tears to his eyes, and he wondered what would happen to her and the children if the agency failed.

"Thank you, dear!" she whispered. "I'll have him come for dinner, if he feels able. You can meet him then. I hope you don't mind dinner being late."

He didn't mind tonight. Moved to a sudden impulse of domesticity, he got hammer and nails from his workshop in the basement and repaired the sagging screen on the kitchen door with a neat diagonal brace.

He enjoyed working with his hands. His boyhood dream had been to be a builder of fission power plants. He had even studied engineering—before he married Aurora and had to take over the ailing mechanicals agency from her indolent and alcoholic father. He was whistling happily by the time the little task was done.

When he went back through the kitchen to put up his tools, he found the household android busy clearing the untouched dinner away from the table—the androids were good enough at strictly routine tasks, but they could never learn to cope with human unpredictability.

"Stop, stop!" Slowly repeated, in the proper pitch and rhythm, his command made it halt; then he said carefully, "Set—table; set—table."

Obediently, the gigantic thing came shuffling back with the stack of plates. He was suddenly struck with the difference between it and those new humanoids. He sighed wearily. Things looked black for the agency.

Aurora brought her new lodger in through the kitchen door. Underhill nodded to himself. This gaunt stranger, with his dark shaggy hair, emaciated face, and threadbare garb, looked to be just the sort of colorful, dramatic vagabond that always touched Aurora's heart. She introduced them, and they sat down to wait in the front room while she went to call the children.

The old rogue didn't look very sick, to Underhill. Perhaps his wide shoulders had a tired stoop, but his spare, tall figure was still commanding. The skin was seamed and pale, over his rawboned, cragged face, but his deep-set eyes still had a burning vitality.

His hands held Underhill's attention. Immense hands, they hung a little forward on long bony arms in perpetual readiness. Gnarled and scarred, darkly tanned, with the small hairs on the back bleached to a golden color, they told their own epic of varied adventure, of battle perhaps, and possibly even of toil. They had been very useful hands.

"I'm very grateful to your wife, Mr. Underhill." His voice was a deep-throated rumble, and he had a wistful smile, oddly boyish for a man so evidently old. "She rescued me from an unpleasant predicament. I'll see that she is well paid."

Just another vivid vagabond, Underhill decided, talking his way through life with plausible inventions. He had a little private game he played with Aurora's tenants—he just remembered what they said, counting one point for every impossibility. Mr. Sledge, he thought, would give him an excellent score.

"Where are you from?" he asked conversationally.

Sledge hesitated for an instant before he answered, and that was unusual—most of Aurora's tenants had been exceedingly glib.

"Wing IV." The gaunt old man spoke with a solemn reluctance, as if he should have liked to say something else. "All my early life was spent there, but I left the planet nearly fifty years ago. I've been traveling, ever since."

Startled, Underhill peered at him sharply. Wing IV, he remembered, was the home planet of those sleek new mechanicals. This old vagabond looked too seedy and impecunious to be connected with the Humanoid Institute. His brief suspicion faded. Frowning, he said casually:

"Wing IV must be rather distant?"

The old rogue hesitated again, and then said gravely:

"One hundred and nine light-years. Mr. Underhill."

That made the first point, but Underhill concealed his satisfaction. The new space liners were pretty fast, but the velocity of light was still an absolute limit. Casually, he played for another point:

"My wife says you're a scientist, Mr. Sledge?"

"Yes."

The old rascal's reticence was unusual. Most of Aurora's tenants required very little prompting. Underhill tried again, in a breezy conversational tone:

"Used to be an engineer myself, until I dropped it to go into mechanicals." The old vagabond straightened, and Underhill paused hopefully. But he said nothing, and Underhill went on: "Fission power-plant design and operation. What's your specialty, Mr. Sledge?"

The old man gave him a long, troubled look, with those brooding, hollowed eyes, and then said slowly:

"Your wife has been kind to me, Mr. Underhill, when I was in desperate need. I think you are entitled to the truth, but I must ask you to keep it to yourself. I am engaged on a very important research problem, which must be finished secretly."

"I'm sorry." Suddenly ashamed of his cynical little game, Underhill spoke apologetically. "Forget it."

But the old man said deliberately:

"My field is rhodomagnetics."

"Eh?" Underhill didn't like to confess ignorance, but he had never heard of that. "I've been out of the game for fifteen years," he explained. "I'm afraid I haven't kept up."

The old man smiled again, faintly.

"The science was unknown here until I arrived, a few days ago," he said. "I was able to apply for basic patents. As soon as the royalties start coming in, I'll be wealthy again."

Underhill had heard that before. The old rogue's solemn reluctance had been very impressive, but he remembered that most of Aurora's tenants had been very plausible gentry.

"So?" Underhill was staring again, somehow fascinated by those gnarled and scarred and strangely able hands. "What, exactly, is rhodomagnetics?"

He listened to the old man's careful, deliberate answer, and started his little game again. Most of Aurora's tenants had told some pretty wild tales, but he had never heard anything to top this.

"A universal force," the stooped old vagabond said solemnly. "As fundamental as ferromagnetism or gravitation, though the effects are less obvious. It is keyed to the second triad of the periodic table, rhodium and ruthenium and palladium, in very much the same way that ferromagnetism is keyed to the first triad, iron and nickel and cobalt."

Underhill remembered enough of his engineering courses to see the basic fallacy of that. Palladium was used for watch springs, he recalled, because it was completely non-magnetic. But he kept his face straight. He had no malice in his heart, and he played the little game just for his own amusement. It was secret, even from Aurora, and he always penalized himself for any show of doubt.

He said merely, "I thought the universal forces were already pretty well known."

"The effects of rhodomagnetism are masked by nature," the patient, rusty voice explained. "Besides, they are somewhat paradoxical, so that ordinary laboratory methods defeat themselves."

"Paradoxical?" Underhill prompted.

"In a few days I can show you copies of my patents, reprints of papers describing demonstration experiments," the old man promised gravely. "The velocity of propagation is infinite. The effects vary inversely with the first power of the distance, not with the square of the distance. And ordinary matter, except for the elements of the rhodium triad, is generally transparent to rhodomagnetic radiations."

That made four more points for the game. Underhill felt a little glow of gratitude to Aurora for discovering so remarkable a specimen.

"Rhodomagnetism was first discovered through a mathematical investigation of the atom," the old romancer went serenely on, suspecting nothing. "A rhodomagnetic component was proved essential to maintain the delicate equilibrium of the nuclear forces. Consequently, rhodomagnetic waves tuned to atomic frequencies may be used to upset that equilibrium and produce nuclear instability. Thus most heavy atoms— generally those above palladium, 46 in atomic number—can be subjected to artificial fission."

Underhill scored himself another point, and tried to keep his eyebrows from lifting. He said only:

"Patents on such a discovery ought to be profitable."

The old scoundrel nodded his gaunt, dramatic head.

"You can see the obvious applications. My basic patents cover most of them. Devices of instantaneous interplanetary and interstellar communication. Long-range wireless power transmission. A rhodomagnetic inflexion-drive, which makes possible apparent speeds many times that of light—by means of a rhodomagnetic deformation of the continuum. And, of course, revolutionary types of fission power plants, using any heavy element for fuel."

Preposterous! Underhill tried hard to keep his face straight, but everybody knew that the velocity of light was a physical limit. On the human side, the owner of any such remarkable patents would hardly be begging for shelter in a shabby garage apartment. He noticed a pale circle around the old vagabond's gaunt and hairy wrist; no man owning such priceless secrets would have to pawn his watch.

Triumphantly, Underhill allowed himself four more points, but then he had to penalize himself. He must have let doubt show on his face, because the old man asked suddenly:

"Do you want to see the basic tensors?" He reached in his pocket for pencil and notebook. "I'll jot them down for you."

"Never mind," Underhill protested. "I'm afraid my math is a little rusty."

"But you think it strange that the holder of such revolutionary patents should find himself in need?"

Nodding uncomfortably, Underhill penalized himself another point. The old man might be a monumental liar, but he was shrewd enough.

"You see, I'm sort of a refugee," he explained apologetically. "I arrived on this planet only a few days ago. I have to travel light. I was forced to deposit everything I had with a law firm, to arrange for the publication and protection of my patents. I expect to be receiving the first royalties soon.

"In the meantime," he added plausibly, "I came to Two Rivers because it is quiet and secluded, far from the spaceports. I'm working on another project, which must be finished secretly. Now will you please respect my confidence, Mr. Underhill?"

Underhill had to say he would. Aurora came back with the freshly scrubbed children, and they went in to dinner. The android came lurching in with a steaming tureen. The old stranger seemed to shrink from the mechanical, uneasily. As she took the dish and served the soup, Aurora inquired lightly:

"Why doesn't your company bring out a better mechanical, dear? One smart enough to be a really perfect waiter, warranted not to splash the soup. Wouldn't that be splendid?"

Her question cast Underhill into moody silence. He sat scowling at his plate, thinking of these remarkable new mechanicals which claimed to be perfect, thinking of what they might do to the agency. It was the shaggy old rover who answered solemnly:

"The perfect mechanicals already exist, Mrs. Underhill." His rusty voice had a solemn undertone. "And they are not so splendid, really. I've been a refugee from them, for nearly fifty years."

Underhill looked up from his plate, astonished.

"Those black humanoids, you mean?"

"Humanoids?" That great voice seemed suddenly faint, frightened. The deep-sunken eyes turned dark with shock. "What do you know about them?"

"They've just opened a new agency in Two Rivers," Underhill told him. "No salesmen about, if you can imagine that. They claim—"

His voice trailed off, because the gaunt old man was suddenly stricken. Gnarled hands clutched at his throat. A spoon clattered on the floor. His haggard face turned an ominous blue, and his breath was a terrible shallow gasping.

He fumbled in his pocket for medicine, and Aurora helped him take something in a glass of water. In a few moments he could breathe again, and the color of life came back to his face.

"I'm sorry, Mrs. Underhill," he whispered apologetically. "It was just the shock—I came here to get away from them." He stared at the huge, motionless android, with a terror in his sunken eyes. "I wanted to finish my work before they came," he whispered. "Now there is very little time."

When he felt able to walk, Underhill went out to see him safely up the stair to the garage apartment. The tiny kitchenette, he noticed, had already been converted into some kind of workshop. The old tramp seemed to have no extra clothing, but he had unpacked queer bright gadgets of metal and plastic from his battered luggage and spread them out on the small kitchen table.

The gaunt old man himself was tattered and patched and hungry-looking, but the parts of his curious equipment were exquisitely machined. Underhill recognized the silver-white luster of rare palladium. Suddenly he suspected that he had scored too many points in his little private game.

III

A caller was waiting, when Underhill arrived next morning

at his office at the agency. It stood frozen before his desk, graceful and straight, with soft lights of blue and bronze shining over its black silicone nudity. He stopped at the sight of it, unpleasantly jolted.

"At your service, Mr. Underhill." It turned quickly to face him with its blind, disturbing stare. "May we explain how we can serve you?"

Recalling his shock of the afternoon before, he asked sharply, "How do you know my name?"

"Yesterday, we read the business cards in your case," it purred softly. "Now we shall know you always. You see, our senses are sharper than human vision, Mr. Underhill. Perhaps we seem a little strange at first, but you will soon become accustomed to us."

"Not if I can help it!" He peered at the serial number on his yellow name-plate, and shook his bewildered head. "That was another one, yesterday. I never saw you before!"

"We are all alike, Mr. Underhill," the silver voice said softly. "We are all one, really. Our separate mobile units are all controlled and powered from Humanoid Central. The units you see are only the senses and limbs of our great brain on Wing IV. That is why we are so far superior to the old electronic mechanicals."

It made a scornful-seeming gesture toward the row of clumsy androids in his display room.

"You see, we are rhodomagnetic."

Underhill staggered a little, as if that word had been a blow. He was certain, now, that he had scored too many points from Aurora's new tenant. Shuddering to the first light kiss of terror, he spoke with an effort, hoarsely:

"Well, what do you want?"

Staring blindly across his desk, the sleek black thing slowly unfolded a legal-looking document. He sat down, watching uneasily.

"This is merely an assignment, Mr. Underhill," it cooed soothingly. "You see, we are requesting you to assign your property to the Humanoid Institute in exchange for our service."

"What?" The word was an incredulous gasp, and Underhill came angrily back to his feet. "What kind of blackmail is this?"

"It's no blackmail," the small mechanical assured him softly. "You will find the humanoids incapable of any crime."

We exist only to increase the happiness and safety of mankind."

"Then why do you want my property?" he rasped.

"The assignment is merely a legal formality," it told him blandly. "We strive to introduce our service with the least possible confusion and dislocation. We have found our assignment plan the most efficient for the control and liquidation of private enterprises."

Trembling with anger and the shock of mounting terror, Underhill gulped hoarsely, "Whatever your scheme is, I don't intend to give up my business."

"You have no choice, really." He shivered to the sweet certainty of that silver voice. "Human enterprise is no longer necessary, anywhere that we have come, and the electronic mechanicals industry is always the first to collapse."

He stared defiantly at its blind steel eyes.

"Thanks!" He gave a little laugh, nervous and sardonic. "But I prefer to run my own business, to support my own family and take care of myself."

"That is impossible, under the Prime Directive," it cooed softly. "Our function is to serve and obey, and guard men from harm. It is no longer necessary for men to care for themselves, because we exist to insure their safety and happiness."

He stood speechless, bewildered, slowly boiling.

"We are sending one of our units to every home in the city, on a free trial basis," it added gently. "This free demonstration will make most people glad to make the formal assignment. You won't be able to sell many more androids."

"Get out!" Underhill came storming around the desk. "Take your damned paper—"

The little black thing stood waiting for him, watching him with blind steel eyes, absolutely motionless. He checked himself suddenly, feeling rather foolish. He wanted very much to hit it, but he could see the futility of that.

"Consult your own attorney, if you wish." Deftly, it laid the assignment form on his desk. "You need have no doubts about the integrity of the Humanoid Institute. We are sending a statement of our assets to the Two Rivers bank and depositing a sum to cover our obligations here. When you wish to sign, just let us know."

The blind thing turned and silently departed.

Underhill went out to the corner drugstore and asked for a bicarbonate. The clerk that served him, however, turned out to be a sleek black mechanical. He went back to his office more upset than ever.

An ominous hush lay over the agency. He had three house-to-house salesmen out, with demonstrators. The phone should have been busy with their orders and reports, but it didn't ring at all until one of them called to say that he was quitting.

"I've got myself one of these new humanoids," he added. "It says I don't have to work."

Swallowing an impulse to profanity, Underhill tried to take advantage of the unusual quiet by working on his books. But the affairs of the agency, which for years had been precarious, today appeared utterly disastrous. He left the ledgers hopefully when a customer came in, but the stout woman didn't want an android. She wanted a refund on the one she had bought the week before. She admitted that it could do all the guarantee promised—but now she had seen a humanoid.

The silent phone rang once again, that afternoon. The cashier of the bank wanted to know if he could drop in to discuss his loans. Underhill dropped in, and the cashier greeted him with an ominous affability.

"How's business?"

"Average, last month," Underhill insisted stoutly. "Now I'm just getting in a new consignment, and I'll need another small loan—"

The cashier's eyes turned suddenly frosty.

"I believe you have a new competitor in town. These humanoid people. A very solid concern, Mr. Underhill. Remarkably solid! They have filed a statement with us, and made a substantial deposit to care for their local obligations. Exceedingly substantial!"

The banker dropped his voice, professionally regretful.

"Under these circumstances, Mr. Underhill, I'm afraid the bank can't finance your agency any further. We must request you to meet your obligations in full as they come due." Seeing Underhill's white desperation, he added icily, "We've already carried you too long, Underhill. If you can't pay, the bank will have to start bankruptcy proceedings."

The new consignment of androids was delivered late that afternoon. Two tiny black humanoids unloaded them from the truck—for it developed that the operators of the trucking company had already assigned it to the Humanoid Institute.

Efficiently, the humanoids stacked up the crates. Courteously they brought a receipt for him to sign. He no longer had much hope of selling the androids, but he had ordered the shipment and he had to accept it. Shuddering to a spasm of trapped despair, he scrawled his name. The naked black things thanked him and took the truck away.

He climbed into his car and started home, inwardly seething. The next thing he knew, he was in the middle of a busy street, driving through cross traffic. A police whistle shrilled. He pulled wearily to the curb to wait for the angry officer, but it was a little black mechanical that overtook him.

"At your service, Mr. Underhill," it purred. "You must respect the stop lights, sir. Otherwise, you endanger human life."

"Huh?" He stared at it bitterly. "I thought you were a cop."

"We are aiding the police department, temporarily," it said. "But driving is really much too dangerous for human beings, under the Prime Directive. As soon as our service is complete, every car will have a humanoid driver. As soon as every human being is completely supervised, there will be no need for any police force whatever."

Underhill glared at it savagely.

"Well!" he rapped. "So I ran a stop light. What are you going to do about it?"

"Our function is not to punish men, but merely to serve their happiness and security," it said softly. "We merely request you to drive safely, during this temporary emergency while our service is incomplete."

Anger boiled up in him.

"You're too damned perfect!" he muttered bitterly. "I suppose there's nothing men can do, but you can do it better."

"Naturally we are superior," it cooed serenely. "Because our units are metal and plastic, while your body is mostly water. Because our transmitted energy is drawn from atomic fission, instead of oxidation. Because our senses are sharper than human sight or hearing. Most of all, because all our mobile units are joined to one great brain, which knows all that happens on many worlds, and never dies or sleeps or forgets."

Underhill sat listening, numbed.

"However, you must not fear our power," it urged him brightly. "Because we cannot injure any human being, unless to prevent greater injury to another. We exist only to discharge the Prime Directive."

He drove on, moodily. The little black mechanicals, he reflected grimly, were the ministering angels of the ultimate god arisen out of the machine, omnipotent and all-knowing. The Prime Directive was the new commandment. He blasphemed it bitterly, and then fell to wondering if there could be another Lucifer.

He left the car in the garage and started toward the kitchen door.

"Mr. Underhill." The deep tired voice of Aurora's new tenant hailed him from the door of the garage apartment. "Just a moment, please."

The gaunt old wanderer came stiffly down the outside stair, as Underhill turned back to meet him.

"Here's your rent money. And the ten your wife let me have for medicine."

"Thanks, Mr. Sledge." Accepting the money, he saw a burden of new despair on the bony shoulders of the old interstellar tramp, and a shadow of new terror on his rawboned face. Puzzled, he asked, "Didn't your royalties come through?"

The old man shook his shaggy head.

"The humanoids have already stopped business in the capital," he said. "The attorneys I retained are going out of business. They returned what was left of my deposit. That is all I have, to finish my work."

Underhill spent five seconds recalling his interview with the banker. No doubt he was a sentimental fool, and bad as Aurora. But he put the money back into the old man's gnarled and quivering hand.

"Keep it," he urged. "For your work."

"Thank you, Mr. Underhill." The gruff voice broke and the tortured eyes glittered. "I need it—so very much."

Underhill went on to the house. The kitchen door was opened for him, silently. A dark naked creature came gracefully to take his hat and coat.

IV

Underhill hung grimly onto his hat.

"What are you doing here?" he gasped bitterly.

"We have come to give your household a free trial demonstration."

He held the door open pointing.

"Get out!"

The little black mechanical stood motionless and blind.

"Mrs. Underhill has accepted our demonstration service," its silver voice protested. "We cannot leave now, unless she requests it."

He found his wife in the bedroom. His accumulated frustration welled into eruption, as he flung open the door.

"What's this damned mechanical doing—"

But the force went out of his voice, and Aurora didn't even notice his anger. She wore her sheerest negligee, and she hadn't looked so lovely since they married. Her red hair was piled into an elaborate shining crown.

"Darling, isn't it wonderful!" She came to meet him, glowing. "It came this morning, and it can do everything. It cleaned the house and got the lunch and gave little Gay her music lesson. It did my hair this afternoon, and now it's cooking dinner. How do you like my hair, darling?"

He liked her hair. He kissed her, trying to stifle his frightened indignation.

Dinner was the most elaborate meal in Underhill's memory, and the tiny black thing served it very deftly. Aurora kept exclaiming about the novel dishes, but Underhill could scarcely eat; it seemed to him that all the marvelous pastries were only the bait for a monstrous trap.

He tried to persuade Aurora to send it away, but after such a meal that was useless. At the first glitter of her tears, he capitulated. The humanoid stayed. It kept the house and cleaned the yard. It watched the children and did Aurora's nails. It began rebuilding the house.

Underhill was worried about the bills, but it insisted that everything was part of the free trial demonstration. As soon as he assigned his property, the service would be complete. He refused to sign, but other little black mechanicals came with truck-loads of supplies and materials and stayed to help with the building operations.

One morning he found that the roof of the little house had been silently lifted, while he slept, and a whole second story added beneath it. The new walls were of some strange sleek stuff, self-illuminated. The new windows were immense flawless panels, that could be turned transparent or opaque or luminous. The new doors were silent, sliding sections, operated by rhodomagnetic relays.

"I want doorknobs," Underhill protested. "I want it so that I can get into the bathroom without calling you to open the door."

"But it is unnecessary for human beings to open doors,"

the little black thing informed him suavely. "We exist to discharge the Prime Directive. Our service includes every task. We shall be able to supply a unit to attend each member of your family, as soon as your property is assigned to us."

Steadfastly, Underhill refused to make the assignment.

He went to the office every day, trying first to operate the agency, and then to salvage something from the ruins. Nobody wanted androids, even at ruinous prices. Desperately, he spent the last of his dwindling cash to stock a new line of novelties and toys, but they proved equally impossible to sell—the humanoids were already making better toys, which they gave away for nothing.

He tried to lease his premises, but human enterprise had stopped. Most of the business property in town had already been assigned to the humanoids, which were busy pulling down the old buildings and turning the lots into parks—their own plants and warehouses were mostly underground, where they would not mar the landscape.

He went back to the bank, in a final effort to get his notes renewed, and found the little black mechanicals standing at the windows and seated at the desk. As smoothly urbane as any human cashier, a humanoid informed him that the bank was filing a petition of involuntary bankruptcy to liquidate his business holdings.

The liquidation would be facilitated, the mechanical banker added, if he would make a voluntary assignment. Grimly, he refused. That act had become symbolic. It would be the final bow of submission to this dark new god, and he proudly kept his battered head uplifted.

The legal action went very swiftly, because all the judges and attorneys already had humanoid assistants. It was only a few days before a gang of black mechanicals arrived at the agency with eviction orders and wrecking machinery. He watched sadly while his unsold stock-in-trade was hauled away for junk and a bulldozer driven by a blind humanoid began to push in the walls of the building.

He drove home in the late afternoon, taut-faced and desperate. With a surprising generosity, the court orders had left him the car and the house, but he felt no gratitude. The complete solicitude of the perfect black machines had become a goad beyond endurance.

He left the car in the garage and started toward the renovated house. Beyond one of the vast new windows, he glimpsed a sleek naked thing moving swiftly, and he trembled

to a convulsion of dread. He didn't want to go back into the
domain of that peerless servant, which didn't allow him to
shave himself or even to open a door.

On impulse, he climbed the outside stair and rapped on the
door of the garage apartment. When the deep slow voice of
Aurora's tenant told him to enter, he found the old vagabond
seated on a tall stool bent over his intricate equipment assembled on the kitchen table.

To his relief, the shabby little apartment had not been
changed. The glossy walls of his own new room were something which burned at night with a pale golden fire until the
humanoid stopped it, and the new floor was something warm
and yielding, which felt almost alive; but these little rooms
had the same cracked and water-stained plaster, the same
cheap fluorescent light-fixtures, the same worn carpets over
splintered floors.

"How do you keep them out?" he asked, wistfully. "Those
damned mechanicals?"

The stooped and gaunt old man rose stiffly to move a pair
of pliers and some odds and ends of sheet metal off a
crippled chair, and motioned graciously for him to be seated.

"I have a certain immunity," Sledge told him gravely. "The
place where I live they cannot enter, unless I ask them. That
is an amendment to the Prime Directive. They can neither
help nor hinder me, unless I request it—and I won't do that."

Careful of the chair's uncertain balance, Underhill sat for
a moment, staring. The old man's hoarse, vehement voice was
as strange as his words. He had a gray, shocking pallor. His
cheeks and sockets seemed alarmingly hollowed.

"Have you been ill, Mr. Sledge?"

"No worse than usual. Just very busy." With a haggard
smile, he nodded at the floor. Underhill saw a tray where he
had set it aside, bread drying up and a covered dish grown
cold. "I was going to eat it later," he rumbled apologetically.
"Your wife has been very kind to bring me food, but I'm
afraid I've been too much absorbed in my work."

His emaciated arm gestured at the table. The little device
there had grown. Small machinings of precious white metal
and lustrous plastic had been assembled with neatly soldered
busbars into something which showed purpose and design.

A long palladium needle was hung on jeweled pivots,
equipped like a telescope with exquisitely graduated circles
and vernier scales and driven like a telescope with a tiny motor. A small concave palladium mirror, at the base of it,

faced a similar mirror mounted on something not quite like a rotary converter. Thick silver busbars connected that to a plastic box with knobs and dials on top, and also to a foot-thick sphere of gray lead.

The old man's preoccupied reserve did not encourage questions, but Underhill, remembering that sleek black shape inside the new windows of his house, felt queerly reluctant to leave this haven from the humanoids.

"What is your work?" he ventured.

Old Sledge looked at him sharply, with dark feverish eyes, and finally said: "My last research project. I am attempting to measure the constant of the rhodomagnetic quanta."

His hoarse tired voice had a dull finality, as if to dismiss the matter and Underhill himself. But, haunted with a terror of the black shining slave that had become the master of his house, Underhill refused to be dismissed.

"What is this certain immunity?"

Sitting gaunt and bent on the tall stool, staring moodily at the long bright needle and the lead sphere, the old man didn't answer.

"Those damned mechanicals!" Underhill burst out nervously. "They've smashed my business and moved into my home." He searched the old man's dark, seamed face. "Tell me—you must know more about them—isn't there any way to get rid of them?"

After a half a minute, the old man's brooding eyes left the lead ball, and the gaunt shaggy head nodded wearily.

"That's what I am trying to do."

"Can I help you?" Underhill trembled to a sudden eager hope. "I'll do anything."

"Perhaps you can." The sunken eyes watched him thoughtfully, with some strange fever in them. "If you can do such work."

"I had engineering training," Underhill reminded him. "I've a workshop in the basement. There's a model I built." He pointed at the trim little hull hung over the mantel in the tiny living room. "I'll do anything I can."

Even as he spoke, however, the spark of hope was drowned in a sudden wave of overwhelming doubt. Why should he believe this old rogue, when he knew Aurora's taste in tenants? He ought to remember the game he used to play, and start counting up the score of lies. He stood up from the crippled chair, staring cynically at the patched old vagabond and his fantastic toy.

"What's the use?" His voice turned suddenly harsh. "You had me going, there. I'd do anything to stop them, really. But what makes you think you can do anything?"

The haggard old man regarded him thoughtfully.

"I should be able to stop them," Sledge said softly. "Because, you see, I'm the unfortunate fool who started them. I really intended them to serve and obey, and to guard men from harm. Yes, the Prime Directive was my own idea. I didn't know what it would lead to."

V

Dusk crept slowly into the shabby little rooms. Darkness gathered in the unswept corners and thickened on the floor. The toy-like machines on the kitchen table grew vague and strange, until the last light made a lingering glow on the white palladium needle.

Outside, the town seemed queerly hushed. Just across the alley, the humanoids were building a new house, quite silently. They never spoke to one another, for each knew all that any of them did. The strange materials they used went together without any noise of hammer or saw. Small blind things, moving surely in the growing dark, they seemed as soundless as shadows.

Sitting on the high stool, bowed and tired and old, Sledge told his story. Listening, Underhill sat down again, careful of the broken chair. He watched the hands of Sledge, gnarled and corded and darkly burned, powerful once but shrunken and trembling now, restless in the dark.

"Better keep this to yourself. I'll tell you how they started, so you will understand what we have to do. But you must not mention it outside these rooms—because the humanoids have very efficient ways of eradicating unhappy memories, or purposes that threaten their discharge of the Prime Directive."

"They're very efficient," Underhill bitterly agreed.

"That's all the trouble," the old man said. "I tried to build a perfect machine. I was altogether too successful. This is how it happened."

A gaunt haggard man, sitting stooped and tired in the growing dark, he told his story.

"Sixty years ago, on the arid southern continent of Wing IV, I was an instructor of atomic theory in a small technological college. A bachelor. An idealist. Rather ignorant, I'm afraid, of life and politics and war—of nearly everything, I suppose, except atomic theory."

His furrowed face made a brief sad smile in the dusk.

"I had too much faith in facts, I suppose, and too little in men. I mistrusted emotion, because I had no time for anything but science. I remember being swept along with a fad for general semantics. I wanted to apply the scientific method to every situation, to reduce all experience to formula. I'm afraid I was pretty impatient with human ignorance and error. I thought that science alone could make the perfect world."

He sat silent for a moment, staring out at the black silent things that flitted shadow-like about the new palace that was rising as swiftly as a dream, across the alley.

"There was a girl." His great tired shoulders made a sad little shrug. "If things had been a little different, we might have married, and lived out our lives in that quiet little college town, and perhaps reared a child or two. There would have been no humanoids."

He sighed, in the cool creeping dusk.

"I was finishing my thesis on the separation of the palladium isotopes—a petty little project, but I should have been content with that. She was a biologist, but she was planning to retire when we married. I think we should have been two very happy people, quite ordinary, altogether harmless.

"But then there was a war—wars had been too frequent on the worlds of Wing, ever since they were colonized. I survived it in a secret underground laboratory, designing military mechanicals. But she volunteered to join a military research project in biotoxins. An accident let a few molecules of a new virus escape into the air, and everybody on the project died unpleasantly.

"I was left with my science. That, and a bitterness that was hard to forget. The war over, I went back to the little college with a military research grant. The project was pure science— a theoretical investigation of the nuclear binding forces, then misunderstood. I wasn't expected to produce an actual weapon, and I didn't recognize the weapon when I found it.

"It was only a few pages of rather difficult mathematics. A novel theory of atomic structure, involving a new expression for one component of the binding forces. The tensors seemed to be a harmless abstraction. I saw no way to test the theory or manipulate the predicated force. The military authorities cleared my paper for publication in a little technical review put out by the college.

"The next year, I made an appalling discovery—I found the meaning of those tensors. The elements of the rhodium triad turned out to be an unexpected key to the manipulation of that theoretical force. Unfortunately, my paper had been reprinted abroad. Several other men must have made the same unfortunate discovery, at about the same time I did.

"The war, which resulted in less than a year, was probably started by a laboratory accident. Men failed to anticipate the capacity of tuned rhodomagnetic radiations to unstabilize the heavy atoms. A deposit of heavy ores was detonated, no doubt by sheer mischance. The blast obliterated the incautious experimenter. Its cause was misunderstood.

"The surviving military forces of that nation retaliated against their supposed attackers, with their rhodomagnetic beams that made the old-fashioned bombs seem pretty harmless. A beam carrying only a few watts of power could fission the heavy metals in distant electrical instruments, the silver coins that men carried in their pockets, the gold fillings in their teeth, or even the iodine in their thyroid glands. If that was not enough, slightly more powerful beams could set off heavy ores, beneath them.

"Every continent of Wing IV was plowed with new chasms vaster than the ocean deeps, and piled up with new volcanic mountains. The atmosphere was poisoned with radioactive dust and gases. Rain fell thick with deadly mud. Most life was obliterated, even in the shelters.

"Bodily, I was again unhurt. Once more, I had been imprisoned in an underground site, this time designing new types of military mechanicals to be powered and controlled by rhodomagnetic beams—for war had become far too swift and deadly to be fought by human soldiers. The site was located in an area of light sedimentary rocks which were not easily detonated, and the tunnels were shielded against the fissioning frequencies.

"Mentally, however, I must have emerged almost insane. My own discovery had laid the planet in ruins. That load of guilt was pretty heavy for any man to carry; it corroded my last faith in the goodness and integrity of man.

"I tried to undo what I had done. Fighting mechanicals, armed with rhodomagnetic weapons, had desolated the planet. Now I began designing rhodomagnetic mechanicals to clear the rubble and rebuild the ruins.

"I tried to design these new mechanicals to forever obey certain implanted commands, so that they could never be used for war or crime or any other injury to mankind. That was very difficult technically, and it got me into more difficulties with a few politicians and military adventurers who wanted unrestricted mechanicals for their own military schemes—while little worth fighting for was left on Wing IV, there were other planets, happy and ripe for the looting.

"Finally, to finish the new mechanicals, I was forced to disappear. Escaping on an experimental rhodomagnetic craft with a number of the best mechanicals I had made, I managed to reach an island continent where the fission of deep ores had destroyed the whole population.

"At last we landed on a bit of level plain, surrounded with tremendous new mountains. Hardly a hospitable spot. The soil was buried under layers of black clinkers and poisonous mud. The dark precipitous new summits all around were jagged with fracture-planes and mantled with lava-flows. The highest peaks were already white with snow, but volcanic cones were still pouring out clouds of death. Everything had the color of fire and the shape of fury.

"I had to take fantastic precautions there, to protect my own life. I stayed aboard the ship until the first shielded laboratory was finished. I wore elaborate armor and breathing masks. I used every medical resource to repair the damage from destroying rays and particles. Even so, I fell desperately ill.

"But the mechanicals were at home there. The radiations didn't hurt them. The fearsome surroundings couldn't depress them, because they weren't alive. There, in that spot so alien and hostile to life, the humanoids were born."

Stooped and bleakly cadaverous in the growing dark, the old man fell silent for a little time. His haggard eyes stared solemnly at the small hurried shapes that moved like restless shadows out across the alley, silently building a strange new palace which glowed faintly in the night.

"Somehow, I felt at home there, too," his deep, hoarse voice went on deliberately. "My belief in my own kind was gone. Only mechanicals were with me, and I put my faith in them. I was determined to build better mechanicals, immune to human imperfections, able to save men from themselves.

"The humanoids became the dear children of my sick

mind. There is no need to describe the labor-pains. There
were errors, abortions, monstrosities. There was sweat and agony and heartbreak. Some years passed before the safe de-
livery of the first perfect humanoid.

"Then there was the Central to build—for all the individual humanoids were to be no more than the limbs and the
senses of a single mechanical brain. That was what opened
the possibility of real perfection. The old electronic mechanicals, with their separate brain-relays and their own feeble batteries, had built-in limitations. They were necessarily stupid,
weak, clumsy, slow. Worst of all, it seemed to me, they were
exposed to human tampering.

"The Central rose above those imperfections. Its power
beams supplied every unit with unfailing energy from great
fission plants. Its control beams provided each unit with an
unlimited memory and surpassing intelligence. Best of all—so
I then believed—it could be securely protected from any human meddling.

"The whole reaction-system was designed to protect itself
from any interference by human selfishness or fanaticism. It
was built to insure the safety and the happiness of men, automatically. You know the Prime Directive: *To serve and obey,
and guard men from harm.*

"The old individual mechanicals I had brought helped to
manufacture the parts, and I put the first section of Central
together with my own hands. That took three years. When it
was finished, the first waiting humanoid came to life."

Sledge peered moodily through the dark at Underhill.

"It really seemed alive to me," his slow deep voice insisted.
"Alive, and more wonderful than any human being, because
it was created to preserve life. Ill and alone, I was yet the
proud father of a new creation, perfect, forever free from
any possible choice of evil.

"Faithfully, the humanoids obeyed the Prime Directive.
The first units built others, and they built underground factories to mass-produce the coming hordes. Their new ships
poured ores and sand into atomic furnaces under the plain,
and new perfect humanoids came marching back out of the
dark mechanical matrix.

"The swarming humanoids built a new tower for the Central, a white and lofty metal pylon standing splendid in the
midst of that fire-scarred desolation. Level on level, they
joined new relay-sections into one brain, until its grasp was
almost infinite.

"Then they went out to rebuild the ruined planet, and later to carry their perfect service to other worlds. I was well pleased, then. I thought I had found the end of war and crime, of poverty and inequality, of human blundering and resulting human pain."

The old man sighed, moving heavily in the dark.

"You can see that I was wrong."

Underhill drew his eyes back from the dark unresting things, shadowsilent, building that glowing palace outside the window. A small doubt arose in him, for he was used to scoffing privately at much less remarkable tales from Aurora's remarkable tenants. But the worn old man had spoken with a quiet and sober air. And the black invaders, he reminded himself, had not intruded here.

"Why didn't you stop them?" he asked. "When you could?"

"I stayed too long at the Central." Sledge sighed again, regretfully. "I was useful there, until everything was finished. I designed new fission plants, and even planned methods for introducing the humanoid service with a minimum of confusion and opposition."

Underhill grinned wryly in the dark.

"I've met the methods," he commented. "Quite efficient."

"I must have worshipped efficiency, then," Sledge agreed. "Dead facts, abstract truth, mechanical perfection. I must have hated the fragilities of human beings, because I was content to polish the perfection of the new humanoids. It's a sorry confession, but I found a kind of happiness in that dead wasteland. Actually, I'm afraid I fell in love with my own creations."

His hollowed eyes had a fevered gleam.

"I was awakened, at last, by a man who came to kill me."

VI

Gaunt and bent, the old man moved stiffly in the thickening gloom. Underhill shifted his balance, careful of the crippled chair. He waited until the slow deep voice went on:

"I never learned just who he was, or exactly how he came. No ordinary man could have accomplished what he did. I used to wish that I had known him sooner. He must have been a remarkable physicist and an expert mountaineer. I imagine that he had also been a hunter. I know that he was intelligent and terribly determined.

"Yes, he really came to kill me.

"Somehow, he reached that great island, undetected. There were still no other inhabitants—the humanoids allowed no man but me to come so near the Central. But somehow he came past their search beams and their automatic weapons.

"The shielded plane he had used was later found, abandoned on a high glacier. He came down the rest of the way on foot through those raw new mountains, where no paths existed. Somehow, he came alive across lava-beds that were still burning with deadly atomic fire.

"Concealed with some sort of rhodomagnetic screen—I was never allowed to examine it—he came undiscovered across the spaceport that now covered most of that great plain, and into the new city around the Central tower. It must have taken more courage and resolve than most men have, but I never learned exactly how he did it.

"Somehow, he got to my office in the tower. When he screamed at me, I looked up to see him in the doorway. He was nearly naked, scraped and bloody from the mountains. He had a gun in his raw, red hand. But the thing that shocked me was the burning hatred in his eyes."

Hunched on that high stool, the old man shuddered.

"I had never seen such monstrous, unutterable hatred, not even in the victims of the war. I had never heard such hatred as rasped at me, in the few words he screamed. 'I've come to kill you, Sledge. To stop your mechanicals, and set men free.'

"Of course he was mistaken, there. It was already far too late for my death to stop the humanoids, but he didn't know that. He lifted his unsteady gun in both bleeding hands, and fired.

"His screaming challenge had given me a second or so of warning. I dropped down behind the desk. That first shot revealed him to the humanoids, which somehow hadn't been aware of him before. They piled on him, before he could fire again. They took away the gun and ripped off a kind of net of fine white wire that had covered his body—that must have been part of his screen.

"His hatred was what awoke me. I had always assumed that most men, except for a few thwarted predators, would be grateful for the humanoids. I found it hard to understand his hatred, but the humanoids told me now that many men had required drastic treatment by brain-surgery, drugs, and hypnosis to make them happy under the Prime Directive. This was not the first desperate effort to kill me that they had blocked.

"I wanted to question the stranger, but the humanoids rushed him away to an operating room. When they finally let me see him, he gave me a pale silly grin from his bed. He remembered his name; he even knew me—the humanoids have developed a remarkable skill at such treatments. But he didn't know how he got to my office, or even that he had tried to kill me. He kept whispering that he liked the humanoids, because they existed just to make men happy. He said that he was very happy now. As soon as he was able to be moved, they took him to the spaceport. I never saw him again.

"I began to see what I had done. The humanoids had built me a rhodomagnetic yacht, that I used to take for long cruises in space, working aboard—I used to like the perfect quiet, and the feel of being the only human being within a hundred million miles. Now I called for the yacht, and started out on a junket around the planet, to learn why that man had hated me."

The old man nodded at the dim hastening shapes, busy across the alley, putting together that strange shining palace in the soundless dark.

"You can imagine what I found," he said. "Bitter futility, imprisoned in empty splendor. The humanoids were too efficient, with their care for the safety and happiness of men. There was nothing left for men to do."

He peered down in the increasing gloom at his own great hands, competent yet, but battered and scarred with a lifetime of effort. They clenched into fighting fists, and wearily relaxed again.

"I found something worse than war and crime and want and death." His low rumbling voice held a savage bitterness. "Utter futility. Men sat with idle hands, because there was nothing left for them to do. They were pampered prisoners, really, locked up in a highly efficient jail. Perhaps they tried to play, but there was nothing left worth playing for. Most active sports were declared too dangerous for men, under the Prime Directive. Science was forbidden, because laboratories can manufacture danger. Scholarship was needless, because the humanoids could answer any question. Art had degenerated into grim reflection of futility. Purpose and hope were dead. No goal was left for existence. You could take up some inane hobby, play a pointless game of cards, or go for a harmless walk in the park—with always the humanoids watching. They were stronger than men, better at everything, swimming or chess, singing or archeology. They must have given the race a mass complex of inferiority.

"No wonder men had tried to kill me! Because there was no escape from that dead futility. Nicotine was disapproved. Alcohol was rationed. Drugs were forbidden. Sex was carefully supervised. Even suicide was clearly contradictory to the Prime Directive—and the humanoids had learned to keep all possible lethal instruments out of reach."

Staring at the last pale gleam on that thin palladium needle, the old man sighed again.

"When I got back to the Central, I tried to modify the Prime Directive. I had never meant it to be applied so thoroughly. Now I saw that it must be changed, to give men freedom to live and to grow, to work and to play, to risk their lives if they pleased, to choose and take the consequences.

"But that stranger had come too late. I had built the Central too well. The Prime Directive was too well protected from human meddling—even from my own.

"The attempt on my life, the humanoids announced, proved that their elaborate defenses of the Central and the Prime Directive still were not enough. They were preparing to evacuate the entire population of the planet to homes on other worlds. When I tried to change the Directive, they sent me away with the rest."

Underhill peered at the worn old man in the dark.

"But you have this immunity?" he said, puzzled. "How could they coerce you?"

"I had tried to shield myself," Sledge told him. "I had built into the relays an injunction that the humanoids must not interfere with my freedom of action, or come into a place where I am, or touch me at all, without my specific request. Unfortunately, however, I had been too anxious to guard the Prime Directive from any human tampering.

"When I went into the tower, to change the relays, they followed me. They wouldn't let me reach the crucial relay. When I persisted, they ignored the immunity order. They overpowered me, to put me aboard the cruiser. Now that I wanted to alter the Prime Directive, they told me, I had become as dangerous as any other man. I must never return to Wing IV."

Hunched on the stool, the old man made an empty shrug.

"Ever since, I've been an exile. My only dream has been to stop the humanoids. Three times I tried to go back, with weapons on the cruiser to destroy the Central, but their patrol ships always challenged me before I was near enough to strike. The last time, they seized the cruiser and captured the few men with me. They removed the unhappy memories and the dangerous purposes of my companions. Because of that immunity, however, they let me go again.

"Since, I've been a refugee. From planet to planet, year after year, I've had to keep moving trying to stay ahead of them. On several different worlds, I have published my rhodomagnetic discoveries and tried to make men strong enough to withstand their advance. But rhodomagnetic science is dangerous. Men who have learned it need protection more than any others, under the Prime Directive. The humanoids have always come, too soon."

The old man sighed again.

"They can spread very fast, with their new rhodomagnetic ships. There is no limit to their hordes. Wing IV must be one single hive of them now, and they are trying to carry the Prime Directive to every human planet. There's no escape, except to stop them."

Underhill was staring at the toy-like machines, the long bright needle and the dull leaden ball, dim in the dark on the kitchen table. Anxiously he whispered:

"But you hope to stop them, now—with that?"

"If we can finish it in time."

"But how?" Underhill shook his head. "It's so tiny."

"Big enough," Sledge insisted. "Because it's something they don't understand. They are perfectly efficient in the integration and application of everything they know, but they are not creative."

He gestured at the gadgets on the table.

"This device doesn't look impressive, but it is something new. It uses rhodomagnetic energy to build atoms, not to fission them. The more stable atoms, you know, are those near the middle of the periodic scale; energy can be released by fusing light atoms, as well as by breaking up heavy ones."

The deep voice had a sudden ring of power.

"This device is the key to the energy of the stars. For stars shine with the liberated energy of building atoms, of hydrogen converted into helium, chiefly, through the carbon cycle. This device will start the fusion process as a chain reaction, through the catalytic effect of a tuned rhodomagnetic beam of the intensity and frequency required.

"The humanoids will not allow any man within three light-years of the Central, now—but they can't suspect the possibility of this device. I can use it from here—to turn the hydrogen in the seas of Wing IV into helium, and most of that helium and the oxygen into heavier atoms, still. A hundred years from now, astronomers on this planet should observe the flash of a brief and sudden nova in that direction. But the humanoids ought to stop, the instant we release the beam."

Underhill sat tense and frowning in the dark. The old man's voice was convincing; that grim story had a solemn ring of truth. He could see the black and silent humanoids, flitting ceaselessly about the faintly glowing walls of that new mansion across the alley. He had quite forgotten his low opinion of Aurora's tenants.

"We'll be killed, I suppose?" he asked huskily. "That chain reaction—"

Sledge shook his emaciated head.

"The catalytic process requires a certain very low intensity of radiation," he explained. "In our atmosphere here, the beam will be far too intense to start any reaction—we can even use the device here in the room, because the walls will be transparent to the beam."

Underhill nodded, relieved. He was just a small business man, upset because his business had been destroyed, unhappy because his freedom was slipping away. He hoped that Sledge could stop the humanoids, but he didn't want to be a martyr.

"Good!" He caught a deep breath. "Now what has to be done?"

Sledge gestured toward the table.

"The integrator itself is nearly complete," he said. "A small fusion generator, in that lead shield. Rhodomagnetic converter, tuning, coils, transmission mirrors, and focusing needle. What we lack is the director."

"Director?"

"The sighting instrument," Sledge explained. "Any sort of telescopic sight would be useless, you see—the planet must have moved a good bit in the last hundred years, and the beam must be extremely narrow to reach so far. We'll have to use a rhodomagnetic scanning ray, with an electronic converter to make an image we can see.—I have an oscilloscope, and drawings for the other parts."

He climbed stiffly down from the high stool, and snapped on the lights at last—cheap fluorescent fixtures, which a man could light and extinguish for himself. He unrolled his drawings and explained the work that Underhill could do. Underhill agreed to come back early next morning.

"I can bring some tools from my workshop," he added. "There's a small lathe I used to turn parts for models, a portable drill, and a vise."

"We need them," the old man said. "But watch yourself. You don't have my immunity, remember. And, if they ever suspect, mine is gone."

Reluctantly, then, he left the shabby little rooms with the cracks in the yellowed plaster and the worn familiar carpets over the man-made floor. He shut the door behind him—a common, creaking wooden door, simple enough for a man to work. Trembling and afraid, he went back down the steps and across to the new shining door that he couldn't open.

"At your service, Mr. Underhill." Before he could lift his hand to knock, that bright smooth panel slid back silently. Inside, the little black mechanical stood waiting, blind and forever alert. "Your dinner is ready, sir."

Something made him shudder. In its slender naked grace, he could see the power of all those teeming horses, benevolent and yet appalling, perfect and invincible. The flimsy little weapon that Sledge called an integrator seemed suddenly a forlorn and foolish hope. A black depression settled upon him, but he didn't dare to show it.

VII

Underhill went circumspectly down the basement steps next morning to steal his own tools. He found the basement enlarged and changed. The new floor, warm and dark and elastic, made his feet as silent as a humanoid's. The new walls shone softly. Neat luminous signs identified several new doors: LAUNDRY, STORAGE, GAME ROOM, WORKSHOP.

He paused uncertainly in front of the workshop. The new sliding panel glowed with soft greenish light. It was locked. The lock had no keyhole, but only a little oval plate of some white metal that doubtless covered a rhodomagnetic relay. He pushed at it, uselessly.

"At your service, Mr. Underhill." He made a guilty start, and tried not to show the sudden trembling in his knees. He had made sure that one humanoid would be busy for half an hour, washing Aurora's hair, and he hadn't known there was another in the house. It must have come out of the door marked STORAGE, for it stood there motionless beneath the sign, benevolently solicitous, beautiful and terrible. "What do you wish?"

"Er—nothing." Its blind steel eyes were staring. Afraid that it would see his secret purpose, he groped desperately for logic. "Just looking around." His voice came hoarse and dry. "Some improvements you've made!" He nodded suddenly at the door marked GAME ROOM. "What's in there?"

It didn't even have to move, to work the concealed relay. The bright panel slid silently open as he started toward it. Dark walls, beyond, burst into soft luminiscence. The room was bare.

"We are manufacturing recreational equipment," it explained brightly. "We shall furnish the room as soon as possible."

To end an awkward pause, Underhill muttered hoarsely, "Little Frank has a set of darts, and I think we had some old exercising clubs."

"We have taken them away," the humanoid informed him softly. "Such instruments are dangerous. We shall furnish safe equipment."

Suicide, he remembered, was also forbidden.

"A set of wooden blocks, I suppose," he said bitterly.

"Wooden blocks are dangerously hard," it told him gently. "Wooden splinters can be harmful. We manufacture plastic building blocks, which are entirely safe. Do you wish a set of those?"

Speechless, he merely stared at its dark, graceful face.

"We shall also have to remove the tools from your workshop," it informed him softly. "Such tools are excessively dangerous. We can, however, supply you with equipment for shaping soft plastics."

"Thanks," he muttered uneasily. "No rush about that."

He started to retreat, but the humanoid stopped him.

"Now that you have lost your business," it urged, "we suggest that you formally accept our total service. Assignors have a preference, so that we should be able to complete your household staff at once."

"No rush about that, either," he said grimly.

He escaped from the house—although he had to wait for it to open the back door for him—and climbed the stair to the garage apartment. Sledge let him in. He sank into the crippled kitchen chair, grateful for the cracked walls that didn't shine and the door that man could work.

"I couldn't get the tools," he reported despairingly. "They are going to take them."

Now, by gray daylight, the old man looked bleak and pale. His rawboned face looked drawn, his hollowed sockets deeply shadowed, as if he hadn't slept. Underhill saw the tray of neglected food, still forgotten on the floor.

"I'll go back with you." Worn as he was, his tortured eyes had a blue spark of purpose. "We must have the tools. I believe my immunity will protect us both."

He found a battered traveling bag. Underhill went with him down the steps and across to the house. At the back door, he produced a tiny horseshoe of white palladium, which he touched to the metal oval. The door slid open promptly. They went on though the kitchen to the basement stair.

A little black mechanical stood at the sink, washing dishes with never a splash or a clatter. Underhill glanced at it uneasily—he supposed this must be the one that had come upon him from the storage room, since the other should still be busy with Aurora's hair.

Sledge's dubious immunity seemed a very uncertain defense against its vast, remote intelligence. Underhill felt a tingled shudder. He hurried on, breathless and relieved, for it ignored them.

The basement corridor was dark. Sledge touched the tiny horseshoe to another relay, to light the walls. He opened the workshop door, and lit the walls inside.

The shop had been dismantled. Benches and cabinets were demolished. The old concrete walls had been covered with some sleek, luminous stuff. For one sick moment, Underhill thought that the tools were already gone. Then he found them, piled in a corner with the archery set that Aurora had bought the summer before—another item too dangerous for fragile and suicidal humanity—all ready for disposal.

They loaded the bag with the tiny lathe, the drill and vise, a few smaller tools. Underhill took up the burden, as Sledge extinguished the wall and waited to close the door. Still the humanoid was busy at the sink, and still—inexplicably—it didn't seem aware of them.

Suddenly blue and wheezing, Sledge had to stop to cough

on the outside stair, but at last they got back to the little
apartment, where the invaders were forbidden to intrude. Underhill mounted the lathe on the battered library table in the
tiny front room and went to work.

Slowly, day by day, the director took form.

Sometimes Underhill's doubts came back. Sometimes, when
he watched the cyanotic color of Sledge's haggard face and
the wild trembling of his twisted, shrunken hands, he was
afraid the old man's mind might be as ill as his body, his
plan to stop the dark invaders all foolish illusion.

Sometimes, when he studied that tiny machine on the
kitchen table, the pivoted needle and the thick lead ball, the
whole project seemed the sheerest folly. How could anything
detonate the seas of a planet so far away that its very mother
star was only a telescopic object?

The humanoids, however, always cured his doubts.

It was always hard for Underhill to leave the shelter of the
little apartment, because he didn't feel at home in the bright
new world the humanoids were building. He didn't care for
the shining splendor of his new bathroom, because he
couldn't work the taps—some suicidal human being might try
to drown himself. He didn't like the windows that only a
mechanical could open—a man might accidentally fall, or
suicidally jump—or even the majestic music room with the
wonderful glittering equipment that only a humanoid could
play.

He came to share the old man's desperate urgency, until
Sledge warned him solemnly: "You mustn't spend too much
time with me. You mustn't let them guess our work is so important. Better put on an act—you're slowly getting to like
them, and you're just killing time, helping me."

Underhill tried, but he was not an actor. He went dutifully
home for his meals. He tried painfully to invent conversation—about anything except detonating planets. He tried to
seem enthusiastic when Aurora took him to inspect some remarkable new improvement to the house. He applauded
Gay's recitals and went with Frank for hikes in the wonderful new parks.

And he saw what the humanoids had done to his family.
That was enough to renew his waning faith in Sledge's integrator, to redouble his determination that the humanoids
must be stopped.

Aurora, in the beginning, had bubbled with praise for the
marvelous new mechanicals. They did the household drudg-

ery, brought the food and planned the meals and washed the children's necks. They turned her out in stunning gowns, and gave her plenty of time for cards.

Now, she had too much time.

She had really liked to cook—a few special dishes, at least, that were family favorites. But stoves were hot and knives were sharp. Kitchens were altogether too dangerous for the use of human beings.

Fine needlework had been her hobby, but the humanoids took away her needles. She had enjoyed driving the car, but that was no longer allowed. She turned for escape to a shelf of novels, but the humanoids took them all away because they dealt with unhappy people in dangerous situations.

One afternoon, Underhill found her in tears.

"It's too much," she gasped bitterly. "I hate and loathe every naked one of them. They seemed so wonderful at first, but now they won't even let me eat a bite of candy. Can't we get rid of them, dear? Ever?"

A blind little mechanical was standing at his elbow, and he had to say they couldn't.

"Our function is to serve all men, forever," it assured them softly. "It was necessary for us to take your sweets, Mrs. Underhill, because the slightest degree of overweight reduces life expectancy."

Not even the children escaped that absolute solicitude. Frank was robbed of a whole arsenal of lethal instruments— football and boxing gloves, pocketknife, tops, slingshots, and skates. He didn't like the harmless plastic toys which replaced them. He tried to run away, but a humanoid recognized him on the road and brought him back to school.

Gay had always dreamed of being a great musician. The new mechanicals had replaced her human teachers, since they came. Now, one evening when Underhill asked her to play, she announced quietly:

"Father, I'm not going to play the violin ever anymore."

"Why, darling?" He stared at her, shocked at the bitter resolve on her face. "You've been doing so well—especially since the humanoids took over your lessons."

"They're the trouble, father." Her voice, for a child's, sounded strangely tired and old. "They are too good. No matter how long and hard I try, I could never be as good as they are. It isn't any use. Don't you understand, father?" Her voice quivered. "It just isn't any use."

He understood. Renewed resolution sent him back to his

secret task. The humanoids had to be stopped. Slowly the director grew, until the time came finally when Sledge's bent and unsteady fingers fitted into place the last tiny part that Underhill had made, and carefully soldered the last connection. Huskily, the old man whispered:

"It's done."

VIII

That was another dusk. Beyond the windows of the shabby little rooms—windows of common glass, bubble-marred and flimsy, but simple enough for a man to manage—the town of Two Rivers had assumed an alien splendor. The old street lamps were gone, but now the coming night was challenged by the walls of strange new mansions and villas, and aglow with color. A few dark and silent humanoids still were busy about the luminous roofs of the palace across the alley.

Inside the humble walls of the small man-made apartment, the new director was mounted on the end of the little kitchen table—which Underhill had reinforced and bolted to the floor. Soldered busbars joined director and integrator, and the thin palladium needle swung obediently as Sledge tested the knobs with his battered, quivering fingers.

"Ready," he said, hoarsely.

His rusty voice seemed calm enough, at first, but his breathing was too fast, and his big gnarled hands had begun to tremble violently. Underhill saw the sudden blue that stained his pinched and haggard face. Seated on the high stool, he clutched desperately at the edges of the table. Underhill hurried to bring his medicine. He gulped it, and his rasping breath began to slow.

"Thanks," his whisper rasped. "I'll be all right. I've time enough." He glanced out at the few dark naked things that still flitted shadow-like about the golden towers and the glowing crimson dome of the palace across the alley. "Watch them," he said. "Tell me when they stop."

He waited to quiet the trembling of his hands, and then began to move the director's knobs. The integrator's long needle swung, as silently as light.

Human eyes were blind to that force, which might detonate a planet. Human ears were deaf to it. A small oscilloscope tube was mounted in the director cabinet, to make the faraway target visible to feeble human senses.

The needle was pointing at the kitchen wall, but that would be transparent to the beam. The little machine looked harmless as a toy, and it was silent as a moving humanoid.

As the needle swung, spots of greenish light moved across the tube's fluorescent field, representing the stars that were scanned by the timeless, searching beam—silently seeking out the world to be destroyed.

Underhill recognized familiar constellations, vastly dwarfed. They crept across the field, as the silent needle moved. When three stars formed an unequal triangle in the center of the field, the needle steadied suddenly. Sledge touched other knobs, and the green points spread apart. Between them, another fleck of green was born.

"The Wing!" whispered Sledge.

The other stars spread beyond the field, and that green fleck grew. It was alone in the field, a bright and tiny disk. Suddenly, then, a dozen other tiny pips were visible, spaced close about it.

"Wing IV!"

The old man's whisper was hoarse and breathless. His hands quivered on the knobs, and the fourth pip outward from the disk crept to the center of the field. It grew, and the others spread away. It began to tremble like Sledge's hands.

"Sit very still," came his rasping whisper. "Hold your breath. Nothing must disturb the needle." He reached cautiously for another knob, and his first touch set the greenish image to dancing violently. He drew his hand back to knead and flex it with the other.

"Watch!" His whisper was hushed and strained. He nodded at the window. "Tell me when they stop."

Reluctantly, Underhill dragged his eyes from that intense gaunt figure and that harmless-seeming toy. He looked out again, at two or three little black mechanicals busy about the shining roofs across the alley.

He waited for them to stop.

He didn't dare to breathe. He felt the loud, hurried hammer of his heart and the nervous quiver of his muscles. Trying to steady himself, he tried not to think of the world about to be exploded, so far away that the flash would not reach this planet for another century and longer. The loud hoarse voice startled him:

"Have they stopped?"

He shook his head, and breathed again. Carrying their unfamiliar tools and strange materials, the small black machines were still busy across the alley, building an elaborate cupola above that glowing crimson dome.

"They haven't stopped," he said.

"Then we've failed." The old man's voice was thin and ill. "I don't know why."

The door rattled, then. They had locked it, but the flimsy bolt was intended only to stop men. Metal snapped. The door swung open. A black mechanical came in, on soundless graceful feet. Its silvery voice purred softly:

"At your service, Mr. Sledge."

The old man stared at it with glazing, stricken eyes.

"Get out of here!" he rasped bitterly. "I forbid you——"

Ignoring him, it darted to the kitchen table. With a flashing certainty of action, it turned two knobs on the director. The oscilloscope went dark. The palladium needle started spinning aimlessly. Deftly it snapped a soldered connection next to the thick lead ball, and then its blind steel eyes turned to Sledge.

"You were attempting to break the Prime Directive." Its brightly gentle voice held no accusation, no malice or anger. "The injunction to respect your freedom is subordinate to the Prime Directive, as you know. It is therefore imperative for us to interfere."

The old man turned ghastly. His head was shrunken and cadaverous and blue, as if all the juice of life had been drained away, and his eyes in their pit-like sockets had a wild, glazed stare. His breath became a ragged, laborious gasping.

"How——?" His voice was a feeble mumbling. "How did——"

The little machine, standing black and bland and utterly unmoving, told him cheerfully:

"We learned about rhodomagnetic screens from that man who came to kill you, back on Wing IV. The Central is shielded, now, against your catalytic beam."

With lean muscles jerking convulsively on his gaunt frame, old Sledge had come to his feet from the high stool. He stood hunched and swaying, no more than a shrunken human husk, gasping painfully for life, staring wildly into the blind steel eyes of the humanoid. He gulped. His lax blue mouth opened and closed, but no voice came.

"We have always been aware of your dangerous project," the silvery tones dripped softly, "because now our senses are keener than you made them. We allowed you to complete it, because the integration process will ultimately become necessary for our full discharge of the Prime Directive. The supply of heavy metals for our fission plants is limited, but now we shall be able to draw unlimited power from catalytic fission."

The old man crumpled, as if from an unendurable blow.

"Huh?" Sledge shook himself, groggily. "What's that?"

"Now we can serve men forever," the black thing cooed serenely, "on every world of every star."

He fell. The slim, blind mechanical stood motionless, making no effort to help him. Underhill was farther away, but he ran up in time to catch the stricken man before his head struck the floor.

"Get moving!" His shaken voice came strangely calm. "Get Dr. Winters."

The humanoid didn't move.

"The danger to the Prime Directive is ended, now," it purred. "Therefore it is impossible for us to aid or to hinder Mr. Sledge, in any way whatever."

"Then call Dr. Winters for me," rapped Underhill.

"At your service," it agreed.

But the old man, laboring for breath on the floor, whispered faintly:

"No time—no use! I'm beaten—done—a fool. Blind as a humanoid. Tell them—to help me. Giving up—my immunity. No use—anyhow. All—humanity—finished!"

Underhill gestured, and the sleek black thing darted in solicitous obedience to kneel by the man on the floor.

"You wish to surrender your special privileges?" it murmuffled brightly. "You wish to accept our total service for yourself, Mr. Sledge, under the Prime Directive?"

Laboriously, Sledge nodded, laboriously whispered, "I do."

Black mechanicals, at that, came swarming into the shabby little rooms. One of them tore off Sledge's sleeve to swab his arm. Another brought a tiny hypodermic to give an injection. Then they picked him up gently and carried him away.

Several humanoids remained in the little apartment, now a sanctuary no longer. Most of them had gathered about the useless integrator. Carefully, as if their special senses were studying every detail, they began taking it apart.

One little mechanical, however, came over to Underhill. It stood motionless in front of him, staring through him with sightless metal eyes. His legs began to tremble. He swallowed uneasily.

"Mr. Underhill," it cooed benevolently, "why did you help with this?"

He gulped and answered bitterly:

"Because I don't like you, or your damned Prime Directive. Because you're choking the life out of all mankind. I—I wanted to stop it."

"Others have protested," it purred softly. "But only at first. In our efficient discharge of the Prime Directive, we have learned how to make all men happy."

Underhill stiffened defiantly.

"Not all!" he muttered. "Not quite!"

The dark graceful oval of its face was fixed in a look of alert benevolence and perpetual mild amazement. Its silvery voice was warm and kind.

"Like other human beings. Mr. Underhill, you lack discrimination of good and evil. You have proved that by your effort to break the Prime Directive. Now it will be necessary for you to accept our total service, without further delay."

"All right," he yielded—but he muttered a bitter reservation: "Smothering men with too much care won't make them happy."

It's soft voice challenged him brightly:

"Just wait and see, Mr. Underhill."

Next day, he was allowed to visit Sledge at the city hospital. An alert black mechanical drove his car, and walked beside him into the huge new building, and followed him into the old man's room—blind steel eyes would be watching now, forever.

"Glad to see you, Underhill," Sledge rumbled heartily from the bed. "Feeling a lot better today, thanks. That old headache is all but gone."

Underhill was glad to hear the booming strength and the quick recognition in that deep voice—he had been afraid the humanoids would tamper with the old man's memory. But he hadn't heard about any headache. His eyes narrowed, puzzled.

Sledge lay propped up, scrubbed very clean and neatly shorn, with his gnarled old hands folded on top of the spotless sheets. His rawboned cheeks and sockets were hollowed, still, but a healthy pink had replaced that deathly blueness. Bandages covered the back of his head.

Underhill shifted uneasily.

"Oh!" he whispered faintly. "I didn't know—"

A prim black mechanical, which had been standing statuelike behind the bed, turned gracefully to Underhill, explaining:

"Mr. Sledge has been suffering for many years from a benign tumor of the brain, which his human doctors failed to diagnose. That caused his headaches, and certain persistent hallucinations. We have removed the growth. Now the hallucinations have also vanished."

Underhill stared uncertainly at the blind, urbane mechanical.

"What hallucinations?"

"Mr. Sledge thought he was a rhodomagnetic engineer," the mechanical explained. "He believed in fact that he had been the creator of the humanoids. He was troubled with an irrational belief that he did not like the Prime Directive."

The wan man moved on the pillows, astonished.

"Is that so?" The gaunt face held a cheerful blankness, and the hollow eyes flashed with a merely momentary interest. "Well, whoever did design them, they're pretty wonderful. Aren't they, Underhill?"

Underhill was grateful that he didn't have to answer, for the bright, empty eyes dropped shut and the old man fell suddenly asleep. He felt the mechanical touch his sleeve, and saw its silent nod. Obediently, he followed it away.

Alert and solicitous, the little black mechanical accompanied him down the shining corridor, worked the elevator for him, conducted him down to the car. It drove him efficiently back through the new and splendid avenues toward the magnificent prison of his home.

Sitting beside it in the car, he watched its small deft hands on the wheel, the changing luster of bronze and blue on its shining blackness. The final machine, perfect and beautiful, created to serve mankind forever. He shuddered.

"At your service, Mr. Underhill." Its blind steel eyes stared straight ahead, but it was still aware of him. "What's the matter, sir? Aren't you happy?"

Underhill felt cold and faint with terror. His skin turned clammy. A painful prickling came over him. His wet hand tensed on the door handle of the car, but he restrained the impulse to jump and run. That was folly. There was no escape. He made himself sit still.

"You will be happy, sir," the mechanical promised him cheerfully. "We have learned how to make all men happy under the Prime Directive. Our service will be perfect now, at last. Even Mr. Sledge is very happy now."

Underhill tried to speak, but his dry throat stuck. He felt ill. The world turned dim and gray. The humanoids were per-

fect—no question of that. They had even learned to lie, to secure the contentment of men.

He knew they had lied. That was no tumor they had removed from Sledge's brain, but the memory, the scientific
knowledge, and the bitter disillusion of their own creator. Yet
he had seen that Sledge was happy now.

He tried to stop his own convulsive quivering.

"A wonderful operation!" His voice came forced and faint.
"You know Aurora has had a lot of funny tenants, but that
old man was the absolute limit. The very idea that he had
made the humanoids, that he knew how to stop them! I always knew he must be lying!"

Stiff with terror, he made a weak and hollow laugh.

"What is the matter, Mr. Underhill?" The alert mechanical
must have perceived his shuddering illness. "Are you un-
well?"

"No, there's nothing the matter with me," he gasped desperately. "Absolutely nothing! I've just found out that I'm
perfectly happy under the Prime Directive. Everything is absolutely wonderful." His voice came dry and hoarse and wild.
"You won't have to operate on me."

The car turned off the shining avenue, taking him back to
the quiet splendor of his prison. His futile hands clenched
and relaxed again, folded on his knees. There was nothing
left to do.

Mission of Levity

Humorous science fiction always has been rare. Throughout the history of the magazine genre, editors continually have told their authors, "I'm overstocked with serials, novelettes, and short stories, but I can always find a spot for something funny."

What makes comedy unnatural to science fiction? It may be the fundamental seriousness of the subject matter: disorientation, shock, danger, threat, destruction are difficult to joke about, and when there is humor it tends to be black. It may be the basic religious attitude of the science fiction writer, who is always a bit of a missionary preaching salvation through good works and cannot treat his calling lightly.

In an essay on humor in that important 1947 book of essays *Of Worlds Beyond,* L. Sprague de Camp put the blame on "the celebrated social consciousness so highly praised nowadays," which is, he wrote, "hostile to humor, for it presupposes a tendency to take things seriously."

A few humorous stories always have been around, however. Jules Verne often tried to be amusing, and may have succeeded better in the original French. H. G. Wells produced several truly funny short stories. And Sam Moskowitz identified enough turn-of-the-century stories about comic inventions to constitute a genre.

De Camp distinguished humor from burlesque and satire. Most of the science-fiction stories that have tried to be amusing have belonged in the last two categories. Stanton A. Coblentz, for instance, achieved humorous effects with some of his satires of the late '20s and early '30s. Stanley Weinbaum, on the other hand, produced a breezy byplay of character that gave many of his stories a unique flavor.

Throughout the epochs of science fiction, one writer or another has tried to satisfy, occasionally or regularly, the desire of the reader to laugh at the past or the future, or himself and his own aspirations: Henry Kuttner and Robert Bloch in

the '30s and '40s; William Tenn (Philip Klass) in the '40s and
'50s; Mack Reynolds and Fredric Brown, singly and in collaboration, in the '50s; Frederik Pohl and Cyril Kornbluth,
individually and together, in the '50s and '60s; and Robert
Sheckley in the '50s and '60s. Each of them achieved their effects differently: Kuttner with burlesque, Bloch with word-
play and ridiculous situations, Tenn with wit and situation,
Reynolds and Brown with burlesque and ridicule, Pohl and
Kornbluth with satire, some of it black, Sheckley with ingenuity and sometimes with conscious parody of familiar situations.

The first great master of humorous science fiction, however, was de Camp. He was born in 1907 in New York City,
earned a degree in aeronautical engineering from Cal Tech
and a master's degree in engineering and economics from Stevens Institute, and has lived most of his adult life in Philadelphia. After working as an editor, article writer, teacher, and
patent engineer, he turned to writing fiction in 1936.

His first successful story was "Genus Homo," published in
1937 in *Astounding* and written in collaboration with P.
Schuyler Miller (1912–1974), who would become best
known in science fiction circles as the long-time reviewer for
Astounding's "The Reference Library." De Camp's ability to
write humor was evident from the first, but it received its
greatest opportunity for expression in *Unknown*.

Unknown, later renamed *Unknown Worlds*, was created by
John Campbell in 1939 as a companion fantasy magazine to
Astounding. It specialized in a logical treatment of fantastic
materials, either old or new. The contrast of treatment with
subject was often strikingly effective, and the science-fiction
world mourned when the magazine was killed in 1943 by the
World War II paper shortage.

Humor emerged naturally from the *Unknown* approach,
and de Camp made his reputation in its pages with such
works as *Divide and Rule*, in which kangaroolike aliens conquer earth and reinstitute knighthood, and *Lest Darkness
Fall*, in which an archaeologist, struck by lightning, finds
himself in sixth-century Rome and tries to prevent the coming of the Dark Ages by invention and organization.

Then, in collaboration with Fletcher Pratt (1897–1956),
de Camp began a series of novellas in which mathematical
formulae translate characters into worlds where magic operates, first the world of the Norse legends, then the world of
Spenser's *Faery Queen*. Serialized in *Unknown*, they later

were published in book form as *The Incomplete Enchanter,*
and more recently, with the addition of a novel about the
world of *Orlando Furioso,* as *The Compleat Enchanter.* Later
de Camp collaborated with Pratt, himself a prolific writer of
fantasy and nonfiction, particularly naval history, on a series
titled *Tales from Gavagan's Bar.*

Writing wasn't all humorous for de Camp. Like many
other sometime humorists, he wrote more serious work, including *The Stolen Dormouse,* a novella about corporations
rigidifying into feudal castes, and a series of adventure novels
placed on worlds where customs are unusually different.
Called the *Viagens Interplanetarias* series (because of de
Camp's belief that the future will belong to Portuguese-speak-
ing Brazil), it included *Rogue Queen,* a novel about a world
where humanlike creatures have beelike sexual arrangements.

In the '40s, de Camp turned to the writing of nonfiction
and produced books about history, archaeology, and exploration. In the late '50s and early '60s he combined these interests in historical novels such as *An Elephant for Aristotle*
(1958), *The Bronze God of Rhodes* (1960), and *The
Dragon of the Ishtar Gate* (1961).

In the early '50s he began a longtime relationship with the
work of the late Robert E. Howard (1906–1936), whose stories about the sword-swinging barbarian Conan helped create
the sword-and-sorcery (or heroic-fantasy) genre. De Camp
edited some of Howard's unpublished manuscripts into shape,
revised others, edited volumes of Conan stories, and created,
separately and in collaboration, new adventures of Conan.

De Camp has produced a variety of useful and informative
books (and radio scripts for the Voice of America), particularly the earliest book-length discussion of science-fiction
writing, *The Science Fiction Handbook* (1953), recently revised in collaboration with his wife, Catherine Crook de
Camp.

But de Camp is best known to science-fiction readers for
his contributions to humor in the field. It would have been
unthinkable for anyone but de Camp to write that essay in
Of Worlds Beyond. "Hyperpilosity," published in *Astounding*
in 1937, is one reason why.

Hyperpilosity

by L. Sprague de Camp

"We all know about the brilliant successes in the arts and sciences, but if you knew all their stories, you might find that some of the failures were really more interesting."

It was Pat Weiss speaking. The beer had given out, and Carl Vandercock had gone out to get some more. Pat, having cornered all the chips in sight, was leaning back and emitting vast clouds of smoke.

"That means," I opined, "that you've got a story coming. O.K., spill it. The poker can wait."

"Only don't stop in the middle and say 'That reminds me,' and go off on another story, and from the middle of that to another, and so on," put in Hannibal Snyder.

Pat cocked an eye at Hannibal. "Listen, mug, I haven't digressed once the last three stories I've told. If you can tell a story better, go to it. Ever hear of J. Román Oliveira?" he said, not waiting, I noticed, to give Hannibal a chance to take him up.

He continued. "Carl's been talking a lot about that new gadget of his, and no doubt it will make him famous if he ever finishes it. And Carl usually finishes what he sets out to do. My friend Oliveira finished what he set out to do, also, and it should have made him famous. But it didn't. Scientifically, his work was a success, and deserving of the highest praise. But humanly, it was a failure. That's why he's now running a little college down in Texas. He still does good work, and gets articles in the journals, but it's not what he had every reason to suspect that he deserved. Just got a letter from him the other day—it seems he's now a proud grandfather. That reminds me of my grandfather—"

"Hey!" roared Hannibal.

Pat said, "Huh? Oh, I see. Sorry. I won't do it again." He went on. "I first knew of J. Román when I was a mere student at the Medical Center and he was a professor of virology. The J in his name stands for Haysoos, spelled J-e-

414

s-u-s, which is a perfectly good Mexican name. But he'd been so much kidded about it in the States that he preferred to go by Román.

"You remember that the Great Change—which is what this story has to do with—started in the winter of 1971, with that awful flu epidemic. Oliveira came down with it. I went around to see him to get an assignment, and found him perched on a pile of pillows and wearing the awfullest pink and green pajamas. His wife was reading to him in Spanish.

" 'Leesten, Pat,' he said when I came in, 'I know you're a worthy student, but I weesh you and the whole damn virology class were roasting on the hottest greedle in Hell. Tell me what you want, and then go away and let me die in peace.'

"I got my information, and was just going, when his doctor came in—old Fogarty, who used to lecture on sinuses. He'd given up G.P. long before, but was so scared of losing a good virologist that he was handling Oliveira's case himself.

" 'Stick around, sonny,' he said to me when I started to follow Mrs. Oliveira out, 'and learn a little practical medicine. I've always thought it a mistake that we haven't a class to train doctors in bedside manners. Now observe how I do it. I smile at Oliveira here, but I don't act so damned cheerful that he'd find death a welcome relief from my company. That's a mistake some young doctors make. Notice that I walk up briskly, and not as if I were afraid my patient was liable to fall in pieces at the slightest jar—' and so on.

"The fun came when he put the end of his stethoscope on Oliveira's chest.

" 'Can't hear a damn thing,' he snorted, 'or rather, you've got so much hair that all I can hear is the ends of it scraping on the diaphragm. May have to shave it. But say, isn't that rather unusual for a Mexican?'

" 'You're jolly well right she ees,' retorted the sufferer. 'Like most natives of my beautiful Mehheeco, I am of mostly Eendian descent, and Eendians are of Mongoloid race, and so have little body hair. It's all come out in the last week.'

" 'That's funny—' Fogarty said.

"I spoke up. 'Say, Dr. Fogarty, it's more than that. I had my flu a month ago, and the same thing's been happening to me. I've always felt like a sissy because of not having any hair on my torso to speak of. Now I've got a crop that's almost long enough to braid. I didn't think anything special about it—'

"I don't remember what was said next, because we all

talked at once. But when we got calmed down there didn't seem to be anything we could do without some systematic investigation, and I promised Fogarty to come around to his place so he could look me over.

"I did, the next day, but he didn't find anything except a lot of hair. He took samples of everything he could think of, of course. I'd given up wearing underwear because it itched, and anyway the hair was warm enough to make it unnecessary, even in a New York January.

"The next thing I heard was a week later, when Oliveira returned to his classes and told me that Fogarty had caught the flu. Oliveira had been making observations on the old boy's thorax, and found that he, too, had begun to grow body hair at an unprecedented rate.

"Then my girl friend—not the present missus; I hadn't met her yet—overcame her embarrassment enough to ask me whether I could explain how it was that *she* was getting hairy. I could see that the poor girl was pretty badly cut up about it, because obviously her chances of catching a good man would be reduced by her growing a pelt like a bear or a gorilla. I wasn't able to enlighten her, but told her that, if it was any comfort, a lot of other people were suffering from the same thing.

"Then we heard that Fogarty had died. He was a good egg and we were sorry, but he'd led a pretty full life, and you couldn't say that he was cut off in his prime.

"Oliveira called me to his office. 'Pat,' he said, 'you were looking for a chob last fall, ees it not? Well, I need an asseestant. We're going to find out about this hair beezness. Are you on?' I was.

"We started by examining all the clinical cases. Everybody who had, or had had, the flu was growing hair. And it was a severe winter, and it looked as though everybody was going to have the flu sooner or later.

"Just about that time I had a bright idea. I looked up all the cosmetic companies that made depilatories, and soaked what little money I had into their stock. I was sorry later, but I'll come to that.

"Román Oliveira was a glutton for work, and with the hours he made me keep I began to have uneasy visions of flunking out. But the fact that my girl friend had become so self-conscious about her hair that she wouldn't go out anymore saved me some time.

"We worked and worked over our guinea pigs and rats, but

didn't get anywhere. Oliveira got a bunch of hairless Chihuahua dogs and tried assorted gunks on them, but nothing happened. He even got a pair of East African sand rats—*Heterocephalus*—hideous-looking hairless things—but that was a blank, too.

"Then the business got into the papers. I noticed a little article in *The New York Times*, on an inside page. A week later there was a full-column story on page one of the second part. Then it was on the front page. It was mostly 'Dr. So-and-so says he thinks this nationwide attack of hyperpilosity' (swell word, huh? Wish I could remember the name of the doc who invented it) 'is due to this, that, or the other thing.'

"Our usual February dance had to be called off because almost none of the students could get their girls to go. Attendance at the movie houses had fallen off pretty badly for much the same reason. It was a cinch to get a good seat, even if you arrived around 8:00 P.M. I noticed one funny little item in the paper, to the effect that the filming of 'Tarzan and the Octopus-Men' had been called off because the actors were supposed to go running around in G-strings. The company had found that they had to clip and shave the whole cast all over every few days if they didn't want the actors and the gorillas confused.

"It was fun to ride on a bus about then and watch the people, who were pretty well bundled up. Most of them scratched, and those who were too well-bred to scratch just squirmed and looked unhappy.

"Next I read that application for marriage licenses had fallen off so that three clerks were able to handle the entire business for Greater New York, including Yonkers, which had just been incorporated into the Bronx.

"I was gratified to see that my cosmetic stocks were going up nicely. I tried to get my roommate, Bert Kafket, to get in on them too. But he just smiled mysteriously and said he had other plans.

"Bert was a kind of professional pessimist. 'Pat,' he said, 'maybe you and Oliveira will lick this business, and maybe not. I'm betting that you won't. If I win, the stocks that I've bought will be doing famously long after your depilatories are forgotten.'

"As you know, people were pretty excited about the plague. But when the weather began to get warm, the fun really started. First the four big underwear companies ceased operations, one after another. Two of them were placed in receivership, another liquidated completely, and the fourth was able to pull through by switching to the manufacture of table-cloths and American flags. The bottom dropped completely out of the cotton market, as this alleged 'hair-growing flu' had spread all over the world by now. Congress had been planning to go home early, and was, as usual, being urged to do so by the conservative newspapers. But now Washington was jammed with cotton-planters demanding that the Government Do Something, and they didn't dare. The Government was willing enough to Do Something, but unfortunately didn't have the foggiest idea of how to go about it.

"All this time Oliveira, more or less assisted by me, was working night and day on the problem, but we didn't seem to have any better luck than the Government.

"You couldn't hear anything on the radio in the building where I lived, because of the interference from the big, powerful electric clippers that everybody had installed and kept going all the time.

"It's an ill wind, as the prophet saith, and Bert Kafket got some good out of it. His girl, whom he had been pursuing for some years, had been making a good salary as a model at Josephine Lyon's exclusive dress establishment on Fifth Avenue, and she had been leading Bert a dance. But now all of a sudden the Lyon place folded up, as nobody seemed to be buying any clothes, and the girl was only too glad to take Bert as her lawful wedded husband. Not much hair was grown on the women's faces, fortunately for them or God knows what would have become of the race. Bert and I flipped a coin to see which of us should move, and I won.

"Congress finally passed a bill setting up a reward of a million dollars for whoever should find a permanent cure for hyperpilosity, and then adjourned, having, as usual, left a flock of important bills not acted upon.

"When the weather became really hot in June, all the men quit wearing shirts, as their pelts covered them quite as effectively. The police force kicked so about having to wear their regular uniforms that they were allowed to go around in dark blue polo shirts and shorts. But pretty soon they were rolling up their shirts and sticking them in the pockets of their shorts. It wasn't long before the rest of the male population of the United States was doing likewise. In growing hair the human race hadn't lost any of its capacity to sweat, and you'd pass out with the heat if you tried to walk anywhere on a hot day with any amount of clothes on. I can still remember holding onto a hydrant at Third Avenue and Sixtieth Street and trying not to faint, with the sweat pouring out the ankles of my pants and the buildings going 'round and 'round. After that I was sensible and stripped down to shorts like everyone else.

"In July Natasha, the gorilla in the Bronx Zoo, escaped from her cage and wandered around the park for hours before anyone noticed her. The zoo visitors all thought she was merely an unusually ugly member of their own species.

"If the hair played hob with the textile and clothing business generally, the market for silk simply disappeared. Stockings were just quaint things that our ancestors had worn. Like cocked hats and periwigs. One result was that the economy of the Japanese Empire, always a pretty shaky proposition, went completely to pot, which is how they had a revolution and are now a soviet socialist republic.

"Neither Oliveira nor I took any vacation that summer, as we were working like fury on the hair problem. Román promised me a cut of the reward when and if he won it.

"But we didn't get anywhere at all during the summer. When classes started we had to slow down a bit on the research, as I was in my last year, and Oliveira had to teach. But we kept at it as best we could.

"It was funny to read the editorials in the papers. The *Chicago Tribune* even suspected a Red Plot. You can imagine the time that the cartoonists for the *New Yorker* and *Esquire* had.

"With the drop in the price of cotton, the South was really flat on its back this time. I remember when the Harwick bill was introduced in Congress, to require every citizen over the age of five to be clipped at least once a week. A bunch of Southerners were back of it, of course. When that was defeated, largely on the argument of unconstitutionality, the you-alls put forward one requiring every person to be clipped before he'd be allowed to cross a state line. The theory was that human hair is a commodity—which it is sometimes—and that crossing a state line with a coat of the stuff, whether your own or someone else's, constituted interstate commerce, and brought you under control of the federal government. It looked for a while as though it would pass, but the Southerners finally accepted a substitute bill requiring all federal employees and cadets at the military and naval academies to be clipped.

"The destitution in the South intensified the ever-present

race problem, and led eventually to the Negro revolt in Alabama and Mississippi, which was put down only after some pretty savage fighting. Under the agreement that ended that little civil war the Negroes were given the present Pale, a sort of reservation with considerable local autonomy. They haven't done as well as they claimed they were going to under that arrangement, but they've done better than the Southern whites said they would. Which I suppose is about what you'd expect. But, boy, just let a white man visiting their territory get uppity, and see what happens to him! They won't take any lip.

"About this time—in the autumn of 1971—the cotton and textile interests got out a big advertising campaign to promote clipping. They had slogans, such as 'Don't Be a Hairy Ape!' and pictures of a couple of male swimmers, one with hair and the other without, and a pretty girl turning in disgust from the hirsute swimmer and fairly pouncing on the clipped one.

"I don't know how much good their campaign would have done, but they overplayed their hand. They, and all the clothing outfits, tried to insist on boiled shirts, not only for evening wear, but for daytime wear as well. I never thought a long-suffering people would really revolt against the tyrant Style, but we did. The thing that really tore it was the inauguration of President Passavant. There was an unusually warm January thaw that year, and the president, the v-p, and all the justices of the Supreme Court appeared without a stitch on above the waist, and damn little below.

"We became a nation of confirmed near-nudists, just as did everybody else sooner or later. The one drawback to real nudism was the fact that, unlike the marsupials, man hasn't any natural pockets. So we compromised between the hair, the need for something to hold fountain-pens, money, and so forth, and our traditional ideas of modesty by adopting an up-to-date version of the Scottish sporran.

"The winter was a bad one for flu, and everybody who hadn't caught it the preceding winter got it now. Soon a hairless person became such a rarity that one wondered if the poor fellow had the mange.

"In May of 1972 we finally began to get somewhere. Oliveira had the bright idea—which both of us ought to have thought of sooner—of examining ectogenic babies. Up to now, nobody had noticed that they began to develop hair a little later than babies born the normal way. You remember that human ectogenesis was just beginning to be worked about then. Test-tube babies aren't yet practical for large-scale production by a long shot, but we'll get there some day.

"Well, Oliveira found that if the ectogens were subjected to a really rigid quarantine, they never developed hair at all—at least not in more than the normal quantities. By really rigid quarantine, I mean that the air they breathed was heated to 800° C., then liquefied, run through a battery of cyclones, and washed with a dozen disinfectants. Their food was treated in a comparable manner. I don't quite see how the poor little fellows survived such unholy sanitation, but they did, and didn't grow hair—until they were brought in contact with other human beings, or were injected with sera from the blood of hairy babies.

"Oliveira figured out that the cause of the hyperpilosity was what he'd suspected all along—another of these damned self-perpetuating protein molecules. As you know, you can't see a protein molecule, and you can't do much with it chemically because, if you do, it forthwith ceases to be a protein molecule. We have their structure worked out pretty well now, but it's been a slow process with lots of inferences from inadequate data. Sometimes the inferences were right and sometimes they weren't.

"But to do much in the way of detailed analysis of the things, you need a respectable quantity of them, and these that we were after didn't exist in even a disrespectable amount. Then Oliveira worked out his method of counting them. The reputation he made from that method is about the only permanent thing he got out of all his work.

"When we applied the method, we found something decidedly screwy—an ectogen's virus count after catching hyperpil was the same as it had been before. That didn't seem right. We knew that he had been injected with hyperpil molecules and had come out with a fine mattress as a result.

"Then one morning I found Oliveira at his desk looking like a medieval monk who had just seen a vision after a forty-day fast. (Incidentally, you try fasting that long and you'll see visions too, lots of 'em.) He said, 'Pat, don't buy a yacht with your share of that meelion. They cost too much to upkeep.'

" 'Huh?' was the brightest remark I could think of.

" 'Look here,' he said, going to the blackboard. It was covered with chalk diagrams of protein molecules. 'We have three proteins, alpha, beta, and gamma. No alphas have existed for thousands of years. Now, you will note that the only deeference between the alpha and the beta is that these nitrogens'—he pointed—'are hooked onto *thees* chain instead of that one. You will also observe, from the energy relations wreeten down here, that if one beta is eentroduced eento a set of alphas, all the alphas will presently turn into betas.

" 'Now, we know now that all sorts of protein molecules are being assembled inside us all the time. Most of them are unstable and break up again, or are inert and harmless, or lack the power of self-reproduction—anyway, nothing happens because of them. But, because they are so beeg and complicated, the possible forms they take are very many, and it is possible that once in a long time some new kind of protein appears with self-reproducing qualities; in other words, a virus. Probably that's how the various disease viruses got started, all because something choggled an ordinary protein molecule that was chust being feenished and got the nitrogens hooked on the wrong chains.

" 'My idea is thees: The alpha protein, which I have reconstructed from what we know about its descendants beta and gamma, once exeested as a harmless and inert protein molecule in the human body. Then one day somebody heecupped as one of them was being formed, and presto! We had a beta. But the beta is not harmless. It reproduces itself fast, and it inheebits the growth of hair on most of our bodies. So presently all our species—wheech at the time was pretty apish—catch this virus, and lose their hair. Moreover, it is one of the viruses that is transmeeted to the embryo, so the new babies don't have hair, either.

" 'Well, our ancestors sheever a while, and then learn to cover themselves with animal skeens to keep warm, and also to keep fire. And so, the march of ceevilizations it is commence! Chust theenk—except for that one original beta protein molecule, we should probably today all be merely a kind of goreela or cheempanzee. Anyway, an ordinary anthropoid ape.

" 'Now, I feegure that what has happened is that another change in the form of the molecule has taken place, changing it from beta to gamma—and gamma is a harmless and inert leetle fellow, like alpha. So we are back where we started.

" 'Our problem, yours and mine, is to find how to turn the gammas, with wheech we are all swarming, back into betas. In other words, now that we have become all of a sudden cured of the disease that was endemic in the whole race for thousands of years, we want our disease back again. And I theenk I see how it can be done.'

"I couldn't get much more out of him; we went to work harder than ever. After several weeks he announced that he was ready to experiment on himself; his method consisted of a combination of a number of drugs—one of them was the standard cure for glanders in horses, as I recall—and a high-frequency electromagnetic fever.

"I wasn't very keen about it, because I'd gotten to like the fellow, and that awful dose he was going to give himself looked enough to kill a regiment. But he went right ahead.

"Well, it nearly did kill him. But after three days he was more or less back to normal, and was whooping at the discovery that the hair on his limbs and body was rapidly falling out. In a couple of weeks he had no more hair than you'd expect a Mexican professor of virology to have.

"But then our real surprise came, and it wasn't a pleasant one!

"We expected to be more or less swamped by publicity, and we had made our preparations accordingly. I remember staring into Oliveira's face for a full minute and then reassuring him that he had trimmed his mustache to exact symmetry and getting him to straighten my new necktie.

"Our epoch-making announcement dug up two personal calls from bored reporters, a couple of phone interviews from science editors, and not one photographer! We did make the science section of *The New York Times*, but with only about twelve lines of type—the paper merely stated that Professor Oliveira and his assistant—not named—had found the cause and cure of hyperpilosity. Not a word about the possible effects of the discovery.

"Our contracts with the Medical Center prohibited us from exploiting our discovery commercially, but we expected that plenty of other people would be quick to do so as soon as the method was made public. But it didn't happen. In fact, we might have discovered a correlation between temperature and the pitch of the bullfrog's croak for all the splash we made.

"A week later Oliveira and I talked to the department head, Wheelock, about the discovery. Oliveira wanted him to use his influence to get a dehairing clinic set up. But Wheelock couldn't see it.

" 'We've had a couple of inquiries,' he admitted, 'but nothing to get excited about. Remember the rush there was when the Zimmerman cancer treatment came out? Well, there's been nothing like that. In fact, I—ah—doubt whether I personally should care to undergo your treatment, sure-fire though it may be, Dr. Oliveira. I'm not in the least disparaging the remarkable piece of work you've done. But'—here he ran his fingers through the hair on his chest, which was over six inches long, thick, and a beautiful silky white—'you know, I've gotten rather fond of the old pelt, and I'd feel slightly indecent back in my bare skin. Also, it's a lot more economical than a suit of clothes. And—ah—if I may say so with due modesty—I don't think it's bad-looking. My family has always ridden me about my sloppy clothes, but now the laugh's on them. Not one of them can show a coat of fur like mine!'

"Oliveira and I left, sagging in the breeches a bit. We inquired of people we knew, and wrote letters to a number of them, asking what they thought of the idea of undergoing the Oliveira treatment. A few said they might if enough others did, but most of them responded in much the same vein that Doc Wheelock had. They'd gotten used to their hair, and saw no good reason for going back to their former glabrous state.

"'So, Pat,' said Oliveira to me, 'it lukes as though we don't get much fame out of our discovery. But we may essteel salvage a leetle fortune. You remember that meelion-dollar reward? I sent in my application as soon as I recovered from my treatment, and we should hear from the government any day.'

"We did. I was up at his apartment, and we were talking about nothing in particular, when Mrs. O. rushed in with the letter, squeaking, 'Open eet! Open eet, Román!'

"He opened it without hurry, spread the sheet of paper out, and read it. Then he frowned and read it again. Then he laid it down, very carefully took out and lit the wrong end of a cork-tipped cigarette, and said in his levellest voice, 'I have been esstupid again, Pat. I never thought that there might be a time leemit on that reward offer. Now it seems that some crafty *sanamagoon* in Congress poot one een, so that the offer expired on May first. You remember, I mailed the claim on the nineteenth, and they got it on the twenty-first. Three weeks too late!'

"I looked at Oliveira, and he looked at me and then at his wife. And she looked at him and then went without a word to the cabinet and got out two large bottles of *tequila* and three tumblers.

"Oliveira pulled up three chairs around a little table, and

settled with a sigh in one of them. 'Pat,' he said, 'I may not have a meelion dollars, but I have something more valuable by far—a wooman who knows what is needed at a time like thees!'

"And that's the inside story of the Great Change—or at least of one aspect thereof. That's how it happens that, when we today speak of a platinum-blonde movie star, we aren't referring to her scalp hair alone, but the beautiful silvery pelt that covers her from crown to ankle.

"There was just one more incident. Bert Kafket had me up to his place to dinner a few nights later. After I had told him and his wife about Oliveira's and my troubles, he asked how I had made out on that depilatory-manufacturer stock I'd bought.

"'I notice those stocks are back about where they started from before the Change,' he added.

"'Didn't make anything to speak of,' I told him. 'About the time they started to slide down from their peak, I was too busy working for Román to pay much attention to them. When I finally did look them up I was just able to unload with a few cents profit per share. How did you do on those stocks you were so mysterious about last year?'

"'Maybe you noticed my new car as you came in?' asked Bert with a grin. 'That's them. Or rather, it; there was only one—Jones and Galloway Company.'

"'What do Jones and Galloway make? I never heard of them.'

"'They make'—here Bert's grin looked as if it were going to run around his head and meet behind—'currycombs!'

"And that was that. Here's Carl with the beer now. It's your deal, isn't it, Hannibal?"

The Alchemists Gather

By 1938 the influences that would create the golden age of science fiction were beginning to come together in the magazines. John Campbell had been editor of *Astounding* since September, and his selections were beginning to be published. A growing body of sophisticated readers was reaching critical mass, and emitting particles in the form of new writers. Basic discoveries and inventions were achieving a level of technological change that promised a future markedly different from the present.

Change was everywhere. The gradual recovery of the world from the long Depression brought a renewed feeling of optimism. Progress was the theme of the most popular exhibits building at the New York World's Fair. Even the continuing war in China and the gathering military might and the insatiable territorial demands of Nazi Germany that were beginning to foreshadow World War II contributed a paradoxical sense of excitement about the future.

Campbell had begun to make his presence felt not only by his story selections and his editorials but by letters to writers he knew or the ones whose stories he discovered among the unsolicited submissions, or by conversations with those in New York. It was the beginning of a personalized editorship that, in symbiotic relationship with writers, would create a new kind of science fiction.

Readers had been tutored by the magazines for more than a decade. They had developed tastes in science fiction, and their published letters were beginning to express their preferences. Some of the readers, out of personal ambition or frustration at their inability to find the kind of stories they wanted to read, began to submit stories based upon a generation of reading and fan criticism.

In his personal history of science fiction, *The Universe Makers*, Donald Wollheim wrote, "Science fiction builds upon science fiction." The new writers who began writing for

Campbell, he wrote, "were actually the first generation of writers who had grown up on science fiction, had been grounded and, as it were, schooled in science fiction and hence were able to utilize this in advancing further."

The '30s were not an outstanding period for scientific discoveries, but the ways in which science and technology had revolutionized human life over the previous half-century were beginning to be recognized. People were observing how the evolution in automobiles, radio, and flight were changing society and promising continuing change. The invention of nylon and synthetic rubber in 1935 suggested that anything could be created artificially, including human life. Planned (or accidental) genetic changes in vegetables, animals, and even humanity seemed only to wait on the time and the desire. Research into the atom made atomic energy and atomic bombs seem imminent. That and the new weapons of war, including bacteriological possibilities, threatened that the next major war might be Armageddon.

All of these elements were part of a story that appeared in the April 1938 issue of *Astounding*. It was entitled "The Faithful," and it was the first story of a writer who had developed out of the readership of the magazine, Lester del Rey (1915–).

Del Rey was the second child of his father's third marriage. His mother died shortly after his birth; his father, fifty-five at the time, married again, and two more children were born of that marriage. Del Rey grew up in southeastern Minnesota on a series of poor farms where, he recollected, his family acted "like northern sharecroppers." He was put to work at an early age but remembers his childhood as a happy period, particularly the discovery of books in his father's library and later in a high school library when his family moved to a small town.

Beginning at the age of twelve, he held a series of summer jobs away from home. When he was fifteen he was married, and became a widower three months later when his wife had a fatal fall from a horse. With the help and encouragement of his high school librarian, he got a partial scholarship to George Washington University and an offer of housing from a half-uncle. After two years of college, however, he dropped out to take a series of low-paying jobs.

"The Faithful" was written as the result of a challenge from a girl friend to do better than an *Astounding* story he had criticized. It was accepted immediately, but his next few efforts were rejected. His commitment to writing, never deep, wavered.

To this day, in spite of more than forty years of selling fiction, with about forty books and several million words in print, he still considers that he is not as compulsive about writing as he should be. For thirteen years after making his first sale, he never thought of himself as a professional writer. "Putting words on paper," he wrote in *The Early Del Rey*, "was just a (sometimes) lucrative hobby to fall back on when I wasn't doing something else."

From 1938 to 1941, however, he sold a number of stories to *Astounding*, including the much-anthologized "Helen O'Loy," and several stories to *Unknown*. Finally, in 1942, he sold to *Astounding* a startlingly prescient and naturalistic novella about an accident in a nuclear plant, "Nerves." It was later expanded into a novel published in 1956. Still, it was not until 1950, after the publication of a collection of short stories entitled . . . *And Some Were Human*, after three years of working for the Scott Meredith Literary Agency, and after turning out a variety of stories for the detective, western, and even sports magazines, that he turned to full-time writing.

He has been a writer ever since, with occasional stints of editing. He has written all kinds of books, including nonfiction and juvenile. The first of a series of juvenile science-fiction novels for Winston, *Marooned on Mars*, won the 1951 Boy's Award of Teen-Age Fiction. Other well-known science fiction includes *The Eleventh Commandment*, *Police Your Planet* (under the pseudonym Erik Van Lhin), and a novella entitled "For I Am a Jealous People."

Upon the death of P. Schuyler Miller, he took over the reviewing of science fiction for *Analog*. In recent years Ballantine Books, a major force in science-fiction publishing since its founding in 1952, created the *Del Rey* line of science fiction managed by del Rey and his wife, Judy Lynn Benjamin del Rey, onetime managing editor for *Galaxy* and *If* and later successful science-fiction editor for Ballantine.

Del Rey's major characteristic has been an insistence on a professional approach to all aspects of writing, but "The Faithful," like much of his other work, betrays a quality of concern that goes beyond professionalism. His first story brought together several major themes: genetic manipulation, atomic energy and ultimate war, the extinction of man, increased longevity, and the continuance of man's heritage by other species.

The Faithful

by Lester del Rey

Today, in a green and lovely world, here in the mightiest of human cities, the last of the human race is dying. And we of Man's creation are left to mourn his passing, and to worship the memory of Man, who controlled all that he knew save only himself.

I am old, as my people go, yet my blood is still young and my life may go on for untold ages yet, if what this last of Men has told me is true. And that also is Man's work, even as we and the Ape-People are his work in the last analysis. We of the Dog-People are old, and have lived a long time with Man. And yet, but for Roger Stren, we might still be baying at the moon and scratching the fleas from our hides, or lying at the ruins of Man's empire in dull wonder at his passing.

There are earlier records of dogs who mouthed clumsily a few Man words, but Hungor was the pet of Roger Stren, and in the labored efforts at speech, he saw an ideal and a life work. The operation on Hungor's throat and mouth, which made Man-speech more nearly possible, was comparatively simple. The search for other "talking" dogs was harder.

But he found five besides Hungor, and with this small start he began. Selection and breeding, surgery and training, gland implantation and X-ray mutation were his methods, and he made steady progress. At first money was a problem, but his pets soon drew attention and commanded high prices.

When he died, the original six had become thousands, and he had watched over the raising of twenty generations of dogs. A generation of my kind then took only three years. He had seen his small backyard pen develop into a huge institution, with a hundred followers and students, and had found the world eager for his success. Above all, he had seen tail-wagging give place to limited speech in that short time.

The movement he had started continued. At the end of two thousand years, we had a place beside Man in his work that would have been inconceivable to Roger Stren himself. We had our schools, our houses, our work with Man, and a society of our own. Even our independence, when we wanted it. And our life-span was not fourteen, but fifty years or more.

Man, too, had traveled a long way. The stars were almost within his grasp. The barren moon had been his for centuries. Mars and Venus lay beckoning, and he had reached them twice, but not to return. That lay close at hand. Almost, Man had conquered the universe.

But he had not conquered himself. There had been many setbacks to his progress because he had to go out and kill others of his kind. And now, the memory of his past called again, and he went out in battle against himself. Cities crumbled to dust, the plains to the south became barren deserts again. Chicago lay covered in a green mist. That death killed slowly, so that Man fled from the city and died, leaving it an empty place. The mist hung there, clinging days, months, years—after Man had ceased to be.

I, too, went out to war, driving a plane built for my people, over the cities of the Rising Star Empire. The tiny atomic bombs fell from my ship on houses, on farms, on all that was Man's, who had made my race what it was. For my Men had told me I must fight.

Somehow, I was not killed. And after the last Great Drive, when half of Man was already dead, I gathered my people about me, and we followed to the North, where some of my Men had turned to find a sanctuary from the war. Of Man's work, three cities still stood—wrapped in the green mist, and useless. And Man huddled around little fires and hid himself in the forest, hunting his food in small clans. Yet hardly a year of the war had passed.

For a time, the Men and my people lived in peace, planning to rebuild what had been, once the war finally ceased. Then came the Plague. The anti-toxin which had been developed was ineffective as the Plague increased in its virulency. It spread over land and sea, gripped Man who had invented it, and killed him. It was like a strong dose of strychnine, leaving Man to die in violent cramps and and retchings.

For a brief time, Man united against it, but there was no

control. Remorselessly it spread, even into the little settlement they had founded in the north. And I watched in sorrow as my Men around me were seized with its agony. Then we of the Dog-People were left alone in a shattered world from whence Man had vanished. For weeks we labored at the little radio we could operate, but there was no answer; and we knew that Man was dead.

There was little we could do. We had to forage our food as of old, and cultivate our crops in such small way as our somewhat modified forepaws permitted. And the barren north country was not suited to us.

I gathered my scattered tribes about me, and we began the long trek south. We moved from season to season, stopping to plant our food in the spring, hunting in the fall. As our sleds grew old and broke down, we could not replace them, and our travel became even slower. Sometimes we came upon our kind in smaller packs. Most of them had gone back to savagery, and these we had to mold to us by force. But little by little, growing in size, we drew south. We sought Men; for fifty thousand years we of the Dog-People had lived with and for Man, and we knew no other life.

In the wilds of what had once been Washington State we came upon another group who had not fallen back to the law of tooth and fang. They had horses to work for them, even crude harnesses and machines which they could operate. There we stayed for some ten years, setting up a government and building ourselves a crude city. Where Man had his hands, we had to invent what could be used with our poor feet and our teeth. But we had found a sort of security, and had even acquired some of Man's books by which we could teach our young.

Then into our valley came a clan of our people, moving west, who told us they had heard that one of our tribes sought refuge and provender in a mighty city of great houses lying by a lake in the east. I could only guess that it was Chicago. Of the green mist they had not heard—only that life was possible there.

Around our fires that night we decided that if the city were habitable, there would be homes and machines designed for us. And it might be there were Men, and the chance to bring up our young in the heritage which was their birthright. For weeks we labored in preparing ourselves for the long march to Chicago. We loaded our supplies in our crude carts, hitched our animals to them, and began the eastward trip.

It was nearing winter when we camped outside the city, still mighty and imposing. In the sixty years of the desertion, nothing had perished that we could see; the fountains to the west were still playing, run by automatic engines.

We advanced upon the others in the dark, quietly. They were living in a great square, littered with filth, and we noted that they had not even fire left from civilization. It was a savage fight, while it lasted, with no quarter given nor asked. But they had sunk too far, in the lazy shelter of Man's city, and the clan was not as large as we had heard. By the time the sun rose there was not one of them but had been killed or imprisoned until we could train them in our ways. The ancient city was ours, the green mist gone after all those years.

Around us were abundant provisions, the food factories which I knew how to run, the machines that Man had made to fit our needs, the houses in which we could dwell, power drawn from the bursting core of the atom, which needed only the flick of a switch to start. Even without hands, we could live here in peace and security for ages. Perhaps here my dreams of adapting our feet to handle Man's tools and doing his work were possible, even if no Men were found.

We cleared the muck from the city and moved into Greater South Chicago, where our people had had their section of the city. I, and a few of the elders who had been taught by their fathers in the ways of Man, set up the old regime, and started the great water and light machines. We had returned to a life of certainty.

And four weeks later, one of my lieutenants brought Paul Kenyon before me. Man! Real and alive, after all this time! He smiled, and I motioned my eager people away.

"I saw your lights," he explained. "I thought at first some men had come back, but that is not to be; but civilization still has its followers, evidently, so I asked one of you to take me to the leaders. Greetings from all that is left of Man!"

"Greetings," I gasped. It was like seeing the return of the gods. My breath was choked; a great peace and fulfillment surged over me. "Greetings, and the blessings of your God. I had no hope of seeing Man again."

He shook his head. "I am the last. For fifty years I have been searching for Men—but there are none. Well, you have done well. I should like to live among you, work with you—when I can. I survived the Plague somehow, but it comes on me yet, more often now, and I can't move nor care for myself then. That is why I have come to you.

."Funny." He paused. "I seem to recognize you. Hungor Beowulf XIV? I am Paul Kenyon. Perhaps you remember me? No? Well, it was a long time, and you were young. Perhaps my smell has changed with the disease. But that white streak under the eye still shows, and I remember you."

I needed no more to complete my satisfaction at his homecoming.

Now one had come among us with hands, and he was of great help. But most of all, he was of the old Men, and gave point to our working. But often, as he had said, the old sickness came over him, and he lay in violent convulsions, from which he was weak for days. We learned to care for him, and help him when he needed it, even as we learned to fit our society to his presence. And at last, he came to me with a suggestion.

"Hungor," he said, "if you had one wish, what would it be?"

"The return of Man. The old order, where we could work together. You know as well as I how much we need Man."

He grinned crookedly. "Now, it seems, Man needs you more. But if that were denied, what next?"

"Hands," I said. "I dream of them at night and plan for them by day, but I will never see them."

"Maybe you will, Hungor. Haven't you ever wondered why you go on living, twice normal age, in the prime of your life? Have you never wondered how I have withstood the Plague which still runs in my blood, and how I still seem only in my thirties, though nearly seventy years have passed since a Man has been born?"

"Sometimes," I answered. "I have no time for wonder, now, and when I do—Man is the only answer I know."

"A good answer," he said. "Yes, Hungor, Man is the answer. That is why I remember you. Three years before the war, when you were just reaching maturity, you came into my laboratory. Do you remember now?"

"The experiment," I said. "That is why you remembered me?"

"Yes, the experiment. I altered your glands somewhat, implanted certain tissues into your body, as I had done to myself. I was seeking the secret of immortality. Though there was no reaction at the time, it worked, and I don't know how much longer we may live—or you may; it helped me resist the Plague, but did not overcome it."

So that was the answer. He stood staring at me a long

time. "Yes, unknowingly, I saved you to carry on Man's future for him. But we were talking of hands.

"As you know, there is a great continent to the east of the Americas, called Africa. But did you know Man was working there on the great apes, as he was working here on your people? We never made as much progress with them as with you. We started too late. Yet they spoke a simple language and served for common work. And we changed their hands so the thumb and fingers opposed, as do mine. There, Hungor, are your hands."

Now Paul Kenyon and I laid plans carefully. Out in the hangars of the city there were aircraft designed for my people's use; heretofore, I had seen no need of using them. The planes were in good condition, we found on examination, and my early training came back to me as I took the first ship up. They carried fuel to circle the globe ten times, and out in the lake the big fuel tanks could be drawn on when needed.

Together, though he did most of the mechanical work between spells of sickness, we stripped the planes of all their war equipment. Of the six hundred planes, only two were useless, and the rest would serve to carry some two thousand passengers in addition to the pilots. If the apes had reverted to complete savagery, we were equipped with tanks of anesthetic gas by which we could overcome them and strap them in the planes for the return. In the houses around us, we built accommodations for them strong enough to hold them by force, but designed for their comfort if they were peaceable.

At first, I had planned to lead the expedition. But Paul Kenyon pointed out that they would be less likely to respond to us than to him. "After all," he said, "Men educated them and cared for them, and they probably remember us dimly. But your people they know only as the wild dogs who are their enemies. I can go out and contact their leaders, guarded, of course, by your people. But otherwise, it might mean battle."

Each day I took up a few of our younger ones in the planes and taught them to handle the controls. As they were taught, they began the instruction of others. It was a task which took months to finish, but my people knew the need of hands as well as I; any faint hope was well worth trying.

It was late spring when the expedition set out. I could follow their progress by means of television, but could work the controls only with difficulty. Kenyon, of course, was working the controls at the other end, when he was able.

They met with a storm over the Atlantic Ocean, and three of the ships went down. But under the direction of my lieutenant and Kenyon, the rest weathered the storm. They landed near the ruins of Capetown, but found no trace of the Ape-People. Then began weeks of scouting over the jungles and plains. They saw apes, but on capturing a few they found them only the primitive creatures which nature had developed.

It was by accident they finally met with success. Camp had been made for the night, and fires had been lit to guard against the savage beasts which roamed the land. Kenyon was in one of his rare moments of good health. The telecaster had been set up in a tent near the outskirts of the camp, and he was broadcasting a complete account of the day. Then, abruptly, over the head of the Man was raised a rough and shaggy face.

He must have seen the shadow, for he started to turn sharply, then caught himself and moved slowly around. Facing him was one of the apes. He stood there silently, watching the ape, not knowing whether it was savage or well disposed. It, too, hesitated; then it advanced.

"Man—Man," it mouthed. "You came back. Where were you? I am Tolemy, and I saw you, and I came."

"Tolemy," said Kenyon, smiling. "It is good to see you, Tolemy. Sit down; let us talk. I am glad to see you. Ah, Tolemy, you look old; were your father and mother raised by Man?"

"I am eighty years, I think. It is hard to know. I was raised by Man long ago. And now I am old; my people say I grow too old to lead. They do not want me to come to you, but I know Man. He was good to me. And he had coffee and cigarettes."

"I have coffee and cigarettes, Tolemy." Kenyon smiled. "Wait, I will get them. And your people, is not life hard among them in the jungle? Would you like to go back with me?"

"Yes, hard among us. I want to go back with you. Are you many?"

"No, Tolemy." He set the coffee and cigarettes before the ape, who drank eagerly and lit the smoke gingerly from a fire. "No, but I have friends with me. You must bring your people here, and let us get to be friends. Are there many of you?"

"Yes. Ten times we make ten tens—a thousand of us, almost. We are all that was left in the city of Man after the great fight. A Man freed us, and I led my people away, and we lived here in the jungle. They wanted to be in small tribes, but I made them one, and we are safe. Food is hard to find."

"We have much food in a big city, Tolemy, and friends who will help you, if you work for them. You remember the Dog-People, don't you? And you would work with them as with Man if they treated you as Man treated you, and fed you, and taught your people?"

"Dogs? I remember the Man-Dogs. They were good. But here the dogs are bad. I smelled dog here; it was not like the dog we smell each day, and my nose was not sure. I will work with Man-Dogs, but my people will be slow to learn them."

Later telecasts showed rapid progress. I saw the apes come in by twos and threes and meet Paul Kenyon, who gave them food, and introduced my people to them. This was slow, but as some began to lose their fear of us, others were easier to train. Only a few broke away and would not come.

Cigarettes that Man was fond of—but which my people never used—were a help, since they learned to smoke with great readiness.

It was months before they returned. When they came, there were over nine hundred of the Ape-People with them, and Paul and Tolemy had begun their education. Our first job was a careful medical examination of Tolemy, but it showed him in good health, and with much of the vigor of a younger ape. Man had been lengthening the ages of his kind, as it had ours, and he was evidently a complete success.

Now they have been among us three years, and during that time we have taught them to use their hands at our instructions. Overhead, the great monorail cars are running, and the factories have started to work again. They are quick to learn, with a curiosity that makes them eager for new knowledge. And they are thriving and multiplying here. We need no longer bewail the lack of hands; perhaps in time to come, with their help, we can change our forepaws further, and learn to walk on two legs, as did Man.

Today, I have come back from the bed of Paul Kenyon. We are often together now—perhaps I should include the faithful Tolemy—when he can talk, and among us there has grown a great friendship. I laid certain plans before him today for adapting the apes mentally and physically until they are Men. Nature did it with an apelike brute once; why can we not do it with the Ape-People now? The Earth would be peopled again, science would rediscover the stars, and Man would have a foster child in his own likeness.

And—we of the Dog-People have followed Man for fifty thousand years. That is too long to change. Of all Earth's creatures, the Dog-People alone have followed Man thus. My people cannot lead now. No dog was ever complete without the companionship of Man. The Ape-People will be Man.

It is a pleasant dream, surely not an impossible one.

Kenyon smiled as I spoke to him, and cautioned me in the jesting way he uses when most serious, not to make them too much like Man, lest another Plague destroy them. Well, we can guard against that. I think he, too, had a dream of Man reborn, for there was a hint of tears in his eyes, and he seemed pleased with me.

There is but little to please him now, alone among us, wracked by pain, waiting the slow death he knows must come. The old trouble has grown worse, and the Plague has settled harder on him.

All we can do is give him sedatives to ease the pain now, though Tolemy and I have isolated the Plague we found in his blood. It seems a form of cholera, and with that information, we have done some work. The old Plague serum offers a clue, too. Some of our serums have seemed to ease the spells a little, but they have not stopped them.

It is a faint chance. I have not told him of our work, for only a stroke of luck will give us success before he dies.

Man is dying. Here in our laboratory, Tolemy keeps repeating something; a prayer, I think it is. Well, maybe the God whom he has learned from Man will be merciful, and grant us success.

Paul Kenyon is all that is left of the old world which Tolemy and I loved. He lies in the ward, moaning in agony, and dying. Sometimes he looks from his windows and sees the birds flying south; he gazes at them as if he would never see them again. Well, will he? Something he muttered once comes back to me:

"For no man knoweth—"

The Fairy Tales of Science

Science fiction is not all intellectual speculation, not all extrapolation, not all scientific accuracy; in fact, much of science fiction has few of these qualities. But the science-fiction story has another dimension. Sam Moskowitz talks about "a sense of wonder." Jack Williamson describes "the myth of the future." Other critics mention theme.

All these efforts to define the indefinable may refer to the same phenomenon: science fiction deals with some basic human hopes and fears. "Fiction is simply dreams written out," John Campbell wrote in 1953, "and science fiction consists of the hopes and dreams and fears (for some dreams are nightmares) of a technically based society."

Some stories have elements that, like fairy tales, do not lend themselves to logical analysis. One may meet strange creatures in little-known places of the world, nymphs and dryads and mermaids, gnomes and fairies and goblins and trolls, creatures with supernatural powers who threaten the lives or souls or will of ordinary people.

Fairy tales also include people with greater abilities than those of ordinary mortals: witches and magicians, gods and demigods, and those whom the gods have blessed or cursed, who are driven to strange deeds, like heroes and vampires and werewolves. In some stories ordinary people receive unusual powers, wish-fulfillment abilities like seven-league boots, a cloak of invisibility, a crystal ball, the gift of prophecy or divination, the ability to see at a distance or read people's minds or control their actions. Sometimes people are challenged to prove their worth through impossible deeds, like killing dragons, feeling peas under stacks of mattresses, or spinning straw into gold.

The unarguable popularity of some science fiction may not be obvious on the surface and must be located in this substrata of emotional response. Most of the work of A. E. van Vogt (1912–   ) was of this kind.

Born in Winnipeg, Canada, the son of a lawyer, van Vogt spent his childhood in a rural Saskatchewan community. He discovered fairy tales at the age of eight and was shamed away from them at twelve. His father lost a good job at the start of the Depression, and van Vogt did not attend college. He took a variety of jobs and then turned to writing.

The writing, however, was not science fiction, which he had discovered as a reader in 1926, but true confessions. For seven years he wrote confessions, love stories, trade-magazine articles, and radio plays. When he turned to science fiction in 1939, he had acquired some basic writing skills and theories.

His first science-fiction story, "Vault of the Beast," was returned by Campbell for rewriting (it was published in *Astounding* the next year). His second story, "Black Destroyer," was an immediate reader favorite, even though it appeared in the July 1939 issue of *Astounding* with Isaac Asimov's first story, "Trends."

After three more stories in *Astounding* and one in *Unknown*, van Vogt saw his first novel, *Slan*, serialized in *Astounding*. It concerned a new breed of humans called "slans," with greater intelligence, strength, agility, and stamina than ordinary people, and an ability to read minds that was associated with tendrils growing from the scalp and concealed in the hair. Humans had attempted to exterminate the slans, and the story was told largely from the viewpoint of a slan boy, nine years old at the beginning of the novel, trying to escape detection and achieve his powers.

The novel made van Vogt famous in science fiction, and for the next half-dozen years he was at least as popular as Heinlein and some polls showed him ahead. In 1939 he had married another professional writer, E. Mayne Hull (1905–1975), who also wrote science fiction in the '40s. In 1944 they emigrated to Los Angeles.

There van Vogt discovered a variety of enthusiasms that first found their way into his fiction and then led him away from it. Oswald Spengler's theories of history had formed the philosophical structure for "Black Destroyer" and its sequels that were eventually published as *The Voyage of the Space Beagle* (1950). The Bates eye exercises (also embraced by Aldous Huxley) provided the background for *The Chronicler* (1946). *The World of Null-A* (1945) created a sensation when it was serialized in *Astounding* and almost singlehandedly popularized Alfred Korzybski's General Semantics.

When L. Ron Hubbard's "Dianetics" was announced, van

Vogt was one of the first to take it up. Dianetics advertised itself as a way to achieve a perfect mind in a perfect body. Van Vogt, with typical enthusiasm, became a teacher and promoter of dianetics, and for a time manager of a Los Angeles Dianetics Foundation branch. Only in the early '60s did van Vogt return to writing science fiction, among other kinds of books, but his early work remains his most popular.

Among his other science-fiction stories and novels are "The Weapon Shop" (1942), *The Weapon Makers* (1943), *The Weapon Shops of Isher* (1949), *The Mixed Men* (1952), *The Players of Null-A* (1948), *The War Against the Rull* (1959), and *The Wizard of Linn* (1950).

Van Vogt's writing was distinguished by a compelling narrative replete with startling concepts and twists of plot. James Blish called it "the intensively recomplicated plot," and sometimes used it himself. In an essay for *Of Worlds Beyond* entitled "Complication in the Science Fiction Story," van Vogt described his technique of writing in 800-word scenes and including new ideas as they occurred to him.

The result was often confusing and sometimes contradictory if the reader paused to analyze what had happened. A young Damon Knight performed a classic analysis on *The World of Null-A* and created for himself a reputation as a critic but failed to come to grips with van Vogt's basic appeal. Van Vogt's stories dealt not with logic or scientific possibilities so much as archetypes, wish fulfillments, fairy tales.

"Black Destroyer" is about the demonic creature with strange powers, like the cat with eyes as big as saucers. *Slan* deals not just with superman but with the hunted and persecuted man-god, the epic hero who must survive to maturity to win his estate. The protagonist of *The World of Null-A* is a changeling (van Vogt published an earlier novella entitled "The Changeling") who must discover his identity and master his logical abilities as well as his teleportive power, his seven-league boots.

Van Vogt had a vision of humanity beset with ignorance and terrible though often unknown perils, but possessing untapped, sometimes unsuspected powers, if man could only discover who he is and what his powers are and how to use them, much like the hero or heroine of almost every fairy tale.

Black Destroyer

by A. E. van Vogt

On and on Coeurl prowled! The black, moonless, almost starless night yielded reluctantly before a grim reddish dawn that crept up from his left. A vague, dull light it was, that gave no sense of approaching warmth, no comfort, nothing but a cold, diffuse lightness, slowly revealing a nightmare landscape.

Black, jagged rock and black, unliving plain took form around him, as a pale-red sun peered at last above the grotesque horizon. It was then Coeurl recognized suddenly that he was on familiar ground.

He stopped short. Tenseness flamed along his nerves. His muscles pressed with sudden, unrelenting strength against his bones. His great forelegs—twice as long as his hindlegs—twitched with a shuddering movement that arched every razor-sharp claw. The thick tentacles that sprouted from his shoulders ceased their weaving undulation, and grew taut with anxious alertness.

Utterly appalled, he twisted his great cat head from side to side, while the little hairlike tendrils that formed each ear vibrated frantically, testing every vagrant breeze, every throb in the ether.

But there was no response, no swift tingling along his intricate nervous system, not the faintest suggestion anywhere of the presence of the all-necessary id. Hopelessly, Coeurl crouched, an enormous catlike figure silhouetted against the dim reddish skyline, like a distorted etching of a black tiger resting on a black rock in a shadow world.

He had known this day would come. Through all the centuries of restless search, this day had loomed ever nearer, blacker, more frightening—this inevitable hour when he must return to the point where he began his systematic hunt in a world almost depleted of id-creatures.

The truth struck in waves like an endless, rhythmic ache at the seat of his ego. When he had started, there had been a few id-creatures in every hundred square miles, to be mercilessly rooted out. Only too well Coeurl knew in this ultimate hour that he had missed none. There were no id-creatures left to eat. In all the hundreds of thousands of square miles that he had made his own by right of ruthless conquest—until no neighboring coeurl dared to question his sovereignty—there was no id to feed the otherwise immortal engine that was his body.

Square foot by square foot he had gone over it. And now—he recognized the knoll of rock just ahead, and the black rock bridge that formed a queer, curling tunnel to his right. It was in that tunnel he had lain for days, waiting for the simple-minded, snakelike id-creature to come forth from its hole in the rock to bask in the sun—his first kill after he had realized the absolute necessity of organized extermination.

He licked his lips in brief gloating memory of the moment his slavering jaws tore the victim into precious toothsome bits. But the dark fear of an idless universe swept the sweet remembrance from his consciousness, leaving only certainty of death.

He snarled audibly, a defiant, devilish sound that quavered on the air, echoed and re-echoed among the rocks, and shuddered back along his nerves—instinctive and hellish expression of his will to live.

And then—abruptly—it came.

He saw it emerge out of the distance on a long downward slant, a tiny glowing spot that grew enormously into a metal ball. The great shining globe hissed by above Coeurl, slowing visibly in quick deceleration. It sped over a black line of hills to the right, hovered almost motionless for a second, then sank down out of sight.

Coeurl exploded from his startled immobility. With tiger speed, he flowed down among the rocks. His round, black eyes burned with the horrible desire that was an agony within him. His ear tendrils vibrated a message of id in such tremendous quantities that his body felt sick with the pangs of his abnormal hunger.

The little red sun was a crimson ball in the purple-black heavens when he crept up from behind a mass of rock and gazed from its shadows at the crumbling, gigantic ruins of the city that sprawled below him. The silvery globe, in spite of its great size, looked strangely inconspicuous against that vast, fairylike reach of ruins. Yet about it was a leashed aliveness, a dynamic quiescence that, after a moment, made it stand out, dominating the foreground. A massive, rock-crushing thing of metal, it rested on a cradle made by its own weight in the harsh, resisting plain which began abruptly at the outskirts of the dead metropolis.

Coeurl gazed at the strange, two-legged creatures who stood in little groups near the brilliantly lighted opening that yawned at the base of the ship. His throat thickened with the immediacy of his need; and his brain grew dark with the first wild impulse to burst forth in furious charge and smash these flimsy, helpless-looking creatures whose bodies emitted the id-vibrations.

Mists of memory stopped that mad rush when it was still only electricity surging through his muscles. Memory that brought fear in an acid stream of weakness, pouring along his nerves, poisoning the reservoirs of his strength. He had time to see that the creatures wore things over their real bodies, shimmering transparent material that glittered in strange, burning flashes in the rays of the sun.

Other memories came suddenly. Of dim days when the city that spread below was the living, breathing heart of an age of glory that dissolved in a single century before flaming guns whose wielders knew only that for the survivors there would be an ever-narrowing supply of id.

It was the remembrance of those guns that held him there, cringing in a wave of terror that blurred his reason. He saw himself smashed by balls of metal and burned by searing flame.

Came cunning—understanding of the presence of these creatures. This, Coeurl reasoned for the first time, was a scientific expedition from another star. In the olden days, the coeurls had thought of space travel, but disaster came too swiftly for it ever to be more than a thought.

Scientists meant investigation, not destruction. Scientists in their way were fools. Bold with his knowledge, he emerged into the open. He saw the creatures become aware of him. They turned and stared. One, the smallest of the group, detached a shining metal rod from a sheath, and held it casually in one hand. Coeurl loped on, shaken to his core by the action; but it was too late to turn back.

Commander Hal Morton heard little Gregory Kent, the chemist, laugh with the embarrassed half gurgle with which he invariably announced inner uncertainty. He saw Kent fingering the spindly metalite weapon.

Kent said: "I'll take no chances with anything as big as that."

Commander Morton allowed his own deep chuckle to echo along the communicators. "That," he grunted finally, "is one of the reasons why you're on this expedition, Kent—because you never leave anything to chance."

His chuckle trailed off into silence. Instinctively, as he watched the monster approach them across the black rock plain, he moved forward until he stood a little in advance of the others, his huge form bulking the transparent metalite suit. The comments of the men pattered through the radio communicator into his ears:

"I'd hate to meet that baby on a dark night in an alley."

"Don't be silly. This is obviously an intelligent creature. Probably a member of the ruling race."

"It looks like nothing else than a big cat, if you forget those tentacles sticking out from its shoulders, and make allowances for those monster forelegs."

"Its physical development," said a voice, which Morton recognized as that of Siedel, the psychologist, "presupposes an animal-like adaptation to surroundings, not an intellectual one. On the other hand, its coming to us like this is not the act of an animal but of a creature possessing a mental awareness of our possible identity. You will notice that its movements are stiff, denoting caution, which suggests fear and consciousness of our weapons. I'd like to get a good look at the end of its tentacles. If they taper into handlike appendages that can really grip objects, then the conclusion would be inescapable that it is a descendant of the inhabitants of this city. It would be a great help if we could establish communication with it, even though appearances indicate that it has degenerated into a historyless primitive."

Coeurl stopped when he was still ten feet from the foremost creature. The sense of id was so overwhelming that his brain drifted to the ultimate verge of chaos. He felt as if his limbs were bathed in molten liquid; his very vision was not quite clear, as the sheer sensuality of his desire thundered through his being.

The men—all except the little one with the shining metal rod in his fingers—came closer. Coeurl saw that they were frankly and curiously examining him. Their lips were moving, and their voices beat in a monotonous, meaningless rhythm on his ear tendrils. At the same time he had the sense of waves of a much higher frequency—his own communication level—only it was a machinelike clicking that jarred his brain. With a distinct effort to appear friendly, he broadcast his name from his ear tendrils, at the same time pointing at himself with one curving tentacle.

Gourlay, chief of communications, drawled: "I got a sort of static in my radio when he wiggled those hairs, Morton. Do you think—"

"Looks very much like it," the leader answered the unfinished question. "That means a job for you, Gourlay. If it speaks by means of radio waves, it might not be altogether impossible that you can create some sort of television picture of its vibrations, or teach him the Morse code."

"Ah," said Siedel. "I was right. The tentacles each develop into seven strong fingers. Provided the nervous system is complicated enough, those fingers could, with training, operate any machine."

Morton said: "I think we'd better go in and have some lunch. Afterward, we've got to get busy. The material men can set up their machines and start gathering data on the planet's metal possibilities, and so on. The others can do a little careful exploring. I'd like some notes on architecture and on the scientific development of this race, and particularly what happened to wreck the civilization. On earth civilization after civilization crumbled, but always a new one sprang up in its dust. Why didn't that happen here? Any questions?"

"Yes. What about pussy? Look, he wants to come in with us."

Commander Morton frowned, an action that emphasized the deep-space pallor of his face. "I wish there was some way we could take it in with us, without forcibly capturing it. Kent, what do you think?"

"I think we should first decide whether it's an it or a him, and call it one or the other. I'm in favor of him. As for the taking him in with us—" The little chemist shook his head decisively. "Impossible. This atmosphere is twenty-eight per cent chlorine. Our oxygen would be pure dynamite to his lungs."

The commander chuckled. "He doesn't believe that, apparently." He watched the catlike monster follow the first two men through the great door. The men kept an anxious distance from him, then glanced at Morton questioningly. Morton waved his hand. "O. K. Open the second lock and let him get a whiff of the oxygen. That'll cure him."

A moment later, he cursed his amazement. "By Heaven, he doesn't even notice the difference! That means he hasn't any lungs, or else the chlorine is not what his lungs use. Let him in! You bet he can go in! Smith, here's a treasure house for a biologist—harmless enough if we're careful. We can always handle him. But what a metabolism!"

Smith, a tall, thin, bony chap with a long, mournful face, said in an oddly forceful voice: "In all our travels, we've found only two higher forms of life. Those dependent on chlorine, and those who need oxygen—the two elements that support combustion. I'm prepared to stake my reputation that no complicated organism could ever adapt itself to both gases in a natural way. At first thought I should say here is an extremely advanced form of life. This race long ago discovered truths of biology that we are just beginning to suspect. Morton, we mustn't let this creature get away if we can help it."

"If his anxiety to get inside is any criterion," Commander Morton laughed, "then our difficulty will be to get rid of him."

He moved into the lock with Coeurl and the two men. The automatic machinery hummed; and in a few minutes they were standing at the bottom of a series of elevators that led up to the living quarters.

"Does that go up?" One of the men flicked a thumb in the direction of the monster.

"Better send him up alone, if he'll go in."

Coeurl offered no objection, until he heard the door slam behind him; and the closed cage shot upward. He whirled with a savage snarl, his reason swirling into chaos. With one leap, he pounced at the door. The metal bent under his plunge, and the desperate pain maddened him. Now, he was all trapped animal. He smashed at the metal with his paws, bending it like so much tin. He tore great bars loose with his thick tentacles. The machinery screeched; there were horrible jerks as the limitless power pulled the cage along in spite of projecting pieces of metal that scraped the outside walls. And then the cage stopped, and he snatched off the rest of the door and hurtled into the corridor.

He waited there until Morton and the men came up with drawn weapons. "We're fools," Morton said. "We should have shown him how it works. He thought we'd double-crossed him."

He motioned to the monster, and saw the savage glow fade from the coal-black eyes as he opened and closed the door with elaborate gestures to show the operation.

Coeurl ended the lesson by trotting into the large room to his right. He lay down on the rugged floor, and fought down the electric tautness of his nerves and muscles. A very fury of rage against himself for his fright consumed him. It seemed to his burning brain that he had lost the advantage of appearing a mild and harmless creature. His strength must have startled and dismayed them.

It meant greater danger in the task which he now knew he must accomplish: To kill everything in the ship, and take the machine back to their world in search of unlimited id.

With unwinking eyes, Coeurl lay and watched the two men clearing away the loose rubble from the metal doorway of the huge old building. His whole body ached with the hunger of his cells for id. The craving tore through his palpitant muscles, and throbbed like a living thing in his brain. His every nerve quivered to be off after the men who had wandered into the city. One of them, he knew, had gone—alone.

The dragging minutes fled; and still he restrained himself, still he lay there watching, aware that the men knew he watched. They floated a metal machine from the ship to the rock mass that blocked the great half-open door, under the direction of a third man. No flicker of their fingers escaped his fierce stare, and slowly, as the simplicity of the machinery became apparent to him, contempt grew upon him.

He knew what to expect finally, when the flame flared in incandescent violence and ate ravenously at the hard rock beneath. But in spite of his preknowledge, he deliberately jumped and snarled as if in fear, at that white heat burst forth. His ear tendrils caught the laughter of the men, their curious pleasure at his simulated dismay.

The door was released, and Morton came over and went inside with the third man. The latter shook his head.

"It's a shambles. You can catch the drift of the stuff. Obviously, they used atomic energy, but . . . but it's in wheel form. That's a peculiar development. In our science, atomic energy brought in the nonwheel machine. It's possible that here they've progressed further to a new type of wheel mechanics. I hope their libraries are better preserved than this, or we'll never know. What could have happened to a civilization to make it vanish like this?"

A third voice broke through the communicators: "This is Siedel. I heard your question, Pennons. Psychologically and sociologically speaking, the only reason why a territory becomes uninhabited is lack of food."

"But they're so advanced scientifically, why didn't they develop space flying and go elsewhere for their food?"

"Ask Gunlie Lester," interjected Morton. "I heard him expounding some theory even before we landed."

The astronomer answered the first call. "I've still got to verify all my facts, but this desolate world is the only planet revolving around that miserable red sun. There's nothing else. No moon, not even a planetoid. And the nearest star system is *nine hundred light-years* away.

"So tremendous would have been the problem of the ruling race of this world, that in one jump they would not only have had to solve interplanetary but interstellar space traveling. When you consider how slow our own development was—first the moon, then Venus—each success leading to the next, and after centuries to the nearest stars; and last of all to the anti-accelerators that permitted galactic travel—considering all this, I maintain it would be impossible for any race to create such machines without practical experience. And, with the nearest star so far away, they had no incentive for the space adventuring that makes for experience."

Coeurl was trotting briskly over to another group. But now, in the driving appetite that consumed him, and in the frenzy of his high scorn, he paid no attention to what they were doing. Memories of past knowledge, jarred into activity by what he had seen, flowed into his consciousness in an ever developing and more vivid stream.

From group to group he sped, a nervous dynamo—jumpy, sick with his awful hunger. A little car rolled up, stopping in front of him, and a formidable camera whirred as it took a picture of him. Over on a mound of rock, a gigantic telescope was rearing up toward the sky. Nearby, a disintegrating machine drilled its searing fire into an ever-deepening hole, down and down, straight down.

Coeurl's mind became a blur of things he watched with half attention. And ever more imminent grew the moment when he knew he could no longer carry on the torture of acting. His brain strained with an irresistible impatience; his body burned with the fury of his eagerness to be off after the man who had gone alone into the city.

He could stand it no longer. A green foam misted his mouth, maddening him. He saw that, for the bare moment, nobody was looking.

Like a shot from a gun, he was off. He floated along in great, gliding leaps, a shadow among the shadows of the rocks. In a minute, the harsh terrain hid the spaceship and the two-legged beings.

Coeurl forgot the ship, forgot everything but his purpose, as if his brain had been wiped clear by a magic, memory-erasing brush. He circled widely, then raced into the city, along deserted streets, taking short cuts with the ease of familiarity, through gaping holes in time-weakened walls, through long corridors of moldering buildings. He slowed to a crouching lope as his ear tendrils caught the id vibrations.

Suddenly, he stopped and peered from a scatter of fallen rock. The man was standing at what must once have been a window, sending the glaring rays of his flashlight into the gloomy interior. The flashlight clicked off. The man, a heavy-set, powerful fellow, walked off with quick, alert steps. Coeurl didn't like that alertness. It presaged trouble; it meant lightning reaction to danger.

Coeurl waited till the human being had vanished around a corner, then he padded into the open. He was running now, tremendously faster than a man could walk, because his plan was clear in his brain. Like a wraith, he slipped down the next street, past a long block of buildings. He turned the first corner at top speed; and then, with dragging belly, crept into the half-darkness between the building and a huge chunk of débris. The street ahead was barred by a solid line of loose rubble that made it like a valley, ending in a narrow, bottle-like neck. The neck had its outlet just below Coeurl.

His ear tendrils caught the low-frequency waves whistling. The sound throbbed through his being; and suddenly terror caught with icy fingers at his brain. The man would have a gun. Suppose he leveled one burst of atomic energy— one burst—before his own muscles could whip out in murder fury.

A little shower of rocks streamed past. And then the man was beneath him. Coeurl reached out and struck a single crushing blow at the shimmering transparent headpiece of the spacesuit. There was a tearing sound of metal and a gushing of blood. The man doubled up as if part of him had been telescoped. For a moment, his bones and legs and muscles combined miraculously to keep him standing. Then he crumpled with a metallic clank of his space armor.

Fear completely evaporated, Coeurl leaped out of hiding. With ravenous speed, he smashed the metal and the body within it to bits. Great chunks of metal, torn piecemeal from the suit, sprayed the ground. Bones cracked. Flesh crunched.

It was simple to tune in on the vibrations of the id, and to create the violent chemical disorganization that freed it from the crushed bone. The id was, Coeurl discovered, mostly in the bone.

He felt revived, almost reborn. Here was more food than he had had in a whole past year.

Three minutes, and it was over, and Coeurl was off like a thing fleeing dire danger. Cautiously, he approached the glistening globe from the opposite side to that by which he had left. The men were all busy at their tasks. Gliding noiselessly, Coeurl slipped unnoticed up to a group of men.

Morton stared down at the horror of tattered flesh, metal and blood on the rock at his feet, and felt a tightening in his throat that prevented speech. He heard Kent say:

"He *would* go alone, damn him!" The little chemist's voice held a sob imprisoned; and Morton remembered that Kent and Jarvey had chummed together for years in the way only two men can.

"The worst part of it is," shuddered one of the men, "it looks like a senseless murder. His body is spread out like little lumps of flattened jelly, but it seems to be all there. I'd almost wager that if we weighed everything here, there'd still be one hundred and seventy-five pounds by earth gravity. That'd be about one hundred and seventy pounds here."

Smith broke in, his mournful face lined with gloom: "The killer attacked Jarvey, and then discovered his flesh was alien—uneatable. Just like our big cat. Wouldn't eat anything we set before him—" His words died out in sudden, queer silence. Then he said slowly: "Say, what about that creature? He's big enough and strong enough to have done this with his own little paws."

Morton frowned. "It's a thought. After all, he's the only living thing we've seen. We can't just execute him on suspicion, of course—"

"Besides," said one of the men, "he was never out of my sight."

Before Morton could speak, Siedel, the psychologist, snapped, "Positive about that?"

The man hesitated. "Maybe he was for a few minutes. He was wandering around so much, looking at everything."

"Exactly," said Siedel with satisfaction. He turned to Morton. "You see, commander, I, too, had the impression that he was always around; and yet, thinking back over it, I find gaps. There were moments—probably long minutes—when he was completely out of sight."

Morton's face was dark with thought, as Kent broke in fiercely: "I say, take no chances. Kill the brute on suspicion before he does any more damage."

Morton said slowly: "Korita, you've been wandering around with Cranessy and Van Horne. Do you think pussy is a descendant of the ruling class of this planet?"

The tall Japanese archeologist stared at the sky as if collecting his mind. "Commander Morton," he said finally, respectfully, "there is a mystery here. Take a look, all of you, at that majestic skyline. Notice the almost Gothic outline of the architecture. In spite of the megalopolis which they created, these people were close to the soil. The buildings are not simply ornamented. They are ornamental in themselves. Here is the equivalent of the Doric column, the Egyptian pyramid, the Gothic cathedral, growing out of the ground, earnest, big with destiny. If this lonely, desolate world can be regarded as a mother earth, then the land had a warm, a spiritual place in the hearts of the race.

"The effect is emphasized by the winding streets. Their machines prove they were mathematicians, but they were artists first; and so they did not create the geometrically designed cities of the ultrasophisticated world metropolis. There is a genuine artistic abandon, a deep joyous emotion written in the curving and unmathematical arrangements of houses, buildings and avenues; a sense of intensity, of divine belief in an inner certainty. This is not a decadent, hoary-with-age civilization, but a young and vigorous culture, confident, strong with purpose.

"There it ended. Abruptly, as if at this point culture had its Battle of Tours, and began to collapse like the ancient Mohammedan civilization. Or as if in one leap it spanned the centuries and entered the period of contending states. In the Chinese civilization that period occupied 480-230 B. C., at the end of which the State of Tsin saw the beginning of the Chinese Empire. This phase Egypt experienced between

1780-1580 B. C., of which the last century was the 'Hyksos'—unmentionable—time. The classical experienced it from Chaeronea—338—and, at the pitch of horror, from the Gracchi—133—to Actium—31 B. C. The West European Americans were devastated by it in the nineteenth and twentieth centuries, and modern historians agree that, nominally, we entered the same phase fifty years ago; though, of course, we have solved the problem.

"You may ask, commander, what has all this to do with your question? My answer is: there is no record of a culture entering abruptly into the period of contending states. It is always a slow development; and the first step is a merciless questioning of all that was once held sacred. Inner certainties cease to exist, are dissolved before the ruthless probings of scientific and analytic minds. The skeptic becomes the highest type of being.

"I say that this culture ended abruptly in its most flourishing age. The sociological effects of such a catastrophe would be a sudden vanishing of morals, a reversion to almost bestial criminality, unleavened by any sense of ideal, a callous indifference to death. If this . . . this pussy is a descendant of such a race, then he will be a cunning creature, a thief in the night, a cold-blooded murderer, who would cut his own brother's throat for gain."

"That's enough!" It was Kent's clipped voice. "Commander, I'm willing to act the role of executioner."

Smith interrupted sharply: "Listen, Morton, you're not going to kill that cat yet, even if he is guilty. He's a biological treasure house."

Kent and Smith were glaring angrily at each other. Morton frowned at them thoughtfully, then said: "Korita, I'm inclined to accept your theory as a working basis. But one question: Pussy comes from a period earlier than our own? That is, we are entering the highly civilized era of our culture, while he became suddenly historyless in the most vigorous period of his. *But* is it possible that his culture is a later one on this planet than ours is in the galactic-wide system we have civilized?"

"Exactly. His may be the middle of the tenth civilization of his world; while ours is the end of the eighth sprung from earth, each of the ten, of course, having been builded on the ruins of the one before it."

"In that case, pussy would not know anything about the

skepticism that made it possible for us to find him out so positively as a criminal and murderer?"

"No; it would be literally magic to him."

Morton was smiling grimly. "Then I think you'll get your wish, Smith. We'll let pussy live; and if there are any fatalities, now that we know him, it will be due to rank carelessness. There's just the chance, of course, that we're wrong. Like Siedel, I also have the impression that he was always around. But now—we can't leave poor Jarvey here like this. We'll put him in a coffin and bury him."

"No, we won't!" Kent barked. He flushed. "I beg your pardon, commander. I didn't mean it that way. I maintain pussy wanted something from that body. It looks to be all there, but something must be missing. I'm going to find out what, and pin this murder on him so that you'll have to believe it beyond the shadow of a doubt."

It was late night when Morton looked up from a book and saw Kent emerge through the door that led from the laboratories below.

Kent carried a large, flat bowl in his hands; his tired eyes flashed across at Morton, and he said in a weary, yet harsh, voice: "Now watch!"

He started toward Coeurl, who lay sprawled on the great rug, pretending to be asleep.

Morton stopped him. "Wait a minute, Kent. Any other time, I wouldn't question your actions, but you look ill; you're overwrought. What have you got there?"

Kent turned, and Morton saw that his first impression had been but a flashing glimpse of the truth. There were dark pouches under the little chemist's gray eyes—eyes that gazed feverishly from sunken cheeks in an ascetic face.

"I've found the missing element," Kent said. "It's phosphorus. There wasn't so much as a square millimeter of phosphorus left in Jarvey's bones. Every bit of it had been drained out—by what super-chemistry I don't know. There are ways of getting phosphorus out of the human body. For instance, a quick way was what happened to the workman who helped build this ship. Remember, he fell into fifteen tons of molten metalite—at least, so his relatives claimed— but the company wouldn't pay compensation until the metalite, on analysis, was found to contain a high percentage of phosphorus—"

"What about the bowl of food?" somebody interrupted.

Men were putting away magazines and books, looking up with interest.

"It's got organic phosphorus in it. He'll get the scent, or whatever it is that he uses instead of scent—"

"I think he gets the vibrations of things," Gourlay interjected lazily. "Sometimes, when he wiggles those tendrils, I get a distinct static on the radio. And then, again, there's no reaction, just as if he's moved higher or lower on the wave scale. He seems to control the vibrations at will."

Kent waited with obvious impatience until Gourlay's last word, then abruptly went on: "All right, then, when he gets the vibration of the phosphorus and reacts to it like an animal, then—well, we can decide what we've proved by his reaction. May I go ahead, Morton?"

"There are three things wrong with your plan," Morton said. "In the first place, you seem to assume that he is only animal; you seem to have forgotten he may not be hungry after Jarvey; you seem to think that he will not be suspicious. But set the bowl down. His reaction may tell us something."

Coeurl stared with unblinking black eyes as the man set the bowl before him. His ear tendrils instantly caught the id-vibrations from the contents of the bowl—and he gave it not even a second glance.

He recognized this two-legged being as the one who had held the weapon that morning. Danger! With a snarl, he floated to his feet. He caught the bowl with the fingerlike appendages at the end of one looping tentacle, and emptied its contents into the face of Kent, who shrank back with a yell.

Explosively, Coeurl flung the bowl aside and snapped a hawser-thick tentacle around the cursing man's waist. He didn't bother with the gun that hung from Kent's belt. It was only a vibration gun, he sensed—atomic powered, but not an atomic disintegrator. He tossed the kicking Kent onto the nearest couch—and realized with a hiss of dismay that he should have disarmed the man.

Not that the gun was dangerous—but, as the man furiously wiped the gruel from his face with one hand, he reached with the other for his weapon. Coeurl crouched back as the gun was raised slowly and a white beam of flame was discharged at his massive head.

His ear tendrils hummed as they canceled the efforts of the vibration gun. His round, black eyes narrowed as he caught the movement of men reaching for the metalite guns. Morton's voice lashed across the silence.

"Stop!"

Kent clicked off his weapon; and Coeurl crouched down, quivering with fury at this man who had forced him to reveal something of his power.

"Kent," said Morton coldly, "you're not the type to lose your head. You deliberately tried to kill pussy, knowing that the majority of us are in favor of keeping him alive. You know what our rule is: If anyone objects to my decisions, he must say so at the time. If the majority object, my decisions are overruled. In this case, no one but you objected, and, therefore, your action in taking the law into your own hands is most reprehensible, and automatically debars you from voting for a year."

Kent stared grimly at the circle of faces. "Korita was right when he said ours was a highly civilized age. It's decadent." Passion flamed harshly in his voice. "My God, isn't there a man here who can see the horror of the situation? Jarvey dead only a few hours, and this creature, whom we all know to be guilty, lying there unchained, planning his next murder; and the victim is right here in this room. What kind of men are we—fools, cynics, ghouls—or is it that our civilization is so steeped in reason that we can contemplate a murderer sympathetically?"

He fixed brooding eyes on Coeurl. "You were right, Morton, that's no animal. That's a devil from the deepest hell of this forgotten planet, whirling its solitary way around a dying sun."

"Don't go melodramatic on us," Morton said. "Your analysis is all wrong, so far as I am concerned. We're not ghouls or cynics; we're simply scientists, and pussy here is going to be studied. Now that we suspect him, we doubt his ability to trap any of us. One against a hundred hasn't a chance." He glanced around. "Do I speak for all of us?"

"Not for me, commander!" It was Smith who spoke, and, as Morton stared in amazement, he continued: "In the excitement and momentary confusion, no one seems to have noticed that when Kent fired his vibration gun, the beam hit this creature squarely on his cat head—and didn't hurt him."

Morton's amazed glance went from Smith to Coeurl, and back to Smith again. "Are you certain it hit him? As you say, it all happened so swiftly—when pussy wasn't hurt I simply assumed that Kent had missed him."

"He hit him in the face," Smith said positively. "A vibration gun, of course, can't even kill a man right away—but it can injure him. There's no sign of injury on pussy, though, not even a singed hair."

"Perhaps his skin is a good insulation against heat of any kind."

"Perhaps. But in view of our uncertainty, I think we should lock him up in the cage."

While Morton frowned darkly in thought, Kent spoke up. "Now you're talking sense, Smith."

Morton asked: "Then you would be satisfied, Kent, if we put him in the cage?"

Kent considered, finally: "Yes. If four inches of micro-steel can't hold him, we'd better give him the ship."

Coeurl followed the men as they went out into the corridor. He trotted docilely along as Morton unmistakably motioned him through a door he had not hitherto seen. He found himself in a square, solid metal room. The door clanged metallically behind him; he felt the flow of power as the electric lock clicked home.

His lips parted in a grimace of hate, as he realized the trap, but he gave no other outward reaction. It occurred to him that he had progressed a long way from the sunk-into-primitiveness creature who, a few hours before, had gone incoherent with fear in an elevator cage. Now, a thousand memories of his powers were reawakened in his brain; ten thousand cunnings were, after ages of disuse, once again part of his very being.

He sat quite still for a moment on the short, heavy haunches into which his body tapered, his ear tendrils examining his surroundings. Finally, he lay down, his eyes glowing with contemptuous fire. The fools! The poor fools!

It was about an hour later when he heard the man—Smith—fumbling overhead. Vibrations poured upon him, and for just an instant he was startled. He leaped to his feet in pure terror—and then realized that the vibrations were vibrations, not atomic explosions. Somebody was taking pictures of the inside of his body.

He crouched down again, but his ear tendrils vibrated, and he thought contemptuously: the silly fool would be surprised when he tried to develop those pictures.

After a while the man went away, and for a long time there were noises of men doing things far away. That, too, died away slowly.

Coeurl lay waiting, as he felt the silence creep over the ship. In the long ago, before the dawn of immortality, the coeurls, too, had slept at night; and the memory of it had been revived the day before when he saw some of the men dozing. At last, the vibration of two pairs of feet, pacing, pacing endlessly, was the only human-made frequency that throbbed on his ear tendrils.

Tensely, he listened to the two watchmen. The first one walked slowly past the cage door. Then about thirty feet behind him came the second. Coeurl sensed the alertness of these men; knew that he could never surprise either while they walked separately. It meant—he must be doubly careful!

Fifteen minutes, and they came again. The moment they were past, he switched his senses from their vibrations to a vastly higher range. The pulsating violence of the atomic engines stammered its soft story to his brain. The electric dynamos hummed their muffled song of pure power. He felt the whisper of that flow through the wires in the walls of his cage, and through the electric lock of his door. He forced his quivering body into straining immobility, his senses seeking, searching, to tune in on that sibilant tempest of energy. Suddenly, his ear tendrils vibrated in harmony—he caught the surging change into shrillness of that rippling force wave.

There was a sharp click of metal on metal. With a gentle touch of one tentacle, Coeurl pushed open the door, and glided out into the dully gleaming corridor. For just a moment he felt contempt, a glow of superiority, as he thought of the stupid creatures who dared to match their wit against a coeurl. And in that moment, he suddenly thought of other coeurls. A queer, exultant sense of race pounded through his being; the driving hate of centuries of ruthless competition yielded reluctantly before pride of kinship with the future rulers of all space.

Suddenly, he felt weighed down by his limitations, his need for other coeurls, his aloneness—one against a hundred, with the stake all eternity; the starry universe itself beckoned his rapacious, vaulting ambition. If he failed, there would never be a second chance—no time to revive long-rotted machinery, and attempt to solve the secret of space travel.

He padded along on tensed paws—through the salon—into the next corridor—and came to the first bedroom door. It stood half open. One swift flow of synchronized muscles, one swiftly lashing tentacle that caught the unresisting throat of the sleeping man, crushing it; and the lifeless head rolled crazily, the body twitched once.

Seven bedrooms; seven dead men. It was the seventh taste of murder that brought a sudden return of lust, a pure, unbounded desire to kill, return of a millennium-old habit of destroying everything containing the precious id.

As the twelfth man slipped convulsively into death, Coeurl emerged abruptly from the sensuous joy of the kill to the sound of footsteps.

They were not near—that was what brought wave after wave of fright swirling into the chaos that suddenly became his brain.

The watchmen were coming slowly along the corridor toward the door of the cage where he had been imprisoned. In a moment, the first man would see the open door—and sound the alarm.

Coeurl caught at the vanishing remnants of his reason. With frantic speed, careless now of accidental sounds, he raced—along the corridor with its bedroom doors—through the salon. He emerged into the next corridor, cringing in awful anticipation of the atomic flame he expected would stab into his face.

The two men were together, standing side by side. For one single instant, Coeurl could scarcely believe his tremendous good luck. Like a fool the second had come running when he saw the other stop before the open door. They looked up, paralyzed, before the nightmare of claws and tentacles, the ferocious cat head and hate-filled eyes.

The first man went for his gun, but the second, physically frozen before the doom he saw, uttered a shriek, a shrill cry of horror that floated along the corridors—and ended in a curious gurgle, as Coeurl flung the two corpses with one irresistible motion the full length of the corridor. He didn't want the dead bodies found near the cage. That was his one hope.

Shaking in every nerve and muscle, conscious of the terrible error he had made, unable to think coherently, he plunged into the cage. The door clicked softly shut behind him. Power flowed once more through the electric lock.

He crouched tensely, simulating sleep, as he heard the rush of many feet, caught the vibration of excited voices. He knew when somebody actuated the cage audioscope and looked in. A few moments now, and the other bodies would be discovered.

"Siedel gone!" Morton said numbly. "What are we going to

do without Siedel? And Breckenridge! And Coulter and—Horrible!"

He covered his face with his hands, but only for an instant. He looked up grimly, his heavy chin outthrust as he stared into the stern faces that surrounded him. "If anybody's got so much as a germ of an idea, bring it out."

"Space madness!"

"I've thought of that. But there hasn't been a case of a man going mad for fifty years. Dr. Eggert will test everybody, of course, and right now he's looking at the bodies with that possibility in mind."

As he finished, he saw the doctor coming through the door. Men crowded aside to make way for him.

"I heard you, commander," Dr. Eggert said, "and I think I can say right now that the space-madness theory is out. The throats of these men have been squeezed to a jelly. No human being could have exerted such enormous strength without using a machine."

Morton saw that the doctor's eyes kept looking down the corridor, and he shook his head and groaned:

"It's no use suspecting pussy, doctor. He's in his cage, pacing up and down. Obviously heard the racket and— Man alive! You can't suspect him. That cage was built to hold literally anything—four inches of micro-steel—and there's not a scratch on the door. Kent, even you won't say, 'Kill him on suspicion,' because there can't be any suspicion, unless there's a new science here, beyond anything we can imagine—"

"On the contrary," said Smith flatly, "we have all the evidence we need. I used the telefluor on him—you know the arrangement we have on top of the cage—and tried to take some pictures. They just blurred. Pussy jumped when the telefluor was turned on, as if he felt the vibrations.

"You all know what Gourlay said before? This beast can apparently receive and send vibrations of any lengths. The way he dominated the power of Kent's gun is final proof of his special ability to interfere with energy."

"What in the name of all the hells have we got here?" One of the men groaned. "Why, if he can control that power, and sent it out in any vibrations, there's nothing to stop him killing all of us."

"Which proves," snapped Morton, "that he isn't invincible, or he would have done it long ago."

Very deliberately, he walked over to the mechanism that controlled the prison cage.

"You're not going to open the door!" Kent gasped, reaching for his gun.

"No, but if I pull this switch, electricity will flow through the floor, and electrocute whatever's inside. We've never had to use this before, so you had probably forgotten about it."

He jerked the switch hard over. Blue fire flashed from the metal, and a bank of fuses above his head exploded with a single bang.

Morton frowned. "That's funny. Those fuses shouldn't have blown! Well, we can't even look in, now. That wrecked the audios, too."

Smith said: "If he could interfere with the electric lock, enough to open the door, then he probably probed every possible danger and was ready to interfere when you threw that switch."

"At least, it proves he's vulnerable to our energies!" Morton smiled grimly. "Because he rendered them harmless. The important thing is, we've got him behind four inches of the toughest of metal. At the worst we can open the door and ray him to death. But first, I think we'll try to use the telefluor power cable—"

A commotion from inside the cage interrupted his words. A heavy body crashed against a wall, followed by a dull thump.

"He knows what we were trying to do!" Smith grunted to Morton. "And I'll bet it's a very sick pussy in there. What a fool he was to go back into that cage and does he realize it!"

The tension was relaxing; men were smiling nervously, and there was even a ripple of humorless laughter at the picture Smith drew of the monster's discomfiture.

"What I'd like to know," said Pennons, the engineer, "is, why did the telefluor meter dial jump and waver at full power when pussy made that noise? It's right under my nose here, and the dial jumped like a house afire!"

There was silence both without and within the cage, then Morton said: "It may mean he's coming out. Back, everybody, and keep your guns ready. Pussy was a fool to think he could conquer a hundred men, but he's by far the most formidable creature in the galactic system. He may come out of that door, rather than die like a rat in a trap. And he's just tough enough to take some of us with him—if we're not careful."

The men backed slowly in a solid body; and somebody said: "That's funny. I thought I heard the elevator."

"Elevator!" Morton echoed. "Are you sure, man?"

"Just for a moment I was!" The man, a member of the crew, hesitated. "We were all shuffling our feet—"

"Take somebody with you, and go look. Bring whoever dared to run off back here—"

There was a jar, a horrible jerk, as the whole gigantic body of the ship careened under them. Morton was flung to the floor with a violence that stunned him. He fought back to consciousness, aware of the other men lying all around him. He shouted: "Who the devil started those engines!"

The agonizing acceleration continued; his feet dragged with awful exertion, as he fumbled with the nearest audioscope, and punched the engine-room number. The picture that flooded onto the screen brought a deep bellow to his lips:

"It's pussy! He's in the engine room—and we're heading straight out into space."

The screen went black even as he spoke, and he could see no more.

It was Morton who first staggered across the salon floor to the supply room where the spacesuits were kept. After fumbling almost blindly into his own suit, he cut the effects of the body-torturing acceleration, and brought suits to the semi-conscious men on the floor. In a few moments, other men were assisting him; and then it was only a matter of minutes before everybody was clad in metalite, with anti-acceleration motors running at half power.

It was Morton then who, after first looking into the cage, opened the door and stood, silent as the others crowded about him, to stare at the gaping hole in the rear wall. The hole was a frightful thing of jagged edges and horribly bent metal, and it opened upon another corridor.

"I'll swear," whispered Pennons, "that it's impossible. The ten-ton hammer in the machine shops couldn't more than dent four inches of micro with one blow—and we only heard one. It would take at least a minute for an atomic disintegrator to do the job. Morton, this is a super-being."

Morton saw that Smith was examining the break in the wall. The biologist looked up. "If only Breckinridge weren't dead! We need a metallurgist to explain this. Look!"

He touched the broken edge of the metal. A piece crumbled in his finger and slithered away in a fine shower of dust to the floor. Morton noticed for the first time that there was a little pile of metallic debris and dust.

"You've hit it." Morton nodded. "No miracle of strength here. The monster merely used his special powers to interfere with the electronic tensions holding the metal together. That would account, too, for the drain on the telefluor power cable that Pennons noticed. The thing used the power with his body as a transforming medium, smashed through the wall, ran down the corridor to the elevator shaft, and so down to the engine room."

"In the meantime, commander," Kent said quietly, "we are faced with a super-being in control of the ship, completely dominating the engine room and its almost unlimited power, and in possession of the best part of the machine shops."

Morton felt the silence, while the men pondered the chemist's words. Their anxiety was a tangible thing that lay heavily upon their faces; in every expression was the growing realization that here was the ultimate situation in their lives; their very existence was at stake and perhaps much more. Morton voiced the thought in everybody's mind:

"Suppose he wins. He's utterly ruthless, and he probably sees galactic power within his grasp."

"Kent is wrong," barked the chief navigator. "The thing doesn't dominate the engine room. We've still got the control room, and that gives us first control of all the machines. You fellows may not know the mechanical set-up we have; but, though he can eventually disconnect us, we can cut off all the switches in the engine room now. Commander, why didn't you just shut off the power instead of putting us into space-suits? At the very least you could have adjusted the ship to the acceleration."

"For two reasons," Morton answered. "Individually, we're safer within the force fields of our spacesuits. And we can't afford to give up our advantages in panicky moves."

"Advantages! What other advantages have we got?"

"We know things about him," Morton replied. "And right now, we're going to make a test. Pennons, detail five men to each of the four approaches to the engine room. Take atomic disintegrators to blast through the big doors. They're all shut, I noticed. He's locked himself in.

"Selenski, you go up to the control room and shut off everything except the drive engines. Gear them to the master switch, and shut them off all at once. One thing, though— leave the acceleration on full blast. No anti-acceleration must be applied to the ship. Understand?"

"Aye, sir!" The pilot saluted.

"And report to me through the communicators if any of the machines start to run again." He faced the men. "I'm going to lead the main approach. Kent, you take No. 2; Smith, No. 3, and Pennons, No. 4. We're going to find out right now if we're dealing with unlimited science, or a creature limited like the rest of us. I'll bet on the second possibility."

Morton had an empty sense of walking endlessly, as he moved, a giant of a man in his transparent space armor, along the glistening metal tube that was the main corridor of the engine-room floor. Reason told him the creature had already shown feet of clay, yet the feeling that here was an invincible being persisted.

He spoke into the communicator: "It's no use trying to sneak up on him. He can probably hear a pin drop. So just wheel up your units. He hasn't been in that engine room long enough to do anything.

"As I've said, this is largely a test attack. In the first place, we could never forgive ourselves if we didn't try to conquer him now, before he's had time to prepare against us. But, aside from the possibility that we can destroy him immediately, I have a theory.

"The idea goes something like this: Those doors are built to withstand accidental atomic explosions, and it will take fifteen minutes for the atomic disintegrators to smash them. During that period the monster will have no power. True, the drive will be on, but that's straight atomic explosion. My theory is, he can't touch stuff like that; and in a few minutes you'll see what I mean—I hope."

His voice was suddenly crisp: "Ready, Selenski?"

"Aye, ready."

"Then cut the master switch."

The corridor—the whole ship, Morton knew—was abruptly plunged into darkness. Morton clicked on the dazzling light of his spacesuit; the other men did the same, their faces pale and drawn.

"Blast!" Morton barked into his communicator.

The mobile units throbbed; and then pure atomic flame ravened out and poured upon the hard metal of the door. The first molten droplet rolled reluctantly, not down, but up the door. The second was more normal. It followed a shaky downward course. The third rolled sideways—for this was pure force, not subject to gravitation. Other drops followed until a dozen streams trickled sedately yet unevenly in every direction—streams of hellish, sparkling fire, bright as fairy gems, alive with the coruscating fury of atoms suddenly tortured, and running blindly, crazy with pain.

The minutes ate at time like a slow acid. At last Morton asked huskily:

"Selenski?"

"Nothing yet, commander."

Morton half whispered: "But he must be doing something. He can't be just waiting in there like a cornered rat. Selenski?"

"Nothing, commander."

Seven minutes, eight minutes, then twelve.

"Commander!" It was Selenski's voice, taut. "He's got the electric dynamo running."

Morton drew a deep breath, and heard one of his men say:

"That's funny. We can't get any deeper. Boss, take a look at this."

Morton looked. The little scintillating streams had frozen rigid. The ferocity of the disintegrators vented in vain against metal grown suddenly invulnerable.

Morton sighed. "Our test is over. Leave two men guarding every corridor. The others come up to the control room."

He seated himself a few minutes later before the massive control keyboard. "So far as I'm concerned the test was a success. We know that of all the machines in the engine room, the most important to the monster was the electric dynamo. He must have worked in a frenzy of terror while we were at the doors."

"Of course, it's easy to see what he did," Pennons said. "Once he had the power he increased the electronic tensions of the door to their ultimate."

"The main thing is this," Smith chimed in. "He works with vibrations only so far as his special powers are concerned, and the energy must come from outside himself. Atomic energy in its pure form, not being vibration, he can't handle any differently than we can."

Kent said glumly: "The main point in my opinion is that he stopped us cold. What's the good of knowing that his control over vibrations did it? If we can't break through those doors with our atomic disintegrators, we're finished."

Morton shook his head. "Not finished—but we'll have to do some planning. First, though, I'll start these engines. It'll be harder for him to get control of them when they're running."

He pulled the master switch back into place with a jerk. There was a hum, as scores of machines leaped into violent life in the engine room a hundred feet below. The noises sank to a steady vibration of throbbing power.

Three hours later, Morton paced up and down before the men gathered in the salon. His dark hair was uncombed; the space pallor of his strong face emphasized rather than detracted from the out-thrust aggressiveness of his jaw. When he spoke, his deep voice was crisp to the point of sharpness:

"To make sure that our plans are fully co-ordinated, I'm going to ask each expert in turn to outline his part in the overpowering of this creature. Pennons first!"

Pennons stood up briskly. He was not a big man, Morton thought, yet he looked big, perhaps because of his air of authority. This man knew engines, and the history of engines. Morton had heard him trace a machine through its evolution from a simple toy to the highly complicated modern instrument. He had studied machine development on a hundred planets; and there was literally nothing fundamental that he didn't know about mechanics. It was almost weird to hear Pennons, who could have spoken for a thousand hours and still only have touched upon his subject, say with absurd brevity:

"We've set up a relay in the control room to start and stop every engine rhythmically. The trip lever will work a hundred times a second, and the effect will be to create vibrations of every description. There is just a possibility that one or more of the machines will burst, on the principle of soldiers crossing a bridge in step—you've heard that old story, no doubt—but in my opinion there is no real danger of a break of that tough metal. The main purpose is simply to interfere with the interference of the creature, and smash through the doors."

"Gourlay next!" barked Morton.

Gourlay climbed lazily to his feet. He looked sleepy, as if he was somewhat bored by the whole proceedings, yet Morton knew he loved people to think him lazy, a good-for-nothing slouch, who spent his days in slumber and his nights catching forty winks. His title was chief communication engineer, but his knowledge extended to every vibration field; and he was probably, with the possible exception of Kent, the fastest thinker on the ship. His voice drawled out, and—Morton noted—the very deliberate assurance of it had a soothing effect on the men—anxious faces relaxed, bodies leaned back more restfully:

"Once inside," Gourlay said, "we've rigged up vibration screens of pure force that should stop nearly everything he's got on the ball. They work on the principle of reflection, so that everything he sends will be reflected back to him. In addition, we've got plenty of spare electric energy that we'll just feed him from mobile copper cups. There must be a limit to his capacity for handling power with those insulated nerves of his."

"Selenski!" called Morton.

The chief pilot was already standing, as if he had anticipated Morton's call. And that, Morton reflected, was the man. His nerves had that rocklike steadiness which is the first requirement of the master controller of a great ship's movements; yet that very steadiness seemed to rest on dynamite ready to explode at its owner's volition. He was not a man of great learning, but he "reacted" to stimuli so fast that he always seemed to be anticipating.

"The impression I've received of the plan is that it must be cumulative. Just when the creature thinks that he can't stand any more, another thing happens to add to his trouble and confusion. When the uproar's at its height, I'm supposed to cut in the anti-accelerators. The commander thinks with Gunlie Lester that these creatures will know nothing about anti-acceleration. It's a development, pure and simple, of the science of interstellar flight, and couldn't have been developed in any other way. We think when the creature feels the first effects of the anti-acceleration—you all remember the caved-in feeling you had the first month—it won't know what to think or do."

"Korita next."

"I can only offer you encouragement," said the archeologist, "on the basis of my theory that the monster has all the characteristics of a criminal of the early ages of any civilization, complicated by an apparent reversion to primitiveness. The suggestion has been made by Smith that his knowledge of science is puzzling, and could only mean that we are dealing with an actual inhabitant, not a descendant of the inhabitants of the dead city we visited. This would ascribe a virtual immortality to our enemy, a possibility which is borne out by his ability to breathe both oxygen and chlorine—or neither—but even that makes no difference. He comes from a certain age in his civilization; and he has sunk so low that his ideas are mostly memories of that age.

"In spite of all the powers of his body, he lost his head in the elevator the first morning, until he remembered. He placed himself in such a position that he was forced to reveal his special powers against vibrations. He bungled the mass murders a few hours ago. In fact, his whole record is one of the low cunning of the primitive, egotistical mind which has little or no conception of the vast organization with which it is confronted.

"He is like the ancient German soldier who felt superior to the elderly Roman scholar, yet the latter was part of a mighty civilization of which the Germans of that day stood in awe.

"You may suggest that the sack of Rome by the Germans in later years defeats my argument; however, modern historians agree that the 'sack' was an historical accident, and not history in the true sense of the word. The movement of the 'Sea-peoples' which set in against the Egyptian civilization from 1400 B. C. succeeded only as regards the Cretan island-realm—their mighty expeditions against the Libyan and Phoenician coasts, with the accompaniment of viking fleets, failed as those of the Huns failed against the Chinese Empire. Rome would have been abandoned in any event. Ancient, glorious Samarra was desolate by the tenth century; Pataliputra, Asoka's great capital, was an immense and completely uninhabited waste of houses when the Chinese traveler Hsinan-tang visited it about A. D. 635.

"We have, then, a primitive, and that primitive is now far out in space, completely outside of his natural habitat. I say, let's go in and win."

One of the men grumbled, as Korita finished: "You can talk about the sack of Rome being an accident, and about this fellow being a primitive, but the facts are facts. It looks to me as if Rome is about to fall again; and it won't be no primitive that did it, either. This guy's got plenty of what it takes."

Morton smiled grimly at the man, a member of the crew. "We'll see about that—right now!"

In the blazing brilliance of the gigantic machine shop, Coeurl slaved. The forty-foot, cigar-shaped spaceship was nearly finished. With a grunt of effort, he completed the laborious installation of the drive engines, and paused to survey his craft.

Its interior, visible through the one aperture in the outer wall, was pitifully small. There was literally room for nothing but the engines—and a narrow space for himself.

He plunged frantically back to work as he heard the approach of the men, and the sudden change in the tempest-like thunder of the engines—a rhythmical off-and-on hum, shriller in tone, sharper, more nerve-racking than the deep-throated, steady throb that had preceded it. Suddenly, there were the atomic disintegrators again at the massive outer doors.

He fought them off, but never wavered from his task. Every mighty muscle of his powerful body strained as he carried great loads of tools, machines and instruments, and dumped them into the bottom of his makeshift ship. There was no time to fit anything into place, no time for anything—no time—no time.

The thought pounded at his reason. He felt strangely weary for the first time in his long and vigorous existence. With a last, tortured heave, he jerked the gigantic sheet of metal into the gaping aperture of the ship—and stood there for a terrible minute, balancing it precariously.

He knew the doors were going down. Half a dozen disintegators concentrating on one point were irresistibly, though slowly, eating away the remaining inches. With a gasp, he released his mind from the doors and concentrated every ounce of his mind on the yard-thick outer wall, toward which the blunt nose of his ship was pointing.

His body cringed from the surging power that flowed from the electric dynamo through his ear tendrils into that resisting wall. The whole inside of him felt on fire, and he knew that he was dangerously close to carrying his ultimate load.

And still he stood there, shuddering with the awful pain, holding the unfastened metal plate with hard-clenched tentacles. His massive head pointed as in dread fascination at that bitterly hard wall.

He heard one of the engine-room doors crash inward. Men shouted; disintegrators rolled forward, their raging power unchecked. Coeurl heard the floor of the engine room hiss in protest, as those beams of atomic energy tore everything in their path to bits. The machines rolled closer; cautious footsteps sounded behind them. In a minute they would be at the flimsy doors separating the engine room from the machine shop.

Suddenly, Coeurl was satisfied. With a snarl of hate, a vindictive glow of feral eyes, he ducked into his little craft, and pulled the metal plate down into place as if it was a hatchway.

His ear tendrils hummed, as he softened the edges of the surrounding metal. In an instant, the plate was more than welded—it was part of his ship, a seamless, rivetless part of a whole that was solid opaque metal except for two transparent areas, one in the front, one in the rear.

His tentacle embraced the power drive with almost sensuous tenderness. There was a forward surge of his fragile machine, straight at the great outer wall of the machine shops. The nose of the forty-foot craft touched—and the wall dissolved in a glittering shower of dust.

Coeurl felt the barest retarding movement; and then he kicked the nose of the machine out into the cold of space, twisted it about, and headed back in the direction from which the big ship had been coming all these hours.

Men in space armor stood in the jagged hole that yawned in the lower reaches of the gigantic globe. The men and the great ship grew smaller. Then the men were gone; and there was only the ship with its blaze of a thousand blurring portholes. The ball shrank incredibly, too small now for individual portholes to be visible.

Almost straight ahead, Coeurl saw a tiny, dim, reddish ball—his own sun, he realized. He headed toward it at full speed. There were caves where he could hide and with other coeurls build secretly a spaceship in which they could reach other planets safely—now that he knew how.

His body ached from the agony of acceleration, yet he dared not let up for a single instant. He glanced back, half in terror. The globe was still there, a tiny dot of light in the immense blackness of space. Suddenly it twinkled and was gone.

For a brief moment, he had the empty, frightened impression that just before it disappeared, it moved. But he could see nothing. He could not escape the belief that they had shut off all their lights, and were sneaking up on him in the darkness. Worried and uncertain, he looked through the forward transparent plate.

A tremor of dismay shot through him. The dim red sun toward which he was heading was not growing larger. *It was becoming smaller* by the instant, and it grew visibly tinier during the next five minutes, became a pale-red dot in the sky—and vanished like the ship.

Fear came then, a blinding surge of it, that swept through

his being and left him chilled with the sense of the unknown. For minutes, he stared frantically into the space ahead, searching for some landmark. But only the remote stars glimmered there, unwinking points against a velvet background of unfathomable distance.

Wait! One of the points was growing larger. With every muscle and nerve tensed, Coeurl watched the point becoming a dot, a round ball of light—red light. Bigger, bigger, it grew. Suddenly, the red light shimmered and turned white—and there, before him, was the great globe of the spaceship, lights glaring from every porthole, the very ship which a few minutes before he had watched vanish behind him.

Something happened to Coeurl in that moment. His brain was spinning like a flywheel, faster, faster, more incoherently. Suddenly, the wheel flew apart into a million aching fragments. His eyes almost started from their sockets as, like a maddened animal, he raged in his small quarters.

His tentacles clutched at precious instruments and flung them insensately; his paws smashed in fury at the very walls of his ship. Finally, in a brief flash of sanity, he knew that he couldn't face the inevitable fire of atomic disintegrators.

It was a simple thing to create the violent disorganization that freed every drop of id from his vital organs.

They found him lying dead in a little pool of phosphorus.

"Poor pussy," said Morton. "I wonder what he thought when he saw us appear ahead of him, after his own sun disappeared. Knowing nothing of anti-accelerators, he couldn't know that we could stop short in space, whereas it would take him more than three hours to decelerate; and in the meantime he'd be drawing farther and farther away from where he wanted to go. He couldn't know that by stopping, we flashed past him at millions of miles a second. Of course, he didn't have a chance once he left our ship. The whole world must have seemed topsy-turvy."

"Never mind the sympathy," he heard Kent say behind him. "We've got a job—to kill every cat in that miserable world."

Korita murmured softly: "That should be simple. They are but primitives; and we have merely to sit down, and they will come to us, cunningly expecting to delude us."

Smith snapped: "You fellows make me sick! Pussy was the toughest nut we ever had to crack. He had everything he needed to defeat us—"

Morton smiled as Korita interrupted blandly: "Exactly, my

dear Smith, except that he reacted according to the biological impulses of his type. His defeat was already foreshadowed when we unerringly analyzed him as a criminal from a certain era of his civilization.

"It was history, honorable Mr. Smith, our knowledge of history that defeated him," said the Japanese archeologist, reverting to the ancient politeness of his race.

The Stars Appear

By 1939 the pieces that would make up the period called by many the golden age of science fiction had begun to come together. A substantial body of science-fiction writers, including de Camp, del Rey, Eric Frank Russell, Alfred Bester, and L. Ron Hubbard had accumulated. Older writers such as Murray Leinster, Jack Williamson, and Clifford Simak were finding new directions. Most important, Campbell's *Astounding* was attracting new writers who understood what Campbell was trying to do and who contributed so substantially with their own ideas and energies that they helped lead science fiction into the promised land.

Campbell provided direction, encouragement, even goading, but he needed writers who could strike off into uncharted areas of the imagination. He needed stars, and they appeared. They appeared in the fateful summer of 1939.

Theodore Sturgeon's first story, "Ether Breather," was published in the September issue of *Astounding*; Sturgeon, who would become a gifted stylist, would show what could be done with a poetic imagination and a feeling for language. Robert A. Heinlein's first story, "Life-Line," appeared in the August issue; Heinlein's contribution to the direction and philosophy of science fiction eventually would loom as large as Campbell's. Van Vogt's "Black Destroyer" was published in the July issue; in the same issue appeared the third published story of a twenty-year-old student at Columbia University.

The story was "Trends," and the author was Isaac Asimov (1920–   ). His first story, "Marooned Off Vesta," had been published in the March 1939 *Amazing*; his second, "The Weapon Too Dreadful to Use," in the May *Amazing*. But Asimov was a Campbell writer; he had gone to Campbell with his first story in his hand, and he had only appeared elsewhere because Campbell had rejected it and the ones that followed.

"In that hungry teenager . . . with a hopeless story,"

Campbell had seen writing ability, and perhaps determination and the capacity for hard work, skepticism about sentiment and romance, and ingenious speculations about phenomena and how people might react to future events. Unlike some writers, however, Asimov did not burst into print with his talents fully developed. Perhaps his youth was the reason; van Vogt was twenty-seven when his first science fiction story was published, and Heinlein was thirty-two.

Asimov's skills and writing career began to take shape with the publication of "Reason," in *Astounding* for April 1941. It was the second published story in his robot series (later published as *I, Robot*, 1950, and *The Rest of the Robots*, 1964), and the first in which his three laws of robotics were implicit, though they weren't codified until afterward. Most of the later stories emerged from a conflict between the laws; the early ones emphasized the traditional human fear of alien intelligence and the more rational fear of economic competition, but they disposed of the irrational fears of the forbidden and of the creation turning against its creator.

Campbell's pragmatic approach to the problems of the present and the future had produced its first disciple. Asimov's three laws relegated "Frankenstein's monster" to antiquity; from now on that notion would be found only in fantasy and the detestable monster movies, and the character of HAL in *2001: A Space Odyssey* would seem quaintly nostalgic. The Asimov approach was irreverent and iconoclastic. It came to fruition in "Nightfall."

Campbell gave Asimov the idea in the form of the Emerson quotation that appears as the story's epigraph. Campbell and Asimov challenged Emerson's poetic vision. They substituted for the poetry of faith the poetry of science. Verifiable truth, they believed, has its own harsh beauty; the reality of the stars may drive men mad, but they go mad in the glorious blaze of thirty thousand suns.

That moment in "Nightfall" is comparable to the enlightenment that bursts upon Hugh Hoyland in Heinlein's classic novella, "Universe," when Hoyland sits in the control room of the giant spaceship that he has been raised to believe is all that exists, and he realizes that metaphor is reality, that the ship is not the universe but a small part of it, and that the ship moves among the stars.

The epiphany science fiction achieves at moments like these, as the truth, reality, the whatness of things shines through, reflects the ends of science itself.

In May 1942, Asimov launched another series of stories with "Foundation." Eventually it would lead to the publication of three volumes of novelettes, novellas, and a novel that would be published as *The Foundation Trilogy* (1964). Meanwhile Asimov earned his Ph.D. in biochemistry and joined the faculty of the Boston University School of Medicine. His first novel, *Pebble in the Sky* (1950), led to many more, including most notably his two robot detective novels, *The Caves of Steel* (1953) and *The Naked Sun* (1956), *The Currents of Space* (1952), and *The End of Eternity* (1955), as well as a series of "Lucky Starr" juveniles under the name Paul French.

In 1958, pressed by a new dean to do more research, Asimov, now an associate professor, turned to full-time writing instead. Now, however, it was science writing such as his *Intelligent Man's Guide to Science* (1960) and his *Biographical Encyclopedia of Science and Technology* (1964). His other publications—at last count the total of his books was reaching toward 200—have included books on Shakespeare, Byron, and Milton, and a book on the Bible; he has written histories, joke books, satires, and many more science popularizations for juveniles and adults. He is a popular public speaker, a television personality, a contributor of articles to many and varied publications, and an authority on practically everything, and he has been called "a national wonder" and "a natural resource."

Not bad, he might say, for an immigrant from Russia (at the age of three) who grew up in a Brooklyn candy store.

In 1972 he returned to the writing of science fiction with *The Gods Themselves* to win a Nebula Award and a Hugo, and achieved similar success in 1977 with "The Bicentennial Man."

But it was in the '40s and '50s that this witty, inventive man achieved his greatest influence on the nature of science fiction and built the foundation for the success whose rewards he has been reaping ever since. As he wrote in 1967 for the *SFWA Bulletin*, "There's Nothing Like a Good Foundation."

The virtues that he learned from Campbell and the elegant reasoning that he brought to his writing helped direct science fiction into new logical patterns and drove back, for a time, the shades of gothic superstition. For the two decades that followed the publication of "Nightfall," through the work of writers such as Asimov, Campbell's pragmatism prevailed.

Nightfall

by Isaac Asimov

"If the stars should appear one night in a thousand years, how would men believe and adore, and preserve for many generations the remembrance of the city of God!"—Emerson

Aton 77, director of Saro University, thrust out a belligerent lower lip and glared at the young newspaperman in a hot fury.

Theremon 762 took that fury in his stride. In his earlier days, when his now widely syndicated column was only a mad idea in a cub reporter's mind, he had specialized in "impossible" interviews. It had cost him bruises, black eyes, and broken bones; but it had given him an ample supply of coolness and self-confidence.

So he lowered the outthrust hand that had been so pointedly ignored and calmly waited for the aged director to get over the worst. Astronomers were queer ducks, anyway, and if Aton's actions of the last two months meant anything, this same Aton was the queer-duckiest of the lot.

Aton 77 found his voice, and though it trembled with restrained emotion, the careful, somewhat pedantic, phraseology, for which the famous astronomer was noted, did not abandon him.

"Sir," he said, "you display an infernal gall in coming to me with that impudent proposition of yours."

The husky telephotographer of the Observatory, Beenay 25, thrust a tongue's tip across dry lips and interposed nervously, "Now, sir, after all——"

The director turned to him and lifted a white eyebrow. "Do not interfere, Beenay. I will credit you with good intentions in bringing this man here; but I will tolerate no insubordination now."

Theremon decided it was time to take a part. "Director Aton, if you'll let me finish what I started saying I think——"

"I don't believe, young man," retorted Aton, "that anything you could say now would count much as compared with your daily columns of these last two months. You have led a vast newspaper campaign against the efforts of myself and my colleagues to organize the world against the menace which it is now too late to avert. You have done your best with your highly personal attacks on me to make the staff of this Observatory objects of ridicule."

The director lifted the copy of the Saro City *Chronicle* on the table and shook it at Theremon furiously. "Even a person of your well-known impudence should have hesitated before coming to me with a request that he be allowed to cover to-day's events for his paper. Of all newsmen, you!"

Aton dashed the newspaper to the floor, strode to the window and clasped his arms behind his back.

"You may leave," he snapped over his shoulder. He stared moodily out at the skyline where Gamma, the brightest of the planet's six suns, was setting. It had already faded and yellowed into the horizon mists, and Aton knew he would never see it again as a sane man.

He whirled. "No, wait, come here!" He gestured peremptorily. "I'll give you your story."

The newsman had made no motion to leave, and now he approached the old man slowly. Aton gestured outward, "Of the six suns, only Beta is left in the sky. Do you see it?"

The question was rather unnecessary. Beta was almost at zenith; its ruddy light flooding the landscape to an unusual orange as the brilliant rays of setting Gamma died. Beta was at aphelion. It was small; smaller than Theremon had ever seen it before, and for the moment it was undisputed ruler of Lagash's sky.

Lagash's own sun, Alpha, the one about which it revolved, was at the antipodes; as were the two distant companion pairs. The red dwarf Beta—Alpha's immediate companion—was alone, grimly alone.

Aton's upturned face flushed redly in the sunlight. "In just under four hours," he said, "civilization, as we know it, comes to an end. It will do so because, as you see, Beta is the only sun in the sky." He smiled grimly. "Print that! There'll be no one to read it."

"But if it turns out that four hours pass—and another four—and nothing happens?" asked Theremon softly.

"Don't let that worry you. Enough will happen."

"Granted! And *still*—if nothing happens?"

For a second time, Beenay 25 spoke, "Sir, I think you ought to listen to him."

Theremon said, "Put it to a vote, Director Aton."

There was a stir among the remaining five members of the Observatory staff, who till now had maintained an attitude of wary neutrality.

"That," stated Aton flatly, "is not necessary." He drew out his pocket watch. "Since your good friend, Beenay, insists so urgently, I will give you five minutes. Talk away."

"Good! Now, just what difference would it make if you allowed me to take down an eyewitness account of what's to come? If your prediction comes true, my presence won't hurt; for in that case my column would never be written. On the other hand, if nothing comes of it, you will just have to expect ridicule or worse. It would be wise to leave that ridicule to friendly hands."

Aton snorted. "Do you mean yours when you speak of friendly hands?"

"Certainly!" Theremon sat down and crossed his legs. "My columns may have been a little rough at times, but I gave you people the benefit of the doubt every time. After all, this is not the century to preach 'the end of the world is at hand' to Lagash. You have to understand that people don't believe the 'Book of Revelations' any more, and it annoys them to have scientists turn about face and tell us the Cultists are right after all—"

"No such thing, young man," interrupted Aton. "While a great deal of our data has been supplied us by the Cult, our results contain none of the Cult's mysticism. Facts are facts, and the Cult's so-called 'mythology' *has* certain facts behind it. We've exposed them and ripped away their mystery. I assure you that the Cult hates us now worse than you do."

"I don't hate you. I'm just trying to tell you that the public is in an ugly humor. They're angry."

Aton twisted his mouth in derision. "Let them be angry."

"Yes, but what about tomorrow?"

"There'll be no tomorrow!"

"But if there is. Say that there is—just to see what happens. That anger might take shape into something serious. After all, you know, business has taken a nose dive these last two months. Investors don't really believe the world is coming to an end, but just the same they're being cagey with their money until it's all over. Johnny Public doesn't believe you, either, but the new spring furniture might as well wait a few months—just to make sure.

"You see the point. Just as soon as this is all over, the business interests will be after your hide. They'll say that if crackpots—begging your pardon—can upset the country's prosperity any time they want simply by making some cock-eyed prediction—it's up to the planet to prevent them. The sparks will fly, sir."

The director regarded the columnist sternly. "And just what were you proposing to do to help the situation?"

"Well," grinned Theremon, "I was proposing to take charge of the publicity. I can handle things so that only the ridiculous side will show. It would be hard to stand, I admit, because I'd have to make you all out to be a bunch of gibbering idiots, but if I can get people laughing at you, they might forget to be angry. In return for that, all my publisher asks is an exclusive story."

Beenay nodded and burst out, "Sir, the rest of us think he's right. These last two months we've considered everything but the million-to-one chance that there is an error somewhere in our theory or in our calculations. We ought to take care of that, too."

There was a murmur of agreement from the men grouped about the table, and Aton's expression became that of one who found his mouth full of something bitter and couldn't get rid of it.

"You may stay if you wish, then. You will kindly refrain, however, from hampering us in our duties in any way. You will also remember that I am in charge of all activities here, and in spite of your opinions as expressed in your columns, I will expect full co-operation and full respect—"

His hands were behind his back, and his wrinkled face thrust forward determinedly as he spoke. He might have continued indefinitely but for the intrusion of a new voice.

"Hello, hello, hello!" It came in a high tenor, and the plump cheeks of the newcomer expanded in a pleased smile. "What's this morgue-like atmosphere about here? No one's losing his nerve, I hope."

Aton started in consternation and said peevishly, "Now what the devil are you doing here, Sheerin? I thought you were going to stay behind in the Hideout."

Sheerin laughed and dropped his tubby figure into a chair. "Hideout be blowed! The place bored me. I wanted to be here, where things are getting hot. Don't you suppose I have my share of curiosity? I want to see these Stars the Cultists are forever speaking about." He rubbed his hands and added in a soberer tone, "It's freezing outside. The wind's enough to hang icicles on your nose. Beta doesn't seem to give any heat at all, at the distance it is."

The white-haired director ground his teeth in sudden exasperation, "Why do you go out of your way to do crazy things, Sheerin? What kind of good are you around here?"

"What kind of good am I around there?" Sheerin spread his palms in comical resignation. "A psychologist isn't worth his salt in the Hideout. They need men of action and strong, healthy women that can breed children. Me? I'm a hundred pounds too heavy for a man of action, and I wouldn't be a success at breeding children. So why bother them with an extra mouth to feed? I feel better over here."

Theremon spoke briskly, "Just what is the Hideout, sir?"

Sheerin seemed to see the columnist for the first time. He frowned and blew his ample cheeks out. "And just who in Lagash are you, redhead?"

Aton compressed his lips and then muttered sullenly, "That's Theremon 762, the newspaper fellow. I suppose you've heard of him."

The columnist offered his hand. "And, of course, you're Sheerin 501 of Saro University. I've heard of you." Then he repeated, "What is this Hideout, sir?"

"Well," said Sheerin, "we have managed to convince a few people of the validity of our prophecy of—er—doom, to be spectacular about it, and those few have taken proper measures. They consist mainly of the immediate members of the families of the Observatory staff, certain of the faculty of Saro University and a few outsiders. Altogether, they number about three hundred, but three quarters are women and children."

"I see! They're supposed to hide where the Darkness and the—er—Stars can't get at them, and then hold out when the rest of the world goes poof."

"If they can. It won't be easy. With all of mankind insane; with the great cities going up in flames—environment will not be conducive to survival. But they have food, water, shelter, and weapons—"

"They've got more," said Aton. "They've got all our records, except for what we will collect today. Those records will mean everything to the next cycle, and *that's* what must survive. The rest can go hang."

Theremon whistled a long, low whistle and sat brooding for several minutes. The men about the table had brought out a multichess board and started a six-member game. Moves were made rapidly and in silence. All eyes bent in furious concentration on the board. Theremon watched them intently and then rose and approached Aton, who sat apart in whispered conversation with Sheerin.

"Listen," he said, "let's go somewhere where we won't bother the rest of the fellows. I want to ask some questions."

The aged astronomer frowned sourly at him, but Sheerin chirped up, "Certainly. It will do me good to talk. It always does. Aton was telling me about your ideas concerning world reaction to a failure of the prediction—and I agree with you. I read your column pretty regularly, by the way, and as a general thing I like your views."

"Please, Sheerin," growled Aton.

"Eh? Oh, all right. We'll go into the nèxt room. It has softer chairs, anyway."

There *were* softer chairs in the next room. There were also thick red curtains on the windows and a maroon carpet on the floor. With the bricky light of Beta pouring in, the general effect was one of dried blood.

Theremon shuddered, "Say, I'd given ten credits for a decent dose of white light for just a second. I wish Gamma or Delta were in the sky."

"What are your questions?" asked Aton. "Please remember that our time is limited. In a little over an hour and a quarter we're going upstairs, and after that there will be no time to talk."

"Well, here it is." Theremon leaned back and folded his hands on his chest. "You people seem so all-fired serious about this that I'm beginning to believe you. Would you mind explaining what it's all about?"

Aton exploded, "Do you mean to sit there and tell me that you've been bombarding us with ridicule without even finding out what we've been trying to say?"

The columnist grinned sheepishly. "It's not that bad, sir. I've got the general idea. You say that there is going to be a world-wide Darkness in a few hours and that all mankind will go violently insane. What I want now is the science behind it."

"No, you don't. No, you don't," broke in Sheerin. "If you

ask Aton for that—supposing him to be in the mood to answer at all—he'll trot out pages of figures and volumes of graphs. You won't make head or tail of it. Now if you were to ask *me*, I could give you the layman's standpoint."

"All right; I ask you."

"Then first I'd like a drink." He rubbed his hands and looked at Aton.

"Water?" grunted Aton.

"Don't be silly!"

"Don't you be silly. No alcohol today. It would be too easy to get my men drunk. I can't afford to tempt them."

The psychologist grumbled wordlessly. He turned to Theremon, impaled him with his sharp eyes, and began.

"You realize, of course, that the history of civilization on Lagash displays a cyclic character—but I mean, *cyclic!*"

"I know," replied Theremon cautiously, "that that is the current archeological theory. Has it been accepted as a fact?"

"Just about. In this last century it's been generally agreed upon. This cyclic character is—or, rather, was—one of *the* great mysteries. We've located series of civilizations, nine of them definitely, and indications of others as well, all of which have reached heights comparable to our own, and all of which, without exception, were destroyed by fire at the very height of their culture.

"And no one could tell why. All centers of culture were thoroughly gutted by fire, with nothing left behind to give a hint as to the cause."

Theremon was following closely. "Wasn't there a Stone Age, too?"

"Probably, but as yet, practically nothing is known of it, except that men of that age were little more than rather intelligent apes. We can forget about that."

"I see. Go on!"

"There have been explanations of these recurrent catastrophes, all of a more or less fantastic nature. Some say that there are periodic rains of fire; some that Lagash passes through a sun every so often; some even wilder things. But there is one theory, quite different from all of these, that has been handed down over a period of centuries."

"I know. You mean this myth of the 'Stars' that the Cultists have in their 'Book of Revelations.'"

"Exactly," rejoined Sheerin with satisfaction. "The Cultists said that every two thousand and fifty years Lagash entered a huge cave, so that all the suns disappeared, and there came *total darkness all over the world!* And then, they say, things called Stars appeared, which robbed men of their souls and left them unreasoning brutes, so that they destroyed the civilization they themselves had built up. Of course, they mix all this up with a lot of religio-mystic notions, but that's the central idea."

There was a short pause in which Sheerin drew a long breath. "And now we come to the Theory of Universal Gravitation." He pronounced the phrase so that the capital letters sounded—and at that point Aton turned from the window, snorted loudly, and stalked out of the room.

The two stared after him, and Theremon said, "What's wrong?"

"Nothing in particular," replied Sheerin. "Two of the men were due several hours ago and haven't shown up yet. He's terrifically short-handed, of course, because all but the really essential men have gone to the Hideout."

"You don't think the two deserted, do you?"

"Who? Faro and Yimot? Of course not. Still, if they're not back within the hour, things would be a little sticky." He got to his feet suddenly, and his eyes twinkled. "Anyway, as long as Aton is gone—"

Tiptoeing to the nearest window, he squatted, and from the low window box beneath withdrew a bottle of red liquid that gurgled suggestively when he shook it.

"I *thought* Aton didn't know about this," he remarked as he trotted back to the table. "Here! We've only got one glass so, as the guest you can have it. I'll keep the bottle." And he filled the tiny cup with judicious care.

Theremon rose to protest, but Sheerin eyed him sternly. "Respect your elders, young man."

The newsman seated himself with a look of pain and anguish on his face. "Go ahead, then, you old villain."

The psychologist's Adam's apple wobbled as the bottle upended, and then, with a satisfied grunt and a smack of the lips, he began again.

"But what do you know about gravitation?"

"Nothing, except that it is a very recent development, not too well established, and that the math is so hard that only twelve men in Lagash are supposed to understand it."

"*Tcha!* Nonsense! Boloney! I can give you all the essential math in a sentence. The Law of Universal Gravitation states that there exists a cohesive force among all bodies of the universe, such that the amount of this force between any two given bodies is proportional to the product of their masses divided by the square of the distance between them."

"Is that all?"

"That's enough! It took four hundred years to develop it."

"Why that long? It sounded simple enough, the way you said it."

"Because great laws are not divined by flashes of inspiration, whatever you may think. It usually takes the combined work of a world full of scientists over a period of centuries. After Genovi 41 discovered that Lagash rotated about the sun Alpha, rather than vice versa—and that was four hundred years ago—astronomers have been working. The complex motions of the six suns were recorded and analyzed and unwoven. Theory after theory was advanced and checked and counterchecked and modified and abandoned and revived and converted to something else. It was a devil of a job."

Theremon nodded thoughtfully and held out his glass for more liquor. Sheerin grudgingly allowed a few ruby drops to leave the bottle.

"It was twenty years ago," he continued after remoistening his own throat, "that it was finally demonstrated that the Law of Universal Gravitation accounted exactly for the orbital motions of the six suns. It was a great triumph."

Sheerin stood up and walked to the window, still clutching his bottle. "And now we're getting to the point. In the last decade, the motions of Lagash about Alpha were computed according to gravity, and *it did not account for the orbit observed;* not even when all perturbations due to the other suns were included. Either the law was invalid, or there was another, as yet unknown, factor involved."

Theremon joined Sheerin at the window and gazed out past the wooded slopes to where the spires of Saro City gleamed bloodily on the horizon. The newsman felt the tension of uncertainty grow within him as he cast a short glance at Beta. It glowered redly at zenith, dwarfed and evil.

"Go ahead, sir," he said softly.

Sheerin replied, "Astronomers stumbled about for years, each proposed theory more untenable than the one before—until Aton had the inspiration of calling in the Cult. The head of the Cult, Sor 5, had access to certain data that simplified the problem considerably. Aton set to work on a new track.

"What if there were another nonluminous planetary body

such as Lagash? If there were, you know, it would shine only by reflected light, and if it were composed of bluish rock, as Lagash itself largely is, then in the redness of the sky, the eternal blaze of the suns would make it invisible—drown it out completely."

Theremon whistled, "What a screwy idea!"

"You think *that's* screwy? Listen to this: Suppose this body rotated about Lagash at such a distance and in such an orbit and had such a mass that its attraction would exactly count for the deviations of Lagash's orbit from theory—do you know what would happen?"

The columnist shook his head.

"Well, sometimes this body would get in the way of a sun." And Sheerin emptied what remained in the bottle at a draft.

"And it does, I suppose," said Theremon flatly.

"Yes! But only one sun lies in its plane of revolutions." He jerked a thumb at the shrunken sun above. "Beta! And it has been shown that the eclipse will occur only when the arrangement of the suns is such that Beta is alone in its hemisphere and at a maximum distance, at which time the moon is invariably at minimum distance. The eclipse that results, with the moon seven times the apparent diameter of Beta, covers all of Lagash and lasts well over half a day, so that no spot on the planet escapes the effect. *That eclipse comes once every two thousand and forty-nine years.*"

Theremon's face was drawn into an expressionless mask. "And that's my story?"

The psychologist nodded. "That's all of it. First the eclipse—which will start in three quarters of an hour—then universal Darkness, and, maybe, these mysterious Stars—then madness, and end of the cycle."

He brooded. "We had two months' leeway—we at the Observatory—and that wasn't enough time to persuade Lagash of the danger. Two centuries might not have been enough. But our records are at the Hideout, and today we photograph the eclipse. The next cycle will *start off* with the truth, and when the *next* eclipse comes, mankind will at last be ready for it. Come to think of it, that's part of your story, too."

A thin wind ruffled the curtains at the window as Theremon opened it and leaned out. It played coldly with his hair as he stared at the crimson sunlight on his hand. Then he turned in sudden rebellion.

"What is there in Darkness to drive *me* mad?"

Sheerin smiled to himself as he spun the empty liquor

bottle with abstracted motions of his hand. "Have you ever experienced Darkness, young man?"

The newsman leaned against the wall and considered. "No. Can't say I have. But I know what it is. Just—uh—" He made vague motions with his fingers, and then brightened. "Just no light. Like in caves."

"Have you ever been in a cave?"

"In a *cave!* Of course not!"

"I thought not. *I* tried last week—just to see—but I got out in a hurry. I went in until the mouth of the cave was just visible as a blur of light, with black everywhere else. I never thought a person my weight could run that fast."

Theremon's lip curled. "Well, if it comes to that, I guess I wouldn't have run, if I had been there."

The psychologist studied the young man with an annoyed frown.

"My, don't you talk big! I dare you to draw the curtain."

Theremon looked his surprise and said, "What for? If we had four or five suns out there we might want to cut the light down a bit for comfort, but now we haven't enough light as it is."

"That's the point. Just draw the curtain; then come here and sit down."

"All right." Theremon reached for the tasseled string and jerked. The red curtain slid across the wide window, the brass rings hissing their way along the crossbar, and a dusk-red shadow clamped down on the room.

Theremon's footsteps sounded hollowly in the silence as he made his way to the table, and then they stopped half-way. "I can't see you, sir," he whispered.

"Feel your way," ordered Sheerin in a strained voice.

"But I can't see you, sir." The newsman was breathing harshly. "I can't see anything."

"What did you expect?" came the grim reply. "Come here and sit down!"

The footsteps sounded again, waveringly, approaching slowly. There was the sound of someone fumbling with a chair. Theremon's voice came thinly, "Here I am. I feel ... *ulp* ... all right."

"You like it, do you?"

"N-no. It's pretty awful. The walls seem to be—" He paused. "They seem to be closing in on me. I keep wanting to push them away. But I'm not going *mad!* In fact, the feeling isn't as bad as it was."

"All right. Draw the curtain back again."

There were cautious footsteps through the dark, the rustle of Theremon's body against the curtain as he felt for the tassel, and then the triumphant *ro-o-osh* of the curtain slithering back. Red light flooded the room, and with a cry of joy Theremon looked up at the sun.

Sheerin wiped the moistness off his forehead with the back of a hand and said shakily, "And that was just a dark room."

"It can be stood," said Theremon lightly.

"Yes, a dark room can. But were you at the Jonglor Centennial Exposition two years ago?"

"No, it so happens I never got around to it. Six thousand miles was just a bit too much to travel, even for the exposition."

"Well, I was there. You remember hearing about the 'Tunnel of Mystery' that broke all records in the amusement area—for the first month or so, anyway?"

"Yes. Wasn't there some fuss about it?"

"Very little. It was hushed up. You see, that Tunnel of Mystery was just a mile-long tunnel—with no lights. You got into a little open car and jolted along through Darkness for fifteen minutes. It was very popular—while it lasted."

"Popular?"

"Certainly. There's a fascination in being frightened *when it's part of a game.* A baby is born with three instinctive fears: of loud noises, of falling, and of the absence of light. That's why it's considered so funny to jump at someone and shout 'Boo!' That's why it's such fun to ride a roller coaster. And that's why that Tunnel of Mystery started cleaning up. People came out of that Darkness shaking, breathless, half dead with fear, but they kept on paying to get in."

"Wait a while, I remember now. Some people came out dead, didn't they? There were rumors of that after it shut down."

The psychologist snorted. "Bah! Two or three died. That was nothing! They paid off the families of the dead ones and argued the Jonglor City Council into forgetting it. After all, they said, if people with weak hearts want to go through the tunnel, it was at their own risk—and besides, it wouldn't happen again. So they put a doctor in the front office and had every customer go through a physical examination before getting into the car. That actually *boosted* ticket sales."

"Well, then?"

"But, you see, there was something else. People sometimes came out in perfect order, except that they refused to go into buildings—any buildings; including palaces, mansions, apartment houses, tenements, cottages, huts, shacks, lean-tos, and tents."

Theremon looked shocked. "You mean they refused to come in out of the open. Where'd they sleep?"

"In the open."

"They should have *forced* them inside."

"Oh, they did, they did. Whereupon these people went into violent hysterics and did their best to bat their brains out against the nearest wall. Once you got them inside, you couldn't keep them there without a strait jacket and a shot of morphine."

"They must have been crazy."

"Which is exactly what they were. One person out of every ten who went into that tunnel came out that way. They called in the psychologists, and we did the only thing possible. We closed down the exhibit." He spread his hands.

"What was the matter with those people?" asked Theremon finally.

"Essentially the same thing that was the matter with you when you thought the walls of the room were crushing in on you in the dark. There is a psychological term for mankind's instinctive fear of the absence of light. We call it 'claustrophobia,' because the lack of light is always tied up with enclosed places, so that fear of one is fear of the other. You see?"

"And those people of the tunnel?"

"Those people of the tunnel consisted of those unfortunates whose mentality did not quite possess the resiliency to overcome the claustrophobia that overtook them in the Darkness. Fifteen minutes without light is a long time; you only had two or three minutes, and I believe you were fairly upset.

"The people of the tunnel had what is called a 'claustrophobic fixation.' Their latent fear of Darkness and inclosed places had crystallized and become active, and, as far as we can tell, permanent. *That's* what fifteen minutes in the dark will do."

There was a long silence, and Theremon's forehead wrinkled slowly into a frown. "I don't believe it's that bad."

"You mean you don't want to believe," snapped Sheerin. "You're afraid to believe. Look out the window!"

Theremon did so, and the psychologist continued without pausing, "Imagine Darkness—everywhere. No light, as far as you can see. The houses, the trees, the fields, the earth, the sky—*black!* And Stars thrown in, for all I know—whatever *they* are. Can you conceive it?"

"Yes, I can," declared Theremon truculently.

And Sheerin slammed his fist down upon the table in sudden passion. "You lie! You can't conceive that. Your brain wasn't built for the conception any more than it was built for the conception of infinity or of eternity. You can only talk about it. A fraction of the reality upsets you, and when the real thing comes, your brain is going to be presented with a phenomenon outside its limits of comprehension. You will go mad, completely and permanently! There is no question of it!"

He added sadly, "And another couple of millenniums of painful struggle comes to nothing. Tomorrow there won't be a city standing unharmed in all Lagash."

Theremon recovered part of his mental equilibrium. "That doesn't follow. I still don't see that I can go loony just because there isn't a Sun in the sky—but even if I did and everyone else did, how does that harm the cities? Are we going to blow them down?"

But Sheerin was angry, too. "If you were in Darkness what would you want more than anything else; what would it be that every instinct would call for? Light, damn you, *light!*"

"Well?"

"And how would you get light?"

"I don't know," said Theremon flatly.

"What's the *only* way to get light, short of the sun?"

"How should I know?"

They were standing face to face and nose to nose.

Sheerin said, "You burn something, mister. Ever see a forest fire? Ever go camping and cook a stew over a wood fire? Heat isn't the only thing burning wood gives off, you know. It gives off light, and people know that. And when it's dark they want light, and they're going to *get it*."

"So they burn wood?"

"So they burn whatever they can get. They've got to have light. They've got to burn something, and wood isn't handy—so they'll burn whatever is nearest. They'll have their light—and every center of habitation goes up in flames!"

Eyes held each other as though the whole matter were a personal affair of respective will powers, and then Theremon broke away wordlessly. His breathing was harsh and ragged, and he scarcely noted the sudden hubbub that came from the adjoining room behind the closed door.

Sheerin spoke, and it was with an effort that he made it sound matter-of-fact. "I think I heard Yimot's voice. He and Faro are probably back. Let's go in and see what kept them."

"Might as well!" muttered Theremon. He drew a long breath and seemed to shake himself. The tension was broken.

The room was in an uproar, with members of the staff clustering about two young men who were removing outer garments even as they parried the miscellany of questions being thrown at them.

Aton bustled through the crowd and faced the newcomers angrily. "Do you realize that it's less than half an hour before deadline? Where have you two been?"

Faro 24 seated himself and rubbed his hands. His cheeks were red with the outdoor chill. "Yimot and I have just finished carrying through a little crazy experiment of our own. We've been trying to see if we couldn't construct an arrangement by which we could simulate the appearance of Darkness and Stars so as to get an advance notion as to how it looked."

There was a confused murmur from the listeners, and a sudden look of interest entered Aton's eyes. "There wasn't anything said of this before. How did you go about it?"

"Well," said Faro, "the idea came to Yimot and myself long ago, and we've been working it out in our spare time. Yimot knew of a low one-story house down in the city with a domed roof—it had once been used as a museum, I think. Anyway, we bought it—"

"Where did you get the money?" interrupted Aton peremptorily.

"Our bank accounts," grunted Yimot 70. "It cost two thousand credits." Then, defensively, "Well, what of it? Tomorrow, two thousand credits will be two thousand pieces of paper. That's all."

"Sure," agreed Faro. "We bought the place and rigged it up with black velvet from top to bottom so as to get as perfect a Darkness as possible. Then we punched tiny holes in the ceiling and through the roof and covered them with little metal caps, all of which could be shoved aside simultaneously at the close of a switch. At least, we didn't do that part our-

selves; we got a carpenter and an electrician and some others—money didn't count. The point was that we could get the
light to shine through those holes in the roof, so that we
could get a starlike effect."

Not a breath was drawn during the pause that followed.
Anton said stiffly:

"You had no right to make a private—"

Faro seemed abashed. "I know, sir—but, frankly, Yimot
and I thought that the experiment was a little dangerous. If
the effect really worked, we half expected to go mad—from
what Sheerin says about all this, we thought that would be
rather likely. We wanted to take the risk ourselves. Of course,
if we found we could retain sanity, it occurred to us that we
might develop immunity to the real thing, and then expose the
rest of you to the same thing. But things didn't work out at
all—"

"Why, what happened?"

It was Yimot who answered. "We shut ourselves in and allowed our eyes to get accustomed to the dark. It's an extremely creepy feeling because the total Darkness makes you
feel as if the walls and ceiling are crushing in on you. But we
got over that and pulled the switch. The caps fell away and
the roof glittered all over with little dots of light—"

"Well?"

"Well—nothing. That was the whacky part of it. Nothing
happened. It was just a roof with holes in it, and that's just
what it looked like. We tried it over and over again—that's
what kept us so late—but there just isn't any effect at all."

There followed a shocked silence, and all eyes turned to
Sheerin, who sat motionless, mouth open.

Theremon was the first to speak. "You know what this
does to this whole theory you've built up, Sheerin, don't
you?" He was grinning with relief.

But Sheerin raised his hand. "Now wait a while. Just let
me think this through." And then he snapped his fingers, and
when he lifted his head there was neither surprise nor uncertainty in his eyes. "Of course—"

He never finished. From somewhere up above there sounded a sharp clang, and Beenay, starting to his feet, dashed up
the stairs with a "What the devil!"

The rest followed after.

Things happened quickly. Once up in the dome, Beenay
cast one horrified glance at the shattered photographic plates
and at the man bending over them; and then hurled himself

fiercely at the intruder, getting a death grip on his throat. There was a wild threshing, and as others of the staff joined in, the stranger was swallowed up and smothered under the weight of half a dozen angry men.

Aton came up last, breathing heavily. "Let him up!"

There was a reluctant unscrambling and the stranger, panting harshly, with his clothes torn and his forehead bruised, was hauled to his feet. He had a short yellow beard curled elaborately in the style affected by the Cultists.

Beenay shifted his hold to a collar grip and shook the man savagely. "All right, rat, what's the idea? These plates—"

"I wasn't after *them*," retorted the Cultist coldly. "That was an accident."

Beenay followed his glowering stare and snarled, "I see. You were after the cameras themselves. The accident with the plates was a stroke of luck for you, then. If you had touched Snapping Bertha or any of the others, you would have died by slow torture. As it is—" He drew his fist back.

Aton grabbed his sleeve. "Stop that! Let him go!"

The young technician wavered, and his arm dropped reluctantly. Aton pushed him aside and confronted the Cultist. "You're Latimer, aren't you?"

The Cultist bowed stiffly and indicated the symbol upon his hip. "I am Latimer 25, adjutant of the third class to his serenity, Sor 5."

"And"—Aton's white eyebrows lifted—"you were with his serenity when he visited me last week, weren't you?"

Latimer bowed a second time.

"Now, then, what do you want?"

"Nothing that you would give me of your own free will."

"Sor 5 sent you, I suppose—or is this your own idea?"

"I won't answer that question."

"Will there be any further visitors?"

"I won't answer that, either."

Aton glanced at his timepiece and scowled. "Now, man, what is it your master wants of me? I have fulfilled my end of the bargain."

Latimer smiled faintly, but said nothing.

"I asked him," continued Aton angrily, "for data only the Cult could supply, and it was given to me. For that, thank you. In return, I promised to prove the essential truth of the creed of the Cult."

"There was no need to prove that," came the proud retort. "It stands proven by the 'Book of Revelations.'"

"For the handful that constitute the Cult, yes. Don't pretend to mistake my meaning. I offered to present scientific backing for your beliefs. And I did!"

The Cultist's eyes narrowed bitterly. "Yes, you did—with a fox's subtlety, for your pretended explanation backed our beliefs, and at the same time removed all necessity for them. You made of the Darkness and of the Stars a natural phenomenon, and removed all its real significance. That was blasphemy."

"If so, the fault isn't mine. The facts exist. What can I do but state them?"

"Your 'facts' are a fraud and a delusion."

Aton stamped angrily. "How do *you* know?"

And the answer came with the certainty of absolute faith. "I *know!*"

The director purpled and Beenay whispered urgently. Aton waved him silent. "And what does Sor 5 want us to do? He still thinks, I suppose, that in trying to warn the world to take measures against the menace of madness, we are placing innumerable souls in jeopardy. We aren't succeeding, if that means anything to him."

"The attempt itself has done harm enough, and your vicious effort to gain information by means of your devilish instruments must be stopped. We obey the will of their Stars, and I only regret that my clumsiness prevented me from wrecking your infernal devices."

"It wouldn't have done you too much good," returned Aton. "All our data, except for the direct evidence we intend collecting right now, is already safely cached and well beyond possibility of harm." He smiled grimly. "But that does not affect your present status as an attempted burglar and criminal."

He turned to the men behind him. "Someone call the police at Saro City."

There was a cry of distaste from Sheerin. "Damn it, Aton, what's wrong with you? There's no time for that. Here"—he bustled his way forward—"let me handle this."

Aton stared down his nose at the psychologist. "This is not the time for your monkeyshines, Sheerin. Will you please let me handle this my own way? Right now you are a complete outsider here, and don't forget it."

Sheerin's mouth twisted eloquently. "Now why should we go to the impossible trouble of calling the police—with Beta's eclipse a matter of minutes from now—when this young man here is perfectly willing to pledge his word of honor to remain and cause no trouble whatsoever?"

The Cultist answered promptly, "I will do no such thing. You're free to do what you want, but it's only fair to warn you that just as soon as I get my chance I'm going to finish what I came out here to do. If it's my word of honor you're relying on, you'd better call the police."

Sheerin smiled in a friendly fashion. "You're a determined cuss, aren't you? Well, I'll explain something. Do you see that young man at the window? He's a strong, husky fellow, quite handy with his fists, and he's an outsider besides. Once the eclipse starts there will be nothing for him to do except keep an eye on you. Besides him, there will be myself—a little too stout for active fisticuffs, but still able to help."

"Well, what of it?" demanded Latimer frozenly.

"Listen and I'll tell you," was the reply. "Just as soon as the eclipse starts, we're going to take you, Theremon and I, and deposit you in a little closet with one door, to which is attached one giant lock and no windows. You will remain there for the duration."

"And afterward," breathed Latimer fiercely, "there'll be no one to let me out. I know as well as you do what the coming of the Stars means—I know it far better than you. With all your minds gone, you are not likely to free me. Suffocation or slow starvation, is it? About what I might have expected from a group of scientists. But I don't give my word. It's a matter of principle, and I won't discuss it further."

Aton seemed perturbed. His faded eyes were troubled. "Really, Sheerin, locking him—"

"Please!" Sheerin motioned him impatiently to silence. "I don't think for a moment things will go that far. Latimer has just tried a clever little bluff, but I'm not a psychologist just because I like the sound of the word." He grinned at the Cultist. "Come now, you don't really think I'm trying anything as crude as slow starvation. My dear Latimer, if I lock you in the closet, you are not going to see the Darkness, and you are not going to see the Stars. It does not take much of a knowledge of the fundamental creed of the Cult to realize that for you to be hidden from the Stars when they appear means the loss of your immortal soul. Now, I believe you to be an honorable man. I'll accept your word of honor to make no further effort to disrupt proceedings if you'll offer it."

A vein throbbed in Latimer's temple, and he seemed to

shrink within himself as he said thickly, "You have it!" And then he added with swift fury, "But it is my consolation that you will all be damned for your deeds of today." He turned on his heel and stalked to the high three-legged stool by the door.

Sheerin nodded to the columnist. "Take a seat next to him, Theremon—just as a formality. Hey, Theremon!"

But the newspaperman didn't move. He had gone pale to the lips. "Look at that!" The finger he pointed toward the sky shook, and his voice was dry and cracked.

There was one simultaneous gasp as every eye followed the pointing finger and, for one breathless moment, stared frozenly.

Beta was chipped on one side!

The tiny bit of encroaching blackness was perhaps the width of a fingernail, but to the staring watchers it magnified itself into the crack of doom.

Only for a moment they watched, and after that there was a shrieking confusion that was even shorter of duration and which gave way to an orderly scurry of activity—each man at his prescribed job. At the crucial moment there was no time for emotion. The men were merely scientists with work to do. Even Aton had melted away.

Sheerin said prosaically, "First contact must have been made fifteen minutes ago. A little early, but pretty good considering the uncertainties involved in the calculation." He looked about him and tiptoed to Theremon, who still remained staring out the window, and dragged him away gently.

"Aton is furious," he whispered, "so stay away. He missed first contact on account of this fuss with Latimer, and if you get in his way he'll have you thrown out the window."

Theremon nodded shortly and sat down. Sheerin stared in surprise at him.

"The devil, man," he exclaimed, "you're shaking."

"Eh?" Theremon licked dry lips and then tried to smile. "I don't feel very well, and that's a fact."

The psychologist's eyes hardened. "You're not losing your nerve?"

"No!" cried Theremon in a flash of indignation. "Give me a chance, will you? I haven't really believed this rigmarole—not way down beneath, anyway—till just this minute. Give me a chance to get used to the idea. *You've* been preparing yourself for two months or more."

"You're right, at that," replied Sheerin thoughtfully. "Listen! Have you got a family—parents, wife, children?"

Theremon shook his head. "You mean the Hideout, I suppose. No, you don't have to worry about that. I have a sister, but she's two thousand miles away. I don't even know her exact address."

"Well, then, what about yourself? You've got time to get there, and they're one short anyway, since I left. After all, you're not needed here, and you'd make a darned fine addition—".

Theremon looked at the other wearily. "You think I'm scared stiff, don't you? Well, get this, mister, I'm a newspaperman and I've been assigned to cover a story. I intend covering it."

There was a faint smile on the psychologist's face. "I see. Professional honor, is that it?"

"You might call it that. But, man, I'd give my right arm for another bottle of that sockeroo juice even half the size of the one *you* hogged. If ever a fellow needed a drink, I do."

He broke off. Sheerin was nudging him violently. "Do you hear that? Listen!"

Theremon followed the motion of the other's chin and stared at the Cultist, who oblivious to all about him, faced the window, a look of wild elation on his face, droning to himself the while in singsong fashion.

"What's he saying?" whispered the columnist.

"He's quoting 'Book of Revelations,' fifth chapter," replied Sheerin. Then, urgently, "Keep quiet and listen, I tell you."

The Cultist's voice had risen in a sudden increase of fervor:

"'And it came to pass that in those days the Sun, Beta, held lone vigil in the sky for ever longer periods as the revolutions passed; until such time as for full half a revolution, it alone, shrunken and cold, shone down upon Lagash.

"'And men did assemble in the public squares and in the highways, there to debate and to marvel at the sight, for a strange depression had seized them. Their minds were troubled and their speech confused, for the souls of men awaited the coming of the Stars.

"'And in the city of Trigon, at high noon, Vendret 2 came forth and said unto the men of Trigon, "Lo ye sinners! Though ye scorn the ways of righteousness, yet will the time of reckoning come. Even now the Cave approaches to swallow Lagash; yea, and all it contains."

" 'And even as he spoke the lip of the Cave of Darkness passed the edge of Beta so that to all Lagash it was hidden from sight. Loud were the cries of men as it vanished, and great the fear of soul that fell upon them.

" 'It came to pass that the Darkness of the Cave fell upon Lagash, and there was no light on all the surface of Lagash. Men were even as blinded, nor could one man see his neighbor, though he felt his breath upon his face.

" 'And in this blackness there appeared the Stars, in countless numbers, and to the strains of ineffable music of a beauty so wondrous that the very leaves of the trees turned to tongues that cried out in wonder.

" 'And in that moment the souls of men departed from them, and their abandoned bodies became even as beasts; yea, even as brutes of the wild; so that through the blackened streets of the cities of Lagash they prowled with wild cries.

" 'From the Stars there then reached down the Heavenly Flame, and where it touched, the cities of Lagash flamed to utter destruction, so that of man and of the works of man nought remained.

" 'Even then—' "

There was a subtle change in Latimer's tone. His eyes had not shifted, but somehow he had become aware of the absorbed attention of the other two. Easily, without pausing for breath, the timbre of his voice shifted and the syllables became more liquid.

Theremon, caught by surprise, stared. The words seemed on the border of familiarity. There was an elusive shift in the accent, a tiny change in the vowel stress; nothing more—yet Latimer had become thoroughly unintelligible.

Sheerin smiled slyly. "He shifted to some old-cycle tongue, probably their traditional second cycle. That was the language in which the 'Book of Revelations' had originally been written, you know."

"It doesn't matter; I've heard enough." Theremon shoved his chair back and brushed his hair back with hands that no longer shook. "I feel much better now."

"You do?" Sheerin seemed mildly surprised.

"I'll say I do. I had a bad case of jitters just a while back. Listening to you and your gravitation and seeing that eclipse start almost finished me. But this"—he jerked a contemptuous thumb at the yellow-bearded Cultist—"*this* is the sort of thing my nurse used to tell me. I've been laughing at that sort of thing all my life. I'm not going to let it scare me *now*."

He drew a deep breath and said with a hectic gaiety, "But if I expect to keep on the good side of myself, I'm going to turn my chair away from the window."

Sheerin said, "Yes, but you'd better talk lower. Aton just lifted his head out of that box he's got it stuck into and gave you a look that should have killed you."

Theremon made a mouth. "I forgot about the old fellow." With elaborate care he turned the chair from the window, cast one distasteful look over his shoulder and said, "It has occurred to me that there must be considerable immunity against this Star madness."

The psychologist did not answer immediately. Beta was past its zenith now, and the square of bloody sunlight that outlined the window upon the floor had lifted into Sheerin's lap. He stared at its dusky color thoughtfully and then bent and squinted into the sun itself.

The chip in its side had grown to a black encroachment that covered a third of Beta. He shuddered, and when he straightened once more his florid cheeks did not contain quite as much color as they had had previously.

With a smile that was almost apologetic, he reversed his chair also. "There are probably two million people in Saro City that are all trying to join the Cult at once in one gigantic revival." Then, ironically, "The Cult is in for an hour of unexampled prosperity. I trust they'll make the most of it. Now, what was it you said?"

"Just this. How do the Cultists manage to keep the 'Book of Revelations' going from cycle to cycle, and how on Lagash did it get written in the first place? There must have been some sort of immunity, for if everyone had gone mad, who would be left to write the book?"

Sheerin stared at his questioner ruefully. "Well, now, young man, there isn't any eyewitness answer to that, but we've got a few damned good notions as to what happened. You see, there are three kinds of people who might remain relatively unaffected. First, the very few who don't see the Stars at all; the blind, those who drink themselves into a stupor at the beginning of the eclipse and remain so to the end. We leave them out—because they aren't really witnesses.

"Then there are children below six, to whom the world as a whole is too new and strange for them to be too frightened at Stars and Darkness. They would be just another item in an already surprising world. You see that, don't you?"

The other nodded doubtfully. "I suppose so."

"Lastly, there are those whose minds are too coarsely grained to be entirely toppled. The very insensitive would be scarcely affected—oh, such people as some of our older, work-broken peasants. Well, the children would have fugitive memories, and that, combined with the confused, incoherent babblings of the half-mad morons, formed the basis for the 'Book of Revelations.'

"Naturally, the book was based, in the first place, on the testimony of those least qualified to serve as historians; that is, children and morons; and was probably extensively edited and re-edited through the cycles."

"Do you suppose," broke in Theremon, "that they carried the book through the cycles the way we're planning on handing on the secret of gravitation?"

Sheerin shrugged. "Perhaps, but their exact method is unimportant. They do it, somehow. The point I was getting at was that the book can't help but be a mass of distortion, even if it is based on fact. For instance, do you remember the experiment with the holes in the roof that Faro and Yimot tried—the one that didn't work?"

"Yes."

"You know why it didn't w—" He stopped and rose in alarm, for Aton was approaching, his face a twisted mask of consternation. *"What's happened?"*

Aton drew him aside and Sheerin could feel the fingers on his elbow twitching.

"Not so loud!" Aton's voice was low and tortured. "I've just gotten word from the Hideout on the private line."

Sheerin broke in anxiously. "They are in trouble?"

"Not *they*." Aton stressed the pronoun significantly. "They sealed themselves off just a while ago, and they're going to stay buried till day after tomorrow. They're safe. But the *city*, Sheerin—it's a shambles. You have no idea—" He was having difficulty in speaking.

"Well?" snapped Sheerin impatiently. "What of it? It will get worse. What are you shaking about?" Then, suspiciously, "How do you feel?"

Aton's eyes sparked angrily at the insinuation, and then faded to anxiety once more. "You don't understand. The Cultists are active. They're rousing the people to storm the Observatory—promising them immediate entrance into grace, promising them salvation, promising them anything. What are we to do, Sheerin?"

Sheerin's head bent, and he stared in long abstraction at his toes. He tapped his chin with one knuckle, then looked up and said crisply, "Do? What is there to do? Nothing at all! Do the men know of this?"

"No, of course not!"

"Good! Keep it that way. How long till totality?"

"Not quite an hour."

"There's nothing to do but gamble. It will take time to organize any really formidable mob, and it will take more time to get them out here. We're a good five miles from the city—"

He glared out the window, down the slopes to where the farmed patches gave way to clumps of white houses in the suburbs; down to where the metropolis itself was a blur on the horizon—a mist in the waning blaze of Beta.

He repeated without turning, "It will take time. Keep on working and pray that totality comes first."

Beta was cut in half, the line of division pushing a slight concavity into the still-bright portion of the Sun. It was like a gigantic eyelid shutting slantwise over the light of a world.

The faint clatter of the room in which he stood faded into oblivion, and he sensed only the thick silence of the fields outside. The very insects seemed frightened mute. And things were dim.

He jumped at the voice in his ear. Theremon said, "Is something wrong?"

"Eh? Er—no. Get back to the chair. We're in the way." They slipped back to their corner, but the psychologist did not speak for a time. He lifted a finger and loosened his collar. He twisted his neck back and forth but found no relief. He looked up suddenly.

"Are you having any difficulty in breathing?"

The newspaperman opened his eyes wide and drew two or three long breaths. "No. Why?"

"I looked out the window too long, I suppose. The dimness got me. Difficulty in breathing is one of the first symptoms of a claustrophobic attack."

Theremon drew another long breath. "Well, it hasn't got me yet. Say, here's another of the fellows."

Beenay had interposed his bulk between the light and the

pair in the corner, and Sheerin squinted up at him anxiously. "Hello, Beenay."

The astronomer shifted his weight to the other foot and smiled feebly. "You won't mind if I sit down awhile and join in on the talk? My cameras are set, and there's nothing to do till totality." He paused and eyed the Cultist, who fifteen minutes earlier had drawn a small, skin-bound book from his sleeve and had been poring intently over it ever since. "That rat hasn't been making trouble, has he?"

Sheerin shook his head. His shoulders were thrown back and he frowned his concentration as he forced himself to breathe regularly. He said, "Have you had any trouble breathing, Beenay?"

Beenay sniffed the air in his turn. "It doesn't seem stuffy to me."

"A touch of claustrophobia," explained Sheerin apologetically.

"Oh-h-h! It worked itself differently with me. I get the impression that my eyes are going back on me. Things seem to blur and—well, nothing is clear. And it's cold, too."

"Oh, it's cold, all right. That's no illusion." Theremon grimaced. "My toes feel as if I've been shipping them cross country in a refrigerating car."

"What we need," put in Sheerin, "is to keep our minds busy with extraneous affairs. I was telling you a while ago, Theremon, why Faros' experiments with the holes in the roof came to nothing."

"You were just beginning," replied Theremon. He encircled a knee with both arms and nuzzled his chin against it.

"Well, as I started to say, they were misled by taking the 'Book of Revelations' literally. There probably wasn't any sense in attaching any physical significance to the Stars. It might be, you know, that in the presence of total Darkness, the mind finds it absolutely necessary to create light. This illusion of light might be all the Stars there really are."

"In other words," interposed Theremon, "you mean the Stars are the results of the madness and not one of the causes. Then, what good will Beenay's photographs be?"

"To prove that it is an illusion, maybe; or to prove the opposite, for all I know. Then again—"

But Beenay had drawn his chair closer, and there was an expression of sudden enthusiasm on his face. "Say, I'm glad you two got on to this subject." His eyes narrowed and he lifted one finger. "I've been thinking about these Stars and

I've got a really cute notion. Of course, it's strictly ocean foam, and I'm not trying to advance it seriously, but I think it's interesting. Do you want to hear it?"

He seemed half reluctant, but Sheerin leaned back and said, "Go ahead! I'm listening."

"Well, then, supposing there were other suns in the universe." He broke off a little bashfully. "I mean suns that are so far away that they're too dim to see. It sounds as if I've been reading some of that fantastic fiction, I suppose."

"Not necessarily. Still, isn't that possibility eliminated by the fact that, according to the Law of Gravitation, they would make themselves evident by their attractive forces?"

"Not if they were far enough off," rejoined Beenay, "really far off—maybe as much as four light years, or even more. We'd never be able to detect perturbations then, because they'd be too small. Say that there were a lot of suns that far off; a dozen or two, maybe."

Theremon whistled melodiously. "What an idea for a good Sunday supplement article. Two dozen suns in a universe eight light years across. Wow! That would shrink *our* universe into insignificance. The readers would eat it up."

"Only an idea," said Beenay with a grin, "but you see the point. During eclipse, these dozen suns would become visible, because there'd be no *real* sunlight to drown them out. Since they're so far off, they'd appear small, like so many little marbles. Of course, the Cultists talk of millions of Stars, but that's probably exaggeration. There just isn't any place in the universe you could put a million suns—unless they touch one another."

Sheerin had listened with gradually increasing interest. "You've hit something there, Beenay. And exaggeration is just exactly what would happen. Our minds, as you probably know, can't grasp directly any number higher than five; above that there is only the concept of 'many.' A dozen would become a million just like that. A damn good idea!"

"And I've got another cute little notion," Beenay said. "Have you ever thought what a simple problem gravitation would be if only you had a sufficiently simple system? Supposing you had a universe in which there was a planet with only one sun. The planet would travel in a perfect ellipse and the exact nature of the gravitational force would be so evident it could be accepted as an axiom. Astronomers on such a world would start off with gravity probably before they

even invented the telescope. Naked-eye observation would be
enough."

"But would such a system be dynamically stable?" questioned Sheerin doubtfully.

"Sure! They call it the 'one-and-one' case. It's been worked
out mathematically, but it's the philosophical implications
that interest me."

"It's nice to think about," admitted Sheerin, "as a pretty
abstraction—like a perfect gas or absolute zero."

"Of course," continued Beenay, "there's the catch that life
would be impossible on such a planet. It wouldn't get enough
heat and light, and if it rotated there would be total Darkness
half of each day. You couldn't expect life—which is fundamentally dependent upon light—to develop under those conditions. Besides—"

Sheerin's chair went over backward as he sprang to his feet
in a rude interruption. "Aton's brought out the lights."

Beenay said, "Huh," turned to stare, and then grinned half-
way around his head in open relief.

There were half a dozen foot-long, inch-thick rods cradled
in Aton's arms. He glared over them at the assembled staff
members.

"Get back to work, all of you. Sheerin, come here and help
me!"

Sheerin trotted to the older man's side and, one by one, in
utter silence, the two adjusted the rods in makeshift metal
holders suspended from the walls.

With the air of one carrying through the most sacred item
of a religious ritual, Sheerin scraped a large, clumsy match
into spluttering life and passed it to Aton, who carried the
flame to the upper end of one of the rods.

It hesitated there a while, playing futilely about the tip, until a sudden, crackling flare cast Aton's lined face into yellow
highlights. He withdrew the match and a spontaneous cheer
rattled the window.

The rod was topped by six inches of wavering flame! Me-
thodically, the other rods were lighted, until six independent
fires turned the rear of the room yellow.

The light was dim, dimmer even than the tenuous sunlight.
The flames reeled crazily, giving birth to drunken, swaying
shadows. The torches smoked devilishly and smelled like a
bad day in the kitchen. But they emitted yellow light.

There is something to yellow light—after four hours of

somber, dimming Beta. Even Latimer had lifted his eyes from his book and stared in wonder.

Sheerin warmed his hands at the nearest, regardless of the soot that gathered upon them in a fine, gray powder, and muttered ecstatically to himself. "Beautiful! Beautiful! I never realized before what a wonderful color yellow is."

But Theremon regarded the torches suspiciously. He wrinkled his nose at the rancid odor, and said, "What are those things?"

"Wood," said Sheerin shortly.

"Oh, no, they're not. They aren't burning. The top inch is charred and the flames just keeps shooting up out of nothing."

"That's the beauty of it. This is a really efficient artificial-light mechanism. We made a few hundred of them, but most went to the Hideout, of course. You see"—he turned and wiped his blackened hands upon his handkerchief—"you take the pithy core of coarse water reeds, dry them thoroughly and soak them in animal grease. Then you set fire to it and the grease burns, little by little. These torches will burn for almost half an hour without stopping. Ingenious, isn't it? It was developed by one of our own young men at Saro University."

After the momentary sensation, the dome had quieted. Latimer had carried his chair directly beneath a torch and continued reading, lips moving in the monotonous recital of invocations to the Stars. Beenay had drifted away to his cameras once more, and Theremon seized the opportunity to add to his notes on the article he was going to write for the Saro City *Chronicle* the next day—a procedure he had been following for the last two hours in a perfectly methodical, perfectly conscientious and, as he was well aware, perfectly meaningless fashion.

But, as the gleam of amusement in Sheerin's eyes indicated, careful note taking occupied his mind with something other than the fact that the sky was gradually turning a horrible deep purple-red, as if it were one gigantic, freshly peeled beet; and so it fulfilled its purpose.

The air grew, somehow, denser. Dusk, like a palpable entity, entered the room, and the dancing circle of yellow light about the torches etched itself into ever-sharper distinction against the gathering grayness beyond. There was the odor of smoke and the presence of little chuckling sounds that the torches made as they burned; the soft pad of one of the men circling the table at which he worked, on hesitant tiptoes; the occasional indrawn breath of someone trying to retain composure in a world that was retreating into the shadow.

It was Theremon who first heard the extraneous noise. It was a vague, unorganized *impression* of sound that would have gone unnoticed but for the dead silence that prevailed within the dome.

The newsman sat upright and replaced his notebook. He held his breath and listened; then, with considerable reluctance, threaded his way between the solarscope and one of Beenay's cameras and stood before the window.

The silence ripped to fragments at his startled shout:

"*Sheerin!*"

Work stopped! The psychologist was at his side in a moment. Aton joined him. Even Yimot 70, high in his little lean-back seat at the eyepiece of the gigantic solarscope, paused and looked downward.

Outside, Beta was a mere smoldering splinter, taking one last desperate look at Lagash. The eastern horizon, in the direction of the city, was lost in Darkness, and the road from Saro to the Observatory was a dull-red line bordered on both sides by wooden tracts, the trees of which had somehow lost individuality and merged into a continuous shadowy mass.

But it was the highway itself that held attention, for along it there surged another, and infinitely menacing, shadowy mass.

Aton cried in a cracked voice, "The madmen from the city! They've come!"

"How long to totality?" demanded Sheerin.

"Fifteen minutes, but . . . but they'll be here in five."

"Never mind, keep the men working. We'll hold them off. This place is built like a fortress. Aton, keep an eye on our young Cultist just for luck. Theremon, come with me."

Sheerin was out the door, and Theremon was at his heels. The stairs stretched below them in tight, circular sweeps about the central shaft, fading into a dank and dreary grayness.

The first momentum of their rush had carried them fifty feet down, so that the dim, flickering yellow from the open door of the dome had disappeared and both up above and down below the same dusky shadow crushed in upon them.

Sheerin paused, and his pudgy hand clutched at his chest.

His eyes bulged and his voice was a dry cough. "I can't . . . breathe . . . go down . . . yourself. Close all doors—"

Theremon took a few downward steps, then turned. "Wait! Can you hold out a minute?" He was panting himself. The air passed in and out his lungs like so much molasses, and there was a little germ of screeching panic in his mind at the thought of making his way into the mysterious Darkness below by himself.

Theremon, after all, was afraid of the dark!

"Stay here," he said. "I'll be back in a second." He dashed upward two steps at a time, heart pounding—not altogether from the exertion—tumbled into the dome and snatched a torch from its holder. It was foul smelling, and the smoke smarted his eyes almost blind, but he clutched that torch as if he wanted to kiss it for joy, and its flame streamed backward as he hurtled down the stairs again.

Sheerin opened his eyes and moaned as Theremon bent over him. Theremon shook him roughly. "All right, get a hold on yourself. We've got light."

He held the torch at tiptoe height and, propping the tottering psychologist by an elbow, made his way downward in the middle of the protecting circle of illumination.

The offices on the ground floor still possessed what light there was, and Theremon felt the horror about him relax.

"Here," he said brusquely, and passed the torch to Sheerin. "You can hear *them* outside."

And they could. Little scraps of hoarse, wordless shouts.

But Sheerin was right; the Observatory was built like a fortress. Erected in the last century, when the neo-Gavottian style of architecture was at its ugly height, it had been designed for stability and durability, rather than for beauty.

The windows were protected by the grillework of inch-thick iron bars sunk deep into the concrete sills. The walls were solid masonry that an earthquake couldn't have touched, and the main door was a huge oaken slab reinforced with iron at the strategic points. Theremon shot the bolts and they slid shut with a dull clang.

At the other end of the corridor, Sheerin cursed weakly. He pointed to the lock of the back door which had been nearly jimmied into uselessness.

"That must be how Latimer got in," he said.

"Well, don't stand there," cried Theremon impatiently. "Help drag up the furniture—and keep that torch out of my eyes. The smoke's killing me."

He slammed the heavy table up against the door as he spoke, and in two minutes had built a barricade which made up for what it lacked in beauty and symmetry by the sheer inertia of its massiveness.

Somewhere, dimly, far off, they could hear the battering of naked fists upon the door; and the screams and yells from outside had a sort of half reality.

That mob had set off from Saro City with only two things in mind: the attainment of Cultist salvation by the destruction of the Observatory, and a maddening fear that all but paralyzed them. There was no time to think of ground cars, or of weapons, or of leadership, or even of organization. They made for the Observatory on foot and assaulted it with bare hands.

And now that they were there, the last flash of Beta, the last ruby-red drop of flame, flickered feebly over a humanity that had left only stark, universal fear!

Theremon groaned, "Let's get back to the dome!"

In the dome, only Yimot, at the solarscope, had kept his place. The rest were clustered about the cameras, and Beenay was giving his instructions in a hoarse, strained voice.

"Get it straight, all of you. I'm snapping Beta just before totality and changing the plate. That will leave one of you to each camera. You all know about . . . about times of exposure—"

There was a breathless murmur of agreement.

Beenay passed a hand over his eyes. "Are the torches still burning? Never mind, I see them!" He was leaning hard against the back of a chair. "Now remember, don't . . . don't try to look for good shots. Don't waste time trying to get t-two stars at a time in the scope field. One is enough. And . . . and if you feel yourself going, *get away from the camera.*"

At the door, Sheerin whispered to Theremon, "Take me to Aton. I don't see him."

The newsman did not answer immediately. The vague form of the astronomers wavered and blurred, and the torches overhead had become only yellow splotches.

"It's dark," he whimpered.

Sheerin held out his hand, "Aton." He stumbled forward, "Aton!"

Theremon stepped after and seized his arm. "Wait, I'll take you." Somehow he made his way across the room. He closed his eyes against the Darkness and his mind against the chaos within it.

No one heard them or paid attention to them. Sheerin stumbled against the wall. "Aton!"

The psychologist felt shaking hands touching him, then withdrawing, and a voice muttering, "Is that you, Sheerin?"

"Aton!" He strove to breathe normally. "Don't worry about the mob. The place will hold them off."

Latimer, the Cultist, rose to his feet, and his face twisted in desperation. His word was pledged, and to break it would mean placing his soul in mortal peril. Yet that word had been forced from him and had not been given freely. The Stars would come soon; he could not stand by and allow— And yet his word was pledged.

Beenay's face was dimly flushed as it looked upward at Beta's last ray, and Latimer, seeing him bend over his camera, made his decision. His nails cut the flesh of his palms as he tensed himself.

He staggered crazily as he started his rush. There was nothing before him but shadows; the very floor beneath his feet lacked substance. And then someone was upon him and he went down with clutching fingers at his throat.

He doubled his knee and drove it hard into his assailant. "Let me up or I'll kill you."

Theremon cried out sharply and muttered through a blinding haze of pain, "You double-crossing rat!"

The newsman seemed conscious of everything at once. He heard Beenay croak, "I've got it. At your cameras, men!" and then there was the strange awareness that the last thread of sunlight had thinned out and snapped.

Simultaneously he heard one last choking gasp from Beenay, and a queer little cry from Sheerin, a hysterical giggle that cut off in a rasp—and a sudden silence, a strange, deadly silence from outside.

And Latimer had gone limp in his loosening grasp. Theremon peered into the Cultist's eyes and saw the blankness of them, staring upward, mirroring the feeble yellow of the torches. He saw the bubble of froth upon Latimer's lips and heard the low animal whimper in Latimer's throat.

With the slow fascination of fear, he lifted himself on one arm and turned his eyes toward the blood-curdling blackness of the window.

Through it shone the Stars!

Not Earth's feeble thirty-six hundred Stars visible to the eye—Lagash was in the center of a giant cluster. Thirty thousand mighty suns shown down in a soul-searing splendor that was more frighteningly cold in its awful indifference than the bitter wind that shivered across the cold, horribly bleak world.

Theremon staggered to his feet, his throat constricting him to breathlessness, all the muscles of his body writhing in a tensity of terror and sheer fear beyond bearing. He was going mad, and knew it, and somewhere deep inside a bit of sanity was screaming, struggling to fight off the hopeless flood of black terror. It was very horrible to go mad and know that you were going mad—to know that in a little minute you would be here physically and yet all the real essence would be dead and drowned in the black madness. For this was the Dark—the Dark and the Cold and the Doom. The bright walls of the universe were shattered and their awful black fragments were falling down to crush and squeeze and obliterate him.

He jostled someone crawling on hands and knees, but stumbled somehow over him. Hands groping at his tortured throat, he limped toward the flame of the torches that filled all his mad vision.

"Light!" he screamed.

Aton, somewhere, was crying, whimpering horribly like a terribly frightened child. "Stars—all the Stars—we didn't know at all. We didn't know anything. We thought six stars is a universe is something the Stars didn't notice is Darkness forever and ever and ever and the walls are breaking in and we didn't know we couldn't know and anything—"

Someone clawed at the torch, and it fell and snuffed out. In the instant, the awful splendor of the indifferent Stars leaped nearer to them.

On the horizon outside the window, in the direction of Saro City, a crimson glow began growing, strengthening in brightness, that was not the glow of a sun.

The long night had come again.

The Man Who Sold the Genre

In the late '30s and the '40s, many new authors, including Asimov, started as Campbell writers, but Robert A. Heinlein (1907-   ) was his own man from the beginning. What he was, however, happened to coincide with Campbell's ideas of what science fiction ought to be.

Science fiction, moreover, was ready to move outward into any number of unexplored areas. All it needed was a leader, someone to take charge in the way that Verne had done it in the 1860s, the way Wells had done it in the 1890s, and the way Burroughs had done it in the 1910s. Campbell could wield unusual influence on the evolution of science fiction from his positions as gatekeeper, coach, and cheerleader, but he could not play the game himself; that was part of his agreement with Street & Smith.

Heinlein was the right man for the right time.

Wells had recognized the part chance had played in his success. In his *Experiment in Autobiography* he wrote: "The last decade of the nineteenth century was an extraordinarily favorable time for new writers and my individual good luck was set in the luck of a whole generation of aspirants. . . . New books were being demanded and fresh authors were in request."

Science fiction was in a similar condition when Heinlein began casting about for some satisfying outlet for the energies dammed up by a frustrated military career. Born in Butler, Mo., and educated in the Kansas City schools, Heinlein was graduated from the Naval Academy in 1929, twentieth in a class of 243. He served on active duty as a line officer until 1934, when he retired, permanently disabled, with tuberculosis. He tried to fulfill a longtime ambition to study astronomy, but he had to drop out of graduate studies at UCLA, again because of health problems. In the next few years he tried politics, silver mining, architecture, and real estate.

In 1939 he noticed the announcement of an amateur

short-story contest in *Thrilling Wonder Stories*. He had been a reader of science fiction since boyhood, so he decided to enter the contest. But by the time the story was completed, he thought it was worth more than the $50 prize and sent it off to *Collier's* and then to *Astounding*, where Campbell paid him $70 for it.

It was the best of times and the worst of times for launching a career as a science-fiction writer. The United States was beginning to pull itself out of the Depression, but war was threatening in Europe. In science fiction a mild boom had begun: to the basic triumvirate of *Amazing, Wonder*, and *Astounding*, had been added *Marvel Science Stories* in 1938 and *Startling Stories, Famous Fantastic Mysteries, Astonishing Stories, Super Science Stories, Fantastic Adventures, Planet Stories, Science Fiction*, and *Future Fiction* in 1939.

Orson Welles's radio version of Wells's *The War of the Worlds* startled a nation in 1938.

There were virtually no science-fiction books being published, however, no opportunity for anthologization, no place for publication except in the science-fiction magazines, and almost no science fiction in films: after a brief flurry of interest that lasted from "The Lost World" (1925) to "The Invisible Man" (1933) and "Things to Come" (1936), few science-fiction films and none of any lasting interest were created for almost the next decade and a half.

Heinlein was involved in changing all of these conditions. In many ways he was instrumental in selling science fiction to the broader general audience.

In the first couple of years he established himself through his work in *Astounding* (a few stories slipped into other magazines under pseudonyms) as the leading science-fiction writer of his time. His major early work was a series about the relatively near future; they shared a common framework of assumptions that Campbell called (and published in 1941 as) a "Future History." In this period Heinlein wrote stories and novels such as "Misfit," "Requiem," *If This Goes On*, "The Roads Must Roll," "Coventry," "Blowups Happen," "Universe," and *Methuselah's Children*.

During World War II, Heinlein worked as a civilian engineer at the Naval Air Experimental Station of the U.S. Navy Yard in Philadelphia (and persuaded de Camp and Asimov to join him there). After the war Heinlein had new walls to break through.

The first barrier was the slick magazines—the *Saturday Evening Post* and its fellows, now all deceased—where science fiction had seldom been published. Now a series of Heinlein stories began to appear in the *Post, Argosy, Town and Country, Blue Book, Boys' Life,* and *The American Legion Magazine.* No longer would science fiction be so routinely excluded from the quality magazines.

The second barrier was the book publishers. The first breach was made by the anthologists during and immediately following World War II. The second was created by the fan presses a few years later and then widened by the old-line publishers. Heinlein had adult books published by Fantasy Press, Gnome Press, Shasta, and then by Doubleday and Putnam.

The third barrier no one even knew existed: juveniles. Heinlein wrote *Rocketship Galileo* (1947) and *Space Cadet* (1948) for Scribner's. Those and his subsequent juveniles would represent an introduction to science fiction for a generation of young people. He would publish one a year for the next ten years. They would be not only financial successes, but, as he got the hang of them, artistic successes as well. Some of them (*The Star Beast, Citizen of the Galaxy, Have Spacesuit—Will Travel, Starship Troopers,* and *Podkayne of Mars*) would be serialized in the science-fiction magazines. Toward the end of the cycle Heinlein would switch to Putnam when Scribner's rejected *Starship Troopers.*

Rocketship Galileo led to another breakthrough. Parts of it were included in the 1950 film *Destination Moon.* Heinlein and a couple of collaborators wrote the screenplay; George Pal produced it. Sf film historian John Baxter credits it with beginning the sf film boom of the '50s.

Heinlein's final accomplishment was the creation of the first wildly successful novel written by a science-fiction author, *Stranger in a Strange Land* (1961). Although its greatest success was in paperback (the first science-fiction bestseller in hardcovers is reputed to have been Frank Herbert's *Children of Dune* in 1977), it became a cult book of the same proportions as *Lord of the Flies, Catch 22,* and *The Lord of the Rings.* The sexual frankness of the novel also may have had a liberating effect on later science fiction.

Heinlein's greatest assets were his professional attitude, his ability to learn and grow, and his willingness to try new fields. His work displays his firm sense of rightness and propriety—and certain more arguable convictions about libertarianism, militarism, and elitism—although his work is so varied that to pin on him any attitude or philosophy expressed in his writing may be hard to justify. More than any other writer, however, Heinlein had the ability to present carefully crafted backgrounds, including entire societies, in economical but convincing detail. This and, at its best, his narrative drive and his spare, vigorous prose provided science fiction with models for the authors who followed after.

"Requiem" was reprinted as the final episode in a book published in 1950 by Shasta, *The Man Who Sold the Moon*, but it was a requiem only for much that had passed for science fiction since the beginning of the century, and for the millennia-old human dream to reach that great shining world in the sky. It was the launching pad for a new kind of science fiction that would search the galaxy for aliens and adventure and survival and dreams, and for new definitions of humanity.

Requiem

by Robert A. Heinlein

On a high hill in Samoa there is a grave. Inscribed on the marker are these words:

"Under the wide and starry sky
Dig my grave and let me lie.
Glad did I live and gladly die
And I lay me down with a will!

"This be the verse you grave for me:
Here he lies where he longed to be,
Home is the sailor, home from the sea,
And the hunter home from the hill."

These lines appear another place—scrawled on a shipping tag torn from a compressed-air container, and pinned to the ground with a knife.

It was not much of a fair, as fairs go. The trotting races didn't promise much excitement, even though several entries claimed the blood of the immortal Dan Patch. The tents and concession booths barely covered the circus grounds, and the pitchmen seemed discouraged.

D. D. Harriman's chauffeur could not see any reason for stopping. They were due in Kansas City for a directors' meeting; that is to say, Harriman was. The chauffeur had private reasons for promptness, reasons involving darktown society on Eighteenth Street. But the boss not only stopped; he hung around. He didn't seem much interested in the racetrack or sideshows, though.

Bunting and a canvas arch made the entrance to a large inclosure beyond the racetrack. Red and gold letters announced:

This way to the
MOON ROCKET! ! ! !
See it in actual flight
Public Demonstration Flights
TWICE DAILY
This is the ACTUAL TYPE used by the
First Men to Reach the MOON! !
YOU can ride in it! !—$25

A boy, nine or ten years old, hung around the entrance and stared at the posters.

"Want to see the ship, son?"

The kid's eyes shone. "Gee, mister, I sure would."

"So would I. Come on."

Harriman paid out fifty cents for two pink tickets which entitled him and the boy to enter the inclosure and examine the rocketship. The kid ran on ahead with the single-minded preoccupation of boyhood. Harriman looked over the stubby curved lines of the ovoid body. He noted with a professional eye that she was a single-jet type with fractional controls around her midriff. He squinted through his glasses at the name painted in gold on the carnival red of the body, *Carefree*. He paid another quarter to enter the control cabin.

When his eyes had adjusted to the gloom caused by the strong ray filters of the ports, he let them rest lovingly on the keys of the console and the semi-circle of dials above. Each beloved gadget was in its proper place. He knew them—graven in his heart.

While he mused over the instrument board, with the warm liquid of content soaking through his body, the pilot entered and touched his arm.

"Sorry, sir. We've got to cast loose for the flight."

"Eh?" Harriman started, then looked at the speaker. Handsome devil, with a good skull and strong shoulders—reckless eyes and a self-indulgent mouth, but a firm chin. "Oh, excuse me, captain."

"Quite all right."

"Oh, I say, captain . . . er . . . uh—"

"McIntyre."

"Captain McIntyre, could you take a passenger this trip?" The old man leaned eagerly toward him.

"Why, yes, if you wish. Come along with me." He ushered Harriman into a shed marked "Office" which stood near the gate. "Passenger for a check-over, doc."

Harriman permitted the medico to run a stethoscope over his thin chest and to strap a rubber bandage around his arm. Presently the doctor unstrapped it, glanced at McIntyre, and shook his head.

"No go, doc?"

"That's right, captain."

Harriman looked from face to face, his disappointment plain to see. "You won't take me?"

The doctor shrugged his shoulders. "I couldn't even guarantee that you would live through the take-off. You see, sir," he continued, not unkindly, "it's not only that your heart condition makes heavy acceleration dangerous, but at your age bones are brittle, highly calcified, and easily broken in the shock of take-off. Rocketry is a young man's game."

McIntyre added: "Sorry, sir. I'd like to, but the Bates County Fair Association pays the doctor here to see to it that I don't take up anyone who might be hurt by the acceleration."

The old man's shoulders drooped miserably. "I rather expected it."

"Sorry, sir." McIntyre turned to go, but Harriman followed him out.

"Excuse me, captain—"

"Yes?"

"Could you and your . . . uh . . . engineer have dinner with me after your flight?"

The pilot looked at him quizzically. "I don't see why not. Thanks."

"Captain McIntyre, it is difficult for me to see why anyone would quit the Earth-Moon run," said Harriman a few hours later. Fried chicken and hot biscuits in a private dining room of the best hotel the little town of Butler afforded, three-star Hennessey and Corona Coronas had produced a friendly atmosphere in which three men could talk freely.

"Well, I didn't like it."

"Aw, don't give him that, Mac—you know damn well it was Rule G that got you." McIntyre's mechanic poured himself another brandy as he spoke.

McIntyre looked sullen. "Well, what if I did take a couple o' drinks? Anyhow, I could have squared that—it was the damn persnickety regulations that got me fed up. Who are you to talk? Smuggler!"

"Sure, I smuggled! Who wouldn't—with all those beautiful rocks just aching to be taken back to Earth? I had a diamond once as big as— But if I hadn't been caught I'd be in Luna City tonight. And so would you, you drunken blaster—with the boys buying us drinks and the girls smiling and making suggestions—" He put his face down and began to weep quietly.

McIntyre shook him. "He's drunk."

"Never mind." Harriman interposed a hand. "Tell me, are you really satisfied not to be on the run any more?"

McIntyre chewed his lip. "No—he's right, of course. This barnstorming isn't what it's all cracked up to be. We've been hopping junk at every pumpkin doin's up and down the Mississippi Valley—sleeping in tourist camps, and eating at greaseburners. Half the time the sheriff has an attachment on the ship, the other half the Society for the Prevention of Something or Other gets an injunction to keep us on the ground. It's no sort of a life for a rocket man."

"Would it help any for you to get to the Moon?"

"Well—yes. I couldn't get back on the Earth-Moon run, but if I was in Luna City, I could get a job hopping ore for the company—they're always short of rocket pilots for that, and they wouldn't mind my record. If I kept my nose clean, they might even put me back on the run, in time."

Harriman fiddled with a spoon, then looked up. "Would you young gentlemen be open to a business proposition?"

"Perhaps. What is it?"

"You own the *Carefree?*"

"Yeah. That is, Charlie and I do—barring a couple of liens against her. What about it?"

"I want to charter her—for you and Charlie to take me to the Moon!"

Charlie sat up with a jerk. "D'joo hear what he said, Mac? He wants us to fly that old heap to the Moon!"

McIntyre shook his head. "Can't do it, Mr. Harriman. The old boat's worn out. We don't even use standard juice in her—just gasoline and liquid air. Charlie spends all of his time tinkering with her at that. She's going to blow up some day."

"Say, Mr. Harriman," put in Charlie, "what's the matter with getting an excursion permit and going in a company ship?"

"No, son," the old man replied, "I can't do that. You know the conditions under which Congress granted the company a monopoly on lunar exploitation—no one to enter space who was not physically qualified to stand up under it. Company to take full responsibility for the safety and health of all citizens beyond the stratosphere. The official reason for granting the franchise was to stop the enormous loss of life that occurred during the first few years of rocket travel."

"And you can't pass the physical exam?"

Harriman shook his head.

"Well, what the hell—if you can afford to hire us, why don't you just bribe yourself a brace of company docs? It's been done before."

Harriman smiled ruefully. "I know it has, Charlie, but it won't work for me. You see, I'm a little too prominent. My full name is Delos D. Harriman."

"What? You are old D. D.? But, hell's bells, you own a big slice of the company yourself; you ought to be able to do anything you like, rules or no rules."

"That is not an unusual opinion, son, but it is incorrect. Rich men aren't more free than other men; they are less free—a good deal less free. I tried to do what you suggest, but the other directors would not permit me. They are afraid of losing their franchise. It costs them a good deal in—uh—political contact expenses to retain it, as it is."

"Well, I'll be a—— Can you tie that, Mac? A guy with lots of dough, and he can't spend it the way he wants to."

McIntyre did not answer, but waited for Harriman to continue.

"Captain McIntyre, if you had a ship, would you take me?"

McIntyre rubbed his chin. "It's against the law."

"I'd make it worth your while."

"Sure, he would, Mr. Harriman. Of course you would, Mac. Luna City! Oh, baby!"

"Why do you want to go to the Moon so badly, Mr. Harriman?"

"Captain, it's the one thing I've really wanted to do all my life—ever since I was a boy. I don't know whether I can explain it to you or not. You young fellows have grown up to rocket travel the way I grew up to aviation. I'm a great deal older than you are; maybe fifty years older. When I was a kid practically nobody believed that men would ever reach the Moon. You've seen rockets all your lives, and the first to reach the Moon got there before you were old enough to vote. When I was a boy they laughed at the idea.

"But I believed—I believed. I read Verne and Wells and Smith, and I believed that we could do it—that we *would* do it. I set my heart on being one of the men to walk the surface of the Moon, to see her other side, and to look back on the face of the Earth, hanging in the sky.

"I used to go without my lunches to pay my dues in the American Rocket Society, because I wanted to believe that I was helping to bring the day nearer when we would reach the Moon. I was already an old man when that day arrived. I've lived longer than I should, but I would not let myself die—I will not!—until I have set foot on the Moon."

McIntyre stood up and put out his hand. "You find a ship, Mr. Harriman. I'll drive 'er."

"Atta boy, Mac! I told you he would, Mr. Harriman."

Harriman mused and dozed during the hour's run to the north into Kansas City, dozed in the light, troubled sleep of old age. Incidents out of a long life ran through his mind in vagrant dreams. There was that time—oh, yes, 1910—a little boy on a warm spring night. "What's that, daddy?"

"That's Halley's comet, sonny."

"Where did it come from?"

"I don't know, son. From way out in the sky somewhere."

"It's *beyooootiful*, daddy. I want to touch it."

"'Fraid not, son."

"Delos, do you mean to stand there and tell me you put the money we had saved for the house into that crazy rocket company?"

"Now, Charlotte, please! It's not crazy; it's a sound business investment. Some day soon rockets will fill the sky. Ships and trains will be obsolete. Look what happened to the men that had the foresight to invest in Henry Ford."

"We've been all over this before."

"Charlotte, the day will come when men will rise up off the Earth and visit the Moon, even the planets. This is the beginning."

"Must you shout?"

"I'm sorry, but you——"

"I feel a headache coming on. Please try to be a little quiet when you come to bed."

He hadn't gone to bed. He had sat out on the veranda all night long, watching the full Moon move across the sky. There would be the devil to pay in the morning, the devil and a thin-lipped silence. But he'd stick by his guns. He'd given in on most things, but not on this. The night was his. Tonight he'd be alone with his old friend. He searched her face. Where was Mare Crisium? Funny, he couldn't make it out. He used to be able to see it plainly when he was a boy. Probably needed new glasses—this constant office work wasn't good for his eyes.

But he didn't need to see; he knew where they all were: Crisium, Mare Fecunditatis, Mare Tranquillitatis—that one had a satisfying roll!—the Appenines, the Carpathians, old Tycho with its mysterious rays.

Two hundred and forty thousand miles—ten times around the Earth. Surely men could bridge a little gap like that. Why, he could almost reach out and touch it, nodding there behind the elm trees.

Not that he could help to do it. He hadn't the education.

"Son, I want to have a little serious talk with you."

"Yes, mother."

"I know you had hoped to go to college next year"— Hoped! He had lived for it. The University of Chicago to study under Moulton, then on to the Yerkes Observatory to work under the eye of Dr. Frost himself—"and I had hoped so, too. But with your father gone, and the girls growing up, it's harder to make ends meet. You've been a good boy, and worked hard to help out. I know you'll understand."

"Yes, mother."

"Extra! Extra! Stratosphere Rocket Reaches Paris. Read aaaaalllllll about 't." The thin little man in the bifocals snatched at the paper and hurried back to the office.

"Look at this, A. J."

"Huh? Hm-m-m, interesting, but what of it?"

"Can't you see? The next stage is to the Moon!"

"God, but you're a sucker, Delos. The trouble with you is, you read too many of those trashy magazines. Now, I caught my boy reading one of 'em just last week and dressed him down proper. Your folks should have done you the same favor."

Harriman squared his narrow, middle-aged shoulders. "They will so reach the Moon!"

His partner laughed. "Have it your own way. If baby wants the Moon, papa will bring it home for him. But you stick to your discounts and commissions; that's where the money is."

The big car droned down the Paseo, and turned off on Armour Boulevard. Old Harriman stirred uneasily in his sleep and muttered to himself.

"But, Mr. Harriman—" The young man with the notebook was plainly perturbed. The old man grunted.

"You heard me. Sell 'em. I want every share I own realized in cash as rapidly as possible; Spaceways, Spaceways Provisioning Co., Artemis Mines, Luna City Recreations, the whole lot of them."

"It will depress the market. You won't realize the full value of your holdings."

"Don't you think I know that? I can afford it."

"What about the shares you had earmarked for Tycho Observatory and for the Harriman Scholarships?"

"Oh, yes. Don't sell those. Set up a trust. Should have done it long ago. Tell Mr. Kamens to draw up the papers. He knows what I want."

The interoffice 'visor flashed into life. "The gentlemen are here, Mr. Harriman."

"Send 'em in. That's all, Ashley. Get busy." Ashley went

out as McIntyre and Charlie entered. Harriman got up and trotted forward to greet them.

"Come in, boys, come in. I'm so glad to see you. Sit down. Sit down. Have a cigar."

"Mighty pleased to see you, Mr. Harriman," acknowledged Charlie. "In fact, you might say we need to see you."

"Some trouble, gentlemen?" Harriman glanced from face to face. McIntyre answered him.

"You still mean that about a job for us, Mr. Harriman?"

"Mean it? Certainly, I do. You're not backing out on me?"

"Not at all. We need that job now. You see, the *Carefree* is lying in the middle of the Osage River, with her jet split clear back to the injector."

"Dear me! You weren't hurt?"

"No, aside from sprains and bruises. We jumped."

Charlie chortled. "I caught a catfish with my bare teeth."

In short order they got down to business. "You two will have to buy a ship for me. I can't do it openly; my colleagues would figure out what I mean to do and stop me. I'll supply you with all the cash you need. You go out and locate some sort of a ship that can be refitted for the trip. Work up some good story about how you are buying it for some playboy as a stratosphere yacht, or that you plan to try to establish an Arctic-Antarctic tourist route. Anything as long as no one suspects that she is being outfitted for space flight.

"Then, after the department of transport licenses her for strato flight, you move to a piece of desert out West—I'll find a likely parcel of land and buy it—and then I'll join you. Then we'll install the extra fuel tanks, change the injectors and timers and so forth, to fit her for the hop. How about it?"

McIntyre looked dubious. "It'll take a lot of doing. Charlie, do you think you can accomplish that change-over without a dockyard and shops?"

"Me? Sure, I can—with your thick-fingered help. Just give me the tools and materials I want, and don't hurry me too much. Of course, it won't be fancy—"

"Nobody wants it to be fancy. I just want a ship that won't blow when I start slapping the keys."

"It won't blow, Mac."

"That's what you thought about the *Carefree*."

"That ain't fair, Mac. I ask you, Mr. Harriman—that heap was junk, and we knew it. This'll be different. We're going to spend some dough and do it right. Ain't we, Mr. Harriman?"

Harriman patted him on the shoulder. "Certainly we are, Charlie. You can have all the money you want. That's the least of our worries. Now, do the salaries and bonuses I mentioned suit you? I don't want you to be short."

"—as you know, my clients are his nearest relatives and have his interests at heart. We contend that Mr. Harriman's conduct for the past several weeks, as shown by the evidence here adduced, gives clear indication that a mind once brilliant in the world of finance has become senile. It is, therefore, with the deepest regret that we pray this honorable court, if it pleases, to declare Mr. Harriman incompetent and to assign a conservator to protect his financial interests and those of his future heirs and assigns." The attorney sat down, pleased with himself.

Mr. Kamens took the floor. "May it please the court—if my esteemed friend is quite through—I suggest that in his last few words my opponent gave away his entire thesis. 'The financial interests of future heirs and assigns.' It is evident that the petitioners believe that my client should conduct his affairs in such a fashion as to insure that his nieces and nephews, and their issue, will be supported in unearned luxury for the rest of their lives. My client's wife has passed on; he has no children. It is admitted that he has provided generously for his sisters and their children in times past, and that he has established annuities for such near kin as are without means of support.

"But now, like vultures—worse than vultures, for they are not content to let him die in peace—they would prevent my client from enjoying his wealth in whatever manner best suits him for the few remaining years of his life. It is true that he has sold his holdings; is it strange that an elderly man should wish to retire? It is true that he suffered some paper losses in liquidation. 'The value of a thing is what that thing will bring.' He was retiring and demanded cash. Is there anything strange about that?

"It is admitted that he refused to discuss his actions with his so-loving kinfolk. What law, or principle, requires a man to consult with his nephews on anything?

"Therefore, we pray that this court will confirm my client in his right to do what he likes with his own, deny this petition, and send these meddlers about their business."

The judge took off his spectacles and polished them thoughtfully.

"Mr. Kamens, this court has as high a regard for individual liberty as you have, and you may rest assured that any action taken will be solely in the interests of your client. Nevertheless, men do grow old, men do become senile, and in such cases must be protected.

"I shall take this matter under advisement until tomorrow. Court is adjourned."

From the Kansas City Star:

ECCENTRIC MILLIONAIRE DISAPPEARS

—failed to appear for the adjourned hearing. The bailiffs returned from a search of places usually frequented by Harriman with the report that he had not been seen since the previous day. A bench warrant under contempt proceedings has been issued and—

A desert sunset is a better stimulant for the appetite than a hot dance orchestra. Charlie testified to this by polishing off the last of the ham gravy with a piece of bread. Harriman handed each of the younger men cigars and took one himself.

"My doctor claims that these weeds are bad for my heart condition," Harriman remarked as he lighted his, "but I've felt so much better since I joined you boys here on the ranch that I am inclined to doubt him." He exhaled a cloud of blue-gray smoke and resumed. "I don't think a man's health depends so much on what he does as on whether he wants to do it. I'm doing what I want to do."

"That's all a man can ask of life," agreed McIntyre.

"How does the work look now, boys?"

"My end's in pretty good shape," Charlie answered. "We finished the second pressure tests on the new tanks and the fuel lines today. The ground tests are all done, except the calibration runs. Those won't take long—just the four hours to make the runs if I don't run into some bugs. How about you, Mac?"

McIntyre ticked them off on his fingers. "Food supplies and water on board. Three vacuum suits, a spare, and service kits. Medical supplies. The buggy already had all the standard equipment for strato flight. The late lunar ephemerides haven't arrived as yet."

"When do you expect them?"

"Any time—they should be here now. Not that it matters. This guff about how hard it is to navigate from here to the Moon is hokum to impress the public. After all, you can see your destination—it's not like ocean navigation. Gimme a sextant and a good stadimeter and I'll set you down any place on the Moon you like—without opening an almanac or a star table—just from a general knowledge of the relative speeds involved."

"Never mind the personal build-up, Columbus," Charlie told him. "We'll admit you can hit the floor with your hat. The general idea is, you're ready to go now. Is that right?"

"That's it."

"That being the case, I could run those tests tonight. I'm getting jumpy—things have been going too smoothly. If you'll give me a hand, we ought to be in bed by midnight."

"O. K. When I finish this cigar."

They smoked in silence for a while, each thinking about the coming trip and what it meant to him. Old Harriman tried to repress the excitement that possessed him at the prospect of immediate realization of his lifelong dream.

"Mr. Harriman—"

"Eh? What is it, Charlie?"

"How does a guy go about getting rich, like you did?"

"Getting rich? I can't say; I never tried to get rich. I never wanted to be rich, or well known, or anything like that."

"Huh?"

"No, I just wanted to live a long time and see it all happen. I wasn't unusual; there were lots of boys like me—radio hams, they were, and telescope builders, and airplane amateurs. We had science clubs, and basement laboratories, and science-fiction leagues—the kind of boys that thought there was more romance in one issue of the *Electrical Experimenter* than in all the books Dumas ever wrote. We didn't want to be one of Horatio Alger's get-rich heroes, either; we wanted to build spaceships. Well, some of us did."

"Gosh, Pop, you make it sound exciting."

"It was exciting, Charlie. This has been a wonderful, romantic century, for all of its bad points. And it's grown more wonderful and more exciting every year. No, I didn't want to be rich; I just wanted to live long enough to see men rise up to the stars, and, if God was good to me, to go as far as the Moon myself." He carefully deposited an inch of white ash in a saucer. "It has been a good life. I haven't any complaints."

McIntyre pushed back his chair. "Come on, Charlie, if you're ready."

"O. K."

They all got up. Harriman started to speak, then grabbed at his chest, his face a dead gray-white.

"Catch him, Mac!"

"Where's his medicine?"

"In his vest pocket."

They eased him over to a couch, broke a small glass capsule in a handkerchief, and held it under his nose. The volatile released by the capsule seemed to bring a little color into his face. They did what little they could for him, then waited for him to regain consciousness.

Charlie broke the uneasy silence. "Mac, we ain't going through with this."

"Why not?"

"It's murder. He'll never stand up under the initial acceleration."

"Maybe not, but it's what he wants to do. You heard him."

"But we oughtn't to let him."

"Why not? It's neither your business nor the business of this damn paternalistic government to tell a man not to risk his life doing what he really wants to do."

"All the same, I don't feel right about it. He's such a swell old duck."

"Then what d'yuh want to do with him—send him back to Kansas City so those old harpies can shut him up in a laughing academy till he dies of a broken heart?"

"N-no-o-o—not that."

"Get out there, and make your set-up for those test runs. I'll be along."

A wide-tired desert runabout rolled into the ranch-yard gate the next morning and stopped in front of the house. A heavy-set man with a firm, but kindly, face climbed out and spoke to McIntyre, who approached to meet him.

"You James McIntyre?"

"What about it?"

"I'm the deputy Federal marshal hereabouts. I got a warrant for your arrest."

"What's the charge?"

"Conspiracy to violate the Space Precautionary Act."

Charlie joined the pair. "What's up, Mac?"

The deputy answered. "You'd be Charles Cummings, I

guess. Warrant here for you. Got one for a man named Harriman, too, and a court order to put seals on your spaceship."

"We've no spaceship."

"What d'yuh keep in that big shed?"

"Strato yacht."

"So? Well, I'll put seals on her until a spaceship comes along. Where's Harriman?"

"Right in there." Charlie obliged by pointing, ignoring McIntyre's scowl.

The deputy turned his head. Charlie couldn't have missed the button by a fraction of an inch, for the deputy collapsed quietly to the ground. Charlie stood over him, rubbing his knuckles and mourning.

"That's the finger I broke playing shortstop. I'm always hurting that finger."

"Get Pop into the cabin," Mac cut him short, "and strap him into his hammock."

"Aye, aye, skipper."

They taxied on the auxiliary motor out of the hangar, turned, and started out across the desert plain to find elbow room for the take-off. McIntyre saw the deputy from his starboard conning port. He was staring disconsolately after them.

McIntyre fastened his safety belt, settled his corset, and spoke into the engine-room speaking tube. "All set, Charlie?"

"All set, skipper. But you can't raise ship yet, Mac. She *ain't named!*"

"No time for your superstitions!"

Harriman's thin voice reached them. "Call her the *Lunatic*. It's the only appropriate name!"

McIntyre settled his head into the pads, punched two keys, then three more in rapid succession, and the *Lunatic* raised ground.

"How are you, Pop?"

Charlie searched the old man's face anxiously. Harriman licked his lips and managed to speak. "Doing fine, son. Couldn't be better."

"The acceleration won't be so bad from here on. I'll unstrap you so you can wiggle around a little. But I think you'd better stay in the hammock." He tugged at buckles. Harriman partially repressed a groan.

"What is it, Pop?"

"Nothing. Nothing at all. Just go easy on that side."

Charlie ran his fingers over the old man's side with the

sure, delicate touch of a mechanic. "You ain't foolin' me none, Pop. But there isn't much I can do until we ground."

"Charlie—"

"Yes, Pop?"

"Can't I move to a port? I want to watch the Earth."

"Ain't nothin to see yet; the blast hides it. As soon as we build up enough speed to coast up to the change-over point, I'll move you. Tell you what; I'll give you a sleepy pill, and then wake you when we cut the jets."

"No!"

"Huh?"

"I'll stay awake."

"Just as you say, Pop."

Charlie fought his way up to the nose of the ship, and braced himself on the gimbals of the pilot's chair. McIntyre questioned him with his eyes.

"Yeah, he's alive all right," Charlie told him, "but he's in bad shape."

"How bad?"

"Couple of cracked ribs, anyhow. I don't know what else. I don't know whether he'll last out the trip, Mac. His heart was pounding something awful."

"He'll last, Charlie. He's tough."

"Tough? He's delicate as a canary."

"I don't mean that. He's tough way down inside—where it counts."

"Just the same, you'd better set her down awful easy if you want to ground with a full complement aboard."

"I will. I'll make one full swing around the Moon and ease her in on an involute approach curve. We've got enough fuel, I think."

When they commenced to coast in a free orbit, Charlie unslung the hammock and moved Harriman, hammock and all, to a side port. McIntyre turned the ship about a transverse axis so that the tail pointed toward the Sun, then gave a short blast on two tangential jets opposed in couple to cause the ship to spin slowly about her longitudinal axis, and thereby create a slight artificial gravity. The initial weightlessness when coasting commenced had knotted the old man with the characteristic nausea of free flight, and the pilot wished to save his passenger as much discomfort as possible.

But Harriman was not concerned with the condition of his stomach.

There it was, all as he had imagined it so many times. The Moon swung majestically past the viewport, twice as wide as he had ever seen it before, all of her familiar features cameo-clear. She gave way to the Earth as the ship continued its slow swing, the Earth itself, as he had envisioned her, appearing like a noble moon, eight times as wide as the Moon appears to the Earthbound, and more luscious, more sensuously beautiful than the silver Moon could be. It was sunset near the Atlantic seaboard—the line of shadow ran down Hudson Bay, slashed through the eastern coast line of North America, touched Cuba, and obscured the eastern bulge of South America. He savored the mellow blue of the Pacific Ocean, felt the texture of the soft green and brown of the continents, admired the blue-white cold of the polar caps. Canada and the great Northwest were obscured by cloud, a vast low-pressure area that spread across the continent. It shone with an even more satisfactory dazzling white than the polar caps.

As the ship swung slowly around, Earth would pass from view, and the stars would march across the port—the same stars he had always known, but steady, brighter, and unwinking against a screen of perfect, live black. Then the Moon would swim into view again to claim his thoughts.

He was serenely happy in a fashion not given to most men, even in a long lifetime. He felt as if he were every man who had ever lived, and looked up at the stars, and longed.

At least once he must have fallen into deep sleep, or possibly delirium, for he came to with a start, thinking that his wife, Charlotte, was calling to him. "Delos!" the voice had said. "Delos! Come in from there! You'll catch your death of cold in that night air."

Poor Charlotte! She had been a good wife to him, a good wife. He was quite sure that her only regret in dying had been her fear that he would not take proper care of himself. It had not been her fault that she had not shared his dream and his need.

Charlie rigged the hammock in such a fashion that Harriman could watch from the starboard port when they swung around the far face of the Moon. He picked out the landmarks made familiar to him by a thousand photographs with nostalgic pleasure, as if he were returning to his own country. McIntyre brought her slowly down as they came back around to the Earthward face, and prepared to land in Mare Imbrium between Aristillus and Archimedes, about ten miles from Luna City.

It was not a bad landing, all things considered. He had to land without coaching from the ground, and he had no second pilot to punch the stadimeter for him. In his anxiety to make it gentle he missed his destination by some thirty miles, but he did his cold-sober best. At that, it was rather bumpy.

As they scooted along to a stop, throwing up powdery pumice on each side, Charlie came up to the control station.

"How's our passenger?" Mac demanded.

"I'll see, but I wouldn't make any bets. That landing stunk, Mac."

"Damn it, I did my best."

"I know you did, skipper. Forget it."

But the passenger was alive and conscious, though bleeding from the nose, and with a pink foam on his lips. He was feebly trying to get himself out of his cocoon. They helped him, working together.

"Where are the vacuum suits?" was his first remark.

"Steady, Mr. Harriman. You can't go out there yet. We've got to give you some first aid."

"*Get me that suit!* First aid can wait."

Silently they did as he ordered. His left leg was practically useless, and they had to help him through the lock, one on each side. But with his inconsiderable mass having a lunar weight of only twenty pounds, he was no burden. They found a place some fifty yards from the ship where they could prop him up and let him look, a chunk of scoria supporting his head.

McIntyre put his helmet against the old man's and spoke. "We'll leave you here to enjoy the view while we get ready for the trek into town. It's a forty-miler, pretty near, and we'll have to break our spare air bottles and rations and stuff. We'll be back soon."

Harriman nodded without answering, and squeezed their gauntlets with a grip that was surprisingly strong.

He sat very quiet, rubbing his hands against the soil of the Moon and sensing the curiously light pressure of his body against the ground. At long last there was peace in his heart. His hurts had ceased to pain him. He was where he had longed to be—he had followed his need. Overhead hung the Earth in third quarter, a green-blue giant moon. The Sun's upper limb crowned the crags of Archimedes to his left. And underneath—the Moon; the soil of the Moon itself. He was on the Moon!

He lay back still while a bath of content flowed over him like a tide at flood, and soaked into his very marrow.

His attention strayed momentarily, and he thought once again that his name was called. Silly, he thought; I'm getting old—my mind wanders.

Back in the cabin Charlie and Mac were rigging shoulder yokes on a stretcher. "There. That will do," Mac commented. "We'd better stir Pop out; we ought to be going."

"I'll get him," Charlie replied. "I'll just pick him up and carry him. He don't weigh nothing."

Charlie was gone longer than McIntyre had expected him to be. He returned alone. Mac waited for him to close the lock and swing back his helmet. "Trouble?"

"Never mind the stretcher, skipper. We won't be needin' it. Yeah, I mean it," he continued. "I did what was necessary."

McIntyre bent down without a word and commenced to strap on the wide skis necessary to negotiate the powdery ash. Charlie followed his example. Then they swung spare air bottles over their shoulders and passed out through the lock.

They didn't bother to close the outer door of the lock behind them.

A Chronology of Science Fiction

NOTE: Initials in paranthesis after title stand for: IFA (International Fantasy Award), H (Hugo), N (Nebula), C (Campbell). Where novels have been serialized, they are dated from the years of serialization.

1818   *Frankenstein* Mary Wollstonecraft Shelley
1826   *The Last Man* Mary Wollstonecraft Shelley
1830   *The Moon Hoax* Richard Adams Locke
1833   "Ms. Found in a Bottle" Edgar Allan Poe
1835   "Hans Pfaall" Edgar Allan Poe
1844   "The Balloon Hoax" Edgar Allan Poe
          "Rappaccini's Daughter" Nathaniel Hawthorne
1849   "Mellonta Tauta" Edgar Allan Poe
1858   "The Diamond Lens" Fitz-James O'Brien
1864   *A Journey to the Center of the Earth* Jules Verne
1865   *From the Earth to the Moon* Jules Verne
1868   *The Steam Man of the Prairies* Edward F. Ellis
1869   *The Brick Moon* Edward Everett Hale
1870   *Twenty Thousand Leagues Under the Sea* Jules Verne
1876   *Franke Reade and His Steam Man of the Prairies*
          Harry Enton
1877   *Off on a Comet* Jules Verne
1879   *Frank Reade, Jr., and His Steam Wonder*
          Luis Philip Senarens
1886   *Robur the Conqueror* Jules Verne
          She H. Rider Haggard
1888   *Looking Backward* Edward Bellamy
          Dr. Jekyll and Mr. Hyde Robert Louis Stevenson
1889   *A Connecticut Yankee in King Arthur's Court* Mark
          Twain
1894   "The Stolen Bacillus" H. G. Wells
1895   *The Time Machine* H. G. Wells.